THE ASSOCIATION FOR SCOTTISH LITERARY STUDIES
NUMBER FORTY-FOUR

MARY PATERSON

OR,

THE FATAL ERROR

*

THE ASSOCIATION FOR SCOTTISH LITERARY STUDIES

The Association for Scottish Literary Studies aims to promote the study, teaching and writing of Scottish literature, and to further the study of the languages of Scotland.

To these ends, the ASLS publishes works of Scottish literature (of which this volume is an example); literary criticism and in-depth reviews of Scottish books in *Scottish Literary Review*; short articles, features and news in *ScotLit*; and scholarly studies of language in *Scottish Language*. It also publishes *New Writing Scotland*, an annual anthology of new poetry, drama and short fiction, in Scots, English and Gaelic. ASLS has also prepared a range of teaching materials covering Scottish language and literature for use in schools.

All the above publications are available as a single 'package', in return for an annual subscription. Enquiries should be sent to:

ASLS, Scottish Literature, 7 University Gardens, University of Glasgow, Glasgow G12 8QH. Telephone/fax +44 (0)141 330 5309 or visit our website at **www.asls.org.uk**

A list of Annual Volumes published by ASLS can be found at the end of this book.

THE ASSOCIATION FOR SCOTTISH LITERARY STUDIES

MARY PATERSON

OR,

THE FATAL ERROR

By David Pae

Edited by

Caroline McCracken-Flesher

GLASGOW

2015

*

Published in Great Britain, 2015
by The Association for Scottish Literary Studies
Scottish Literature
University of Glasgow
7 University Gardens
Glasgow G12 8QH

ASLS is a registered charity no. SC006535

www.asls.org.uk

ISBN: 978-1-906841-20-1

A catalogue record for this book
is available from the British Library.

The Association for Scottish Literary Studies acknowledges
support from Creative Scotland towards
the publication of this book.

Typeset by AFS Image Setters Ltd, Glasgow
Printed and bound by Bell & Bain Ltd, Glasgow

Contents

Acknowledgements

This editing project began with my research into Burke and Hare and the retellings of their tale. Thanks for *Mary Paterson*, then, belong first to everyone who assisted with *The Doctor Dissected*, and especially to my partners in any Edinburgh venture, Valerie Ludlow and Penny Fielding. Anyone studying *Mary Paterson* also owes much to pioneering work on David Pae by William Donaldson and Graham Law. The National Library of Scotland, the Edinburgh Room of the Edinburgh Central Library, the British Library and the Dundee Central Library are primary resources for research on Pae. My work benefited greatly from the knowledge of librarians, and those who staff these archives. The Dundee staff, in particular, made the impossible happen not once but many times, finding and making available the most obscure of materials. The Caitlin Long fund in the College of Arts and Sciences helped with the purchase of digitised materials. And for those of us who struggle in archives, access to memorabilia carefully preserved by families is a remarkable gift. I owe sincere thanks to Judith and Anthony Cooke for their hospitality on a cold Dundee day. It is to them and to the DCL that I owe my sense of Pae and Leng as people, not just as historical figures.

My thanks, of course, to the ASLS, including supportive colleagues Jim McCall and Ian Brown, and to Duncan Jones— who patiently listened to my first enthusings about a little-remembered yet fascinating novel, ready for its twenty-first-century rebirth.

Abbreviations

Courant	*Edinburgh Evening Courant*
DCL	Dundee Central Library
DPJ	Dundee *People's Journal*
ECL	Edinburgh Central Library
Mercury	*Caledonian Mercury*
Pae Papers	Pae family papers (Judith and Anthony Cooke)
SDT	*Sheffield Daily Telegraph*
Sharpe	MS collection, ECL YRA 637

Language Resources

CSD	*Concise Scots Dictionary*
DSL	*Dictionary of the Scottish Language*
EDD	*English Dialect Dictionary*
MMS	*Manual of Modern Scots*
OED	*Oxford English Dictionary*, online resource www.oed.com

Permissions

Leng Papers:	Dundee Central Library
Pae Papers:	Judith and Anthony Cooke
Sharpe Collection:	Edinburgh Central Library

Introduction

By the time *Mary Paterson* began publication in 1864, David Pae was already a very successful novelist—though few people knew it. The son of an Amulree miller, who died when he was six weeks old, Pae was a Scottish "lad o' pairts". He progressed from the local school at Coldingham, where his mother had moved, to Edinburgh, where he worked as warehouseman for Thomas Grant, printer, publisher and bookseller. While in Edinburgh, he wrote drama criticism, and had his first piece published in *The Theatre*, which he subsequently edited. He moved on to novels, beginning with the short volume *George Sanford: Or the Draper's Assistant* (1853), and caught major public and commercial attention with *Jessie Melville, or the Double Sacrifice* (first titled *Jessie the Bookfolder*), which ran in the *North Briton* newspaper in 1855.[1] By 1858, the success of *Jessie Melville* was driving serial fiction in Scotland and encouraging Pae's concurrent publication in numerous papers (Law, *Serializing Fiction in the Scottish Press*, 160). *Lucy, the Factory Girl* (also known as *The Factory Girl*) in 1858 ran first in the *North Briton* and earned him another £21 when almost simultaneously serialised in the *Glasgow Times* (Pae, *Lucy*, xv). Despite what seem to be numerous publications in the interim, including a book edition, *Lucy* was considered still a desirable item in 1863, when John Leng of the Dundee *People's Journal* proposed to republish it for ten guineas so long as "the Story shall not appear in any other paper in Scotland while we are publishing it" (John Leng letter, 13 July 1863, Pae Papers). So it was for his talents as a successful—if anonymous—writer of serial fiction for the burgeoning popular newspaper trade that Pae joined Leng's Dundee operation.[2] Eventually, he would edit the spin-off *People's Friend* (as would his son), and he made a further step towards that opportunity

---

1. Biographical information is drawn from the obituary by Pae's colleague Andrew Stewart in the *People's Friend*, 21 May 1884. Law includes this obituary in *Lucy*, 301–06.

2. See Law in Pae, *Lucy*, for a bibliography of Pae's works (345–51).

with *Mary Paterson, or, The Fatal Error*, first published in the weekly *People's Journal* from 1864 to 1865.

Mary Paterson's story was already well known. The scandal of Burke and Hare, who murdered to supply Edinburgh anatomist Robert Knox, had resonated internationally since 1828. It had dominated the newspaper press of late 1828 and early 1829; persisted in extensive trial accounts from publishers Thomas Ireland (*West Port Murders*) and Robert Buchanan (*Trial of William Burke and Helen M'Dougal*), both 1829; thrilled in the London true crime *Murderers of the Close: A Tragedy of Real Life* (1829), and been recently remembered in Alexander Leighton's 1861 *The Court of Cacus: The Story of Burke and Hare*.[3] Pae himself had included a lightly fictionalised Doctor Knox in *Lucy*.[4] Why, then, revisit the tale? From a serial fiction perspective, it could have no surprises, none of the cliffhangers which were a staple of the developing genre and favoured, indeed, in *Lucy*.[5]

Here, it is worth considering the nature of the Dundee *People's Journal*, and the character of David Pae. The *Journal* was overtly a paper for the people. Whatever the true state of education in nineteenth-century Scotland, as William Donaldson says, it seems clear that by mid century, "The gradual invasion of society by the printed word itself prompted the urge to read, and people often taught themselves from whatever came to hand" (*Popular Literature in Victorian Scotland*, 18). In 1855, the removal of the Stamp Tax on newspapers encouraged sales among the poorer but rising classes. Thus the *Journal*, in its first issue, situated itself against "cheap papers which have sprung up since the abolition of the stamp ... utterly unworthy of the intelligence and character of the respectable portion of the working-classes" and aimed "not to write *down*, but to write *up* to the good sense of the working-classes, whose interests will be carefully considered, and a

---

3. For newspapers see McCracken-Flesher, 313–19; for *Murderers of the Close*, see 15, 38, 40, 57, 69, 77; for Leighton, see 64–70.

4. See Pae, *Lucy*, and McCracken-Flesher, 70–75.

5. Wilkie Collins (following Charles Reade) is said to have declared "Make 'em cry, make 'em laugh, make 'em wait—exactly in that order." (See Rachel Ihara, "Novels on the Installment Plan." Diss. City University of New York, 2007, p. 20 n. 6.) Collins's novel *The Woman in White*, published as a serial from 1859 to 1860 in *All the Year Round*, provides numerous examples, as does Pae's own *Lucy* (1858).

considerable portion of space devoted to the discussion of questions in which they are specially concerned" (11). John Leng's socially conscious paper, with its informational articles, letters columns, and dialect opinions from working man "Tammas Bodkin" (pseudonym for weaver and editor William Latto), met, encouraged and directed popular demand through a deliberately improving conversation with its readers. Changes in transportation and the canny exploitation of networks expanded sales far beyond Dundee[6] until, by 1864, such was the *Journal*'s reputation and its role in the rise of working men and women that Garibaldi wrote from Italy lamenting his inability to visit Scotland, and asking Leng to deliver his address to the Working Men's Committee (Garibaldi to Leng, 1 June 1864, DCL).

David Pae perfectly aligned with these circumstances as a literary working man making his way in the world—and with a point to get across. In fact, Pae had quite a few distinct opinions that, early in his career, he hoped to share. As a millenarian, in 1853 he had published his version of musings by Christadelphian John Thomas (McCracken-Flesher, 86–87). This extensive disquisition on how contemporary international politics pointed to the end of times for Pae was both a sublime truth to communicate as widely as possible and an opportunity to make money. He wrote to an emigrant cousin at the end of 1852: "You mention your intention to Speculate, now what would you think of beginning with me, I have at present in the printer's hands, a sixpenny pamphlet, which I believe will sell as well in America as in Britain ... I would like you to risk an edition of 1000, in America, and let you have half of the profit" (to "Dear Tom", 12 December 1852, Pae Papers).

According to extant letters, Pae had equally strong feelings on the Masons (he considered them political and blasphemous) and on intemperance. In 1858 he mocked the "five-act melodrama performed in the Masonic Lodges" as "Vulgar ... and highly profane".[7] Interestingly, his editors had reservations on how such ideas, when published, might impact their cause and, perhaps more importantly, his reputation and sales. To Pae's lengthy attack on the Masons, his publisher cagily replied: "It is very good, but I am afraid that it will call forth

---

6. See Donaldson, 23–24.
7. Pae Papers, "Freemasonry: Its Nature and Character", MS.

a great deal of ill will" (Thomas Grant to David Pae, 20 July 1858, Pae Papers). A few days later, Grant impressed further on his recalcitrant author: "I do not apprehend any personal mischief from the publication of Freemasonry but just a great deal of ill-will, and I am not much more reconciled to it with your name. For I doubt they would attempt to clamour down the merit of your writings which might be injurious to you" (28 July 1858, Pae Papers). That same year J. G. Bertram, Pae's editor at the *North Briton*, advised the author, evidently keen to push temperance as a topic: "The kind of paper you would like the N. B. to become is no doubt a good kind, but my dear friend it wouldn't pay" (6 August 1858, Pae Papers). The author might have understood, for he had been caught out by his enthusiastic communication of John Thomas's sermonising—that worthy accused his admirer of plagiarism, and noted the "Seventy-three thousand sterling six-pences" Pae had gained (McCracken-Flesher, 86).

What to do? To some extent, *Mary Paterson* is the answer, provided by the opportunity of the Dundee *People's Journal*, with its wide circulation among the classes Pae wished most to impact. Alongside the articles on working conditions ("A Calendar Man on Calendar Works", 27 August 1864: 2), politics ("The Best Means of Acquiring Reform", 4 February 1865: 2) or improving discourses ("Meanness", 21 January 1865: 2), readers write in with their thoughts on "Church Psalmody" (19 November 1864: 2) or "The Temperance Club" (24 December 1864: 2). Here the story of Burke and Hare, already notorious as a cycle of murder and drunkenness, could fit right in as a tale at once historical and admonitory. Depending on the incapacity of victims through drink, with the doctor's payments for corpses exacerbating the alcoholism of the perpetrators and the alcoholism in turn driving the quest for money-making victims, it was inherently an argument for temperance.

Yet for all Pae's commitment to worthy ends, what makes *Mary Paterson* such a strong novel, and worth reprinting here, is the degree to which he manages to allow the story to speak for itself. He certainly does thematise in the direction of his interests. Building his newspaper story towards three-decker novel style, he envelopes the short history of Mary Paterson and her unfortunate association with Burke and Hare within Mary's prehistory and the subsequent tale of those she left behind. Resisting spoilers, let me point simply to how Mary's fall from her father's house is a fall into sin but also into drunkenness. Moreover, those whose irresponsibility precipitates or assists her fall share the same vice and ultimately suffer its consequences for themselves. Pae is of course prone to the occasional authorial pointing of a moral. Mary "fell— 'fell by her own consent' " (chapter 1); when one of the book's deceivers ponders marriage and escape from ignominy, Pae opines: "False hope. Bet and Dick ... are steeped in vice; they are subject to no moral principle, the elements of pure enjoyment are not in their natures" (chapter 38). He draws direct parallels between crime and retribution—it is one year after the first murder that Burke is found guilty, and one year after another that he is hanged. And the novel ends with the earnest invocation: "Lead us not into temptation." But Pae for the most part does a remarkable job of energising rather than simply appropriating this twice-told tale—consider how, for all his religious morality, he develops a complex character in the fallen Mary Paterson, and allows the recuperation of Jessie Brown. And by displacing the story before and after, expanding its causes and working out its effects through marginal and invented characters, Pae both defamiliarises the tale and gives it a driving narrative logic. In one striking example, Pae ties the historical figure of a young man inciting the crowd at Burke's execution—a face in the crowd actually remarked upon by the *Caledonian Mercury*—to Mary's fictional lost love, James. Then he ties James forward through love to Lizzie, the forlorn sweetheart of another actual victim, Joe the miller. Similarly, he intensifies his tale by giving the Grays, who did in reality expose the crime and do so here, a backstory in love, drunkenness and loss that echoes the experience of Joe and Lizzie.

Such loose relationships woven into tight thematic parallels point towards melodrama. Pae (anonymously) had quite a reputation in the genre already, his novels being full of lost children, usurped inheritances, Newgate criminality and stunning self-sacrifice. But on the one hand, Pae himself draws attention to coincidence through his characters and as narrator—note Bet's amazement at meeting James Crawford twenty years after the story's main events, and Pae's deliberate invocation of a justice so coincidental it is poetic. And on the other hand, in his newspaper introduction (cut from the

1885 book), Pae engaged current biases about the sensation
novel, arguing a case both literary and religious that "when
sensation novels are so popular, and so vehemently denounced
... the narrative should be reproduced of deeds so utterly surpassing in atrocity anything described in nature, if for no
other purpose than to show that the sensation novels of the
present day do not present such gross exaggerations of human
wickedness as their decriers assert" (Preface). These deeds,
he thought, for their very reality needed to be told, "*provided
they carry faithfully and prominently their lessons with them*".

The realities of the Burke and Hare story, however far they
align with melodrama (usually through the leering Hare),
indeed echo powerfully into Pae's fictive past and on into his
recuperative future. Lively characterisation and astute use of
Scots and Irish dialect help—though the dialect energises
mostly lower-class and minor characters, as per contemporary
convention. Characters swear liberally for Victorian times.
And Pae gives an unflinching description of contemporary
sexuality. The Burke and Hare ménage lie down "promiscuously" after a binge and Mary's fallen life is expressively rendered—something so shocking to one Yorkshire audience
that their local paper announced "We have been compelled
to withdraw the story ... in consequence of the unusual sensational character of some of the incidents, and the repeated
remonstrances of our subscribers."[8] Pae's characters are vocal,
colourful and human in their contradictions. Drawn widely
from Scotland in the story's first movement, then wound
tightly together into the reality of Burke and Hare, only to be
dispersed again and entwined once more as their various fictional tales play out, they both entice and challenge audience
investment.

The success of Pae's strategies in reaching a large audience
is attested to by circulation figures from the *People's Journal*.
Every Saturday, the weekly touted its previous issue's accomplishments in sales. By its own reporting, in the week before

---

8. Reported in Alexander Andrews (ed.), *The Newspaper Press: A Medium of
Intercommunication Between All Parties Associated with Newspapers and a Record of
Journalistic Lore* (London: E. W. Allen, 1867), 177. The matter seems to have been
a *succès de scandale*, for it is also reported in the *Dundee Courier and Argus*, 28 May
1867, and *Aberdeen Journal*, 29 May 1867.

Mary Paterson commenced publication, the *Journal* sold 61,200 copies—already, be it noted, a substantial circulation.[9] By the last number, sales figures had attained 85,670. The *Journal* was on an upward trajectory—but it seems that Mary, in her life, demise and next-generation recuperation, may have actively helped.

Whether it was for the sexuality or the swearing (both routinely dropped in the 1885 novel), the melodrama or the vibrant characters, Pae's story caught the popular imagination. Upon Mary's death, one reader of the *Journal* circulated a poetic response that concluded:

> In grief she went to Edinburgh,
>   And lived a life of shame,
> Until that murderers, Burke and Hare,
>   Extinguished her name.
>
> All ye young maidens beware
>   How youth's gay moments fly;
> And you should have yourselves prepared,
>   *Ere* you in dust do ly.[10]

Perhaps now, as Pae had hoped in the newspaper preface, through this ASLS version *Mary Paterson* can once more exercise its "power to fascinate and instruct".

---

9. Donaldson tracks the *Journal*'s rise from a claimed circulation of 7,000 per week in 1858 to a broader regional sale of 58,000 at the start of 1864 (23–26). Within two years, it was at 100,000. In 1861, the census showed the Scottish population at approximately 3,050,000 adults. For comparison, in the 1860s Dickens's *All the Year Round* averaged 100,000, peaking at Christmas to 300,000. See www.victorianweb.org/periodicals/ayr.html

10. Dundee *People's Journal*, 8 October 1864. Mary had died in the 1 October issue.

Textual Essay

Mary Paterson, or, The Fatal Error is extant in four forms: the first serial publication, which ran in John Leng's Dundee *People's Journal* from 9 July 1864 to 22 April 1865; a serial publication that ran in the *Sheffield Daily Telegraph*, edited by Leng's brother, W. C. Leng, from 28 October 1865 to 4 August 1866; an illustrated book published in London by Fred Farrah, 1866; and an 1885, posthumous, book version published in Dundee and London by John Leng, in association with John Menzies of Edinburgh and Glasgow, Westwood & Son in Cupar, Fife, and W. & W. Lindsay in Aberdeen. The DPJ (missing dates 17 September 1864, 25 February 1865 and 8 April 1865—chapters 11, 35 and 41) and final novel are available at the Dundee Central Library; the Sheffield newspaper and the Farrah edition are in the British Library.

All four versions have been consulted to derive this edition, but it is based on the first newspaper publication supplemented for the missing dates by the Aberdeen, Banff, and Kincardine edition of the *People's Journal*, collated against the 1885 novel (by Juxta). This choice was determined by the fact that we have no paper trail for author revisions between versions. The comparison, then, indicates most reliably a shift in editorial perceptions and public sensibilities between the relatively racy serial with its 1866 reprint, and the more restrained 1885 novel.

The introduction to this edition assesses the substantive differences between the newspaper and the 1885 book.

For the most part, chapters are aligned between the two main stages of publication. However, in two places they are out of step: newspaper chapters 14 and 15 (maintained in 1866) are partly merged in the 1885 book, which starts its chapter 15 at the break in the newspaper chapter. The newspaper's last three chapters are rearranged in the novel such that what takes four chapters in the 1864 newspaper takes two in the 1885 book—a change also visible in the *Sheffield Daily Telegraph* and Farrah editions. The newspaper's chapters 40 and 41, "Happiness at Kirkton" and "Triumph", merge as chapter 40, "Triumph", in 1866 and 1885, with only 1866

indicating a previous break; chapters 42 and 43, "After
Twenty Years" and "The Fate of Hare—Conclusion", merge
as chapter 41, "After Twenty Years—The Fate of Hare—
Conclusion", with no indication of a break in 1866 or 1885
(but half a sentence is excised in both novels that points to a
concluding newspaper instalment: "We shall, in our turn,
relate it to the reader in our own words, and it will be found
to form a natural conclusion to the tale"). Three serial chapters that break between movements of the story show no
breaks in 1866 and 1885—chapters 4, 14, 17, though 14
breaks in 1866—and one uninterrupted newspaper chapter is
broken in the later book—chapter 40. Chapters 24 and 25
make up one number of the story for the newspaper. And, in
an indication of serial publication, chapters get longer around
Christmas. Pae tended to huddle up his endings—his *North
Briton* editor, J. G. Bertram, complained when he abruptly
wrapped up the 1858–59 novel *Lucy, the Factory Girl*, leaving
the newspaper without copy—so perhaps not surprisingly, the
final chapters of *Mary Paterson* are short (just over a column
for 41, 42, 43, and right at a column for 40).[1] Pages 385 and
386 are misbound in the 1885 book.

Given that the story starts as a newspaper serial, and ends
as a book almost twenty years later, many of the small differences between versions are surely due to house styles and compositors' preferences. For instance, generally, the newspaper
hyphenates nouns such as fire-side, key-hole, the book less so;
generally the book hyphenates phrases like "half-a-mile",
"one-and-six", and the newspaper does not. Yet both versions
favour to-night, to-morrow, to-day, and no system seems to
maintain throughout for either text. Indeed, in both we can
occasionally see the effect of shifting compositors—at times
one is comma light, the other heavy, but then the situation
reverses; one clearly favours "Dr.", another Dr, but Doctor
and doctor are also in play, and the four-way squabble can go
on within a chapter in the newspaper as much as it can prove

---

1. James G. Bertram to David Pae, 6 April 1859, Pae Papers. Bertram complained: "This is very strange, after the conversation I had with you about a
fortnight ago when you said that the story would last for at least two months &
probably longer. You know so well how necessary it is that a new story should
be a good way on before the old is dropped."

a tussle between the 1860s and 1880s versions of the tale. Katy and Lizzy vary in spelling within numbers of the newspaper; the old woman from Gilmerton is "rale weel" as she anticipates Burke's "rael Irish potheen" (though dialect may play a role here). And on one occasion, a new newspaper compositor proves unable to keep characters' names straight, confusing Tom with Dick (chapter 31) and Tibb with Bet (chapter 34). Some naming errors (Bell for Bet) persist from newspaper through to the 1885 book (Chapter 27).

Still, there are some clear trends; the early editions prefer "aint" and "wont" to "ain't" and "won't", and they steadfastly write: "have'nt", "would'nt", "is'nt" and "its", not "it's". The 1885 book chooses "grey", not "gray", eschews italics, and doesn't much like dashes. Accents and dialects are best maintained in the newspaper, and these too have distinct flavours: when rendering Irish accents, the newspaper prefers "ould" and "tould", the book goes for "owld", "towld" and "cowld". But here too there is some variability. For instance neither generation of compositors is able to maintain for long "tae" against "to".

One consistent and surprising difference arises in paragraphing. Contrary to what we might expect, the newspaper runs long paragraphs, whereas the 1885 book breaks long sections repeatedly. What is at stake here? Letters suggest that Pae was paid by the task and by sales, rather than by the line, so padding the text by excessive paragraphing would make no difference to the author.[2] But why paragraph the novel so much? A question to ponder.

An answer may lie in small but persistent substantive changes: "shocked extremely" becomes "shocked", "most fatal" becomes "fatal"—clearly, there is some tidying up and streamlining in process here. Since, however, there are more losses than gains to meaning by such changes—a raw and

---

2. An agreement between Thomas Grant and David Pae for weekly numbers of *The Merchant's Daughter; or Love and Mammon* is negotiated at "3 of a number if under 4,000 and 15/– additional for every thousand ... The author to receive payment monthly" (Grant to Pae, July 1856, Pae Papers). A plan for the novel carries a word count on the back (1 July 1856, Pae Papers). For *The Heiress of Wellwood*, Pae received from the *North Briton* "One pound one Shilling per week—payment weekly—the Copy right of the tale belonging to the Author" (J. G. Bertram to David Pae, 5 November 1859, Pae Papers).

dangerous "she-tiger" in 1885 becomes a clichéd "tigeress"
(chapter 12)—the short paragraphs may stand as a program-
matic but uninspired attempt to energise the text in line with
the unimaginative line editing.

It is for these reasons, in the end, that the present volume
chooses the newspaper text. Bowdlerised for the 1885 reader-
ship, with its sexual references and oaths excised, when
addressed to the working class and Scottish educated audience
in the Dundee *People's Journal*, the story races along, given
character even by its imperfections. In headlong paragraphs
not stopping for a comma, leaping ahead across dashes, intensified by italics, and raw with dialect, Pae tells his unvarnished
tale.

This ASLS volume silently emends a very few distinct mistakes: errors in character names are corrected; Mary's fear of
"his" father is corrected to fear of her own, as makes sense in
context; a dropped ! is reinstated; typos ("up-paralleled")
are corrected; variations on —" (interrupted speeches) are
standardised; names are regularised (daft Jamie is corrected to
the more frequent Daft Jamie); spellings not a matter of dialect are standardised; and ;" becomes "; in all cases. Readers
can thus experience the novel largely as it first came into
nineteenth-century hands—missing only the smell of fresh
newsprint and the unwieldiness of the period's massive papers.

MARY PATERSON

OR,

THE FATAL ERROR

A Story of the Burke & Hare Murders

(By the Author of " The Factory Girl.")

Preface

Thirty-six years ago—in the month of November 1828—Edinburgh and the whole of Scotland was thrown into a state of the most unparalleled excitement by the discovery of a series of atrocious and brutal murders which had been perpetrated in a house situated in one of the dark and dirty closes of the Metropolis. For some months before, several people had at short intervals gone amissing, and no trace could be had of them. In a most sudden and mysterious manner they disappeared from the streets, and were never again heard of by their anxious and distracted friends. So great was the commotion and terror caused by these disappearances that the idea generally prevailed that an organised band existed in the city for the purpose of kidnapping the inhabitants for purposes too horrible to be even imagined. But when the truth did come out, it was so appallingly worse than anything that had been conceived that the whole country was petrified with horror, and the names of Burke and Hare became a terror in every district. Those who are old enough to remember the time will readily testify that a sensation equal to that which the discovery of these murders produced has never occurred since, and we doubt much if it has its parallel in any past age; while at the present day, after the lapse of nearly forty years, the names of Burke and Hare are invested with horror, though the nature and details of their crimes are but partially known to this generation.[1]

In the following story the history of these crimes will be fully embodied. It seems fitting that at a time when sensation novels are so popular, and so vehemently denounced by certain critics as monstrous conceptions, utterly untrue to nature, that the narrative should be reproduced of deeds so utterly surpassing in atrocity anything described in nature, if for no

---

1. In the course of a year Burke and Hare, abetted by Hare's wife and Burke's mistress Helen McDougal, committed sixteen murders and sold the corpses to Dr Knox the anatomist. See Lisa Rosner for an extensive account, and her website burkeandhare.com. The *Sheffield Daily Telegraph* serialisation of 1865 sensibly adjusts the opening phrase to "thirty-seven years ago".

other purpose than to show that the sensation novels of the present day do not present such gross exaggerations of human wickedness as their decriers assert. In fact, after such atrocities as the Burke and Hare murders, it is impossible for any romance writer to depict either fabulous or exaggerated deeds of human crime; and, *provided they carry faithfully and prominently their lessons with them*, the production and popularity of stories of this character is not to be deplored. Human nature is not to be improved by "concealing its worst deformities". Let these be presented; not, certainly, in such a way as to invest the tale with a mere morbid fascination, but as Shakespeare, and Milton, and the great masters represented them—with power to fascinate and instruct.[2]

This object we shall keep carefully in view in the present story. There will be not a little in it of what Burns designates as the "horrible and awfu' ";[3] but all those portions, the reader will bear in mind, are strictly *historical*—due not to the fancy or heated imagination of the writer, but to absolute fact, which is not only incapable of being exaggerated, but which can never be described with a full measure of truth or accuracy. We shall endeavour, however, not to let these dark deeds lie in their native darkness. We shall bring them to the light to show to what lengths man can go in wickedness, and to what a fearful extent temptation may have power over him.

There is also a good deal of pathos and beauty, and tender affection, surrounding the murderous history; for evil always brings out its opposite, and we shall do our best to illustrate these finer and more attractive traits. So that if we can but

---

2. Sensation fiction's most famous examples had just been published: Wilkie Collins's *The Woman in White*, 1860; Mrs Henry Wood's *East Lynne*, 1861; and Mary Elizabeth Braddon's *Lady Audley's Secret*, 1862. As *Mary Paterson* began publication, the *Christian Remembrancer* considered the "indispensable point" of such novels to "contain something abnormal and unnatural; something that induces ... a sort of thrill". A sensation novel "stimulates a vulgar curiosity, weakens the established rules of right and wrong, touches ... upon things illicit ... and draws a wholly false picture of life". Unsigned review, "Our Female Sensation Novelists", *Christian Remembrancer* 46.121 (July 1864), 209–36; see 211 and 236.

3. From Robert Burns, "Tam o' Shanter", describing the artifacts upon the altar at the witches' sabbath: "mair o' horrible and awfu', / Which ev'n to mention wad be unlawfu'." See *Burns Poems and Songs*, ed. James Kinsley (Oxford: Oxford University Press, 1969), 446, lines 141–42.

realise the ideal we have set before us, we have great hope
that the story will contain the elements of real good; and while
affording a melancholy testimony to the degradation, the
cruelty, and brutality to which our race can descend, that it
will also contain lessons of important instruction, and scenes
of fairest beauty, to prove the more glorious truth that man's
origin is divine, and his true aspirations heavenward.[4]

4. This preface does not appear in the 1885 edition. The Dundee *People's
Journal* for 9 July 1864 gives the preface, then chapter 1; the 1866 novel changes
the preamble to "Thirty-eight years ago", adjusts tense to express the novel's
completion, and dates the Preface "May, 1866".

CHAPTER I

THE HOUSEHOLD AT BRAESIDE—AN OLD STORY OF SELFISHNESS AND SIN

A more respectable or a better respected man than old Andrew Paterson did not live in or near the village of Kirkton. This little Scotch village is to be seen from the battlements of Stirling Castle by any one who looks in a south-westerly direction. Being very near the centre of Scotland, and in close proximity to scenes consecrated for ever to the memory of the nation's struggle for independence, many of its inhabitants were strongly tinged with the nobler Scottish characteristics—religious and national.[1] Andrew Paterson was a man of this stamp. Living near to Bannockburn on the one hand, and the moors and mountains where the Covenanters fought and fell on the other, he was deeply imbued with that spirit of staunch stern independence which caused the men of these times to stand out so bravely for their rights, and dare with equal heroism the invader and the persecutor. Had Andrew lived in these troublous years, he would assuredly have been a follower of Wallace and Bruce, or a houseless Covenanter, worshipping God according to his conscience in the solitary glen, or on the lonely mountain top under the midnight stars. But it was Andrew's fortune to live in a more peaceful age, when the sturdy Scottish spirit was free to develop itself after its own fashion, and hold a creed and maintain a worship according to its own liking. After the most strait sect of his religion, Andrew lived a Seceder. He was an elder in the quaint old-fashioned burgher meeting-house at the end of the village, and at the time our story opens had held this office for

---

1. Braeside and Kirkton (and later, Mount Cairn) are used as generic Scottish names, signifying a hillside, a town with a church, and a hill with a stone marker. Stirling Castle was a favoured home for Scotland's monarchy from the time of Alexander I to the Union of the Crowns in 1603. Stirling is strategically and symbolically important, but not geographically central. Three miles north of the castle, William Wallace defeated the English army at the Battle of Stirling Bridge (1297). Three miles south, King Robert the Bruce defeated England's King Edward II at the Battle of Bannockburn (1314).

nearly forty years, no one being able to remember a single Sabbath day on which he was absent from ordinances.[2]

He was an old man now, and his hair was thin and grey, nevertheless he was hale and hearty, of fresh ruddy complexion, and full countenance. He had never known sickness, and the chief trouble he had experienced was in the death of his wife, which sad event occurred long years ago, and had for a length of time made his home desolate. The neighbours thought he would have married again, if only for the sake of his little infant daughter; but Andrew declined to put another in the place of her he had loved so fondly, and took a distant relative to be his housekeeper, under whose care and his own his only child was reared.

His circumstances in life were of a very comfortable character. The little farm which he cultivated was his own. It was not large, but it was sufficient to keep what is termed "a rough house,"[3] and to enable Andrew to save a small sum every year, which he placed in the hands of Mr Leech, the lawyer.[4] By his neighbours Andrew was looked upon as extremely "well to do," though he was of too reserved a nature to speak of his circumstances to any one, and nobody could make so free with him as to ask him concerning them.

For Andrew was somewhat austere and forbidding in his manner, as Scotchmen of his stamp are apt to be. He was neither communicative nor demonstrative, but most just and upright in all his dealings, and even charitable in his own way, though

---

2. Covenanters took their name from the religious and political National Covenant of 1638, and the Solemn League and Covenant of 1643. They were strict Presbyterians. At the Battle of Stirling (1648), Covenanters in rebellion against the Scottish Parliament and aligned with Cromwell attacked Stirling. They were routed in a skirmish. Presbyterianism was eventually established in Scotland, but the Restoration brought government back into Church decisions. As a result, a number of groups seceded from the Church of Scotland, starting in 1733. The schism of 1747 turned on whether to swear support of established religion. Burghers took the oath; Anti-Burghers did not. Burghers and Anti-Burghers both split into "Auld Licht" (conservative, holding to the Solemn League and Covenant) and "New Licht" (more liberal) factions at the turn of the nineteenth century.

3. CSD gives "a guid rouch house", meaning well supplied "with good plain fare".

4. Mr Leech the lawyer: this name places the lawyer in a tradition of stock characters and caricature revived in the comic and sentimental novel (consider Dickens's Wackford Squeers, the schoolmaster at Dotheboys Hall).

little country village, where everybody's affairs were discussed by everybody. The reason of this is easy of explanation. The place of meeting was a wood at one side of Andrew Paterson's little farm. The wood was on the confines of Captain Grahame's property, and as no one had a right to visit it, or to go in that direction at all, the stolen interviews of the lovers were held all unseen by human eye. They took place at an hour when honest old Andrew was enjoying his well-earned repose. He never failed to retire to rest at an early hour in the evening, and deemed that the other two members of his household were in bed like himself. Sometimes they were, but sometimes not; for when Mary went to meet her lover the indulgent Peggy remained up to re-admit her without noise.

Thus it was that the mischief was accomplished—a mischief which must soon come to light, as Mary had for some time sadly and anxiously comprehended. Her gaiety and thoughtlessness had by this time received a check, for now that the consequence of her guilt was in a slow but sure manner bringing that guilt to public knowledge, the shame it must entail, and the awful severity of her father's godly ire, were forcing her to deep regret and sorrowful reflection.

As yet no one—not even Peggy—suspected her situation, though the time was coming very near when she would become a mother, and concealment was no longer possible. Her confidence in Duncan was as great as ever. To her repeated solicitations for the fulfilment of his promise he had always a plausible excuse ready, and her devotion to him was so great that, for his sake, and for the securing of his interests, she was ready to make any sacrifice.

Had she known the truth; had she known what his interests really were, according to his own nature, she would doubtless have acted differently. Could she have but got a glimpse into the black corrupt bosom on which she so fondly reclined, and seen the rottenness and deceit that there abode, she must have fled from him in horror and despair. But to her he was as yet all fair and honourable, and though present circumstances prevented him from giving her the honoured name of wife, she was ready to wait till he was free and personally independent, a position which he assured her he should reach in a year, or two years at the most.

But what was the truth as regarded this base deceiver? He was betrothed to another, and had been so all the time that

he did not forget to accompany the charity with moral and spiritual advice. When we said that he was respectable, and greatly respected, we went to the full boundary line of truth. It would be too great a stretch of statement to say that he was loved, for he wanted those softer, tenderer, and kindlier qualities which could draw towards him the affections of his neighbours.

His daughter Mary was the most beautiful girl in the village, aye, or within many miles of it. Her form was symmetry itself—her features faultless; and she possessed a gracefulness in all her movements which was the unstudied attribute of nature. Not that she was by any means unconscious of her beauty. She had been told of it too frequently, and by too many people for that; especially had she heard her loveliness extolled, almost daily, and in the most unqualified terms, by Peggy M'Naughton,[5] her father's housekeeper and her own feminine guardian from childhood. Peggy's pride in, and fondness for, her master's only child knew no bounds; and it was her custom, unknown to Andrew, to indulge her in many things which the strict notions of the elder would not have countenanced. So far as matters fell under his own eye, Andrew held Mary under the tight reins of discipline, but she was necessarily left much to the care of Peggy, who did not approve at all of the old man's severity, and encouraged by all means in her power the natural gaiety and waywardness of Mary's temper and disposition.

Under the influence of these extreme modes of management, Mary grew up beautiful, high-spirited, and self-willed. She received a plain, yet good education. Peggy wanted her to learn the modern accomplishments of music and dancing, but Andrew sternly set his face against those profanations. Nevertheless, though wholly untaught, Mary could sing and dance too, and, with Peggy's connivance, had many opportunities of indulging in these pastimes, of both of which she was passionately fond.

Of course, a girl of Mary Paterson's attractions had many admirers among the village rustics. One only was, however, seriously considered to be her sweetheart, and that was James

---

5. M'Naughton: Mac and Mc (an abbreviation) were commonly represented as M' in nineteenth-century Scottish texts. Henry Beadnell's *Guide to Typography* (London: F. Bowering, 1859) states that the inverted comma "is used in place of a *c*, in proper names having the prefix *Mac*, contracted into *Mc* or *M'* ... where ... no space intervenes between the two parts of the word" (1.172).

Crawford, a neighbouring farmer's son. That this youth loved Mary with all the ardour of his nature there could be no doubt, and, being in all moral and social respects a suitable suitor for her hand, Andrew looked favourably on his attentions, and let it be understood that his consent to the marriage would not be withheld.

Mary herself did not say much about the matter. James Crawford was a solid, sensible young man, and of his fondness for herself she had ample proof. She also "liked" him well enough, and for a considerable time was kind and frank to him, and by her conduct gave him and others to understand that she would by and by become his wife.

Gradually, however, a change came over her; a coldness towards James, a shunning of his society, and a marked dislike to speak in any way of a marriage between them. James noticed this change at once, and asked her to explain it; but she would not, and laughingly asked him if she had not a right to change her mind. Her father did not remark it for some time—not indeed till James spoke of it, and then he rebuked her for her levity and fickleness, but failed to elicit any explanation, or to effect a change in her behaviour. Perhaps the only one who knew anything of its meaning was Peggy M'Naughton, but Peggy was careful not to let her knowledge be suspected.

Peggy did know a little, but only a very little portion of the truth, and did not even dream of the grievous error which by this time Mary had committed.

Vain, giddy, and thoughtless, the girl had given her heart to one who moved in a higher station, who had been smitten by her charms, and who had wooed her clandestinely for the basest of all purposes. Flattered by his attentions, deceived by his promises, beguiled by his protestations, and seduced by his arts, she fell—"fell by her own consent."[6] What can be said in extenuation of her folly, her crime? Not much. After all that could be said, it was crime and folly still. Nevertheless, it is crime and folly which is as old as humanity. Mary

Paterson was very young, very unsuspicious, and very t[rust]ing; and of these things her heartless seducer took full ad[van]tage, and through them ultimately effected her ruin.

He was young—young in years, but old in the knowl[edge] of sin. He had been two sessions at the Edinburgh Unive[rsity] and there had this knowledge been acquired. There had [the] purity and simplicity of his nature been effectually remo[ved] there had he been initiated into many mysteries of iniq[uity] and long before he was ready to graduate professionally [he] had graduated in sin.

The name of this destroyer of female innocence and bl[ighter] of the hopes and reputation of Mary Paterson was Du[ncan] Grahame, the only son of Captain Grahame, a retired [mili]tary officer who resided at Mount Cairn, in the neighb[our]hood of Kirkton, and at no very great distance from Brae[head] the peaceful and happy home of Andrew Paterson—pea[ceful] and happy till the destroyer came and made it desolate.

The youth was a medical student, sure of an appoint[ment] in the army or navy, through his father's influence, whe[n he] had received his diploma; and being connected with a fa[mily] of distinction, his friends, and he himself, looked forward [to a] high and brilliant career.[7]

His intrigue with Mary Paterson was on his side, and f[rom] the very first, of a dishonourable character. He mean[t to] seduce her, and he meant nothing more. The idea of marr[ying] with her was something he laughed at, but her excee[ding] beauty excited his determination to possess her. To succee[d in] his base undertaking, he required to assume a mask of hy[poc]risy and falsehood, and he simulated so well an ardent [love] and devotion that the unsuspecting girl, believing all, cam[e to] her ruin.

So secret were these interviews that the intimacy betw[een] them was not suspected even by the prying gossips of [the]

---

6. In early Calvinism, the elect are made so not by their own worth, but by God's grace. Yet God does not foreordain. Paradoxically, reprobate and elect voluntarily pursue the path for which they are chosen. Pae, however, did subscribe to the idea of general atonement—though characters like Burke and Hare test that notion.

---

7. Since the mid eighteenth century, Edinburgh had been a leader in m[edi]cal teaching. However, the profession was not regulated in behaviour, trai[ning] or practice until the 1850s, and it was only with the development of a[naes]thesia and antisepsis that doctors started to cure people and gain resp[ect] about 1865. Medical students were notorious for "immorality", inferred [from] their heroics as bodysnatchers and their necessary carnal knowledge. [Alex]ander Leighton's *The Court of Cacus* (1861) had recently described this ki[nd of] student.

he was engaged in seducing her. Lucy Grahame was his father's ward, and his own half-cousin. She was an heiress, and it had been early arranged by the Captain that she and Duncan should be united. The marriage would keep the family property in the family name, and would besides give to Duncan a good social position. This arrangement was one to which the young people themselves readily consented. Lucy Grahame was a proud girl, and too strong-minded to fall into the weakness of love. She liked her cousin Duncan, and he being as good as herself in point of family, the union was, in her eyes, quite suitable.

Duncan himself was only too ready to vault into a position such as a marriage with his wealthy cousin would command. He had no notion of foregoing his profession; on the contrary he was much in love with it. It was, in fact, the only thing he was in love with, and he had an ambition to distinguish himself in it. But at the same time he knew that an independence otherwise would assist him not a little in climbing the ladder, and he threw no obstacle in the way of his father's matrimonial proposition.

So Lucy and Duncan were betrothed. This also was unknown to the good folks of Kirkton. Lucy resided with a female relative in a distant part of the country. She was unknown in the neighbourhood of Mount Cairn, therefore the engagement between her and the young student was unheard of.

This was fortunate for Duncan's designs against Mary Paterson, but unfortunate for Mary herself. The knowledge of his engagement with Lucy would have saved her from her guilt, and the misery and awful fate which followed; and instead of becoming what she did become, she might have remained true to James Crawford, and become settled in the comfortable position of a Scottish farmer's wife. But the voice of the serpent only was heard, and the lie of the serpent believed.[8]

The seducer was little less alarmed than his victim at the prospect of discovery. Not that he minded either the shame or the sin, but he dreaded the consequences as regarded his engagement with Lucy Grahame. Lucy's proud spirit, he

---

8. Pae makes Mary a new Eve.

knew, would never brook the insult implied in his intrigue with another; and if she came to know of it previous to their marriage, that marriage, he was well assured, would never take place.

This was a catastrophe which must be avoided at whatever risk, and Duncan's chief care now was directed to the manner by which the secret was to be kept. His task was a difficult one. He had Mary still to deceive—an easy matter hitherto, but it might be hard to persuade her to keep the secret as concerned him when shame and scorn had overtaken herself. His influence over her, he knew, was very great, and he trusted to that influence to induce her to go to another part of the country, where he was aware he could obtain shelter for her with a woman, who, for payment, would nurse her, and keep silence for the present.

For the present. It was only for the present that he cared; only until his marriage with Lucy was over. Then the discovery might take place without damaging him in the only way he dreaded being damaged. True, Lucy might storm and be furious; but what of that? The fault was a pre-nuptial one, not to be made anything of in a legal sense; and as for the domestic disturbance to be created, he trusted to time to get over that. For the present, however, concealment was of the very utmost importance. All his prospects in life depended upon it, therefore every possible means must be taken to preserve his character in the eyes of his father and of his betrothed.

Of course Duncan Grahame was a youth utterly selfish. A man who would betray a girl as he had betrayed Mary Paterson can be nothing but selfish. He acts for the gratification of his own pleasure, and for that alone. The consideration of the feelings and circumstances of another never intrudes. Thus Grahame consulted his own interests alone, and cared not though these were to be secured by blighting the young life of the unsuspicious being who had so fatally trusted him. Her beauty having bloomed for his unholy gratification, it might now wither and be trampled under foot. Her anguish, her misery, her despair were nothing to him. Her after fate might be as wretched as a broken reputation and a cruel world could make it; but if he, the author of her ruin, could escape evil consequences, that was all he cared for.

Knowing that but a very short time remained till discovery

became inevitable, and that the sharp eyes of Mary's neighbours might detect her situation any day, he found means of
conveying a note to her, asking her to meet him in the wood
at the old trysting place, on a certain evening and at a certain
hour. His purpose was to induce her to quit her father's roof,
and make a secret journey with him to the residence of the
woman he knew of, where she would remain till after she had
become a mother; and in the interval he would do his utmost
to celebrate his marriage with Lucy. After which, he would
be free to lay aside his mask, and show himself to Mary in his
true character as a vile, base, heartless deceiver, letting her
understand the depth of hopeless ruin into which she had been
brought.

Mary received his note in safety, read it with sparkling eyes,
and burned it according to his directions, but not before she
had covered it with many kisses.

"To-morrow night," she murmured, with a happy smile.
"Oh, I shall see my darling to-morrow night!"

CHAPTER II

THE ELDER AT HOME—THE BETRAYER AND HIS VICTIM—MARY'S DEPARTURE FROM HER FATHER'S HOUSE

Andrew Paterson, the douce, grave, serious, and pious elder sat in the sanded parlour of his little cottage of Braeside, poring over the Bible by the somewhat dim light of an oil lamp. He was alone. The usual evening worship of the family was over. Peggy and Mary were supposed to have retired to rest, and Andrew, as was his wont, tarried by himself to study a portion of the contents of the Divine Book, which has been an exhaustless mine of strength, comfort, direction, guidance, and consolation to pious souls in all generations.

The door was on the latch, not having been locked for the night, this being the last thing the old man did ere entering his solitary sleeping chamber, that had been solitary to him now for nearly twenty years. Solitary, and yet sacred to the memory of much deep and holy spiritual communion; for the God-fearing man, though alone was yet not alone, the *Father* being with him.

As he sat with his venerable head bent over the open volume, a slow and light footstep came to the outer door, the latch was lifted, and some one entered. So deeply absorbed was Andrew in his meditations, that the noise, which was indeed but slight, did not disturb him, nor was his attention even caught by the quiet appearance in his chamber of a young man dressed in hodden grey,[1] who, the moment he saw how Andrew was occupied, took off his bonnet[2] and silently regarded him.

This youth had a broad, sunbrowned brow, the heat of summer (for it was now close upon autumn) had made his honest, intelligent countenance swarthy, as through the long sultry days he had toiled industriously in his father's fields. It was a countenance honest, as we have said, yea, honesty was

---

1. Coarse homespun woollen fabric, undyed.
2. Brimless woollen cap; particularly Scottish.

stamped upon it with a force and power which could not be mistaken, the features were so open, and the eye, albeit at the moment somewhat sad, was clear, its glance being indicative of the consciousness of rectitude.

There was a sadness on the youth's face, however; and as he stood contemplating the aged student of the best of all Books, he, without knowing it, gave utterance to a heavy sigh.

This sigh the old man heard, and he slowly raised his head, manifestly not a little surprised, when his calm eye fell on the form of the youth.

"Jimes Crawford, is that you?" he asked, in a tone of astonishment.

"Deed is it, Andrew; and nae doot ye wadna be expectin' tae see me here at this untimeous oor," answered the young man, coming slowly forward and taking a seat at the other side of the little white wooden table.

"Na, Jimes, lad, I wasna expectin' ye. I hope there's naething wrang up bye at the Knowe?"

"Oh, naething ava. They are a' sleepin' there by this time; but I hae come doon tae speak tae ye aboot Mary. I sair dreed that Mary disna want tae sweetheart me ony mair; for o' late she has been anxious tae haud oot o' my road,[3] and whan I chance tae find her alane, and speak tae her in the auld langsyne way, she shakes her heid and rins awa', wi a blush on her face and the tear in her e'e."

"I'm concerned aboot that, Jimes," returned Andrew. "I wad fain believe that it's naething mair than yer ain imagination; but, sooth tae say, I hae noticed a change in her mysel', though I ne'er said a word aboot it, thinkin' it tae be but a young lassie's glaikitness. Mary, puir thing, is no jist so douce as I wad like, and hisna had a mother's counsels tae guide her. I hae dune my best, Jimes, tae bring her up in the richt way, but a faither canna dae a mither's pairt."

"Mary is everything that's guid," put in the young man, as the colour deepened on his brown cheek, and his round blue eye sparkled brightly. "She's merry, nae doot, and lichthearted, but I like tae see that in a lassie. Tell me this,

---

3. Stay out of my way.

Andrew, if ye can. Dae ye think there's—there's ony ither that she has taken up wi'?"

"Ony ither, Jimes!" repeated the old man. "Na, ye can keep yersel' easy on that score. There's no a lad in Kirkton or roond aboot that she muckle as speaks tae."

"Then maybe there's a hope o' her comin' round again," remarked the youth. "Ye see, Andrew, dearly as I lo'e her, I wadna force mysel' upon her if she didna like me. She's the only ane that ever I could marry, and a sair job it would be for me if the lang courtship breaks up; but—better that than waur."

"Ye are a sensible lad, Jimes," returned Andrew; "an' there's no anither in the parish that I wad like tae see my dochter married tae but yoursel'. And I hope and pray that the lassie hersel' will turn into the same way o' thinkin'. I could speak to her and advise her. I wadna like tae gang ony farrer than that. Some parrants order and command in a case o' that kind; but I think that's clean contrary to what is richt —and—"

"So it is—so it is," said the youth, hastily. "If Mary tak's me, it maun be oot o' her ain free will. Muckle as I want tae hae her for my wife, a forced marriage can never be a happy ane."

"There can be no happiness where there's no a blessin' frae abune," said Andrew, as he solemnly cast his eyes upward. "It's oors for tae wush and tae pray, Jimes; and my wushes and prayers are that you and Mary may be man and wife; but if it's sae ordained that it's otherwise tae be, we maun bend without a murmur tae His will."

"I wad try, Andrew, I would try," said James, with a sigh; "but I doot it would be a hard fecht."

A breathless listener at the outside of the half-open door had caught nearly every word of this conversation. From her little casement above, Mary had seen James approach the house, and wondering exceedingly at his presence there at such an hour, being alarmed, moreover, lest he had discovered her intimacy with Duncan Grahame, and was about to communicate the same to her father, she waited till she heard him enter the little room below, where she knew the latter still sat, and throwing a shawl over her arm, she slipped stealthily down the stair and stood still as a statue in the passage, close to the door, where every word came distinctly to her ear.

What she did hear was a great relief to her fluttering heart. Her secret was still unsuspected, and she had the satisfaction of learning that her father meant to leave her free in making choice of a husband. No sooner had she heard the last words we have recorded than, with a lightened heart, she turned away, and with noiseless movement, proceeded to a back door, where she let herself out into the soft silence of the summer night.

Close by the rear of the cottage was a little field of green pasture, bounded by a tall, thick hedge of hawthorn; and Mary had but to pass within the little gate and be concealed from view. Keeping within the shadow of the overhanging hedge, she drew the shawl she carried close round her head, and proceeded in the direction of the wood, whose distant outline could be seen against the western sky.

"Poor James!" murmured Mary, with the faintest feeling of regret. "I liked him well enough till I met Duncan, and then I knew that it was only liking, not love. He hopes to win me still. Oh! if he only knew—if any of them knew; but they will—they must soon; the truth cannot be concealed much longer, and I dread my father's displeasure when he knows the worst. Oh! if Duncan would but consent to a private marriage; that would save me from all the reproach and shame. Perhaps he will; perhaps it is to arrange for this he has asked me to meet him to-night. Oh! the dear, noble, generous fellow, how I long to see him."

Her half-murmured soliloquy was suddenly interrupted by a hare starting from the side of the hedge and bounding away across the field. For a moment only Mary was startled by this breaking of the universal stillness. Having been reared in the country, she was not frightened to walk in its solitude, even at that late hour of the night; and recently she had been abroad on that very footpath at even a later hour. The starting of the hare was rather assuring than otherwise, as it gave her to understand that no human being but herself was in the vicinity.

The night was lovely. It was, as we have said, on the eve of harvest. The broad moon, which ripened the whitening grain, hung far up in the blue sky, and bathed the landscape in a flood of soft, silver light. The dew was gathering on the grass, and the corn in the fields, now bending its heavy ears, rustled faintly in the gentle air that floated from the hills, whose round outlines could be seen as they towered in motion-less silence in the calm moonlight, with streaks of shadow lying on their slopes, and patches of white rock glittering between.

After nearly half an hour's walk, Mary came to the edge of the wood, the low fence of which she had just crossed, when a tall handsome youth sprang forward, and clasped her in his arms.

This was Duncan Grahame, her seducer and betrayer—the smooth-tongued tempter, whose arts had robbed her of virtue, and whose cruelty meditated her desertion.

"My own sweet darling Mary," he said, in a rich and finely-modulated voice.

Mary murmured his name in fondest accents, and laid her head with pride and joy upon his bosom, while his false lips were pressed to hers, and their breaths mingled together.

"Oh, Duncan, I am so glad we have met to-night," said Mary, when the first minute of caressing had passed.

"Ah, you are lonely, I daresay, down at the old cottage," he rejoined. "I don't wonder at that, for there is nobody there at all like yourself. You can't but mope and be melancholy."

"Oh, I am not melancholy," answered Mary, smiling up at him; "but when I am alone I am always thinking of you."

"You are!" cried the hypocrite, with pride and exultation, as again he kissed her.

Oh, what a clear, trusting, unsuspicious smile she sent up into his handsome countenance. It was full of love, and cloud-less and boundless trust. Not the faintest shadow of suspicion dimmed the brightness of her glance.

"I wish I could only have you always beside me," he observed.

"Do you really wish that?" she asked, with a sparkling smile.

"*Do* I wish it? Can you doubt it?"

"No; for you tell me it is so, and your assurance makes me very, very happy. We must now be all in all to each other, dear."

"So we must—so we shall," he rejoined; "and it was to speak of this that I asked you to meet me to-night."

"Ah, our marriage!" she quickly rejoined. "Have you seen your way to effect that?"

"Not quite," he basely answered. "My father is so irascible

and unreasonable that it is in vain to hope for his sanction. But the time will soon come when I shall be able to act independently, and if we can get safely through our present circumstances, all will be well."

"Oh Duncan, I do fear for my father's anger," said Mary. "I will brave anything for your sake—the world's shame, the scorn of my acquaintances—but my father's displeasure, I greatly dread that. He is so strict, you know, and—"

"I know he is very tight-laced, and bigoted, and all that sort of thing," rejoined Grahame, "and on that account, more than anything else, I was worried about my inability to make things all right. Of course, if you insist on it, we could be married in spite of everything—only that would knock up my prospects entirely."

"No, no; you know I would not do that," said the devoted girl. "I will suffer anything rather than you should be injured. But don't you think, dearest, that we might be privately married?"

"I have thought of that," returned the dissembler, quite readily. "I have thought it all over most anxiously, and fear, my darling, that it cannot be done. We would have to trust several people with the secret, and thus it would not be safe. It would have every chance of coming to my father's ears—in which case I am ruined for life."

"Oh, no! this must not, must not be," cried Mary, who implicitly believed his word. "I would never forgive myself if I were to be the cause of misfortune to you."

"Nay, I would brave everything, sacrifice everything for you; and if I were to be the only sufferer by my father's displeasure, this would not cause me a moment's hesitation. But it is of your benefit I am thinking."

"Oh, kind, generous Duncan," exclaimed Mary. "Why should others be so cruel as to be a bar to our happiness? Why should your father be so proud and inflexible? It is true, I am poor and lowly born, but—"

"But you are the sweetest angel that ever lived," cried the deceiver; "and if my father only knew you as I do, he would be delighted to have you for his daughter. He may, he will, in time; and then I am sure his prejudice and anger will vanish before your beauty and goodness. In a year or two, darling, I shall have finished my studies, and my profession will make me independent of my father. Then we shall be married

openly and publicly, and before the world will I with pride
take my Mary to my heart and home."

He drew her to his bosom, and there she nestled with loving
fondness. He was with skilful art working upon her heart and
feelings to make her ready to comply with the cruel and heartless scheme he had devised. Quickening her love for himself
by a show of tenderness, he was obtaining an unlimited sway
over her will, that he might have her thoroughly under his
influence, and ready to act as he dictated.

"Are you willing to wait for these better days?" he gently
asked, impressing at the same time a Judas kiss upon her
lips.

"Can you doubt it?" was her proud reply.

"You will sacrifice all others for me?"

"All!" she rejoined, turning up to him a face of beaming
affection, whose loveliest beauty the moon revealed in all its
bewitching enchantment. A heart and soul less callous and
debased than that of Duncan Grahame would have been smitten with repentance when gazing on such love and trust; but
he was untouched with either pity or regret.

"No, dearest, I do not doubt it," he returned. "But the
present must now be thought of, for that, too, threatens us
with trouble."

"Alas, yes," she sighed, brought by his words to the remembrance of her painful situation. "The world's scorn I can bear
with comparative indifference, but I tremble for my father's
anger."

"You must escape both, my darling," he whispered, in a
low tone.

"Oh, if I only could!" she sighed.

"You can—you shall," he rejoined. "Be guided by me,
and all evil results shall be avoided."

She raised herself from his bosom and looked at him inquiringly. The shawl fell back from her head, and the flowing
tresses of her magnificent hair fell like a cataract upon his
arm.

"Tell me how, Duncan?" she eagerly said, after a moment's
silence, which he did not interrupt.

"It is a sacrifice you must make," he said; "and if I did
not fully trust in your love I should not propose it. But, Mary,
darling, we are now all in all to each other. The world, our
friends, must be given up, if necessary. Have you the courage,

for my sake—for both our sakes—to quit your father's house?"

"Leave my father!" she repeated, in alarm.

"It is the only method I can think of," he went on, without allowing her time for reflection. "The world's scorn and your father's anger are the worst, but not the only evils to be dreaded. Our fond, true love has hurried us to a position which the prejudiced world, in its cold, unfeeling ignorance, stigmatises as folly, and visits with a senseless reprobation. Unfortunately, we cannot be independent of the world, and require to be careful not to offend it. Now, Mary dear, depending on your love for me, I have secured an asylum for you in a part of the country twenty miles from this, with a poor but honest woman, who will nurse you and tend you as if you were her own daughter. The cause of your flight, or the place to which you have gone, no one in Kirkton must know—not even your father. Leave a few lines for him to let him know that you are safe, but write not a word to give him a clue to your whereabouts; and when all danger is past, when I am free to make you my wife, we shall re-appear together. The past will be unknown, and, therefore, overlooked. Your father will rejoice at beholding you again, and a life of happiness shall be before us."

In speaking these words Grahame threw much tenderness into his tone. His whole chance lay on this moment, and he had previously calculated it well. When he uttered the last words he glanced at Mary's fair, moonlit face, and saw with triumph that there was no promise of opposition there.

"You are right, dear Duncan," she observed. "We are all the world to each other, and must cling together. I never thought to leave my father in this way; but it is for the best, and, as you say, we shall hope for better days."

Mary was the more easily led into the snare because her lover's proposal afforded the prospect of escaping her father's severe reproaches, and these she dreaded more than all else. She had an affection for the old man—an affection which, had it not been interfered with by the passion that now possessed her, would have seemed strong and sacred. But the selfishness and vanity of her nature had been aroused by the love she had for Duncan Grahame; and then its consuming force swallowed up and absorbed all opposing feelings, and she was ready to sacrifice even her father to her infatuation.

The youth's dark eye gleamed with triumph when she spoke the words of consent to his proposal. He had gained his purpose. The danger to his prospects was averted, and time was given him to make all secure by his marriage with Lucy Grahame.

"When must I go?" inquired Mary, as he kissed her again.

"Immediately, dear. Not a day is to be lost, for a discovery may take place at any moment. Meet me here to-morrow night at eleven. I shall have a fly[4] waiting down in the road."

"So soon," she murmured.

"The sooner the better; you will thus have less time to think of it. But cheer up, my Mary. We are in trouble now; a little patience and all shall be well."

All shall be well! Oh! the mockery of these heartless words of cruel betrayal. It would be "well" for him, according to his own desire, but for Mary herself and for her future they signified a brutal indifference—the extreme of utter selfishness.

Such was the youth who had gained the poor girl's whole heart—a possession of which he was altogether unworthy—a youth devoid of principle, of honour, almost of humanity itself.

They parted that night, she nothing doubting, only, as she softly and noiselessly entered the little cottage that had always been her home, and called to mind that she would be but another day beneath its roof, she became sad and heavy of heart. Yet she turned her eye from the painful present to the future, and persuaded herself that all was bright and happy there.

All the following day she was engaged in making preparations for her departure. According to her lover's instructions, she conducted these preparations with utter secrecy. Not a single hint was given to Peggy of what was intended, and the latter took no heed of Mary's movements, though afterwards she remembered that she did wonder what Mary was doing in her bed-room all day.

The evening came, and brought old Andrew in from the fields; Mary was peculiarly kind and tender towards him, and that night, when the little household knelt at the altar of

---

4. Hired light horse carriage.

worship, the old man was very fervent in his supplications in her behalf. It was with great difficulty that Mary could restrain her sobs, and to conceal her emotion she bade him a hurried good night the moment they rose from their knees, and ran up the little stair to find the solitude of her own apartment.

Here she had little time to indulge in reflection. It was near the hour when they must depart. She listened anxiously to hear Peggy retire to her sleeping closet, for on this occasion she was as desirous of concealing her out-going from the housekeeper as from her father, and Peggy she knew would not suspect that she meant to meet her lover that night, seeing that she had met him on the previous evening.

Mary had waited long till Peggy entered her sleeping place, and the house became entirely silent. With a beating heart the ill-fated girl drew writing materials toward her, and, lighting a candle, sat down and penned the following lines:—

Dear Father, —Forgive me. I have left you for a time, but only for a time, and the step I have taken is for the best. Do not seek me, for the search will be fruitless; but in due time and in happy circumstances I shall appear and ask your forgiveness and your blessing. Till then, my father, farewell. Do not grieve. I assure you that I am quite safe. Love me still, and till we meet again, pray for your affectionate daughter Mary.

She folded the slip of paper on which these words were traced, and writing on the back, "To my Father," she placed it on the window sill. Then lifting the bundle she had tied up, she blew out the light, crept from the room, and noiselessly descended to the front door. This being still unlocked, she had but to lift the latch, and the next moment she was in the open air, under the soft light of the moon. She looked in at the little window, and saw her father bending over the Bible; one long lingering look she bent upon him, then heaving a sigh, she turned away, and passing round to the rear of the cottage, directed her steps towards the place of rendezvous.

She never looked upon her father's face again.

CHAPTER III

THE NIGHT RIDE—THE QUIET COTTAGE— FIRST APPEARANCE ON THE SCENE OF HELEN MACDOUGAL AND BURKE— DR FORD ENGAGED

Duncan Grahame was at the trysting-place some time before Mary appeared. The horse and gig were in the narrow lane at the corner of the wood, and everything was prepared which would save him from the consequences of his *liaison*. If he once had Mary safely in the gig, and the horse's head turned across the country, all would then be secure; but he did not know what had occurred since he parted with Mary on the previous evening. Perhaps a discovery had taken place. The slightest accident, he knew, might reveal the girl's situation, in which case all his plans would be frustrated and his grand prospects ruined. Most impatiently, therefore, did he pace to and fro within the fence, keeping his eye fixed on the footpath by which Mary was to come, wrapped up, as he always was, in his own intense selfishness.[1]

It was a close and sultry summer night. Not a breath of air stirred the trees, and the corn stalks, with their heavy heads, stood silent in the fields, under the ripening moon, which was floating among fleecy clouds above the distant battlements of Stirling. It was a rich mellow scene of peace and of beauty. Heaven and earth seemed to hold sacred communion, and silence and immensity embraced the universe.[2]

"She comes not," muttered the youth. "By Jove! I fear there's something up. Perhaps she has taken ill. In her nervous state she isn't to trust to a moment. Gad! I wish I had made this arrangement a fortnight ago, and the danger would have been past. Ha! I see a speck in the distance now."

Far off, on a footpath which ran by the side of the hedge, a small dark moving object had become visible to his eager

---

1. The 1885 book drops reference to Duncan's selfishness.
2. 1885 cuts this sentimental and religious sentence.

gaze. For a time he could not make out whether it might not be fancy, but gradually it enlarged and came nearer, till he could distinguish a female form, and recognised Mary by her figure and her walk.

" 'Tis she, and she comes alone!" he exclaimed, with boundless satisfaction. "Heavens! what a relief does that sight give me! I am safe. Lucy is mine, and a bright course is before me!"

Yes; but what course was before the girl he had wronged and was about to desert? Not one thought did he bestow upon her possible fate; her he sacrificed without a pang or a regret, leaving her to helplessness, shame, and scorn.

Nearer and nearer she came towards the wood, and it seemed with a slow and languid step. In one hand she carried a bundle wrapped in a cotton shawl, and with the other she gathered her dress together, to free it from the briars that grew by the wayside. Ah, poor girl, had she been as careful to save her heart and conscience from the more destructive briars of the path of life, a different and happier fate would have awaited her.

Duncan Grahame stood within the shadow of the wood, smoking a cigar and awaiting her approach. The time had been when, at the first glimpse of his idol, he would have rushed to meet her, and lavished upon her the most tender caresses; but his passion was cooled now. She was the idol of his fancy no longer, and he was not enticed to the same demonstrations of regard.

And yet Mary had not perceived the change in him; she deemed him as fond and loving as ever. Ah, she was bound to him now. Her honour, her virtue, her all, she had given him; and, trustful in her own simplicity, she saw not the change that had taken place.

Not until she had come close to the fence did he move forward to meet her. Then he threw away the end of his cigar, emerged from under the umbrageous tree, and came to the gap which led from the field into the wood.

Mary started at his abrupt appearance.

"Oh, Duncan," she exclaimed, "I am so glad to see you. I feared you had not come."

"All right, my darling, but the horse is down in the lane, and I have had him to look after. Why, what ails you, dear, you are trembling?"

"Oh, I am so tired and so nervous," she returned, leaning heavily on his arm.

"Silly girl," he whispered, as he assisted her through the gap.

"I am not so strong as I once was," she returned, with a weary smile.

"I know, I know, but you will get over it soon. Cheer up. In an hour or two you will be in a place of safety, where no cold look or cruel word will ever reach you."

"I am thankful when I think of that," answered Mary, "but it cuts me to the heart to leave my father. Oh, what will he say in the morning when he finds that I am gone?"

"Not so much as he would have said if you had remained," suggested Duncan, artfully leading Mary to thoughts which reconciled her to the course she had taken.

"Come," he added, "a few steps farther and your fatigue will be over."

It was not without great difficulty that Mary managed to cross the strip of plantation, assisted even as she was by the strong arm of her companion. The long walk she already had, and the excitement under which she laboured, made her weak and tremulous, so that Duncan had her almost to carry to the spot where the vehicle waited.

In a few moments they were seated, and, the horse flying forward, the wood was quickly left behind them. Where they were going Mary knew not. She had never in all her life been out of the district. Stirling was the largest town she had seen, and the view from the castle was the largest she had ever obtained of the wide world into which she was soon to be cast.

Yet, though she knew not where she was going, she was in no respect anxious on that score. Her trust in Duncan being implicit, she doubted not the refuge he had secured was one of safety and comfort. The journey occupied them more than three hours; it was therefore more than two hours after midnight when they came to the end of a straggling village, lying in the midst of a wide, open country.

Duncan did not drive up the street of the village, but turned sharp off to the left into a dusty lane which led to a quaint, old, isolated house, from one of the small windows of which a light glimmered.

"You see Helen is up; she expects us," remarked Duncan.

"Oh, this is the place, then," said Mary, with some degree

of interest, casting her eyes at the same time over the dim scene.

"This is the place," repeated Duncan. "It was here I served my apprenticeship to Doctor Ford; nice fellow the doctor. He'll be very attentive to you, and see you all right. I'll speak to him before I go."

"But you'll visit me often, won't you, dear?" said Mary. "I shall be so lonely here among strangers."

"My darling, I shall be prevented from seeing you for some time. I go to Edinburgh to-morrow to resume my studies. I must push up hill you know, and the faster I work the sooner shall I be able to make you my wife."

"Oh, Duncan! how shall I ever bear the separation?" sighed Mary, as the tears gathered in her eyes. "Without you I shall be miserable."

"Nonsense," he returned. "You will find Helen M'Dougall[3] a very agreeable companion, and in the circumstances you will require always to keep indoors. No one must know that you are here. But I know you will be cautious for both our sakes."

"I will, indeed, dear Duncan. But you will write often?"

"Oh, of course," promised the deceiver, though at the moment he mentally resolved to furnish no such dangerous evidence against himself as a letter would afford. He was inwardly congratulating himself with the thought that, in an hour or two more, all his trouble in the matter would be over, for he meant never to see Mary again, and would make it certain before he left that she should be allowed no means of communicating with any one till it was no longer against his interest that she should do so. It was very much in the form of a prisoner that he was now consigning her to the woman of this house, and the latter understood full well the part she had to play. Not that Duncan had trusted her too far either. He had by no means given her to understand what his game was, further than that he wished Mary to be carefully watched, and allowed no real freedom till he sanctioned it.

It was a lie he told Mary when he said he was to depart immediately for Edinburgh. The classes did not open till

---

3. Helen begins as Macdougal, then is M'Dougall through this chapter, but generally M'Dougal thereafter.

November, and he did not require to return to the metropolis
till that month. His real purpose was to go that very day to
the house of the relative with whom Lucy Grahame resided,
and begin the effort he meant to make to precipitate his marriage with the latter—an event which he determined should,
if possible, take place before the opening of the college, so that
he and his bride might spend the winter in Edinburgh.

Ah me! more duplicity—more selfishness and cruelty. What
a revelation for the poor, forsaken, and deserted girl when
the truth shall burst upon her! The gig pulled up at the door
of the humble, old-fashioned house, which seemed to be the
only residence to which the lane led. At that early hour not
one of the villagers were astir; indeed, they had not seen a
human being throughout the journey. Duncan helped his
companion to alight, and so little noise had the wheels made
on the dusty ground, that their arrival had not been heard
within.

It was from a window on the ground floor of the building
that the light spoken of came, and Mary, as she descended
from the vehicle, glancing through the casement, saw that it
proceeded from an oil lamp burning on the mantel shelf, and
that in front of the fire—or rather the fireplace, for no fire
seemed to burn in the grate—sat a woman with her arms
folded on her breast, and her head leaning thereon, asleep.

Her companion had made the same observation, and no
sooner were they both on the ground than he approached the
window and tapped with the handle of his whip.

The woman heard the noise at once, and sprang rather
wildly to her feet, rubbing her eyes and looking round her in a
bewildered way.

Duncan tapped on the window again, and this seemed to
make her regain her recollection thoroughly, for she snatched
down the light and came and opened the door.

Mary naturally viewed with some curiosity the woman
who was to be her companion and nurse. She was stoutly
made, somewhat soft looking, and coarse and heavy of fea-
ture. She had a round eye, of no great brilliance or expression,
and a countenance neither repulsive nor attractive. There
was more of hardness and callousness in it than Mary liked,
but even to her view it was not destitute of feeling. She saw at
a glance, however, that the woman was of a very different
stamp from Peggy M'Naughton, who had been to her as a

mother—not always judicious, but faithful and devoted as mother could be.

"I'm sure I beg your pardon for having kept you waiting," said the woman, as she stood aside to let them pass.

"You were asleep, I saw, Helen," remarked Duncan.

"I was indeed, sir, and the fire has gone out, and the young lady must be cold."

"No, thank you," returned Mary, "I am not at all cold, only tired—very tired and wearied."

"Take her to her room at once, Helen. Good-bye, Mary."

Mary turned towards him with a look of startled anxiety.

"Shall I see you in the morning?" she quickly asked.

"To be sure, silly one. There, go up stairs with Helen, and get to bed and sleep soundly."

He kissed her lightly on the forehead. She returned his kiss, and with a fond, loving look, went up the narrow wooden stair after the woman, little dreaming that he and she had parted for ever.

Duncan went outside when she left, and walked to and fro in front of the house, watching the light which glimmered now in the upper window—the only upper window in the building, and half-buried among the black thatch of the roof.

He had walked for some time in this manner, growing every moment more impatient, till at length he gave vent to his irritation in short whispered sentences.

"Confound it, why need she stay so long up there, when I want to leave this before daylight? And I have to see Ford too. Thank goodness, Mary is off my hand now, at all events. That source of trouble and danger is removed. Not an eye has seen us on the road to-night, so no one can suspect. I'm safe, quite safe for a month or two, and before the end of that time I hope to call Lucy mine. Curse the hag, is she not coming down yet?" The light at length began to move in the window, then it vanished from the room and appeared on the stair. Duncan stepped in to the house, closed the front door, and entered the kitchen, followed in a moment or two by the woman herself.

"How long you have kept me," he muttered, "I thought you would never come."

"I waited till she was asleep, poor thing. How pretty she is; and what grand hair! I never saw anything to equal it."

"She is sleeping, then," said the youth, interested only in her first remark.

"As sound as an infant. She is quite done out, and no wonder, after such a long ride in her state. It is my opinion, Mr Duncan, that she won't be long."

"Perhaps. But tell me, have you any people about you just now—any lodgers?"

"Only one," returned Helen, colouring a little.

"Man or woman?" asked the youth.

"A man; a labourer on the canal."

"A sweetheart, perhaps," remarked the other.

"We live very pleasant together, at all events," remarked Helen; "he is a blythe, cheerful, open-hearted fellow, an Irishman, William Burke by name, as merry, happy, and good-natured a man as—"

"Oh, never mind about that. Is he safe to trust in this business? Have you told him anything?"

"Nothing particular."

"Then don't mention my name at all. Now you know your instructions. Don't allow Mary to communicate with any one, and say nothing about her to any one yourself. Nobody has seen us come here, and nobody need know that she is here. When she turns ill send for Ford. You'll manage all the rest. I gave you ten pounds the other day; here is ten pounds more. Be faithful to my instructions, and you will be still better paid."

"It's all right, Mr Grahame," said the woman, as with sparkling eyes she took the notes he handed her. "I will be attentive to everything. You may fully depend on me."

"I will. O, by the by, Mary expects to see me in the morning. Tell her I think it best for both of us I should not return."

"Very well, sir. She'll feel it hard at the time, but as you say, it will be for the best."

To this the youth made no reply, but walking quickly out of the house, he unfastened the horse's rein, sprang into the gig, and drove furiously away.

Helen watched him as he rushed down the lane in the moonlight, till he turned the corner, when she heard the wheels of the vehicle rattle loudly over the rough village street; then she closed and fastened the door, and returned to the kitchen.

In the passage, and close to the door of the opposite room, stood a short, thickset man, in his trousers and shirt. He had a round, good-humoured face, a pair of small, twinkling eyes, a short nose, and large mouth—in short, a regular Irish countenance.

"Begorra, but it's yerself, Helen, me darlint, that can make money while other people are sleepin'," he exclaimed. "Sure now it isn't every one that has made ten pounds this mornin' afore breakfast."

"I should think not," returned Helen, with a laugh. "But what are you doing there, William? I thought you would be lying sound asleep."

"Bedad, I was asleep every inch uv me, but somehow I waked and missed you, and I heard ye afther spakin to some one in the kitchen. Throth, and wasn't it jealous I was, and wouldn't I have knocked the fellow to smithereens intirely, if he had been makin' love to ye."

"Oh, how can you speak that way," returned Helen, with a laugh. "You know well enough that I don't allow anybody to make love to me but you."

"Faith, and I believe yez, me darlint, and it's our own two selves that will stick together through life, and devil a need for a praist to tie us. Och, but Helen, avic,[4] wouldn't I like to earn tin pounds as aisy as you've done this mornin'. It isn't workin' at the canal like a horse I'd be. But what's the mainin' of it at all, at all?"

"Hush, speak lower. There's a girl in the room above, and she may hear us. She is going to have a young one, and *he* has brought her here to get it over in quiet."

"*He?* The gint that tipped you the tin pounds?"

Helen nodded.

"They've made a bit uv a mistake—got out uv their reckoning loike?" said Burke, with a facetious chuckle.

"Yes, but for any sake don't say a word about it, or I'll see no more notes like these."

---

4. *avic*: "my son". Clearly, as the *Fortnightly Review* noted, "Well-known to all readers of Irish stories are the terms of endearment. ... Here, however, mistakes are frequent, *e.g.*, *'avic'* (my son) addressed to a girl." Mary Hayden and Marcus Hartog, "The Irish Dialect of English", *Fortnightly* NS 85 (1909): 775–85; see 783–84.

"Divil a word will I spake," returned the other. "But what are you going to do wid all the money?"

"I'll share it with you, William. We'll have a jolly blow out first of all, and we'll keep the rest, and when we go to Edinburgh in the winter it will set you up as a travelling merchant, and we shall live together quite comfortably."

"Och, musha, but isn't it yerself that's a sinsible ould lass," cried Burke, in the greatest of glee. "Comfortable—was it comfortable ye said? Bedad, thin, that's too poor a word entirely. It's blessed we'll be every day uv our lives. I'll buy a beautiful new flute, and that and a drop o' the craythur[5] will make the nights pass like glory. Och, sure, our lives will go mighty pleasant together, me darlint."

Helen replied by a responsive sentiment. This was their imaginary future—not a very fair or spotless one certainly, but still without the faintest foreshadow of that which was to be so horribly realised.

*

While this couple were holding the above conversation, Duncan Grahame was closeted with Doctor Ford. The doctor lived in a two-storey house at the head of the village. The house stood within its own grounds, surrounded by a high wall, pierced by a large wooden door for the entrance and exit of the doctor's family and his many callers. The doctor's family was not large, consisting only of his sister, who kept house for him, one female servant, and an elderly man, who acted in the double capacity of groom and gardener.

This latter personage slept in a little loft above the stable, close to the door which entered from the road. It was his duty to attend to the summons of the night-bell, and carry the messages to the doctor, whose sleeping apartment could be approached without disturbing the other inmates of the house.

Grahame, who had served his apprenticeship with the doctor, and knew the ways of the house, drew up at the great door, and gave a vigorous pull at the night-bell, when, in less

---

5. A drink—particularly of whisky (or whiskey, for the Irish).

than a minute, out pops a white head from a square cavity in the stable wall just overhead.

"What's the matter?—wha wants the doctor?" was the inquiry put by the owner of the head.

"Open the gate, John," said the youth.

"Gi'e me yer message first," returned John.

"Oh, bother, man; don't you know me?"

"Eh—what? I daur say I should ken that voice," cried John, bending down towards Duncan's face.

"Of course you should. Come quick; I have no time to spare."

"Guid gracious! is it Maister Grahame?"

"Yes, yes, old fellow."

"The like o' that!"

The head disappeared in a twinkling, and a few moments after the gate was opened.

"What's wrang, that ye are here at this oor?" asked the greatly wondering John.

"Nothing wrong, John; but I am on my way south, and want to have a chat with the doctor for a minute or two."

As Duncan said this, he led the horse and gig within the gate, which John very hastily closed the moment they had got into the interior.

"Is this anither o' *yon* jobs?" asked the old man, in a fearful whisper, as he peered anxiously into the gig.

"What do you call '*yon*' job, John?" asked the youth, with a laugh.

"Oh ye ken what I mean—when ye sent the lang, black, fearsome-lookin' chap out frae Embro."

"Ye mean Merry lees—Merry Andrew, as we call him."[6]

"Eh, mercy! Maister Grahame, he's a queer man yon. Is—is he here wi' ye the night?"

"No, no; I am on no such errand. Have you got a liking for night visits to the churchyard?"

---

6. Alexander Leighton's 1861 fictionalised history *The Court of Cacus: The Story of Burke and Hare* had featured numerous actual bodysnatchers, in particular "Merrylees, or ... Merry-Andrew, a great favourite with the students" (Leighton, 45). He was renowned for playing the grieving relative to make away with unclaimed corpses from the infirmary and rumour had it he snatched his own sister from her grave in Pennicuik (46, 67–76).

"Oh, Lord, no!" answered John, with a shudder.

"I hope I'll ne'er hae a hand in sic a job again. I dreamed about it every nicht for sax weeks after."

"Pooh! What is there in a dead body to make any one afraid? Just give me the key of the doctor's room, and hold the rein till I return. I'll not be over a minute or two."

John handed him the key, and the youth, crossing the little lawn, went to the door of a low wing at the side of the house. Here he gave himself admittance, and with the movements of one quite familiar with the locality he threaded a long passage, and entered a small closet, in which stood a night-lamp. Lifting this and turning it full up, he crossed to a door opposite, pushed it open, and was in the doctor's bedroom.

The latter lay upon a curtainless bed sound asleep, with an empty bottle and glass on a table near.

"So he has been jolly last night," muttered the youth. "If it had not been for this one failing, Ford might have been the rival of Monroe."[7]

He went to the bedside and gave the sleeper a rough shake.

The doctor stirred at once.

"Who is it, John? Has Mrs Corbet taken ill at last?"

"Come, wake up, doctor, I want to speak to you!"

At the sound of the youth's voice the doctor opened his eyes with an astonished jerk.

"Bless my heart and soul, Grahame, is that you? Another subject wanted? Sorry you came so far; nothing available at present. Fact is, my boy, the risk is greater than I care to run. If the thing got wind the people here would tear me piecemeal."

"Keep yourself easy. I'm not here at present on staff duty, but on a private matter of my own. There is a girl down at Helen M'Dougall's; she will have a child soon; I want you to take up the case, and say nothing about it."

---

7. The variously spelled Monro dynasty of Edinburgh doctors started with the current surgeon's grandfather (dubbed *primus*), who founded the Edinburgh Medical School, and included his father (*secundus*). The strain of brilliance and knowledge had waned by the time it got to *tertius*, so the fictional Ford might well have rivalled Monro (as did Robert Knox, who figures centrally in *Mary Paterson*).

"Whew! You've been poaching during the Christmas holidays over at Mount Cairn. Wild dog. You should have known better. Unsafe doings in the country."

"You'll do me a great service by observing secrecy in the matter. The fact is, were it to come out, I would be seriously compromised with the governor. But I know I can count on you as a friend in the affair."

"So you can, my boy. I'll see the girl through it. What's the time?"

"In a week or two; not more than a month at farthest."

"All right. They'll send for me, of course. But, I say, you must get into bed. You know the way."

"Nay, my gig is in the yard. I must be miles from this by breakfast time, so I'll not keep you from sleep any longer."

"What! you are going, are you? Bless me, man, when I wake in the morning I'll think your visit has been a dream."

"Then ask John about it; he'll put you right. Good-bye, old fellow."

"Good-bye. Don't poach at Christmas again."

CHAPTER IV

MARY AND HER COMPANIONS IN THE COTTAGE—THE CHILD OF SHAME— FATAL TIDINGS

In the little box-bed of that quaint and humble attic room in the cottage, Mary Paterson slept soundly, and when after many hours of profound repose she awoke it was to contemplate a flood of brightest sunshine streaming through the narrow window upon the wooden floor.

The place was, as we have said, humble—humbler than Mary had been accustomed to, but it was very clean, and, in the radiance of the summer light, looked cheerful. The furniture was scanty, and what was of it was of the very plainest description, but it and the floor had all been recently scrubbed; the walls had been washed, and everything had been made tidy by Helen M'Dougal for her expected guest.

Mary awoke greatly refreshed, and the gladsomeness of the sunny day made her glad also. She did think of her father and Peggy. They would have discovered her departure now, and her father would have got the letter she had left behind. What would they think? Would a suspicion of the truth occur to them?—would her father be angry beyond forgiveness? This last thought reconciled her at once to the step she had taken. She had escaped all scorn and reproach, and ere long she would return in circumstances that would entitle her to hold up her head without a blush. So with this prospect before her, she gave herself up to the most pleasant thoughts of the present.

By the angle of the streaming sunshine she calculated it to be late in the day, and, remembering that her hostess told her that she would not awake her, but allow her sleep to have its own time, she gave a smart tap on the little table that stood by her bedside.

"Duncan will be waiting for me," she murmured, "and I must ask Helen to tell him that I shall be down immediately."

Helen entered at the moment, her round, heavy face encompassed by the border of a clean cap.

"Ah! and don't you look a deal better this morning, miss?" she cried, when she caught sight of Mary's sparkling eyes.

"Oh, I have had such a sound and long sleep," said Mary. "I am sure it must be late, and Mr Grahame will be impatient. Please to tell him that I shall be down in a very few moments."

"Oh dear! Mr Duncan is away, and he said—"

"Away!" echoed Mary. "Oh, why did you not wake me? It was very cruel of you."

"Don't fret, miss. He didn't stay more than a few minutes after I went down, just as you fell asleep. He said it would be better that you shouldn't see him in the morning. The pain of parting might hurt you."

"He meant it, then," said Mary, as the tears gathered in her eyes. "He meant to leave without saying farewell. Oh, this was deceiving me!"

"I knew you would feel it hard at first, and told him so; but I think it was quite right of him after all, for to part with him to-day would have done you harm. Cheer up, like a good girl, and I will bring you up your breakfast."

And deeming that no more comfort was needful, the woman departed on the errand she had named.

This was Mary's first positive disappointment, and she felt it very bitterly. Never having known it before, she was not schooled to bear it; and when Helen returned she found her weeping violently.

Ah! this was to the poor helpless girl only "the beginning of sorrows."[1] Having "loved not wisely but too well," the cup of her folly was rising to her lips, to be drunk to the dark dregs.[2] She was sad as yet, and only sad, for she suspected no baseness or deceit on the part of her lover. But the terrible truth will ere long reach her mind, and then—

---

1. Jesus describes the results of following false prophets in Matthew 24:8, translated as "All these are the beginning of sorrows" (King James version of the Bible).

2. Shakespeare's hero so characterises his folly in *Othello*, V:ii:344. The "cup of folly" was one cup too many, as translated from Euboulus's Greek by R. Cumberland: "The third and last to lull him to his rest, / Then home to bed! But if a fourth he pours, / That is the cup of folly"; *Scots Magazine* 50 (January 1788): 146. Psalm 75:8 promises that from God's cup "the dregs thereof, all the wicked of the earth shall wring *them* out, and drink *them*" (KJV).

She felt very lonely in that strange and quiet house, with no companion but Helen M'Dougal, a woman whom she soon found was not suited to her tastes and feelings. She did not find her ill-natured or vicious, but she was coarse, and had no great feeling. She also soon came to see that she liked whisky, and was not unfrequently to a considerable degree under its influence. At these times her coarseness of nature was doubly manifested. She would have Mary to take a little whisky along with her, lauding it as a grand cure for care, but Mary would not be prevailed on to drink it. The taste repelled her, and care had not yet become so cankering to her heart as to induce her to seek refuge from it in oblivious intoxication.

With the other inmate of the cottage—William Burke—Mary became very friendly. Burke was a happy, cheerful being, as most Irishmen are. He was always hearty and always sociable, proud of singing a good song, and able to do it with not a little pathetic power. He had his faults, too, the chief being that he was fond of idleness, and also, like his companion, fond of whisky. The hard work he had to undergo, as a labourer at the canal—which was being constructed between Edinburgh and Glasgow—was by no means to his taste, and he meant to make a change after the autumn was over, hoping to hit upon some easier way of making a living.

The relation which existed between him and Helen M'Dougal was not understood by Mary just at first; but she did find it out by-and-bye, and the knowledge of it coming gradually to her mind, it did not shock her so much as it would have done had she made the discovery abruptly. Though they lived together without the sacred tie of marriage, yet they lived happily and comfortably, and this reconciled Mary to the immorality of the affair. Alas! had she not been let down to the platform which this couple occupied by her own lapse from virtue! The time had been when she, the godly elder's daughter, would have been shocked extremely by an arrangement of such a nature.

As for Burke and Helen themselves, they were in no way ashamed of their position and connection. They had come to look at it and think of it as quite a matter of course—or more probably they had come not to look at or think of it at all. Helen was a widow, and Burke had a wife in Ireland; but they had a real affection for each other, and allowed no moral considerations to be a bar in the way of their inclination.

Days and weeks went by, and Mary received no letter from Duncan. This pained her exceedingly. She was loth to bring against him the charge of unkindness and neglect; but when several weeks had elapsed without his silence being broken, she could not forbear.

Helen tried to soothe her by suggesting that he would be so hard kept at his studies as to be unable to find time to write, and Mary tried to make herself believe that this must be the case. Yet, do as she would, a shadow fell and gathered round her heart—a shadow of fear and foreboding, and all the more gloomy that it was indefinite.

In this way passed the time of harvest, a time which had always been very happy and animating in Mary's experience. Helen did not find the instructions given by young Grahame difficult to fulfil. Mary never spoke of going out; she did not even wish it and the cottage being isolated from the rest of the village, no one knew of her presence there.

At length, late on an October night, Mary was taken ill, and Burke went for Doctor Ford. The latter, true to his promise to the young man, came at once, and prepared to give the case his best attention.

Burke sat in the kitchen alone, Helen and the doctor being in the room above. He sat by the side of the fire smoking his pipe, and thinking of nothing in particular.

Presently there was a footstep on the stair, and the doctor entered.

"Well, the girl is to be in no hurry to let me home," he remarked, as he drew a seat to the opposite side of the fire and sat down.

"Och, then, just make yourself aisy," returned Burke. "A seat by a blazin' fire on a cowld October night aint the worst thing one can have at all, at all."

"No more it is," rejoined the doctor, with a laugh; "but there's such a thing as improving it. There's half a crown. Don't you think you could knock up old Corbet at the inn, and get a bottle of whisky?"

"Devil a doubt uv that!" exclaimed Burke, starting up with great alacrity; "and as you observe, doctor, a drap o' the crayther makes a mighty increase to the comforts o' the fireside. It completes the thing intirely. The fire gives the heat outside, and *it* gives the heat inside."

"That's sound philosophy, Burke," responded the doctor,

"and the sooner you are back to apply it the better, for my stomach wants heat at this moment. I've had a long cold ride to-night, and want something to warm me."

"Faix, thin, ye'll have it in the twinkling uv a bed-post," rejoined the Irishman, as with a bound he disappeared.

He did not return just so soon as he said, for the inn was some little distance off, and the landlord had to be roused from his bed. His absence lasted fully a quarter of an hour, at the end of which time he reappeared with the liquor, which he had no difficulty in procuring. Forbes Mackenzie was not heard of in those days.[3]

The doctor had not been idle in the interval. He had rummaged Helen's cupboard, and got a jug, spoons, glasses, and the sugar basin, and these he had arranged on the table. The kettle, which had been hung on the fire for another purpose, was boiling. Therefore everything was ready for the making of toddy, and in a very few minutes the doctor and the Irishman were seated each with a smoking tumbler before them.

As Duncan Grahame had remarked, this was Doctor Ford's failing. He loved a glass, and frequently descended from his level to gratify this inclination. He would associate with persons quite beneath him in social life, and of course as they could not come up to his place, he had to go down to theirs, and it therefore often happened, as on this occasion, that he made boon companions of those who were no proper associates for him. This failing did not only lower his character, but it was a bar to his professional advancement.[4]

"By the powers! doctor," cried Burke after they had "fraternised" for some time over the toddy, "is't true what ould Corbet tould me just now—that there's been a murder up in the Longbank wood, and that the man's body was got this afternoon?"

---

3. Scottish Conservative MP for Peeblesshire and temperance reformer. He introduced the 1853 Public Houses (Scotland) bill, which as the Licensing (Scotland) Act instituted Sunday and late night closing. It was dubbed the "Forbes Mackenzie Act". Mackenzie died in 1862.

4. The 1885 book cuts previous paragraphs from "The latter, true to his promise" through to "professional advancement", inserting the transition paragraph: "It was while Dr. Ford was seated with Burke in the kitchen that the following conversation ensued." Burke's preparation to drink, and mention of Dr Ford's predilection, is all excised.

"A man's body has been got," replied the doctor; "but as for murder, that's a different thing. There's not one mark on the corpse, for I was up examining it."

"Och, thin, sure it can't have been murder, for murder always marks itself."

"So it does," returned the doctor; "but that is because the murderer doesn't know how to do the deed without making a mark, and it is a mercy he doesn't, for then it might never be found out."

"But doctor, dear, you don't mane to say that such a thing could be done?" said Burke, rather astonished.

"Couldn't it?" returned the doctor, whose discretion the toddy had overcome. "Were I a stronger man than you, or had I another to help me, I could have you dead in a quarter of an hour, and leave nothing by which the best doctor in the country could say how you had died."

"Musha, then, how can that be at all at all?" asked Burke, more and more astonished.

"Bah! the thing is as simple as the alphabet. All that I would have to do would be to press my hand firmly on your nose and mouth, so that no breath could escape, and no air find entrance. Then I would leap upon your breast with my knees, bringing the whole weight of my body to press upon your chest. This would prevent your lungs from having room to play. In a quarter of an hour, I tell you, you would die for want of air."[5]

"Yes, if I was fool enough to lie still and let you do it," laughed Burke, as he tossed off his glass.

"Oh, I assumed the matter of superior strength," observed the doctor, as he followed the example.

"Begorra! it would be hard work to murder a man in that way, anyhow," said the Irishman.

"It would, unless the victim were helplessly drunk. In that case the difficulty would not be great."[6]

"Doctor, you are wanted," exclaimed Helen at this moment

---

5. The book speeds this up to "two minutes".

6. Burke's confession claims that "suffocation was not suggested to them by any person as a mode of killing, but occurred to Hare" (Buchanan, Appendix 36).

from the top of the stair. With a hasty gulp the doctor tossed
off the remaining contents of his glass, then starting to his feet,
made his way hurriedly up the stair to his patient.

"They're mighty queer devils them doctors," said Burke to
himself when again he was left alone. "I've heard that they
know a man's inside as well as any other body knows his outside. Well, I don't think I would like to be one for all that.
By the powers, I would as soon work on the canal at three
shillings a-day, and the Lord knows it's not fond I am of that
either."

This conversation with Doctor Ford made no impression
on Burke's mind at the time. By the following day he had
forgot all about it; but it was most fatal seed sown in his
memory, and was destined to bear terrible fruit hereafter.

*

Before sunrise Mary Paterson was thrilled with the pride
and joy of a mother. She heard with feelings not to be
described the cry of her first-born, and her pride and joy were
deepened when she was told it was a boy. She took it to her
bosom, kissed its soft, velvety cheek, and murmured the name
of its father.

"Oh, if Duncan were here—if he only knew!" she sighed.
"How shall I get the glad tidings conveyed to him? Surely he
will write soon—or perhaps be means to come. Oh! what joy
to see him take our boy in his arms, and behold the sparkling
of his happy eye as he gazes on his own image!"

Her recovery was safe and rapid, and the child was healthy
and strong, its likeness to its father being extreme, and to
Mary gratifying.

But of that father there was still no tidings, and but for
Mary's attention being taken up with her new charge, her
anxiety would have been harrassing.

Helen M'Dougal began now to have her own thoughts
about the matter. She came to the conclusion that Duncan
had cast Mary off, and did not mean to concern himself any
more about her. His utter silence since he brought her there,
and his hurrying away without bidding her farewell, were
proof sufficient that this was the case. If his love for Mary continued, he would not have acted as he had done through all
these weeks. He would have both written to her and visited

her, and the fact that he had done neither showed that he had deserted the girl who still trusted him.

This was a matter of particular interest to Helen. If he had deserted her he would pay no more money on her account, and every day she and the child remained this was at Helen's expense. Now the truth was, the money she had got from the youth was wearing done. She had spent a deal of it in drink, which Burke and herself had consumed, and in a week or two longer there would not be sufficient left to put Burke into business, as they contemplated on their removal to Edinburgh in the end of November.

From the time that Helen came to the conclusion that the girl was forsaken, she became to her an object of dislike, and there was formed in her mind the wish to get rid of her. It was a swindle, of which she had been made so far the victim, and she had no wish to be further victimised. No doubt the twenty pounds she had received was good payment for any trouble or expense she had been at as regarded Mary, but the nature of the service rendered made exorbitant payment an expectation. In fact, Helen felt that she ought now to make the best of it, and the best was only to be made by getting Mary away. A tender-hearted woman would have cherished the forsaken one as long as she could, but, as we have already remarked, Helen had little tenderness about her. She had a great deal more consideration for herself than for any other body, unless perhaps for Burke, to whom she was really devoted, and for whom she was prepared to make any sacrifice.

And yet she did not know how to let Mary understand that she wished her to depart. It was evident that she did not as yet believe herself to be abandoned, and unfeeling as Helen was, she had not the heart to hasten the agony which she knew would follow the discovery. She talked to Burke about it, and he was even more averse than herself to undeceive poor Mary, though he also fully believed that the youth had deserted her.

He advised Helen to say nothing to Mary but that they were to remove to Edinburgh in a month, and she hoped she would have got over her troubles before that time.

Things were in this position when one afternoon the postman came to the cottage with a newspaper—the first time perhaps that such a personage had been over its threshold.

"A paper for you," he said, handing it to Helen.

"For me!" echoed Helen, in amazement.

"Yes, your name is on it—Helen M'Dougal."

"Who is it from?" asked the woman, in unmitigated surprise.

"How should I know?" returned the official with a smile. "Here, take it, for I have no time to stand here."

He had not gone more than a few moments, and Helen stood still in the kitchen, looking in a sort of bewildered way at the paper, particularly the address, which was Hebrew to her, when a fleet footstep descended the stair, and Mary ran in much excited.

"O Helen! what is it?" she exclaimed. "Anything from Duncan?"

"It's a newspaper," replied Helen; "but who was to send a newspaper to me?"

Mary glanced at it, and giving a slight scream, snatched it eagerly out of Helen's hand.

"Oh, it is Duncan's writing!" she wildly exclaimed. "He has sent it: it must contain something about him. I'll run upstairs and open it up."

Helen made no objection to this, believing that, since it was from the youth, it must be for Mary and not for herself; and she was busy conjecturing whether her idea of his intention was wrong after all when a piercing shriek sounded from the room above, accompanied by the noise of something falling heavily on the floor.

"My gracious! what is it?" exclaimed Helen, as she rushed up.

Mary lay extended on the floor where she had fallen, motionless and insensible. Her right hand grasped the open newspaper. Her face was white and bloodless, and her eyes closed.

Helen lifted her up, propped her head and shoulders against the side of the bed, and ran for water to bathe her face, but all her efforts to restore animation were vain. Fortunately at this moment Burke came in from his day's work, and she despatched him for Doctor Ford. The doctor was not in, but was expected every minute, and he would be sure to come down the moment he returned.

"What can be the meaning of it?" said Helen. "It is something she has seen in that paper, and something about Mr Duncan, I am sure."

"Indade. Then it's meself would like to know what it is," observed Burke, as he tried to take the paper from Mary's clutched hand. This he could not do, for the fingers had stiffened in their grasp, and no effort short of rough force could release it.

It was now dark, but a candle burned in the room, and Burke, taking it in his hand, knelt down where Mary lay against the bed, and ran his eye over the paper. A large cross mark in red ink caught his glance, and bending forward he slowly spelled out the following paragraph:—

"At Castle Bank, Ayrshire, on the 28th instant, Duncan Grahame, only son of Captain Grahame, Mount Cairn, Stirlingshire, to Lucy, only daughter of the late Francis Grahame, Esq."

"His marriage!" ejaculated Helen, as she stared at her companion with open mouth.

"Be jabers, but that's enough to make her faint," remarked Burke, as he rose again to his feet. "It wouldn't be any wonder if it kills her outright. It's a crying shame o' the young gent to lave a purty girl like that. He couldn't have got a swater or a smarter colleen in all Scotland."

"But she wants the money, William, and what will any one not do for money?"

"Thrue for it, me darlint. Money plays the devil wid everything. There's the doctor."

"What's the matter?" asked the latter, as he came into the little room and saw Mary in her recumbent position.

"She's seen something in that paper that's given her a shock. Mr Duncan's married."

"Oh—ah! I got cards this afternoon. Never had a hint of it before. H'm—let me see—pity the girl got to know it so abruptly—a sore disappointment for her, I fancy—poor girl, and her so pretty too—splendid figure—quite a model—and what magnificent hair. Poor creature! we must do what we can to get her roused. Ah! she is coming to; I see a flutter in her eyelids."

The doctor applied a bottle of strong salts to Mary's nostrils. She heaved a long sigh, gave a low, protracted, plaintive moan, and slowly struggled back to consciousness.

The blow had fallen.

CHAPTER V

THE WANDERING OUTCAST

Poor Mary awoke to utter misery. When she opened her eyes she was for a moment or two bewildered, and remembered nothing, but a glance at the newspaper, which she still tightly held in her hand, served to recall the terrible truth that Duncan Grahame was married.

"Do you know anything of this, doctor?" she asked, in a tone the strange distinctness of which startled every one.

"Of what, Mary?" asked the doctor, evasively.

"Of Duncan's marriage," she pointedly returned.

"Well, yes," said the doctor, thinking it best to give a direct answer. "I got cards this afternoon—the first hint I had of the matter."

"It is true, then—quite true," murmured Mary; and though she spoke audibly, she seemed to be speaking to herself. "I thought it might be a mistake—some other person of the same name. But no, no; it is real, it is true—true."

"You feel better now, I hope?" said the doctor, in a kind tone.

"Better?" repeated Mary, with a bitter ghastly smile. "Oh, yes, yes; I am better. I shall not faint again."

"That's a brave girl. It is a trial for you, no doubt, and for a time you will feel it keenly. But bear up, make up your mind to endure what is inevitable, and by-and-bye you will get over it."

The doctor said this in a hurried way. The case was one in which he had no skill, and what little advice he thought it best to give he gave rapidly, not knowing really what to say.

Mary replied by another wan, silent, ghastly smile, but uttered no word. The doctor took his leave, saying that he would be glad to return if his services were required.

After he was gone, Helen began to give comfort in the way that she thought best, and this was by railing in un-measured terms against Duncan Grahame. It seemed to her that in the circumstances she could give pleasure to Mary only by reviling the author of her ruin.

Such coarse and vulgar invective as that in which she

48

indulged was as distasteful to Mary's bleeding heart as was
Dr Ford's superficial chatter, and she made no reply to it.
Feigning to be overcome by sleep, she asked Helen to leave
her for the night, and drawing her child to her bosom, she
passed the night in perfect silence.

But she slept not, even for a moment. Her mind was busy
with its bitter, bitter thoughts. Duncan Grahame was unveiled
to her now in all his vileness, selfishness, and deceit. The fair
covering of love and nobleness with which her fancy and affection had invested him was utterly torn away. She now saw
his worthless character in its very nakedness. There was
nothing to cling to—no possibility of mistake. There he was—
a revealed hypocrite, deceiver, and betrayer.

She had been duped and basely and heartlessly deserted.
Not only had she been ruined by the man she trusted, but he
had sacrificed her to his own interests. Her sequestration in
the cottage was not for the purpose of sheltering her from
shame and reproach, but to keep the matter secret till its discovery could not injure himself. His silence, his absence were
fully explained now.

That night of silent thought and bitter reflection effected
in Mary a complete separation between the present and the
past. In the morning she was altogether another creature. Her
very character seemed changed. The cruel blow which her
confiding trust had received destroyed the woman's weakness
she formerly possessed, and a hard, fierce, rugged recklessness
came in its place. There were just two issues which experience
like hers could reach—she must either have been crushed and
broken-hearted or roused to fierce, indignant, self-reliance.
This latter was the actual result. That grief which dissolves in
tears did not come to her. Her misery did not reduce her to
despair, as it would have reduced thousands. On the contrary,
it produced in her a certain strength of resolution which she
had not before manifested, and her course was taken.

The following was a cold and dark November day, and at
an early hour in the afternoon she surprised Helen M'Dougal
extremely by intimating that she was that very afternoon
going away.

The intelligence, though it astonished, did not grieve Helen;
in fact, she had just been thinking that, now that Duncan
Grahame's intentions were revealed, the sooner she was free of
her lodger the better.

"But where are you going?" asked Helen, in a tone which betokened more of curiosity than of sympathy.

"I cannot say yet," she answered; "only I must leave you, for I have no means of paying you. Tell me this—Have you been paid up to this time?"

"Yes, that is paid in a certain way, though, to tell you the truth, I expected more. But I free you of it. It was the young lying blackguard that—"

"Then," interrupted Mary, "to prevent you from being at further loss, I shall leave at once."

The woman made no opposition to this proposal, and Mary went away up stairs to make ready.

Her few preparations did not occupy much time, and when she came down again, with her baby wrapped in a shawl and sleeping in her arms, Burke was in the kitchen.

"And is it yerself that's going to lave us?" exclaimed the Irishman, when Mary appeared.

"Yes, I am going away," answered Mary, quite calmly. "There is no need for me remaining here any longer."

"Be jabers! but I'd have someting out ov the young gint anyhow. He's bound to pay swately for the child, and—"

"Good-bye," said Mary, holding out her thin, white hand.

"Take a drop of the craythur afore you go," said Burke, pouring out a glass of whisky.

"Yes, do," urged Helen. "It will put some heat in you this cold afternoon, and make you strong for your walk."

"Uv coorse it will," seconded the Irishman. "Nothing like the potheen[1] for puttin' away grief and keepin' up the spirits."

Mary hesitated a moment, then she quickly raised the glass to her lips, and with a desperate impulse drank it off.

She said good-bye again, and then parted in a kindly manner. Then she drew the child closer to her bosom, passed over the threshold, and began her weary wandering.

At the end of the lane she did not turn up into the village, but turned to the right along the road she had, months before, come with Duncan.

For the first few miles she felt neither fatigue nor depression. The whisky she had drunk made her feel wildly excited, and

---

1. Highly alcoholic Irish spirit, home distilled from barley or potatoes, and illegal in Ireland from 1661.

banished the bitterness and sadness from her heart. She began for the first time to have faith in its power to banish care, so highly extolled by Helen and Burke.

The short twilight soon came on, and night began to settle down. The day had been extremely cold and very lowering. A chilling wind had swept along the unsheltered road, driving the withered leaves before it, and passing through the bare, black hedges and across the stubble of the shorn fields; and as daylight faded this piercing wind brought with it hard, battering rain-drops out of the leaden clouds that hung in the sky.

Mary was but thinly clad. The shawl which should have protected her from the cold was, with a mother's self-sacrifice, wrapped round the baby, and, as the heavy drops came splashing in her face, her chief thought was how she might save her helpless infant from the storm.

She was now becoming weary and depressed. The stimulating influence of the whisky had departed, and its corresponding power of wretchedness had supervened. The darkening night, the lonely road, the bitter blast, the weariness of her limbs, and the desolation of her heart, made the poor girl miserable indeed.

Where was she going?—Home—to the place of her happy childhood and girlhood—to the place where once she had known peace and dreamed not of sorrow. She was going there, and yet not to rest. It was to be no longer a home for her. The shame and punishment she must now bear she would not bear in the sight of those who knew her. The fierce spirit that had been roused within her would not brook that, and she had resolved to go to Edinburgh. What she would do when she got to Edinburgh she had no distinct or definite idea of. She would work—work for herself and her child—that was her thought; but of the kind of work, or how she was to procure it, she was ignorant.

She would not go, however, without having a last look at the old, dear place. She had no wish to speak to her father, or that he should know of her visit; but she had a strong desire to look upon him unseen, and to have an interview with Peggy M'Naughton. To Kirkton, then, she was wending her way. She hoped to reach it unseen, and to be away from it for ever ere the morning light.

Fiercer blew the wind, and faster beat the rain against poor

Mary's shivering form, as she tottered forward carrying her motionless burden. The night was every moment growing darker and wilder, making the progress of the weary one very slow and very painful.

At a late hour she crawled forward to the outskirts of Kirkton, and looked for the light from the parlour window in the cottage of Braeside. She looked with eager anxiety, but saw it not. The rain and the wind, she thought, must be blinding her, or perhaps her father had now retired to rest. She stood still a moment, and wiped away the rain that trickled down her face, and peered steadily through the darkness in the direction where she knew the cottage lay.

Alas! the cottage was shrouded in ominous gloom. The gleam of light which used on winter nights to send its cheering ray far over the country was extinguished, and Braeside lay enveloped in the universal November darkness.

Mary tried to hasten her steps through the village. She could have reached the cottage without going near the houses, but the path was circuitous, and the poor girl was now wet to the skin and nearly exhausted.

As she crept painfully along the silent, deserted street, and saw the dim shadow of the houses she knew so well, the sense of her degraded position deepened on her spirit. She was wandering as an outcast in the village street where she had once played in all the guileless innocence of childhood. Once these houses had all an open door for her, and smiling faces to welcome her over the threshold, but now both houses and hearts were shut against her, and she crept past in the darkness of night like a guilty thing. Never till that moment had her error, her crime, been so deeply realised, for now she felt how completely it had shut her out from the fellowship of those she had known all her days.

Heaving a long, heavy sigh, she passed the last of the buildings, and turned her weary feet into the lane which led to her father's cottage. Her heart now beat very fast, her head swam round, her knees trembled, and she grasped a gate to keep herself from falling. The long walk, the battling with the wind, and her excessive agitation, had completely worn out her strength.

After standing for a few moments, she quitted the support of the gate, and tottered forward. By-and-bye the form of the cottage and the out-buildings near loomed through the darkness. Amid the most perfect silence, she approached, and stood by the closed door of her early home.

No light, no sound. The silence and darkness of the grave seemed to rest upon the spot; only at intervals the gusts of wind came wailing against the gable, and the heavy rain-drops battered upon the walls.

Mary made her way round to the rear of the cottage, and her heart bounded with thankfulness when she saw a gleam of light come from the kitchen window. The curtain was drawn, but at the side she got a glimpse of the interior, and saw Peggy M'Naughton seated before the fire, busy knitting— her favourite occupation in her hours of leisure.

Satisfied that no one was in the kitchen but the old woman, Mary gave a feeble, timid tap upon the glass.

Peggy heard it, raised her head, and listened.

"That weary rain," she muttered, bending to her work again.

Mary would have tapped again immediately, but the melancholy change which had passed on Peggy's face since last she saw it startled and shocked her so much that she had not the power. For one thing, Peggy looked twenty years older. Her face had grown withered and wrinkled, but the sad and sorrowful expression of it was what chiefly frightened Mary. Grief of the most hopeless kind was pictured on it, as if some dreadful mental suffering had lately been endured, the dark shadow of which abode as if never to depart.

The weary wanderer tapped again, and this time a little louder, and again Peggy raised her head and listened.

"Peggy," said Mary, in a faint, husky tone.

Peggy threw down her knitting, clasped her hands, and looked in terror towards the window.

"Guid be aboot us!" she ejaculated. "Is that a wairnin'?"[2]

"Peggy," said Mary, once again in the same weak, tremulous tone, "it's me; pray open the door; I am Mary."

The old woman gave a shrill scream, and bounded across the kitchen floor. The bolt of the back door was withdrawn, the door itself was pulled quickly back, and a pair of eager arms were stretched forward, which clutched Mary's figure as she tottered into the passage.

---

2. Peggy imagines a "warning", or spiritual visitation.

"My bairn, my bairn! Oh! is it you, my bairn?" sobbed
Peggy, in wildest excitement.

"Yes, Peggy, it is me," answered Mary, gulping the words
out hysterically, and staggering forward into the lighted
kitchen.

"Thank God, ye hae come at last!^{3} Oh! Mary, Mary!
But, my ain darlin', ye are wat and weary, and—Gracious
Providence!"

The poor girl had sunk down on the nearest chair, in a
half-fainting condition, and her benumbed arms relaxing in
powerless weakness from the child which they had held so
long to her bosom, it rolled upon her knee, and would have
fallen to the floor if Peggy had not instinctively caught it in
her arms. As she did so, the shawl which covered it fell aside,
and the sweet, rosy face of the infant was revealed, eliciting
from Peggy the ejaculation we have recorded, and then striking her utterly dumb.

The sight of the child took away the power of speech, but
it quickened the power of thought. At one glance, as it were,
Peggy saw all—Mary's betrayal and desertion—her trust and
her ruin. She stood with the child in her arms, gazing upon
it in a kind of stupefaction, when it opened its large blue eyes
and laughed up in her face. That laugh won Peggy's entire
heart. She snatched it to her lips, and kissed it with vehement
emotion. Then she took away the wet shawl which enveloped
it, and wrapped it in a blanket which hung near the fire.

Meanwhile Mary's prostration increased. The heat of the
kitchen overpowered her, and faintly she cried for water.

This turned Peggy's attention from the child to its mother,
and the white, wan face and sinking form of her loved one
gave her a terrible shock. Quickly she laid the child into an
easy chair, and rushed to where Mary sat.

"My darlin', my dawtie," she fondly murmured. "Oh, but
ye are sair forfouchten. Hae ye come far in the wind and
rain?"

"I have been walking for the last nine hours," gasped
Mary.

"God help ye! an' ye are as wat as muck."

"Oh, Peggy," murmured Mary, anxiously, "is my father

---

3. The book gives "Thank Heaven".

very angry? I don't want him to see me; I don't want him to know if I have been here; but oh tell me is he well?"

Such a look of agony passed over Peggy's face! She tried to speak twice, and failed. At the third effort she managed to articulate—

"Ay, he's weel."

This was followed by a groan; then she hastily went on to take away Mary's wet clothes.

"Oh, I am so glad he is well, Peggy! I thought I might see him in at the front window; but I suppose he has gone to bed, so I shall not see him at all. But I deserve it all. Do not take off these things, Peggy, for I must soon be away again."

"Away!" echoed Peggy. "Whaur are ye gaun away to!"

"Hush! I cannot, will not live here. I am ruined, Peggy—ruined. He has betrayed, deserted me. Oh, what a poor mad dupe I have been!"

"The scoundrel!" groaned Peggy; "and has he really refused to marry ye?"

"Oh, he deceived me up to the last moment, and now he has married another."

"Wae's me, wae's me!" wailed the old woman. "I canna help takin' blame to mysel' for lettin' ye carry on wi' him. I've had a sair sair heart sin' that awfu' mornin'. Oh, Mary, what for did ye leave us?"

"He persuaded me that it was for the best," answered Mary, "and that it would save me from open shame. I believed him then, but I know his object now. Oh, he was false, false. But I have been the dupe, and I have made up my mind to be the victim. No, Peggy, do not undress me, for I have not long to remain."

"Lord bless us, lassie, what dae ye mean?" exclaimed Peggy, in astonishment. "Noo that ye are come back ye'se never get awa' again, but ye'll just bide wi' me and—"

"Peggy, do not madden me!" cried Mary, with passionate vehemence. "Never will I stay here to face the scorn of my acquaintances. I have brought my own fate upon me, and I mean to endure it; but not here—no, not here."

"The lassie's dementit!" ejaculated Peggy, staring in wonder at Mary's reddening cheeks and flashing eyes. "Gang awa! And whaur wad ye gang tae?"

"To where I am not known," returned the girl; "to Edinburgh. There I will work for bread to myself and my boy."

"Tae Edinburgh!" repeated Peggy, in a tone of saddest pity. "That's perfect nonsense, my darlin', perfect nonsense. No, no, ye'll just stay beside me, noo that I am left my lane, and—"

She stopped suddenly, for she had unwittingly said more than she intended. Mary's quick apprehension caught in alarm at her words, and a fearful terror rushed to her heart.

"Merciful heaven! what mean you?" she asked, clutching at Peggy's arm, and gazing with searching eagerness into her face. "My father!" she gasped; "you—you said he was well."

"Sae he is, dear, sae he is," returned Peggy, with quivering lips. She tried to allay Mary's quickened anxiety, but her great grief was stronger than her power of control, and she burst into tears.

"My God!" screamed Mary, clutching the old woman's arm more vehemently than before.[4] "What is it—what has happened? My father—where is he? Do not deceive me. It would be cruel to deceive me. Tell me the truth. Oh be quick and tell me."

"O Mary, Mary, yer father's deid," sobbed Peggy, unable longer to keep back the sorrowful truth.

"Dead!" echoed Mary, recoiling at the awful shock. Her form seemed suddenly to pass into the rigidity of marble. She stood straight up, her face grew fearfully white, a glaze of stony horror settled in her eyes, and for some moments it seemed as if a statue, and not a living form, stood in the apartment.

Peggy's burst of grief merged into terror at the change which passed over Mary. She rushed towards her, and cast her arms wildly round her.

"Oh, I did wrang tae tell ye sae sune. I didna mean it. But dinna tak on sae. I said yer father was weel, and sae he is—far better and happier than ever he could be on earth. And he suffered naething, but just swaffed awa' in the fit four hours after he took it. He never spak', and the doctor said he wasna sensible. Sae he wan quietly till his rest, and that was a great blessin'."

"Dead!" repeated Mary. "Dead! and I have killed him."

"No, no; dinna say that, Mary, for that's no richt. His

---

4. Again, the book drops the invocation of God.

time was come, puir man, and ye ken he was weel prepared."

"My poor, poor father!" cried the remorse-stricken girl, as
a sudden but blissful[5] revulsion of feeling assailed her. Her
burning brain found sudden relief in a flood of tears, and,
throwing herself back in the chair, she wept with the wildest
vehemence.

That outburst of sorrow probably saved her reason from
being overturned, or prevented a brain fever. She wept herself
into quiet sadness.

"When did it occur?" she asked, turning towards Peggy,
who, almost equally distressed, was striving to soothe her by
all the means she could think of. "When did it happen? Tell
me all."

"It all happened in the mornin', when we found out that
ye was awa'," replied Peggy. "Nae suner had yer faither read
yer letter than he gied a deep groan and fell back in his chair.
He had taen a stroke o' deid palsy, and ne'er spak' again. In
four hoors he breathed his last."

"At least, then, he did not curse me," groaned Mary;
"and he has been saved from the sorrow which my shame
would have caused him."

"But, wae's me," added Peggy, who did not hear these
words, "my ill news is no a' telt yet. On the funeral day, what
did that vagabond, Leech the lawyer, dae but produce a
paper which he ca'd a bond for twa thousand pounds that he
said yer faither was awn him. It's as great a lee as ever man
telt, for weel dae I ken that yer faither wasna awn a fardin tae
ony body, and he had a lot o' siller lyin' in Leech's hands
forby. But there's nae proof for it, and the paper was signed
by yer faither, and naebody can say onything. Sae at Martinmas here we hae tae flit, and the rubber taks Braeside and a'
that belangs tae it. But he'll never thrive; the defrauder o' the
faitherless and the orphan can never thrive."

"For my sake it matters little," sighed Mary. "But you—
what is to become of you in your old days?"

"Fortunately, my darlin', I hae my bit siller in the bank

---

5. "blissful" presumably in the sense of holy, blessed, transfiguring (all now
obsolete).

at Stirlin'. It's no very muckle, but it will keep you and me
and the bit bairnie in a plain way."

"No, no, Peggy; I cannot, will not, be a burden on you. If
you promise to keep my presence here a secret from the neighbours, I'll stay for a day or two, but no longer. I am resolved
on that, and nothing will turn me."

*

For four days Mary and her child remained in great seclusion at Braeside. Not a soul in Kirkton knew that she was
there. During these four days Peggy used every effort to
induce her to forego her intention of departing to Edinburgh,
but to all her solicitations Mary turned a deaf ear. The wilfulness of her disposition was as great as ever, and a certain
bitter recklessness was now added to it.

She would not change her purpose, but she did at length
consent to allow Peggy to keep the child. The little fellow had
by this time taken to the old woman most surprisingly. The
exhaustion of the foot journey, and the shock received by the
news of her father's death, had made Mary incapable of suck-
ling the child any longer, but the system of feeding to which
Peggy resorted turned out most successful, and the infant
seemed to be in such good hands that the mother's heart was
constrained to admit that for the little fellow's good it would
be better that he should remain with his faithful nurse.

So at an early hour on the fifth morning Mary bade her
sleeping infant farewell. To the weeping Peggy she also bade
adieu, and in the darkness which preceded a November dawn,
she again left her home—and left it, as it turned out, for ever.
She had come unnoticed, and unnoticed she left. Towards
evening weary and footsore she entered Edinburgh, and when
she had entered the great city she had unconsciously come to
the brink of her final and awful ruin.

CHAPTER VI

BURKE AND HARE IN TANNER'S CLOSE— THE MOCK FUNERAL—THE FIRST VISIT TO SURGEONS' SQUARE—THEY RESOLVE ON MURDER

Two years have come and gone, and once more it is an autumn day—a day of blue sky and bright sunshine—a day when throughout the whole extent of broad and bonny Scotland the reapers are in the fields cutting down the yellow grain, enlivening their toil by laughter and song. In all the vales and in all the uplands of the mellow landscape are many bands to be seen, with their bright hook-blades flashing in the sun as they bury them among the shocks of corn, while on the still and sultry air the sound of their happy voices are wafted among the woods and over the slopes of purple heather, and down the smiling course of the crystal stream, where the latest wild flowers of the year are blooming in richest loveliness, and where woodland warblers are swelling the thanksgiving song which universal nature is raising to the beneficent creator who has crowned the year with his goodness.[1]

But this same autumn day can show another and darker scene than this. In the dingy, dirty closes of old Edinburgh there is to be seen little of the blue sky and less of the bright sunshine, and there the faintest echo of the reaper's song is not heard, and the happy harvest joy is unknown.

In a little dingy room of a house in one of the narrowest and dirtiest closes in the West Port, a group of four living persons are assembled. Two of these were Burke and Helen M'Dougal. Burke sat in a corner near the window on a cobbler's stool, mending a shoe, and Helen, and another

---

1. The book drops "and where woodland warblers are swelling the thanksgiving song which universal nature is raising to the beneficent creator who has crowned the year with his goodness", perhaps for its gushing natural and religious sentiment.

woman were huddled together on stools, near the embers of a fire which had cooked the breakfast they had just eaten.

Burke had much more of a broken-down appearance than when last we saw him as a day-labourer in Stirlingshire. He and Helen had come to Edinburgh as they proposed, but idle inclinations and drunken habits had prevented them from prospering much in the world. With the last remnant of Helen's money Burke became a travelling merchant, in which occupation he succeeded but poorly. Then he wrought at various country places, and finally he took to shoe-mending, and he and Helen became lodgers in this house in Tanner's Close, West Port.

The woman with whom Helen huddled on the hearth was the landlady of the house, a dirty, slattern, sensual, hard-featured woman, with an Irish cast of countenance; her hair seemed red, so far as the colour could be determined through the dirt; her face had a bold, masculine expression; and her whole appearance denoted less of the woman than of the virago.

Her protector, the lord and master of the establishment, sat on a higher stool at the other side of the fire, moodily smoking a black short pipe. A more repulsive-looking wretch than he was, mortal eye could scarcely look upon. His small head sloped away back from the brow to the crown, very much like an idiot's. The face below the brow, however, was not idiotic in its expression, but it was worse. To use a good Scotch term, it was "gruesome" to look at. There was a huge mouth, high cheek bones, and small oval grey eyes, a most extraordinary distance from each other. They seemed little other than horizontal slits in the skin of the face, into which a little grey glancing ball had been inserted. But the horrid, loathsome leer which was their natural and almost invariable expression, made one uncomfortable, even by looking at them, and suggested ideas of a disposition of the cruelest character. This man was *Hare*.

On a low, curtainless, and filthy-looking bed behind the group lay a coffin of blackened deal, very plain and coarse-looking. It contained the body of a lodger who had died a day or two before, and who was that day to be buried. He had been an old soldier, a pensioner, whose quarterly allowance was nearly but not quite due, and would not, therefore, now be paid.[2] Hare had been looking forward to this money as the means wherewith he was to be paid what the old man owed him; and the latter having died just a little too soon, this hope of satisfaction was thereby taken away, and it was this disappointment which made Hare moody and sullen as he sat silently smoking his pipe.

"A penny for yer thoughts, me boy," said Burke, breaking the silence that had for some time prevailed.

"Faix, then, ye may hand it over at wonst," replied Hare, as he slowly took the pipe from between his teeth. "I was thinking what a mighty shame it was uv the ould vagabond to go off in such a spiteful hurry. If his soul and body had hung together till next week, it's his quarter's pinsion I would have got, and then he might have gone to Purgatory[3] and wel-come—the sooner the better afther that. But divil a farden will I get now, and him next to four pounds in my debt. Bad luck to him, the ould Highland thief!"

"Be jabers, thin, couldn't the money be got out uv him yet?" said Burke, speaking like a man to whom a sudden idea had occurred.

"What the divil do ye mane?" asked Hare, as a look of wonder issued from his ill-favoured eyes.

"Troth, thin, and wouldn't the doctors be afther buyin' him. I've heard as how they employ men to take bodies out uv their graves; and what would be the differ to them if the body has never been buried?"

"By the powers, but that's an illigant idea intirely," exclaimed Hare.

"And so it is," added his wife. "The devil a funeral he should have at all, at all, if his old bones would bring money."

"But how could it be done," suggested Helen, who relished the idea no less than the others. "You know he is to be buried

---

2. After reform in 1806, military pensions rewarded service and supported disability. The disabled could receive a shilling a day. The 1816 register of mili-tary pensioners suggests that six out of seven Scottish soldiers from the Napo-leonic era returned to Britain, but often to England or the lowland cities. See J. E. Cookson, "Early Nineteenth-Century Scottish Military Pensioners as Homecoming Soldiers", *The Historical Journal* 53.2 (June 2009): 333, 323, 327.

3. Pae signifies Hare's Catholicism by his invocation of Purgatory, a doc-trine not shared by most Protestant churches.

to-day at one o'clock, and the people are asked. If the neighbours came to know we sold him to the doctors, they would make an awful noise about it."

"Och, and wouldn't we get mighty aisy over that, Nelly," observed Burke. "Sure, the coffin full uv that tanner's bark[4] out there would be just as heavy as if ould Donald was in it; and couldn't we bury it like a Christian, and never a sowl the wiser?"

"Uv coorse, we could," cried Hare, starting up and giving a low, satirical laugh, while the horrid leer broadened on his inhuman countenance. "But," he added, "how are we to get the bargain made wid the doctors?"

"We'll find that out up in Surgeons' Square," rejoined Burke. "It's there I've heard the bodies are taken to. We'll go up to-night, Hare, me boy, and do the best we can wid the queer devils."

This arrangement being deemed every way satisfactory, Burke and Hare went to the back of the neighbouring tannery, where lay an immense heap of bark, and a quantity of this they managed to bring into the house unseen. Without ceremony, the body was drawn from the coffin, and, enveloped as it was in the shirt which formed its shroud, it was carried into a little room adjoining, and pushed under the bed out of sight. For greater security against discovery, the door of the room was locked, and Hare put the key in his own pocket.

The work of stuffing the coffin with the bark was now quickly proceeded with, and when the gloomy receptacle was filled, the lid was screwed down, and the coffin was laid on the bed as before.

The trick succeeded to the entire satisfaction of those concerned. At one o'clock the funeral proceeded from the house to a neighbouring churchyard, and the coffin was interred with the usual formalities, no one but Hare and his accomplice having the slightest suspicion that a fraud had been perpetrated.

At dusk the worthies set out to pay a visit to Surgeons'

---

4. Tanner's Close, beneath the west side of Castle Hill, was named for its local industry, in this period the tannery of Allan Boak. Tanning used tannins derived from tree bark. RCAHMS website record NT27.

Square. The business being utterly new to them they were at a loss how to proceed. Burke left Hare in the Cowgate, and proceeded alone to open negotiations.

The little melancholy square was silent as the grave, but a light glimmered in one of the windows of Doctor Knox's class-rooms, and from that window a young man was at the moment gazing upon the gathering twilight of the autumn night. Burke, as he sauntered hesitatingly along, eyed this youth with a sly and stealthy glance. The errand on which he had come had made him nervous a bit, and he didn't know "at all, at all" how he was to make known his business.

While directing his side-long glances, he observed the youth quit the window, and presently appearing at the entrance door below, he beckoned to Burke to come forward.

The latter obeyed, and for a moment the two stood silently confronting each other, the youth curiously scanning the man before him to see if the guess he had made as to the object of his presence there was correct, and Burke absolutely blushing in his awkward bashfulness.

"Well, my man, what do you want?" asked the young doctor, pretty sure that his conjecture was correct, though he knew that the man before him was not one of their regular body-snatchers.

"Want," repeated Burke sheepishly; "I—I don't know."

"Oh, come—you do want something; tell me what it is."

Just then a footstep was heard in the square, and Burke started and looked nervously round in the direction whence the sound came.

"Och, musha, there's somebody coming," he whispered.

"See, come along here," said the youth, taking Burke by the arm, and half pulling him up the stair.

He led him into a room where other three youths seemed at work, for their coats were off, and they wore cotton sleeves on their arms.

Large tables stood everywhere in the room, and on the tables lay bundles covered by dirty cloths. The atmosphere of the room was close and full of heavy odours. Burke shuddered as he looked at the awful bundles, and, turning to his con-ductor, said, hastily—

"Might I make bould to ask if you are Doctor Knox?"

"Oh, no; but I am one of his assistants, and will do just the same."

The other assistants, smelling business, came eagerly forward.

"Got 'the *thing*' for us—eh?" asked one.

Burke looked dubious, and still hesitated. He did not exactly know if he understood what was meant by "the thing."

"Oh, speak out; don't be afraid. You are all safe here," said his first interrogator, encouragingly. "Have you a body to dispose of?"

"Yes," answered Burke, immediately relieved by being able to come to the point.

"That's right; this is the place to sell such an article."

"And what do you give for wun?"

"It depends much on the condition of the subject. Six, seven, eight, and sometimes as high as ten pounds."

"The wun I've got is fresh and beautiful," returned Burke, whose eyes sparkled at the prospect of so much cash.

"Well, when you bring it we shall see what it is worth. Can you have it here to-night at ten?"

"Och, sure and I can."

"Then bring it at that hour, in a box; and it may be as well to let no one see you—you understand?"

"I take you," said Burke, with a nod of intelligence. "Sure, now, I've got a tea-chest[5] nate and handy; might that do to hould it in?"

"Nothing could be better. Remember the hour. I shall be here to receive the subject and pay you."

Burke went down the stair highly elated. He had succeeded in his mission beyond his expectations, and was delighted to find that no unpleasant questions were asked.

Hare was waiting anxiously for him in the Cowgate.[6]

"Have you seen the doctors, thin?" he eagerly inquired in a hurried whisper.

"Indade, and I have, whole four o' them, me boy. It's all right. We are to take the body up at tin o'clock to-night, and they'll pay us for it."

---

5. Plywood box, lined with metal, about 20 × 30 inches, used to ship tea to Britain.

6. Street running under the South Bridge—another dark and crowded slum where Hare could skulk.

"Och, murther, isn't that beautiful," said Hare, with one of his most frightful leers; "and did they say what they would give for it?"

"They have to see it first; but they towld me they sometimes gave as much as tin pounds for a good wun."

"Thunder and turf! tin pounds!" ejaculated Hare, in joyful amazement.

"Isn't that illigant?" added Burke.

"Be jabers, and it's twice as good as the ould boy's pension."

"Uv coorse, the half is mine," said Burke, as he shuffled along.

"We'll share it to a farden, me boy; and a mighty jolly blow-out we'll have afther we come back."

Arrived at Tanner's Close, they acquainted the women with their prospect, and the tea-chest of which Burke had spoken was emptied of its miscellaneous contents, and the body of the old pensioner packed into it. This matter required silence and secrecy, for some of the lodgers had come in for the night, and it was necessary that none of them should have a suspicion of what was going forward. But the little room in which the body lay was well adapted for this object. It was the room which Burke and Helen occupied. It was on the other side of the passage, and isolated from the rest of the house—a solitary back room, with a small window, opposite which was a high grey dead wall.

It was not without considerable difficulty that the old man's body, now stiff in death, was bent and packed into the tea-chest. The actors in the scene were far from being at ease in the doing of their work, for it was the first time they had been engaged in such a matter, and the nature of it was such as to make the hardest hearts quiver. But the expectation of the gain to be derived made them go through with it; and what will not the hope of gaining money tempt man to do? It is this hope that has led to the worst crimes by which humanity has been disgraced. The love of money is truly the root of all evil,[7] and how deep this root goes down into the sinner's soul we shall yet find exemplified in the history of these four who are

---

7. 1 Timothy 6:10: "For the love of money is the root of all evil."

now in the little room packing up the cold clay of their dead fellow-being, to be sold like merchandise.

The task was done, the tea-chest was made secure, and the hour appointed was near. The burden was hoisted on the broad shoulders of Burke, who made his way with it up the narrow close, through the Grassmarket, and by way of Candlemaker Row into Bristo Port. Mindful of what the assistant at Surgeons' Square had told him of the necessity of using caution so that no one should see them, Burke took this circuitous route. At Bristo Port, Hare received the burden, and by this division of labour they got safely and comfortably into Surgeons' Square.

Still timorous, through inexperience, they did not march boldly into the dissecting hall, but laid the chest down close to a cellar door, and gave information of its arrival.

"Here with it," said the assistant, who, with the other three were still at work in the room. It was a mere common-place matter of business with them, and they neither felt nor manifested any scruples of delicacy.

The next minute Burke and his companion brought the box into the room, and the *piece of goods* was displayed. The merchants did not exactly discant on the excellence of the commodity, but the purchasers examined it with a keen eye to its commercial value.

Without saying a word, one of the students left the hall, and almost immediately a smart, fussy, self-consequential man, wearing spectacles entered. This was Doctor Knox, who rapidly ran his eye over the body, and simply said—

"Seven pounds ten."

Burke and Hare were a little disappointed at the sum named. They expected near ten pounds at least. But to such men seven pounds ten was a large sum, and their mode of earning it very easy, so without a word they pocketed the price, took up the empty tea-chest and departed.

"Perhaps we shall be able to give you more for the next," said the assistant, as they were going out at the door. "Such a thing as that is always welcome here."

And thus the transaction was finished, and Burke and Hare went home to Tanner's Close, with their first earnings in Surgeons' Square.

Who can forbear remarking the fatal facility for the disposal of human bodies which the history of this transaction discloses?

We designedly and deliberately say a *fatal facility*. Here was a man, a perfect stranger to these doctors, who offered a dead body for sale, and it was bought and no questions asked—not one simple interrogation as to how the body had been procured; and not only so, but an invitation was given to bring more. Was this not, *at the least*, presenting a very strong temptation? Was it possible that the idea never occurred to the doctors that the subjects which they bought so freely, and paid for with a comparatively large sum, might have been got in a criminal way? Was their faith in the men who engaged in such traffic so great that they considered them incapable of doing anything worse than robbing a churchyard or purchasing unburied bodies from needy relatives? We cannot think so. We are forced to believe that with them the exigencies of science were made paramount, and that they made it a point to ask no questions, lest they should be put in possession of dangerous knowledge. But the fact is, the principle of their procedure was immoral. They based the claims of their humane science on a practice not only at variance with honesty, but abhorrent to all human feeling, and it was impossible that a system, illicit in every sense, should not lead to crimes of the worst description; and of these crimes we must consider the doctors *presumptively guilty*, inasmuch as they carefully abstained from satisfying themselves that they were not committed. When the fearful truth did come to light, the doctors tried to clear themselves by protesting their ignorance. In our opinion, it was this ignorance which constituted their greatest guilt.

"Well," remarked Hare, as they made their way home by the Cowgate, "we haven't got so much as we expected, but by the powers, it's a lot o' money for carrying a full tea-chest the matter uv three-quarters of a mile."

"Thrue for it," returned Burke, "it's a mighty long time we are in making as much at hawking or mending shoes. Come, let us share in Rymer's, and take in a bottle a-piece to make a night uv it."

Acting on this suggestion, Burke and Hare entered a public-house not far from their residence, and in a back room there, over a glass of whisky, they divided the spoil. Then, taking each a quantity of liquor with them, they made their welcome appearance in Tanner's Close.

Money earned in such a way, and by such men, could not

possibly be well spent. A very carnival of alcoholic revelry
began. Work was not to be thought of while the money lasted,
and the reckless mode of disposing of it was not calculated to
make it last long. Several days of feasting, drinking, quarrelling, and fighting ensued, till the last shilling of the seven
pounds ten was done, and then the wild revelry was, per force,
brought to an end.

After the carouse, work was of course more distasteful than
ever, and on the first day of enforced sobriety Burke sat down
in his cobbler's stall with very great reluctance. He was sitting
alone in the afternoon (all the others being out) listlessly
mending a shoe, when Hare came in. He had been hawking a
little, but to no great purpose, and was in a correspondingly
dissatisfied mood. But he sat down in silence, and meditated
with the air of one who revolved a thought in his mind.

"I say, Burke, me boy," he observed, after a long pause,
"this is mighty poor work for both uv us. I made only two-
pence with the hurley to-day."

"Faix, thin," answered Burke, "it's meself that's not much
better. This bit uv a job won't turn in more than sixpence. I
was just thinking to meself what a lucky thing it 'ud be if
another lodger would be kind enough to die in the house."

"Och, sure, and I've thought that a thousand times," said
Hare. "But there's no appearance uv that luck comin'—*unless
we make it.*"

The last words Hare uttered in a whisper, and the moment
he had done so he rose and looked into the other apartment
to see that no one was listening.

The room in which they were was the small back room
which looked out upon the dead wall. Helen and Mrs Hare
had both come in, but, Hare closing the door, they could not
hear the conversation.

Burke eyed his companion's proceedings with some interest,
and when the latter returned to his seat, he had ceased to
work, and was looking fixedly at him.

"And how could we make the luck to come?" he asked, in
reference to Hare's last words.

"Aisy enough. Give one a knock on the head. The tramps
that come here to lodge would never be missed."

"Thrue for it, but the doctors would see that the body had
been murdered, and wouldn't that be afther bringing us into
a purty scrape?"

"Begorra, thin, it's a pity it couldn't be done without making a mark at all, at all," observed Hare.

The words went like an electric current into Burke's memory, and roused from thence, with the rapidity of lightning, the information he had two years before received from Doctor Ford.

"Thunder and turf! but it *can* be done," he exclaimed, in great excitement. "I was towld of a way that doesn't lave a scratch."

And throwing down his work, he rose and came close to Hare, and repeated what Doctor Ford had said.

Hare listened with ferocious eagerness, and the dreadful leer became more than ever diabolic. He comprehended the horrible *modus operandi* almost by instinct.

"Och, thin, it's the beautiful luck that will come to us afther all," he exclaimed. "Sure, we can't try it too soon, and maybe it's tin pounds we'll get this time up by at the Square. They tould us they would be glad to see us again."

"Troth and they did, and I didn't forget it," said Burke.

This, then, was the fruit of that first visit to Surgeons' Square. The welcome they had there received, and the profitable transaction they had negotiated, coupled with the indiscreet communication formerly made to Burke by Dr Ford, made these two men resolve on the crime of murder.

Murder, in the year 1827, was no new crime, nor was the motive for its commission which actuated these men new, for to obtain money the darkest deeds of crime have been done in all ages of the world, and this was precisely the object which Burke and Hare had in view. But the mode of murder they resolved on was entirely new, and the sale of the body of their victim was also an unheard-of mode of making the crime yield its expected fruit; and but for the system of secret body-buying pursued by the doctors, the terrible crimes whose history we are now to record would never have been committed.

Weeks passed without a lodger coming to Hare's house, and they grew impatient for a victim—so impatient that Hare resolved to go to the streets and seek out some poor wretch whom no one would miss, lure him or her to the house, and put in practice the scheme on which they had resolved.

CHAPTER VII

THE FIRST VICTIM—A LOST MOTHER

On a hard frosty morning in the month of December 1827, an old woman and a young good-looking girl came slowly out of the village of Gilmerton, and turned into the road leading to Edinburgh.

The girl was bare-headed and in her house dress, and did not seem to be going any distance, but the old woman had on her bonnet and shawl, and in her hand she carried a black can. She was neatly but very humbly attired. Her garments were of the plainest and coarsest description: a green faded bonnet, an old-fashioned shawl, and a black merino gown, industriously darned in various places, all gave evidence that her circumstances in life were not by any means affluent.

On the brow of the height they stood still.

"I dinna think I'll gang ony far'er, mother," said the girl. "I find it gey cauld wantin' bannet or shawl."

"Very weel, Jenny lass," responded the old woman. "Gang yer ways back tae the hoose. I'll be hame aboot the darkenin'. Ye can hae the kettle boilin'. I'll bring hame a pickle fine tea oot o' Melrose's shop."[1]

"Very weel, mother," returned the girl. Then fixing a somewhat anxious look on the old woman, she added, "And dinna tak' whisky the day tae dae ye harm."

"Na, na, lass; I'll tak' care o' that. I maun hae a wee drappie just tae keep oot the cauld, but I'se no hurt mysel'. Eh, na, I'se no hurt mysel'. Dinna be the least feared o' that."

The girl did not seem to be quite satisfied by the assurance thus given, and when she parted with her mother she gazed after her with a misgiving look and sighed. She knew how often the same pledge had been given and broken. It was her mother's one failing—a liking for whisky. She had acquired

---

1. Andrew Melrose founded his tea company in the Canongate in 1812, and three years later opened an establishment on the South Bridge. Other stores followed.

the liking in the house of a gentleman where she had long been nurse, and it grew upon her with years, so much so that when the opportunity occurred she generally yielded to the temptation. Such an opportunity her daughter knew would occur that day, for she was going to receive money from a gentleman in Heriot Row.[2] This gentleman she had nursed, and he allowed her a little annuity, which saved her from want in her old age. She drew it in weekly sums of one and sixpence, and this was her errand to Edinburgh that day.

Before turning into the village street the young girl stood and watched her mother trudging slowly down the hill. Beyond the bare, black, wintry woods rose, in the clear frosty air, the tower of Liberton Church, and over against it appeared the rounded crest of Arthur's Seat, with the houses of Auld Reekie[3] clustering on the ridge at its base. Through the pure atmosphere the buildings of the city could be distinctly seen—the castle on its craggy height, the grey crown of St Giles, with the tall lands[4] of the High Street rising between. The pointed spire of the Tron was not erected till the following year. The splendid villas to the south which now form such a large portion of the view from the same spot were then unbuilt. The Grange and Newington were green meadows and open fields, with a house here and there which claimed to be a residence in the country.

Beyond the picturesque ridge of gables and spires the Forth gleamed in the sun, and the hills of Fife lay sharp against the sky; while stretching eastward was a blue, bright expanse of sea, indented by the irregular coast, and dotted by the distant outlines of the Bass and North Berwick Law.

It was not much of this noble and splendid scene that the girl saw. She was more occupied in watching the lessening form of her old mother as she wended her way to the city. At length a turn of the road hid her from sight, and the girl went

---

2. Heriot Row was built in the early 1800s, so the old lady worked for a well-to-do family in the New Town.

3. Nickname for Edinburgh, that references its smoky atmosphere.

4. A "land" was a tall tenement building, originally with shops on the ground floor, well-to-do in the middle, and poorer classes at the top. These ran along the High Street up the spine of the Castle Hill. By the 1820s they were in disrepair, with the rich moved to the New Town on the north side.

into the house, little dreaming that she would never see her mother again.

*

In the afternoon, when it was wearing towards dark, the old woman made her appearance in the Grassmarket. Probably she was there so far on her way home. Alas! she had broken the pledge she had given to her daughter, and was considerably the worse of liquor. She was not quite drunk, but was so far influenced by what she had taken that her sober judgment was gone. In her hand she held the same black can, but it was now filled with dripping which she had got at Heriot Row.

As she wandered somewhat aimlessly to and fro, little noticed by the crowd that thronged the Square, a malignant eye fell upon her. Hare was prowling about that afternoon in search of a victim, and no sooner had his gaze lighted on the old woman than his fiendish heart bounded with the thought that at length a suitable one had turned up. He saw at a glance that she was half drunk; by her dress he knew she was from the country; and she was evidently alone. Poor and friendless, who was to make inquiries after such an one? If he could lure her quietly to the house in Tanner's Close, there would be little danger of discovery.

He dogged her footsteps for some time till she came to a quiet corner, and then he accosted her.

"Och, musha! and is this yer own self?" he exclaimed, pretending to recognise her.

The old woman turned round, and fixed her unsteady eyes on him inquiringly.

"Why, thin, don't you know me?" he added.

"Na, I dinna ken ye," she returned. "Ye maun be mistaken."

"Divil a bit o' me. Don't you remember me being at the harvest at your place?"

"Up bye at Gilmerton?" she said.

"Uv coorse; where should it be but at Gilmerton?" returned Hare, catching readily at the revelation of her residence.

"Maybe ye was ane o' the Irish chields that lodged next door wi' Katey Finlayson."

"Shure and I was. I thought you would remimber me."

"'Od, man, I canna just say I mind o' ye," returned the unsuspicious, half-drunken woman. "You Irish are a' sae like ilk ither. Though, after a'," she added, taking another look at him, "ye hae a gey kenspeckle face. I might hae minded ye by yer een."

"Och, now," returned Hare, "and isn't it mighty glad I am that I've met ye. Come along wid me to my house up the street, and I'll give ye a glass o' the best whisky that's to be had in Edinburgh."

"Eh, man—I—I sud be gaun awa' hame," she returned.

"What? It isn't proud ye are?" he said, in a half-offended tone.

"Eh, na, I'm no proud; and it's very guid o' you; but I'm thinkin' it wull sune be dark, and I hae a lang road afore me."

"And wouldn't the whisky put heat in you this could night, and help ye to go over the road?" added the wily villain.

"Deed wad it. As ye say, it's very cauld, and there's naething like whisky for heatin' a body's stamach. If ye liket tae gie me a dram in this public-hoose."

"Och, what for would I do that, when the stuff I have at home is tin times better than anything to be got in there? It's the rael Irish potheen—the best in the world. Come along, me darlint, and drink my health in it."

He took her by the arm and drew her forward in the direction of the West Port. She was only too ready to accompany him. The prospect of getting the whisky was a temptation not to be resisted.

It was now getting dusk; the lamps were not lighted; and in the narrow, dingy West Port they passed along without attracting observation.

Most carefully did her companion assist her down the few steps which led from the street into the close, and down the narrow close itself, which was already cast in deep twilight.

"Preserve us a'! but this is a queer place tae live in," remarked the old woman, as, upheld by Hare, she staggered down the steep declivity. The other was too excited to make any reply to this. Having got her so far, unseen by any one, as he thought—and he had all the way carefully watched if they had become objects of observation to a passer-by—he was exulting in anticipated success.

At some distance down the close they came to a low, isolated house, the door of which stood open, and from one of
the windows the bright fire-light flickered cheerfully.

Hare led the old woman across the passage, and into the
front room. His wife and Helen M'Dougal were there, and
Burke lay indolently on a wooden settle against the wall.

"Man alive!" exclaimed Hare, "get up wid ye and wilcome
an ould friend. Ye mind uv her when you and I lodged next
doure to her house at Gilmerton, when we harvested there.
Sure ye have'nt forgotten the honest, dacent craythur?"

"Och, by the powers! and how are ye?" said Burke, starting
up in full understanding of the wink which Hare gave him.

"I'm rale weel, I thank ye," answered the old woman.

"I've brought her in to have a glass afore she goes home,"
said Hare.

"Throth and ye couldn't have done less," remarked Burke.
"Sure many a one we had together at Gilmerton."

"Ay, that wad be in Katey Finlayson's."

"To be sure it was—in the public-house yonder."

"Eh, mercy, no; Katy has nae public-house."

"Sure now yer forgetting intirely," cried Hare. "It was
Katey Finlayson's house we lodged in."

"And isn't that just what I mane?" responded Burke, with
ready alacrity. "Didn't Katey get in the whisky at night to
help to make us merry after the hot day's shearing?"

"Ay, she's a hearty body, Katey," said the old woman;
"and she'll be glad tae hear that I've fa'en in wi' twa o' her
auld lodgers. Maybe she'll gi'e ye a ca' when she's in the
toon."

A candle was lighted, and Helen M'Dougal was despatched
with their last shilling to procure whisky. It was brought in,
and they gathered round the table to consume it. The first
glass, added to what she had partaken of before, made the old
woman very merry and garrulous.

"Eh, but it's a grand thing pleasant company," she cried.
"My dochter Jenny wull be expectin' me hame aboot this
time; but de'il care, it's no every nicht I meet wi' sic kind
freends. She's a guid wench, though, is Jenny, and she's as
bonnie as she's guid."

"Bonnie!" cried Hare, eulogistically. "She's the purtiest,
swatest craythur ever I saw. Upon my sowl, she took away
me heart intirely."

"Hoots, but she's far bonnier sin' ye saw her, and a better wife is no tae be had in a' the Loudens."

"Faix and it's meself that thinks that same," responded Hare, "and if ye wouldn't have any objections to me as a son-in-law, by the powers, I'll marry her meself."

"I've nae objections ava," exclaimed the inebriate. "Ye're a rale kind chield, and I like ye mysel'."

"Then, by the powers, ye'll live wid us, me darlint, and it's the jolly divils we'll be for ever and ever."

"Be me sowl, Hare, but it's in luck ye are now intirely," cried Burke. "If I wasn't a married man meself, I would be afther fightin' ye for the purty colleen."

"Thin it's well for ye that ye are married," responded Hare, "for, be jabers, the boy that came between me and my wife that is to be I would sind into smithereens in no time. Here, mother, dear, take up yer glass, and drink to our happy marriage."

"Ay wull I, lad. Lord, I'm gettin' fou! But deil ane o' me cares. Jenny will say naething when she hears I've gotten a man for her. Here's tae her and you, ye Irish chield."

"That's the last uv the whisky," whispered Mrs Hare, as the old woman was tossing off her glass.

"Thin go out for more," returned Hare, with fierce rapidity.

"Haven't another farden to get it wid."

"The divil—is there no way uv getting it?"

"There's the ould woman's can uv kitchen-fee," suggested Mrs Hare. "I could sell it."

"That's the thing," whispered her husband; "away wid ye at wonst, and come back directly wid the whisky."

The old woman was now very drunk, and wildly happy. The others had partaken much less freely of the liquor, but they had pressed glass after glass upon her, and she drank without any objection. Suddenly, in her drunken glee, she started a song. Burke joined in with an exuberant chorus, and a scene of the most noisy merriment followed, in the midst of which Hare's wife quietly left the room with the woman's black can, and the empty bottle. The can with its contents she managed to dispose of quite readily; then with the proceeds she got the bottle refilled, and returning to the house, set it on the table.

The old woman had just at the moment finished one of her songs, and in her mad excitement she seized the bottle,

and, pouring out another glass for herself, drank it off at a
gulp.

More songs followed, more laughter, more wild and frantic
merriment, till the old woman's tongue refused further utterance, her eyes closed, and her head fell helplessly on her
breast. She had reached the stage of drunken insensibility.

Burke and Hare watched her keenly. They had watched
her all along, and certain significant glances had passed
between them. But only glances. They had not ventured to
exchange words, though their mutual understanding was
pretty complete.

"She's stopped up at last," whispered Burke, after bending
over her for some moments, and satisfying himself that she
was quite unconscious.

"And a mighty long time it has took to do it," remarked
Hare. "She's a tough ould screamer."

"But what does it all mane?" asked Mrs Hare, looking
half curious, half angry. "Uv coorse it was all blarney about
marrying her daughter."

"It was blarney ivery bit uv it," said Hare, with one of his
most frightful leers.

"You don't know her then," remarked Helen.

"Divil a bit uv it. Neither William nor I ever set eyes on
her afore."

"Troth an' we didn't. I don't know her from my great-
grandmother."

"Thin, what's the manin' uv it?" asked Mrs Hare again.

Hare looked at Burke.

"Out wid it," said the latter.

"Any lodgers come in to-night?" asked Hare in a whisper,
as he looked cautiously round.

"Not one."

"So much the better. This one is worth five hundred."

"Go along wid ye. She don't look as if she had a farden to
bless herself wid."

"But hasn't she good flesh and bones, and won't she bring
something heavy up at the Square?"

"Is it to murder her ye mane to be afther?"

"Arrah, now, don't spake so loud," said Hare, angrily.
"Shure, if we mane that, we needn't cry it out to let everybody in the close know."

"Oh, don't think of it!" exclaimed Helen, greatly horrified.

"It will be sure to be found out. The doctors will see that she has been murdered, and—"

"Keep yourself aisy, Nelly," observed Burke. "Dr Ford tould me uv a way that doesn't lave a mark, and sure we want money mighty bad. Hare and I will put the breath out uv her, and when you see her you'll not know anything has been done—no more than if it was the ould Highlander that died in the natural way."

"Och, thin, that makes a mighty differ," said Hare's wife. "Sure if it can't be found out there isn't an easier way uv gettin' money."

Thus the feeble scruples of the women were overcome, and with no great shock of recoil at the cruelty or the crime, they tacitly acquiesced in the horrid design.

The old woman still lay with her head on her breast, and was breathing heavily. Burke and Hare took each an arm and lifted her into the little back room. Here they laid her on the bed, shut the door, and stood looking at each other.

The near prospect of what they meant to do appalled both of them, and they had not courage to try the experiment. If it should fail—if they could not accomplish it—if the deed when done revealed itself on the body, how should they dispose of it?

It was the risk of detection that made them pause, and not a relenting of heart. There was no compassion for the old helpless woman whose life they designed to take away, nor for the daughter at home of whom they had heard her speak, and who would vainly look for her return. No; all their concern was lest their adventure should miscarry, and so land them in jeopardy.

"Now, thin," said Hare, after a pause, "let us do what the doctor tould yez. It won't take much to stop her windpipe."

"Troth, thin," returned Burke, "it's myself that daren't do it just at wonst. If we miss the way and don't kill her."

"Begorra, thin, sure we'll kill her another way," rejoined Hare, ferociously. "We'll put a prattie down her throat, and say it choked her."

Burke looked at the senseless form lying on the bed, and stood hesitating. Finally he returned to the other room, and left the deed undone.

Hare followed. His nature was cruel enough to have strangled the victim at once, but he was too cowardly to run the risk of putting his single neck in the noose, and so he refrained, grumbling, however, at the other's timidity.

The women met them in the passage, scared and frightened. Murder was new to them likewise, and they laboured under all the nervousness of inexperience.

A word or two growled by Hare let them understand that the woman still lived.

Besides the little back room, there were two sleeping apartments in the house, and while the women went into one, Burke and his associate entered the other. Burke, without undressing, threw himself on the dirty bed, and Hare lay down by his side, and so they fell asleep.

Burke was a heavy sleeper, and his slumber was unbroken till the morning, before it was quite daylight, when Hare disturbed him.

"Arrah, now, me boy, isn't it two mighty big cowards we are, to let our fine plan go down just for the thrying. Sure, afther the ould woman has been so nately trapped, and when we have got nothing to do but press the wind out uv her, it isn't ourselves that's going to let her away. Man alive, she may be as good as tin pounds to us, and neither you nor me has a farden to cross ourselves wid."

Burke sprung up, with an oath. "Come on then and we'll do it at wonst," he said. "Give me a glass o' potheen, and I'm bould for the divil himself."

Hare rose with great alacrity, lighted a candle, and handed his companion a glass of the whisky. He drank none himself; he was ready to do his part of the murder without such priming.

They entered the little back room, and found their victim still asleep. But she awoke as they went in, and immediately complained of being sick and ill—the effects of the great quantity of drink she had imbibed the previous night.

"Och, sure now," said Hare, "wan glass will put you all right."

"Oh dear," whined the old woman, "what will Jenny be thinkin'? I maun awa hame directly."

"Uv coorse ye will, but ye'll not refuse a glass."

He held it to her lips, and the temptation was more than she could resist. She drank, and the yearning to be home gave place to a renewed elevation of spirits. She grew exhilarated and extravagant as before, and drank glass after glass as they handed them to her. In a very short time she was again drunk to unconsciousness.

"Now for it," said Burke, who seemed determined to act this time without taking time for reflection.

"All right, me boy," returned his instigator and accomplice, setting down the glass and taking his place at the head of the bed.

The old woman was turned with her face uppermost. Hare pressed his hands firmly on her nose and mouth, and Burke threw himself upon her breast, causing his whole weight to bear upon her lungs.

Overcome though she was by the whisky, she struggled violently. The thread of human life sometimes snaps very easily when Nature herself is the minister of death; but when it is not Nature, but violence, life makes a most determined resistance before its citadel is taken. Let the contest be ever so unequal, it never accepts it as hopeless, but fights strenuously to the last. For a full quarter of an hour these human butchers felt the writhings of their victim as they mercilessly suffocated her. Heart and lungs were faithful to their duty, and strove to the utmost of their power to perform their functions; but air, the vital principle of their operation, being withheld, they were reluctantly compelled to give in.

It was a sorry, sickening sight if anybody had been there to see it. It was a spectacle of humanity in about as brutal a form as it had ever manifested itself. The divine element was extinguished, and the diabolic ruled supreme.

Successful! Oh, yes, the experiment was only too successful. When, at the end of fifteen minutes, Burke rose from the now motionless body, and Hare took away his villainous hands from the face, their infernal hope was gratified, and Dr Ford's theory proved to be correct. The old woman was now dead, and little or no marks of murder were to be found remaining on the body. The chin was bruised and ruffled a little by Hare's murderous grasp, and one or two blue marks appeared on the body, but nothing to indicate death by violence.

Burke sat down in a chair to catch his breath, which had been not a little disturbed by his exertions, and, to calm his shaking nerves, he gulped down another glass of whisky. Hare needed no such sedative. He it was who carefully examined the body, and the chuckle and leer with which he reported that all was right were frightfully hideous.

The tea-chest was now brought in, and the corpse, still warm, was undressed and packed into it. The green bonnet, the old-fashioned shawl—which she had probably got for her wedding—and the well-worn black gown, were thrown into one corner, along with the rest of her clothes, and the tea-chest, with its ghastly contents, was placed in another, to stand till night.

To the four occupants of the house that day seemed a long one. Unused as they were, *as yet*, to the commission of the darkest and worst of crimes—murder—their dread of detection was extreme. Should the old woman be searched for by her friends, as undoubtedly she would, they might track her to Tanner's Close. Perhaps some casual observer did notice her in Hare's company, or perhaps some of the neighbours saw the two enter the close or the house together, and thus a clue might be obtained which would lead to a search, and then—

Their apprehensions were imaginary. The career of slaughter now begun was not destined to be so soon terminated. No one came to inquire at the house for the old woman, and at dark Burke went up to the Square.

All right! He had but to bring the body at a later hour, and it would be bought and paid for. Still it was not without a fast beating of their guilty hearts that the murderers entered the hall with their burden. The body they knew must be inspected, and that inspection might result in the detection of the murder. Groundless fear! The inspection which was dreaded was not for the purpose of satisfying the doctors that the subject had died a natural death.

Oh dear, no. It was to discover how far it was suited to their professional purpose. Had there been a red gash across the throat, or had the skull been beaten in, these might have suggested murder, as they would have done to anybody; but anything short of obvious butchery was quite safe under their eye, for the very sufficient reason that their examination had nothing judicial about it.

"A good subject," said Doctor Knox, with a nod of approval; "fresh and firm—ten pounds."

The price was paid, and the murderers left the Square almost frantic with delight.

*

Shall we say a few words about the grief, the distraction, the anguish and despair of the young girl at Gilmerton—how she sat in the lonely village dwelling waiting all that night for the mother that never came—how, on the following morning, she sought for her in the village, along the Edinburgh road, and through most of the streets of the city? All that she could learn was that on the previous day she had been at Heriot Row, had received her money, and got the can filled with kitchen-fee. No further trace of her could be discovered; no one had noticed her—no policeman, no friend, no passenger through the streets. Days and weeks of anxious, sorrowful, but vain search followed, and the bereaved daughter felt her disappearance to be not only an overwhelming grief, but a perplexing mystery. Ultimately the distracted girl concluded that her poor mother had somehow come to an untimely end, and she often murmured in plaintive tones—

"Oh, if I only kenned hoo and where it was, it wad be some consolation!"

Alas! when she did, many months afterwards, come to know where and how it was, the knowledge added tenfold to her heavy grief.

CHAPTER VIII

THE DOUBLE "SHOT"

The successful issue of their first murder made the occupants of the house in Tanner's Close wildly happy. It opened up to them a prospect of affluence—of indolent ease. Work was the abhorrence both of Burke and Hare, and nothing but the incumbent necessity for supplying their physical wants would have caused them to undertake any employment at all. Here there was a way by which they could get plenty of money without requiring to labour. They had reached a veritable El Dorado[1] in one of the dingy Edinburgh closes. It was a risky business certainly; but if, by care and caution, they secured and disposed of their victims, neither want nor work were contingencies they had longer to dread.

So they concluded among themselves as they caroused and revelled most riotously with the ten pounds which they got for the old woman's body. The women bought gaudy clothes, and began to carry their heads much higher towards their neighbours. The men also arrayed themselves in smarter garments, and lounged at the top of the close with their hands in their pockets—those hands now reddened by the indelible stains of human blood.

And did the deed they had done not haunt them with remorse? Apparently not, else they could not have so easily looked forward to others of the same character. The fact was, the natural brutality of their natures, together with that lowest form of mammon worship of which they had become the votaries, had extinguished or smothered any spark of feeling. In all cases the murderer must first murder himself. Burke and Hare could never have strangled the old woman from Gilmerton if previous to that their own humanity had not been strangled out of them. This was not difficult to do, inasmuch as its proportion, along with the brutal and the devilish in their natures, had been originally small, and what was of it strong drink and a loose and degraded life had hardened

---

1. City of gold (from the conquistadors' view of the Americas).

and blunted. In Burke, as we shall afterwards find, a very small remnant of it did still linger, which required to be continually drowned in potations of whisky. But Hare had no such fitful qualms. On the contrary, the chief element of his nature seemed to be cruelty. Beyond the pecuniary profit of the crime, he had a ferocious pleasure in committing it. It was with something of a savage delight that he clutched at the throat and mouth of the victim. The nerves of his murderous hands were as cold and as firm as iron, and the leer of his disgusting face was at the moment frightfully malicious.

Well, the whole four of them, though they suffered no remorse sufficient to deter them from further deeds of the same nature, were yet quite conscious of the peculiar source from which the money in their possession had come, and that very consciousness made them spend it in feverish and frantic debauchery. Have our readers ever reflected on the relation which exists between gaining and spending? If they have they must have perceived that it is only the earnings of a healthy and honest industry that are judiciously expended. "Ill got ill gone," as the proverb says. He who gets money as the fair return for legitimate and useful labour—he alone, we think, can spend it with profitable economy. The inheritor of a fortune he never wrought for becomes for the most part either a miser or a spendthrift, while the man who obtains money by crime finds it absolutely to burn away in his possession. The fruit of murder is proverbially bitter and profitless, and so these people found it. For days and weeks riot was the order of the house; so much so that the neighbours noticed it, though they little imagined its cause.

And so it came to pass that in a short time the price of blood was gone. All that it had done was to procure them a week or two of wild, almost insane, indulgence of the lowest animal life, in the midst of which pound after pound disappeared rapidly, and only a few shillings remained amongst them.

"We'll have to be on the outlook again, me boy," remarked Hare when this fact dawned upon their half-drunken minds. "It's a mighty pity that we should want the tin when so many shots are to be got on the streets."

"Uv coorse, it is," responded Burke; "and it would be as mighty a pity for you to go about starving wid a barrow, and me to break me back bending over ould shoes when money

is to be had in an aisier way. So look alive, ye divil, and bring
in another ten pounder."

"Throth then I'll tell ye what. I've been afther thinking
that Mary Haldane is just the shot for us. Ye know ould Mary
that's niver sober when she can get a drop to drink."

Burke knew Mary well, and he gave it as his opinion that
she was a most likely woman for their purpose. So it was
resolved that Hare should be on the outlook for her in the
Grassmarket, in which place of thoroughfare she was commonly to be found.

*

It was a cold dry night in January, and the lamps of the
streets shone clear in the frosty air. A great crowd was collected at the east end of Princes Street, for the people were
coming out of the theatre, and as the house had been densely
filled in all parts, the crowd which it emptied into the street
was large and noisy.[2] But hundreds were there besides those
who had been in the theatre, and about the box entrance a
mass of people had collected to see the fashionable people quit
the house and drive away in their carriages. Among the crowd
were not a few of those unfortunates who had fallen from
virtue—poor miserable creatures whom a thousand various
circumstances had brought into their degraded position. Pretty
some of them were—nay, beautiful in a physical sense. Most
of them no doubt had the stamp of their vice and misery
clearly impressed upon them, but others there were, the bloom
of whose maiden loveliness had not yet vanished—who still
preserved the personal beauty which had been the primary
cause of their ruin, and enabled them now to draw with
comparative ease the thoughtless and unprincipled into their
snares.

Two of these girls stood close to one of the pillars arm in
arm, and the light from a lamp fell full upon their faces. One
of them was tall and stately, and strangely beautiful. Her
figure was faultless, her features most regular, her eyes large
and lustrous, and masses of the richest hair hung about

---

2. The Theatre Royal, built in 1769, stood at the north end of the North
Bridge.

her temples, and showed itself in wavy curls beneath her bonnet.

Ah! that face—that figure. We have seen them before. This is Mary Paterson—once the innocent, the virtuous, the guileless and pure, and now, alas! she had come to this. Two years' familiarity with Edinburgh life has made her an associate of the degraded and the fallen. Her first grievous error has brought her step by step to the worst position which a woman can reach, and a bolder or more regardless girl of her class was not to be found in the city.

Her companion was named Jessie Brown, a plainer and more timid girl, but otherwise as vile and degraded. She and Mary were constant companions. They lodged together in one of the closes which run from the High Street, and when they went to the streets they generally went in company. Thus it chanced that on this occasion they stood together watching the gay and fashionable people as they left the theatre.

Suddenly, as a gentleman emerged from the building with a dark-haired lady on his arm, Mary clutched convulsively at her companion's arm and gasped for breath. Jessie hastily looked at her and saw that she was deadly pale.

"What's the matter, Mary—are you ill?" she hurriedly asked.

Mary answered not, but continued to gaze most fixedly at the pair. Their carriage had not come quite forward, and they had to stand a moment waiting for it.

As they thus stood Mary unconsciously pressed forward, and at the same moment the gentleman turning his head in her direction, his eyes fell upon her. The moment he saw her he started violently, and staggered a step back; then he stood for a moment rooted to the spot as rigid as a statue, still gazing at her.

The carriage drew up, but he made no motion to hand the lady into it.

"This is our carriage, dear," whispered the latter, tapping him gently on the arm.

He started again, and in nervous haste assisted her into the vehicle. He sprang in after her, and kept his head steadily directed towards the Register Office till the carriage rolled away.

"My gracious, what is it, Mary?" asked her companion again. "Do you know the gent?"

Mary shivered, and drew her associate out of the crowd.

"My betrayer," she whispered. "That, Jessie, is the man who ruined me and made me what I am."

"The base deceiver," returned Jessie, warmly.

"He *was* a deceiver," rejoined Mary. "But for him I might have been—Yet why need I say what I might have been? I strive never to think of that; it does no good, only vexes me. I say, Jessie, we'll not stay out any longer to-night. I've got ten shillings, let us go in and be jolly, for the sight of—of—him has ruffled me a bit, and I want a glass or two to steady my nerves."

"Was that his wife along with him?"

"I should say so."

"What a dowdy. How on earth did the man come to prefer such a lump of grey skin and bone to you?"

"She was *gilt* and I was only plain," returned Mary, bitterly. "My charms did well enough for the passing hour, but her gold was a loadstone of life. But come, I must not speak any more of it or I shall get wild; my brain is getting hot already—whisky will cool it. Come, we and the Marys will have a night of it."

And have two years produced this terrible change?

Yes, two years can do much when the path is a down-hill one, as Mary's was. She came to Edinburgh with a dream of honest labour in her soul; but by that time she had become the sport of circumstances, and a desperate recklessness, born of her betrayal and abandonment, made her only too ready to fall into a course which was speedily suggested to her by poverty and friendlessness in a great city. She had many bitter regrets at first. Visions of Braeside and her godly father, with his grey locks and the Bible on his knee, would intrude upon her degradation, and fill her soul with the most poignant anguish. But a refuge from these was always at hand and eagerly rushed to. That refuge was intoxicating drink—the Lethe river which drowns so much human remorse and prevents repentance.

Fortified by the wild excitement which it produced, and further debased by the companions she now mingled with, and the moral suicide of the life she led, she soon ceased to think of her home and Peggy, and even of her child, whom she resolved never again to see. That feeling of propriety was still left in her seared soul. No one whom she had once known and loved would ever see her in her misery and shame, or know the dark course she had entered. Her very child she would not pollute by a kiss from her unholy lips. There was a sealed packet which she had given in charge to her companion, Jessie Brown, with instructions for the latter to open it, if she should suddenly die, and forward it to the address which she would find beyond the outer envelope; but beyond this, and telling Jessie how she had been first betrayed, Mary never adverted to her former life of innocence.

Amid this fierce feverish existence Mary's person grew more remarkably striking. Her figure developed in faultless proportions, her complexion preserved and even increased its bloom, and her face grew more attractive. Her undeniable beauty had, however, assumed a bold, rude character. The materialism of beauty was there, but its soul was gone. The gentleness and meekness of virtue had departed with virtue itself, and the deep discerner of beauty who looked beneath the fair exterior would have found its subtle essence awanting. The eye of the libertine, however, was by that fair form immensely pleased, and Mary found no difficulty in captivating. If honest labour had failed to procure her a livelihood, dishonest idleness had done so to her satisfaction.

The two girls gained the High Street by way of the North Bridge, and entered one of the closes which ran down towards the Cowgate. About the middle of the close they entered a narrow doorway, and groped their way without difficulty— for they were familiar with the place—up a narrow, well-worn stair, till they came to the very top. Here they entered a room, where the only light came from a few red embers that glowed in the grate. Crouching in silence over these embers were two naked-looking figures, who moved not when the girls went in.

"Haven't you got a candle to-night, Mary?" asked Jessie.

"Not a morsel," replied a husky voice.

"And no money either?"

"Not a farthing. Mary is in the sulks to-night, and would'nt go out."

"And so I may," said a younger voice, in a querulous tone. "I have hardly a rag to cover me, and who can stand about the streets naked in a cold night like this?"

"Well, here's money," cried Mary. "Run out one of you for coals, candles, bread and cheese, and two bottles of whisky. We'll have a blow out for once."

The elder of the two rose with alacrity, and came eagerly forward.

"You are a good, kind soul, Mary," she huskily said. "Two bottles—did you say two bottles?"

"Ay, two; they will serve the longer. Now make haste, for both Jessie and me are very cold."

The woman needed no second bidding. She took the money—wages of iniquity—out of Mary's hand, and the next moment they heard her hustling down the stairs.

It was not long till she returned, but Mary sat impatient and fierce of heart and soul. In the dark, the form of Duncan Grahame came more vividly before her, and she longed to banish it. It was the first time she had seen him since their parting at the cottage, and the sight had brought to her mind, in all its strength, the recollection of all the wrongs she had endured at his hands—her misplaced love, and his selfish treachery and desertion. A fierce war of passion raged in her soul, to escape which she wished to rush into the excitement and forgetfulness of drunkenness.

The scene which ensued when the drink was brought in we shall not describe. All the four drank of it greedily, for between vice and intemperance there seems to be an inevitable connection. Suffice it to say that long before the morning light they were all lying on the floor of that miserable room, in the helplessness and unconsciousness of the most excessive intoxication.

Regarding the other two women, we now require to speak. They were mother and daughter. The old woman's name was Mary Haldane. She was now a poor drunken sot, but had once been very different. A youth of purity and innocence had been hers. Once she had been a father's pride and a mother's joy, and at the Sabbath school a pastor's hand had been laid lovingly in blessing on her head. But it was the old story of misplaced love, temptation, and fall. "The serpent beguiled her, and she did eat."[3] She was deserted and cast upon the city, with her child of shame. She fell lower and lower, and she brought up her daughter—called Mary, too—to the same life of vice and misery. The latter, like her mother, was a drunkard, and had early taken to a course of open vice.

---

3. Eve's excuse in Genesis 3:13.

It could not be said that she fell from virtue, for she had never been familiar with anything but a life of sin. Her mother sometimes, in lucid moments of remorse, let fall in her hearing a truth she had learned at the Sabbath school, but she had never been the subject of regular instruction, and her ignorance and moral turpitude were extreme.

Old Mary Haldane was two or three days under this debauch, during which she did not appear in her usual haunt—the Grassmarket. But when the drink was done she crept away down the close, and with red eyes and quivering nerves wandered up the Cowgate to her accustomed beat.

She had not been long here when she was accosted by Hare. This monster was an old acquaintance, for Mary had at one time lodged in his house.

"Top of the evening to yez," said Hare, making up to her as she stood at the foot of a close.

Mary returned his leer with a broad grin.

"Aha, William Hare," she remarked. "Things are looking up with you. You've got a better coat on your back than ever I saw you wear before."

"Thrue for it," he returned. "It's in luck I am intirely. But for all that I never forget ould friends. But what has come over yez at all, at all—have ye been down wid the fever?"

"Oh, I'm mortal bad to-day. We had a spree up in the house, and the drink is done."

"Is that all, my cushla machree? Come up wid me to the house, and I'll put you right. There's prime potheen in the cupboard, and a glass or two uv it will firm yer legs a bit."

"Are you in earnest?" asked Mary, as with her bleared eyes she gazed on him in considerable astonishment at such an unexpected offer.

"Uv coorse I am. Aren't you and me ould friends, and didn't I always like ye? and now that I am in luck I want you to come and drink to its remainin'."

And these words Hare accompanied with another frightful leer. He had been on the outlook for Mary for a day or two, and was overjoyed at meeting her in a frame of body and mind so suited to his purpose. The offer of a dram at any time, but especially in her present state of feverish reaction, was a bribe not to be resisted; and without requiring one word of entreaty, she was drawn away to the slaughter-house.

Poor Mary had always been the butt of the boys and girls

of the street, and as she and Hare went up the West Port a group of urchins followed at their heels, to tease and vex the wretched creature. This secretly enraged Hare, for it brought so many eyes upon them; and his fingers itched to clutch some of the offenders by the throat and strangle them. But in the open street and under the light of day he durst not so manifest his wrath. Just as they were gathering at their heels like a cluster of bees, Burke came down the street, and it did not require Hare's peculiar wink to let him know how matters stood.

"Arrah, get out wid ye, ye little wicked devils, to trate a decent ould woman in that manner," he exclaimed, making a rush at the group, and scattering them in terror. Away they ran scampering down the street, and Hare and his companion were free to proceed towards Tanner's Close unmolested.

Another quick private signal passed between the murderers, and Burke continued his walk, while the decoyer lured their victim into the shambles.[4] He did not go far, however, but, turning into the first byepath, made his way rapidly to the close. Mary was there all safe, or rather for herself all unsafe. They had got her into the little back room, and the whisky was already produced. She drank greedily, drank largely—drank "to the point."[5]

And then followed the tragedy. We need not repeat the description, for it was the same process. In this case, however, nature was more tenacious than in the former, for when the struggles had ceased, and all seemed over, the murderers released the body, under the idea that death had ensued. But it was not so, for she began to breathe again, and life, almost chased out of its citadel, would have returned, if more violence not been used. Again, however, were Hare's murderous hands pressed upon nose and mouth; again did Burke throw his brutal body upon the prostrate woman; and the soul of Mary Haldane, all impure as it was, was driven into the presence of its Maker. Her wretched, outcast life on earth was ended, and her poor, miserable body was sold for a sacrifice to the Moloch of science.

A third time was there a transaction in Surgeons' Square. The draft drawn on Death & Co. was promptly honoured,

---

4. Meat market; where slaughterers work (figurative).
5. To the point of intoxication.

and the forgery never suspected, though the signature must have presented clumsy signs of it. Ah, but then the bankers had no interest in discovering a forgery; nay, their interests lay the other way, for the draft was of equal value to them whether forged or genuine.

Thus another mother was lost, and another weeping daughter went on the following morning through the streets in search of her. For Mary Haldane the younger had this virtue left in her nature—she loved her mother, and was plunged into the wildest sorrow by her unaccountable disappearance. She had not sought long till she heard tidings of her in the Grassmarket. She had been seen going with Hare in the direction of the latter's residence, and with joy and hope the afflicted daughter went to make inquiries of her there.

"Is my mother here?" she eagerly asked, as, entering the front room, she presented herself before Mrs Hare and Helen M'Dougal.

The guilty women were for some moments thunderstruck and terror stricken; but Hare's wife immediately met the question by a bold denial.

"Faix, thin, and she isn't. What would she be afther here?"

"A pretty piece of impudence it would be for a beggar like her to come to a respectable house like this," said Helen, with an air of great indignation.

"Oh dear! she is lost, and the people told me they saw her on the street yesterday with William Hare."

"Och, musha, sure that has been a lie intirely," protested the virago.

"Sure, thin, it wasn't," said Hare himself, coming from the back room. "You two weren't in the house, and don't know about it at all, at all."

"Oh, then, she was here?" cried the girl.

"Uv coorse she was," rejoined the murderer, at the same moment managing to convey a significant signal to his wife.

"And where is she now? Oh, tell me where she is!"

"Didn't she be afther telling yez she was going to see her friends at Mid-Calder?"

"No, she never said a word about that."

"Och, thin, it was too bad uv her intirely to go away without lettin' on. But she tould me, and I gave her a glass to help her on the road. More by token, I've got some uv the same beautiful stuff in the room beyont, and if ye'll come in I'll give you a glass uv it too."

This temptation was as irresistible to the daughter as it had been to the mother, and, overjoyed at hearing news of her mother's safety, she complied with the invitation, and entered the fatal room.

The drink was set before her, and she, having no power of resistance, drank glass after glass as they were pressed upon her. When she was considerably intoxicated, Burke came in, and the wink of intelligence passed between the human butchers. The appetite for murder, growing on both of them as it was fed, made them resolve to despatch the daughter as they had done the mother.

And they did it—yes they did it; and that very night mother and daughter lay side by side, stiff and cold, in the dissecting room of Dr Knox. Still no questions asked, and no hesitation manifested, though on two consecutive nights the same men brought a dead body to dispose of—two *healthy bodies*, free of disease, and both reeking with the fumes of whisky. What a beautiful and sublime faith in humanity these doctors must have had! There might be a raising, and there might be selling, but murder, oh fie, murder? Who could possibly dream of such a thing being done? Wasn't the Scotch a whisky-drinking people, and hadn't these creatures died of *delirium tremens*?

Undoubtedly; and their friends, as great drunkards as themselves, had sold the bodies to these two enterprising and speculating Irishmen, to avoid the expense of burying them, and to obtain at the same time the means of continuing their debauch.

"Gentlemen of Surgeons' Square, what is your verdict?"

The surgical jury, without retiring, find unanimously that the deceased died of *delirium tremens*.

Meanwhile Burke and Hare are returning in boisterous glee to Tanner's Close, chuckling facetiously at the successful issue of what they called their "double shot."

CHAPTER IX

THE MILLER'S SON

Four bodies having now been disposed of at Surgeons' Square—three of them murdered—with perfect safety, the butchers congratulated themselves on the profession they had taken up. It was easy, profitable, and the market promised ever to be a ready one, for at all their visits to the hall they were informed they might come again whenever they got hold of "the thing." Now, "the thing" referred to could be got hold of at any time, for tramps and wanderers were constantly coming to lodge in the house in Tanner's Close, whose presence no one would notice, and whose disappearance no one would mark. And then there were the streets, swarming with vagrants and poverty-stricken wretches, who might vanish and never be inquired after, for in these days the police system had not attained to anything like its present efficiency; and when any one did disappear, and could no longer be seen or heard of, it was conjectured that they had either departed from the city or had got drunk and fallen into the canal; and so in a very little time they passed away from the recollection of the few neighbours who knew anything about them.

So, encouraged by past success, and seeing such prospects before them, Burke and Hare were highly elated, and resolved to devote themselves to the promising career they had begun. Their notion of life was to eat, drink, fight, swear, and sleep, and their traffic with Surgeons' Square promised to supply them abundantly with these, their essentials. Surgeons' Square was their bank, and a dead body was a ten pound draft, which they had but to present at any time, and as often as they chose, to receive the money. Was not this about the most convenient way of getting a living which they could have fallen upon? To "get a living" is just what everybody is trying for. There is, of course, an honest and a dishonest way of doing it, and people of principle will try the honest way, while people without principle will take a dishonest course if it be presented and seems to be moderately safe.

Now, the dishonest course consists of infinite degrees, and those who enter it have no security that they shall stop at any one point. They have slipped their cable, and are drifting along the current of crime, which becomes stronger and swifter as they advance, and it depends more on circumstances than themselves whether they shall not go to the furthest and darkest limits. Burke and Hare found that they could get a living, and a jolly one too, by murdering people and selling their bodies. The offence and atrocity of the crime lay, of course, in the murder, not in the sale; but the murder was committed for the purpose of sale, and if the sale had not been possible, they would not have murdered. Depend upon this— that these men did not suffocate their victims for the pleasure of doing it. Hare did, indeed, manifest a fiendish eagerness for the frightful work, and his butcher nature had no compunction. Still money, not murder, was his aim. Burke, his associate, was more nervous, and remorse did haunt him, so much so that he required to have the whisky bottle constantly at hand, and a lighted candle always by his bedside. What we want to bring out is this: that circumstances and temptation, more than a peculiar cruelty and ferocity of nature, caused these men to do what they did. They, and they alone, so far as we know, despatched living men and women, that they might sell their dead bodies; but the question might very pertinently be asked, Would none but them have yielded to the same temptation if laid in their way? The records of crime and the career of criminals warrant us in believing that hundreds would have done it. In the days when coining and forging of bank notes were capital offences, and when the Mint gave a large reward to informers and captors, the criminals themselves have been known to get bad coin or false notes conveyed to the possession of innocent persons, whom they denounced, and who, being apprehended, were hanged, while the wretches got the reward. What better were those than the West Port murderers? or what better is any murderer who murders for gold? The motive is the same, and the crimes are very much alike.

Still the peculiar character of the Burke and Hare murders, the mode in which they were committed, their number, and the sale of the bodies, mark them out as monsters of the very worst description. Humanity shudders at the thought of their deeds, and their butcheries won't stand a repeated description. It was always the same sickening and disgusting business— the luring of the victim into the house, the plying with whisky,

the dragging into the back room, the smothering, the packing
of the body into box or barrel, and its conveyance to Surgeons'
Square, where it brought its price. It would be loathsome to
us, and, we are sure, distasteful to our readers, to go over the
several murders in detail; but, inasmuch as several of the cases
were surrounded by sad and touching circumstances, we shall
select these from the black list and weave them into our
story.

*

In a sweet, secluded spot, far from the haunts of vice and
crime, at the foot of a deep-wooded dell, shut in on three sides
by rocky heights, and fronted on the other by the blue, far-
stretching sea, stood a mill. At a few yards' distance from the
mill was the miller's house, a little red-tiled dwelling, with a
stable and one or two small outhouses attached. There was no
other building near, and no other human habitation in sight.
A more rural, beautiful, and retired spot can scarcely be
imagined. At this hour it stands in the same solitude that it
did then; and a few weeks ago, when, on a bright summer
day, we emerged from the deeply wooded dell, and came
upon it nestling in the midst of the valley, we thought it
hardly possible to gaze upon a scene of deeper peacefulness.
The whirr of the mill wheel was the only sound that broke the
summer stillness, for the sea, sometimes so angry with that
rocky shore, was smooth as an unruffled lake, and smiled in
silence to the bending heaven. The sultry woods and slopes
lay around in hushed repose, and the spray and water drops
which the wheel cast up in its ponderous revolutions flashed
like gems in the golden sunlight. It is one of the few nooks of
nature on which the last fifty years of human progress have
wrought little or no change. At one point, at the top of the
little valley, a few yards of the North British Railway are to
be seen, and frequently during the day the smoking engines
flash past, visible but for a moment, and then gone, leaving
their white smoke to curl for an instant among the trees, and
sending down an echo of the nineteenth century's sounding
activity into the secluded vale. But, beyond this glimpse of the
rushing world without, the place preserves its old and primi-
tive retirement, being nothing changed to outward appearance from what it was on a clear summer morning in the year

1828, as a young man emerged from one of the outhouses and, without going into the dwelling, walked slowly away towards a plank which spanned the stream which gave water to the mill.

The youth was about to step upon this plank for the purpose of going across, when an elderly man, white with flour, came from behind the wheel and confronted him.

"Oh, you are there are you, Joe!" said the latter, sternly, the moment he caught sight of the young man. "Are you not ashamed of yourself? Never came home last night—drunk of course, as usual."

Joe hung his head. He had nothing to answer, for he had been drunk, as usual, and had crawled into the outhouse to sleep among the straw.

"I tell you what it is, Joe," said the old man, more angrily, "this sort of thing won't do. If you don't mean to behave yourself, and give up drinking, you can go away, and not remain a burden upon me. You have been the vexation of my heart for many a day, and I am not going to put up with it any longer."

"Where would you have me to go to, father?" asked the youth, as a deep flush suffused his already ruddy cheek.

"Go where you like," was the reply. "But if you don't mend your ways, you'll never come to any good. If it hadn't been for your drunken habits, you might have been very comfortable in this mill, and made me comfortable too. I looked forward to your marrying Lizzy Fairbairn,[1] and making the old house pleasant and cheerful. But that is all at an end now, and I don't want to have you any longer here to disgrace me."

At mention of Lizzy Fairbairn's name Joe raised his head, and looked not a little astonished when his father spoke of all being ended between them. He loved Lizzy most devotedly, and for her sake, as well as his own, he made many a resolution to give up drinking; but the moment temptation came in his way he yielded to it, and degraded himself below the level of the beasts.

"I'll give it up, father, I promise you I will," he said in an earnest tone. "Lizzy and I will get married immediately, and

---

1. Another symbolic name: fair child.

this will keep me to the house. It's the want of company at home that takes me up to the village; but when I have Lizzy to talk to, I'll never think of the public-house."

"You can't have Lizzy, I tell you," returned the miller. "She and her father came past the public-house last night, and saw you drunk and fighting before the door; and it so angered him that he told Lizzy she wasn't to think of you any more, and she promised she wouldn't. He came down when it was late to tell me, and I couldn't say he was doing wrong, for if I had a daughter I shouldn't allow her to marry a drunken, good-for-nothing fellow like you. Lizzy has kept long by you, in the hope that you would mend, as you promised, but what she saw last night has settled her."

"You don't mean that?" said Joe. "You are joking."

"Am I? Then you can go to James Fairbairn and ask him, or to Lizzy herself, for that matter. She'll never marry you now, and she'll do quite right. It would be like going into the fire when she saw it. What lassie would take for a husband a man that couldn't keep himself sober? She could look for nothing but misery and starvation. Lizzy is quite right, I say. No one connected with you can put up with you any longer, and neither will I."

The angry father turned on his heel as he said this, and went back into the mill, leaving Joe standing alone with one foot upon the plank. He stood thus for some moments, motionless, looking in the direction of the mill door; then putting his hands into his trousers pockets, he crossed the stream and sauntered down to the sea beach.

Joe was a big, well-made, and well-favoured youth. He was large every way—large in body and large in heart, good-natured and most obliging. But his besetting sin was the fatal sin of drunkenness, so besetting and so fatal to one of his temperament and disposition. He was social, liked company, and could not resist the offered dram. He sorely lacked firmness. He knew he was going down hill, and hundreds of times he resolved to give up the glass, and promised Lizzy Fairbairn that he would; but his resolutions and promises were like the morning cloud and early dew—they speedily vanished before the solicitations of a boon companion.

Those who knew Joe intimately and loved him truly were deeply grieved at the ruin he was bringing upon himself. If he could have conquered his weakness and laid aside his besetting sin, a nobler fellow could not have been found in all the parish. Most generous in soul and sympathetic in heart, and obliging in disposition, he would, by steadiness, have gained a most respectable and popular position, but the demon-spell was upon him, and blasted all his goodliness. He was one of many thousands whom strong drink has enchained and destroyed.

In his sober moments no one was more sensible of his folly than was Joe himself, and now, as he wandered down to the beach, he was one of the most miserable beings. The intelligence communicated by his father had stunned him. Lizzy had seen him in his state of intoxication, and had promised to her father to give him up. Her father had often urged her to do this, but Lizzy's loving woman's heart was loth to lose its faith in her lover's amendment. He had promised so earnestly, and with so much sorrowful contrition, that he would eschew his drunken companions and the public-house, that she fondly believed what she so fondly wished, and again and again she smiled through the tears he kissed away, and put her trust in his word.

Joe sat down on a large stone a yard or two from the edge of the water, and communed with his miserable heart and conscience. His head ached frightfully and his nerves were all quivering with his recent debauch, but the cool sea breeze which fanned his temples revived and refreshed him. His mental wretchedness, however, was beyond description. So far as he was aware, Lizzy had never seen him intoxicated, and he had led her to believe that he was not so bad as had been represented to her. But now she had beheld him in his degradation, and, if his father's report was true, the sight had disgusted her to that degree that she had finally resolved to cast him off.

"I must see Lizzy at once," he said, as he rose from his rocky seat. "If it is true that she is done with me, I will leave the place as my father wishes, and what becomes of me after that I don't care. I daresay they'll take me for a soldier."

He bent down and laved his face and head in one of the many crystal pools which the tide had left on the sand; then turning eastward, he struck upon a winding path that led up the height.

Away on the breezy upland, where the bracing air from the sea swept over the wide fields, the heather-crested hills, and open moor, there stood, between two green swelling knolls, a set of farm offices, and in the direction of these Joe made his way. He did not proceed direct to the dwelling-house, but turned aside and entered one of the fields, where cows were grazing. In the corner of this field, near the hedge, a girl was milking a cow, and Joe, even at that distance, saw that it was Lizzy.

As he approached, she saw him coming, but did not raise her head, or even turn round her face to greet him, but if he had been a little nearer he would have seen that her hands trembled and her face flushed and paled by turns.

"A fine morning this," said her lover, as his shadow fell upon her kneeling figure.

"Yes—very fine," returned Lizzy, in a low voice, but still without looking up.

"What's the matter with you, Lizzy?" asked Joe, as he caught sight of great round tears running down her cheeks. "Something has vexed you—something about me. My father has told me this morning that you and your father saw me last night up at the—at the village."

"Yes, Joe, we did," was Lizzy's mournful reply; "we saw you in front of the public-house."

"And I suppose I was touched a bit. Well, I did meet a few lads, and we had a glass too much; but that won't occur again, Lizzy. I am going to break off from the drink now entirely."

Lizzy shook her head, and the tears fell faster than before.

"You have promised that so often, Joe," she sadly murmured, "that I have lost all hope in it. Did your father not tell you what my father said to him last night?"

"Yes, he told me; but it cannot be true that you mean to forsake me."

"Not forsake you, Joe!" said the girl, turning her tearful and sorrowful eyes towards him. "You know I never would do that. But you have forsaken yourself. You are not the Joe I promised to marry, and I cannot, will not embrace certain misery. No, Joe, everything is done between us now."

"You *do* mean to cast me off, then," he said, as a tremble went through his strong frame.

She rose from her kneeling posture, and turned her grief-stricken face full upon him.

"What would you have me do, Joe?" she calmly asked,

but in accents full of anguish. "You love me—I believe that; but you love drink better, or you would have given it up long ere this for my sake. That you have not done so is a proof that the habit is one that has obtained full mastery over you, and, like all who yield to it as you do, it will bind you closer and closer with its bitter chain, till it destroys everything that is good in you. Would you, then, have me link my fate to yours?—would you drag me down with yourself?"

"I swear to you, Lizzy, I will not be tempted to taste drink again!" cried Joe, vehemently.

"You have sworn that a thousand times," rejoined the girl. "I believed you once—I believed you often; but I have lost all faith now. Have I not clung to you for years? have I not pled with you and prayed for you? But all in vain. My father and all my friends have long urged me to give you up. I refused, for my love made my faith strong and my hope tenacious; but last night, after seeing what I did, I promised my father that I would, so you and I must—must part now, Joe."

She burst into a flood of tears, and, pressing both her hands upon her face, sobbed violently. Joe was in a moment at her side, and was passing his arms tenderly around her, when she quietly but firmly withdrew from him.

"You won't be so cruel as you say, Lizzy?" he said, and his own voice trembled with emotion. "Try me once again, and you will see me keep my word."

"The old, old promise, Joe, so often, often broken. My promise I count more sacred, and that which I made my father last night I will keep. I will not reproach you, Joe; I will not speak of the grief and disappointment you have occasioned me. Let us part without a word of recrimination. Good-bye, Joe—may God bless you. I will never cease to pray for your reformation."

She said this in a hurried way, as if forcing herself to say it firmly. Then she took up her pitcher to return to the house.

"If you cast me off in that way I will go right on to ruin," blurted out Joe. "My father has told me this morning to leave the place, and I will. I don't care what comes of me now, since you have turned your back on me. I am weak and foolish, I know, but if I had some one beside me who cared for me I would keep right; but, now that I am left to myself, I don't give three straws whether I sink or swim."

"Oh, don't talk like that, Joe," returned Lizzy, looking back. "You might make a man of yourself if you would only give up the drink, for no one has a better head or a warmer heart. Do bethink yourself, Joe, if not for my sake, yet for your own; and if you do go away from here, keep clear of all companions who would lead you to the public-house, and you will redeem yourself."

"I see how it is, Lizzy," said Joe with great bitterness; "you wish to get rid of me that you may marry another. Young Wilson of the Hill is a richer man than me, and I know he wants you. To be sure, his moral character is not the most spotless, but his money will make up for that."

"Joe, that is cruel—it is insulting," answered Lizzy. "If I give you up, I will never, never marry another."

"And is this, then, to be the end of all our company-keeping?" said the youth, as Lizzy moved slowly away.

"Alas, yes," sighed the wretched girl; "your own conduct has made it so."

"Then, farewell," he cried. "You will never see me again."

And turning round, he walked with the air of a desperate man in a direction different from his father's house. Lizzy stood gazing after him till he turned the shoulder of a hill, but he never looked back. When his tall form vanished over the height a long wail of agony broke from the maiden's lips, and, clasping her hands together, she sat down upon the grassy bank, and gave way to the most poignant grief. To give him up thus had cost her a fearful struggle, for she loved him fondly and truly, and had clung to him, hoping against hope, when all her friends advised and urged her to give him up.

After she had wept long and sore, she again took up her pitcher, and wended her way with a sorrowful heart to her peaceful home.

Her discarded lover wended *his* way to a more peaceful home still—to a small and ancient churchyard which stood on one of the heights close to the sea. On this wild and lonely spot was a little enclosure full of mounds and gravestones, and at one side the ruins of what had once been a chapel, whose roofless aisle the wind now swept through with mournful sound. Close to the mouldering wall of this hoary ruin Joe went, and threw himself down by the side of a grassy grave, whose thick turf showed that the tenant below had long slumbered in that place of dreamless repose. It was the grave of his mother, who had died when he was quite a boy.

"Oh, mother, mother," sobbed the strong yet erring man, "if I had not lost you, I would not have so lost myself. You were my best, my kindest friend, and for want of you I have been led to this ruin of my life."

Much more he muttered as he lay prostrate above his mother's hallowed dust, and gave way to a grief which in its vehement sobs, shook all his frame. Then he threw his arms across the matted mound, and, burying his face among the tall rank grass, lay for some moments quite still. Suddenly, he started up, and, rushing through among the moss-covered stones, sprang over the low wall, and went at a very rapid pace across the fields towards the highway.

*

Two nights after this Joe was wandering sad and dejected about the streets of Edinburgh. The previous night he had lain in a field in the suburbs, but that night he longed to sleep under the shelter of a roof, for his limbs were aching and his body shivering with fatigue and exposure. Yet all the money he had was fourpence, and he was aware that such a small sum would not procure for him very comfortable quarters.

He was sauntering dejectedly in the High Street, the desperate nature of his condition being only too clearly stamped on his crouching, creeping form, when some one close to his side accosted him in a broad Irish accent—

"Ye seem mighty sore knocked up, me boy. What's the matter wid yez?"

Joe turned to the speaker, and though the face that met his gaze was far from prepossessing, yet the man was the first who had spoken to him of all that had passed by, and he was grateful.

"I am tired," answered Joe. "I have walked all to-day and yesterday, and I'm like to drop."

"Man alive, why don't ye go to yer lodgings, thin?" asked the stranger, who was no other than Hare.

"Because I have no lodgings to go to. I am quite a stranger in Edinburgh."

"And haven't ye got any friends?"

"No," answered Joe, gloomily; "not one."

"Och, musha, but yours is a hard case intirely. Sure it's the luck uv ye that made ye fall in wid me. I keep a clane, purty lodging-house in a street along there. Come along, and it's proud I'll be to put ye up."

"I—I'm much obliged to you," said Joe, hesitatingly, "but my funds are low just now. I don't think I have any more than fourpence."

"Och, be my sowl, what's about the money?" cried Hare, with an apparent burst of generosity. "It goes to me heart to see a dacent boy like you wanderin' about widout a place to put his head in. Come along, and I'll make ye comfortable for to-night at any rate."

Joe went with all readiness. He was weary beyond description, and, besides, he felt ill. A cold, icy shiver ran down his back, his head throbbed violently, and his whole body was stiff and sore. He was, in truth, miserable and wretched in the extreme, and he longed just to lay himself down somewhere to enjoy quiet repose.

So he went with Hare to the fatal house in Tanner's Close. He was a waif cast up by the troubled ocean of life—a poor, homeless, friendless one—the victim of his own weakness of will—made an outcast by his folly and his love for the low socialities of the public-house.

Burke and the two women were in the house when he went in, but he was too exhausted and unwell to notice anybody or anything. He could not even eat anything, though for two days he had scarcely tasted food. He was only too glad to crawl, at Hare's bidding, into the back room, and there throw himself on the miserable bed.

How different was the heavy-smelling atmosphere of that dirty, dingy chamber from the pure, sweet country air that floated round the old mill, and over the heath-clad heights, and through the leafy woods of his distant home? But Joe was too exhausted and ill to make the comparison. He stretched himself out among the filthy straw, and was soon asleep.

"Be jabers, but he's too strong intirely," said Burke, as he and his murderous associate conversed together in one of the outer rooms. "He must have the drink in him afore we try it on."

"Man alive! he's as wake as a child," urged Hare. "He could scarcely crawl through the Grassmarket."

"It's only tired he is, not wake," remarked Burke, "and he would make a terrible struggle."

"You won't do it then?" returned Hare, disappointed.

"Not to-night. Arrah, now, can't you wait till to-morrow night. He'll drink like a fish, and then we'll do it aisy. It's mighty pleasant for you that has only to hould yer hand on their mouth. If ye had my hard work to do, ye would take good care they hadn't much strength left in them."

By the morning Joe was in a raging fever, and in his ravings he let his listeners understand his story. By these they learned more fully how safe it would be to make him one of their victims.

For three days he was furious, and Burke would not attempt his murder, though Hare, with his usual eager cold-blooded cruelty, frequently urged its commission. On the fourth morning Joe was prostrated by exhaustion, and then they deemed their opportunity had come.

So the monsters entered the little back room, prepared for their horrid work.

Joe lay perfectly still, with his eyes closed. His breathing was scarcely audible, his ruddy face was now pale and pinched, and his light hair lay in tangled masses on his brow. He was alike unconscious of, and helpless to avert, the fate in store for him.

The deed was quickly done, though with a slight change in the *modus operandi*. Hare, instead of pressing his hand on nose and mouth, took a pillow and laid it over the face, bearing at the same time the weight of his arms upon it. We don't suppose he had ever read Shakespeare, or heard of Othello: it was, therefore, no plagiarism on his part—it was purely his own devilish invention.

Poor Joe was easily overcome. Burke had not to complain of hard work in his case. The fever had helped them, by taking the strength out of their victim. A few spasmodic motions of the limbs, a great gurgling in the chest, and all was over. The hapless, misguided youth, who might have been the happy husband of a true-hearted girl, was betrayed to violent death; *but his body brought a pound more than the rest at Surgeons' Square.*

CHAPTER X

THE HELPLESS WANDERERS

In one of the wildest Irish counties a small rude cabin stood at the side of an immense tract of black bog. It was a solitary habitation, and the only thing of its kind to be seen in the bleak district. A small village or hamlet did indeed lie on the other side of the distant hill that cast its bare round top up against the western sky, and was on fine summer evenings crowned by the glorious hues of sunset. But this hamlet could not be seen from the cabin in question; it stood alone upon the wide waste—a speck of human life in the midst of chaos. It was lonely in the summer stillness, and doubly lonely in the winter desolation.

Nevertheless, humble though it was, it was the abode of contentment and love. Dennis O'Shea lived in it, with his warm-hearted wife and his old mother, and his little deaf and dumb boy—the silent wistful one whose life was shrouded from human gaze and cast into the dim dark region of silence. How the father and the mother and the old grandmother lavished their love and tenderness on the stricken one! Though nine years of age he had grown very little, and the deprivation of his two senses had made all his ways most innocently infantile. He had evidently a great love for his three relations, whose centre of affection he was, and he seemed to receive great pleasure from basking in the summer sun and gathering wild flowers near the cabin door. Beyond this he was a sad and hopeless mystery, as all deaf and dumb people are, to whose shrouded fettered mind little access has been had. Had poor little Dennis—he bore his father's name—been put into some training school, and there subjected to the patient instruction conveyed in these institutions, the seal upon his soul might have been removed and the springs of intelligence opened up.[1] But in the wastes of benighted Ireland forty years

---

1. Dr Johnson visited Thomas Braidwood's Edinburgh school for the deaf and dumb (est. 1760) in 1773. That school moved to London by 1783. Deaf and Dumb institutions opened in Edinburgh in 1810, then Aberdeen and Glasgow

ago such a benevolent institution had never been heard of, and the poor mute was left alone in his sepulchre, the stone of which no one knew how to roll away.

But otherwise the helpless one was a blessing to the little household. He was there a centre of love, which is always a centre of harmony, kindly feeling, good humour, forbearance, and peace. His affliction brought out a whole host of soft feelings and tender emotions, and these in turn modified the natures and sweetened the dispositions of those who cherished them. Dennis, the father, might have been as wild a fellow as lived in the district, as fond of drinking and quarrelling and fighting as any of the boys of the village; but he was not. At night, after he returned from his work, instead of going to the public-house, he remained at home with little Dennis on his knee, and a great deal of humble but sweet domestic enjoyment in his heart; his little pale-faced and rather delicate wife engaged in mending his clothes or her own, and the old woman busy knitting for him a pair of coarse-ribbed stockings. Dennis had sense enough to know that the quiet happiness of evenings so spent was preferable to the boisterous merriment of the social gatherings at the village—ending, as they often did, in bloody heads and broken bones. For, previous to his marriage and the birth of this his only child, he had been like the other boys of the place, and had gone to patterns,[2] and fairs and faction fights, and come in for his share of the results of such doings. But little Dennis and his deep affliction had caused him to lose relish for such rough and dangerous amusements, and a more sober and industrious fellow was not known for miles around.

Of course, sobriety and industry do not mean among the peasantry of Ireland what they mean among the peasantry of Scotland or England—the absence of deep poverty. Let an Irish working man be as saving and economical as he can, he is never anything but poor—he doesn't expect to be, and therefore he is quite contented with his lot. With his potato-

---

in 1819, and Dundee in 1846. Edinburgh's Donaldson's Hospital (1850) accepted children aged seven to nine, and worked with them till they turned fourteen. Iain Hutchison, "Early Institutional Provision in Scotland for Disabled Children", *Scottish Journal of Residential Child Care* 3.1 (Feb/March 2004): 31–43; see 32.

2. OED gives: Irish, patron saint's days, with associated festivities.

patch and his pig, and a few days of labouring work here and there, the wages of which procure meal and tobacco and whisky for daily consumption, he counts himself prosperous, and lives on in his smoky cabin, attending chapel and going periodically to his "duty" to the priest, having no wish to be anything higher than what he is.[3]

Dennis O'Shea was therefore a poor man, and poverty was the order of his household. They generally found the means to satisfy the wants of each day that dawned, but a shilling or two of reserve was a thing never dreamed of, far less realised. The rent had to be met regularly, but then the pig paid that, though always under vehement protest. So there they lived on the side of the great black bog, with a mysterious providence in the midst of them, operating as a bond of love, and keeping their affections fresh and glowing.

But, alas! the dark cloud of sorrow and desolation suddenly gathered and burst upon them. One morning Dennis left the cabin to go to a large village twelve miles distant, where a fair was to be held. His wife when he left did not counsel him to keep free of drinking, quarrelling, and fighting, knowing she did not require to do so. He kissed her and little Dennis and was gone. Ay, and as it turned out, gone, never to return. There was plenty of quarrelling and fighting at the fair that day, with none of which Dennis was connected. There was also a most ferocious faction fight, which brought the hot passions of the combatants up to the most bitter pitch, and there was much blood shed, and on one side a man was killed.[4] Darkness separated the combatants; but on the side where the loss was greatest the most deadly revenge was

---

3. The Popery Act 1703/09, which required that when a Catholic died his property must be divided equally among his male heirs (unless the eldest converted), had long-term pauperising effects.

4. Civil unrest was rife in Ireland between Catholics and the Ango-Irish ascendancy, and between Catholics and Protestants. Factions were complex: Ireland had gained an independent but limited parliament in 1782; this produced the rebellion of 1798 (led by Protestant liberals as the Society of United Irishmen) and the Act of Union in 1800. The British establishment encouraged factionalism to disempower all sides: in 1797 the Dungannon commander plotted a show (but not the reality) of general disarmament "to increase the animosity between the Orangemen and the United Irishmen" (Lecky, 7: 312). In the late 1820s, factionalism built in the lead up to the Roman Catholic Emancipation Act of 1829.

cherished, and they repaired by twos and threes to the outside
of the village to lie in wait for any of their foes who might be
returning home alone.

The moon did not rise till an hour or more after dark, but
the night being a clear one, it was certain to be light, and
Dennis O'Shea, counting on this, did not leave the village till
after twilight. About half a mile onward the road passed
through a dense wood, and here Dennis was fallen upon by
nearly a dozen savage men, who, taking him for the actual
murderer of the man who had come to his death in the fray
that afternoon, beat him with ferocious brutality on the head
with bludgeons fresh cut from the trees. The first blow stunned
him and he fell, and it is to be hoped that he was mercifully
saved from the pain of the rest of the blows. When they left
him poor Dennis lay on the road a mangled corpse, and it was
not till the following morning that he was found stiff and cold
by some men who had come in search of him. His alarmed
wife, finding that he did not return, ran to the village and
reported his unaccountable absence. Dennis, though not a
boon companion, was respected by all, and a band of willing
searchers went off on the instant. They proceeded for more
than eleven miles, and then they found him lying on the road
under the deep shadow of the trees. He was scarcely to be recognised, so bruised and battered was his face by the murderous
blows. They knew him, however, by his garments, and con-
structing a litter of branches, they laid the body thereon, covered
it with an old cloak, and carried it mournfully homeward.

When they reached the village they rested in the public-
house, and Bridget Docherty, an elderly woman and intimate
friend of the O'Sheas, went across the common to break the
fatal tidings. Need we describe the heartrending scene that followed? A husband's loss falls with as heavy a stroke in an
Irish cabin as in a British mansion; and never did wife of fox-
hunting squire who broke his neck in leaping a fence receive
with a wilder burst of grief and woe the dead body as it was
carried into the hall than did the stricken widow rush to meet
the cold clay of her murdered Dennis.[5] She cast herself on

---

5. A cliché of the Anglo-Irish ascendancy. In his 1776–1779 tour, Arthur
Young observed these bucks "hunt in the day, get drunk in the evening, and
fight the next morning". They are "the pest of society" (Lecky, 2: 324 n.i.).

the body in frantic agony, and wailed over him the most endearing appellations. The old woman, too, was plunged into excessive grief, but hers took a sterner form, and with clenched hand she called down curses on the murderers of her brave and noble boy. Poor little Dennis, the mute, no one could tell how he thought or felt. Probably he did not comprehend the nature of the calamity, and did not recognise the bloody mass which lay on the floor, for with a look of fear he ran and hid himself in the folds of his grandmother's gown.

This melancholy tragedy took place in spring time, and before the height of summer the broken-hearted widow slept side by side with Dennis in the rude village churchyard. To stay with her helpless boy, or to join her lost husband, was an alternative which, if left to her choice, she would never have settled; but it was settled for her, and death fulfilled his not always unkind commission. Thus the old grandmother was left alone with the poor deaf and dumb boy, and with no means for his or her support. Before the mother closed her eyes in death, she advised the old woman to go to Scotland and seek for a brother of hers who resided there. Perhaps he would be kind to them, perhaps he would take pity on the helpless orphan, and for the sake of its mother, whom he once loved, would give them some assistance. It was a poor hope, but still it was the only one, and a few days after the sod was laid upon the mother's breast, they left the cabin and went forth on their wanderings.

The warm-hearted villagers, when they bade them adieu, blessed them and gave them what little they could spare. Bridget Docherty was the last to leave them, and in parting instructed her to tell her son Terry, who was somewhere about Edinburgh, that she too meant to come over to Scotland in the fall of the year.

Who can imagine the deep and keen sorrow of the old woman as she crossed the threshold of the little cabin, where they had known so much love and peace, and closed the door for ever behind her? What desolation of heart could be greater than hers? Left alone in the world, with the charge of that stricken child, who would never be able to make his own way in life—old, feeble, and with the prospect of want and death before herself—truly her case was pitiable in the extreme. Most bitter and sad were the blinding tears through which she looked back for the last time on the solitary cabin, and with its image in her lonely heart, so full of all she had enjoyed and loved and lost, she turned away into the wide, the cold, and the unknown world.

A week from thence, and the vessel in which she came across landed her at Greenock, where her slow and painful foot-wandering in Scotland began. Along the wet and dirty roads she trudged, with the boy by her side. Having her alone to cling to now, he seemed to love her with all the intensity of his shrouded nature, and would put his little hand in hers and gaze up to her wrinkled face with his great round wistful eyes, and smile confidingly. Poor boy! His soul in its imprisonment knew nothing of anxiety or care. The past, the present, and the future were alike unscanned by him. He loved his grandmother, he liked always to be near her, and this seemed to constitute all the enjoyment of his limited life.

Before they reached Glasgow the little money and other things received from the kind-hearted villagers were done, and the old woman had to ask for doles from the cold hand of the world's charity. This was not so hard to her as it would have been to some. The Irish nature is not so independent as the Scotch, and is more easily bent to the solicitation of alms—besides it was for the helpless boy as much as for herself that she begged, and she could present him as the most eloquent appeal to the generosity of strangers.

Still, at the best, it yielded but a scanty and precarious support, and at night, for want of a few pence to pay for shelter, she had often to lie down under a hay rick, or under an overhanging hedge. Fortunately the nights were warm and dry, and with the boy folded to her aged bosom, the old woman would go to sleep under the midnight stars, and dream of the bright and happy days of old spent in the green isle of Erin.

It was only a simple unsophisticated woman who would have come hopefully in search of a man whose name alone she knew, and expect to find him in such a city as Edinburgh. She was not even sure that he was there. Some one who had come from Scotland many months before reported that they had seen him in the Cowgate, and that he had said he was working somewhere in the town, but whether he was there still, or in what part of the city he lodged, she knew not.

At length, however, she entered the city from the west, passed through the Grassmarket, and, missing the Cowgate, of which she was in search, came up the Bow to the High Street.

As she passed the Cross, the welcome tones of the Irish tongue struck upon her ear, and turning round she saw two men standing together in close conversation.

One was weak and delicate-looking, evidently in bad health. The other was a stout man, pretty well dressed, and with an unmistakeable Irish countenance, though the features thereof were the opposite of attractive. Still he was her countryman, and in a strange land she had no hesitation in accosting him.

"If ye plaise, could ye be afther tellin' me where the Cowgate is?" she asked.

The man turned quickly round, and quitting his hold of the arm of his companion, ran his two ill-favoured eyes over the old woman and the boy. At the brief survey a gleam twinkled in the horizontal orbs, and a sinister smile broadened on his thick, sensual lips.

"Och, be me soul, and its from the ould counthry ye are!" he cried, with a warmth of feeling and animation which his cold, cruel features belied.

"Throth, and its that same," returned the poor, sorrowful creature. "It plaised God to take to himself my purty son, the father of this poor boughal, and his mother wasn't long going afther him, and as I hadn't another soul to care for us two in the ould counthry, we've come over to seek out an uncle uv the helpless alanna—one Michael Curran. Maybe its yourself would know where he stops?"

"Devil a doubt but I'll find it out any way," replied the other, who seemed a friend raised up in the hour of need. "But there's time enough for that anyhow. Sure it's tired ye are and hungry both?"

"Och, thin, ye are only spakin' the blessed truth," sighed the old woman. "We haven't seen the inside uv a house for two days, and it's not much mate we have had to ate either."

"Arrah, now, don't ye hurt me heart entirely," responded the good Samaritan. "I have a house in one uv the streets beyont, and a bite and sup, wid a cruskin of skalteen, and a bed for the night, ye are mighty welcome to."

"O may the Lord be good to yez all yer days," exclaimed the old woman in a transport of gratitude. "Sure he sint us up here to meet wid you and"—

"Faugh shana nis," interrupted the other. "Sure it's but

my duty to help a poor distressed country-woman, and I wouldn't be an Irishman at all at all if I didn't."

Of course the reader suspects that this generous stranger is Hare, and understands his intentions in reference to the poor old unsuspecting woman. He was that afternoon prowling for a victim, and the weak ailing man with whom he was in conversation was one whom he was trying to lure to the shambles. Fortunately for *him* was the approach of the old woman, and no sooner had Hare begun to speak to the wanderer than he crept away, all unconscious of the escape he had made.

To the West Port then went Hare and the old woman by his side, leading the deaf and dumb boy by the hand—she all gratitude and thanks, and the monster chuckling at the expectation of another "shot."

Burke stood at the mouth of Tanner's Close as they approached, and Hare, with his frightful leer, which served as a signal to his already wide-awake accomplice, introduced the old woman as from the old country, come over in search of Michael Curran.

"Caed mille failthe," cried Burke, warmly shaking her by the hand. "Sure and I saw Michael just the other day, and its proud I'll be to find him for yez. But what's the matter with the little boughal?"

"Plaise God, he's dafe and dumb," answered the woman, looking down to the little boy.

"Och musha, and is'nt he to be pitied?" said Hare, in a sentimental tone. "But come down to the house wid me. Its meself, William, that's going to give the dacent craythur a bed and a bite till she has time to get spache of Michael."

"Sure, now, ye was always the big-hearted Christian," rejoined Burke, "and when ye die, if they take ye to the dure of Purgatory in a mistake, the keeper won't take ye in, but sind ye to glory at wunst."

"Oh, go along wid ye," said Hare, pretending bashfulness, and at the same moment leading the way down the close.

The old woman and her charge were conducted over the fatal threshold. A few words of introduction caused the women to receive them with all cordiality, and they were shown into the back room at once. Food was what they sorely needed; but while a biscuit was got for the boy, drink was offered first to the old woman, with the assurance that it would revive her quicker than anything else. How could she doubt the word of such good friends? She drank up her glass, and the whisky following upon hunger and emptiness, made her intoxicated in a very few minutes, and when the glass was re-filled she drank again, so that the confederates saw she would very soon reach "the point."

Mrs Hare coaxed the boy to the front room, and sitting down with him near a large fire, the heat acting upon his weary frame set him asleep. She laid him down on one of the comfortless beds, and scarcely had she done so when the entrance of Helen M'Dougal from the back room gave her to understand that the tragedy was to begin.

The two sat down together by the fire and remained perfectly silent. They did not once look at each other. Mary Hare sat gazing unconsciously at the fire, but Helen covered her face with her apron.

In a few minutes the stillness was broken by suppressed sounds from the back room—strange sounds of hard breathing, voiceless struggling—violent wrestling, choking, gasping, gurgling—sounds which would have chilled with horror any listener, even though they knew not their cause.

Helen shuddered and pressed her hands upon her ears. The other bestowed upon her a look of sneering contempt. On the dirty bed lay the boy calmly sleeping—the most touching picture of the dark and terrible scene.

At the end of fifteen minutes there was perfect stillness again, and the women knew that the deed was done. Helen drew a long sigh of relief, and uncovering her head met the cold, cruel look of Mrs Hare.

"Sure, thin, how mighty squeamish ye are getting," remarked that virago. "Isn't it better for poor craythurs like that to get out uv a world they have no way uv livin' in, and don't their bones, which they can make no use uv, bring us bread?"

"I know that," returned Helen; "but I am always afraid we shall be found out."

"Devil a found out we'll be at all at all, if we keep quiet ourselves," rejoined Mary, angrily; "Who's to find us out, I would be afther axin'? Nobody's here to see it done, and the tramps are never missed. You'd better give up yer soft ways, or I'll maybe give Burke the wink, and then you are sure uv a wallopin'."

"You needn't do anything of the kind, Mary," responded

Helen. "I am not squeamish any more than you, but I know it is possible for the thing to be discovered. There is the boy. What is to be done with him? Surely they don't mean to—to murder him also?"

"Faix, then, I never thought uv that. I suppose he is too small for the doctors to buy. I suppose we'll have to take him down to the Canongate and lave him in the street. There's one good thing—he can't spake, to tell anything."

By-and-by Burke came out of the back room whistling, and Hare followed with a sardonic grin on his hideous face. They came and sat down beside the women round the fire. It was growing dark now, and lights from upper windows flickered in the narrow close.

"Be jabers, but there's another good job done," remarked Hare, with a ferocious chuckle. "This is one of our tin pound days."

"Won't the boughal count for something?" said Burke.

"Faix, thin, the doctors might think him too small entirely," observed Hare.

"Mary thinks we might stray him in the Canongate," remarked Helen. "He can't speak, you know—so we are safe."

"Small ones are just as good as large ones to the doctors," said Burke.

The others, who believed more in size than form, did not think this, and there being a difference of opinion, the matter was suffered to drop for the present. Burke immediately cried out for whisky, as he always did after the commission of a murder, and Helen was sent out for it. The next hour or two passed in wild debauchery, the noise of which disturbed not the slumber of the deaf and dumb boy. During the evening, however, he awoke, and looked all round for his grandmother. Not seeing her in the room, he looked wistfully in every face, then went to the door of the back room as if to enter. Mary pulled him back, and by signs made him understand that his grandmother was sleeping.

Yes, she was sleeping the long, dreamless sleep of death. Another victim had been added to their black list; another "thing" was got for Surgeons' Square. The monsters had no pity for her age—no compunction for her nationality. Old and wearied though she was, she struggled desperately in their grasp, when she realised the danger of her position and their intentions towards her. Probably the conviction flashed upon her at the same moment that the boy would be murdered too, and it was her love and fear for him that made her struggles so desperate. But her wild, frantic resistance was of no avail. She, an old worn-out woman, in the hands of two strong human butchers, was powerless to save herself, and did finally succumb. The moment she was dead they stripped her, and flung her on the bed till a box was got for her conveyance to the Square.

At a late hour in the evening Hare went out to procure this box. Mrs Hare and Helen were also out, and Burke sat alone in the room with the dumb boy. Then the demon came anew into the bad brutal heart, and he debated within himself the propriety of murdering the child. What good would it do to let him live? He had nobody to take care of him, and he would never be able to care for himself. Then the doctors would be sure to buy him, and a few pounds might as well be made out of him as not.

In this way he seconded the promptings of his diabolical heart, till his resolution was taken; and, gulping up a large draught of whisky, he took the boy in his arms and carried him into the fatal room. There he laid the poor helpless one on the floor, placed his broad bloody hand on the little nose and mouth, and his knee on the chest. Just as he was about to crush the life out of the boy, the victim looked up at him with his great wistful eyes, and gave a confiding smile. That look and smile went to the monster's heart, and for the first time touched it with pity and remorse. It was a look and smile which haunted him through the rest of his guilty life.

But it did not cause him to relent or change his purpose. He shut his eyes to hide the sight, and pressed the more firmly on mouth and breast. When he looked again the great round wistful orbs were covered with the film of death, and the little lamb had passed from the butcher's gripe, we trust into the blessed fold of the Good Shepherd.

CHAPTER XI

A MISADVENTURE ON THE WAY TO SURGEONS' SQUARE—A COUNTRY EXCURSION—THE ITALIAN BOY

Burke had just gulped down a quantity of whisky to steady his nerves, which the look of the dumb boy had shaken so much, when Hare returned with an empty box.

"Faix, thin, that is too small entirely," said Burke.

"Sure and it isn't," replied his confederate. "We've packed as big a wun as that ould woman into a tay chest."

"Thrue for it, but there's more nor the ould woman to go."

Hare looked round the room, and missing the boy, fixed his alarmed eyes on the other inquiringly.

"You've done it then?"

"Nate and aisy. But, och musha, if ye had seen the look the boughal give me! Be me soul, I would give all we'll get for him up at the Square to get it out uv me head."

In reply, Hare carelessly remarked that a sleep would do that, and looked at the box reflectively.

"There's no way o' makin' it hould them both," he muttered. "Begorra, we'll just have to carry thim up at twice."

"Haven't ye got an empty herring barrel in the stable?" inquired Burke.

"So I have, and that would hould thim beautiful," cried Hare with sudden animation. "And couldn't we put Donald into the cart to-morrow night, and make him draw the barrel up to the Square?"

"Uv coorse we could, and that will save both uv us a sweatin'."

Hare gave one of his frightful leers, and taking down a heavy rusty key, which hung above the fireplace, went out, returning in a minute or two with a large herring barrel. This was taken into the back room, and after much difficulty the two bodies were crammed into it, and the lid fastened down. Burke then *rolled* it out into the close to the door of a small stable which stood a few yards up the close.

Between the door of the house and the stable door they encountered one of the neighbours.

"Dear me, that's surely a heavy barrel," remarked the woman, who had some difficulty in getting past them.

"A barrel of herrings is always heavy," replied Burke.

"I hope it will be lighter when I come home with it to-morrow night," remarked Hare, facetiously.

"Eh me, are ye gaun tae sell herrin' noo?" said the woman.

"Anything to make a dacent living," answered Hare.

"Oh aye, tae be shure. Folk sud dae a' they can tae earn an honest penny. Bide a wee and I'll bring oot a plate for a wheen. What are they the dizzen?"

"Faix thin," replied Hare, quite composedly, "it's meself that's sorry I can't give ye thim, for the barrel isn't broken up, and I don't mane to do it till I get down to the Canongate to-morrow. Tin thousand thanks to ye all the same."

Without the faintest shade of suspicion the woman passed on, and the barrel was rolled into the stable and covered up with some dirty straw. The only other object in the stable was the miserable skeleton of a brown horse, the mere frame of an animal, reduced literally to skin and bones. Before this breathing anatomical specimen a little dry, dirty straw was placed, which, hungry though it was, it did not attempt to eat.

It was scarcely dark on the following evening when the old worn-out hack was put into Hare's ricketty cart, and the barrel being placed in it, away they went down the West Port, Hare at the horse's head, and Burke following behind. So long as they were going down hill old Donald managed to keep his feet and let the cart shove him forward, though he staggered painfully from side to side, and occasionally gave a deep groan. But when they entered the Grassmarket and came upon even ground, where he required to pull, he came to a stand-still. Hare had no stick, and could not therefore urge him on, but he tugged desperately at his head, and Burke pushed as desperately behind. It was of no use. The worn-out animal had come to his last legs, and could not move a foot. This threw the two murderers into the greatest alarm, for while they tugged and strained the people on the street began to congregate around them. Should the police come and make inquiries as to what was in the barrel a discovery would be made, and their crimes brought to light.

"I say, Paddy, it's no use trying to make that beast go," said the ostler of the White Hart, who came forward among the rest. "The hack is done—hasn't the strength of a fly left in him."

"He's not done, he's only obstinate," said Hare savagely. "Lind me a stick, one uv yez, and ye'll see him go off like the mail coach."

A stick was handed to him by some one in the crowd, and with this he rained a storm of unmerciful blows on the dry hard ribs of the poor beast, making them rattle under the strokes.

The result of this was that, instead of going off like the mail coach, the beast's unsteady legs gave way, and he fell with a crash to the ground.

"I told you so," cried the ostler. "That horse has pulled his last load, and you may take him to the tanyard when you like. My eye! look at the hole in his shoulder."

He put out his hand and pulled away a square piece of skin, which had been patched on by some knavish horse-dealer, and underneath was a deep hole in the flesh, stuffed with tow.

"I'm blessed if ever I seed the match of that," said the amazed ostler. "I say, Paddy, the man you bought the beast from sold you as well as the horse."

Hare paid little attention to these remarks, being more occupied in stealthily noticing the proceedings of Burke, who, while all were engaged with the fallen horse, got the barrel quickly rolled from the cart, and engaged a porter to take it away in his hurley. Hare was immensely relieved when he saw the porter move off with the burden, and Burke in his company.

At the top of the High School Wynd Burke paid the porter, and, lifting the barrel in his arms, carried it into the Square. Several students were in the hall when he staggered in with it. The assistant who usually transacted the business came forward with a familiar nod the moment he entered.

"Got another thing?"

"Throth, sir, I've two things this time," answered Burke.

"Two bodies in that barrel?"

"Wun o' them is a small wun—a little slip o' a boughal."

"A what?"

"A boy, if it plaise ye. But maybe ye don't do anything wid little wuns."

"Oh yes, we do. Small as well as large are useful here, so out with them."

This was, however, a matter of great difficulty. The bodies had become stiff and rigid, and it seemed as if the barrel would require to be broken to pieces. They did at length, however, manage the matter, and the old woman and her grandson lay side by side on the dissecting table.

The assistant looked at both approvingly. "Of course," he remarked, "we can't give as much for the boy as for the full grown body. Here is sixteen pounds for the two."

"Thank ye, sur," said Burke, as he counted the money, and shouldered the empty barrel.

"Six pounds for the boughal," he said to himself, as in great exultation he went down the wynd. "Be jabers, and wouldn't we have lost that intirely if I hadn't stood out for thim both. Be jabers, but that ould devil uv a horse was near bringing the ruin on us."

"Holy Mother! is it all right?" asked a voice at his elbow, and at the same moment Hare came from out the shadow of a dark entry.

"Keep yourself aisy, me boy. I saw you were in a mighty shake when Donald gave in, and be gorra so was I, for I thought the ould baste was going to turn witness against us."

"It's a pity the doctors don't buy dead horses as well," returned Hare. "I took the ould thief to the tanyard, and they only gave me tin shillings for him—him that cost me two pounds, bad luck to him."

"Never mind, me boy," returned Burke. "We can stand the loss uv the horse. I got sixteen pound for what was in the barrel."

"Thunder and turf! Sixteen!" exclaimed the astonished Hare. "Thin they do buy little wuns?"

"I tould ye so. A little one is just the same as a big one, only smaller."

"Sure, thin, it's glad I am wid all my heart that the horse is dead, for I've got no more use for him. It's a mighty big fool I wid be to go about wid a cart or a barrow selling fish or apples, when we have such a thriving trade to stick to."

"Uv coorse you would," responded his companion. "I mane to keep the cobbler's stall in the house, just to keep the neighbours from wondering, but devil a shoe I'll mend as long as shots turn in. I say, me boy, there's M'Callum's, let's go in and have a glass or two. We need it after the fright the baste gave us."

The amazing success which these men met with in their unparalleled career of crime made them bold and confident. They did not go sneaking along to Surgeons' Square as they did at first—taking byepaths and going at a late hour. They took their way through the busiest thoroughfares, and at an early hour of the evening when the streets were crowded. Familiarity with murder and the impunity with which they perpetrated one after another made them almost forget the necessity of secrecy, and they looked forward to years of the same profitable work. The poor of the streets had come to be looked on as their natural prey, and the means of revelry and material gratification. In their low brutal minds there were no limits set to their operations, and they began almost to leave out of view the contingency of discovery and the consequences which would follow it, looking only to the never-failing supply of victims which the city afforded, and to the ready market which existed for them in Surgeons' Square.

And so days and weeks passed on, and the fatal back room in Tanner's Close witnessed repeated tragedies of the same horrid character as those we have described. Poor houseless wanderers going about the country begging, would come for a night's lodgings to Hare's house, and never leave it, except in a box. They were made drunk and suffocated. The inveterate love of drink which characterised wanderers was a great aid to the murderers. They never attempted the deed till the victims were helplessly intoxicated—a state into which it was never very difficult to bring them.

But they did not confine themselves to the stray victims who came in as lodgers. These were too few and irregular to satisfy the demon lust that had been roused within them. Poor wretches were lured in from the street and cruelly despatched. The house in Tanner's Close was the very portals of the grave. A likely individual once across its threshold was doomed. The dark, dirty, foul-aired back room was a chamber of horrors such as human imagination had never pictured. Murder after murder committed within its four walls, while a few yards off there was on all sides a city full of teeming life, no one dreaming of the human butcheries which were weekly, almost nightly, perpetrated in their very midst.

The life which their atrocities enabled these wretches to live was, as might have been expected, one of riot and drunkenness. Notwithstanding the large sums they received for the bodies, they saved nothing, nor did they add to the decency or the comfort of their miserable dwelling. All the money was spent in extravagant or wasteful indulgence. It could not be otherwise. Brutal and debased natures such as theirs, capable of doing the deeds they committed, were utterly incapable of rising above the very lowest debauchery. Their very crimes chained them down to the most beastly indulgence. Humanity having gone out of them, their existence had scarcely any human features about it.

Burke and Helen were the only ones who sometimes felt ill at ease in the midst of their wild, frenzied revelry. Helen was never free from fear. She felt no remorse for the cruelty and accumulated crime, but the possibility of detection was always present to her more than to the others, and it made her continually anxious and nervous. Burke's discomfort of mind proceeded from another cause. More intelligent than the others, the weight of blood did press upon his soul, and he began to be haunted by superstitious fears. He could not be for a moment in the dark, his sleep grew troubled, and fearful dreams would cause him to awake in terror. But a draught of the raw whisky, which stood continually by his bedside, drowned his fears for the time. This, however, was the shadow of retribution hovering near his soul. The murder of the dumb boy stuck to his memory, and his last look was frequently before his sight.

Hare and his wife had no fears to haunt and no feelings to annoy them. The cold cruelty of the one and the fierce passion of the other was of a type so low as to preclude them from feeling anything like a soft emotion. Murder was to them, even at the first, a thing of no great horror, and when they grew familiar with it by repetition, they looked upon it as they looked on any ordinary occurrence of life, and any thought of consequences, apart from the visitation of human justice in the event of discovery, never seemed to intrude on their brutified understandings.

About the middle of summer Burke felt an inclination to pay a visit to the country. What prompted him to this we have no means of knowing. Probably it was with a view to get rid of the unpleasant restlessness that his crimes occasioned, or perhaps it was only to gratify an inclination for wandering which is generally possessed by his countrymen of the same class. He had been accustomed for years to roam from place to place, and now that the bright summer days were visiting the earth, the desire might come upon him with increased force. Be this as it may, the inclination did seize him, and as he had the means of gratifying it he resolved to go along with Helen to pass a few days at the village in Stirlingshire where they first became acquainted and first lived together. So one morning they set out on foot from Tanner's Close, Burke having his share of the money got for the last murdered body in his pocket.

What their sensations might be when they passed from the smoky streets and came amidst the pure, peaceful innocence of nature who can tell? but was not every sight that met their eye, and every sound that greeted their ear, calculated to bring their guilt home to their conscience? In the dirt, and darkness, and drunkenness of Tanner's Close they had little to remind them of the terrible wickedness of their career; but out in the centre of the summer landscape, with the blue sky overhead and the fragrant sunlit air around them, and the beauty and melody of a crimeless creation revealed on every side, how full of accusation and how suggestive of their atrocious criminality was everything they beheld. Unless the blood upon their souls had seared and hardened into an impenetrable crust, one cannot imagine how they could feel anything but misery in the country scenes through which they wandered. But when humanity reaches their debased and degraded level it gets out of the sphere of moral cognisance altogether, and we lose the very data of induction.

Left to themselves, Hare and his wife revelled and rioted together, and soon managed to squander the few pounds which was their share of the last payment at Surgeons' Square. One night when Hare tossed the last guinea into Mary's lap, and told her to go out for the materials for the night's feast, he remarked—

"If William doesn't come soon it's ashore we'll be intirely. I wonder what's keeping him so long."

"Faix, thin, it's meself that knows that same," returned Mary in an angry tone. "It's Helen that's keepin' him, and tryin' to persuade him not to come back at all at all. She's been mighty squaimish all along, because she's Scotch and hasn't pluck in her, and I know she's wanted Burke more nor wunce to give up our purty schame. She's not to trust to, the mane, dirty, Scotch crayther, and now that she has got Burke

in the counthry and all to herself, it's a thousand chances if
she lets him come back."

"Faugh shana nis," returned Hare, sharply. "William is a
true broth uv a boy, and has got more spirit in him than let
her keep him out o' the way o' makin' money aisy. It's not
out-door work he'll go to again, or patching shoes for sixpence
a day, as long as tin pound notes can be had up at the Square;
and if Helen was to ax him to do it, be jabers the thrashing
she'd get would lave aching bones for a week afther it. Devil a
fear but he'll come back when his money is done, and I hope
that will be at wunst, or we'll be in a purty fix."

"What need for waitin' till he come?" suggested Mary.
"Couldn't we manage wun ourselves?"

"Begorra, I niver thought uv that," returned Hare, with
animation. "But could you hilp me, for I wouldn't be strong
enough to do it all meself?"

"Uv coorse I could hilp you, if you'll only tell me the
way."

"Hush," said Hare, as a footstep sounded in the passage,
and as fate would have it, a small, white-faced, Italian boy
came in to lodge for the night. He carried under his arm a
wire cage, which contained two white mice, which he had
taught to perform certain little tricks, the exhibition of which
on the streets brought him a scanty and precarious livelihood.
He had just come from Glasgow, and found his way to
Tanner's Close, having lodged there before.[1]

Immediately on his appearance a quick meaning glance
passed between Hare and his wife, and in answer to his question, expressed in broken English, if he could have a bed for
the night, the virago, with an air of great cordiality, assured
him that he could.

The poor boy thanked them in his simple, earnest way,
and glad to find repose after his weary day's wandering, he
sat down by the fire and drew forth a parcel of provisions,

---

1. Pae weaves together Burke and Hare and a story of the London murderers Bishop, Williams, May and Shields, who in 1831 were tried for the
copy-cat crime of killing Carlo Ferrari, an Italian boy who performed on the
street with white mice. This crime was discovered by the anatomists. See
Sarah Wise, *The Italian Boy: Murder and Grave-Robbery in 1830s London* (London:
Jonathan Cape, 2004).

with which he made his simple supper, sharing it with his two mice, who came from the cage and ate out of his hand. The lad seemed very fond of his four-footed companions, and chatted to them in his own language, and they ran about on his breast and nestled in his bosom with evident delight. Then he put them back into the cage and asked to be allowed to go to bed. At a signal from Hare, Mary led him into the fatal back room, and pointing to the bed, left him to retire to his anticipated repose.

"Och, by the powers, but there's a piece uv luck for us," said Hare, when she returned to the front chamber. "A better wun couldn't have turned up."

"How will we do it?" asked Mary, her red eyes sparkling with a fiendish light.

"With the tick o' chaff[2] on that bed," answered Hare. "All we have got to do is to put it on the top uv him and keep it there till he's dead."

"Well, that's mighty aisy any way," returned the woman with the utmost coolness, and she went away to purchase whisky and other things for a night of rioting.

By the time she returned Hare had satisfied himself that the Italian boy was fast asleep, and he was eager to do the diabolical deed they meditated. His companion was as ready as himself for the bloody work, and between them they carried the bundle of chaff from one of the beds in the front chamber into the back room. True enough, the poor boy slept soundly, and never moved as they laid the heavy mass above him. Before he could have time either to cry or struggle, Hare and his wife sprang upon the top and pressed with all their weight. There was for a few moments desperate motion underneath, and sometimes the murderers were almost tumbled on the floor; but they grasped the wooden frame of the bed and kept their place.

The woman was as ferocious and cruel in the perpetration of the deed as Hare, to whom the work was nothing new. She kept her place with a firm and unhesitating determination, and even after all had become quiet, and Hare had risen, satisfied that the murder was consummated, she lay still, and her eyes gleamed with the light of savage fury.

---

2. Straw-stuffed mattress.

"Maybe he isn't dead," she said, in answer to Hare's beckoning signal.

"He's dead, if he had got double life in him," rejoiced the other. "Get off wid yez and hilp me to put him into the box."

They lifted the chaff-tick, and there lay the boy, still and motionless, with his face downwards, and his head buried among the straw. He had turned himself round in the desperate struggle he had made for breath.

"Bring the tick along to the other room at wunst," said Hare, and before touching the body they did as he suggested, carrying the bedding back to its place. Returning to the room immediately, they approached the body, and were about to undress it, when, to their amazement, the boy sprung up and gazed at them with bloodshot eyes and a face of white pale horror. He was not dead—having managed to turn on his face, his mouth came opposite a crevice in the wood of the bottom of the bed, and by this means he had inhaled a sufficient quantity of air to keep him alive—though he was bewildered and nearly insensible. During the few moments that elapsed while they were carrying away the tick he revived somewhat, and the full horror of his position coming upon him, he sprung wildly up and confronted his amazed murderers.

Uttering a loud, shrill cry, he leapt from the bed and rushed to the door before Hare had sufficient presence of mind to move. But as the youth flew past, he gave a fierce oath and sprang upon him, clutching him by the throat on the threshold and dragging him back. There was only one way to do the work now—the old way of holding down and pressing on the chest.

"Hould his nose and mouth," cried Hare, as he threw him on the floor. The woman knew as if by instinct what was to be done, and she pressed her two hands on his face with a gripe which savage fury alone could maintain. The struggle was a terrible one, and once or twice Hare was about to get a knife and accomplish the murder in an easier way, but he remembered that this would make the body unpresentable at Surgeons' Square, and with renewed ferocity he pitted his strength against the despairing strength of his victim.

The latter at length succumbed. He was a slender delicate boy, and the frames of his assailants were both brutally strong.

After nearly a quarter of an hour of hard wrestling the citadel of life yielded and the usual signs of suffocation were manifested. Then came perfect silence, broken only by the hard breathing of the two butchers and the shrill squeaking of the two mice in the cage, who seemed to witness with agony the murder of their young master.

All was over some time before they quitted their hold.

"It's all right now," said Hare, as at length he rose. "The breath is out uv him at last, but by jabers it has been hard work. It's all along uv the want uv the drink. It's as aisy as anything when they are drunk."

Mary took her hands cautiously from the nose and mouth, and blood and froth came gurgling forth. This the monster in woman's form wiped away with her palm without a shudder, and yet she was about to become a mother!

Next evening the body was left in Surgeons' Square, and Hare returned with nine pounds in his pocket. Poor wandering boy! Perhaps he looked forward to spending the winter in his own sunny south, and perchance a fond and loving mother awaited his coming.

CHAPTER XII

BURKE AND HELEN RETURN TO TANNER'S
CLOSE—THE QUARREL AND THE FIGHT—
CHANGE OF SCENE—MARY PATERSON AND
HER FRIEND LURED TO THE HOUSE IN
GIBB'S CLOSE

On the following evening, as Hare and his wife were sumptu-
ously regaling themselves with beefsteaks, shortbread, and
whisky, Burke and Helen made their appearance.

"Och, be the powers, and there ye are at last," cried Hare.
"What the deuce[1] have ye been afther so long in the counthry
at all at all? Mary and I were beginning to think you had
given us the slip entirely."

"Ye don't seem to have missed us much thin," returned
Burke, nodding his head in the direction of the table, where
the incongruous eatables were piled up.

"Faix thin, and there ye are mighty far wrong," rejoined
Hare. "I was just afther saying to Mary this blessed moment,
that she had bought thim things wid our last fardin, and if
ye didn't come back purty smart I would have to go out
wid the barrow, to thry for a copper or two to keep us
livin'."

"And haven't ye been doin' anything in *our* line thin?"
remarked Burke, in a tone of surprised interrogation.

"Indade and I haven't," answered Hare, with brazen
effrontery, for he and his wife had agreed that they would
conceal from their confederates the murder of the Italian boy,
lest Burke should claim the half of the money.

The new comers were asked to sit down and partake of
the feast. They did so; but Burke kept moody and silent, and
in a very short while he rose and went out, saying he would
be back soon.

He took his way to Surgeons' Square. He suspected that
Hare was deceiving him, and he was going to inquire if he

---

1. "the deuce", is changed to "the devil" in 1866; even though euphemistic, it
is dropped in 1885, as is the more straightforward "the devil" on almost every
occasion.

had been at the hall with a "shot" during his absence. In answer to his inquiry, Dr Knox's assistant told him that Hare had been with a body on the previous evening, and got nine pounds for it.

"Thank ye, sur," said Burke, grinding his teeth as he turned away. He strode back to Tanner's Close in a furious rage, and entering the room where Hare and the women still sat round the table, he gave the latter a tremendous kick with his foot, which sent it to splinters, and made what was upon it fall with a crash upon the floor.

"Man alive! is it mad ye are?" shouted Hare, starting to his feet in amazement, as did the others.

"Ye mane, dirty, lying blackguard!" roared Burke. "Ye would be afther cheating me."

"Macree aisthig! How could ye think such a thing?" rejoined Hare, determined to stick to his lie.

"Didn't ye tell me ye had not had a shot when I was away?"

"Troth, and I only tould yez the blessed truth. Ax Mary."

"Arrah, and ye did now," exclaimed Mary promptly. "We haven't had wun lodger in the house if ye had thought uv doin' it by yerself."

"It's lyin' ye are, both uv ye," shouted Burke. "Ye was up at the Square wid wun last night, and got nine pounds for it."

"Holy Mother! how did ye know that?" ejaculated Hare, so surprised to be thrown off his guard.

"I knew it whenever I saw you and Mary sittin' at such a mighty fine supper; for sure now, sis I to meself, their money is gone by this time, and if they hadn't a shot, they could not ha' been atin' and drinkin' like that. And didn't I just go up to the Square and find it out?"

"Och murder, then it's thrue, afther all," acknowledged Hare. "But for what did ye send the ould table to smithereens and spill the good skalteen?"

"Because I was mad at ye decavin' me, and thrying to chate me out uv four pounds tin."

"Och, musha!" cried Hare, "but that's mighty fine intirely. Is it chatin' to keep what I made meself? and would ye have the half uv the shot that ye never fingered? Didn't Mary and me do it our two selves, and hard work it was to us, and you goin' about the counthry like a gintleman?"

"Faugh shana nis," broke in Burke impatiently.[2] "Who was it that got the half o' the little boughal? And did you so much as lay a finger on him? Give me the four pounds tin, I say."

"I won't then," answered Hare doggedly.

"You won't?" shouted Burke.

"I tell ye, I won't."

Burke's eyes emitted one bright flash, and springing on Hare he clutched him by the throat. Hare was ready for him, and caught him by the breast in turn. They wrestled fiercely for some moments without either gaining the advantage, when Burke quitted his hold and dealt Hare a thundering blow in the face. Hare retaliated by one equally effective, and a regular battle ensued.

It was like a struggle of wild beasts, so ferociously did they smash at each other, and their yelling oaths and imprecations were like the howls of infuriated animals. Hare was not so strongly built as Burke; but he was half drunk, and the peculiar ferocity of his nature being fully roused, he fought with savage determination. Blood soon began to flow down both their faces, and one of Hare's almond eyes was shut up. Mary no sooner saw this than she leapt on Burke like a she-tiger, and she would have torn his hair off by handfuls with her claws if Helen, whose Scotch blood was by this time up too, had not pulled her away. The two women then set at each other after the peculiar fashion of female combatants. In a moment or two both their caps were torn to shreds, and purple marks showed the course of their nails over each other's faces, while their hair hung in blinding masses over their eyes.

Helen was by far the stronger, though not the most vicious. What Hare's wife wanted in strength she made up by ferocity, and shrieking, yelling, and scratching like a fiend, she finally closed with her antagonist, and fastened her teeth in her cheek. The excruciating pain caused Helen to lift her foot, on which was the heavy shoe with which she had walked the country, and with this she gave the other a fearful kick in the side, which made her drop with a groan upon the floor.

Hare was by this time having the worst of it also, and with

---

2. Phrase is dropped from 1885.

a sudden bound he rushed into the back room and closed the door.

"Come out uv this, Nelly avourneen, and devil a wun uv us will darken their doure again," exclaimed Burke, taking Helen by the arm and dragging her away. Hare, through the key-hole, saw them depart, and also observed Mary lying on the floor in a state of great pain.

"Oh, mercy! what will I do?" she groaned.

"What's the matter?" asked Hare, coming forth from his retreat.

"Oh, musha, I'll need Mrs Prior at wunst. The pains are on me.[3] Oh, wirra, wirra! it's meself that will die this night."

Hare ran for a woman who lived in the next house, and sending her in as present aid, he next proceeded up the close, and crossing the street entered another dark, dirty alley, in one of the houses of which lived Mrs Prior, who acted as mid-wife among the poor of the locality. This important personage was a tall masculine-looking woman, with a red face and cherry cheeks, separated by an immense Roman nose—also, red, especially at the point. A hint from Hare was enough for the midwife, and she went at once to the house in Tanner's Close. Before midnight Mary Hare gave birth to a child—a boy, and on the very bed where two nights before she had assisted in murdering the Italian lad.

Talk of the accident of birth! Into what a fearful sphere of vice, wickedness, and crime had this infant come, and of what brutal, debased parentage was it the offspring. Why, the very source and circumstances of its birth doomed it to ignorance and debasement. With professional murderers for parents, and a place of squalid wretchedness and misery for its nursery, how could it possibly escape being vicious and abandoned? Heaven help it, for there seems no human hope for such an one, and if the iniquities of parents are visited on the children, what a terrible legacy of evil and retribution shall it have for its inheritance. Yet, though it saw the light in such untoward circumstances, it was a strong healthy child, and its brutal mother, like the wild beasts to which she was in nature so

---

3. Reference to labour is dropped from 1885, and the midwife becomes a "nurse".

closely allied, was in a few days going about as if she had
never passed through a mother's dangers.

On quitting the house in Tanner's Close, Burke and Helen
proceeded to Gibb's Close, in the Canongate, where lived a
brother of Burke's—Constantine by name, who earned his
livelihood by working as a city scavenger. Here, though the
hour was late, they obtained shelter, and resolved to take up
their abode till other arrangements could be made.

*

This quarrel between Burke and Hare, resulting in the
transference of the former from the West Port to the Canongate, was destined to have a tragical effect on the poor, unfortunate, misguided, and infatuated girl whose name our story
bears—Mary Paterson.

Mary appeared now to be hopelessly lost. The abandoned
career she had entered on is one from which reclamation is
seldom effected, and forty years ago the class of unfortunates
to which she belonged were very much left alone to sink in the
deep, bottomless mire. No one seemed to care for them, their
misery, or their ruin. Society proscribed them, and they
revenged themselves as they do still, by pestering and corrupt-
ing as far as their influence reaches the society from which
they have become outcasts.

Mary Paterson was one of the least likely to escape from
the slough of despond and despair.[4] Her pure, fair girlhood
was against it; the wilfulness of her disposition was against it;
the bitterness of her betrayed heart was against it; and, last
of all, the scorn and neglect of society operating on her
passionate nature, closed the gates effectually against her
return to virtue. That one deep error of her life had done it
all—the listening to, believing in, and yielding to the tempter.
We are apt, in our sympathy, to say it was weakness rather
than guilt; that the tempter took advantage of the holiest feeling in her soul, and turned her very excellence into shame
and crime. Most true that he, the instigator of the evil—he,
the deliberate and designing seducer, we cannot reprobate too
much; but on her part it was a grievous error, and known to

---

4. From John Bunyan's 1678 allegory *The Pilgrim's Progress*.

be such. The daughter of the God-fearing Scotch elder[5] was not ignorant that she yielded to what was sin, and what no love could sanction or cover, and the Divine law of consequence recognises no palliation in the betraying circumstances.

Nay, Mary's former innocence, the brightness of her childhood, the religious influences by which her early youth had been surrounded, and the keen strength of thought and feeling which she possessed, served to render her degradation all the severer and deeper. These, which were restraining influences in the path of virtue, became goading forces in the downward road after the barriers of virtue were broken through. The memory of a happy past always serves to make the guilty present more guilty still.

Mary Paterson was known among her companions for her boldness and recklessness. The most shameless girl who walked the streets was not more wild or impudent in behaviour, because Mary seldom went about without being under the influence of drink. In her moments of sobriety she had often times of wretchedness and anguish, but these did not drive her to repentance; they rather operated in an opposite direction. She rushed to deeper potations and wilder revelry as an escape from them. Her great beauty made her comparatively independent, for, while her more faded companions found it often difficult to earn the wages of shame, she never lacked admirers(?) when she chose to put herself in their way.[6]

Her chief companion was Jessie Brown, a quieter and more timid girl. After the unaccountable disappearance of Mary Haldane and her daughter, Mary and Jessie continued to live by themselves in the same house. Some months had passed now, and the two girls had heard no tidings of them. They made what inquiry they could, but girls in their position could do little in the matter. Moreover, they concluded that mother and daughter had quitted Edinburgh to gratify some wandering inclination, and that when they were tired of rambling they would return. So, after the first week or two,

---

5. Mary's father is an ordained office holder in his local presbytery—presbyteries, through their elected "elders", call and ordain their own ministers, and administer their church.

6. This inserted question mark is in the newspaper. So it stands either as a wry comment on the term "admirer", or as an author's note to self in the MS inappropriately transcribed by the compositor.

their interest in the matter lessened, and they went on in their dark and wicked career.

One beautiful summer night, at a late hour, Jessie and Mary were at the foot of the High Street, near to the Canongate, when Jessie got into dispute with another girl—a fury in temper—who, after a volley of abusive names, struck Jessie a severe blow on the face. Mary, who stood by, could not see her friend thus ill-used, and, springing forward, she dealt the striker a *thud* in the breast. This brought on a fierce battle between the two, and screams, yells, oaths, and blows ensued, in the height of which a couple of constables arrived, and marched the party to the Police Office.

They were locked up in a cell, and liberated at an early hour in the morning. None of the shops were open but the public-houses, and the two girls went into one of these in the Canongate, and asked for a glass of whisky at the counter.

There was one man in the shop having a glass—a broad-shouldered, thick-set man, shabbily dressed, to whom neither of the girls paid any heed, though he was eyeing Mary with a look of earnest curiosity. At length the latter chanced to turn her eye on him, and recognised him.

It was Burke.

At sight of him Mary reddened not a little, for he brought the past strongly to her mind, and recalled the terrible scenes in the house of Helen M'Dougal.

"My goodness! Mary Paterson, is it yerself or yer ghost?" exclaimed Burke.

"Do I look like a ghost?" returned Mary, with a saucy toss of her head. Her confusion had been but momentary. Burke was the first person she had seen since she came to Edinburgh, whom she had known in her better life, and there was the shame of discovery in the recognition. But she reflected that Burke and Helen had themselves lived in a way not the most virtuous, and this thought brought back her usual audacity.

"Do ye look like a ghost?" repeated Burke. "Well, yer purty enough for wun, only I never saw a ghost come into a public-house for a glass afore. It's a mighty dale improved ye are since ye left us up at the ould cottage."

"Ah! many things have come and gone since then," remarked Mary, with something like a sigh.

"Thrue for it. And have ye been long in Edinburgh, if I may be as bould as to ask?"

"Ever since that time," answered Mary, hurriedly. "And a jolly life I've had of it," she added, with a bold, reckless laugh.

"Uv coorse ye will," assented Burke. "Edinburgh is the place for fun and devarsion—though maybe yer long-faced counthry friends don't like it."

"My friends know nothing about me, and never will if I can help it," said Mary; "so I hope you won't blab."

"What! me?" cried Burke. "Och, be the powers, and wouldn't I be the last boy to do that same. Shure, now, I'm too proud to have met yez, and you and yer purty friend will just go wid me to my lodgings over there and see Nelly. She'll be delighted to see yez."

"Ah, is Helen with you still?" cried Mary, her face lighting up with interest.

"Uv coorse she is. Nelly and I mane to stick together, and shure we're man and wife entirely, barrin' the blessin' o' the praist, and that isn't much. Come along wid ye."

"Will you go, Jessie?" asked Mary, turning to her companion.

"I think we had better go home," said Jessie. "We've been out all night, you know, and I'm hungry."

"Och, thin, is it hungry ye are?" cried Burke. "Shure, now, and wouldn't we get breakfast for ye in the twinkling of a bedpost—a jolly good breakfast, and plenty of potheen to wash it down."

This promise decided the matter, and Jessie consented to go.

"Give me two bottles uv yer best whisky," said Burke, throwing half a sovereign on the counter.

The whisky was brought, and handing a bottle to each of the girls to carry, Burke led the way from the shop to Gibb's Close, and Mary and Jessie followed unsuspiciously behind him. The house was by itself, at the top of a long stair. The opposite house on the same flat was at the time shut up.

On entering, Constantine Burke, his wife, and Helen were in the front room, and the fire was not yet kindled.

"Nelly, me darlint, here's an ould friend come to see yez this morning," cried Burke, with peculiar animation.

"My gracious! Mary Paterson, is it you?" exclaimed Helen, greatly astonished. "Where have you come from?"

"From the Police Office," answered Mary, "where Jessie here and I were put last night for a row."

"And what have you been about since I saw you last?
How's the child?"

These and many other questions Helen asked, and Mary
answered them in a frank, careless manner. How different
from the girl who in the bitterness of grief left the cottage in
Stirlingshire with her babe in her arms! But Helen M'Dougal
never thought of that, at least in the way of moral reflection.
She too was changed, fearfully changed since then. Her
woman's heart, not quite dead then, was dead now, and
buried too—buried beneath crime and blood—else how could
she have responded as she did to the private signal given her
by Burke—the signal which intimated that these girls were to
be made their victims! She was in nowise shocked at the
thought of murdering the girl whom she had nursed and
tended, roughly yet faithfully, for the temptation which operated now was unknown then, else, undoubtedly, Mary would
have been despatched at that time, when the deed could have
been done with impunity. But here she had turned up again,
in circumstances much the same, and when their traffic with
Surgeons' Square was at its briskest. No compunction, therefore, was felt in numbering her among their increasing list of
victims. There was no hesitation felt on the score of friendship
or acquaintance. One would have naturally thought that
Mary, with whom they had been on kind and friendly terms,
would have been spared. But no! Their inhuman crimes had
left them without the capacity of regretful feeling, and Mary
and her companion were as coolly devoted to death as the
others had been.

One thing, however, did give Helen anxiety. Could Constantine Burke and his wife be trusted? They knew nothing
about the deeds which had been done in Tanner's Close, and
might not be brought over to consent to the same being committed in their house. Would it not, therefore, be unwise and
highly dangerous to run the risk? Burke evidently thought
there was no danger, for he was now plying the two girls with
whisky, with the obvious view of bringing them to "the
point"; but she was resolved to suggest the difficulty to him if
she could get the opportunity.

A sumptuous breakfast was soon prepared, and the party,
some of them now considerably intoxicated, gathered round
the table to partake of it. Before they were quite done Constantine had to leave to go to his work, and after he was gone

the whisky was again brought out, and the wild revelry was resumed.

Mary drank eagerly and recklessly, but Jessie was more guarded. She could on certain occasions make herself intoxicated enough, but at that early morning hour she had no inducement, and drank but sparingly, notwithstanding the assiduity with which Burke pressed the whisky upon her.

But poor Mary had no such scruples. She was excited, and at such times she always drank readily, greedily. The meeting with Burke and Helen had brought the bitter past full into her mind, and when that past intruded itself she invariably drowned it with potations of strong drink. The man who pressed it upon her now was the man who had first prevailed upon her to take it to cheat the heart of its sorrow. She had tested his statement to the full, and found that it did cause the grief and pain of the heart to give place to a wild, frenzied indifference; but, oh! it was but a temporary deception. It was no cure—no lasting balm for her chafed and accusing spirit, and it carried her only further and further along the downward road to ruin.

Very soon on this occasion she was helplessly intoxicated, and past all motion and consciousness. Jessie had not so lost the command of herself, and would on no account be prevailed on to drink as much as Burke wished. She was also concerned and alarmed about her friend, and expressed her anxiety in words.

"Och, and won't she soon come all right again," said Burke. "Sure it isn't every day she meets with ould friends, and you and her are just as much at home here as if ye were in yer own house. So take up yer glass and be jolly."

"No more drink," returned Jessie. "It doesn't agree with me in the morning, and I wish Mary hadn't taken so much either."

"Be jabers, thin, it isn't so much uv the drink she has had; it's the want uv sleep. If she was put to bed for an hour or two she would waken up as fresh as a sparrow."

"What's to hinder her being put to bed in the next room?" suggested Helen.

This was the very proposal which Burke wished made, and he warmly seconded it. Jessie thought it was the best thing that could be done, and she and Helen between them carried Mary into the back room and laid her on the couch. Helen pressed Jessie to lie down beside her, but this she refused to do. She said, however, that she would sit on a seat by the bedside and wait till Mary awoke.

Helen left her, and returned to the room where Burke was.

"Now, ye devil," whispered the latter, "keep thim snug and aisy in there till I go up to the close for Hare."

"But what if *she* blab?" said Helen, pointing to Constantine's wife, who was putting the dishes away in a closet.

"Be aisy about that. Shure a few shillings will make her quiet enough. Away back to that room wid yez, and take the whisky. Try her again, for we'll want her drunk too. As for Mary, devil a fear uv her coming to for six hours at laste."

Having given these instructions, Burke went away, and strolled with an apparently indifferent step towards the West Port. He had not seen Hare since the night of their quarrel, and did not know whether he might be inclined to renew the connection.

But Hare welcomed his appearance with great cordiality. He as well as Burke felt that they were necessary to each other. They were linked together by a chain of crime and mutual interest. They could not afford to dissolve partnership, so they agreed to laugh at the fight they had had, and in a glass of the strongest mountain dew they drunk to their reconciliation and their *future prosperity*.

The intelligence brought by Burke, that two victims were ready for them down in Gibb's Close, was received by Hare with fiendish exultation. Nothing delighted the monster so much as the prospect of a "shot," and here was a double one. Twenty pounds at least to be got for them in Surgeons' Square.

In a few minutes the two butchers were proceeding through the Grassmarket, and down the Cowgate, to perform their murderous work in the new shambles. To look at them as they went along, no one would have deemed them capable of such atrocities. Hare was ill-favoured enough, and absolutely loathsome to look upon; but Burke was a quiet, inoffensive-looking man, and, if dressed in black cloth, might have been taken for a Methodist parson. Had a phrenologist, however, examined the huge head that lay like a bullet on his short, thick neck, he would have found behind his ears the organ of destructiveness enormously developed.

They gained the Canongate, entered Gibb's Close, and went up the long stair to the house of Constantine Burke, where Mary Paterson and Jessie Brown still remained.

CHAPTER XIII

THE MURDER OF MARY PATERSON

On the arrival of Burke and Hare in the house in Gibb's Close they found, as was to be expected, that Mary was still help-lessly prostrated under the influence of the whisky she had imbibed. But Jessie Brown, her companion, was still in the possession of her faculties, and was even soberer than when Burke left, for not all the entreaties of Helen M'Dougal could prevail on her to drink any more.

"What the devil is to be done wid that?" said Burke, turning to his associate.

"Is it much strength she has in her?" asked Hare, peeping through the key-hole of the door leading to the back room.

"Faix," said Burke, "it's more nor I would like to meet wid wantin' the whisky."

"She's sleepin'," whispered Hare, as he rose from his knees.

"Sleepin', is she?" rejoined the other, taking his place and putting his eye to the key-hole.

Jessie lay back on the stool, with her head leaning against the wall. Her eyes were closed, and she did seem to be slumbering. Poor Mary lay upon the bed in the same position in which she had been placed. Her power of motion, as well as her consciousness, was entirely gone.

Burke scanned Jessie's form with a critical eye. She was not a big girl, but neither was she weak; and he resolved not to attempt her murder without first making her intoxicated. He by no means despaired of being able to do this. She belonged to a class who he knew indulged in habits of intemperance, and once get her so far under the influence of drink, she would easily be constrained to go on to "the point." For the present, however, she was there an obstacle in their way, and must for a time be got rid of.

"Nelly," he whispered, "you'll be after taking her out for a walk. Half an hour will do."

"Faix, thin, but be sure to bring her back," said Hare, who would rather have kept her in their power, only he saw with Burke that they could not despatch her in her present state, nor while she was there murder Mary.

Helen M'Dougal comprehended only too clearly what was required of her, and was ready to play her part in the dark drama. Burke and Hare withdrew into a closet, so that Jessie might not be aware they were in the house, and the moment they were concealed Helen went into the back room and made the proposition to Jessie that they should have a turn and get a mouthful of fresh air. The girl, utterly unsuspicious, readily assented, as Mary was still unconscious, and was likely to be so for some time.

They went away, and the murderers came out from the closet to do their fell work. Constantine's wife had gone out a message, so that there was no human eye to witness the deed. Hare's first care was to fasten the outer door, and while he was doing this Burke was nerving himself for the deed by quaffing a large quantity of whisky. Then they entered the room where Mary lay.

"Be jabers! what a purty colleen," said Hare, as he looked at the silent form on the bed. And Mary was beautiful, even as she lay there in her degradation. The magnificent tresses of her glossy hair lay in luxuriant disorder upon the dirty pillow, and though her face was flushed and red with the fiery fluid, and though thereon the past two years of vice and dissipation had set their impress, yet the features were regular as ever, and even more completely developed. To see one so young and fair lying in such wretched abandonment was a sight to make the angels weep; and then it added tenfold to the sadness of the spectacle to know that the two men who now stood over her had come to take her life away, and destroy for ever any possibility of her reformation. Out of that drunken stupification it was destined that she should pass into the awful future, covered with the sin and shame of her abandoned life. Ah, who that saw her bright and happy morning of existence could dream of a close so dark and dreadful? Oh, the region of evil is so near as to be within the reach of every one; and whoso deliberately wanders away into that region goes within the range of unknown possibilities, and may incur a fate the nature of which can seldom be anticipated. How the first fatal error brought this hapless girl step by step into the valley of guilt and shame, till her career was suddenly and sickeningly terminated!

Let a veil be drawn over the last act of this melancholy tragedy. We know the time of its duration, and the horrible circumstances constituting it. It was made up of the fatal fifteen minutes which it took these murderers to perform their butcherly work. They never departed from their mode of practice, and the case of poor Mary was not different from that of any of their previous victims. Nature made the same protest and resistance. The power of life, though weakened beforehand, would not be quietly or passively crushed out, the faithful organs struggled against a death which was none of Nature's producing, and ceased to work only when their latest strength was gone.

It is sickening enough to describe, or in imagination to contemplate these fiends crushing the life out of wandering wretches, with whose history we are little acquainted, but it is doubly painful to think of them laying their foul and murderous hands on one with whose sad story and bitter experience we are acquainted, and perchance have been interested in. Poor Mary had indeed by this time fallen low enough—but for the sake of the past we pity her still and are deeply touched by her tragic fate. Since, however, from that fate we cannot save her, we can at least—and we will—avoid a description of the scene.

At the end of fifteen minutes she lay far stiller than before, with the colour already fading from her cheek, and her bright, round eyes widely open, but covered with the film of death. All her earthly shame, sorrow, and sin were at an end, and she was beyond the reach of repentance and reformation.

When the deed was done, Burke applied again to the whisky, but Hare, whose callous heart needed no such opiate, very coolly dragged the body from the bed and thrust it underneath out of sight. Then with a fiendish chuckle, and one of his most horrible leers, he sat down to wait the arrival of the other victim.

"Begorra, here they come," he whispered, as footsteps were heard on the stair. "I'll be afther hiding in the closet again, and lave you to manage the girl wid your blarney."

The closet was near to the outer door, and as Hare stepped into it he drew the bolt with which the latter was fastened. He was but a moment or two out of sight when Helen and Jessie made their appearance.

Burke seated himself by the fire in the front room, and appeared to be half asleep, but roused up at the entrance of the women. Helen gave him a private glance of anxious inquiry, which he returned with another which assured her that the deed was done.

"Is Mary awake yet?" was Jessie's first question.

"Och, thin, and haven't ye seen her?" rejoined Burke.

"Seen her?" repeated the girl. "No; is she away?"

"Throth and she is. Ye hadn't been gone two minutes when she came round beautifully, and got up. Her and I were talking over ould stories at the fireside here, when who should come in but a packman that Mary seemed to know, and was mighty glad to see. He asked her to go out and have a dram wid him, and she went away, saying that if she wasn't back before you to tell you to wait for her, and she wouldn't be long."

This lie told well enough to deceive Jessie, and at Burke's invitation she sat down, and the whisky bottle was once more put upon the table. Beyond a single glass, however, the girl would not partake of the noxious beverage. Burke plied his every art to persuade her, and in this he was assiduously seconded by Helen, but all their solicitations proved fruitless. Whether from prudence or from instinct, or from a natural obstinacy of disposition, she steadily refused to taste the glass which had been refilled, and sat waiting impatiently for the return of her friend, whose stiffening corpse was lying within a few feet of her.

Nearly half an hour passed in this manner, and then Constantine's wife came in. This was a dangerous circumstance, for, inasmuch as she was not in the conspiracy, she might say something to betray them, or she might enter the closet where Hare was concealed, which would produce a result equally unfortunate. Burke was about to draw her into the back room and take her into their confidence, when Jessie rose, declaring that she would go up to their house, where she was sure Mary must have gone.

"Och, sure, it's not there you'll find her," said Burke hastily. "The packman and her haven't got done wid their glass yet, and when they do, it's here she'll be sure to come to."

The girl, however, was so persuaded that Mary must have gone home, that she was determined to leave, and Burke, finding no plausible means of detaining her, suffered her to go.

Of course, when she reached their humble abode in the High Street Close, Mary was not there, and everything was just as when they left on the previous evening. Jessie waited for some time, and still Mary came not. In the afternoon she went out again, with the intention of going in search of her to the house in which they had been in the morning.

But when she reached the Canongate she suddenly discovered that she had taken no notice of the close in which that house was situated, and she spent an hour or two in seeking for it. The Canongate closes are, however, so much alike in their general features of narrowness, dirtiness, and darkness, that she failed to light upon the one of which she was in search, and weary and disappointed she was retracing her footsteps homewards when her eye lighted on Constantine Burke entering Gibb's Close with a broom and shovel under his arm. She recognised him in a moment, and following after, overtook him at the foot of the stair which she had sought so long.

Constantine had not been home since the morning, and could therefore tell her nothing about Mary, so she ascended the stair with him, and they entered the house together.

Helen and the other woman sat at the fire alone, but as they went in Burke came hurriedly out of the back room and closed the door.

"Och, thin, there you are," he cried; "but what the devil has Mary not come back for? Shure Nelly and myself are hurt entirely at her leaving us in such a way."

"Gracious me! has Mary not been here yet?" exclaimed Jessie.

"Never a footstep," answered Burke.

"Haven't you seen her?" asked Helen.

"I have not," replied the girl. "She has never been up at the house, and I hoped to find her here. What ever can have come over her?"

"Gone off wid the packman, I'll bate a guinea," cried Burke.

On this occasion there was no attempt made to detain Jessie. She was now quite sober, and the opportunity of murdering her was lost. Hare, who was in the back room, was loth to let her out of his clutch, but as there seemed no help for it, he had agreed with Burke that she should not be murdered. She therefore departed again, wondering much at Mary's unaccountable desertion.

Burke watched her down the stair, and by hanging over a

window saw her go up the close. He then returned, and taking
Constantine by the arm, led him into the back room, where
to his horror he saw the body of Mary lying naked on the bed,
and Hare sitting by the side of an empty tea chest.

"Holy Mother!" ejaculated Constantine, standing stock still
and staring with open eyes and mouth at the corpse.

"She tuk a fit," whispered Burke, "and died in it."

"And what for didn't ye tell the girl that?" asked his
brother.

"Shure, now, where would have been the good uv that?
Wouldn't ye have had all the trouble uv burying her? and
now wid all the aise in life we'll get quit uv her and make a
shilling or two for aich uv us forby."

"Och, murder! and how's that?" inquired Constantine,
who was all in a fluster.

"William there," replied Burke, pointing to Hare, "has
heard by chance that the doctors buy dead bodies, and it's
there we mane to take her, and devil a sowl will ever know
about it at all at all."

Constantine's wife had been told the same story, and the
two implicitly believed it, and for the sake of the few shillings
they expected to get promised to keep the matter secret.

The body, still warm, was packed into the box, and no
sooner had the shadows of twilight shrouded the streets in
semi-darkness than the two wretches shouldered their burden
and went by way of St Mary's Wynd to Surgeons' Square.

The hall was very brisk that evening. Numerous students
were at the various tables busy in the pursuit of their scientific
investigations, and Dr Knox himself was, with cotton sleeves
and knife in hand, bending over a piece of mortality which
lay on one of the marble slabs.

The single eye of the Professor gleamed through his clear
spectacles as it fell on Burke and his companion entering with
their burden. They came into that hall now with all the familiarity and confidence of regular frequenters. The fear and
shame which they manifested at first had long since passed
away, and they put the box on the floor and pulled out the
body with quite an air of business promptness.

The corpse was cold now, but not stiff, and when the murderers tossed it roughly upon a dark table, it lay there like a
reclining marble statue, beautifully faultless in all its proportions, while the long tresses of hair, which had once been the

pride of the wearer and the admiration and envy of friends and acquaintances, lay coiled upon the snowy neck, and trailed half-way along the table.

One of the assistants came forward, and at the first glance could not suppress an exclamation. This caught the attention of Knox, and he too came forward.

"There's a purty wun, sur," said Burke, who was always spokesman on these occasions.

Knox said nothing, but ran his eye slowly over the motionless form.

"She has been a *very* pretty girl that," he remarked, after several moments of silent inspection. "Upon my soul, I never saw a more beautiful body."

By this time several of the students had surrounded the table, and among the rest a tall, fair-haired lad, who, the moment his gaze rested on the features, started back with an ejaculation of horror.

"Good gracious! I know that girl," he exclaimed. "I was with her only two nights ago, and she was then in perfect health."[1]

"What body is that, and where did you get it?" asked Knox, turning to Burke.

"Plaise, sur, it's the body of a woman that got peppered in a row in a house in Hackerton's Wynd, and they sold her to huz, for they wanted money to carry on the spree."

This was Burke's ready answer, coolly given, *and it sufficed.* Not another question was asked; not one suspicion raised. If the girl had been killed in the manner Burke declared, would not the body have presented proof of the fact? Yet there was no wound or mark of a murderous blow—nothing whatever to corroborate the lie which had been told them, and which so easily satisfied them.

At the far end of the hall a youth was busy at a table alone, and he was the last to approach the slab on which the body lay. He came carelessly forward, and leaning over the head of a very short student, obtained a full view of the face. It was

---

1. This moment echoes a story of the times that held Knox's assistant had recognised Mary (Edwards, 89). The later edition of Pae's novel drops this sentence—perhaps because it invokes consideration of how a medical student might know a prostitute. The 1866 edition begins the comment with "Good God!"

a sight that transfixed him and froze the very blood at his heart. Ah! well did he know that face, and many a time had it reclined confidingly on his bosom, while he toyed with the magnificent hair, and whispered in her ear the words of honied deceit. That youth was Duncan Grahame, and the white dead face he gazed upon was the face of the poor, simple, loving girl whom he had ruined, betrayed, and deserted. Callous as was the heart, and seared the conscience of the selfish libertine, this was a sight which gave him a terrible shock. He staggered back against one of the tables, and covered his face with his hands, to shut out that white, fixed countenance, and the dull, glassy eyes, that seemed staring full at him.

No one noticed his emotion, for all were engaged in contemplating the finest specimen of the human form that had ever been seen in that hall. So pleased was Dr Knox with the "thing" that he told his cashier to give fourteen pounds for it—the largest sum that these men had yet received for the articles in which they trafficked.

"What glorious hair!" observed one of the students, as he lifted the long, soft tresses, which lay in all directions round the head.

"Superb. Worth a pound at least if it were sold," remarked the assistant, as he counted out the money.

Burke pricked up his ears when he heard this.

"And here it will be thrown away," added the first speaker.

"Wouldn't ye be afther lettin' me cut it out?" said Burke, eagerly.

"Oh, by all means," answered Knox. "The hair is not of the slightest use to us, and if you can get a few shillings for it, why shouldn't you?"

A pair of large scissors were handed to him, and he deliberately cut the hair away, tress by tress, till it lay a shining heap upon the table. Then he took a dirty handkerchief from his pocket, and tying it into the form of a bundle, he bid Hare take up the empty box. With a brutal grin the fellow did it, and they departed, highly elated at this additional stroke of business at the Square.

"By jabers," said Hare, as they made their way down to the Cowgate, "I thought it all up wid us when yon spalpeen said he knew the 'shot.' By the powers, but ye had the answer nate and handy. Devil a one of them doubted yez."

"Begorra, thin, it didn't nade much larnin' to decave them," rejoined Burke. "But, throth, it was myself that was shakin' a bit too, for I hadn't a moment to think how to get up the blarney."

As they crossed the Cowgate, a youth clad in dark clothes, who had come down the Wynd at a rapid pace, turned to the right and walked on in the direction of Holyrood. His step was wild and vehement, and his face, revealed in glimpses by the light from the shop windows as he rushed past, was white and scared-looking. It was Duncan Grahame. So great was the shock he received at sight of Mary's dead body that, finding it impossible to conceal his emotion, he threw off his cotton sleeves, seized his hat, and left the hall, to go he hardly knew whither.[2] That white, dead face and ghastly eye haunted his vision, and seemed as if photographed on his brain.[3] Though he pressed his two hands upon his face, it was there still, as distinctly perceived by him as when he first looked upon it, and he was now making his way to darkness and solitude, to hide from human observation the agitation he could not otherwise conceal.

He passed the Palace of Holyrood, and clambered the steep slopes of Arthur's Seat. He was alone now; the great city lay at his feet; the soft, blue sky, with its brightening stars, hung above, and the dark shadowing of the hill rose up against it. But the youth saw neither the twinkling lamps, nor the beaming stars, nor the mountain crest; for wherever he turned his gaze that white, still face filled up the view, and remorseful memories crowded up from the rocky sepulchre of his heart. He could not shut out the truth from his conscience that he it was who had laid poor Mary dead and degraded upon the dissecting table. He had made her the victim of his selfish gratification. He had set himself to win her heart only that he might rob her of her virtue, and then desert her. He had done

---

2. Anatomists and surgeons of the period typically wore morning attire, not concerned with infection or dirt; concern with cleanliness for patient or doctor came much later in the period. See Adam Jones, "Bare Below the Elbows: A Brief History of Surgeon Attire and Infection", *BJUI*, 102.6 (September 2008). Wiley Online Library.

3. Thomas Wedgewood made "sun pictures" in 1800, and in 1822 Nicéphore Niépce created the first permanent image. The word "photograph" was coined in 1839 by John Herschel, so not available to Grahame's self-perception in 1828.

these things with the most ruthless indifference, and having left her alone in her ruin and her shame she had fallen into that abandoned career which had brought her to such an untimely and dishonourable end.

Oh, if this youth had possessed anything like a heart of flesh in his bosom he might well have been tortured to madness by the agony of remorse at the thought of what he had done. But for him Mary Paterson might have been the happy, honoured wife of a man who loved her, and who would have shielded her with his noble heart from the rude winds and rough blasts of the world. But for him she might at that moment have been the joyous centre of a joyous Scottish home, far away from the shadow of that sphere of vice which had encircled her. But there she was, and he was the author of it all. He felt this, and it greatly annoyed him; but his was a heart incapable of deep sorrow, and in the feelings which now moved him there was little either of sorrow or repentance.

He wandered for more than an hour upon the silent hill, then he went home to his splendid residence at the west end of the city. In the drawing room his wife was seated, with their boy, a child of nearly two years, in her lap. She was a plain, though sweet-looking being, not capable herself of deep love, and not requiring it in her husband, else she would not have been satisfied with the measure of affection bestowed upon her by Duncan. Without very strong regard on either side, they managed to get quietly enough along together, and she being rich, Duncan was able to pursue his surgical studies under great advantages.

On his appearance in the well-lighted drawing-room, Lucy noticed that he was pale and haggard, and she remarked it.

"Yes," he returned, "I feel tired and jaded."

"Oh, worried, no doubt, with hard study. Do let us go to the country for a few weeks, dear. You need a change. You work far too close."

The proposition was too much in accordance with his present feelings to be rejected. He could not, he felt, go to the Hall till that faultless form had served the purpose for which it had been brought. He therefore assented to the proposal, and on the following day he was miles away from Edinburgh.

CHAPTER XIV

MORE VICTIMS—THE MURDER OF
DAFT JAMIE

And when is these men's terrible career of blood and crime to be terminated? is a question which, we doubt not, has long ere this risen in the reader's impatient and indignant heart. While one is fascinated by the horrible details as by a spell, there also comes a feeling of mingled disgust and anger. The repetition of the same scenes of butchery—the process followed almost weekly by which human beings were killed like sheep, and disposed of with as little ceremony as attends the buying and selling of an animal's carcase—this, we say, cannot be thought of without stirring in the heart the deepest indignation, and the earnest desire, when the discovery of the horrible truth is to be made, to know that vengeance may overtake the murderers, and that society may be rid of such prowling and destroying beasts of prey.

Clearly, so far as we have yet gone in the history of the dark and frightful business, the end is not visible. There is, we see, no likelihood of the discovery being made by the doctors, for though we cannot say they are positively cognisant of what is doing in Tanner's Close and elsewhere, yet they are, we cannot help thinking, wilfully shutting their eyes, lest they should see. Most assuredly, in the transactions which Dr Knox and his assistants have up to this point had with Burke and Hare, there was abundant room for suspicion, and suspicion honestly entertained would speedily have brought the atrocities to light. But, as we before remarked, the doctors had no *desire* to suspect, and therefore, so far as they are concerned, the butcheries threaten to go on long enough.

Nor is there any likelihood of a discovery resulting from the upbraiding consciences of any of the four wretches who are concerned in the murders. Instances have been known where the weight of blood grew so heavy on the criminal's soul, and produced such an agony of remorse, that, in order to get rid of it, confession has been made of deeds which would otherwise never have been made known. But neither Burke nor Hare, nor the two women who are their associates, are persons capable of feeling this remorse. They have got beyond that, else they could not have gone on from one murder to another; and every new murder made the probability of repentance and remorse less.

Still the conviction is forced upon us that a discovery *must* come. Both heart and mind revolt from the idea that such a black career of wickedness can be long protracted. Let the doctors continue to present the same facilities and the same temptation—let the consciences of the criminals remain seared and unimpressible—yet our natures feel assured that in some other way the crimes will become known and be put an end to. Humanity, we are convinced, is too sacred, and human life too precious, to be thus preyed upon with impunity.

Most true. In the nature of things, the frightful doings of these men cannot be long protracted. One murder, it has been remarked, will scarcely hide—how then shall a series of murders remain concealed? and how shall professional murderers continue in their career of crime. The universe and all its laws are against them—physical, social, and moral philosophy are all working towards detection. The very success which has attended and is attending their deeds shall in due time lead to discovery. Every fresh murder is giving them a careless confidence, which is certain to merge in a growing imprudence that shall bring suspicion upon them—a suspicion which once aroused shall never be allayed, but shall unveil the secret horrors of Tanner's Close, and make the country and the world at large shudder with horror, and burst forth in one universal shout of execration.

Still the end is not yet. The cup of their iniquity is not full. Discovery and the vengeance to follow is but a question of time, but the time is still somewhat in the distance, and other deeds of atrocity require to be recorded. Justice is sure, but sometimes it mysteriously tarries.

*

Burke and Helen M'Dougal did not go again to lodge with Hare in Tanner's Close. The quarrel was made up, and they were all friends again, so far as such wild beasts could be friends; but for some reason or other they thought it best to live separate.

Not far separate, however; for Burke and Helen took up

their quarters in a "land" a little to the east of Hare's dwelling, in a house occupied by one Broggan, a relative of Burke's. Between this house and the old shambles in Tanner's Close there was free and easy access, so that it is probable it was with a view to the convenience of their operations and the extension of their *business* that a separate residence was decided upon. Broggan and his wife did not remain long in the house after Burke and Helen took up their abode in it. They almost forthwith departed, being moved to go with fear at what they one day saw.

It was a few days after their new lodgers had come to them that they were both working out, and Burke and Helen were in the house alone. About mid-day a tap was heard at the door, and Helen, opening it, beheld a cousin of her first husband—a woman called Ann M'Dougal. She had come from a far-off country village for the sole purpose of paying her distant relative a visit. She was invited in, and cordially welcomed by both Helen and Burke, who at once resolved to make her one of their victims. For this purpose, the necessary adjunct—strong drink—was procured. Hare was communicated with, and dropped in as if by chance. The drink then went round, the visitor was pressed to partake, and this she freely did, till she reached "the point." Then came the old, familiar process—the process which, however often repeated, never lost any of its horror—and the country cousin lay dead upon Broggan's bed.

This was the first murder that was committed in Broggan's house, and as both he and his wife were ignorant of the diabolic deeds that went on in Tanner's Close, the murderers thought it better that the corpse should be got rid of before they came in from the fields; so, although it was yet early in the afternoon, Burke went to the Square, to ask if a body could be received before dark.

"O yes," replied the assistant; "there is not the slightest objection to that, if you are ready to risk carrying the box in daylight. People, you know, have a very absurd prejudice against bodies being brought here, and loiterers in the wynd might annoy you."

"Och, by the powers, I'll risk it, sur," rejoined Burke, quite boldly.

"Well, to make the danger less, I can give you a nice brass-nailed leather trunk to bring it in. Will you have it?"

"Throth and I will, and take it mighty kind uv ye too."

"Come this way, then," said the doctor; and, opening a trap door, he descended by a ladder to an apartment beneath.

Burke followed. The place was almost in total darkness, and Burke thought it must be the wine cellar, for it had a strong odour of whisky. Just as he stepped off the last round of the ladder, the young man put up the gas, and Burke saw they were in a low-roofed apartment, in the centre of which was an immense circular vat, which he was barely tall enough to see into.

"Och, murder, what a thundering big tub," he observed. "What do ye hould in it, sur, if I might be so bould as ax?"

"It is there where we preserve the bodies till we need them," was the answer. "See, there is the last you brought us as fresh as the hour she died."

The assistant, as he spoke, lighted a gas-jet which overhung the vat, and pointed to a couple of steps where Burke might stand and look in. The latter did so, and saw that the vat was nearly full of whisky, and there, near the bottom, lay the white stiff body of poor Mary Paterson, cold and beautiful as the chiselled marble.

The murderer felt a tremor strike through his hardened soul as his eye encountered the ghastly sight, and he quickly drew back.

"Begorra, and is that all whisky?" he observed. "Och, but wouldn't that make a boy jolly for many a month to come?"

He got the trunk—a large, clean, and almost new leathern box, and carrying it to the West Port, he and Hare packed the body of the woman into it. They had scarcely got it stuffed in when to their confusion Broggan and his wife entered the room.

"Och, musha, where have you got that purty trunk, and what's in it?" asked Broggan.

"Sure and I bought it from a broker in the Cowgate to hould our clothes in," replied Burke.

"Be jabers, then the trunk is better than the clothes," laughed Broggan, as he went forward and suddenly tossed back the lid.

The moment he did so the laugh vanished from his face, and he grew white as a sheet, for in the open trunk he beheld a dead body.

"Holy powers!" he ejaculated, and staggered back unable
to utter another word.

"Well, thin, ye needn't be afther sayin' anything about
what ye have seen," said Burke, "and I'll give ye a pound or
two to kape the secret."

Broggan accepted the pound or two, but he had got such
a fright that he could not remain longer in the house, and
Burke being only too anxious to get rid of him, gave him some
more money, and he and his wife immediately left Edinburgh.

Burke and Helen had now the house to themselves, and
they were free to pursue their murderous career without
observation. To facilitate operations they turned the place
into a lodging-house, and any poor tramp who came for a
night's shelter was drugged with drink and smothered. Sometimes the deed was done in the old back room in Tanner's
Close, and sometimes in Burke's new residence. And if lodgers
did not present themselves in sufficient numbers to satisfy the
growing rapacity of the wretches, one or other of them would
prowl about the streets and lure victims to their dreadful fate.
They grew every day more bold and audacious through the
success which still attended them, and planned and executed
their crimes with almost reckless rapidity.

An old washerwoman, who washed at houses in the neighbourhood, came one day to the house. She had been in the
habit of washing for Broggan's wife, and was not aware they
had left.

"Och, never mind," cried Burke, "you'll not lose a farden
by that, for sure we'll want our clothes washed too, and you're
the dacent woman that will do it. Come in wid yez and drink
a glass to our long acquaintance."

The woman complied; she sat down and drank. Like many
of her class, she liked whisky, and as it was here pressed upon
her, to all appearance without money and without price, she
drank freely, became first merry, then wildly excited, and
finally dead drunk. When she had reached this stage Hare
was sent for, and—*that night the body was sold in Surgeons'
Square.*

Shortly after this, as no lodgers turned up, and the monsters
wanted money, Burke rose early one morning, and went out
to the streets in search of a victim. It was in the grey light of a
September morning, and he sauntered away by the back of
the Castle. At the foot of the Lothian Road an old, shrunken

woman was stirring with a short stick a heap of ashes which
had been thrown from a house near at hand. She was what in
Edinburgh is known as a cinder-gatherer. In the early morning, before the dust carts came round to remove the heaps of
ashes which the occupants of the houses empty in the streets, a
few poor creatures, generally old women, sunk in the deepest
poverty, come forth and make an examination of these heaps,
gathering therefrom the cinders that may be mixed with the
ashes, and sometimes lighting upon articles of value that may
have been inadvertently thrown out with the dust.

It was one of these miserable beings on whom the baleful
eye of Burke lighted, as her withered form bent over the ashes
she stirred.

"The top o' the mornin' to yez," said the prowler, going
forward and accosting her. "Sure it's cowld work that, anyhow."

"O, deed ay, my gude lad," returned the woman, in a
mournful tone. "It's a puir job this, but ane's glad to dae onything to get a wee bit fire. I've seen the day when I didna
need to come oot this way; but, waes me! there's a sair change
cam' owre my lot."

"Haven't ye got some friends to be good to yez in yer owld
age?" inquired Burke.

"No ane," returned the woman, with a sigh. "I had three
sons and a dochter, but twa o' my sons are in Ameerika, and
it's mony a year sin I heard word frae them. My ither son
and my dochter are baith deid, and sae I'm left alane, and
I'm rale ill aff."

Burke's heart beat with joy. Where could a more likely
victim be had?—an old, lonely woman, steeped in poverty,
who had no one to care for or to miss her. It would be a
charity to herself and everybody, as well as a profit to him
and his associate, to rid her of her wretched life. And forthwith words of sympathy, pity, and commiseration flowed from
his lips, concluding with an invitation to breakfast at his house
in the West Port.

The poor creature gladly listened to words of kindness, for
these she had seldom heard of late, and gratefully accompanied her new friend. *That night she too lay stiff and dead in
Surgeons' Square.*

It is scarcely to be wondered at if the ease and safety with
which they had committed their numerous crimes made these

men imagine that there was really little danger in the lucrative profession they had adopted, and that they might go on luring people from the street, and killing them off hand. Had they not reached some such idea as this they would never have fixed their murderous choice on the being whom they made their next victim.

Almost every village in the land has its idiot, simpleton, or half-witted person. In Edinburgh, at that time, there were two or three, but notably one who was known throughout the city as "Daft Jamie." This natural was known to, and liked by everybody. He was "the only son of his mother, and she was a widow."[1] Ay, and never did mother love a son more— never did son evince greater affection for a mother.

Their love for each other was indeed proverbial. The poor mother doted on her boy the more because of his great affliction. It was her pride to keep him clean and comfortable, and every morning when he left home for his daily rambles through the city—for, like most of his kind, he was a great wanderer—she would see that his clothes were properly put on, and that his face shone as bright and clear as soap and water could make it.

Jamie was full of good nature, and possessed a shrewdness and a wit which often cast ridicule on those who attempted to play upon him. His very simplicity of nature prevented any one from getting the advantage of him, for, not knowing the sarcasm or banter of others, he never grew angry at what was said to him; while, at the same time, no feeling of propriety or delicacy kept him from giving the most pungent retorts, not known by himself to be such, but clearly appreciated by those who heard them.

No one was better known or better liked in the town than Jamie. He was a universal favourite, and the donations he received kept himself and his mother out of want. He was a strong young fellow, constantly wandering about the streets, bare-headed, and might be seen smiling to all well-dressed people as he went along, and taking snuff from a brass box, which he carried in one hand, with a little horn spoon in the other. Jamie's smile was irresistible, it possessed such happiness and contentment, and probably a happier being, or one

---

1. Luke 7:12. Jesus goes on to raise the deceased son of the widow.

more free from care, was not to be found in all the city. He was disturbed by nothing. In sunshine and rain he went about all the same, without shoes and stockings, and without a hat; and wherever anything of interest or importance was going on Jamie was sure to turn up.

Now, one would suppose that this was a person who would have been the last thought of as a victim by Burke and Hare, and yet they marked him out, and resolved to decoy him to the shambles—a convincing proof that imprudence was coming on as the result of success. No one was likely to be more missed, sought after, or avenged, for Jamie was the care and the charge of everybody, and his disappearance would be certain not only to be at once generally noticed, but would create an actual want among the citizens. To present him at Surgeons' Square was even an act of the greatest temerity, for there, too, he was well known, and would be immediately recognised.

The murderers, however, seemed to be oblivious to all this. Mammon and crime had blinded them, and the brutal, animalised life they had led had almost destroyed any little judgment that had been left them. So Jamie was pitched upon as a victim to be secured, and the first favourable opportunity of getting him to Tanner's Close was to be seized.

This opportunity was not long in arriving. One day Hare's wife was coming out of a tobacconist's shop in the Grassmarket, when her evil eye fell on Jamie going to and fro among the people as if looking for some one. She made her way towards him, and took hold of his arm.

"Sure now, Jimmie, you seem to be wanting somebody," she said, with an insinuating smile.

"Ay, I am wantin' somebody," replied Jamie, continuing to look anxiously up and down the street.

"And who is it ye're wanting now?"

"Eh?"

"Who is it you are afther looking for?"

"I'm looking for my mither. Hae ye seen her ony gait?"

"Uv coorse I have. She's in my house, and sent me to bring you to her."

"Very weel, ye micht ha'e telt me that half an hour syne, for I've been gaun aboot here and ither places seekin' her. Tell her tae come awa' hame, and there's a snuff tae yersel'."

He held out his brass box, with its lid open, and the woman took a pinch.

"But she tould me to bring you up to my house along wid me, for she wants to see you there," was the ready lie that came next.

"Oh, very well then, I'll gang wi' ye," returned the simple creature; and with the utmost docility he walked along by her side towards the West Port.

Alas, that was the last time he was destined to walk on the streets of Edinburgh—those streets which he had traversed daily for many years. The poor, happy, half-witted lad was being led to his death, and the bait which lured him to his doom was the holy divine feeling which lived so strong in his nature, where reason was mysteriously shrouded—his filial love. In the hope of finding his mother he went with all readiness to the fatal Tanner's Close.

Most terrible was the leer which Hare gave when his wife entered accompanied by the "shot" which they had all been on the outlook for. A word or two let him up to the deception, and, receiving Jamie with the utmost cordiality, he said that his mother had just gone into a neighbour's house, but would return soon, and she had left word that he was to wait for her there.

"Very weel, I'll dae that," said Jamie, sitting down composedly, and applying again to the box and the spoon.

The woman was going out again, when Hare thrust a shilling into her hand.

"Bring whisky," he muttered.

She nodded intelligently, and went away. She did not proceed at once up the close, but, by going down a common stair in a "land" further down, reached a long, dark passage which communicated with Burke's house. Her object was to acquaint him with the fact that Jamie was trapped, and send him up to assist in his murder.

Burke was not in, and Helen did not know where he might be found. He had gone out only a little before, and could not therefore be far off.

Nor was he. When Hare's wife went into the public-house in the West Port for the whisky, Burke was drinking at the counter. He had, in fact, seen Hare's wife go up the street with Daft Jamie, and knowing the deed that was to be done, he was preparing himself for it. It did not, therefore, require the wink with which the woman favoured him to let him understand that he was wanted.

"All right," he whispered; "I'll be down immediately."

She went away before him, and when, a few minutes later, he sauntered down the close, and entered Hare's house, Jamie was sitting with a broken cup in his hand half full of whisky.

"Weel, cummer, dae ye no see my mither comin' yet?" was the question he put to Burke the moment he appeared.

"Faix and I did. I spoke to her this minnit in the close and tould her you were here, and—"

"That's a man," exclaimed Jamie, rising quickly and making towards the door. "I wad gie ye a snuff if my mither wasna waitin' for me."

"Och, don't be in a hurry at all, at all," said Burke, with perfect coolness. "When I told yer mother ye were here she said you must wait till she came."

"Oh, vera weel. Will she be lang?" said the obedient fellow, returning and sitting quietly down again.

"She may be a minute or two, but we can enjoy ourselves till she come."

"Hae, there's a snuff then," rejoined Jamie, holding out the shining box.

It being about the middle of the day, and there being people going up and down the close, they quietly shut and secured the outer door, and the two murderers set themselves to make Jamie drunk. This they deemed would be a very easy task, but found themselves quite out in their calculations. Beyond about half a glass of whisky Jamie would not go. They pressed, and urged, and persuaded to no effect.

"Na, na," he said, "I'se tak nae mair whusky. I dinna like it. It gies me aye a sair heid, but I'll snuff as muckle as ye like, if the snuff's guid."

Intemperance in snuff, however, would not suit their purpose, and, as a last resource to induce him to drink, Burke declared that his mother had enjoined him to do so. But Jamie had sense enough not to believe this. His mother had always cautioned him against drinking, and he was sure she would not send such a message.

This was a serious difficulty in the way of their intention. Jamie was a strong fellow, and to encounter him as he was, involved a terrible struggle. Seeing it was quite in vain to endeavour to make him intoxicated, they wiled him into the back room, and got him to lie down on the bed, Hare lying down beside him in front. In a very little the small quantity of whisky he had taken set him asleep. The butchers now looked at each other in silent perplexity.

"Shall we try it now?" whispered Burke.

Hare rose cautiously from his place by Jamie's side, and looked at the sleeper.

"Begorra, he's a strong devil to fight wid," he observed, "but uv coorse we must have him."

Burke's eyes gleamed with deadly light, and with set teeth he put off his coat, and laid it on the floor.

Then he stood looking irresolutely at the large form on the bed. Common prudence would have caused him to abandon the intention altogether, but a fierce thirsting spirit was roused within him, and he actually trembled with excitement and eagerness.

At length, in an instant, and with something like a frantic bound, he threw himself on the top of the sleeper, calling on Hare to do his part of the work.

Jamie was awake in a moment, and with superhuman strength flung Burke from above him and leapt upon the floor. By instinct, or in some other way, he seemed to understand his danger and their murderous intentions towards him, for he stood glaring at them with excited eyes for a moment or two, then with a tremendous roar he sprang forward to the entrance of the room.

Burke made a dash at him, and got between him and the door, calling with an oath upon Hare to come and help him. But Hare's cowardly nature shrank from the encounter, and he became so terrified that he thought of making his escape. At this juncture Burke seized Jamie in his powerful arms, and threw him heavily on the floor, pinning him down with his arms and pressing his heavy body on his chest.

The poor simpleton, as he fell, cried piteously "Mither, mither," and began again to struggle with frantic desperation. Terror and madness gave him double strength, and once more he dashed Burke from above him, and bounded to his feet, the foam of rage fleeing from his lips, and his eyes flashing with burning light. It was clearly now a life-and-death struggle for Burke. Jamie, in his fury, had become as much the assailant as the assailed, and when Burke rushed at him again he closed with him in a desperate wrestle, Hare still standing back, afraid to take part in the struggle.

Locked in this mortal embrace, they were driven from side to side of the little room, smashing the furniture that was in it, Burke roaring forth oaths all the time, and Jamie making occasionally a bellowing noise. They came to the floor again, and Burke uppermost as before; but he felt that, without assistance, he would be overcome, and swearing a dreadful oath, he roared out to Hare that if he did not come to his aid he would stick him with a knife.

This threat brought Hare's courage up, and, throwing himself on his knees, he seized Jamie's head, and pressed his hands with savage ferocity on nose and mouth. This for some moments increased the victim's frantic efforts, and with gigantic force he once more threw Burke off him. Hare, however, kept his hold, and in a moment Burke was again in his place, pressing with all his might and all his weight on the victim's chest.

Poor Jamie's strength was now waning; nevertheless he resisted still with fearful tenacity, and when he lay still for a few moments, and the butchers thought he was nearly gone, he suddenly renewed the struggle almost as vigorously as at first.

This continued for about twenty minutes, when the nature which had so faithfully defended the threatened life succumbed, and the weakness, stupor, and exhaustion of death came on. There was the usual internal noise, the choking in the throat, the spasmodic heaving of the chest, and the quivering of the limbs—all which signs grew fainter and fainter, till they ceased altogether.

Even then the murderers did not rise up from their victim. So terrible had the battle been, that they were afraid it might be renewed. Ah, no! The poor simple youth, whose glimmering reason taught him only to be happy and contented, had reached the goal to which all are going. Daft Jamie was dead.

CHAPTER XV

DAFT JAMIE MISSED, AND SOUGHT FOR IN VAIN—THE STORY OF WALTER GRAY

The struggle with Daft Jamie was the most terrific which these monsters had encountered in their murderous practices. A strong young man, full of health and strength, and not under the influence of strong drink when he was assailed, he made a wildly frantic resistance; and it must have been peculiarly touching to hear him, in those moments when he got his mouth free, call piteously for his mother—the only being on earth who devotedly loved him, and whom he so deeply loved in return. But the only ears who heard his dying cries were deaf to the mercy which their very simplicity would have stirred even in hearts hard and cruel. Burke and Hare had long ere this got beyond the region of feeling and emotion. A superstitious fear did most certainly possess the soul of the former, sufficient to cause him restlessness and rob him of even the peace of the wicked. His moral nature was not so utterly dead as was Hare's, but its capability of relenting or of turning seemed to be past. Therefore the frantic cries of the poor idiot awoke no sympathy or compassion in the bosom of his murderers, who wrought with all their brutal strength to overcome him and crush out his shrouded life.

When the bloody work was accomplished, and the body of their victim lay still in death, Burke was breathing hard, being thoroughly exhausted. The moment he was certain that death had really ensued, he rose from the body, and, with glaring eyes, turned fiercely on Hare.

"Why the deuce didn't ye strike in at wunst, ye mane, cowardly spalpeen?" he savagely exclaimed. "It's just about too much the crayter was for me, and, by jabers, it isn't much I have you to thank for, at all, at all. Faix, then, ye won't be so backward in wantin' yer half up at the Square."

"Aisy now, William dear," returned Hare, who was conscious that the reproach was merited. "Sure, I was watching all the time to get hould uv him, and couldn't make it out, for him and you wheeled about so much. But you fought him the bouldest ever I saw. Sure never a boy in Ireland could

have done it so illigantly. It was just admirin' ye I was all
the time."

"Faith, thin," returned Burke, drily, "I could have wanted
yer admiration if I had got yer hilp. But devil another will I
try that hasn't got the power taken out uv them by whisky."

"Indade, and that's thrue intirely," said Hare. "Bedad, it's
the whisky that does the most uv the work for us."

While Hare was speaking Burke was rifling the pockets of
the poor murdered youth. In one was the favourite brass
snuff-box and spoon, and in the other a few shillings and
coppers which had been given him in his wanderings that
day. The money was fairly divided, and Burke gave Hare the
spoon and kept the box.

That night the body was taken in a box to the Square,
and, *after being examined*, was paid for with the sum of ten
pounds.

In regard to this murder, we do not know whether to
wonder most at the hardihood of the murderers or the com-
plicity of the doctors. It was a convincing proof of the recklessness which success in sin had occasioned, when they ventured
unhesitatingly on a victim so well known in the city as Daft
Jamie. They must now have departed from the cautious principle followed at the beginning of their career, of making
away with none but those not likely to be missed. They must
have known that Jamie, whose presence was so familiar in the
streets, would not disappear without inquiry or comment. He
was likewise so well known to everybody that, unless they
could now securely count on the connivance and winking
silence of Dr Knox and his assistants, they durst not have presented his body at the Square, where it was certain to be at
once recognised.

We can account for the imprudence of this deed only on
the principle that a repetition of crime blunts the criminal's
every sense. Success in iniquity makes the sinner doubly pre-
sumptuous in its commission, and leads him to adopt fewer
and fewer means of precaution against its discovery. We must,
of course, in this recognise the providential condition of ultimate detection, and read the important truth that in this universe of divine organisation it is the tendency of hidden crime
to reveal itself.

Surely, however, the doctors in Surgeons' Square were
resolved to give no assistance to this natural law, for when the

well-known body of Daft Jamie was laid before them they bought it and said nothing. Well, we shall here record the fact, and say nothing either.

The first to miss the poor simpleton was of course his mother. Great as were his wanderings through the city, he never failed to enter his humble home by an early hour in the evening; but for the first time he came not, and knowing his habits so well, his mother wondered much at his non-appearance. Wonder very soon gave place to anxiety and alarm, as hour after hour passed without his footstep being heard on the stair, or his voice crooning a song, as he came gaily home for the night. When it began to grow late, the dwelling of the poor widow became suddenly desolate, for the mother's heart was quick to imagine the worst, and she at once connected his absence with his utter loss.

No sooner had this sad idea entered her mind and settled there than she began a wild search for her missing boy. With wringing hands and frantic voice she proclaimed his disappearance, and ran hither and thither in search of him, calling on him by name, and asking all she met if they had not seen him.

The excitement at once spread. The news flew fast that Daft Jamie was lost; and so great a favourite was he with young and old that hundreds eagerly joined the weeping mother, and before morning the whole city was examined from one end to the other. Very few could remember seeing him that day, and those who did so were unable to recall the place or the time at which they noticed him. No cue could, therefore, be found by which to trace him, and his disappearance seemed an inexplicable mystery.

Now it was that strange vague fears and rumours flew through the town of various people having disappeared in the same unaccountable manner, and in addition to certain authentic facts, the grossest exaggerations grew into shape, and stories of the wildest improbability gained belief. It was reported that there was in existence in the city a secret society, composed of fearful men, whose work it was to decoy people to some dreadful fate, the nature of which was quite indefinite. Some said they were sent abroad and sold as slaves, and others that they were murdered and eaten. Nothing, in short, was too extravagant or too horrible for the credulity of the people, and a general terror spread through the community.

In the midst of this excitement and outcry no sign came
from Surgeons' Square, though the doctors there must have
known that the body of the idiot whose disappearance had
caused such commotion was lying in their dissecting room.
They had it in their power to throw light on his unknown fate,
but *in the interests of science* they held their peace, and thus
claimed for their idol the sacrifice of human life. The poor
mother was doomed to mourn in despair for her lost son, who
was all the dearer to her because of his helplessness and depen-
dence. With him vanished the sad and sole comfort of her
lonely life, and her silent hearth was now cold and desolate
indeed.

But while all things seemed conspiring to prolong the
unparalleled career of these monsters in Tanner's Close,
Heaven was in its own way preparing the means of their
detection. The cup of their iniquity was now nearly full, and
the hour of discovery and the beginning of retribution was
near at hand. The agency by which this was to be accomplished introduces a short story of life's trials and failings, and
love's tenderness and devotion, and ultimate triumph over
temptation. This little story forms a fitting sequel for the
present chapter.

*

In a sweet sequestered village, not many miles from Edinburgh, lived Walter Gray and Rose Mowbray, and these two
young people were lovers. Beneath the shadow of the grand
old woods, in the half hidden walk which skirted the little
river as it flowed through the deep rocky ravine, on the brink
of which the village stood, their hearts grew with delicious
joy into the deepest and truest mutual affection. The parents
of both were well-to-do people in the village, and in point of
social position the young folks were pretty equally matched.
Walter was the son of the principal carpenter, and the father
of Rose had long been the head gardener on the estate which
surrounded the village. This entailed estate was, at the time
of which we write, possessed by General Stewart, who, having
retired from the army, brought with him into private life
many of the notions which, as a military officer, he had
imbibed. He was for one thing a stern disciplinarian, and
stood out for unhesitating and implicit obedience on the part

of those in his service, his idea of authority extending even to their family arrangements.

One day, Walter Gray was executing some little repairs in the General's mansion, and as he was a great favourite wherever he went, the cook had, as a manifestation of her goodwill, given him a glass of whisky. Now we have to remark that Walter was in many respects like Joe the miller's son, whose sad fate we recorded in a former chapter. He was, like him, ardent and generous in heart, frank in manners, and kindly in disposition; and, like him also, he was only too apt to yield to the temptation to take too much strong drink. It had, in short, begun to exert its power over him, and though he had not as yet gone the length of being considered a drunkard, there were whispers in the village about him, and sundry ominous shakings of heads in connection with his name, and words of foreboding spoken in reference to Rose Mowbray, to whom, it was well known, he was engaged to be married.

The glass of whisky he had received from the cook was not exactly calculated to strengthen his prudence, and it so happened that when the General came to inspect his work, and found fault with something he had done, or perhaps failed to do, the youth answered him rather rudely. For a moment or two the General was struck dumb with surprise at the young man's horrible audacity, then growing purple with rage, he burst out upon him as he would have done with a private soldier under his command. This sort of treatment was what Walter Gray was not disposed to submit to in silence. His ideas were rather liberal and democratic, and these being at the moment stimulated by the drink he had partaken of, he was not slow to give expression to them. In short, he gave the General a bit of his mind, and the result was that he was ordered from his presence, and commanded never to come near the mansion again. With a contemptuous toss of his head, Walter gathered up his tools and went whistling from the room.

That afternoon the General's carriage stopped at the door of Mr Gray, sen., and its august occupant having alighted, and been shown into the best parlour, the carpenter was summoned to his presence, and informed in words of sternest indignation that he must banish his son from the place. As was natural, the father was not a little astonished at this, and even after being told the reason of such a command he was not inclined to yield to it till the General haughtily told him that, if he did not do as he demanded, he himself should remove from the estate.

This was a serious matter. Unfortunately the General had the power to order his removal; and as the whole village stood on his property, Mr Gray's entire business was thereby imperilled. Still he was not inclined to comply with such an arbitrary injunction, and would probably have given a refusal, accepting the consequences, had not the youth himself, who had overheard the conversation, come quietly into the room at this juncture, and, with quiet dignity and firmness, intimated his resolution to depart.

This resolution he kept; for that very week he went into the city and obtained work in a large carpentry establishment, there engaging to enter on this employment in the beginning of the week following.

Next to himself the person most interested in his change of situation was Rose Mowbray. She, along with Walter, had looked forward to a happy married life in the village where they had been both brought up, where they would be near their parents and all their friends. But this pleasant anticipation must, for the present at least, be abandoned.

After many tears on the part of Rose, and many manly protestations of love on the part of Walter, they separated, and the youth went for the first time from home, and into the dangers and allurements of a great city. Oh, what a testing time is this for a young man! How many fail to keep their integrity under such an ordeal. Freedom from restraint and the presence of seductive temptations combine to draw the feet away from the path of virtue, and not unfrequently the giddy youth enters a downward course from which he is never rescued, finding, it may be, an early death and a premature grave.

In his betrothal to Rose Mowbray, Walter Gray was under a blissful restraining influence. His pure and ardent attachment to Rose kept him from that vice and gross impurity into which youth in the city is so ready to fall; but his natural leaning towards intemperance was increased, and ere long he was drawn under the influence which has proved fatal to thousands—the insidious, ensnaring, and destroying influence of strong drink.

News of this sad fact reached the village, and lost nothing

by the way. It came to the ears of the father of Rose, who was not slow to mention it to Rose herself. The girl with her true, brave, loving heart, would not credit the report, at least in all its extent; and with flushed cheeks defended her absent lover. Nevertheless, on the following day, when by appointment they met in the woods, she spoke to him of what she had heard, and anxiously looked in his face for a reply.

Walter coloured. "Do they really say such things as that of me?" he rejoined.

"Yes, dearest, but it is not true. I well know it is not true," said Rose, with an air of beaming confidence.

"Of course, it isn't true," returned Walter; "at least nothing like what is reported. I do take a glass occasionally, but not to do me harm; and I can take it or want it just as I like. You see, the truth lies here, Rose: I am lonely in my lodgings of an evening, and go out sometimes to meet a friend or two. We have a bit of supper, and perhaps something to drink along with it. But, Rose, darling! I'll tell you what will prevent all that sort of thing. Be my wife, and we will take a nice little house to live in, and I shall then never think of going out of an evening, and, of course, will never take drink at all. Promise to do this, Rose. My wages will keep us in a plain comfortable way, and my father will furnish the house for us. Will you do it, Rose dear! and we shall be so happy?"

Rose listened to his words with pleasure, for they made her warm, loving heart beat fast and joyously. She believed all he said, and never doubted but her influence would be amply sufficient to keep him in the path of sobriety, so she hid her blushing face in his bosom, and promised to be his wife at an early date.

In a transport of happiness Walter caught her to his heart, and the next minute was one of absorbing bliss. When they looked up they were startled to find General Stewart standing within a few feet of them, gazing with a frowning countenance.

"So, young woman," he pompously exclaimed, "you are allowing that good-for-nothing fellow to court you. Be thankful that I have come upon you to prevent you making a fool of yourself. The fellow, I am told, is a drunken rascal; so go home and have nothing more to do with him."

"General Stewart," said Walter, angrily, "I am a poor man, and you are rich; but that is all the difference between us. In everything else I consider myself just as good as you, and it is gross impertinence in you to speak as you have spoken."

"What do you say, fellow—what do you say?" fumed the General. "Impertinence; did I hear you right? You actually had the audacity to use the word impertinence to me?"

"Yes, and I would use it to any man who dared to act to me as you have acted."

"Begone, sirrah," roared the General. "Decamp from this wood, or I will give you in charge to the constable."

"Try it," sneered Walter; "that would be the dearest order ever you gave. This path is public, and you have no more to do with it than I have. I will thank you therefore to leave us to ourselves."

"Girl," sputtered the now furious General, "go home instantly, and I will follow and see you safe under your father's roof, and I'll take care that he looks after you for the future."

Rose had been accustomed to regard the General with the greatest awe and fear; but ever since he had insisted on Walter being sent from the village, she had regarded him with feelings of indignation, and his imperious interference on this occasion made her bravely angry.

"I am quite safe with Walter, sir," she replied, putting her arm confidently within that of her lover.

"More insubordination, by Jove," roared the General, fairly boiling over with wrath. "Very well, young woman. I shall go to your father and direct him to have you thoroughly restrained. This is the last time you shall meet that drunken rascal."

He turned, and was about to walk off, when Walter stepped into the narrow path before him, and blocked up the road.

"Out of my way," thundered the irate officer.

"Not till I have told you a bit of my mind," rejoined the youth.

The General held up his stick as if to strike.

"Take care," said Walter, as his eye emitted one gleaming flash. "Touch me ever so lightly with that stick, and were you ten times a General, I shall knock you down. Now, sir, you have chosen to interfere in my affairs in a way most tyrannical and unjustifiable. You insisted on me leaving the village, and now you would endeavour to separate Rose and me. This time, however, you shall fail. Rose has promised to be my wife, and she has got too true and noble a heart to be false to me at your imperious bidding. Let me advise you not to meddle any more with things and persons that do not concern you, and learn this, that poor folks have rights, and spirit, and feeling as well as you."

Having delivered himself thus, the youth stood aside to let the General go forward, which the latter did in speechless rage. He went at once to the father of Rose and forbade him to allow his daughter to marry Walter Gray. Rose, however, was faithful to her plighted troth, and they were married immediately, and went to a small but comfortable home in Edinburgh.

For a time all went well with them. They lived as happily together as a married couple could; but by degrees Walter was tempted to spend his evenings in his old haunts, from which he generally returned home intoxicated.

Poor Rose did her utmost to wean him from these habits. By loving, tender solicitations, she entreated him to shun the course he was pursuing in time, for she saw the misery and wretchedness to which it would lead. Walter laughed at her fears, and to show her, as he said, that he was quite able to restrain himself, would remain at home for an evening; but when on the following day a companion met him and urged him to return to the social gatherings at the public-house, he weakly yielded, and returned with his manhood degraded as before.

The downward course of a drunkard has been often depicted, and need not be repeated here. Surely and fatally the love for drink grew stronger than every other passion, and ate out the tenderness and affection of his heart, the frankness and generosity of his nature. Nay, in proportion to these qualities which he once possessed, was the evil change which drink made upon him. It became his master, and he became its utter slave.

The usual consequences soon followed. He became idle as well as dissipated, and of course when he did no work he received no wages. They fell into poverty, their furniture was sold bit by bit, and by-and-bye they were reduced to the deepest destitution. A daughter had been born to them, and the sorest part of the trial for Rose was that she had often no nourishment for her little one, whom she saw pining away

day by day for want of support. This was torture to her
mother's heart, and it served to make her appeal the more
earnestly to Walter to abandon his downward course, which
had brought them all into such misery. Her love for him had
been proof against all his unkindness and cruelty. She would
not forsake him, she would not give him up, but continued to
hope even against hope for his reformation. She did, indeed,
grow pale, and thin, and melancholy, but no bitter reproach
ever passed her lips.

No one but the bond slave of strong drink would have cherished the habit which brought such degradation on himself
and such desolation on his household. But Walter Gray,
though he saw the dire effects of his intemperance, had not
strength to shake off the fetters. In his lucid moments his
remorse was most poignant; but this remorse instead of causing him to forsake its cause, only drove him deeper into the
mire, for to escape from it he rushed the more wildly into the
oblivion of intoxication.

At length he caught a fever, and for weeks was delirious.
When he recovered his reason, it was to learn from the white
trembling lips of Rose that their little one had died. The intelligence went to his heart like a dagger, and he became conscious of his infatuation and his guilt as he had never been
before. The weeks of convalescence which followed were weeks
of deep silent reflection and heartfelt repentance; and on the
bosom of his weeping wife he vowed never again to let strong
drink pass his lips.

In process of time he was able to leave his couch and move
about, but they were now houseless and penniless. All their
furniture, and nearly all their clothes, were gone, and though
Walter readily obtained work—to be accomplished as he had
strength to do it—yet, having now no home of their own, they
required to go into lodgings.

And, alas! it was lodgings of the very poorest kind they
could take, and they wandered many hours in the lowest parts
of the town before they could find shelter. At last they succeeded in obtaining lodgings in the West Port—*in the house of
Burke.*

The very consideration of their obvious poverty and helplessness, which prevented others from taking them in,
prompted Burke and Helen M'Dougal to receive them. The
poorer and more friendless their lodgers were, the better for

their purpose, and in the poor emaciated youth, and patient, worn-looking wife, they anticipated victims for Surgeons' Square. A few days passed away quite comfortably, Walter's strength slowly returned, and he was able to work a few hours every day. Rose trembled lest he should revert to his former course of intemperance. If his former companions asked him to join their dissipated society, she greatly feared his inability to resist that temptation; in which case revived hope would vanish, and a cloud of hopeless darkness would settle over their lives.

But this fear eventually promised to be groundless. Walter's good resolution was not forsaken, as in the sad time that was past. His old companions did gather round him, and did seek to induce him to go to the tavern, but he steadily and firmly refused. Burke, too, on various occasions sought to make him intoxicated, and failed. Walter Gray's manhood had asserted itself. Love had triumphed, and days of happiness might yet be in store for them.

CHAPTER XVI

THE LITTLE OLD WOMAN

It was the morning of the last day of October 1828—a dull, raw, drizzly morning—when business or necessity, and not pleasure, drew people abroad. The narrow streets of the old town of Edinburgh were wet and greasy, and a dull grey haze rested on the house tops, and on the distant openings between the houses. Everything wore a chill and cheerless aspect, and the little groups that used to gossip at the "close mouths" were nowhere visible, so that the thoroughfares were almost silent, save for the slow, melancholy rumble of an occasional cart, drawn along by a listless horse, which seemed to be depressed as its driver by the dull coldness of the day, containing, as it seemed to do, the prelude of approaching winter, and of the dismal November days just at hand.

Among the very poor people to be seen in the West Port on that comfortless morning was a little quick-motioned woman, very barely and shabbily dressed, and to all appearance sorely reduced in circumstances, for she was engaged in the unenviable work of soliciting charity. A most wonderful elasticity of nature that little old woman must have had, for even in these melancholy circumstances she walked along with a brisk, almost nimble step; and when she met with a denial, as for the most part she did at the shops she entered, she turned away with undimmed eye, and gave vent to no murmur of discontent.

In this manner she entered a public-house, and made her appeal to a stout red-faced man, who was busy behind the counter burnishing a pewter vessel.

"Och, sur, and might it plaise ye to help a poor wandering woman that hasn't a bite to put in her mouth this cowld morning?"

"Never serve beggars," was the gruff reply. "Got too many taxes to pay for that, and heavy poor's rates into the bargain. Haven't you got a parish?"

"Throth, thin, and I suppose I have, sur; but it's many a weary mile from this, across the wather in ould Ireland. I've just come over to seek for my son Terry, and oh, wirra,

I've sought four days for him and can't find him at all, at all."

"Can't help that. You Irish should stay in your own country. We've got plenty of poor of our own to support."

The little old woman made no reply to this, she did not even heave a sigh, but turned silently round and went out again with hungry heart to face the raw morning chillness.

She had not gone many steps from the door when a hand was laid upon her arm, and turning round she encountered the face of a man she had seen in the shop, but from whom she did not think it worth while to ask help.

"God save ye, ould mother, but it's a poor trade ye've taken up this morning anyhow," said the man.

"Jasus[1] be wid yez, and it's the true word yer spakin," responded the beggar, her eye brightening at the kind address of her countryman.

"And so ye are just from the ould counthry. Bad luck to the boy that wouldn't be kind to wun that's like his own flesh and blood. Sure now ye won't refuse to take a bit uv breakfast from me in my own house down the close on the other side."

"Is it refused you said?" cried the little old woman, with sudden animation. "Troth, thin, it's proud and thankful I am for the offer, and may the Holy Virgin bless ye for the makin' uv it. Och, musha, the days are past for ould Bridget Docherty to be proud."

"Docherty! Did you say Docherty?" exclaimed the other, with an appearance of much interest.

"Indade I did, and sure that is my name."

"Och, come along thin, and maybe it will turn out that it's friends we are. Why, woman alive, my mother was a Docherty."

"And did she come from Ballydun?"[2]

"In coorse she did, only it's many a long day and year sin'. But, cushla machree, don't stand out any longer in the cowld and wet when a warm fire-side is waitin' for ye to step into."

They crossed the street and entered Tanner's Close. The

---

1. References to Jesus and God are commonly excised in the 1885 book.

2. Ballydun is near Kilkenny, but the name is also generic Irish: place/ homestead with a fort. Note that Dennis (fictive son of the old woman and father of the dumb boy) dies at Kilkenny.

old woman closely followed at the heels of her conductor, who was no other than *Burke*, and his purpose in inviting her to his house was the old object of murder. They had not secured a victim since Daft Jamie was despatched, and here by a happy accident one had turned up whom there would be no difficulty in managing. He did not lead her into Hare's house, but down a common stair, and along a dark passage into his own, and a private signal sufficed to let Helen M'Dougal understand his fatal intention regarding the stranger. Helen interpreted the signal without the slightest emotion. Murder had now become so familiar to her and all of them, that the contemplation of it scarcely fluttered or excited them. She understood the part she had to play, and received the old woman as her husband's unfortunate country-woman with every show of kindness, hastening to prepare a warm and comfortable breakfast, while Burke and the wanderer sat by the fire engaged in conversation. It was conducted by Burke in a gay, hilarious tone; but it took a turn which caused even his cruel heart to feel a pang of momentary fear.

"Och, thin," said the woman, "and wouldn't it vex the heart uv my boy Terry entirely, if he knew his poor ould mother was wanderin' through this mighty big town seekin' for the son she couldn't find, and forced to ask hilp from strangers."

"And so it would," rejoined Burke; "but as sure as my mother was a Docherty, it's here ye'll stay till Terry is found."

"The Blessed Virgin give ye glory," cried the old woman, in a burst of gratitude. "Shure now, Terry half expects me about this time, for when the mother uv Dennis O'Shea came over three months sin', I towld her to tell him I wad set out afore winter set in. Ye wouldn't be afther seein' the ould woman? She had a poor deaf and dumb boughal wid her, for ye see Dennis was killed up at Kilkenny, and his poor purty wife broke her heart for him, lavin' the helpless innocent to the care uv ould Biddy, and she came over here wid it along wid her to find out Michael Curran, the only relation they had in all the world."

Burke winced at this incidental revelation; for this, he doubted not, was the old woman and the dumb boy who had been made their victims, and it was startling to know this acquaintance turning up to be disposed of in a like manner. Beyond a momentary twinge of feeling, however, Burke was in no ways moved, but in a jocular tone hoped that the old woman had found Michael, and that she and the dumb boy were provided for.

Breakfast being discussed, it became necessary that Helen should understand the mode of procedure to be adopted, and entering the next apartment he privately beckoned her to follow him.

"It can't be done till night," he whispered; "but don't for the sowl uv yez let her over the dure."

"But the Grays," remarked Helen, anxiously. "How is it to be done and them in the house?"

"Faix they must be got out uv the house somehow. Lave that to me. I'll go up and tell Hare about the shot, and we'll be back after it's dark."

As the best means of keeping the little woman in-doors all day, Helen set her to clean the house, and most willingly did the grateful and unsuspecting creature labour at this work, for she was so thankful to have reached a kindly shelter, and did her utmost to acknowledge, if she could not repay, the hospitality which had been extended to her.

So they wrought side by side at house cleaning all the day, and gossiped together as women always do with each other, and yet all the time Helen M'Dougal knew that the poor woman was doomed; that she had but a few hours to live; that when the darkness of night came on she was to be barbarously murdered. One cannot get a better glimpse of the callousness of heart reached by the companion of Burke than this fact affords. With this terrible knowledge in her bosom, she could gossip familiarly all day with the intended victim, and give no sign of it. There was neither nervousness nor restless-ness—no pity and no compunction; but with Judas-like friend-ship she maintained a pleasant, kindly exterior, waiting till the butchers should arrive to do their bloody work.

Thus in happiness and active exertion the little brisk-hearted old woman passed the day which was to prove the last of her life. The young melancholy wife of Walter Gray spent the same time alone in the dark dingy room which formed the lodging for Walter and herself. She noticed the presence of the little old woman, but paid no particular heed to her, being more deeply occupied, it is likely, in sad thoughts of the fair but vanished past, and the dark disheartening present, and yet not disheartening altogether, for Walter was now giving signs of amendment, and there was a promise and a prospect of better days to come. Oh, how fervently she prayed that the prospect might be realised! It was no small aggravation of her misery that she who had lived so long in a clean sweet country home should be compelled to exist amongst dirt and squalor; but she was content, nay glad, to endure the present discomfort and privation, if it should prove the threshold to a bright future in which she should again have a husband she could respect and admire as well as love.

There was even now a token of this, hence her lonely days spent in the house of Burke were days not wholly dark and cheerless. They were gilded by hope, and where hope is, gladness also lingers.

The lamps had not long been lighted in the streets when Burke and Hare and Hare's wife came in from Tanner's Close, and with them a supply of whisky, wherewith to produce the revelry which always preceded the butchery of the victims. They were gathered round the fire, and the little old woman in the midst of them, the object of universal attention and friendly solicitation, when Walter Gray came in from his work. He required to pass through the front room in which they were seated to reach the little apartment where he and his wife lodged, and was doing so with all the greater haste when he saw how they were engaged, and smelt the fumes of his old enemy—whisky. But Burke came in his way, with a full glass in his hand.

"Throth, now, you'll not refuse to drink the hilth uv this dacent ould friend uv mine, that has come from Ireland all the way."

"No whisky—no drink," said Walter, hastily, as he pushed aside the glass which Burke thrust almost in his face.

"Man alive, it won't bite you. Take it up, and be friendly."

"For God's sake don't tempt me!" returned Walter, with quivering frame. "If you knew what wretchedness and misery drink has done to me and mine you would not offer it to me."

"Och! by the powers you'll get over all that. Sure a dhrop of the real potheen is the greatest blessing uv life. Just a mouthful, to drink the ould woman's hilth."

"No, no," returned the young man, good-humouredly, but firmly. "You mean it in kindness; but I assure you you could

not do me more harm in this world than by persuading me
to do what you ask. I wish your friend health and happiness
as sincerely as if I drank the liquor. There now, let me
pass."

And, with a quick motion, Walter glided past Burke, and
entered the little back room, closing the door behind him.

Rose was waiting for him with outstretched arms, and
threw herself fondly on his bosom.

"Oh, I am so glad, so happy that you resisted. I stood
behind the door, trembling lest he should get you to drink;
but you stood out nobly, manfully. Bless you, Walter; God
bless and strengthen you always. You have conquered now.
Oh, yes, you have conquered!"

He bent his head upon her cheek and sobbed, while his
whole body shook with strong emotion.

"Heaven help me, Rose!" he gasped. "It was almost more
than I could stand. The demon was rising within me, tempting me to swallow the drink; and even now every nerve in my
frame is quivering with agitation. Oh, do not praise me, Rose,
for I do not deserve it. Another such temptation, and I feel
that I shall fall, and if I do there is no further hope for I shall
then go to utter destruction."

"But you will not fall, Walter," returned Rose, in a hopeful
tone, as with loving hand she lifted the damp hair from his
hot brow. "Your triumph to-night will give you strength for
the future. Come, dear, and have tea, it will do you good."

Her sweet, cheering words soothed and calmed him, and
the first rays of returning hope entered his soul, even as they
sat together in that dirty, squalid chamber, whose poverty-
stricken appearance reminded him so forcibly of the dire result
of his weakness, folly, and guilt. Out of the depths of his
degradation he lifted his eyes to the heights of respectability,
and resolved by God's strength to climb these again. Hitherto,
though he ardently desired to redeem himself, he had almost
despaired of doing it, but to-night, under the smiling hopefulness of Rose, his own hopefulness grew likewise, and he contemplated the day when he should again hold up his head
among his fellows, and restore to Rose the comforts of which
he had so cruelly deprived her. So much for the blessed influence of a true, loving, and devoted wife.

They spent the rest of the evening in sweet communion with
each other, hardly heeding the noisy revelry which was going

forward in the next apartment. That noise was increasing every moment as the whisky circulated more freely and made its influence the more felt. The party seemed also to grow very merry, as the orgie proceeded, for they occasionally burst out into snatches of song, and the shrill voice of the little old woman was as loud as the rest, as she executed in great glee several favourite Irish ditties.

When it was wearing late, Burke came into the back room and asked the Grays if they would, as a favour, sleep that night in Hare's house, as the little woman was to stay with them, and they had no bed to offer her but the one in that room.

Walter was a little surprised at this request, but made no objection, and about eleven o'clock he and Rose were conducted by Hare's wife to the house in Tanner's Close, and shown into the awful back room there which had been the scene of so many dreadful tragedies. In happy ignorance of the murders which had recently been perpetrated within its four walls, they retired to rest, and slept in peace, dreaming of no harm.

Let us return to the house they had just left. Everything was in full preparation there for the murder that was meditated. The departure of the Grays removed the only barrier which stood in the way of its commission; and now that they were gone, the murderers resolved to get their bloody work expeditiously done.

The little old woman was much excited by the whisky she had partaken of, but she was not drunk, nor would she be prevailed upon to drink in a sufficient quantity to bring her to "the point." She rather chose to be wildly elevated, and danced and sung with uproarious delight. Thinking that by humouring her they would induce her to drink more freely, the others joined in the wild frenzy of the hour, and a very saturnalia ensued.

In the midst of the noise and shouting, there entered Mrs Connoway—a woman who lived on the other side of the passage, and who, being Irish, was attracted by the Irish airs which were being sung.

The little old woman, finding in her another country-woman, fraternised with her at once, and insisted on accompanying her into her own house. Burke and Hare and the women followed, taking the whisky with them, and for another hour the revelry was kept up in Mrs Connoway's, at the end of which time they left the latter to herself, and returned to the house of Burke.

The old woman was still not sufficiently drunk for their purpose; but the murderers had by this time become fiercely impatient, and would do the deed at once. By a private arrangement, Burke and Hare got up a pretended quarrel between them, which came to a sham fight, supposed by the intended victim to be a real conflict. She was naturally alarmed, and her sympathies being enlisted in behalf of Burke, who had been so kind to her, she took his part in the quarrel. At this point the two women, knowing what was coming, ran into the passage, closing the door which led into the room.

The pretended fight between the two men became to all appearance fiercer, and the little woman coming between them, was thrown violently to the ground, and, very much to her astonishment, found Burke kneeling on her breast, and Hare holding her nose and mouth. The terrible change in the eyes of Burke, which now glared with his horrible purpose, revealed to her, as she gazed up into them, that they meant to murder her, and, with a frantic effort of despair, she tore Hare's hands away, and uttered a loud piercing shriek of mortal terror. The cry might have been repeated if Burke had not clutched her throat in a gripe of iron, and held it till Hare refastened his hold, and that with a strength which the weak frame beneath could not resist. The poor victim, now fully conscious of her position, writhed in their suffocating grasp, and gazed up at them with eyes which seemed about to burst from their sockets with agony. She did her best to cast them off, and so long as the least strength remained in her, she struggled to the utmost of her power, for nature, in its extremity, will not cease to resist, however hopeless the effort. For full fifteen minutes they held her. Her struggles had ceased, and, in the belief that she was dead, they rose. But she was not dead yet, for her bruised chest gave one long, deep inspiration, and she would, in all likelihood, have recovered, if the startled murderers had not thrown themselves upon her again, and kept their place till the fact of death was beyond all doubt. When they rose up the second time the little old woman had passed from pain and fear on earth into the presence of her Judge.

A tea-box, in which to put the body, had been procured in the afternoon, and had been used as a seat during the evening. The old woman herself had sat upon it for some time, little imagining that in an hour or two it was meant to contain her dead body. It was at once brought forward by Hare, and the women being called in from the passage, they very coolly stripped the rags from the still warm and almost quivering corpse, and Burke and his accomplice tried to stow it away in the box. The box, however, proved much too small, and, do as they would, the body could not be got into it. This brought matters to a stand-still for the present. Another box could not be procured till morning, so, with an oath of impatience, Burke doubled the body up and threw it a crevice between the bed and the wall, where it was covered up with some dirty straw.

It was now past twelve o'clock, and Burke proceeded to the residence of the keeper of the doctor's rooms in Surgeons' Square. This official lived in a house quite near; and Burke brought him down to show him the body, which, he said, would be ready for delivery at the Square in the morning. A portion of the straw was pulled aside, and the man looked carelessly at "the thing," saying at the same time that the rooms would be open at nine, but that neither the professor nor his assistants would be there till ten, and that it might be as well not to bring the body till that hour.

When this man went away, the four wretches resumed the revelry which had been interrupted by the horrible tragedy we have described. The ghastly object in the corner was no hindrance to their merriment—the fact that the little old woman who but an hour before was the happiest and most gleeful of the party, was now a bruised and breathless corpse, did not in the least interfere with their enjoyment. They drank, and laughed, and joked with the most ribald brutality, for was not the sum of ten pounds sure for them on the following day.

In the midst of their noisy sociality, and somewhat to their alarm, a footstep sounded in the long, dark passage, and a young man walked in. He was a nephew of Brogan, the former occupant of the house, and had just come through from Glasgow, where his uncle had gone.

"Man alive, John Brogan, is it you?" cried Burke, who, with the others, was now considerably intoxicated.

"Indade, and it's just the same, and a weary man I am after more nor a forty miles' travel."

"Faix, thin, that manes Glasgow."

"Shure an' it does."

"And is Barney there?"

"Throth an' he is. He has got on to clean the streets. What a mighty hurry he was in to get out uv Edinburgh. But Uncle Barney was always soft and nervous. Be jabers, but it isn't much uv the Brogan blood he has got in him anyhow. It wouldn't have been the sight uv a dead body that would have frightened me."

"I believe ye, me boy," returned Burke, with a wink of approbation.

Hare got up and looked close into the young man's face with his gruesome eyes.

"Is it the thruth ye'r spakin' now?" he said.

"The thruth it is, and devil a lie in it at all at all," was the rejoinder.

"Then come and sit down and have a glass o potheen. There's a stool among yon straw; bring it and sit down alongside ov us."

Brogan went to the end of the bed, and groped in the straw for the stool. He touched something that made him start, but, instead of running back, he pulled the straw away, and saw the naked body of the murdered woman.

"Thunder an' ouns, it's another body!" he exclaimed, more surprised than dismayed. "Begora! but it's a mighty queer stool you've sint me for. Where do you get thim all?"

"What do you want to know for?" asked Hare.

"Because I'd like to get hold uv them, too. I've been tould the doctors pay well for them."

On hearing this answer Hare looked at Burke, and the latter nodded intelligently. The same idea had occurred to both. Hare had often spoken of extending their *business*, and, by means of a new partner, this might be done. Brogan might, they thought, be safely let into the secret, and made their associate and accomplice; and he was given to understand that by-and-bye he would be told a thing or two. So he covered up the body again, and, sitting down beside them, joined in the revelry, which went forward with increased animation.

Towards daylight, Hare and his wife went to their own

house, and Burke, Helen, and Brogan lay down promiscuously, to sleep off the effects of their carousal.[3] They were all
three sunk in deep slumber about eight o'clock, when Walter
and Rose came in to have breakfast, and it was not till after a
long and loud knocking at the outer door that they could gain
admittance. It was Helen M'Dougal who at length opened
the door for them, and, when they entered, Burke and Brogan
rose from their lairs.

"I suppose we can't get into our own room, as your friend
won't be up yet," said Walter.

"Oh, yes; she's up and away two hours ago," said Burke,
hurriedly. "Come, stir yourself, Nelly, and let us be afther
havin' breakfast."

The young pair went into the little apartment at the back,
both of them wondering at the old woman's sudden departure.
This wonder was increased when Rose made the discovery
that the bed had not been slept on. It was precisely the same
as when they left the house the previous evening.

They stood looking at each other in silent astonishment for
some moments.

"There's a mystery here," said Walter, at length. "The
whole thing has a queer look, which I don't like. I tell you
what, Rose, I shan't go to my work to-day. I could not be
easy, leaving you here, till we find out what has become of the
old woman."

"Merciful heaven! they cannot have harmed her," whispered Rose, growing pale with apprehension.

"I hope not," returned her husband; "but the whole thing
is suspicious, and we shall watch them to-day."

"So we shall," added Rose quite nervously. "That man
Hare, who was here last night, is a fearsome-looking creature.
I could not help shuddering when I looked at him."

"It may be all right enough," observed Walter; "but, to
say the least of it, these people are queer and mysterious. The
man Burke does nothing, so far as I can see, yet they are
always flush of money. They live in a royal fashion, and must
squander every week on meat and drink as much as would
keep a large family very comfortably. If they get it honestly
it's more than I can see how."

---

3. 1885 deletes "promiscuously", probably for its sexual reference, which
increased over the century.

"Oh, Walter!" faltered Rose, "what you say frightens me very much. I have had strange thoughts about them myself, and now I am positively nervous."

"Nay, there is no ground for fear. I shall not leave you alone with them again till I am satisfied that there is nothing to conceal. To-day's watching will do it. Before night I am certain we shall get to know what has become of the little old woman."

At last, then, O reader, light begins to break upon the darkness of this long and murky tunnel in the railroad of social life. Suspicion has entered a genuine, honest heart, and on the result of that suspicion hangs the momentous issue of these men's career of crime being continued uninterrupted or brought to a speedy and eternal close. Unconsciously, therefore, Walter Gray had the most tremendous human interests in his keeping, and, though he knew it not, the lives of his fellow-beings were depending on the result of his watching that November day Burke and his ill-favoured associates.

CHAPTER XVII

WALTER GRAY AND HIS WIFE DISCOVER THE BODY OF THE LITTLE OLD WOMAN— JUSTICE AWAKENED AT LAST

Rose's first act in their little room that morning was to proceed to light the fire, that she might prepare their frugal breakfast. There was fuel enough lying about, but a little straw was wanted to set the fuel in a blaze, and, knowing there was a quantity in the front room, at the end of the bed, she went there to procure a handful.

This was what she did every morning, without requiring to ask permission, and on this occasion she went forward as usual to where the straw was lying, and was about to bend down to lift some, when Burke suddenly and roughly pulled her back, and stept between her and the bed.

"Keep out o' there," he said, with a significant nod, and a fierceness which frightened Rose.

"I merely want a little straw to light the fire," she faltered, utterly at a loss to account for his violence.

"And couldn't ye be afther takin' it out uv yer own bed?" he snarled. "There," he added, snatching up a handful and giving it to her; "take that, and go away wid yez."

Rose took the straw mechanically, and returned to the back room, wondering much at the man's anger, but setting it down to the account of drink—for he seemed still to be under the influence of the previous night's dissipation.

She found Walter standing near the door, rigid and ghastly. He had seen Burke's movement and heard his words, and they suggested to him a horrible suspicion. There must, he thought, be something particular amongst the straw; and his flesh crept as he conjectured what that something might be. So plainly was his inward horror marked in his countenance that Rose stood still to look at him; and the expression in his face suggested the same terrible idea to her own mind.

"Oh, Walter!" she gasped. "Can there be anything hid among the straw?"

"It looks very like it," he returned; and, as he whispered the words, his lips became firmly pressed together.

"The—the—little old woman!" added Rose, in the extremity of apprehension, clutching Walter's arm at the same moment with her shaking hand.

"That is my impression," was his reply.

"Merciful heaven! let us quit the house," whispered the trembling girl.

"Not yet, dear. I must be satisfied first. Possibly our suspicion may be groundless; but if not, it is our duty to know the truth and disclose it, for, if it be as we think, then a murder has been committed, and the perpetrators must be brought to justice."

"Oh, dear, how stupid and terrified I am," said Rose, sinking helplessly upon a stool. "I feel as if I could not breathe. The air of the house feels thick and heavy. Whatever are we to do?"

"Watch," replied Walter, in a stern tone; and again his lips were unconsciously compressed.

Burke and the others had now seemingly become alive to the necessity of keeping every one from approaching the straw, and the young man Brogan was commissioned to sit on a chair in front of the bed for this purpose—a post which he was quite ready to fill.

He had not sat very long when he felt, or imagined he felt, a bad smell come from the body, and communicated this fact to Burke.

"Begorra! thin we must take out the smell wid one that's stronger," returned the latter; and, taking up a bottle more than half full of whisky, he dashed its contents over the bed and all round the room. He was in the act of doing this when Mrs Connoway came in.

"Musha, thin, is it deprived o' yer raison ye are?" exclaimed the woman, standing amazed at his procedure.

"You may say that," spoke up Helen M'Dougal. "He got more drink last night than was good for him, and he's just crazy this morning."

"Divil a bit o' me," cried Burke. "The whisky is bad, and the sooner it's made away wid the sooner I'll get the bottle filled wid better. And more nor that, isn't this the way to encourage trade?"

"And where is Mrs Docherty this morning?" asked Connoway, looking round in search of the little old woman.

"She's away," answered Helen in a moment. "I packed

her out of the house pretty smart this morning when I found her making rather too friendly with my husband."[1]

"Hould yer tongue, Nelly," laughed Burke. "The dacent woman meant it all in kindness; and ye got jealous in a mighty hurry intirely. It was a big shame o' ye to put the ould crayter to the door in the way ye did."

"It was high time," rejoined Helen, with pretended anger.

"Be my sowl but she's a canty ould body," observed Connoway. "The skalteen made her as wild as a kitten. What a power o' noise ye made in here after ye left my house. Was it fightin' ye was?"

"Throth, and we was just that same," answered Burke. "Hare said something to me that wasn't purty, and I knocked him down for it. Uv coorse that put his blood up, and we had an out-and-out set-to. But five minutes' good fightin' made us friends again, and afther that, bedad, the potheen wint faster than ever."

To this conversation Walter and Rose listened in the next room with breathless attention. Here was a different account given of the departure of the little old woman, and, from the allusion made to a fight which had taken place they drew dark conclusions. Everything tended to strengthen the suspicion they entertained; and they thought they understood only too well the object Brogan had in view in keeping sentinel in front of the straw.

So the hours of the day passed. Burke and the others were evidently flustered; Hare and his wife looked in occasionally, and Burke and Helen sometimes went out with them, but the young man Brogan never moved from his chair. The Grays, though keeping a close watch on all that went forward, did not show that they were doing so. There was a crevice in the partition wall between their room and the front apartment, and through this they could obtain a view of that apartment without being themselves seen.

About the middle of the afternoon, when every one chanced to be absent, Brogan suddenly left his seat, and he also went out. Walter from his place of view observed this, and hastily

---

1. "with my husband" is deleted in 1885 edition, perhaps as suggesting sexuality.

acquainting Rose with the fact, opened the door of communication and passed into the front room.

Rose followed with beating heart. There was perfect
silence in the place; but some of them might return, therefore
not a moment was to be lost. Casting a quick but searching
glance all round, and listening intently, till satisfied that no
footstep was in the passage, the youth approached the bundle
of straw, and, not without a tremor, began to overturn it,
Rose watching his motions with bated breath and strained
eyeballs.

He had not groped two moments when he started back with
an exclamation of horror, which made Rose give utterance
to a suppressed scream. Though he really expected to find
there the dead body of the little old woman, yet, when his
hand grasped another hand that was cold and stiff, he was
startled beyond measure at the touch, and, in the impulse of
the moment, sprang back in dismay.

"Oh, Walter, what is it?" gasped Rose, who felt very like
to faint. "Is—is she there?"

"Yes," answered the other in a fearful whisper.

Then with a desperate resolution, and in energetic haste,
he tossed aside the straw, and there lay the body before them
entirely naked, doubled up, rigid and distorted. There was
blood round the mouth and over a part of the face, but they
at once recognised the features as those of the brisk, happy
creature who on the previous evening took such an active part
in the wild merriment that then went forward.

"For God's sake, Walter, let us fly from this place," screamed
Rose, dragging frantically at her husband's arm.

"First go and bring Mrs Connoway to see this," said Walter
quickly.

Rose was gone in a moment, and immediately Mrs
Connoway burst in highly excited.

"Holy Mother, and they've murdered her," she exclaimed,
holding up her two hands in horror when her eyes fell on the
body.

"It seems only too like it," said Walter.

"Merciful heaven, they are coming," cried Rose distract-
edly, as a footstep was heard without.

In a moment Mrs Connoway rushed back to her house,
and Walter and Rose ran into the passage. There they
encountered Helen M'Dougal alone.

"Where are you going?" she asked.

"Out of your house for ever," replied Walter. "We have seen the body."

"What body?" demanded Helen, in pretended astonishment.

"The body among the straw—the body of the old woman. It's no use denying it any longer, for we have seen and examined it."

"John Brogan," cried Helen, in great alarm.

"Brogan is not in," said Walter. "He went out, and that is how we got an opportunity of looking among the straw."

"But you'll hold your tongue," said Helen, now greatly terrified. "For God's sake say nothing about it. It will be as good as ten pounds a week to you."

"God forbid that I should keep the secret of murder on my conscience," returned Walter, rushing past her, and hurrying away, dragging Rose with him.

They had scarcely got out of the close when Burke and Hare came in, the latter carrying a large tea-chest in which to pack the body. To them Helen told what a discovery the Grays had made, and great was their wrath against Brogan.

"Let us murder them both," suggested Hare, with a frightful leer.

"But they are gone," exclaimed Helen, "and they will tell what they have seen."

"Thin, by the powers, it's time we had the shot up to the Square," said Burke. "In wid it, William, as fast as ye can, and I'll go for M'Culloch the porter to carry it."

They fancied that if once the body was got rid of, and in the hands of the doctors, all would be right, yet a sort of infatuation appears now to have come over them, for when, a few minutes after, Burke returned with the porter, the body still lay among the straw, and Hare and Brogan, who had now come in, were quarrelling about what the latter had done in deserting his post.

This Highland caddy must either have been very stupid or very ready to wink at what was most suspicious, for he unhesitatingly assisted them to press the body into the box, and was even careful to push in some straggling locks of hair that hung over the lid.

All being secured, the box was lifted upon his back, and he trudged off with it, having received instructions to go by

the Cowgate and up the High School Wynd, where Burke
would meet him.

Both Burke and Helen met him there. For the first time
in the history of these dark transactions, Helen accompanied
him, nay more, at the entrance to the Square, Hare and
his wife stood waiting for them, so great was the anxiety of
all four, and so eager were they to share the price of the
crime.

As fate would have it, the dissecting room was shut, and
Dr Knox and his assistants gone. The attendant was, however,
still on the premises, and he received the body and deposited
it in the cellar. Then be intimated to them that they would
require to go with him to Newington to the house of the Professor in order to get their money.

They went, and the porter accompanied them, for he was
to receive five shillings for carrying the box from the West
Port to the Square. When they got to Newington the official
went in to Dr Knox and got a portion of the price only, as the
doctor required to see the body before he could say what
should be given for it. The sum now paid was £7 10s, and the
party entered a public-house near, where it was shared, and
a glass apiece drunk in the way of friendship. Then they
returned in a band to the city, where the train was already
begun to be laid which was to result in their well-merited
destruction.

*

Walter Gray and his wife, on emerging from Tanner's
Close, crossed the street and took up a position in a dark doorway opposite. Here they saw Burke and Hare enter with the
tea-chest, and witnessed the rest of their proceedings till the
porter departed with his load, followed at a little interval by
the four associates.

They were both very much excited, though Walter was by
no means agitated with the fear and terror which almost overwhelmed Rose. The poor girl was naturally enough unhinged
by the discovery they had made; but in his breast a feeling of
indignation mingled with excitement, and thoughts of justice
and punishment joined with his pity and commiseration for
the old helpless woman who had, he doubted not, been barbarously murdered.

"Come, Rose," he remarked, "we need not stand any longer here."

"Where shall we go?" inquired his trembling wife.

"To the Police Office," was his answer. Then more tenderly and kindly he added, "My poor lass, how you tremble and shake. It is a desperate business, but who knows if this is the first person those people have murdered; others have been missed in the city of late, and perhaps they went the same way. Think of Daft Jamie that nobody knows what came of. 'Twas only the other day in the shop that I heard the doctors had got him. Now I have no doubt they have just taken that old woman's body to the same place."

"Oh, it is dreadful, Walter—it is very dreadful, and they should be punished for murdering the poor unsuspecting old woman. But yet I wish some other persons than us had made the discovery. It will bring the eyes of everybody upon us."

"Can't help that now, Rose dear," he rejoined. "We have made the discovery, and our duty is to bring the deed to light."

Walter Gray was young, ardent, and generous still. Strong drink had not deprived him of his noble nature. It had, indeed, enslaved and degraded him to a sorrowful degree; but now that he was determinedly freeing himself from the bonds of his tyrant, his wide and warm heart and true feelings were asserting their presence again.

In carrying out his present purpose he did not at first find the work so personally easy as he anticipated. Justice he found at the first approach to be suspicious, and that to a very unpleasant extent.

When they got to the Police Office they had to wait a considerable time in a large room amongst a noisy crew ere they could get speech of one of the officers; at length they obtained an interview with one named Fisher.

"Well, my man, what is your complaint?" asked the official, in rather an off-hand and careless tone.

"We have come to let you know of a murder that we strongly suspect to have been committed in the West Port."

"A murder?" repeated the officer, running his eye quickly and inquiringly over the persons of Walter and Rose.

"Yes, a murder."

"In what house, and by whom?"

"In a lodging-house off Tanner's Close, kept by an Irish-

man named Burke. He and another Irishman named Hare
have, I believe, murdered an old woman."

"Burke—Hare—never heard of them. But tell me all about
it."

Walter did so, relating all the particulars of the last
twenty-four hours. The officer listened with rather an incredu-
lous air, and scanned again and again the figures of his infor-
mants, evidently drawing an inference from these of no
favourable kind. The dress of Walter and Rose bespoke the
very deepest poverty; but, more than this, Walter's whole
appearance gave indication of the intemperance which had so
sorely reduced them.

"Now, then, how came you to be lodging in a house of this
kind?" asked the officer sharply.

Walter coloured deeply, and Rose hung her head in
silence.

"Who are you? What are you?" demanded the man, with
increasing severity.

"I am a joiner," answered the youth. "But what has this
to do with what I have told you?"

"A joiner. And are you at work?"

"Yes."

"And lodging with this girl in such a low house. Pray, is
she your wife?"

"Look ye," said Walter, with flashing eyes and angry countenance, "I came here to disclose what I believe to be a great
crime, and you have no right to insult me by such questions.
If you choose to examine into the matter, I am ready, for the
sake of public safety, to assist you; but I shall not submit to
annoyance or impertinence. Come, Rose."

"Oh, stop a bit. You have said too much to be allowed to
go away in that fashion. You must accompany me to the
house of this man Burke."

"Well, I am quite ready to do so; but ten chances to one
if you find any of them there. Knowing the discovery which I
have made, it is not likely they will return to the place."

In this Walter was mistaken. Notwithstanding that they
knew the body of the old woman had been discovered by
Gray, they manifested a most unaccountable indifference to
the fact—an indifference which can be explained only on the
principle that past success had destroyed prudence altogether.
When the officer and the Grays reached Tanner's Close,

Burke and Helen were sitting by the fire alone; and even when they saw their two lodgers enter with the policeman they were not dismayed.

"You keep a lodging-house," said the officer, looking round the apartment.

"Sure and I do."

"Where are all your lodgers?"

"Faix, thin, you've got two uv them wid yez; and bad luck to thim, for it's meself had to put thim away this afternoon for bad conduct."

"Oh, that's the way of it, is it?" said the officer, deeming that the tale told him by Walter had been invented out of spite.

"It is false, and you know it," said Walter, sternly.

"Where are your other lodgers?" asked the policeman.

"Haven't got any more."

"Where's the woman who was here last night?"

"She went away this morning. Hare, a neighbour of mine, was in the house at that time, and he'll sware to what I say."

"Have you any more witnesses to that fact?"

"Oh, more nor half a dozen."

Fisher was more and more convinced that Gray's story was nonsense, but, for form's sake, he began to examine the apartment more particularly, and, among other things, he looked at the bed, turning down the dirty clothes as he did so. On the undermost sheet he was startled to observe large splatches of dried blood.

"What's this—blood!" he exclaimed.

"I can explain that," cried Helen, in great haste, and with unmistakeable perturbation. "One of our lodgers, a young woman, a tramp, was confined here some weeks ago, and the bed was not cleaned. But about the old woman, she can easily be got if you want her. I know where she lives, and saw her on the street not an hour ago, shortly after she left."

"When did she leave?"

"At seven o'clock to-night."

"To-night! Your husband said she left in the morning."

"Oh yes, by-the-bye, it was the morning, now when I mind."

Guilt and fear had made Helen M'Dougal entirely lose her self-possession, and, in her eagerness to clear herself and Burke, she overshot the mark. The officer did not fail to notice her confusion, and for the first time a suspicion against them entered his mind.

"Oh, well," he observed, "if you can find her it is all right; only this young man tells me that he and his wife saw her dead body lying in the room this afternoon."

"Och, the dirty, mane lying blackguard!" exclaimed Burke, while Helen became pale as death, and said nothing.

Walter firmly and boldly persisted in his story; and Fisher, chiefly on account of the woman's evident confusion, resolved to take both her and Burke to the Police Office, though he was still inclined not to think seriously of the affair.

But his superior, the Superintendent of Police, entertained a different opinion when the parties appeared before him, and when he had heard Walter's story and Fisher's report of the visit he had paid to Tanner's Close. He ordered Burke and Helen to be locked up in the meantime, and set off himself to Tanner's Close, taking Fisher and Walter with him, also Mr Black, the police surgeon.

A more minute search of Burke's house was now instituted, and, while this was going on, Mrs Connoway came in and informed them that she had been brought by the Grays to see the body, recounting also what she had been cognisant of as to the proceedings of the previous evening.

"And sure now," she added, picking up something which lay among some rags in a corner, "sure that's the striped short-gown the little ould woman had on."

The Superintendent took it from her and looked at it.

"You can swear to that?" he said.

"Indade and I can, for as thin and dirty as it is it was the only decent thing the poor crayter wore."

"That looks like blood, Doctor," observed the Superintendent, pointing to a dark stain on the sleeve of the miserable-looking garment.

"It is blood," returned the Doctor, after a moment's examination.

The short-gown was taken possession of, but the rest of the rags could not be identified. The straw in which the body had lain was now under the bed, but they pulled it out, and found amongst it a quantity of blood mixed with saliva, which, the Doctor conjectured, might have come from the throat of a corpse, especially if death had been the effect of strangulation.

There was sufficient evidence now to warrant the fullest investigation; but as the hour was late, nothing further was done that night. On the following morning the same party proceeded to the rooms of Dr Knox in Surgeons' Square. Neither the students nor the professor had yet arrived, but the curator was there, and him the Superintendent began to interrogate.

"Was there a body brought here last night?"

"Yes," answered the man quite frankly, for, as he suspected nothing, he had nothing to conceal.

"What sort of a body is it?"

"Don't know. The box has not been opened. It is standing in the cellar."

"Do you know the party who brought it?"

"I do. His name is Burke. He lives in Tanner's Close, West Port."

"Show us the box."

The curator led them to the cellar, and the box was opened.

"There's the body I saw among the straw," said Walter Gray, the moment the lid was taken off. "That is the body of the little old woman."

The surgeon bent down and examined it.

"I observe some contusions," he said, "and certain marks of violence."

"Enough," returned the officer. "It must go at once to the Police Office." Then, turning to the curator, he asked, "Has that man Burke brought bodies here before?"

"O yes, freq—"

The word was arrested on the man's tongue by a loud, authoritative "Hem" behind them, and turning round, they beheld Dr Knox standing in the cellar.

"What's the matter, gentlemen?" he asked, bowing to the Superintendent and the surgeon, both of whom he knew.

"We have come about this body which was brought here last night," replied the former. "There is a suspicion that it has been murdered."

"Murdered!" echoed Knox. "Oh, nonsense!—ridiculous!"

"I am sorry to say that various things point to such a crime. The man has been arrested, and a strict investigation must take place. This box will have to go to the Police Office just as it is."

"Certainly, if you require it," said Knox, coldly.

"May I ask, Doctor, if you have got any other bodies from this man?"

"I decline to answer the question," was the answer, very stiffly delivered.

"But the ends of justice may require an answer," observed the Superintendent.

"Once for all, sir, allow me to say that I decline answering all questions," said the Professor, in a cold and haughty manner.

The other bowed in reply, and, procuring two men, removed the body to the Police Office. Justice was awaked at last.

CHAPTER XVIII

A POST-MORTEM EXAMINATION—
APPREHENSION OF HARE—IMMENSE PUBLIC
SENSATION—HARE AGREES TO BECOME
KING'S EVIDENCE—THE RAGE OF BURKE

The officers of justice immediately procured the services of
two of the most eminent medical men in Edinburgh, who,
along with the police-surgeon, made a *post-mortem* examination
of the body. The latter told his coadjutors nothing as to the
facts of the case—he revealed none of the circumstances
attending the discovery of the corpse—he stated no reason
why such a *post-mortem* examination was being made. The
examiners did, indeed, in all likelihood, conjecture that it was
in the interests of justice they were called in; but they conducted their examination in utter ignorance of the suspicions
which had been aroused.

And what was the result of their unbiassed and independent
investigation? To what opinion did they come concerning the
death of the little old woman?

It was this, that her death had been the result of violence.
There were marks and bruises on various parts of her body—
on the legs, on the shoulder, and on the head. There was a
cut on the inside of one lip, and the skin of the throat under
the chin was blue and ruffled, as from a gripe of great ferocity.
There was an effusion of blood among the spinal muscles,
and blood was also slowly coming from nose and mouth.

Looking at all these things, to what conclusion could the
examiners come but this, that the woman had been murdered?
She had not died a natural death, for all her organs were
healthy, and these various marks pointed significantly to violence and strangulation.

No sooner was this report given in than Hare and his wife
were apprehended. Who may tell how these wretches passed
the hours which intervened between the seizure of Burke and
Helen and the moment when the representatives of the law
came to Tanner's Close to secure them likewise? Their guilty
minds must have expected such a visit, yet they had taken no
means to escape—they were found together in their dingy

house, and carried off to the Calton Jail. By this time, and in spite of the endeavours of the authorities to keep the matter secret, the story had spread through the city, and with an effect positively electrical. The town was roused at once, from one end to the other, to an excitement never before paralleled. The news went that two Irishmen in Tanner's Close, along with their wives, had been taken up for murdering people and selling them to the doctors, and from that moment the names of Burke and Hare became names of horror, terror, and dread throughout the land. The wildest talk of their deeds which fear could invent were circulated and shudderingly credited. Young and old were stricken with consternation and dismay, and the public mind was roused to a pitch of the most dangerous indignation and fury. The people clamoured, nay howled, less for justice than revenge. The general popular feeling was that such monsters should have no trial, but should be given to the fury of an incensed populace, and torn to pieces in their hands.

It was now only too clearly understood how so many persons had disappeared of late and particularly what had become of Daft Jamie. Every one who had relative or friend missing came at once to the conclusion that they had been kidnapped and smothered by these fearful men, and the most exaggerated ideas of the number they had murdered prevailed in all parts of the country.

It was one of those occasions in which the deep universal heart of humanity asserts itself. The horror and indignation, the rage and fury, which culminated in an insatiable thirst for vengeance was not discreditable to the community. Indifference or common excitement in such a case would have been one of the most deplorable facts to put on record. The intense agitation, the roaring, rushing storm of unmodified wrath which raged in the heart of the populace was healthy and true in its character. Its very fierceness was a human triumph, a satisfactory testimony to the abhorrence which man feels of crimes so monstrous. If ever there was a time when the door of human mercy required to be shut and an unmitigated thirst for retribution experienced, it was when the discovery of these atrocities was made, and, accordingly, the great social heart beat with one universal, burning, throbbing desire that a terrible doom should at once overtake the West Port butchers.

Like every one in the city and throughout the country,

Jessie Brown was horrorstruck by the discovery which had been made; but her horror was doubly paralysing, for it was accompanied by the revelation of the dreadful fate of her lost friend, Mary Paterson. The disappearance of Mary, so mysterious and unaccountable, was unaccountable no longer. It was patent to her now that in the house in Gibb's Close she had been murdered by Burke, and sold, as the other victims had been, to the doctors. No sooner had this conviction forced itself upon her than she ran to the Police Office and told all she knew and all she suspected. The Police Office with the entrances to it was the scene of great popular commotion. A violently-excited crowd had assembled, whose agitation and extravagant behaviour gave token of the intensity of feeling which had been roused. The authorities were busy listening to the stories of those who came with names of missing relatives and friends; and every fresh tale, circulating through the throng, increased the ferment, till dangerous consequences began to be apprehended.

As was most natural and inevitable the public rage was vehemently directed against the doctors in Surgeons' Square. The people would not for a moment believe that they were ignorant of the murders—in fact, it was believed by not a few that Dr Knox had instigated Burke and Hare to commit the deeds, and had taught them the art of smothering, and loud voices rose on every side asking why Knox and his assistants were not apprehended.

It was through this excited multitude that Jessie Brown made her way, and not without difficulty did she struggle into the presence of the superintendent. To him she told all the particulars regarding poor Mary's disappearance, and he heard her with more interest than he had manifested in the other numerous stories which had been brought to him, the features of which he at once saw were coloured, if not altogether created by the imaginations of those who told them. But Jessie's narrative was too circumstantial and probable to be thrown aside, and he took her address, and told her that an investigation would at once be made into the matter. The investigation was made, and the girl's story was only too fully substantiated.

The authorities soon found themselves in a quandary. While they had plenty evidence to convince them that Daft Jamie, Mary Paterson, and the woman Docherty had been

murdered by those now in custody, that evidence was extremely weak as regarded its legal conduct. The doctors, in
consistency with their character all along, refused to give any
information, and as the bodies of the two first had not been
seen, there was no direct proof that they were murdered. One
very natural and significant piece of evidence had, indeed,
been obtained. When Burke was searched, Daft Jamie's brass
snuff-box was found upon him, and identified by his weeping
mother. But in a criminal court a brass snuff-box could do
little to convict of murder. As regarded the case of the little
old woman, the evidence was much more ample, but not such
as to bring home guilt to any particular person.

In these circumstances, the Lord Advocate and those
charged with the interests of justice felt themselves in a most
perplexing situation. The enraged people were calling for
vengeance, and if, for want of evidence, the law failed to
secure within its retributive grasp those of whose guilt every
one was assured, the mob would in their rage be certain to
break out in open and dangerous riot.

Things were in this position when one afternoon Fisher,
the detective,[1] entered the Superintendent's room in the Police
Office, and informed the chief of the establishment that the
Lord Advocate desired to see him in his chambers. The Superintendent at once put on his hat, and went round to Parliament Square. Sir William Rae sat in his private room alone,
and wore an air of gravity and anxiety. Before him lay all the
papers connected with the Burke and Hare case. Having
motioned to the Superintendent to take a chair, he thus
addressed him—

"I wish to consult you about these West Port murders. I
have just gone over the papers, and find that the evidence is
most unsatisfactory—in fact, worthless as it stands. If we put
these four persons at the bar without more proof than we now
have, the jury cannot convict them. Now, an acquittal would
be a palpable failure of justice, and in the present inflamed
temper of the people, would be sure to produce the most
serious consequences. Something really must be done."

---

1. Anachronistic. OED specifies "detective" does not come into use until
1843.

"Would your lordship think of securing one of them as a *socius criminis?*"[2] asked the chief of police.

"My very idea," returned Sir William. "But two will be required. In fact, two only would be practicable. If, for instance, one of the women were tried, she would not consent to criminate her husband; but if both husband and wife were taken, their evidence would convict the other two, and this, I believe, is all that justice can accomplish."

"I have no doubt whatever, Sir William, that you have suggested the only way out of the difficulty," returned the other. "Which prisoner would your Lordship advise should be first tried?"

"I think Hare. I have no doubt that the whole four of them are guilty. Still, there are probably degrees of guilt attaching to each, and it strikes me that Burke, who I am told is the strongest man, would have the largest share in the actual murder. I would advise, then, that you should first apply to Hare and his wife."

"It shall be done immediately," returned the Superintendent, starting up.

"Of course, if Hare should refuse, then attempt Burke. Promise immunity as the price of information."

The Superintendent nodded and took his leave. "Fisher is the man for this mission," he muttered, as he crossed the Parliament Square.

Fisher was soon found, and a few words sufficed to let him understand what was wanted by the Lord Advocate. As in duty bound, he was quite ready to take the matter in hand, and departed at once to the jail.

The four prisoners were confined apart, and the jailer led him to the cell occupied by Hare, into which he introduced him, and left the two together.

Hare sat on the side of his wooden bed, and as Fisher looked at his sloping forehead and small oval eyes, set far apart, his high cheek bones, and frightful mouth, he thought he never had beheld such a loathsome and repulsive countenance. The mixture of cunning, brutality, and cruelty which the gruesome face exhibited was sickening even to this police officer, who had come in contact with criminals

---

2. Associates in crime.

of all degrees of guilt and ferocity, and it was not without a cold shiver creeping over him that he opened the conversation.

Hare on seeing him gave a scowl. The days which he had passed in that silent cell in enforced sobriety had given him time and opportunity to reflect on his position, and his coward heart trembled with apprehension. The sight of the officer who had apprehended him and his wife was most unwelcome—hence the scowl.

"Well, my man," began Fisher, "you and your companions have got into a pretty mess. You are charged with more murders than that of the old woman."

"Indade," rejoined Hare, sullenly. "What others, might I ax?"

"Daft Jamie and Mary Paterson," answered Fisher, with intended bluntness, scrutinising at the same time with great keenness Hare's vile and villainous countenance.

The wretch winced but remained silent. He was cunning enough to say nothing which would criminate himself or any of the others.

"Might it not be as well for you to make a clean breast of it?" suggested Fisher.

"Och, go along wid yez," returned Hare, with another scowl. "Isn't it a mane and dirty thing uv ye to thry to get round me in that way. Ye needn't bother yerself at all, at all, for divil a word will ye get out uv me to carry back to them that sent ye."

"Oh, very well," said Fisher, carelessly. "The offer I was going to make you I shall make to Burke, and I think he'll jump at it pretty smart."

On hearing these words Hare's eyes gave an unmistakeable twinkle, which Fisher saw, but without noticing it he turned and walked leisurely towards the door of the cell.

"Well, thin," said Hare, in a changed tone, "ye needn't be in such a mighty hurry. Sure if ye have anything to say to me ye might be afther doin' it plump and plain."

"I will," said Fisher, wheeling suddenly round, and confronting him. "I will be plain and frank both. The fact is, the evidence we have got is not sufficient to convict any of you of these murders, and the Lord Advocate has resolved to admit one of you as evidence against the others. I have come to you to give you the first chance; but as you incline to refuse,

I'll give it to Burke, and I know he'll not be such a fool. He'll save his own neck and make you swing for it."

The wily detective turned again towards the door, and made as if he was about to knock for the turnkey to let him out; but, as he expected, Hare spoke in time to prevent this.

"Och, now, this is some blarney uv yer own yer spakin'," he said, with an air of eagerness which Fisher did not fail to observe, and which convinced him that his object would be accomplished.

"No, it is the truth," resumed the officer; "on condition that you tell all about the business, you'll get off with nothing done to you. Do you agree to this?"

Hare remained silent for some minutes, and Fisher stood patiently waiting for him to answer, watching narrowly all the while the expression of his loathsome countenance. That expression gradually grew into something fiendish, for a horrible leer proceeded from the large mouth—the old leer of satisfaction which the monster never failed to manifest at the prospect of anything personally profitable.

"Would ye be afther takin' my wife as a witness, too?" he at length asked.

"Yes," returned Fisher. "Whoever I make the bargain with, the woman is included."

"And nothing will be done to us?"

"Nothing. If you tell the truth, and give full information against Burke and his wife, you will after the trial be set free."

"Begora thin, I'll do it," said Hare with another leer. "It was Burke that murdered all the three."

"Stop, stop," interrupted Fisher. "You will give your information only under examination, and that will be to-morrow."

And as he spoke he knocked loudly at the door of the cell.

At this Hare's cowardly heart took alarm, and he hastily exclaimed—

"It's a bargain, thin. You don't mane to go back?"

"Don't be afraid. I am only going to see that your wife is confined in the same cell with yourself. To-morrow morning you will be both ready for your examination."

"Throth and we will," responded Hare, chuckling now with satisfaction. The thought that his own neck would escape the gallows made his craven nature merry. Of course he had no compunction at giving up Burke to the hangman. The tie that bound these men together was a tie of crime only, not of friendship, still less of affection. It is probable that Burke would have hesitated more on the score of consideration for his accomplice had the same offer been made to him, but there is little doubt that he, too, would have saved himself by turning informer against the other.

The Lord-Advocate, as we have seen, decided on giving Hare the chance of escape in preference to Burke, on the supposition that the largest share of guilt attached to the latter. Here, however, he was mistaken. If any difference of degree in criminality existed between wretches so horribly guilty, Hare was the worst of the two. He it was who originally suggested the idea of murder, and he was the chief instigator to every separate crime. There was also this difference between them, that whereas Burke required whisky to nerve him to the bloody work, and to drown the terror which reflection brought, Hare had no need for drink either for the one purpose or the other. He was so utterly callous and hardened, so cruel and pitiless, as to be able to do his part of the deed without either a previous stimulant or a subsequent sedative. There was still a faint shadow of humanity in Burke's soul, but none in his—he seemed to be wholly a fiend.

The day following, Hare and his wife were examined, both of them said much to criminate Burke, but not a word against themselves. According to Hare's account, he was only cognisant of, not a participator in, the murders. He had seen Burke commit them, he had sat in a chair in the room while he smothered the victims, and he had received a portion of the money got from the doctors for the bodies, but this was all he had to do with the matter—nothing more—neither him nor his wife, who never saw anything of the kind going on.

Of course, the authorities saw that this was a most evident falsehood, so far as regarded Hare's share in the deeds, and they looked forward with much misgiving to the effect such gross perjury would have on the jury at the trial. But bad as Hare's evidence was, they were shut up to present it, for without it no conviction could possibly take place, and should the law be unable to punish the doers of atrocities whose horrible character had roused Scotland to its centre, a fierce outbreak of the people was to be apprehended. So they had but one choice for their adoption, and preparations were made to try Burke and Helen M'Dougal, with Hare and his wife as the chief witnesses against them.

*

It was on a dark, gloomy November day that the citation was served on Burke to stand his trial for three different murders before the High Court of Justiciary on the 24th day of December. He took the paper quite carelessly from the hands of the officer, and without any emotion began to read it.

A year's idleness and rioting had made him fat, and having been deprived of whisky since his incarceration, he had regained his natural freshness of complexion, so that those who saw him now looked upon a strong, large-boned, fleshy man, a trifle under the middle size, of a countenance not unpleasant, and with manners that were even polite. At times, in the solitude of his cell, he was observed to give way to irritation and to become restless, as if mentally ill at ease, but for the most part he maintained a quiet composure, and looked anything but the ferocious murderer that he was.

At night, however, in the utter darkness by which he was surrounded, he had many wakeful and wretched hours, for then memory rose up, darker a thousand times than the murkiness of night, and the many murders of the bygone year crowded their terrible scenes upon his recollection. He saw the starting eyeballs of the victims glaring up at him as they lay upon the floor; he heard their stifled cries and the choking noise in their throats; but above and before all, he saw the white face and wistful look of the poor helpless dumb boy, which had never ceased to haunt him since the hour when he had crushed out his young innocent life, and laid him on the bed by the side of his dead grandmother.

The wretched man would lie on his hard pallet trembling with superstitious terror, and when at length he fell into a slumber it was troubled by frightful visions, and in an agony of terror he would awake and start up, with the fear-sweat standing in beads on his burning brow. Truly the serpent of retribution was beginning to coil itself round his soul, and send its pangs into his guilty conscience.

By day, however, and while the eyes of others were upon

him, he managed to maintain an air of calmness and even indifference. The fact was, he was shrewd enough to know that the evidence against him and the rest was scanty, and in a legal sense deficient. He, therefore, entertained the idea that they would get off, and this it was which kept him cool and apparently unconcerned.

When he opened the citation which had been served on him, the jailor and officer lingered in the cell, anxious to see what effect would be produced when he read the names of the witnesses. Their curiosity was fully rewarded, for no sooner had he caught sight of Hare's name and that of his wife than a look of amazement came into his face.

"What the devil does this mane at all, at all?" he inquired. "Begora, thin, they've got Hare and Mary among the witnesses."

"Of course," remarked the officer; "they are the principal witnesses against you."

"Against me!" repeated Burke, utterly aghast.

"Yes; Hare and his wife have turned king's evidence."[3]

A roar of rage and a tremendous oath burst from Burke's lips at the same moment, and starting to his feet he stood glaring with eyes that blazed like candles. He was like a wild beast suddenly lashed to fury and brought to bay.

"King's evidence!" he shouted. "He's going to give me up, is he?"

"He's going to save his own neck by putting the rope round yours," added the officer, with a significant nod.

Burke's face became fearfully distorted, his broad chest heaved convulsively, his eyes rolled wildly to and fro, and shot forth flashes of lurid fire, and his hands clenched together, till the paper he held rustled in his grasp. Then, with another roar of foaming fury, he threw himself on the pallet, and gave vent to a torrent of frantic curses.

---

3. Witness for the state, thus exempt from prosecution.

CHAPTER XIX

THE TRIAL OF BURKE AND
HELEN M'DOUGAL

Early on the morning of Wednesday, the twenty-fourth of December, there was a great stir in the High Street of Edinburgh. By seven o'clock, and ere the grey, cold winter dawn had broke in silence on the city, many people might be seen by the hazy light of the street lamps converging towards one point—viz., Parliament Square. There was eager excitement in their faces and gestures, and a general manifestation of intense agitated interest, that showed how strongly moved they were in prospect of the event which was that day to take place.

That event was the trial of Burke and Helen M'Dougal.

The people as they entered Parliament Square took up their position in front of the door of the High Court of Justiciary; and as the morning wore on, and the light of day began to steal over the scene, it fell upon a large compact crowd, which every moment was augmenting, the purpose of whose individual constituents was to gain admittance to the Court-room when the door should be opened.

Long before the hour at which this was done, the multitude assembled in the Square was large enough to fill the small Court-room several times over, and it became apparent that those only who were near the door would obtain an entrance, and fewer even of those than might have been anticipated, for a large number of persons who had influence with the officials of the Court were—all unknown to the promiscuous mass in the Square—being admitted by another and more private door in a distant part of the building, so that even before the doors were opened at all the place was nearly filled. The jurymen and witnesses were also admitted by a private door out of sight of the multitude.

The popular excitement being so great, the authorities were apprehensive of a riot, and a strong body of police and the military at the Castle were kept in readiness to restrain any outbreak that might take place.

At length the doors were opened, and a fearful rush took

place. Women screamed, men cursed and swore, and tremendous efforts were made by every one to accomplish what was really impossible. In a very few moments, and while the struggle was at its height, the doors were closed again, and the announcement made that the Court was full. This seemed incredible, and the swaying crowd would not believe it. But it was true, nevertheless. Those who had managed to wriggle through the open doors almost immediately filled up the remaining seats, and the place was crammed, nay choked, in every part.

A more splendid bar never assembled to conduct a trial. The poverty of the prisoners did not permit of their feeing counsel for their defence; but their peculiar notoriety had prompted the most eminent advocates at the bar to defend them without money and without price. On behalf of Burke there appeared Sir J. Moncrieff, who was then Dean of faculty, and Mr P. Robertson, afterwards known as Lord Robertson, while Helen M'Dougal had for her powerful defender, Henry Cockburn, who subsequently, as everybody knows, was also elevated to the bench.

The prosecution was of course conducted by the Lord Advocate, Sir Wm. Rae, assisted by his advocates-depute, among whom we believe was Alison, the future historian of Europe. The Judges who sat to try the case were Lord Justice-Clerk Boyle, and Lords Meadowbank, M'Kenzie, and Pitmilly, and so, in the hands of the most eminent legal talent of Scotland, one of the most important and exciting trials that ever took place in any country was proceeded with.

When the prisoners made their appearance in the dock, the sensation throughout the Court was extreme. It was with something like breathless horror that the densely packed mass looked upon the man whose name had for weeks been a fearful household word in every house in the city, and yet the being presented to their gaze had by no means the appearance of the monster which their imaginations had pictured. They looked upon a quiet, composed, and not unpleasant-faced man, between thirty and forty years of age, who had a decided Irish cast of countenance, but which presented little appearance of cruelty or brutality. It was even mild, good-natured, and intelligent. The people were evidently non-plussed. They expected to see a loathsome, savage-looking, repulsive wretch; and, instead, there was presented to their

view a short thick-set man, dressed in a threadbare blue
surtout, who seemed little moved by his awful situation.
His companion was much more agitated than himself.
Helen M'Dougal, dressed in a checked shawl and faded green
bonnet, looked wildly and fearfully round upon the hundreds
of eyes that glared upon her, and gave evident signs of terror
and dread.

When the indictment was about to be read, the junior
counsel for Burke objected to this being done; but Lord Boyle
having repelled the objection, it was read out at full length
amid the most breathless silence, every ear being strained to
catch the minutest word.

It charged Burke with the murders of Mary Paterson, Daft
Jamie, and Mrs Docherty—Helen M'Dougal being indicted
for the last-named crime alone.

When the reading was finished, Burke's counsel spoke up
again, contending that it was contrary to the law of Scotland
for two panels to be tried under an indictment containing
three charges against one, and one charge only against the
other. A long argument ensued, ending in this that the Judges
recommended the Lord Advocate to waive the two first
charges against Burke in the meanwhile, and lead proof concerning the last—the murder of Docherty, with which both
prisoners stood equally charged. This the prosecutor agreed
to, and the examination of witnesses began.

There was the publican in the West Port, who told that,
on the morning of the last day of October, the little old
woman came into his shop asking charity. He did not say how
gruffly and peremptorily he had refused her request, but he
stated that Burke was in the shop at the time, and went out
immediately behind the beggar woman. He saw Burke accost
her, speak with her for a minute or two, go across the street,
and enter the close leading to his dwelling, the little old
woman following close behind him.[1]

There was Mrs Connoway, who lived on the opposite side
of the passage, and she told how on Hallowe'en night she
heard a great singing of Irish songs in Burke's house, and
much mirth and revelry going on, whereupon, being Irish
herself, she went in and saw the little old woman dancing and

---

1. It was the shop boy who testified.

singing under the influence and excitement of liquor. She recounted how they became very friendly at once—how the little old woman accompanied her to her own house, the others following—how they danced and sang there for an hour, and then returned to Burke's, where subsequently she heard a great noise of struggling and fighting, accompanied with one or two fearful shrieks. She continued her evidence by telling how she went in next morning and found Docherty gone, being told by Helen M'Dougal that she had ejected her, as she had got impudent and too familiar with her husband;[2] and, finally, she related how in the evening of that day Mrs Gray rushed into her house greatly excited, and asked her to come and see the little woman's dead body lying naked among the straw.

The interest of the listeners in the Court became more intense as the chain of evidence led nearer and nearer to the murder. Previous to the trial the facts had been kept as private as possible, and to the people they were almost new. The reading of the indictment gave them to understand what to expect, and as the proof began to give promise of bearing out the indictment, which stated the fact, the mode, and the purpose of the murder, the attention of the crowded Court became fascinated as by a spell.

The evidence of the Grays deepened and intensified the universal interest still more. There was a perfect hush of silence as, falteringly and low, yet with distinctness, Rose told all the particulars she knew—how the little old woman had been brought into the house by Burke in the early part of the day— how Helen M'Dougal had set her to clean the house, and that the two women were thus engaged till the evening, when Burke and Hare and Hare's wife came in, and forthwith a scene of revelry began, which continued till near midnight, when Burke came and said that she (the witness) and her husband would require to sleep in Hare's house that night, as the little old woman must have their bed. Then Rose went on to speak of their going to Hare's house, and returning in the morning, when the little old woman was no longer to be seen; and when such contradictory accounts of her departure were given by Burke and Helen that their suspicions were

---

2. Again, reference to familiarity with Burke is cut in 1885.

roused, and they resolved to keep watch. The tragic element became to the listeners something almost unbearable as Rose detailed the succeeding circumstances—the incident which directed their attention to the straw, and made them think the body was concealed there—the watch set upon that particular spot by Burke in the person of the youth John Brogan, who ultimately in the afternoon, when all the others were out, deserted his post, and left the watchers free to examine the straw. The stealthy entrance of the watchers into the apartment, their approach to the straw, Walter bending down to examine it, and the cold, horrible touch of the dead hand, were all details which wound the audience up to the highest pitch of excitement; and then when the description was given of the straw being hurriedly tossed aside, and the naked, bruised, distorted body fully revealed, a thrill of unspeakable horror ran through every frame.

Walter's testimony served to relieve the mental tension, for, being to the same purport, a repetition of the facts already known allowed the effect of the first disclosure to modify itself. As the young man proceeded with his evidence he grew into the hero of the hour, for it became clearly apparent that he it was who had brought the series of unparalleled atrocities to light, and by terminating the career of the murderers had in all probability saved many lives. He was looked upon, therefore, with immense favour by the people, and when he left the box, after recounting the course he took in making the matter known to the authorities, a cheer that would not be repressed rang through the Court.

Next came the police officials, the curator of the hall in Surgeons' Square,[3] and M'Culloch the porter, by whose evidence the body of the murdered woman was traced to the hands of Dr Knox, where, only too obviously, other victims had gone.

By this time the hours of the short December day had passed, and the twilight of the Christmas eve began to cast the Court-room into deepening shadow. These hours had passed like so many minutes, so absorbed were the people in the revelations of the trial. The place was now lighted up, and a

---

3. There was debate at the time as to whether David Paterson was more than a door-keeper for Knox (McCracken-Flesher, 42).

strange, weird aspect it presented. The Judges on the bench in their gaudy robes; the advocates in their black gowns and grey horse-hair wigs; the two mute statues of flesh and blood at the bar; and the sea of faces in the background, made up a picture of the most impressive description.

The next witness was one whose appearance was wildly looked for, and received with a shudder of loathing abhorrence. It was *Hare*, and as he ascended the witness box, and the light shone strongly on his repulsive countenance, revealing it in its hideousness of expression, the people instinctively thought that the ideal of a murderer stood before them.

Burke had manifested no feeling or emotion till now, but when his eyes fell on Hare a red gleam flashed from them, and he regarded his associate and instigator and prompter in crime with a fearful scowl. It was then that those who looked upon him could see the fiend in his nature, and understood how he could clutch a helpless fellow-being by the throat, and ruthlessly crush out the life. Had he been free at the moment, and with Hare in his power, there is little doubt but he would have killed him in his fury.

The traitor looked everywhere but at the dock where the prisoners sat. Evidently he dreaded to catch sight of Burke, and stood looking round the crowded Court, meeting with his horrid leer the looks of hate and terror which his presence inspired. For a full minute he stood thus under the silent universal gaze. The very Judges regarded him with fixed attention and something like curiosity, while all the advocates and officials made him the object of their undisguised scrutiny.

Then the mockery of administering the oath was proceeded with, and, without the least compunction or hesitation, the wretch swore to "tell the truth, the whole truth, and nothing but the truth."

We shall not here repeat the tissue of manifest lies of which his evidence consisted, in verbatim form, but shall give the substance of his story as drawn forth by the questions of the Lord Advocate, and to avoid his Irish phrases we shall put the account in the third person.

According to Hare's statement, then, he and Burke met on the street in the West Port on the last day of October, and Burke asked him into a public-house to have a glass. When there Burke told him that there was an old woman at home whom he was going to murder—that he had lured her from the street for this purpose, and that she would be a good *shot* to take to the doctors. He then asked Hare to go down with him to the house and see her. He went, and saw her washing a gown. He remained about five minutes, and then went home. After dark he returned, and there was a jolly party in Burke's house—drinking, singing, and dancing. They all went to Connoway's house across the passage, and remained there a while, after which they returned to Burke's house. Hare did not imagine Burke was going to murder the little old woman that night, but just after they had got in from Connoway's, all at once Burke got angry and insolent, asked Hare what business he had in his house, and struck him. Hare immediately struck back, and a bit of fighting ensued, when immediately the little old woman came between them to separate them, and got knocked over. At this moment Hare gave up fighting, and went and lay down in the bed, when Burke in a moment sprang upon the woman ere she had time to rise from the floor, and lay heavily down upon her. She gave a loud shriek, and at the same instant Helen M'Dougal and his own wife ran into the passage. Burke now laid himself more firmly down upon the woman, pressed her head with his breast, laid one hand on her nose and mouth, and gripped her throat with the other, holding her thus for fifteen minutes, at the end of which time she was dead. All this time Hare did nothing. He merely rose from the bed, sat down on a chair, and looked on. He laid not a finger on the woman in the way of violence, but waited and saw Burke rise from her dead body, strip her naked, double her up, throw her down by the end of the bed, and put straw upon her. After this the women returned, and the party had more drink, when Burke went and brought in the attendant at the rooms of Dr Knox. After this they all lay down and fell asleep, and the night following they got a box and took the body to Surgeons' Square, then went to Dr Knox's house at Newington, got five pounds, and divided it between them.

Such was the incredible tissue of falsehoods told by the leering, infamous miscreant. Not one of these hundreds of listeners but saw that he was lying, and not a doubt was felt that he was as much concerned in the murder as was Burke. The counsel for the prisoners subjected him to a searching cross-examination, and in various ways strove to get him to admit that he and Burke had been engaged in other murders besides this; but he was told by the Bench that he need not answer such questions unless he chose, and he was cunning enough not to choose. He remained silent, but his silence was as convincing to those present as his confession would have been.

Once only when he was delivering his fabrication his eyes met those of Burke, and instantly quailed before their scorching glare. He turned white, and for a moment trembled; but instantly averting his gaze he recovered his audacity.

When he left the Court it was in charge of an officer, and his exit was greeted by the hisses and groans of the spectators, which the Bench immediately suppressed.

Hare's wife followed, and her appearance also produced the strongest aversion. A more dirty, slatternly, sensual, passionate-looking woman eye could not look on. She carried her child in her arms, and simpered and smiled in the most disgusting fashion. She was the very incarnation of debased womanhood. Her small, twinkling eyes, bleared and red; her freckled, loathsome face, and matted, sandy hair, made her an object of unmitigated detestation.

Her story was a corroboration of Hare's. They had concocted their lie well, and stuck to it with malignant tenacity. The counsel for the defence did, indeed, tear her answers to pieces, and hold them up to withering scorn. She was surprised into an acknowledgement of having seen "such tricks" before, and in various respects showed yet more clearly that the whole four were equally guilty.

It was near midnight when the evidence was completed. Through the whole day the people kept their seats, and seemed to feel neither hunger nor fatigue, so intensely absorbed were they in the trial and the horrors it revealed. Outside the excitement had been of the most tremendous description. Occasionally a scrap of information as to the proceedings of the Court found its way to the Parliament Square, and flew like wildfire over the city. Exaggerations, too, and false rumours were spread, which made the people think the murderers would get off, and this so roused the popular indignation that the authorities had the utmost difficulty in keeping the city quiet.

The night was cold and frosty, but multitudes waited on at the entrance to the Court to learn the issue. Hour after hour passed, the dawn of another day drew near, and still the doors were closed. One or two, unable longer to bear the suffocating atmosphere and the protracted confinement, made their way out, and communicated to the heaving mass of people that the advocates were addressing the jury, and the multitude kept hanging on expecting every minute that the trial would close and the verdict be declared.

The speeches of the Crown prosecutor and the counsel for the prisoner occupied six hours. That of the Lord Advocate, though strongly worded, was not vehement. He pressed for a verdict of guilty against both prisoners, as one who spoke from a thorough consciousness of their guilt, and who personally felt the deepest abhorrence of their crimes. He looked and spoke as one under a pressing sense of responsibility and anxiety—he was then and there the guardian of human life and public safety, as well as the accusing angel of justice; and if these prisoners at the bar escaped the punishment which they so clearly merited, then he feared, and justly feared, that the public demand for justice and retribution would be manifested in scenes of wildest violence. But, convinced himself beyond all shadow of doubt that they were guilty, the strength of that conviction caused him to assume the same fact as regarded the jury, and he felt that the cause he had to sustain was not one which he required to plead for. His chief anxiety was about the evidence of Hare and his wife. He could not suppose for a moment that one of the fifteen who listened to him believed that the *socii criminis* spoke the truth, and if they should on that account reject their evidence, then that which remained would not be sufficient for conviction. He set himself, therefore, to anticipate the objections which were sure to be taken by the prisoners' counsel, and to satisfy the minds of the jury themselves, by labouring to show that Hare's testimony, though suspicious, and as regarded himself not trustworthy, yet there could be little doubt indeed that Hare told the truth as to Burke's own share in the crime. He might not have done the deed without assistance, as Hare represented, but assuredly he was the principal criminal. To that extent Hare's evidence and the evidence of his wife was to be credited.

The speech of the Dean of Faculty in behalf of Burke was powerful and trenchant. He addressed himself chiefly to the weak point in the prosecutor's case—the want of good independent evidence, and the presence of the bad incredible testimony of the two participants, which, the speaker contended, was not worth the slightest particle of consideration, and which the jury should scornfully and indignantly reject.

Mr Cockburn followed in behalf of Helen M'Dougal and it has been often said that a more brilliant display of forensic eloquence was never made in a Court of Justice. He likewise tore the evidence of Hare and his wife scornfully to tatters, and spoke of themselves in the following terms:—

"A couple of such witnesses, in point of mere external manner and appearance, never did my eyes behold. Hare was a squalid wretch, on whom the habits of his disgusting trade, want, and profligacy, seem to have been long operating in order to produce a monster whose will, as well as his poverty, will consent to the perpetration of the darkest crimes. The Lord Advocate's back was to the woman, else he would not have professed to have seen nothing revolting in her appearance. I never saw a face in which the lines of profligacy were more distinctly marked."[4]

The effect of these two powerful speeches, in as far as they might work on the feelings, and even mislead the judgment of the jury, was corrected by the summing up of the Lord Justice-Clerk, who took the same view of the evidence of Hare and his wife as the Lord Advocate had done. He also gave a masterly analysis of the whole evidence, and that in a manner so strongly against both parties that every one in the Court felt that they must be condemned.

The jury then retired, and there followed that period of awful suspense for the prisoners, and of intense, impatient restlessness for the spectators, called "waiting for the verdict." Burke, cool and indifferent as he had been throughout the trial, was the same still; but Helen was strongly agitated now.

"Arrah, don't be afther breakin' down that way, Nelly," whispered Burke, in her ear. "It's all up wid both uv us, and whin the Judge passes sentence just look at me all the time and do as ye see me do."

"Oh, William!" sobbed the wretched woman; "I always dreaded that this day would come."

---

4. Buchanan, 182.

The momentous minutes passed, and half-suppressed whis-
perings were heard in all parts of the Court. The light of the
Christmas morning, which had been for some time struggling
in through the high windows, and trying to conquer the
yellow artificial light within, was growing stronger every
instant, and making the flame of the candles look sickly and
feeble. The advancing daylight also revealed the wan and
worn faces of those who, for twenty-four hours, had watched
through the long trial. Pale, colourless and almost ghostly
many of the countenances were, but the eyes were bright with
fierce expectancy, and every one, probably even the prisoners
themselves, were longing for the return of the jury, that the
unbearable suspense might be ended.

At length the bell rang, and a violent sensation passed like
an electric shock through the crowded Court. Every eye was
turned to the open door, and when the jurymen appeared one
by one, grave and solemn, people strove to read the result in
their faces.

The few moments they took to get seated seemed ages to
the feverishly excited people, but at length the last was in his
place, and amid breathless silence the foreman rose to deliver
the verdict—

"The jury unanimously find the libel against Helen
M'Dougal NOT PROVEN."[5]

"Nell, you are out of the scrape," said Burke, with the
utmost coolness, and in a tone loud enough to be heard over
all the silent Court.

"The jury unanimously find the prisoner, William Burke,
GUILTY as libelled."

Like the rush of a pent-up stream when the sluice is raised,
the announcement of the verdict produced a sudden, vehement,
indescribable sound in the Court. Every breast seemed to have
given a full sigh of relief and satisfaction, and the word Guilty
passed as on swiftest wings to the outside, where the dense
multitude waited, and immediately the air was rent by the
most tremendous shouts, which must have startled the echoes
of old St Giles, and might almost have penetrated the stony

---

5. A verdict peculiar to Scotland that does not prove a case but finds
enough evidence to withhold the determination "not guilty".

ears of King Charles' statue. The shouts, many times repeated, were taken up by the people on the High Street, and in a few minutes the welcome news flew through the city, and produced a fierce, stern, universal pleasure.

CHAPTER XX

THE BEGINNING OF RETRIBUTION

GUILTY! That word sounding through the hushed and breathless court was the first stroke of retribution. It had been long delayed, and the crimes to be avenged had accumulated to a fearful extent; but it had come now, and its first blow was at an hour of solemn and emphatic significance. It was precisely one year before—on the Christmas morning of 1827—that Burke and Hare had murdered their first victim— the old woman from Gilmerton.[1] A year had run its course since then—a year crowded with black atrocities—sixteen in number, at least; and there stood one of the murderers, at the end of the completed cycle, pronounced guilty, and set aside to undergo the law's heaviest doom. At that dread moment it is not likely that Burke's mind reverted to this fact; but shall we not look upon it as more than a coincidence—as the spirit of sternest outraged justice marking with its deepest seal of reprobation the unparalleled and fiend-like crimes—connecting in an unmistakeable way the guilt with the punishment? Ay, and in a very little we shall find a further and still more striking manifestation of the same retributive significance.

Burke heard that part of the verdict which sealed his fate with the same coolness and indifference which he had displayed through the whole twenty-four hours—for that was the exact period which the trial had occupied. Not a muscle of his face moved, neither did the colour of his countenance change. He remained calm and composed—the least agitated, in fact, of any in that assembly. He had, in truth, days before, made up his mind as to the result. From the moment he knew that Hare and his wife were to appear as witnesses against him, he had not the slightest doubt but he would be condemned. Hence he indulged in no hope, and when the word "Guilty" was pronounced he was neither surprised nor dis-

---

1. Burke's confession to George Tait, Sheriff-Substitute, gave old Donald as dying naturally "about Christmas 1827", and the old woman from Gilmerton as murdered "early last Spring" (Buchanan, Appendix to the Supplement, 32–33).

appointed, but heard it with an outward equanimity which surprised every beholder—disgusting as well as surprising them, for it gave a still more terrible idea of his hardened and brutified nature.

His companion did not show the same absence of emotion. She started wildly round to the jury, and seemed about to make a frantic appeal to them. Her strong affection for Burke was the only redeeming quality in this woman—the only lingering trace of something human in her; and now, careless of the fact that she herself was saved from the gallows, she was wildly agitated by the declaration which she full well knew consigned her companion to death.

Before she had time to utter a word Burke touched her arm and whispered something in her ear, which restrained her, and, burying her face in her hands, she burst into tears.

When the verdict was recorded, and the Lord-Advocate moved for sentence, the latter was proposed by Lord Meadowbank, and the following is a part of his address:—

"My Lord,—I am confident that there is no chance of my being contradicted when I say that in the history of this country—nay, in the whole history of civilised society—there never has been exhibited such a system of barbarous and savage iniquity, or anything at all corresponding in atrocity to what this trial has brought to light. Individual murders have been committed, crimes of all descriptions have been perpetrated; but that there should, at this time of day, in this country, have been found to be regularly organised and established a system of cold and premeditated murder such as we have now heard of was, I am sure, beyond the imaginations of your lordships to have conceived. Had one individual been found so utterly divested of all human feeling as to have been guilty of the offences here brought to light, your lordships might have well been amazed and horrified; but that there should have existed in this great and populous city not one individual only, but apparently a number of individuals, both male and female, leagued and combined together for the purpose of sacrificing their unoffending fellow-citizens, for the sordid purpose of selling their bodies, is inexpressibly horrible, and to one feeling for the character of his country, in the last degree humiliating. It would be in vain that I should search for words to express the ideas which the general announcement of such a system of horrible atrocity must necessarily create, but your lordships are bound, for the sake of public justice, to express the feelings which you entertain of one of the most terrific and monstrous delineations of human depravity that has ever been brought under your consideration."[2]

The other assistant judges briefly endorsed Lord Meadowbank's sentiments, and the sentence of death which he proposed, when the Lord Justice-Clerk assumed the black cap that he might officially pronounce it.

"*William Burke*," said the Judge, in a grave and solemn tone.

Burke at once rose to his feet, and stood straight and firm in the dock, calm and stoical as ever.

His Lordship prefaced the sentence by the following appropriate remarks:—

"You now stand convicted by the verdict of a most respectable jury of your country of the atrocious murder charged against you in this indictment, upon evidence which carried conviction to the mind of every man that heard it in establishing your guilt of that offence. I agree so completely with Lord Meadowbank, who has so fully and eloquently described the nature of your horrid crime, that I will not occupy the time of the Court in commenting upon it further than by saying that one of a blacker description—more atrocious in point of cold-blooded deliberation and systematic arrangement, and where the motives were so comparatively base—never was exhibited in the annals of this or any other court of justice. I have no intention to detain this audience by repeating what has been so well expressed by my brother. My duty is of a different nature, for if ever it was clear beyond all possibility of a doubt that the sentence of a criminal court will be carried into execution in any case, yours is that one, and you may rest assured that you have now no other duty to perform on earth but to prepare in the most suitable manner for appearing before the throne of Almighty God, to answer for this crime and for every other that you have been guilty of during your life. The necessity of repressing offences of this most extraordinary and alarming description precludes the possibility of your entertaining the slightest hope that there will be any alteration upon your sentence. In regard to your case, the

---

2. Pae merges speeches reported in Buchanan, 195–96, and 197.

only doubt that has come across my mind is whether, in order to mark the sense the Court entertains of your offence, and which the violated laws of the country entertain respecting it, your body should not be exhibited in chains, in order to deter others from the like crimes in time coming. But, taking into consideration that the public eye would be offended with so dismal an exhibition, I am disposed to agree that your sentence shall be put in execution in the usual way, but accompanied with the statutory attendant of the punishment of the crime of murder—namely, that your body shall be publicly dissected and anatomised. And I trust that if it is ever customary to preserve skeletons, yours will be preserved, in order that posterity may keep in remembrance your atrocious crimes. I would entreat you to betake yourself immediately to a thorough repentance, and to humble yourself in the sight of Almighty God. Call instantly to your aid the ministers of religion of whatever persuasion you are. Avail yourself from this hour forward of their instructions, so that you may be brought in a suitable manner urgently to implore pardon from an offended God. I need not allude to any other case than that which has occupied our attention these many hours. You are conscious in your own mind whether the other charges that were exhibited against you yesterday morning were such as might be established against you or not. I refer to them again merely for the purpose of again recommending that you may devote the few days that you are on earth to imploring forgiveness from Almighty God. The sentence of the Court is that you, William Burke, be taken from the bar back to the Tolbooth of Edinburgh, there to be fed on bread and water only, until Wednesday the 28th day of January next, and upon that day to be taken forth from the Tolbooth to the common place of execution in the Lawnmarket, and there, between the hours of eight and ten o'clock before noon, be hanged by the neck until you be dead, and your body thereafter to be delivered to Alexander Monro, to be by him publicly dissected and anatomised. *And this I pronounce for doom.*"[3]

The Judge delivered the sentence, with its accompanying

---

3. Buchanan, 198–99.

remarks, in a clear, firm, impressive, and withal a stern tone. For the most part, the dread sentence of death is pronounced with much feeling and emotion. There are few murderers who do not receive pity from the representative of justice when pronouncing doom; and the faltering voice and glistening eye attests the sorrow and pain experienced in sentencing a fellow-creature to be deprived of life, and sent into the dread, eternal, irreversible future! But that feeling seemed to be quite absent in relation to Burke. The bench seemed to share the strong feelings of detestation, abhorrence, and indignation felt by all ranks of the people. The character of his crimes precluded compassion for himself, and produced a bitter, fierce, hatred against him.

And this feeling was no doubt increased by the utter want of any proper feeling on his own part. He had sat during the whole trial with apparent unconcern and indifference, and stood now receiving his sentence with the same callous composure. Had he given evidence that he entertained a sense of his awful position, the strong public rage against him might have been a little modified, for sorrow and remorse go far to disarm resentment. But he showed neither the one nor the other, and when the last words of the sentence were uttered, and he was motioned to leave the bar and descend to the cells below, he walked away with an unmoved air, followed by the groans and execrations of the excited people.

The latter now poured in a tumultuous stream from the stifling Court into the clear frosty air of the Christmas-day, and were individually beset by the crowd outside eager to receive particulars of the proceedings. The excitement grew every hour, and along with it a strong popular cry of indignation at the thought that Hare should escape. Also the verdict of "Not proven" against Helen Macdougal[4] was scornfully condemned; and the angry shout was raised that justice was being defrauded, and that nothing would satisfy its just requirements, or the hungry public craving for vengeance, but the execution of all the four.

_____

4. The third variant on the name: M'Dougall becomes typically M'Dougal and now for a moment Macdougal.

This feeling grew stronger still as the newspaper reports of the trial were read in the city and throughout the country. It was then the people obtained a pretty accurate notion of the numerous and terrible crimes which had been committed; and the thought that one only of the criminals should be hanged, while three were let off, positively maddened the people. Nay, the cry was raised that the doctors should be brought to trial too, for the public would not believe but they had full knowledge of the murders, and even instigated to their commission.

Public feeling grew so fierce in this direction that, towards evening, a crowd, chiefly composed of young lads, marched up Leith Street, carrying a gibbet, with the figure of a man hanging from it by the neck.

This figure bore a strong enough resemblance to Dr Knox to be recognised as such, and it was received with shouts of approbation by the passers-by.

The crowd, swelling as it went, proceeded along the Bridge towards Newington, and came to a halt in front of Knox's house in Minto Street. There, amid frightful yells, a burning torch was applied to the hanging figure, and the effigy was speedily consumed.

Meanwhile, the police authorities, receiving notice of what was going forward, collected a strong force, and, marching by a back way, got entrance at the rear of the doctor's house, and issuing out by the front upon the astonished crowd, dispersed them before they had time to proceed to a more violent demonstration.

At a later hour, however, the crowd returned, greatly increased and differently constituted. It was no longer composed of mere lads, but of full-grown, fierce-hearted men, in whose determined breasts there burned a strong and, on the whole, a just indignation. When this crowd came surging and roaring in front of the house, Dr Knox had the temerity to appear at one of the upper windows with a pistol in his hand, and threatened to fire upon the multitude. This injudicious piece of bravado put the spark to the explosive material, and immediately a shower of missiles flew through the air, and came crash against the windows, shattering the glass in each into thousands of pieces. The roadway having been recently macadamised, stones were to be had in plenty, and in a very few minutes every window in front of the building was in ruins.[5] This was all the damage the mob thought proper to do on that occasion, for, after riddling the sashes, the shouting multitude quietly dispersed.

Very many of those who made this violent demonstration were no doubt mere lovers of mischief, but there is no doubt the majority meant to express thereby their sense of the doctor's conduct in relation to the Burke and Hare murders. It was an honest, irrepressible outburst of their outraged feelings, healthy at bottom, and not, in a certain sense, to be condemned, though we confess it would have been better had the public resentment shown itself in a more dignified way. But the mob, whether excited in a right or a wrong cause, manifests its feelings always roughly and violently, and in the howls of execration and the smashing of his windows Dr Knox might have learned more clearly than he did before how culpable he had been.

The trial and the reports of it circulated in the newspapers made a revelation at which the whole country stood aghast. The London papers took the matter up at once, and the authorities were severely charged with mismanagement in being able to bring to justice only one of the four wretches who made up the infamous gang. Amid the excitement and indignation of the moment, much was said foolishly and unwarrantably. The fear was even generally expressed that the three who had escaped were let loose upon society to resume the same murderous practices. This was a peculiarly foolish and short-sighted idea. After the exposure which had been made, the same crimes were made for ever impossible. The doctors, for instance, would never again purchase bodies in the same careless and negligent way, and thus all temptation to the committal of such murders was removed, even if Hare and the others had desired to renew their atrocities. But even this was by the trial rendered so improbable as to have become virtually impossible. The gang was most thoroughly broken up, and the two women, with Hare, were to be sent into a world raised in arms against them. In the midst of a furious and enraged populace, where could they have

---

5. Scot John McAdam had invented a way of packing grades of stones for durable roads, which was coming into use in the 1820s and 1830s. Pae places Edinburgh at the forefront of technology.

further opportunity of entrapping and murdering victims?
Nay, there was but shallow philosophy in the cry which was
raised that they had escaped punishment. In an earthly sense,
their punishment was greater far than that of Burke. He was
kept out of the reach of popular fury, and promptly despatched, while they became wanderers and vagabonds upon
the earth, hunted like wild beasts, refused food, rest, or shelter,
doomed to linger out a wretched existence under a heavy
ban of social reprobation. Burke's death was a death of
minutes, but they had to endure a death of years, and experience an amount of wretchedness compared with which Burke's
punishment was a blessing.

We do not see either how the authorities were to blame in
the course they pursued. It is almost certain that had the four
criminals been placed at the bar not one of them would have
been convicted, nor would the extent of their crimes ever have
come to light. The jury were of course responsible for their
verdict of "Not Proven" in the case of Helen M'Dougal. If
the evidence did not bring out active participation on her
part, it clearly established a guilty knowledge and connivance
fatal enough to her in the eye of the law, and perfectly sufficient to justify a verdict of condemnation. But the jury, loath
to send a woman to the scaffold, sent her forth in *their* mercy
to a still worse fate.

This story we are writing is a story of crime and retribution.
Had it been one of crime only, and not of retribution also,
we should never have penned it, for crime which is not succeeded by visible punishment cannot carry in its narration
any beneficial lesson. It is, of course, true that all crime has
retribution for its shadow, only the shadow is sometimes not
revealed, and unthinking people may on this account imagine
it is absent altogether, and the idea may be entertained that
it is a possible thing to do evil and escape with impunity.

Possibly some of the readers of this our tale may deem that
the relation and description of these Burke and Hare tragedies
can serve no good purpose. Now, we say in answer to this that
humanity is none the worse of knowing its capacity of evil. If
this narrative were a pure fiction, the idea might be correct,
but inasmuch as the whole thing is a matter of history, we say
it is good for people to know it. The Lord Justice-Clerk hoped
that the skeleton of Burke would be preserved, in order that
posterity might keep in remembrance his atrocious crimes,

and we but give effect to his proper wish in presenting this account of these crimes in detail.

But all along we have had in view the retribution which followed them, and we now gladly leave the crimes, with all their hideous enormities, to picture forth the retribution as faithfully as we can. What we have now got to do is to follow the after fate of these four criminals, and in the suffering, shame, and ignominy which overtook them, the reader will see most vividly illustrated the solemn declaration of Holy Writ—"Though hand join in hand, yet the wicked shall not be unpunished."[6]

As Burke was the first to suffer, and as his punishment was most public and prominent, we shall first relate the circumstances accompanying his execution, and then devote a chapter or so to each of the other three, showing how they wandered separate outcasts over the earth, and drank to the bitter dregs the cup of their terrible iniquity.

6. Proverbs 11:21.

CHAPTER XXI

BURKE IN THE CONDEMNED CELL—HEAVY TIDINGS FOR LOVING HEARTS

With a firm step and unmoved countenance, Burke descended the stairs from the Court to the rooms below. He never spoke a word; and the officer did not care to break the silence he maintained by addressing any remark to him. A conveyance was got, and he was taken from the building by a private door, and by back streets to the Calton Jail, in which place he was lodged ere the populace had time to recover from the first excitement produced by the knowledge of his conviction, and thought of watching for his removal.

He was taken direct to the condemned cell, a cold, dark, gloomy compartment, across which stretched a thick iron rod, on which hung a heavy chain. This was called the "gad"; and to the chain all prisoners under sentence of death were fastened.

No sooner was Burke introduced to this dreary place than he shivered, and said in an irritable tone—

"This is a d——d cowld place ye've brought me to."

The officials were shocked beyond measure at such profanity in one who was now in the very shadow of death, and one of them gravely rebuked him. The reproach caused the pent-up flood of passion in his soul to burst forth; and he broke out into a bitter reviling of Hare, who had betrayed him. For many minutes he was like an enraged wild beast; and those who looked on him then saw in him the capacity of all the murders he had committed. With the most frightful oaths he expressed his intense regret that he had not strangled Hare as he had done the others. The fit of awful passion having spent itself, he threw his chained limbs upon the stone couch, and gnashed his teeth and twitched his clenched hands convulsively.

Such a fit of raging passion did not again return upon him. By degrees he began to realise a sense of his position, and to make up his mind for the fate which was inevitable. The shadow of death in which he lay settled consciously down upon his spirit, and calmed and sobered him. And then it was that the best part of his nature came out; and to the few visitors who were admitted to see him he appeared a wonderfully gentle, intelligent, and polite man. These few—such as Professor Wilson and others who had sufficient influence with the authorities to be permitted to see him—were amazed to find such a wholesale murderer so quiet, docile and *conversible*. He was by no means the brutal wretch they expected to see. There was no appearance of ferocity about him, either in his aspect or bearing. Phrenologists did, indeed, see in his short bull-dog neck, and the large development behind the ears the great possibility of a cruel and remorseless nature; but his small eye, smooth speech, and polite demeanour seemed opposed to any natural theory of his murderous character.[1]

But really in this there was nothing inconsistent with the deeds he had committed. He murdered—not out of passion, revenge, or blood-thirstiness—but positively out of a love of laziness. By murder he found he could live without constant hard work or steady application of any kind, and moral principle being wanting, and selfishness supreme, he could murder without compunction, but also without much murderous feeling.

As was most natural, great efforts were made to get him to confess his crimes, but at first he showed no signs of doing this. On the contrary, he denied his guilt, much in the same way as Hare had done, and declared that the latter was the actual murderer, particularly that it was him alone who had murdered Daft Jamie.

As the days passed, however, which brought nearer the fatal morning for which he said he "would not greatly weary," a change was wrought upon his feelings. The Catholic priest who attended him wrought so far on his religious hopes or fears as to induce him to confess all; but we are inclined to think that the thought of retaliating on Hare prompted him as much as any other feeling to make a clean breast of it. For himself he had no longer anything to hope or fear in this

---

1. The *Caledonian Mercury* reported Burke's phrenological measurements, noting the areas that denoted destructiveness "very large" (31 January 1829: 3), but the *Edinburgh Evening Courant* summed up: "There is nothing in his physiognomy, except perhaps a dark lowering of the brow, to indicate any peculiar harshness or cruelty of disposition" (25 December 1829: 2).

world. Confession, therefore, would, without injuring himself, gratify in some degree his revenge.

And so he did confess, and those who received his confession were horrified beyond measure to find him give the particulars of no fewer than sixteen murders, including of course every one which we have detailed in previous chapters. Had Burke not made this confession the terrible truth would never have been known, and most of the frightful tragedies enacted in Tanner's Close would have been for ever concealed.

His full account was shudderingly taken down in writing, and was attested by himself in a few lines written by his own hand, and signed with his name in full. The paper was then given in charge to the editor of the *Courant* newspaper, to be published immediately after his execution. Forthwith there appeared in that paper an intimation that such a confession had been made, with the promise of its appearance on Thursday, the 29th of January, the day after the murderer's sentence should be carried out.

*

Let us leave for a little the doomed wretch, for whose execution an infuriated people waited with greedy expectation, and pass to the scene of the early chapters of our story.

The red December sun had set behind the western mountains, and the shadows of twilight were settling silently down upon the little village of Kirkton and the landscape which surrounded it. The country was now cast into the bleak and desolate embrace of winter. Trees and hedges were leafless, fields were bare, or black with new ploughed furrows, and at night the stars shone with clear frosty lustre, while the bright firelight gleamed from cheerful cottage windows, indicating snugness and comfort within.

On the southern slope which overlooked the village there stood a comfortable farmhouse, with its attendant outbuildings and barnyard filled with neatly-built stacks, whose pointed tops looked straight up to the clear and cloudless sky, in which the stars were brightening as the twilight deepened. From the window of the dwelling there streamed a ruddy blaze of glittering firelight, which sent its cheering illumination far across the valley. Inside, in the clean well-sanded kitchen, sat an old woman—not old beyond the power of activity, for she seemed a little wiry creature, though her grave wrinkled face showed many signs of grief and care. On her knee sat a sprightly boy of three years, whose large blue eyes, round open face, and curly ringlets of golden hair, presented a fine specimen of beautiful and innocent childhood. It was, in truth, a lovely face to gaze upon, and went far to warrant the fond looks of pride which the sad eyes of the old woman bent upon it, as its owner prattled away to her, asking, with infantile eagerness, if "dada" would soon be home.

"Yes, ma bonnie lammie," returned the old woman, as she tenderly lifted the clustering locks from the boy's white smooth brow; "dada wunna be lang noo, and he'll be sure tae hae a horsie for his little pet." The child clapped his hands in delight, and looked eagerly through the window upon the darkening landscape as if to watch the approach of the expected one.

The woman is the reader's old acquaintance, Peggy M'Naughton. The place where we now find her is not the cottage at Braeside, where Andrew Paterson lived and died. Oh, no. Peggy was turned out of that cottage at the November term which followed the old man's death. Leech, the lawyer, in virtue of the bond for two thousand pounds which he produced when the old man was no more, took possession of the property, and, putting in a tenant of his own to occupy it, Peggy had to quit the old well-loved place, where she had hoped to spend her days.

She had made up her mind to take one of the houses in the village and live there, devoting herself to the upbringing of the infant which poor Mary had given her in charge; but a few days before she required to remove, James Crawford entered the cottage at Braeside, and asked her to come and live with him, and be a housekeeper to him as she had been to old Andrew.

Peggy was thrown into complete astonishment by this offer—request rather—for James Crawford was the last person whom she expected would befriend her. She judged so because of the way Mary had treated him; but she began dimly to comprehend that it was even out of his still-cherished love for Mary that he had made the proposition, when he took in his arms the babe which slumbered on her knee and bent his face over it to kiss it and hide the tears that sprang from his eyes.

"Ye'll no refuse me, Peggy," he said, looking up at her, and revealing his agitated face.

"Refuse ye, Jimes!" returned Peggy, speaking herself in a voice faltering with emotion; "God bless ye for sic unexpected kindness. I never wud hae thocht o' sic a thing after the grief ye've had frae puir Mary—"

It required but this to make the youth break down entirely, and hastily laying the infant in her lap, he threw himself on a seat, and gave way to a great burst of grief, in which Peggy heartily joined.

"I hae lost Mary," sobbed James, "but, oh, I hivna lost my love for her. I'll never marry noo, Peggy, never—never, and it wad be a comfort tae hae ane in my hoose that loved her tae, and that could speak to me about her."

Peggy pointed to the babe on her knee. "I hae promised to bring it up, the puir wee lammie."

"And sae ye shall," cried James. "We'll baith bring it up, and be as guid to it as if it was our ain."

This touching proof of the young man's deep affection Peggy could not resist, and when the flitting day came, she and little Duncan removed to James's house at Southfield, and took up their permanent abode there.

As the child grew it entwined itself closer and closer round the hearts of those two who loved it so dearly—first for its mother's sake, and then for its own. The passing months developed it into a fine beautiful boy, with Mary's likeness vividly stamped on its young face. It became the joy and gladness of their two solitary hearts, and the drop that sweetened the sorrowful cup of their lonely lives.

Every day they expected to hear news of Mary, either to hear from her or to see her return; but months and years passed away, and no tidings reached them. They were all that time kept in merciful ignorance of the abyss of degradation into which she had descended—of the wretched miserable lost life she was leading in Edinburgh, and of the dreadful way in which that hopeless life had been ended. While her body lay stiff and cold in the huge vat in Surgeons' Square, they spoke of her as a wanderer whose return they still expected. Alas! the time was now come when the overwhelming truth was to be made known to them.

"Dada now, dada now," exclaimed the little Duncan, clapping his hands with renewed glee, as the sound was heard of a horse galloping up the rough hard road towards the house.

The child bounded away through the open door, and Peggy hastened to spread the table with the evening meal. She had nearly completed this when James came in, wrapped in his riding dress, with Duncan perched on his shoulder, and already the delighted possessor of the painted horse which "dada" had brought him from Stirling.

"Ye'll hae had a cauld ride frae the market the night, James," remarked Peggy.

"I never felt the cauld, Peggy," responded James, as he kissed the child and set him down on a stool near the fire, where he was at once absorbed in the gratifying contemplation of his new toy.

The strange tone in which James uttered the words caused Peggy to look at him, when, to her dismay, she saw he was white and agitated.

"Preserve us a'! what's the matter?" she ejaculated. Then her mind leaping at once to the centre of its thoughts, she exclaimed, "Ye hae heard news o' Mary, I'm shure ye have. Oh, tell me what they are. Is she weel—have ye seen her?"

"I hae heard news o' a Mary Paterson," faltered James, "but, oh, I hope it's no her."

"Mercy me, what for, James? Is it bad news?"

"Waefu', waefu'," groaned the young man, his strong tender heart quivering within him. "But, in the name o' a guid God, I hope it's no oor Mary."

Peggy's tongue clove to the roof of her mouth, and she was unable, through fear, to frame the question which her whole soul strove to utter. James saw the mute intensity of her wish, and with a trembling hand took from the inside pocket of his greatcoat a newspaper.

"The haill trial o' Burke is in here," he said; "and a young lassie ca'ed Mary Paterson is ane o' them he murdered. It may no be her," he added, as in speechless agony Peggy dropped upon a stool. "The chairge for that murder and for the murder o' Daft Jamie wasna gane into, for the monster has been condemned for the puir auld Irishwoman."

"Alack, alack!" moaned Peggy. "It's like eneuch tae be her. Oh, my puir bairn, and hae ye come tae sic an end—you that was sae licht-hearted and sae happy."

"Dinna speak that way," said James, bursting into tears.

"There's like tae be mony ane in Edinburgh o' the same name."

"May be sae, may be sae; but"—and here Peggy's voice failed of utterance, and she wrung her hands and wept in wildest grief.

The violence of her wailing attracted the attention of the child from his toy, and, looking for a moment or two in childish wonder and dismay, he got up, flew towards her, and climbed upon her knee, flinging his little arms round her neck, and crying for company.

The presence of the child seemed but to add to the violence of the old woman's grief, for, snatching the little thing to her heart, she burst out in more vehement lamentations, which James did his best to assuage by repeating his hope that the murdered girl was not their Mary.

"James," said Peggy, looking suddenly up, and making a great effort to suppress her grief, "I am gaun to tell ye the nicht what I never yet breathed tae mortal. It was ower at Redding, in the woman M'Dougal's house, that Mary had her wean."

"Mercy me!" ejaculated James. "Hoo did she come to think o' gaun there?"

"*He* took her—the blackguard."

James started up and walked across the room several times, and whenever his face was turned towards the firelight, it reflected itself in the deep flashing of his eyes.

"Peggy," he said, at length, "I never asked ye yet *wha* was the villain that ruined her; but I ask ye now. Will ye tell me?"

"Yes, James, I wull," cried Peggy impulsively. "It was Duncan Grahame."

"The Captain's son, at Mount Cairn?"

"Ay, just him."

No sooner had Peggy given this information than she repented it, for the expression of concentrated wrath which it brought upon the young man's face made her fear the consequences.

"Oh, what hae I dune?" she wailed, wringing her hands again. "Ye'll no dae onything wrang, Jimes? Promise me that ye wunna. Duncan, I hear, is a great man noo—a doctor in Edinburgh, and married to his cousin."

"Ay," rejoined James with angry bitterness, "and where is

the puir trusting creature he ruined? What business had he tae come wi' his false tongue atween her and happiness? Say nae mair, Peggy, say nae mair. I'm aff tae Edinburgh the morn; an', please God, I'll no come back till I find oot whether it is oor Mary or no."

"But ye'll no be heidstrong, Jimes—ye'll no be heidstrong?" pleaded Peggy, who was terrified lest he should seek out Duncan Grahame, and in his rage do something to bring himself into trouble.

"Dinna be fear'd," answered the youth with stern gravity. "I'll no break the law either o' God or man."

*

On the afternoon of the following day James Crawford stood in the High Street of Edinburgh. He was almost a stranger in the town, had visited it but once or twice, and that when he was but a mere boy. In those days of stage-coaches, when railways were almost unknown in Scotland, travelling was, of course, a much more serious and difficult thing than it is now, and much seldomer undertaken. But, besides this, James was a youth of a sober, steady disposition, not given to rambling; hence it was that for many years he had not been to the city, and was almost wholly unacquainted with its streets.

By dint of inquiring he made his way to the Police Office, and being shown into the presence of the Superintendent, he went straight to his point by asking who the Mary Paterson was which Burke had murdered.

The official looked at him angrily at first, but kindly when his keen eye detected the honesty and sincerity of his purpose.

"It was not proved that he murdered Mary Paterson at all," he replied. "That case did not go to trial."

"I ken that; but ye wad hae a' the evidence that was tae be brocht forrit."

"True; but I can give you no information about that. It is quite against the rules."

"Oh, sir, dinna mind the rule in a case o' this kind. It's oot o' nae idle curiosity I'm askin. I kenned a Mary Paterson ance—I loved her, sir, but I lost her. A villain cam' atween me and her, and brocht her tae shame. She left her faither's house three years syne, and we hae heard naething o' her sin syne. But, sir, though it's a' ower atwixt us, I love her still, and wad dae onything tae help her. Ye may ken, then, how anxious I am to find oot that the victim o' Burke is no her, and for ance ye'll surely break through yer rule, and tell me."

The Superintendent was touched by this simple avowal of the youth, and felt inclined to favour him.

"I have not got the evidence," he said, "but I can give you the address of the chief witness, a Jessie Brown, with whom the girl lived."

"Oh, thank ye," returned James. "That wull dae."

The official turned up a large book, till he found the address he sought, which he noted on a slip of paper, and gave to the youth. The next minute James found himself again on the High Street, with the cold December air fanning his fevered brow.

It was not without great difficulty that he found the close marked on the paper, and even after he did he wandered up and down its dingy length, looking in dismay at the dark doorways on either side, and uncertain which of them to enter. At length, a policeman came in view, and he asked him if he could show him the house where Jessie Brown lived.

The policeman turned sharp round upon him.

"What business have you with Jessie Brown?" he quickly asked. "That's the way you country fellows lose your money, and give us so much trouble to find it again. You go to the houses of girls like Jessie Brown and get robbed, and then come complaining to the Police Office. Take my advice, and go home without seeing Jessie Brown, or any of her kidney."

James stared at the speaker in bewilderment. He had not the slightest idea what he meant, and told him so.

"Stuff—you're not so green, or why would you ask for the address of a common street girl?"[2]

The youth's eyes were opened now, and he stood dumb with horror, utterly unable to speak, till the policeman, with a grunt, was moving away, when he laid his hand on his arm to arrest him.

"Guid God! is this Jessie Brown ane o' that kind?" he ejaculated.

---

2. 1885 drops the reference to Jessie's profession.

"Oh, go along—if you are not a fool yourself, you must not take me for one."

"Look," returned James, holding out the paper. "Maybe ye ken that hand o' write."

The policeman looked at it.

"Why, the Superintendent wrote that," he observed, in a tone of surprise.

"Yes, he kens what I am ca'in' on this woman for, and he gied me the address."

"Oh, that makes all the difference in the world," remarked the officer in an altered tone. "Do you see yon third entry on the right hand side?—that is the place. Go up the stair to the very top, and the door to the left is the door of her room."

The youth mechanically walked down the close to the doorway indicated. Within its dark threshold he leant his throbbing head upon a cold stone, and groaned in mental agony.

"Oh, if it is indeed Mary, I hae warse tae learn than that she has been murdered," he moaned. "Lost, lost, lost! but, no, I winna believe it till I ken mair than I dae yet."

With a desperate resolution he groped his way up the greasy stair, which was shrouded in almost total darkness with its circular turnings, and the damp dirty smell, which was very strong to him, all used as he was to the sweet breath of the open landscape. He was sick and giddy when he reached the top, and paused for some moments at the door to which he had been directed.

There was a suffocating feeling in his throat, and his heart beat wildly with its emotion. He dreaded to go in, fearing, with a very shrinking of soul, what he might have to learn from the girl he had come to see.

He knocked upon the door, and for some moments his knock was followed by perfect silence. Then there was a rustle made by some one moving within, and the door was opened.

The eyes of the youth reeled, and a mist came before them as he caught a glimpse of a slender naked-looking girl,[3] rather under the middle height.

"Are you Jessie Brown?" he gasped.

"Yes; will you come in?"

---

3. In the older meaning of wearing only her undergarment, here likely her shift.

The voice was gentle enough, and the girl's appearance was not repulsive, as James expected it would be. He therefore walked into the little room, and sat down on the first seat he saw, for he was so agitated as to be unable to stand.

Jessie stood regarding her visitor with a puzzled look, because for some moments James did not speak.

"Ye'll wonder wha I am," he at length said in a sad trembling voice. "I hae comed tae ask ye a question or twa aboot Mary Paterson."

"Oh, indeed! You knew poor Mary?" said Jessie, a tear coming into her eye.

"I hope no," returned James. "I hope in God's name it's no the Mary I kenned; but if ye could tell me whaur she belanged to. Was she a toon's lassie?"

"No—a country girl, as many of us are."

"And—dae ye ken—what pairt o'—o'—the—country she cam' frae?"

Jessie regarded him for some moments with fixed countenance, and then she asked a question which came to the young man like a thunderbolt—

"Is your name James Crawford?"

"Mercifu' Providence!" he gasped, and could say no more.

"I am right. You are James Crawford."

"I—am."

"*Then poor Mary was the girl you knew!*"

A sharp agonising cry broke from the poor lad's lips, and, sliding from the seat, he fell heavily on the ground, insensible.

"My God, he has fainted!" exclaimed the girl, rushing forward and trying to raise his head.

It was true. The strong man, whose heart still cherished its first and only love, lay helpless and unconscious, stricken down by the heavy tidings of woe that had fallen on his ear.

CHAPTER XXII

A GLIMPSE OF HOPE STRIKES INTO THE DEPTHS—THE SORROW OF LOVE—MORE RETRIBUTION

Say not that the poor unfortunates of our cities have lost all the tenderness and gentleness of their sex! Who that has read the autobiography of De Quincey does not call to mind the reason he had for knowing otherwise—how, when he was wandering hungry and penniless through the streets of London, he was relieved and cherished with all a sister's pure devotion by a girl named Anne—how the memory of that noble lost girl dwelt passionately in his imagination; and how years afterwards he sought her to save her, but found her not![1]

And on this occasion, too, James Crawford had reason to know that vice and an abandoned career had not utterly destroyed the womanly nature; for when he returned to consciousness it was to find his head supported in the lap of Jessie Brown, and her hot tears of pity and sorrow falling on his face. She could not raise him from the ground, but she had taken his head from the dirty floor and loosened his neckerchief, and was bathing his temples with water, while, as we have said, the warm tears of sympathy flowed from her eyes.

Poor James. It was the sudden realisation of his worst fears that overwhelmed him—the awful certainty that Mary had been in the worst sense lost. Anything like this he had not dreamed of, and the assurance of it, which he could no longer doubt, had given him a shock which for a time o'ermastered his strong and simple manhood, making the world for one moment a reeling chaos, and the next blank nothingness.

Under Jessie's simple ministrations he soon revived; his youth, and health and vigour of body could not long remain under the dominion of mental night. Aided as much by these as by the remedies employed, his consciousness returned; and,

---

1. Thomas De Quincey, "Confessions of an English Opium Eater", *London Magazine* 4.22 (October 1821): 354–79. See 377.

after a few wondering moments of struggling recollection, he
rose, remembering and understanding all.

"And she had come tae this," was all he could say, as, with
a long, agonising groan he re-seated himself, and covered his
face with both his hands.

"Don't think *too* hard of Mary, sir," Jessie ventured to say.
"If you knew how she was ruined and deserted you would pity
more than blame her. Alas, she suffered the full penalty of
her errors, as we all do sooner or later; and then to think that
she was so cruelly murdered. Oh, I have not known a moment's
peace since I knew, and have seldom left the house."

James listened eagerly, and greedily drank in every word
the girl uttered. He looked at her, too, and was touched with
pity rather than with a feeling of disgust at her appearance.
The face he looked upon was a sad suffering face—not the
bold face of the wanton, or the luring, smiling countenance of
the "strange woman."

"You and Mary were cronies," he said, softly and sadly.

"Yes, for more than a year."

"And did she tell ye her history?"

"Not till recently. And, oh! that reminds me," cried Jessie,
starting suddenly up, and opening a small box that stood in a
corner of the room. "That reminds me that some time before
her cruel end she gave me a sealed packet, which I was to
open after her death. I remembered nothing more about it,
for I thought I would be dead first. Here it is."

She brought from the box a long thin packet, tied with a
string and sealed with a piece of red wax. A light was struck
and the outer envelope torn away, when there appeared
another envelope sealed in the same way, and addressed "To
Peggy M'Naughton, Kirkton, Stirlingshire." Within the string
of this inner envelope was a slip of paper with a few lines in
Mary's handwriting, asking Jessie to have the packet conveyed to the address it bore.

James took the packet, and dashed the tears away as he
recognised the handwriting. Jessie knew it could not be in
safer keeping than in his, and she entrusted him with its delivery to Peggy.

With faltering voice the youth now inquired how Mary
had fallen into the hands of the miscreant Burke, and Jessie
related all she knew of that terrible story—beginning with
their meeting with Burke in the public-house in the Canon-

gate, and being invited by him to the house of Constantine Burke in Gibb's Close, where they were plied with drink till Mary was beyond the power of helping herself. Then she told how, when she herself would not drink to the same extent, she was lured out for a walk with Helen M'Dougal, and on returning was told that Mary had departed in the company of a packman.[2]

"I thought this very strange," Jessie went on to say, "for when I left, poor Mary was so helpless that she could not recover so soon; but, oh! dear, I never once thought of foul play. How could I? Who would have believed such wretches lived on earth? I expected her to return every day, but the moment I heard that Burke was taken up for killing people and selling them to the doctors, I knew that she had been murdered."

James listened to the sad, sad story, and sobbed like a child.

"And is that a' that has been discovered?" he asked. "Will the doctors tell me nothing?"

"I hear that Burke has confessed everything since he was sentenced to be hanged," suggested Jessie; "and his confession will be published in the *Courant* after his execution. But, perhaps, if you call at the office they will give you a sight of it."

"I'll gang there this very nicht!" exclaimed the youth, rising to his feet, "and mony thanks tae you for yer kindness."

"My kindness," sighed Jessie. "Oh, sir, I wish I was only worthy of showing kindness to any one; but I am not—I am a degraded and abandoned creature, and my last hope is but to die."

"Wad ye wush tae leave the life ye lead if ye had the chance?" asked James, looking at the girl with kind commiseration.

"To leave it, sir; oh, how gladly," she returned. "But the wish is a vain one—the chance is impossible. Every avenue of return to virtue is shut against such as I am. The world unites to keep us in the mire of our degradation. We have all to realise this, sir, that to fall from virtue is to fall for ever."

He took out his pocket-book and handed her a five pound note.

---

2. 1885 deletes "in the company of a packman" here and subsequently, either because irrelevant or perhaps because implying Mary's promiscuity.

"Tak' this," he said; "it will keep ye frae the streets for a while, an' afore it is dune I shall see ye again, and think what can be dune tae save ye."[3]

Jessie took the note mechanically, and stood looking at him in speechless amazement. Then, in a transport of gratitude, she seized his hand, and passionately kissed it, covering it at the same time with a shower of tears. The fountain of the girl's better nature was re-opened. Kind words of hope and promise, to which she had long been a stranger, removed the stone from the door of her heart's sepulchre, and, in the deep valley of her sin and misery, she obtained a glimpse of the blue and holy heaven.

The tears of a Magdalene, who shall despise them? Have they not been hallowed now for eighteen hundred years— hallowed and made precious since the time they washed the Saviour's feet, and soothed the weariness of the Friend of sinners? Who shall dare despise them when *He* accepted them? Who shall, by words of harshness and scorn, dry them up, and so seal again the fountain from whence they flow?

Jessie Brown had fallen very low. She had lived in much vileness and sin, but she too could tell a story of misplaced love—of man's faithlessness and desertion—of the world's cruelty and scorn—of desires cherished and efforts made to quit the miserable life in which she had got entangled; but which desires had been weakened, and efforts baffled by a society which dooms her class to perpetual abandonment.

Let us not be mistaken here. We have not gone out of our way to touch on this subject. The course of our story has directly led us to it, and we would be as careful to divest false pity and sympathy from these "unfortunates," as we are to record our protest against the false admiration with which it is sought to surround them by certain anonymous writers, who have of late written most pernicious books pretending to be the history of certain fashionable frail women in the metropolis. In no sense whatever is the position of these women free from blame or worthy of envy. The leading of such a life is in all of them a deep crime against virtue, whatever may have been the nature of their first temptation, or however strong

---

3. 1885 deletes references to Jessie as a girl of the street, and a few paragraphs later to the "vileness and sin" of her profession.

the barriers which society present against their return to a virtuous course. And on the other hand, the life called "jolly" and "exciting," which many of them lead, and which the books in question do their best to make seductive by investing it with a desirable pleasure, is in reality and at the best miserable. It is feverish existence even when "jolliest," and has its regular and frequent intervals of painful reflection—of suffering, remorse, misery, and despair. Let us never be induced to grant anything opposed to this. Once separate vice from its inevitable penalty, and the sluice-gates of social immorality are thrown wide. Above all, let those who are to a great extent the guardians of virtue—the popular writers of the day—avoid the mischievous deadly error of putting a gloss of any kind upon vice, and avoid saying one word to indicate that it is viewed as in the least degree desirable. Rather let them be the benefactors of the species by being true to this point of their mission—the exhibition of the solemn salutary truth that departure from virtue in any sphere brings only evil, and that continually, so long as the fatal downward course is persisted in.

*

James Crawford descended the stair with a bosom full of mixed feelings of pity and anguish. He felt so strange as to be unable to know how he felt. He was stunned and paralysed. The experience of the last hour was like living in a dream. He knew that a great sorrow had come upon him, but also that he was unnaturally calm under it—that its very magnitude had robbed him for the time of the power of feeling. In this state he asked and found his way to the *Courant* office.

A few sentences of explanation were sufficient to enlist the feelings of the editor in his behalf, and the latter taking from a drawer a folded manuscript, read from it that portion of Burke's confession which related to Mary Paterson. It contained a full acknowledgment of her murder in the house in Gibb's Close, and the disposal of her body at Surgeons' Square.

The voice of the editor as he read the paragraph sounded in the ears of James Crawford like the knell of doom. The words burned into brain and heart like a stream of molten fire, and incoherently thanking the reader for his kindness, he rushed from the office, and strode in semi-unconsciousness down the High Street.

The street lamps were now lit, and that busy thoroughfare was full of people passing to and fro, and the rushing din of city life sounded deep among the high quaint houses and down the narrow closes that opened their black mouths on either hand.

The youth was but faintly conscious of the flaring light and the noisy crowd, and hurried on he knew not, thought not, whither. Down the Canongate he walked at a rapid, almost headlong pace, and people instinctively moved out of his path, and stood looking at his tall manly figure till it was lost to view. Still he pursued his way, knowing and heeding nothing, till the lights grew thinner and the streets less frequented. In this heedless aimless way he passed into the ghostly silence and solitude of the Palace Yard at Holyrood, where the ancient home of Scotland's kings threw its black shadow on the frosty ground, and lifted its turrets to the calm night sky. Passing the south end of the venerable pile he kept his way into the open park. The lighted city with its bustle and turmoil was now left behind, and he was alone with his rushing thoughts amid the silence of earth, under the shining stars.

Then it was that the great love of his anguished heart came out in a passionate wail of sorrow. He thought of the happy sunny past, when he and Mary played in the bright summer days among the flowers of the grassy meadow, or by the banks of the crystal stream—the glad joyous days when their young hearts knew no care, and had not even dreamed of sorrow. He thought of a still later time when, the days of childhood past, they had grown into youth and love—when his pretty playmate had become his heart's idol, and a radiant vision of life enraptured all his being. Then the deep dark shadow fell on the field of his retrospection, answering to the time when the idol fell from its shrine, ceased to be a bright hope, and became but a sad memory. But now the shadow had deepened into the blackness of darkness, and he had to mourn his Mary lost and murdered. What wonder if the strong resolute heart was torn almost to bursting, and if his faith and trust in the God which old Andrew Paterson served so long wavered for a moment in his soul?

For hours during that still frosty evening James Crawford

roamed heedlessly over the slopes and knolls of Arthur's Seat, absorbed in those torturing feelings of sadness and anguish— kept from sinking into despair only by the fierce revengeful thoughts which crept in to mingle with the sorrow—the thought of Mary not lost and abandoned by herself merely, but ruined and destroyed by others, and in the bitterness of his soul he cursed her betrayer and her murderer in a frame of mind which his strictly religious spirit had never before manifested. He felt that he did well to be angry at the wanton destruction by selfish sinful man of one of the fairest beings— one, too, round whom his heart's love twined as round a natural centre. He thought of what might have been, and contrasting that with what was, his soul was stirred by the very bitterest desires.

By accident rather than intention he reached another outlet from the park, and entered again the lighted streets of the city. He was now in its southern suburb, where the airy well-built houses were occupied by the better classes. He was listlessly walking along one of the quietest of these streets, where no one but himself chanced for the moment to be. But presently a quick light footstep came from the opposite direction, and James was dimly conscious that a human figure was approaching him. This figure he was heeding as little as he had done the crowds in the Canongate, but just as it was passing he chanced to look up, and the face that met his gaze under the light of a lamp made his heart leap wildly in his bosom.

It was a face which he knew—the face of one of the only two men in the world he hated—Duncan Grahame the author of the terrible calamity which tore his heart with anguish.

Grahame was past in a moment. If he looked at James at all he gave merely a casual glance and went his way. Not so the other. He stood still and gazed after Duncan till he saw him go up a step or two and pull the door-bell of one of the fine houses.

In a moment or two the door was opened, and a flash of bright light struck out upon the dark street. By the aid of this illumination James saw Duncan enter as one who went into his own house. The door was immediately shut, and the gloom of the street returned.

With an uncontrollable impulse the youth went back and stood before the door which had just been opened and shut.

On a brass plate in the centre he read the name, and knew that it was Grahame's house.

Hesitating not a moment, he gave a violent jerk at the bell, and the peal which followed was loud and vehement. While it yet continued to sound through the house, the door was again opened, and the same stream of light shone out on the youth's face.

The girl who opened the door looked at James expecting his message, but he seeing Duncan in the hall hanging his coat upon a peg, stepped in, and went right towards him.

"A word wi' you, sir, if ye please," was his curt salutation, delivered in a thick voice, hoarse with emotion.

"Well, my man, what's the matter?" asked Duncan, thinking his visitor was wishing to consult him professionally.

"Can we no get into a room by oorsels?" said James.

"Oh, certainly, if necessary. Is it anything particular?"

"Yes," was Crawford's laconic response.

"This way, then," rejoined Duncan, and crossing the hall he entered a most comfortably furnished parlour, followed by his visitor.

"Now, then, tell me your case, and we'll see what can be done for you."

"My case is beyond your poo'er tae mend," said James, in the same peculiarly hoarse voice.

Grahame turned sharply round and looked at him. The strange answer made by the youth caused the doctor to think he was mentally affected; but to his professional eye there were no signs of insanity in the figure which stood before him. There was health in the ruddy countenance, and strength in the robust frame. The eye, though clear and bright, was steady and perfectly intelligent; but there was an expression of deep concentrated passion which Grahame did not fail to notice.

"Why, then, do you come to me?" he asked.

"Because," returned James, sternly, "ye are the author o' a' the wrang and sorrow. Ye divna ken me, sir; but I ken you, and that muckle better than ye think. My names[4] is James

---

4. Colloquial with distress, James gives his plural names—James and Crawford.

Crawford. I'm a farmer near Kirkton, and that, as ye ken, is no far frae Mount Cairn."

"And what of that?" demanded Grahame.

"I'll tell ye. Atween Kirkton and Mount Cairn there's a place they ca' Braeside—you ken it?"

"Suppose I do, what then?" rejoined Grahame, curtly, yet unable to keep from slightly changing colour.

"It was there was born and brought up ane whose name was never spoken there but wi' a blessin'—*Mary Paterson.*"

Grahame started, and blazed up angrily. "I have no time to attend to such a silly story," he snappishly said.

"Hiv be no.[5] I'm thinkin' the story is no sae silly as it is unpleasant. But I hae come tae speak aboot it, and speak aboot it I will."

"Look you, fellow," returned Grahame; "I shall not suffer myself to be so addressed by such as you. Quit this house instantly, or I shall take measures to have you forcibly expelled."

"Sic as me," repeated James, with proud indignant disdain. "Man, learned and rich as ye are, I wad be ashamed tae pit mysel' on your level. If I had dune what ye hae dune, I couldna show my face either in toun or country."

"This is most insufferable insolence," hissed Grahame, in a suppressed tone. "By what right do you speak in that impudent way to me?"

"By the richt that the wranged has to speak to the wrangdaer. I loved Mary Paterson, sir, and we wad hae been married and lived happy if ye hadna comed, like the blackhearted villain that ye are, and deceived her by yer leein' promises. She believed ye, and ye ruined her. If yours had been honourable love I could hae seen her yer wife, and keepit my heart's sadness to mysel'; but wi' you it was a' deception thegither. Frae the very first, sir, ye meant tae ruin her, and when yer bad purpose was served, and she was brought tae shame, what did ye dae? Ye lured her frae her friends, took her under nicht amang strangers, and there deserted her; wi' her kiss o' truthfu' love yet on yer lip ye went and married anither."

"For God's sake, speak low," said Grahame, in great alarm.

---

5. Meaning, "Perhaps not".

"Ay, ye're frichtened that yer wife sud hear this. Man, what a thing o' selfishness ye are. For yer cruelty and sin tae that puir lassie ye ha'ena even ae faint regret; but the fear o' detection mak's yer bad heart trimmle, and so it may, for if the woman that is noo yer wife kenned that ye cam' tae her fresh frae the side o' a guileless lassie that ye wranged and left tae starve or dee—her and the bairn that was aboot tae be born tae ye—it's like the news wad mak' a change atween her and you."

"Forbear," said Grahame, in a whisper of terror.

"Forbear," cried Crawford; "and what forbearance dae ye deserve? What mercy had ye for Mary Paterson or her auld faither, whase grey hairs ye brought wi' sorrow tae the grave? After robbin' her o' a' that was dear and precious to her, ye took her among the fremmed, and there left her intendin' never tae see her again, and her just aboot tae become a mother; and what was the consequence? When she learned your treachery and desertion she couldna face her faither and the neebors, though, waes me, she didna ken that she wadna face her faither till the great day, for the shock o' her gaun awa' killed him. But the scorn o' her acquaintances was mair than she could thole, and tae escape it the puir lassie cam' tae this big toun o' Edinburgh a' by hersel', and tae save hersel' frae want she gaed tae the streets. It was you that drove her there, sir—it was you that sent her, body and soul, doon tae destruction—it was you that put her into the hands o' that monster, Burke—it wasna his hands alone that murdered her, it was yours. And yet here ye are livin' in this fine hoose wi' a wife that honours ye because she disna ken ye, and among folk that count ye respectable, little thinkin' that the death o' a ruined victim lies on yer conscience. Hech, man, if this toun o' Edinburgh kenned the story o' this Mary Paterson, whase murder a' body has heard o', what a hissin' and groanin' wad follow ye, like yer shadow where'er ye gaed, and honest men and women wad say that you and Burke sud hang on the same gallows."

"See here," said Grahame, as in great agitation he took a pocket-book from his bosom. "If a twenty-pound note will keep you quiet—"

"A bribe tae hide the truth!" exclaimed James, with withering scorn. "Man, I wadna dae that for twenty thousand pound notes. But I see hoo it is—ye judge a' body by yersel'.

However dinna let yer bad cooard's heart fear that I shall publish your guilt and puir Mary's weakness to a cauld uncharitable world. I leave it now tae yer ain conscience. If ye can live at ease, dae sae; but there's a day comin' when you and Mary Paterson will meet, and the great God shall judge atween ye."

As he uttered these last words, James Crawford turned loftily round, and throwing open the door of the room passed into the lobby. Grahame, anxious to keep the servants or his wife from meeting him there, ran hastily past him, and held wide the street door for his exit, and with swelling heart the injured and bereaved youth strode over the threshold, and was once more on the pavement of the silent street.

Most thankful was Duncan Grahame at his departure, and inwardly congratulating himself on his narrow escape from discovery, he returned to the room they had just left. But no sooner had he crossed the threshold than he beheld a sight which froze him with horror. At an open door between that room and a back apartment stood his wife, white, cold, implacable. One glance at her countenance showed him that she had heard all.

And so she had. In the little bedroom beyond, where Duncan had never dreamed of her presence, she had listened to every word of the conversation, and had thus come to a knowledge of her husband's perfidy, cruelty, and guilt. Like a statue of marble she now stood, and bent upon him a look which showed him she was offended past all forgiveness. Indeed, he felt it could not be otherwise. He knew well her proud spirit would not brook the slight which had been put upon her, and it did not require any words on her part to express the anger of her feelings.

"Sir, we immediately part," she said, in a low tone, but in clear distinct accents.

"You have heard all, then?" he faltered.

"All," she deliberately repeated, and her passionless face was fixed as adamant.

"Well," he returned, striving desperately to recover himself, "I would much rather that it had been otherwise, but since accident has you acquainted with what had much better have remained concealed, I may as well admit that I was guilty of a youthful indiscretion, such as most young men fall into, but which are not thought to be very—"

"Silence, sir; varnish not your crime in my hearing. Offer no excuse; hint at no palliation. The die is cast—we separate."

"Oh, ridiculous, Lucy," said Grahame. "You view the matter in a wrong light entirely. This affair took place before our marriage. There is no ground for a separation."

"No *legal* ground, perhaps," she coldly rejoined. "But I shall seek no release from a court of law. We part, *in fact*, without the aid of the bench, and that is the separation with which I must be content."

"I will not agree to it," said Duncan, doggedly. "Why, such a thing would entirely ruin my professional prospects."

"Your professional prospects are not to be supported at the expense of my honour," she calmly and haughtily observed.

"Lucy, this is absurd," said Grahame. "You are angry now, and are saying what you do not mean. A night's reflection will cause you to think differently."

"You are mistaken—quite mistaken. No amount of reflection will cause me to feel and resolve otherwise than I do now. We part to-night and for ever."

"But I repeat I will not agree to such a thing. You are my wife, and we cannot separate without mutual consent."

"Not if I claim to be supported by you; but you forget that my fortune is settled on myself. I thank Heaven that it is so, and next to Heaven I thank my father that it is so, for otherwise I should have been one of the most miserable of women. The tie that binds us cannot be lawfully severed; but our marriage in the sight of Heaven is null and void, and our marriage life has terminated."

"You have not the heart to do this," he pleaded.

"The heart," she bitterly repeated.

"The cruelty, then."

"It is not cruelty, it is simple justice and propriety. It is what is due to myself. Were I to remain a day longer with you I would become a participator in your iniquity. But let us end the discussion, for farther words are useless. My resolution is taken, and no earthly considerations can shake it."

She swept past him, ascended the stair to her own apartment, and locked herself in against his intrusion.

Thus the sin of Duncan Grahame was finding him out, and bringing upon him the only form of retribution which was to him a punishment.

CHAPTER XXIII

EXPIATION

Slowly but inevitably the 28th day of January approached—the day of doom—the day of final retribution to Burke—it was the day for which he said he should not "greatly weary." Yet, as it drew near, he became fearfully impatient for its arrival. We suspect it is so in the case of most condemned criminals who have no hope of a respite. The appalling prospect before them is so torturing to contemplate that they long to escape from it, even though the avenue of release is constituted by the scaffold.

At the same time it is wonderful how a man is able to resign himself to the inevitable, even in the worst of all circumstances. Once assured that his doom is as certain as fate, he makes up his mind for it, and meets it with greater or less firmness. Burke did this in no common degree. Not for one moment did he indulge the hope that his sentence would be mitigated, and those few who were allowed to see him were amazed at his calmness and freedom from agitation. But really there was no wonder in it at all. The manifestation is common, and has its explanation in the philosophy of human nature, especially brutified and deeply criminal human nature.

There is room in these days for much to be said on the religious state of criminals between sentence and execution. That stoical resignation of which we have spoken is taken as a token of much that it does not mean. It is considered to be due to religious influence, and to be the effect of the pious instruction of priests and ministers. Far be it from us to say that Heaven's grace cannot and does not enter the condemned cell; but we fear a great deal is mistaken for grace that is not grace at all. For instance, the young man Bryce, who was lately executed in Edinburgh, declared the evening before his death that the period he had spent in jail had been the *happiest* period in his life.[1] This was taken as an unequivocal proof of the triumph

---

1. George Bryce, "the Ratho Murderer", was the last person executed in Edinburgh, 1864.

of religion and of its saving power in his soul; but really we fail to recognise it as such. Conversion would, we think, in such a case, have produced anything but *happiness*, for all conversion is, we know, preceded by repentance and a deep abiding sense of sin, which by no means produces happiness. Blessedness may succeed as flowing from a sense of divine pardon and peace; now, significantly enough, though we heard of this young man's "happiness," we heard nothing of his apprehension of sin.

Will Burke was by no means a likely candidate for repentance. The sentence of death and the view of death can change no one's nature, and three weeks of priestly ministration is not warranted to overcome more than thirty years' growth in sin and crime. From all the testimony we can gather, Burke was callous and indifferent to the last. His restless broken sleep by night was haunted by horrid dreams, which made him groan and writhe, and brought the sweat in drops upon his face, and these were the only times when he showed terror and dread. The moment he awoke and collected his faculties he was cool as before, and sat in the shadow of death with a heart of stone.

His chief anxiety was to get a decent suit of black clothes in which to appear on the scaffold, and he actually reminded his jailors that Dr Knox owed him five pounds on the last body he had got, which sum he thought he was entitled to receive.

The last day he spent on earth was spent, not in the condemned cell, but in the lock-up, near Liberton Wynd, where the scaffold was to be erected. At the early hour of four o'clock on the Tuesday morning he was taken off the "gad," and conducted to the entrance of the jail, where a vehicle stood to convey him to the High Street. It was a clear frosty morning, and he cast his eyes to the bright stars shining in the far deep blue, and to the rounded crest of the Calton Hill, which rose close above him. The glimpse he had of this earthly scene was but brief, for he was quickly thrust into the van, and driven rapidly through the silent streets.

Few people were abroad at that hour, and the few solitary wanderers who chanced to be on the Bridge little dreamt that the vehicle which rattled past them bore the notorious Burke to the spot of expiation. It was to avoid all interruption from the infuriated populace that the authorities had him removed so soon, and they perfectly succeeded in their object. The van in due time reached the entrance to the Police office, and Burke was safely transferred to the strong room at the back of the Advocate's Library, which was used for prisoners the night preceding their execution. Burke felt it a great relief to be free from his chains, and in a few minutes after his arrival he was stretched on the hard couch fast asleep.

The most of the following day was spent with the ministers of religion, and ofttimes as its hours passed Burke expressed an intense wish for the arrival of the moment that should separate him from the world. He was paler now—perhaps this was the result of confinement and low diet—but he had lost no bulk, and seemed as fat and muscular as ever.

Twilight came, the last twilight ever his eyes should behold, and gradually it absorbed the light of the dim cell, and shut in the world with the darkness of his final night.

At ten o'clock, when he was preparing to retire to rest, a knocking sound from without began to penetrate into the room. Burke's attention was arrested, and for a moment or two he stood listening.

The keepers heard it likewise, and knowing what it meant half averted their faces from his and kept an ominous silence.

"Faix, then, that's my platform they are afther putting up," he remarked, with a sickly smile. Then he turned deadly pale and shuddered, for at the moment the sound of shouts and hurrahs came distinctly from the street, telling him with what a jubilee of exultation the people were awaiting the spectacle of his execution.

This shook him more than anything had yet done, and in silence he lay down to compose himself if possible for his last sleep. In this he succeeded, for in about ten minutes he was breathing heavily; and when one of the attendants looked at him he was sunk in slumber.

A very curious phenomenon this, and one which almost never fails. The first night after a murderer's trial and condemnation he rarely sleeps at all; but the last night preceding his execution he generally enjoys a long sound slumber. Here is more of the philosophy of human nature, but we shall not pause to consider it further.

He slept very calmly for more than three hours, when he began to move restlessly on his couch, to toss his arms about, and to groan as one labouring under a horrid dream. A vision of his crimes was evidently haunting his guilty soul, for the sweat drops gathered thick upon his face, and his hands and arms moved about convulsively.

"Hilp, Hare, hilp!" he gasped, "for the devil uv an idiot is too sthrong for me. Hould him off, I tell yez—there—choke him, choke him—quick, or he'll be up again!"

"He's dreaming of the murder of Daft Jamie," whispered the half-frightened watchers to each other.

He did not awake just then; he fell quiet again, but only for a short time. This dream was followed by another more horrible still, for his countenance became distorted, and manifested an expression of indescribable terror.

"Begorra there's the boy's big eyes again! Don't be afther looking at me that way! Och, musha, it takes the strength from me intirely, they burn into my sowl like coals uv fire. Lave me, lave me, lave me!"

His paroxysm became so frantically vehement that the jailors shook him till he awoke, when he gazed at them for several moments with distended eyes, in which the glare of horror still lingered; but immediately he grew calm, and asked what hour it was.

"Two o'clock," was the reply.

"Thin I have six hours yet," he returned, laying himself down again to sleep.

Just then another round of loud cheering broke the night's stillness, and was prolonged for several minutes. Burke heard them again, and again he shuddered, but this time the shudder was followed by a scowl. Finally he fell asleep once more, and slept on till seven o'clock pealing from the tower of St Giles proclaimed that he had but an hour longer to live.

*

Let us change the scene for a little from the interior of the lock-up to the streets outside. Scarcely had the darkness of the evening of Tuesday come on when the High Street and Lawnmarket became unwontedly animated with groups of people highly excited, and manifesting much eager loquacity. These groups rapidly increased as the hour grew late, till from St Giles' Church to beyond Bank Street a dense crowd had congregated, full of wild eager expectation for the scene of the following morning.

On the eve of an execution in Edinburgh this locality is always astir, but on no previous or subsequent occasion has there been such a gathering or such excitement as was witnessed on this Tuesday evening. It seemed as if a very jubilee had come. Shouts of joy rent the air, mingled with fierce anathemas against the three murderers who had escaped.

One figure was very prominent in the throng. It was that of a tall stout young man, dressed in a drab overcoat, whom no one knew, but who showed a peculiar and savage interest in the subject which was occupying everyone's attention. Wherever a knot of people were discussing the Burke and Hare tragedies, and giving vent to their strong vengeful feelings, he would join them and inflame them still more by his strong wrathful denunciations.

This youth was James Crawford, and of all the thousands who had assembled to behold the execution of Burke, perhaps he had the greatest cause to cherish feelings of personal bitterness and revenge. Within the last few days James' character seemed utterly changed. Formerly the quietest and most equal of men—sad and melancholy he had of course been for years—he now seemed to be possessed with a passion of the most intense character. It was more than excitement, it was rather a fever of the brain—a veritable thirst of vengeance against Burke, which had prompted him to come from Kirkton to witness his execution, and it was with greedy ear that he heard the people's fierce breathings of indignation, for these fed the fury of his own soul, and made him feel all the more satisfaction in his anger.

It was now ten o'clock, and suddenly a great uproar was heard at the lower part of the Lawnmarket, coming from the direction of the Tron. Loud shouts—yells rather—rose above the general din, and with one accord the crowd rushed downwards.

"It's him, it's Burke; they are bringing him to the lock-up," was the general cry, and like howling fiends they rushed to see him, James Crawford rushing and howling as madly as any of them.

It was not Burke, but it was something little less satisfactory—it was the scaffold, which was being conveyed on a cart to the top of Liberton Wynd. The frantic multitude demanded that the horse should be taken out, which was at once done, when a dozen hands seized the cart, and bore it, amid loud exclamations, up towards the Lawnmarket.

James Crawford was the foremost in this demonstration, which was truly with him and with all a work and labour of love. In a twinkling the black beams were lifted from the cart upon the pavement, where the carpenters already stood, tools in hand, to erect the (in this instance) welcome instrument of death.

The first thing to be done was to establish a wooden barrier to keep off the crowd, a very necessary precaution at all executions, but doubly so in this case, when the popular indignation against the prisoner ran so high. The noise of the hammers was like music to the crowd, and the shouts and hurrahs grew so loud as to reach—as we have seen—the interior of the lock-up, so as to be heard by the murderer himself. Then the expressions of joy and rejoicing were redoubled when any portion of the scaffold was finished, and when the transverse beam was put in its place, and the whole set up, the rounds of cheers became deafening, and woke the echoes of the distant streets. And here again did James Crawford take a prominent part. With hat in hand he wildly moved his arm in the air, and literally shrieked his huzzahs, creating quite a furor in those who surrounded him, who little knew the cause he had for all that bitter ferocity.

It was near two o'clock, and rain had begun to fall heavily, accompanied with fierce moaning gusts of wind, as if nature itself was expressing its detestation of the foul crimes for which Burke was to suffer. The keen frost of the previous day had given place to a raw chilly atmosphere, and the wind and rain which supervened made it bitterly cold, dreary, and dismal.

Furiously beat the great rain-drops on the pavement and against the wall and the dark gloomy scaffold, while the wind rushed in passing gusts down the narrow closes, and rattled upon the window boards, and made the lamps flicker like torches, giving to the street a wild, weird, and dismal aspect.

The heavy blast sent many home, while others crowded into the stairs and passages which were open, but the greater portion of the crowd remained around the scaffold, determined to brave the fierce and drenching hurricane, so that they might have a good stance for beholding the spectacle of the morning.

The hours which now elapsed before day dawned were

spent in comparative quietness by the people. The discomfort caused by the storm subdued their boisterous demonstrations, and they waited with what patience they could muster for the morning light.

Just as day was about to break, the wind fell and the rain ceased, and immediately the crowd swelled rapidly, receiving large accessions every moment from all the streets and avenues that opened on the scene. The roads in the neighbourhood of the city began about the same time to swarm with country folks, pouring in to witness the sight; and when the grey light of the new day was strong enough to render objects visible, it fell upon a dense mass of human beings packed firmly together, and extending from the Tron Church to the Castle Hill, probably reaching the extraordinary number of thirty thousand. Every inch of space commanding a view of the scaffold was occupied. Door-ways, windows, railings, and house-tops were actually covered with clusters of human beings, while the level space contained a literal sea of human faces, all turned towards one object—the grim black painted scaffold, which stood close to the corner of the County Buildings at the top of Liberton Wynd.

All ranks and classes were there. It was no vulgar multitude that had come to gratify a morbid curiosity. The crowd was composed of far other than the off-scourings of the city. These, of course, had crept in large numbers amongst the thousands which crammed the space; but the immense majority was composed of respectable and intelligent people, come there not to gloat over the spectacle of a human being put to death, but to satisfy their indignant and outraged feelings. Women were there, many of them even in the centre of the mass, and their screams as they were crushed in the press rose above the general hum.

And where was James Crawford now? Not in the thick of the crowd, where he could not be certain of having a near and sufficient view of the execution; but perched in a window on the second storey of a house in the Lawnmarket, directly opposite Liberton Wynd, where, without the slightest obstruction, he immediately overlooked the scaffold, and would be sure to see most minutely everything as it went forward.

Between six and seven o'clock a strange dark figure appeared upon the scaffold. It was Williams, the hangman, and for once that universally execrated personage was received with favour,

for when he was seen fixing the rope to the beam, the performance elicited tremendous shouts of approbation.

In a lull which succeeded a clear voice rang out over the
heads of the people—

"Gie him nae rope."

And instantly that suggestion was vehemently seconded by
the thousands below, who took up the cry, and "no rope,
hangie," "Burke him," "choke him," "strangle him," rose from
many lips, followed by a perfect Babel of furious sounds.

The hangman nodded acquiescence, and most intense was
the satisfaction when he adjusted the rope at a very short length.

Not the least satisfied with this arrangement was James
Crawford. He it was who first made the suggestion, and a
grim smile of triumph spread over his face when the people
caused the hangman to follow it out.

And now the appointed hour drew near. The dim yet distinct light of a dull, cold, cheerless morning showed the face of
St Giles' clock and the hands creeping round to the fatal hour.
How intently James Crawford and the thousands more of the
impatient throng watched the dial and the slow motion of
the brazen pointers, which seemed to their feverish gaze to lag
purposely in their course. Not so. Minute after minute was
told with inevitable accuracy, and as the third quarter rung
out, the now familiar cheers proclaimed the general joy.

For three-quarters of an hour before this, Burke had been
engaged in preparation for his dreadful fate. At seven the
jailors roused him from a sound and peaceful sleep, and when
told that it wanted but one hour to eight, his countenance
never changed, but without a word he sat up and partook of a
hearty breakfast.

While engaged in eating this, his final meal, the priests,
ministers, sheriffs, and bailies arrived to do the last offices for
him, and see the sentence of the law carried out. He readily
engaged with attention in the devotional exercises which
ensued, and once or twice sighed heavily, but never lost firmness, and manifested no deep emotion.

Requiring to go to another apartment, he was on his way
thither, when in the passage he was confronted with a silent,
motionless apparition—the hangman. Even this sight did not
dismay him, for he merely motioned him aside with the
remark:—

"I am not ready for you yet, me boy."

In a minute or two, however, he was ready, and quietly submitted himself to the operation of pinioning—a process which the finisher of the law performed without much ceremony or delicacy. The fact was that the hangman shared in the universal detestation with which the criminal was regarded, and had a savage pleasure in making his death-punishment as severe as he could.

Since his condemnation Burke had not asked for pity, and he got none. The officials of the jail had shown him the usual attention, but denied to him what they had freely given to others—sympathy and commiseration. His crimes forbade it, and his callous indifference had sealed up still further the fountain of human pity.

Eight o'clock struck, and at the first solemn toll of the bell Burke rose to his feet, eager now to pass the awful ordeal. A glass of wine was offered him, which he accepted, and drank to the toast—"Farewell to all my friends." The procession was then formed, and they passed out to tread the dolorous way to the gibbet.

Still no manifestation of weakness on the part of Burke. Quiet, docile, and perfectly tractable he was, but with no sign of penitence. He had confessed his crimes, but neither with regret nor remorse. Humanity, which he had crushed out of him, did not return even at this last hour of retribution.

Pen cannot describe the roar of thunder which burst forth when the crowd caught sight of him ascending the scaffold. It was at that moment that for the first time he winced and showed signs of agitation. The effect, however, was to make him hasten up the steps, and presently he stood beneath the beam, in view of the yelling multitude, whose storm of concentrated wrath belched forth in howling execrations. In all that immense assemblage not one heart throbbed with compassion. All, all, leapt with fierce vengeful triumph; and deeming it mockery to favour such a wretch with devotional exercises even at such a moment, they continued to curse and yell as he knelt with his back to them in prayer.

These devotions occupied only a minute or two, and Burke rose and stood near the bottom of the steps which led to the trap below the dangling rope. The hangman's assistant, seeing him hesitate, pushed him rather roughly, towards the stair, when instantly Burke turned towards him with a fearful scowl, and the next moment *ran* up to the fatal spot.

His face was now towards the raging crowd, and as fresh
and if possible still more furious bursts of execration were
thundered forth, his eye glared over the sea of faces, and was
caught for an instant by the wild gesticulations of James
Crawford at one of the windows opposite, who was striving
with all his might to incite the crowd to further demonstrations of hatred.

"Quick!" said Burke, with his white, quivering lips, as
Williams fumbled at his throat to remove the neck-cloth.

"Quick!" he repeated, "the knot's behind."

Roughly the hangman wrenched the cloth away, and sub-
stituted the noose of the rope, adjusting it so that the knot,
instead of being directly at the back of his ear, was *behind*—a
fearful difference for the criminal when he was suspended.

All was now ready; the white handkerchief was placed in
Burke's hand, the priests withdrew, the cap was pulled over
his face, and he stood upon the drop—*alone*.

At this moment the tremendous noise of the crowd was
hushed, and a breathless sensation held every heart. Suddenly
the handkerchief was seen to flutter away from his hand, and
at the same instant a creaking noise was heard, and the murderer was swinging and struggling in the air, the last sound
he heard on earth being the concentrated roar of thirty thousand throats as the people shouted with joy to see him
launched into eternity.

He was strangled—literally suffocated, as he had suffocated
his victims. Having little or no fall, and the knot of the rope
being behind, his neck was not dislocated, as is usually the
case, nor was the cord sent tightly round the windpipe to
choke him at once, so that he must have died a slow and horribly painful death, fully conscious for some time of the sense
of suffocation, and experiencing the agony which he had so
ruthlessly inflicted on others. Call this poetical justice if you
will; certainly it was a most striking fulfilment of the words
of Holy Writ—"With what measure ye mete it shall be
measured to you again."[2]

For many minutes the dying wretch struggled violently. At
first, indeed, he tried to catch with his feet for support, but
Williams, who was now below, drew him up close to the

---

2. Matthew 7:2.

beam, where he writhed convulsively, each violent motion calling forth renewed shouts of triumph.

James Crawford from his perch in the window clapped his hands with frantic vehemence, and sent forth shouts at the utmost pitch of his voice. So marked was his demonstration of satisfaction that the reporter for one of the papers—the *Mercury*—noticed him, and in the account of the execution related how a young man from a window on the second storey, and clad in a drab greatcoat, led the populace in their outbursts of feeling, and seemed extraordinarily eager to show his detestation of the criminal who was at the moment expiating—so far as man could exact expiation—his unparalleled crimes.[3]

Burke's last struggle, it was remarked, took place *fifteen minutes* after he was thrown off, the precise time it generally took him to murder his victims. At the end of that period all quivering motion ceased, the head fell listlessly to one side, and the body swayed gently to and fro in the cold winter wind—*Burke was dead.*

Now let us mark again at what a significant hour the final stroke of human retribution fell. On that same morning, twelve months before, he had murdered Mary Haldane the younger. Her mother he had despatched the previous evening, and when the poor girl came into Tanner's Close in search of her, she was lured into the fatal back room, and there despatched. And now it came to pass that, on the anniversary of the day and hour of her death, her murderer was being suffocated by the hand of justice for that and other atrocities.

And so the first of the four West Port murderers met his fate. He was the only one of the four whom justice overtook in a legal form. Notwithstanding which it may be said that his fate was not the least enviable. It may also be said that never was a death on the scaffold more amply merited.

The greater portion of the assembled multitude remained

---

3. The *Caledonian Mercury* indeed remarks "a person dressed in a drab great coat hallooing and encouraging the mob to persevere in these manifestations of their feelings, from a window on the second floor of a house, a little to the eastward of the scaffold, on the opposite side. This individual, who seemed anxious to render himself conspicuous by prompting fresh ebullitions of the popular sentiment, persevered indefatigably in his exertions until the body was cut down" (*Caledonian Mercury*, 29 January 1829: 3).

till nine o'clock, when the body was cut down and taken within the precincts of the police buildings. Then they dispersed, the scaffold was removed, and the space into which the thirty thousand people was packed was an open thoroughfare once more.

The public death of Burke did not satisfy popular fury, even as concerned him. A demand was made for a public exhibition of his body; and so determined were the people to obtain this that they threatened the destruction of the College if they were refused. It was granted, and the body was laid naked on a marble slab in the dissecting room of Dr Munroe, and for six or eight hours a stream of people, entering by one door, and leaving by another, glided past it, to the number, it was estimated, of thirty thousand—the same number as that present at his execution. On the following day crowds flocked to the College gates expecting to be admitted again, but in this they were disappointed. We need scarcely say, however, that on the first day James Crawford was among the earliest to pass by the marble slab to gratify, though he could not quench, his insatiable feeling of hatred against the murderer of the girl he so passionately loved.

Burke's skeleton is still preserved in the College, and may be seen by any one who desires to behold the bones of a murderer whose name has for nearly forty years been a fearful household word in the whole kingdom.

CHAPTER XXIV

SAD AND HAPPY EFFECTS

A few days after the execution of Burke, the confessions he had made were published, and contained a revelation of terrible import to many. It was then that Mary Simpson of Gilmerton knew for certain what had become of her mother; for in these confessions it was declared that she was the first victim. Her sorrow and anguish we shall not venture to describe.

But great as was her distress, it was little in comparison with that of the relatives of Joe, the miller's son, whose death was not even suspected till the truth was made known from the condemned cell by the murderer, in all its circumstantial horror.

After he had been turned off by his father, and had quitted the rural spot where his youth had been spent, in the manner described in a former chapter, poor Joe had of course never been heard of. His stern and severe father secretly mourned him, though to the neighbours he had never uttered a word of lamentation. He cherished the hope that one day he would return a wiser and a better man, and be his successor yet in the old mill, after he had, with filial hand, closed his own eyes in death, and lowered his head into the grave by the side of his wife, near the lonely, sea-beaten ruin.

Lizzy Fairbairn, the girl to whom Joe had been betrothed, also cherished his memory with secret sorrow, and grew pale and sad after he was gone. It was a sore trial to her to give him up as she had done—but, deeply as she grieved, she did not reproach herself for that act. She had clung to him through much of his degradation, and again and again renewed her hope of his amendment; and it was not till such hope was no longer possible that she brought the engagement to a close.

Even then, in the depths of her devoted heart, she could not banish a faint gleam of hope that lingered. She was not without an idea that, after his departure, the consequences of his folly would accomplish what hitherto kindness and forbearance had failed to effect—that he would redeem himself and return to claim her yet, when she would joyfully become his wife, and experience happiness again.

When months passed and brought no tidings of him, she concluded that he had left the country and gone abroad, and every time she went to the village expected to find at the Post-Office a letter for her bearing some foreign post-mark, and containing some glad intelligence for her sinking heart.

Guess then her grief and anguish when the fatal tidings reached her that poor Joe had been one of Burke and Hare's victims. The shock of the intelligence left her with a stricken heart. To say she was stunned and paralysed is to say very little; the misery and horror of her soul threatened to dethrone her reason, and for some time it was feared she would become a mindless maniac. She did not become insane, but from the hour when the tidings reached her, she became a prey to the deepest melancholy, and from this nothing could rouse her. The music of her life was gone, and there seemed no prospect of its harmony and melody being restored. It was most touching to behold her pale sorrowful face, most beautiful still, as she mechanically went about her daily work, refusing to be beguiled into a smile, and seldom into a word of conversation. Doubtless the only wish of her heart, under the first weight of its crushing calamity, was to die.

No one knew from any words which he uttered how the shock struck the miller; but it was observed that from that day his hair grew rapidly white, his once tall form became bent, and a deep shadow of silent grief settled on his stern face. He withdrew almost entirely from society, and lived in utter loneliness in his little cottage on the solitary shore.

It seems difficult to conceive that these Burke and Hare atrocities should bring anything but misery to whosoever was connected with them; and yet, even as regards them, the Scottish proverb has its illustration—"It's an ill wind that blaws naebody guid." The dark and tragic business brought good to Walter Gray and his wife Rose. The public, sensible that they had been the means of bringing the career of the murderers to light and to a termination, showed their appreci-ation of the service by raising a small sum of money and pre-senting it to them. This enabled them to furnish a small house in Causewayside, and Walter's good resolution to ab-stain from drink being the more firmly established, the prospect was opened before them of a return to social comfort and domestic happiness. Their experience had been bitter but salutary, and Rose, when she looked back upon it, and reflected what a blessing had accrued, was thankful for its severity.

One day Walter was on his way home to dinner, and while going down the Crosscauseway, a carriage met and passed him. He did not notice it, and therefore did not observe the head of an elderly gentleman thrust from its window to gaze fixedly after him. Presently, in obedience to a sharp order from the interior, the coachman wheeled his horses round, and pulled up at the door which Walter had entered.

The latter had just thrown aside his cap, and was about to seat himself at the humble table where the smiling happy Rose presided, when a shadow fell upon the floor, and, looking up, they were amazed to behold the form of General Stewart standing within the threshold.

"Well," said the General, in his prompt off-hand manner, "you two have been much before the public of late, and people talk well of you. I am pleased myself—much pleased at what you have done. It was your duty, and you did it well. But how did it come that you were lodging in the house of those wretches?"

They were both silent. Walter's face reddened, and Rose hung her head.

"Oh, I see how it is," resumed the General. "My prophecy turned out a true one. You became the slave of drink, and reduced yourself and your wife to beggary."

"Oh, sir, don't speak so to Walter," cried Rose, hastily. "He doesn't deserve it; indeed he doesn't. If you knew how bravely he has overcome temptation, how kind and loving he is now, and how happy we are together—"

"General Stewart," said Walter, rising and speaking respectfully, yet with quiet manly dignity, "the last time we met, I uttered words which I now regret having spoken. I have learned and experienced much since then, especially have I learned much about myself. What you said turned out only too true. I did become a drunken, good-for-nothing fellow—"

"Oh, Walter!" interrupted Rose, in great distress.

"Nay, let him speak," said the General approvingly.

"I gave myself wholly up to the power of strong drink," added the youth; "for it I sacrificed everything—my honour, my manhood, my independence, and brought Rose along with myself to poverty and misery. We went to lodge in Burke's

house because we could command no other shelter; but thank
God a sense of our desperate condition, and my responsibility
for it, struck my soul with shame and remorse, and on my
knees I sought pardon, and asked help to resist the devil who
had enthralled me. I am doing my best, sir, to rise from my
degradation. My darling wife has been my guardian angel in
my weakness, and with God's help and the support of her
love, I feel that I am conquering my foe."

"I see you are," returned the General, with a nod of approbation, "or you would not have borne so meekly the words I
addressed to you just now. Well, young man, I think I did
you injustice. I was hasty and harsh with you. I forgot that
you was not a soldier, and that I was not your General. But,
after all, what took place has turned out for the best. Your
conduct in turning out that nest of murderers deserves more
recompense than it has yet got. The fact is, we were both
wrong, and we both own it. Come back and work with your
father again. I have erected a cottage not far from his, and
you and Rose shall have it. Will you come?"[1]

Need we say that this offer on the part of the General was
cordially accepted, and that shortly after Walter and Rose
went back to their native village, where they lived in love,
gladness, and honour, and where children were born to them
to increase and intensify their earthly happiness? We shall
have no occasion to advert to them again. They came acci-
dentally, as it were, into our story, by being the means of
bringing to light the crimes of Burke and Hare; and having
traced their connection with that tragic history, and told how
that connection issued in the long run for their benefit, we
shall leave them to the enjoyment of their simple and now
uneventful village life, and return to the more prominent
personages of our tale.[2]

---

1. In fact, whatever efforts were made to reward the Grays, the Edinburgh
Central Library includes an 1829 letter from Ann Gray (Pae's "Rose") to James
Stephenson reading: "as you are the only friend that I have in this place &
have no other person to apply to I am sorry to inform you that my husband
has been in great distress ever since I seed you and died—yesterday morning
... Ann Gray widow of James Gray." She asks for support. The letter is bound
with materials by Charles Kirkpatrick Sharpe relating to the *West Port Murders*,
see Sharpe.
2. Chapters 24 and 25 make up one number in the Dundee *People's Journal*.

CHAPTER XXV

HELEN M'DOUGAL BECOMES A VICTIM OF POPULAR FURY

When Helen M'Dougal was by the verdict of the jury dismissed from the bar of the High Court, she was kept in the lock-up till the night of the following day, and then set at liberty.

She stood upon the High Street. It was Saturday night, and she knew not where to go. Everywhere the people on the street were talking of the trial, and she heard enough to show her that her escape from the gallows was considered a foul defrauding of justice.

Gathering her thin shawl closely around her, to protect her shivering form from the winter's cold, she crept down a close, and by various byepaths reached the Calton Hill, on the southern brow of which she stood, gazing wistfully at the gloomy jail below. Burke was there, condemned to die, and her affection for him was the only human thing remaining in her heart. They had sinned together, and were now separated for ever. In a week or two he would be dead—she would never see or speak to him again—without him, henceforth, she must live in the world.

And what was she to do? *How* was she to live? A few coppers was all she had in her possession; these would serve her but for a day, and then—what then?

Naturally enough she thought of the time at which, and before which, she met with Burke, and formed her dishonourable connection with him. She then wrought in the fields, and this she would have to do again. Ah, she was comparatively innocent then; but what was she now? A guilty knowledge of, and consent to all the murders which Burke and Hare had committed in Tanner's Close made her as much a murderess as if her own hand had done all the deeds, and she was not so destitute of reflection as not to know this.

She looked down on the countless lights of the great city, and felt that she had not one friend among its thousands of inhabitants. Her crimes had made her an outcast. Retribution, long delayed, had overtaken her and those associated

with her in their commission, and she was now beginning to
endure the bitter experience of such an unparalleled course of
wickedness.

She sat on a cold stone on the brow of the hill till she
shivered in the piercing wind. Then she bethought herself that
she would find shelter in the house in the West Port which
she and Burke had occupied when they were apprehended.

So, after casting another long wistful glance at the heavy
walls of the prison, she left the hill, and managed to reach the
West Port without being recognised.

She had got the key of the house returned to her when she
was set at liberty, and with a stealthy step she crept along the
passage, and noiselessly let herself in.

All was dark, damp, and comfortless, and the solitude of
the place with its terrible associations filled her with terror.
There was a little bit of candle stuck in the bottle, and a
tinder-box was on the cold clammy shelf above the fire-place.
With much difficulty, and after many vain attempts, she succeeded in striking a light, which served only to shew her the
darkness of the place. The grate was empty, and she had not
an ounce of coal with which to kindle a fire. Through the
broken panes of the window the frosty wind streamed coldly
in, causing the candle to flare and flicker, and making moving
shadows in the dingy room, suggestive of fearful things to a
guilty mind. Everything too served to remind her of the horrid
deeds which that room had witnessed. There was the bed on
which some of the victims were laid, and there lay the straw
in the corner where the old woman Docherty had been
thrown. She seemed to hear anew the agonising shriek of the
little old woman, her gasps, and panting for the breath which
was being choked out of her, the gurgling in the throat, and
all the other sounds accompanying the monstrous deed. And
as imagination, assisted by the dreary solitude and desolation,
conjured up these impressions, the wretched woman muffled
her head in the shawl she wore, as if expecting to see some
frightful apparition rise to confront her.

Wretched and terror-stricken though she was, she grew
hungry, and longed for some whisky to warm her and give a
little courage to her trembling soul. The few coppers she had
would procure a small piece of bread and cheese and a gill.
She therefore resolved to venture into the West Port to procure them.

Scarcely had she emerged from the mouth of the close when she met in the face a woman who knew her, and who, after the first moment of breathless surprise, exclaimed at the utmost pitch of her voice, "Eh, mercy! Lucky M'Dougal.[1] Oh, ye cursed wretch. Hoo daur ye come here?"

The words were heard, and the news flew like wild-fire. The denizens of the West Port rushed in furious excitement out of their houses, and with yells and curses of execration flocked about the shivering wretch.

"Tear her to pieces," roared some.

"Burke her," shouted others.

"Throttle her," shrieked more.

"Droon her in the Nor' Loch,"[2] exclaimed a woman's voice, rising shrilly above the din of Babel sounds.

This suggestion was received with a deafening shout of approbation, and meanwhile handfuls of mud and filth were thrown upon M'Dougal till she was bespattered from head to foot.

She sought to find shelter in some of the shops, but those within thrust her out. She tried to rush down an open close, but was met in the face by other faces yelling with fury. On all sides she was surrounded, and nearly blinded by the dirt and stupefied by the shouting. She staggered here and there, hustled violently from side to side, and more than once nearly thrown to the ground. Had she actually fallen, she would assuredly have been trampled to death by the fast increasing and terribly excited crowd, who were every moment growing more clamorous and vindictive.

When the commotion was at its height two policemen forced their way into the centre of the mass, and dragged her, though with the utmost difficulty, to the neighbouring police station.

Thither the crowd followed, shouting and yelling as furiously as before; and if the doors had not been shut and barricaded, the people would have forced themselves in. As it was, the demonstration of popular fury grew so alarming that

---

1. "Lucky" was a Scots familiar term for an old woman.

2. Anachronistic. The Nor' Loch, running along north of the castle, had been drained in 1759, though the area did continue to flood for a time. Perhaps the woman is knowingly hinting to a prior use of the loch for ducking witches.

a *ruse* was adopted to disperse the crowd. A ladder was set up against one of the back windows, and this being discovered, the intended effect was produced. It was believed that M'Dougal had escaped in this direction, and with renewed yells of rage the people rushed away in all directions in search of her.

Advantage was immediately taken of this clearance in the street to get the terrified object of the popular wrath conveyed to the Central Police Office, where she was securely lodged in one of the cells.

Before break of day a plate of porridge was set before her, and she was advised to partake of them and quit the city before it was light, by which course alone she might hope to escape from the hands of those who seemed determined to destroy her. She silently consumed the food, and drawing once more her tattered shawl close to her shaking body, was conducted, weeping bitterly, to the street entrance and there set adrift.

Adrift—truly adrift. Neither home nor resting-place had she in the wide world, the humanity of which was in arms against her. With a friend nowhere, and with enemies everywhere, to which quarter should she turn? It mattered little, for every place was void of promise, nor was she capable of making any choice, yet she wandered away in a direction the very worst she could have taken. She crossed the Mound, traversed the long length of Princes Street, and took the road westward, her intention being to go to Redding—the village where she and Burke first began to live together.

She got clear of the city without being recognised, and in the darkness began to plod her weary way along the solitary country road.

It was the mirky hour before the dawn—the darkest hour in all the night. The face of the sky was obscured with one universal cloud, and a keen cutting frost wind swept through the gloom. This biting breeze she had to face and strive against as she pressed painfully forward. Heaven and earth seemed joined with man to testify their indignation and hatred.

By the time the grey light of the holy Scottish Sabbath began to pluck the near objects out of the power of night, she had placed several miles between her and the city, and seeing a half-ruined shed standing at a little distance from the road-

side, she crept towards it for rest and shelter. Here, among a
quantity of straw close to the north wall of the hut which was
still entire, she lay down, and with a long weary sigh of
exhaustion fell soundly asleep.

When she awoke the first sound that fell on her ears was
the sweet sacred sound of a Sabbath bell, so full of peace and
quiet joy to hearts weary with the world's toil. A Scottish
Sabbath! What a sweet outward beauty prevails over our land
on the weekly day of rest. We say nothing of the reality of
the worship or the devoutness of the worshippers who, with
sober feet, go up to the house of prayer and bow themselves
before the Most High God. We give no commendation to the
intensely rigid observance of the day, which was more peculiar to the past than the present; nor do we make an invidious
comparison between the religion of Scotland or that of other
countries; but this we say, and we glory in the fact, that a
Scottish Sabbath has a fullness of meaning in it such as the
Sunday of no other country can claim. There is in Scotland a
most marked and delightful distinction between the Sabbath
and other days of the week such as we cannot find in other
parts of the world. Go to England or Ireland and the line of
demarcation is considerably fainter. Go to France or any of
the continental countries and it is fainter still, almost to invisi-
bility. Outwardly, the seventh day is more a Sabbath in
Scotland than anywhere else. Often has it seemed to us that
the sun is brightest and the landscape fairest on that hallowed
day. Over moor and field and forest a calm stillness rests.
There is Sabbath everywhere—Sabbath in the city with its
closed workshops and smokeless chimneys; its sonorous bells
and throngs of well-dressed worshippers—Sabbath in the
woods, where nature, animate and inanimate, sends up to
heaven a blended song of praise, uniting in its strain the voices
of bird and insect, stream and tree and flower—Sabbath in
the meadow, where the cattle roam unharnessed, and enjoy
their weekly period of repose—Sabbath in the field where the
plough stands in the furrow, and the whistle is unheard on
the lea—Sabbath on the mountain where the shepherd lies
beside his dog with his flock around him, and his broad serious
face bending between an open Bible and an open heaven—
Sabbath far away in the glen where the cottager sits by the clear
brook, and the Highland maiden reclines among the heather,
listening not to the sound of Sabbath bells, but to the gladsome

notes of the lark as he floats high in the blue ether, singing his Sabbath hymn at the gates of heaven. Real indeed, and as beautiful as real, is the Scottish Sabbath. It lays its loving spell on all things; shuts out earth from view, and sheds upon the path a soft and streaming radiance from heaven. Long may the sons of Scotland love and cherish their Sabbath in the liberal spirit of the Sabbath's Lord!—long may it stand as a blessed bulwark against the overwhelming flood of labour and toil—hedging round for human spirits a sacred sanctuary of rest, in which they may for a brief season lift their thoughts to a higher and more blessed life, and in the calmness of the breathing time catch a view of their glorious destiny.

But what has guilt and fear to do with Sabbath beauty and peace? Helen M'Dougal, if she once felt the influence of the sacred day, had long since lost the pleasure and the peace it yielded; and now when the Sabbath bell greeted her ear as she rose from her weary couch among the straw it only brought to her recollection the miserable position in which she was placed.

As she listened it ceased, and she knew that the worship to which it called was begun. She went to the front of the shed and looked forth. The sun was shining now in a sky of cloudless clearness, and in the distance was a village whose church spire pointed heavenward. From where she stood she could command a view of its porch, and saw one or two of the latest worshippers pass into it. No other human being was within sight, and she quitted her rude place of shelter, regained the highway, and proceeded forward towards the village. She was very hungry, and thought of asking food at some open door.

The church itself was the first building she reached. It stood at a little distance from the village, in the centre of a little churchyard crowded with memorial stones, separating the grassy mounds and individualising the handfuls of human dust which lay beneath.

The large iron gate being open, Helen entered, conscious of no object she had in doing so. She even approached the building itself, the porch of which stood wide, and listened to the solemn song of praise that swelled within. The measured music brought up many memories of the past—days and years when she, too, went to the House of God and raised her voice in prayer. What a fearful separation there was between that time and now! Between the past and the present there was a great gulf fixed—a gulf of deepest guilt and crime, which could never be bridged over, and never filled up, but which must yawn there in bottomless blackness.

The psalm ceased, and she heard the minister announcing his text—

"Whoso sheddeth man's blood, by man shall his blood be shed."[3]

The words sounded in her ear like the voice of doom, and with a great shudder she turned away and entered the village.

Here she was fortunate enough to procure food, and proceeded on her way westward, until weary, foot-sore, and ready to drop from exhaustion, she arrived in the gloaming at Redding.[4]

From the window of the little cottage which she once inhabited there came the ruddy lustre of cheerful firelight, and noiselessly she approached and looked in.

A young mother sat on the hearth nursing her child, while at the opposite side of the fire a man was proudly dandling an older boy on his knee. Helen knew that man and woman well. They were engaged to be married when she left the place three years before, and there they were living in domestic felicity in the home which had once been hers.

The woman chancing to look up, saw the face at the window—and saw it clearly in the bright firelight which fell upon it.

"Nell M'Dougal!" she screamed, with a great start; and before Helen had time to draw back, the man also looked round, saw, and recognised her.

"The wretch! what does she want here?" he cried, as, hastily setting down the child, he hurried to the door.

Instinctively Helen ran down the lane, and scarcely knowing what she did, she turned up the long village street. It was silent when she entered it. One or two people standing at their doors saw a woman hurry past, but did not know her in the darkness. Soon, however, there was a stir behind, and the cry was raised that Nell M'Dougal, the murderess, was there.

Like bees the villagers flocked into the street, and the same shouts of fury and rage which the night before had filled the

---

3. Genesis 9:6.
4. Village twenty-four miles west-north-west of Edinburgh, close to Falkirk.

West Port broke the Sabbath stillness of Redding. The
wretched woman shuddered as she heard them, and her weary
feet, now winged by fear, swiftly carried her to the further
extremity of the village.

On came the excited villagers like a pack of blood-hounds
in full cry. In a few moments they would be sure to overtake
her. Dr Ford's garden door stood open, and darting in she
closed it behind her. Scarce had she done so when the yelling
crowd rushed vehemently past.

CHAPTER XXVI

THE FATE OF HELEN M'DOUGAL

Scarcely had Helen M'Dougal disappeared within the door, and found shelter in Dr Ford's courtyard, than the yelling villagers went rushing past in full pursuit. She heard their fierce determined threats of vengeance in voices which she well recognised—hoarse, angry voices of men and women who, in former days, had been her obliging neighbours and acquaintances, but who now uttered their bitterest curses against her.

Sick at heart, weak with hunger, exhausted with fatigue, and trembling with fear, the miserable wretch tottered towards the door of an outhouse, and tried to gain admittance. It was only hasped, not locked; and raising the hasp, a slight push caused the door to open inwards. To the shivering woman, whose limbs were stiff with cold, the interior felt warm and comfortable. It was Dr Ford's stable, but seemed to be empty, for all was silent. In the darkness she groped her way forward, and entering an unoccupied stall, sunk down upon a heap of hay, where she found a dreamy rest in her state of utter prostration.

In this retreat the sound of distant shouts and cries reached her, showing that the people were still in pursuit, and enraged at being unable to find her. Presently the brisk sounds of wheels came rattling along the road, and a vehicle pulled up at the doctor's gate.

"Dick—halloa, Dick," exclaimed a voice, which she recognised as the doctor's.

A window was pulled up, and a woman called out—

"Dick isn't in, sir; Helen M'Dougal has come to the village, and the people are all after her, and Dick has gone too."

"Stupid fools," muttered the doctor; then in a louder key he cried, "Bring me a lantern then, Martha, and I'll put up the horse myself."

They are coming here; I shall be discovered, thought Helen; yet she made no farther effort at concealment. She was, in truth, benumbed and unable to move.

The great gate creaked on its hinges, and horse and gig

were brought into the courtyard, and put back under the shed which adjoined the stable. Then, in a little while, a horse's footsteps approached the stable door, which was pushed open, and the beast entered. The expectation of being trampled on flashed in terror through Helen's mind, yet she had no power to cry out. Fortunately the animal found its way in the darkness, and entered the stall next to where the woman lay.

The doctor followed, and was fumbling with the buckle of the harness, when his housekeeper came in with a lantern, which cast a weird mixture of light and shadow over the stable.

"Have the idiots gone out of their senses?" asked the doctor, in an impatient tone. "I met a crowd of them whooping and yelling along the road like fiends."

"Didn't they tell you who they were after?" said the housekeeper, in a severe tone.

"Why, yes; I stopped the gig—or rather they stopped it by filling up the road in front of the horse, and the questions came like a shower from their gaping throats—Have you seen her? Where is she? Is she far before us?

"Not a soul had I seen on the road for the last two miles, but they wouldn't believe me, and rushed on, shouting something about Helen M'Dougal. Had I known that rascal Dick was among them, I should have collared him and brought him back."

"Indeed then it's no wonder they are after the murdering wretch," answered the housekeeper. "I'm sure I don't know how she had the impudence to come among decent people."

"But is she really here?"

"To be sure she is. Tom Lorrey and his wife saw her looking in at their window, and the moment she was discovered she took to her heels up the village. I hope they'll catch her and tear her in pieces or drown her in the pond."

"I hope they'll do nothing of the sort," returned the doctor. "Why should they kill the woman?"

"Because she has committed murder!" answered the irate Martha.

"Well, that's no reason why they should commit murder too."

"Yes it is," maintained Martha, stoutly. "If you read the Bible more than you do, doctor, you would know that it

says—'Whoso sheddeth man's blood, by man shall his blood
be shed.'"

"But the jury found that it wasn't proved that she has shed
blood," suggested the doctor, with a smile.

"The jury told a lie then," returned Martha, in a great
heat. "She was as bad as any of them; they were all alike, and
should be hanged, every one of them; and so should Doctor
Knox for that part of it, for it is my opinion he knew all about
their crimes."

"Nonsense," laughed the doctor; "I know Knox as well as
I know you, and am quite certain he had not the faintest
suspicion of it."

"You'll not get anybody to believe that though," said the
housekeeper incredulously.

"Oh, that's possible, for the public is the most unreasonable
animal alive; but we'll not discuss this matter any further just
now. What is of more importance to me at this moment is to
know if the kettle is boiling."

"It's been boiling, but I set it off."

"Then go in and put it on again, for I want a hot tumbler
after my cold ride. I'll follow you in a minute."

Martha, whose temper was still ruffled by the little discussion that had taken place, set down the lantern on the corn
bin, and went away without a word.

The doctor had now got the harness off his horse's back,
and having hung it up, he came round into the empty stall for
a handful of hay that lay there. Stooping down he touched,
not the hay, but the arm of a human being.

"God bless us, what's that?" he ejaculated.

"It's me, doctor," was the answer, in a feeble voice.

"You! Who are you?"

"Don't you know me? I am Helen M'Dougal."

"Good heavens, what are you doing there?"

"I came in to escape from the people. I could not run a step
further, for I have walked all day, and haven't had a bit of
food."

"Gracious me, that's dreadful. Why did you come here
where you are so well known?"

"I don't know. I had nowhere else to go, and no money.
They would not let me stay in Edinburgh; I was nearly
murdered last night. Oh, doctor, take pity on me, and give
me some food, or I shall die of want."

The doctor stood looking down upon her in puzzled silence.

"A pretty pass you have brought yourself to," he observed. "It would have been infinitely better for Burke and you if he had remained here working for a half-a-crown a day."

"It would, indeed," moaned Helen. "A thousand times have I rued the day we left Redding."

"What on earth tempted you and the others to commit such horrible crimes?"

"Hare was the worst—him and his wife. It was all lies he told at the trial. He helped Burke and always got him to do it, and then he went and told upon him."

"To save his own neck," added the doctor. "Of course he would. No honour in a felon of that kind. But what's to be done? You can't remain here, for if Martha comes to know it she'll alarm the village, and the incensed people will kill you."

"Oh, I must rest a while," wailed the miserable wretch. "I have travelled all day, and haven't tasted anything since one o'clock."

"Horrible!" murmured the doctor. "Yet I don't wonder at the rage of the people, for the murders were most inhuman. It's a million pities Dr Knox had anything to do with the bodies."

"He didn't know they were murdered," returned Helen. "People may say as they like, but he didn't know it."

"Of course he didn't; I was quite sure of that."

"You had more to do with them than he had," added Helen.

"Me!" ejaculated the amazed doctor. "What on earth do you mean?"

"You once told Burke the way to do it, and he never forgot it."

"What a monstrous falsehood!"

"It is no falsehood," said Helen M'Dougal. "It was yon night in our house when you were waiting on the girl Duncan Grahame brought to be confined. You told Burke how people could be murdered without leaving a mark on their body, and he and Hare did it in the way you said."

Dr Ford was struck dumb. The woman's words caused the conversation he had that night with Burke to flash vividly into his recollection, and he did remember speaking of that particular mode of death, though little dreaming to what abuse the information would be put. He felt that, however unintentionally, he was remotely connected with the Burke and Hare murders.

"Has Burke told this to the authorities?" he asked, in a rather anxious tone.

"No, he has not. He never said a word about it, and never will. Poor fellow! they are going to hang him."

"And very properly too," thought the doctor, but did not say so. Just at this moment someone came running into the court-yard and approached the stable.

The doctor wheeled suddenly round and in haste snatched up the lantern, just in time to meet Dick as he rushed in at the door.

"So, you rascal, you have been running after that woman too."

"Yes," replied Dick, quite unabashed, for nobody was afraid of the doctor. "But we couldn't catch her. She must be hiding somewhere. If we had got her, what rare fun we would have had."

"Why, what did the people mean to do with her?"

"Hang her on a tree. Tom Lorrey got a halter out of Aleck Swansen's stable to do it."

"Then it's as well for Tom Lorrey that the woman has not been got," remarked the doctor. "You need not go in, Dick. I have suppered the horse myself. Take in the lantern, and tell Martha I shall be in presently."

Dick departed with the light, and the doctor turned back into the stable.

"In an hour or so," he said, "I shall bring you some food. But you must be gone before morning, for if you remain you will be sure to be discovered, and I can't save you from the fury of the villagers."

"Oh, yes," answered the woman, "if I had a few hours' rest I will leave. Oh, dear, where I am to go I know not."

The doctor did not wait to hear more, but, locking the door of the stable, he deposited the key in his pocket, and entered the house in a very thoughtful and abstracted mood.

Within the period he named he returned to the stable with food enough to make one substantial meal.

"I would have brought you more but for two reasons," he explained to the famished wretch, who began voraciously upon it. "In the first place, very much would hurt you; and, in the second place, I could not abstract more from Martha's pantry without rousing her suspicion. But here are a few shillings with which you can buy food when you are at a distance from this; only I warn you again to place yourself a long way hence before the morning light, and not come back here again if you wish to live. I hear the villagers mean to hunt about for you early in the morning, and if they find you in their present state of hatred and fury your death is certain."

"Where am I to go to?" whined the woman, with a burst of tears.

"That I know not. I should say where you are not known. You are strong, and may work for your bread."

He flung a handful of silver into her lap and went away.

"I will leave the stable door unfastened," he added, "and the small door in the wall will be only bolted, so you will easily find the way to the road."

These last words he spoke in a whisper, for he had stepped into the courtyard, and had no wish that any body should hear him but the person he addressed. This sort of concealment was something quite new to the doctor, for his life was a peculiarly open one, and secrecy in anything was quite foreign to his nature. But pity for the wretch from whom all human pity was withheld, and a self-reproach produced by what she had told him, caused him to succour her for the night, and facilitate her escape from popular vengeance.

Helen M'Dougal rapidly consumed the food, and her ravenous appetite was far from satisfied. She had, however, for the present to be content, and cowered down again among the hay. She grew drowsy, but durst not sleep, for she knew that if she gave way to slumber it would continue for many hours, and the fear of being seized by the villagers made her shudder with apprehension.

When she became warm in her lair, and experienced that lassitude of repose which was so much needed, the temptation to remain was almost resistless, and she was just sinking into an overpowering slumber when a loud noise made by the horse in turning himself made her start, and conscious of the narrow escape she had made, she resolutely left the place among the hay, and made her way to the outside of the doctor's premises.

Oh, how the bitter punishment of her crimes was now

overtaking this guilty woman. Allowed to obtain no rest, an object of unpitying obloquy and vengeance, doomed to wander in the cold and darkness of midnight, moneyless, shelterless, and without a place of security to which she might direct her steps, with what bitter, bitter regret did she look back on the past year of her life, filled with the black deeds of cruelty and blood, whose consequences had now come upon her in the form of fearful retribution. What would she now have given to have stood as clear of blood as she did the last time she walked along the road she was now traversing? But her regret was vain and altogether hopeless. She had sown the wind and must reap the whirlwind. She found no mercy from man, and durst not even ask mercy from God. Truly "the way of transgressors is hard."

The next two or three days were passed by Helen M'Dougal in miserably wandering to and fro, she scarcely knew where, but chiefly in rural districts, sleeping in sheds and outhouses, where, being thinly clad, she nearly perished with cold. In the villages or hamlets through which she passed, she bought food with the money she had received from Dr Ford—food to sustain her miserable life, and also whisky to make its misery less felt.

Having spent three or four days in this manner, she was creeping along a road in a part of the country utterly unknown to her, as it was drawing towards the gloaming of a bitterly cold January day. The keen frost wind came sweeping from the north, where the sky seemed black with a coming tempest, and spread like the fiend of desolation across the bleak wintry landscape, cutting the wanderer to the bone, and making the rags to flutter from the trembling limbs.

The night grew wilder as the darkness fell, and now and then a rattling hail blast showered its hard stones in the wanderer's face, heralding the storm that was about to burst. The miserable half-faint outcast looked wistfully around on all sides for some shelter, but none could she descry. The level road ran through an open piece of country black and bare. Not a wood, nor a hedge, nor even a wall was there to put between her and the furious wind. A desolate heath or moor seemed to stretch in all directions till it met the frowning sky. There was nothing for it, therefore, but to persevere or sink down and die.

On and on toiled the hapless wayfarer, sometimes brought

to a stand-still, and sometimes even sent a step backward by the force of the blast, till after, as it seemed, an age of desperate struggle, her weary, despairing heart was cheered by a strong light flickering through the gloom, and as she proceeded still further near the crest of the height, other lights beamed from below. Then she knew that there was a valley before her, and in the valley a village, where innocent hearts were sheltered in peaceful homes against the biting cold of the winter's tempest.

For her there was no such home and no such shelter. Her evil deeds had made her an outcast from her kind, and she could have again no comfort or peace.

The strong light she first saw gleamed by itself above the village, and in the extremity of her suffering she thought she would direct her steps towards it and seek refuge for the night.

When she drew near she found it to be the cottage belonging to a farm place. The outhouses were at one side, but shrouded in darkness; and it was from the kitchen window on the ground floor that the bright light came. The wanderer crept towards the window and gazed in. An elderly woman sat knitting in the firelight, and on a stool at her feet was a child amusing itself with some toy. To the eye of the starving woman the place was a paradise, and she gazed with wistful longing through the open window, lacking the courage to enter.

While hesitating thus, a loud, fierce barking burst forth at her feet, and a dog bounded from a kennel, and, leaping forward, would have seized her, but the strong chain dragged him back. The old woman within, attracted by the dog's furious barking, came to the door, and saw the crouching form of Helen M'Dougal, as revealed by the ruddy light from the window.

"Mercy preserve us, woman! wha are ye staunin' there in sic a night?"

"I am a poor houseless wanderer," answered Helen. "I have just crossed the moor, and am nearly dead with cold and hunger."

"Puir creature," said the other; "this is no a nicht for a brute beast tae be abroad, let alane a human being. Come awa in by, and we'se try and pit ye up till the mornin'."

"Oh, heaven bless you for your kindness!" faltered Helen

through her blue stiff lips, as she tottered forward to the threshold.

The dog's loud fierce bark had sunk into silence when the woman came to the door, and the sagacious animal, seeing that the wanderer was received with favour, wagged his tail and crept back into the kennel, where, after having so faithfully done his duty, he buried himself over among the straw.

"Dear me," observed the woman of the cottage, as she set a chair at the side of the fire, and not too near it, lest the heat should injure the half-frozen wanderer. "Dear me, ye are shurely very ill aff tae be wanderin' aboot at sic a time o' the year. Hae ye nae hame ava?"

"None," replied Helen; "I am a poor miserable creature, compelled to seek my bread from door to door."

"Hech me, and that's a cauldrif job at the best. Bless me, dawtie, what's the matter wi' ye? Dinna be frightened, the puir body will no meddle ye."

These last words were spoken to the child, a sharp bright-eyed boy, who, as soon as he had seen the face of Helen M'Dougal, gave a cry of terror, and clinging to the old woman hid his face in her gown.

She tried to reassure him and to coax him with courage, but the more she spoke the more did he cling to her, and regard with dread and aversion the face of the stranger.

"Did ever anybody see the like o' that," said his protector, in a disappointed tone. "Ma darlin', that's no like ye ava; ye used tae be as bauld as a lion when a stranger ca'd in."

"It's my rags that frighten him," said the wanderer. "He is not accustomed to see such as I am."

"Oh, deed there's mony a puir wanderin' body comes to oor door, and I never saw him sae unco as that. But dinna tak' notice o' him, and he'll sune come tae."

With a sigh of unspeakable satisfaction, Helen M'Dougal sank wearily into the chair that had been set for her, and eagerly consumed a cog of porridge which the woman had just made for her own supper.

"The maister man is no at hame," the latter remarked, as she sat down and resumed her knitting, the child still keeping close to her, and ever and anon casting terrified looks at the stranger.

"He's no at hame," repeated the woman. "He's at Embro.

Awfu' daeins there enoo. Nae doot, you that's gaun
aboot the kintra wull hae heard o' the Burke and Hare
murders."

"Ye—yes; oh, I have," faltered Helen. "The—the country
is full of it."

"And nae wonder. Eh, the blackguards! they sud be hanged
every ane o' them. And yet they tell me there's nane but
Burke tae swing for it. Is that no shamefu'?"

Helen's tongue clave to the roof of her mouth, and she
could not frame a word in reply.

"I'm sayin', is that no shamefu'?" repeated the old woman,
looking up from her knitting. "And they no a' to be hanged.
And what for did they let awa' that hizzy M'Dougal?"

"God knows," gasped her listener, with a desperate effort.

"Oh, the cruel, heartless monsters," the old woman went
on. "Tae tak' the lives o' the puir things—the auld woman
and the helpless simpleton, and that young lassie they ca'
Mary Paterson. Hech," she added, as if speaking to herself, "I
wuss Jimes was hame, tae let me ken the best or the warst
aboot her. Oh, my bairn! my bairn! my puir lost wanderin'
bairn! I hope it's no you!"

She laid her knitting in her lap, and sat silent, gazing
mournfully into the fire, busy with her sad and sorrowful
thoughts. When she recovered from her abstraction she found
that the wanderer had fallen sound asleep in her chair, and
the child was also slumbering with his head laid upon her
knee.

She gently and tenderly undressed him and laid him in
bed, and was about to resume her seat by the fire, when a
well-known footstep approaching the door made her start in
eager surprise and run into the passage, when she met the tall
muffled-up form of James Crawford, white with the snow
which was now falling heavily.

"Oh, Jimes, ma man," she cried, "I'm glad tae see ye,
though I didna expect ye in sic a nicht. And what news hae
ye brocht? It's no her—it's no Mary—tell me it's no
Mary!"

James was now in the kitchen, and his eye fell in surprise
on the wretched figure sleeping by the fire.

"It's a puir wanderin' woman," Peggy M'Naughton hastened
to explain. "She cam tae the door just after the darkenin',
cauld, and wat, and hungry, and I couldna turn her awa' tae

starve.[1] She's sleepin' there as sound as a stane. But ye hinna
telt me the news, ye hinna—Mercy, James, what is it?"

"Oh, Peggy, the warst, the warst," groaned James, turning
towards her his white anguished face.

"It *is* oor Mary?" was all that Peggy could gulp out, her
own face turning white and bloodless likewise. "Oh, the
murderin' wretches, did they tak' the life o' a puir helpless
lassie?"

And Peggy, sitting down covered her head with her apron,
rocked her body to and fro, and sobbed forth her bitter grief.

When she had calmed somewhat, she asked James to tell
her the particulars, which he did, *hiding nothing*. The life of sin
and shame into which Mary had fallen was not kept concealed. It was spoken of with all subdued restraint, for he who
told it was the one of all others whose heart prompted him
to spare the character of her of whom he spoke, and to none
but Peggy would he breathe the terrible truth. But she, he was
aware, ought to know; for Peggy had stood to Mary in the
room of a mother, and the story of Mary's fall and degradation would be kept in her bosom with all a mother's jealousy
of concealment.

So he told her, and the intelligence, softened though it was
as far as possible, froze her stricken heart with horror, and
after a long time of silent agony the first words she uttered
were—

"Oh, thank the Lord that her faither didna live tae hear
o' this."

"Weel, Peggy," sighed James, "if she sinned she has suffered, for that monster, Burke, and his hellish crew murdered
her."[2]

And forthwith he related all that he had learned from Jessie
Brown and at the *Courant* office, drawing forth from his bosom
the packet which the girl had given him and handing it to
Peggy, to whom it was addressed.

"Open it yersell, Jimes," said Peggy; "I havena strength
tae dae it."

The youth did so, and within the outside covering was a
folded sheet of parchment constituting a duly executed deed,

---

1. Scots: to die, or perish.
2. As usual, 1885 drops the reference to hell.

making her child the lawful heir of whatever might be hers. Pinned to the parchment was a slip of paper on which the following was written in Mary's own hand:—

"Dear Peggy,—When this reaches you I shall be no more. It may prove to be of no use, for my father's property seems to have gone into the hands of another; but in case the future should bring to light anything like fraud or mistake, I take the precaution to secure for my boy that which, alas! the law does not allow him to inherit. Farewell, dear Peggy. If you loved me seek not to know my history after I left Braeside. Forget me if you can; and never, never let my boy hear the name or know the fate of his wretched and unhappy mother,—MARY."

James read this aloud in a voice broken by emotion, and for some time they could do nothing but mingle their tears together. Then in order to divert their hearts from the overwhelming sorrow the youth related his interview with Duncan Grahame, and intimated his resolution to go back to Edinburgh to see Burke hanged.

Here the attention of the speakers was arrested by the sleeping wanderer, whose slumbers, hitherto profound, were strangely disturbed. She seemed to be labouring under a fearful dream, and her face bore an expression of intense agitation. Peggy was about to awake her, and thus relieve her from her imaginary terror, when her lips began to move, and words came rapidly forth. "Don't hang him, my Lord. Hare was worse than him. It was all lies Hare told. He helped to murder the whole of them, and his wife knows it as well as me."

"Lord a mercy! wha can she be?" ejaculated Peggy. James Crawford, to whom the words brought a startling suspicion, sprang forward and glowered into the sleeper's face.

The latter, as the scene of her dream changed, cowered back in her chair, and held up her hands before her.

"Don't murder me!—oh, don't murder me. Oh, policeman, save me from these people."

"By a' that's horrible," roared James, "that's Helen M'Dougal!"

His loud voice roused the sleeper, and she started up in wild terror.

"Yes, yes," she cried. "But let me go; do not meddle me, good folks; let me go."

She uttered these frantic words ere she had come to the recollection of where she was. Then, looking wonderingly round, she gazed inquiringly on James and Peggy.

"It's just her," shouted James. "They chased her out o' Redding last Sabbath nicht."

"Oh, the murderin' limmer; and she had the impertinence to come here," shrieked Peggy—"here, after killin' puir Mary."

"Wretch!" hissed the youth; "I kenna what hinders me frae chokin' the black soul oot o' ye; but if ye dinna gang oot o' the hoose this moment *I'll* dae it. Do ye hear; awa wi' ye."

"There's the door," added Peggy, in a shrill scream. "Off wi' ye, or I'll tear yer e'en oot."

The miserable woman waited to hear no more, but rushed through the open door which James had made ready for her exit—rushed out into the midnight darkness and the blinding drift.

This was the last time that human eye beheld the living form of Helen M'Dougal. Weeks after, when the heavy and long-continued snow storm vanished before the softer breath of the returning spring, the dead emaciated body of a woman was found lying on the ground far across the moor, about a mile from James Crawford's cottage. It was impossible to identify the body, for the hungry rats or other vermin had eaten away the flesh off the face; but the rags which partially covered her both James and Peggy recognised, and knew it was the body of Helen M'Dougal.

But they kept their knowledge to themselves, and the parish authorities laid the corpse in a pauper's grave, and recorded the funeral as that of a nameless and unknown wanderer.

CHAPTER XXVII

WHAT BEFELL HARE'S WIFE

That same stormy snowy night in which Helen M'Dougal was driven from the cottage of James Crawford, Hare's wife was liberated from the Calton Jail, where the authorities had kept her since the trial, till the popular fury should have somewhat calmed.

She could not, however, remain there always, and she was set at large, with the advice given her to get out of Edinburgh as quickly and secretly as possible. She heard this recommendation, and gave little heed to it, but with her child in her arms went forth from the prison, and took her way openly towards Waterloo Place.

The wintry wind swept ruthlessly along the Regent Road, dashing the hard snow flakes against the prison wall. The black mass of the Calton Hill was fast whitening under the falling snow, and on the streets, close by the kerb stones, little drifts had gathered to the depth of some inches, while the northern sides of the lamp-posts were also clad in cold ghostly white.

Mary Hare, highly elevated at being once more free, went briskly along, past the Post Office and the theatre, and turned up the North Bridge. Neither shame nor remorse had a place in her bosom, for had not she and Hare got out of the scrape very cleverly? *He* was not liberated yet, but would be soon, when they would join each other, congratulate each other on having got so nicely out of the difficulty, and live together as before.

The loathsome woman's elation and triumph were suddenly disturbed as she passed a well-lighted window on the bridge, by a loud exclamation from a ragged boy, of—

"There's Hare's wife."

It is wonderful how rapidly a crowd can gather on the streets of a city. Let anything extraordinary or sensational occur, and the thoroughfare, which the moment before was almost deserted, is filled by an eager agitated assembly. It was so now. When the boy's exclamation was uttered, the bridge was almost free of passengers, yet, in a few seconds, quite a throng had surrounded the woman, and savage cries of rage and hatred mingled with the blast.

The crowd was of a higher grade than that which had assailed Helen M'Dougal in the West Port, but it was not one whit less ferocious, and a pelting shower of snowballs was hurled against the cowering form of Mrs Hare. But for the child she carried in her arms, her experience at the hands of the enraged people would have been of a character most frightful, but some of the more humane shouted not to hurt the bairn, and she, taking advantage of the caution, crouched down by the wall and held the child in front of her to be screened from the descending snowballs.

At this juncture a body of policemen came down from the High Street, and, placing her in the midst of them, conveyed her to the office, receiving many hard blows as they performed this protecting work.

Once lodged within the walls of the office, she was for the time secure from further molestation, and, half dead with fright and pain, she sat weeping in one of the guard-rooms, scarcely heeding the cries of the infant that clung to her breast.

But this asylum could be nothing more than temporary, and in a day or two thereafter she was set adrift, as Helen M'Dougal had been, a few hours after midnight, to go where she might.

Behold, then, this second member of the murderous West Port gang sent forth a hunted fugitive, under the righteous laws of society, trying to escape from the ruthless vengeance of that humanity which by their hands had been so atrociously destroyed. Shall we say that the universal feeling of intense hate and abhorrence was too cruel or too vindictive? We dare not say so. The crimes had been without a parallel in magnitude, number, and character, and the criminals were so base and brutal as to put them beyond the pale of sympathy, sentimental feeling, or forbearance. Humanity would not have been true to itself if it had acted towards these wretches in any other way—especially those of them whom the law could not reach. Their crimes had been without palliation, their retribution must therefore be measureless. Incapable of repentance or remorse, they were utterly undeserving of pity, not so much for the sake of justice as for the sake of that human nature which they had so foully destroyed. The inevitable law of adjustment required to operate in the fearfully disturbed balance, and the process of adjustment was as sacred as the law to which it belonged.

Into the cold bleak winter world, then, went Hare's wife, her cruel heart and passionate nature cowed by the circumstances in which she was placed. In this, the beginning of her retributive experience, let us remember her prominent share in the West Port butcheries. She it was who lured many of the victims into the fatal room. She it was who had led Daft Jamie like a sheep to the shambles, and with her own hand she had assisted Hare to smother the Italian boy. The fierce and brutal nature of the murderess was in her. Woman she was not—she was more a wild beast or a fiend.

And it was like a hunted wild beast that she now began her wanderings. Shaking her clenched hand wildly in the air, as she looked up and down the empty High Street, she poured forth blasphemous curses on the people who had assailed her; then tucking her sleeping child under her arm, she went away by the back of the Castle, and so out into the country westward.

Her object was to reach Ireland, where, in her native country, she hoped to find an asylum. The way to Glasgow was a long and painful one, for the roads were now heavy with snow, and the child at her breast was burdensome to carry. Once, as she sat resting on one of the canal bridges, she thought of dropping the child into the water and so getting quit of it, but the surface was covered with a crust of hard, impenetrable ice, and that mode of riddance was not available. She went once more on her way, and at length entered Glasgow in a state of utter exhaustion.

Having been frequently in Glasgow, she knew a beggar's lodging-house not far from the Broomielaw,[1] and thither she directed her weary steps, having just procured by begging a few pence to pay for supper and bed. Little did those who, in the pity of charity, dropped a copper into her hand, know that they were giving succour to the notorious woman, Hare's wife.

The lodging-house to which she repaired, though situated

---

1. By the river, and close for ships departing to Ireland.

in one of the lowest localities, and dirty in the extreme, was a place of nightly joy and feasting, for it is well known that no class lives better in regard to food than the street beggar.

In a back court, having an entrance from two different streets, it was reached by descending six or eight stone steps, the door at the bottom of which gave immediate entrance to a large low-roofed place, crossed by heavy beams above, and supported by black iron pillars. It had once been a cellar, and had bare, unplastered walls, and for a window an iron grating, which let in both light and air. At one end, however, was an immense fire-place, which gave room for a deal of contemporary cooking, and along the base of the back wall was a layer of straw, half hidden by a series of filthy coverlets. This served as a common bed for the lodgers.

When Hare's wife crawled in here for rest and shelter, but a few of the lodgers had come in for the night, but they continued to arrive one by one till the place was quite full. Having brought in her supper with her she squatted down on the floor, in the shadow of one of the iron pillars, fearful lest she should be recognised by any person who might have lodged in her house in Tanner's Close. Being in that position nearly out of sight, she was taken little or no notice of, and, utterly exhausted by fatigue, she leaned her back against the pillar, and fell asleep, the increasing sound of the revelry even failing to disturb her.

The scene was now approaching to something like a carnival. On the long glowing grate pots simmered and pans hissed, sending forth a most tempting flavour. On the rough deal tables, too, bottles of all sorts and sizes were placed, and cracked jugs and broken glasses, mingled with piles of bread and cheese, eggs, bacon, boiled fowls, fish, and an immense collection of miscellaneous edibles. The liquor in the bottles was of various kinds, chiefly ale, porter, and whisky, but even wine was not absent.

The groups assembled to partake of this good cheer were of the most extraordinary and varied character. All the individuals were nondescripts in point of dress. Most were in rags, and not one had an appearance in keeping with the profusion of luxurious provision under which the tables groaned. During the day they had been spread over the city plying their avocations of begging, singing, organ-grinding, and, in some instances, stealing and pocketpicking, and their efforts had been so successful as to provide a supper which no honest industrious working man ever dreamed of sitting down to.

Amongst the motley crew of villanous-looking men and
dirty degraded women we require to notice but three individuals. The first was a young man whose appearance was
greatly above the others; in fact, he had little in common with
the rest except seedy, patched, and ragged clothes, and a certain manifestation of vagrancy in his looks and general
appearance. He was one of the most boisterous of the
company, and, asserting that he had met with rare good luck
that day, he was liberally treating the rest to the contents of
two or three bottles which he had brought in with him.

"Draw it mild, Dick, my lad," rcmarked an elderly man,
who, with a female companion, were enjoying a substantial
but not particularly extravagant supper at the table nearest
the fire. "Draw it mild, my boy," he added, with a sagacious
nod. "Rare good luck don't come every day, and it's as well
to keep as much to-night as will make the pot boil to-
morrow."

"Hang it, old Bowser, don't preach to me," returned the
youth, who was excited to recklessness by the drink he had
swallowed. "That sort of thing won't suit my notions at all.
My motto is to be merry when I can, and let the morrow take
care of itself."

"Why, then, you've got a bad motto, that's all," said the
other, who had been called Bowser.

"Have I?" exclaimed the youth. "It's to be found in the
Bible, and most people say that's a good book."

"Too good for the likes of us," rejoined Bowser, with a
slight laugh. "But take my word for it, Dick, lad, a fellow is
the better of having a shilling or two in his pocket *in the
morning.*"

"Won't do, I tell you," roared Dick. "Them's the sort of
counsels the old folks at home tried to palm on me, but not
suiting my spirit I came off to enjoy life in my own way, and
I mean to do it too. Now, look ye, every soul in the house
has got to drink a glass of my whisky. It will stand one a-piece
all round."

"Hurrah! hurrah!" shouted in approbation those who were
thus to share in the youth's generosity.

"When Dick aint in drink he's precious hard though,"
observed Bowser's female companion, in that worthy's ear.

"Why, in course he does know what he's about there," acquiesced Bowser. "But you see, Tibb, I wants him to go home with us, and if he gets on the batter he's fixed here for a fortnight at least."

"I wish we could get away home," answered the woman. "I'm sure Bet will be letting everything go to the dogs, for she's too soft in the crib. But here we have been nearly a week in Glasgow and no baby turned up."

"Don't despair," whispered Bowser. "You saw how near I was to nipping one yesterday. Luck may serve me better the next time."

The man and woman who carried on this whispered conversation were somewhat noteworthy in appearance. The woman was tall and bony, and had one of the biggest noses ever seen on a human face. A most determined-looking woman she was, and one that no man would care to encounter—there was something so calm and resolute about her. Clearly she was a woman born to command, and she did command in a sphere of her own, from which she was at the present time absent.

Bowser was her husband, and he, too, was noteworthy. His face said, as plainly as face could say, that he was cunning and calculating. The very glance of his small grey eye impressed one with the idea that he was always looking after the main chance, and would very likely not be troubled with any scruples of conscience in the mode of getting the main chance looked to. He was a powerfully-built man, though now, like the woman beside him, turned on the shady side of the hill of life.

Dick, true to his half-drunken promise, went round the company, bottle and glass in hand, and made every one drink it from full to empty—a work in which he met with no opposition, for all were eager enough to accept a gift so much to their liking, and the popular enthusiasm produced by Dick's free-heartedness grew noisily vehement, till a very Babel of sound shook the cellar, and would have brought interference from above, if the rooms there had not been used as storehouses, and were at that hour shut up.

"I'm blessed if that ain't awful," said Tibb, turning to Bowser, after sending a watchful glance over the scene. "Catch our crib in Dundee ever breaking out into howls like these; wouldn't we just silence the idiots?"

"In course we would," returned Bowser; "but old Bess, here, don't care what goes on, so long as the browns tumble in."[2]

"Has everybody got a glass round?" asked Dick, flourishing the bottle, and looking round him in all directions.

"That woman sleeping at the foot of the pillar hasn't tasted," cried some one.

"By Jove, and she hasn't," said Dick, pouring out another glass. "Poor devil, she looks as if she needed a drop to warm her. Here, mistress, wake up and take this to put some heart in you."

It was Mrs Hare to whom he spoke, and he enforced his words by bending down and shaking her by the shoulder.

"My eye! what a sound sleep she's in," remarked the youth, as his rough shaking failed to rouse her. "She looks as if she hadn't been at it for a week. Come, mistress, rouse up and take this to make your sleep all the better."

"Who is she, Bess?" asked one at an old woman, the keeper of the house.

"Don't know," replied the crone; "a shrimp, I fancy. Anyhow she's Irish, and she paid her money for the night."

"Let us have a look at her," said a weather-beaten old hag. "If she's from Belfast I should know her fr—Why, as I'm alive, its Hare's wife!"

"Hare's wife!" shouted every one, and in a moment the sensation in the place was indescribable.

"Ay! Haven't I lodged in her horrible house in Tanner's Close."

"And so have I," cried one and another flocking round the prostrate sleeper, and peering into her face. They at once recognised her, and frantic cries of "choke her," "Burke her," "smother her," burst forth.[3]

The fiendish yells broke the wretch's slumber, and she rose to her feet in bewildered consternation and dismay, to meet a score of faces glaring vengeance upon her.

"Hang her to that hook," exclaimed Dick, pointing to an iron rivet in one of the cross-beams.

---

2. Browns are copper coins.

3. Burke gave his name to murdering by his technique—suffocation. OED gives the first use of the phrase as at his hanging.

"No, no! smother her as they did in Tanner's Close," shouted a number all at once. "Burke her and her brat too. They killed children there!"

This proposal seemed to meet with most general favour, and in a trice the woman was thrown on the floor with her child, now crying in her arms, and those who held her shouted for the others to bring bedding to lay upon her.

She shrieked wildly for mercy, but her frantic prayer was in vain, and half-a-dozen willing hands began to drag from its corner the only stuffed bed-tick which the place contained.

They had not got it more than a yard or two out of its place when, being rotten with damp, it suddenly gave way, scattering the chaff upon the floor, and prostrating those who were so eagerly dragging it.

"There's our chance now," whispered Bowser to Tibb; these two having taken no part in the storm which raged. "There's a kid for us at last."

"But how can we get it?" asked Tibb, as raising her tall form she looked over the others' heads at the woman they meant to despatch.

"We must get her out of this," was Bowser's hurried reply. "Stand by me, and if we once get her clear of the door, I'll manage it."

Whereupon while those who had been overturned were still sprawling on the floor, and everything was in the most frightful confusion, Bowser thrust aside those who were between him and the intended victim and exclaimed—

"Don't be idiots. The worse she is, the less is she worth hanging for."

"It's not murder, it's justice," cried Dick.

"Justice or not, the law will call it murder, and hang us all. Now I for one won't risk the noose for such as her. Let us turn her out."

"No, no; smother her," was again the cry, and more vehement than before, and in the midst of the renewed hubbub Bowser, making a signal to Tibb, laid about him vigorously with his arms, sending the astonished beggars rolling one upon the other on the ground, while Tibb, understanding what was wanted, lifted Hare's wife from the floor, and bore her towards the door, and up the steps which led to the court.

The moment she had cleared the threshold with her burden, Bowser sprung after her, and snatching the key of the door from the inside placed it in the outside, and closing the door with a bang, locked it, and was up the steps in an instant.

Tibb stood in the court, and Hare's wife, whom the danger and terror had infused with energy, was looking wildly round her to see in what direction to run.

"Follow me—quick, before they get out," whispered Bowser.

He darted across the court, and into the street, closely followed by Tibb and the other. He led them by various turnings to the Broomielaw, where they took refuge in one of the sheds in the quay, and were safe from pursuit.

"Och sure and ye've saved me life this terrible night," said the trembling wretch.

"We have," said Bowser. "But you are not safe so long as you are in Glasgow, you should cross to Ireland immediately."

"Musha thin, and that's the very thing I want to do; but where am I to get the passage money?"

"Never mind passage money," said Bowser; "the Fingal sails just in an hour. She's lying just along there. Here's half-a-crown for you; that will buy as much food as you'll want on the voyage. Get it as you go along, and creep on board without letting any one see you. Hide somewhere on deck all night, and when they find you in the morning they can do nothing but carry you across."

She clutched the half-crown, and had turned to fly, when Bowser grasped her by the shoulder.

"Stop," he said; "better give Tibb there your child. You'll have enough to do to take care of yourself. It would only cry in the ship, and so you would get turned out."

"Will you keep it then?" asked the callous wretch.

"We will. Tibb and I will bring it up."

Without a word, the unnatural mother handed the infant to Tibb, giving it no parting kiss, not even a farewell look, and quitting the shed, hurried as fast as she could towards the vessel, which was about to start for Belfast.

The half-crown was spent in purchasing bread and cheese and a small bottle of whisky, and, having secured these about her person, she crossed again to the quay, and crept along, avoiding observation till she came to the Fingal, where the stir of embarkation was going forward.[4]

In the bustle and confusion which prevailed at the moment she managed to steal on board unperceived, and making her way to the fore part of the vessel, got under a heap of wrappings, took a long pull at the whisky, and fell asleep before the vessel had left her mooring.

"Now then, Tibb, can't you keep the brat from squalling?" said Bowser, as he and his female companion made their way up the Saltmarket, the latter carrying the child, which cried vehemently.

"Not till I have something to stuff its mouth with," returned Tibb. "Why, bless me, it aint nothing more nor skin and bone; it's as light as a feather. I wouldn't have believed a starved thing like that could cry so wicked."

"Ah! it will have a spice of the devil in it; it has come of a bad kind," remarked Bowser.

"There—why, if it hasn't got the hooping cough!" cried Tibb, as the infant laboured under a most distressing fit of coughing.

"So it has, and so much the better. People pity a sight like that and fork out. The kid should be worth ten bob a week more to Bet."

"I hope we'll start to-morrow," said Tibb, in a grumbling tone.

"No mistake about it if we can get Dick to move, and I think we shall, for he is sure to be cleaned out to-night, and he hasn't a rag of toggery to raise the wind with."

"I've seen him pawn his flute afore this," observed Tibb.

"Ha, ha! but I've taken care of that," rejoined Bowser with a chuckle, as he drew the end of an ebony flute from his sleeve, and pushed it up again the moment that Tibb's sharp eye had seen it.

About half-way up the Saltmarket they turned into a dark dirty close, and entered another low lodging-house of a character very similar to that they had just quitted. The scene

---

4. An 1828 advertisement shows the *Fingal*, captained by Hugh Price, as a Belfast steamer run by G. and J. Burns, along with her sister ship, the *Eclipse*. They departed from the Broomielaw and from Greenock, near Glasgow. Wednesday departures were at 4 p.m.—after dark in the Scottish winter. Online at www.theglasgowstory.com/image.php?inum=TGSE00228.

within we shall not describe, but there they slept for the night, and a fearful night of wind and rain it turned out to be.

At a somewhat late hour on the following day the youth who has been named Dick was sauntering aimlessly along the Trongate when a heavy hand fell upon his shoulder, and, looking round, his bloodshot eye fell upon Bowser.

"Well, my hearty, what's trumph?" was that worthy's question.

"The ace of nothing," was the answer, in a desponding tone. "I made an ass of myself last night—haven't even a copper left! and, curse it, I've lost my flute somewhere or other."

"It's not lost that a friend has," said Bowser, as he pulled forth the flute, to the youth's no little satisfaction.

"But I say," cried the latter, as a sudden recollection came upon him, "what for did you and Tibb bolt with Hare's wife last night? The wretch has got no right to live."

"Perhaps not; but don't you twig—I wanted the kid."

"And have you got it?"

"Tibb has it safe, along at Verger's in the Saltmarket."

"And where's its precious mother?"

"Half-way to Ireland by this time, if the Fingal hasn't gone to the bottom in last night's wind."

"Then you've got your errand served?"

"Yes, and we must be off to Dundee this afternoon. You'll come, won't you?"[5]

"Don't care if I do, for I'm tired of Glasgow. But, I say, I'm cursed dry."

"I'll stand a calker."

"That's the sort. Bowser, you're a brick."

*

Let us put back the wheel of time for a few hours, and return again to the darkness of the previous night. It was just upon the verge of dawn, and the Fingal was tossed fearfully upon the billows of the raging sea. A tremendous storm had

---

5. Dick, Bowser and Tibb are moving from one centre of Scotland's international export business to another. Glasgow focused on the tobacco trade, Dundee on linen and jute.

come on just as she reached the lower part of the river, and there was nothing for it but the brave ship to plough her way in the face of the hurricane towards the open sea. Higher and higher rose the white-crested waves, and the spray and foam flew in clouds through the rigging. Every sail was reefed, and the bare masts creaked and bent till the test of their soundness was beyond all dispute.

Suddenly a mighty wave came like a mountain towards the vessel's bows, and broke with a roar of thunder, sweeping over the deck like a rushing flood. The wretched fugitive, who had for some time been trembling in her place of conceal-ment, was forced therefrom by terror, and with a wild shriek rushed out to a shelter more secure. It was a fatal course. Not for one moment could she keep her feet on the sloping deck, which the wind swept with all its force, and another wave breaking at the moment over the ship, it caught her in its resistless course, and carried her aft over the bulwarks into the frowning deep.

One wild, death-shriek she uttered, as she was being whirled to destruction—a shriek of horror and despair, which rose, if not above, yet in contrast to, the deep hoarse roar of the storm, and it struck upon the startled ear of the man lashed at the helm, who looked hastily forward, and saw a woman's form in the white foam of the flood which was rush-ing towards him.

He was nearly powerless to help, for the unexpected sight of a woman there paralysed him with horror, and besides, for his own safety, he was lashed to the wheel. Yet, instinctively, he threw out his hands and tried to clutch her as she was borne past. Hopeless effort! He but saw for a moment her white face of despair turned frantically towards him, and the next instant she was swept into the boiling surge.

He shouted vehemently, "A woman overboard!" but no one could hear his words, even if it had been possible to render any assistance.

In half an hour the hurricane suddenly ceased, and the man told his tale to the officer of the watch.

The passengers were mustered, and no one was missing; it was therefore considered to be a freak of the man's excited imagination, and he was himself forced to consider it so. Still, the white face of horror haunted him by its vividness, and he superstitiously cherished the belief that he had seen a spirit.

Thus, though she had escaped all punishment from the law of man, this brutal woman very speedily met with a violent death. No trace of her body was ever found. The great ocean grave retained it; but on that day when the sea gives up its dead, she shall come forth with the thousands who have slept their long sleep in its depths, and shall stand with her guilty associates before the bar of a universal and unerring judgment.

CHAPTER XXVIII

HARE

We now come to describe the retribution which overtook the last and worst of the four associated criminals—the arch-murderer Hare. When we say the worst, we mean the most ferocious, the prime instigator to the crimes, and the cruelest in their commission. In a moral point of view, we think Burke was *really* the worst, because he sinned against the greatest light. He had more intelligence than Hare, and the shadow of humanity still lingered in his soul, visiting it, if not with compunction, at least with fear, and compelling him to fortify his evil nature with strong drink.

While he had to darken the little light that was in him, and banish the faint traces of his better nature that hovered about his heart, Hare had apparently no light to darken, and no better nature to destroy. This made him at once worse and better than Burke—worse as a human being, but better as a criminal, for he did not need to struggle in any way against the angel of virtue.

In popular estimation, however, and also in the eye of the law, had the truth been fully known, Hare was the greater fiend; and while he had sufficient cunning to concoct a story, by which the guilt of Burke was declared, while his own share in the murders was denied, yet he was not intelligent enough to deceive a single listener as to his own participation in the crimes. Everybody saw clearly that he had saved his own neck by betraying his accomplice; and the dissatisfaction at his escape was even fiercer and greater than the satisfaction felt at Burke's punishment.

After giving his perjured evidence in the Court, he was led away, still in custody, to a back entrance, where a cab was got, and, accompanied by two jailers, was driven back to the Calton Hill prison. As the cab rattled along the lighted streets, the jailers were not a little astonished to hear him chuckle, and to observe a leer of great satisfaction on his gruesome countenance.

"Faix, then, it's meself that's done it nate and clever," he observed, with an air of great delight.

"Done what?" asked one of his attendants.

"Got meself off," added the monster, with another gleeful leer.

"Ay, by putting the rope round Burke's neck," returned the warder, in a tone of disgust.

"Thrue for it," said Hare, with another horrible chuckle.

The question of his escape from legal justice was not yet quite settled however. The public howl for his punishment grew louder every hour. The people were enraged beyond measure at the thought that the greatest of all these atrocious murderers should escape, and clamoured with the wildest determination for his trial for others of the murders that had been committed.

In this wish and cry all classes, high and low, educated and uneducated, joined, but the Lord Advocate gave it to be understood that the compact which had been made with him barred all further proceedings against him. The Crown had taken him as King's evidence, promising that he should not be punished, and the Crown was bound to implement its agreement, however guilty he might have been.

The more astute of the people reasoned that this might be true so far as the murder for which Burke had been convicted was concerned, but that it did not apply to the case of Daft Jamie, which had not come to trial. In answer to this, it was stated that the fact of this case not coming to trial was no fault of Hare's, or of the public prosecutor either. Hare had given his information about it, and was ready to give his open testimony, and the Lord Advocate had the case in the indictment, which was departed from only at the request of the judges. To all intents and purposes, therefore, Hare had done his work, and was entitled to the immunity under the promise of which that work had been performed.

Foiled in this, another suggestion was made, viz, that a private prosecution might be raised against him by a relative of one of the victims—the mother of Daft Jamie, for instance, who could claim compensation for the loss of her son. Wherefore a fund was raised, and several of the more active and influential citizens undertook to manage the case in the woman's name, and Francis Jeffrey (afterwards Lord Jeffrey) was engaged to conduct it in the Court.

This proceeding pleased the public immensely, and it was hoped this human wild beast would still be trapped. The matter involved one or two nice points of law, and these being considered by the gentlemen of the long robe of infinitely greater importance than the punishment or liberation of Hare, his interests were espoused by no less a person than Duncan M'Neill, then an advocate at the bar, now the Lord President of the Court of Session.

Counter-action was at once taken, and while witnesses were being got up against Hare, a petition was presented by him praying to be liberated from prison. This petition was, of course, presented to the Sheriff, who refused it until it was settled whether a private party had a right to prosecute him, this being a question which the High Court of Justiciary alone could decide.

Meanwhile, Hare was kept in prison, and was loathed and detested even by the worst criminals there. Like as the poet has represented the traitor Judas in hell was Hare's treatment by his fellow-prisoners.

"The common damned shunned his society,
And looked upon themselves as fiends less foul."[1]

When taking his walks in the exercise yard, visitors to the prison would be standing at the grating wishing to see him, and lest any one should mistake another for him the rest of the prisoners pushed him forward and pointed him out. And to show the moral perversion of the wretch's nature, he was gratified at being thus lionised. Never once did he manifest the slightest spark of shame; on the contrary, he was proud of the interest he created, and was fond of showing himself to the eager yet horrified onlookers. It was even said at the time that when an artist, who was introduced to the grating when he was in the yard, was busy taking his likeness, Hare observed him, and came and stood full in his view till the sketch was done, and then asked a shilling for being so obliging.

It was now near to the day of Burke's execution, and the *Courant* had intimated that in the paper which had an account

---

1. Adapted from Scottish poet Robert Blair's poem "The Grave: Self-Murder", published 1743. Blair wrote: "The common damned shun their society, / And look upon themselves as fiends less foul."

of his execution there would also be given his confession, which intimation was no sooner brought under the notice of Hare's legal agents than an application was made for the court to prohibit the publication of such a confession, previous to the settlement of the question at issue; as it might subsequently prejudice Hare's interests.

The prohibition was made, and the *Courant* obeyed it, for when the paper appeared on the day of the execution it did not contain the confession, but explained why it had in the meantime been withheld.

Some four days after Burke was hanged, Hare's case came on for adjudication before the High Court, and it was considered so important that all the judges sat on the bench.

We need not here give the arguments for and against, but the decision was in Hare's favour, the principle being laid down that the Lord Advocate, representing the Crown, represented also the whole community, and the pledge given by him to a criminal who turned King's evidence was virtually a pledge given by the nation, collectively and *individually*. The Lord Advocate then, in representing everybody, represented, amongst others, *the mother of Daft Jamie*, and his lordship's pledge of immunity was her pledge also.

So Hare was free.

Ay, and in freeing Hare—guilty though he was—the law asserted its honour and inflexible integrity. It allowed itself to give no weight to popular feeling. It sheltered with its justice the head of the vilest criminal, to whom, otherwise, it would have awarded the heaviest punishment. It was not Hare's deep guilt it had now to take into account, it was its own dignity and truth, and it vindicated these, though, in doing so, it freed from its clutches one of the most abandoned wretches who had ever lived. And we repeat that the law never dealt out more even-handed justice than when it opened the doors of the Calton Hill Jail to Hare, and said he was at liberty to depart.

To depart, but *whither?* That was a question not for it, but for Hare, and for Hare alone, and it was a question which he could not answer. Indeed, he seemed never to have given it a thought, for his brutal nature was not capable of imagining that he was in any danger from public vengeance. Now that the law had cleared him, he supposed that he was now perfectly safe, and might go where he pleased. But the officials knowing how his wife and Helen M'Dougal had been mobbed, and being well aware that if he fell into the hands of the people he would be torn limb from limb, gave him to understand the necessity of getting away from Edinburgh incog,[2] and concealing himself from public recognition. And in order that a town riot might be prevented, they took measures to send him away by the night mail, which went by way of Dumfries.

On the afternoon of the very day on which the High Court pronounced the decree of his liberation, a place was taken on the outside of the coach for a "Mr Black." If the name had been chosen by design it could not have been more appropriate. *Black* he certainly was beyond all earthly degree, and to have matched him in this one would have had to produce a fiend direct from the regions below.

The coach started at eight, and some ten or fifteen minutes before the hour Hare and an officer dressed in plain clothes came quietly out from a side door in the prison, and moved hastily along towards Waterloo Place. Hare's form was enveloped in a huge dark cloak, the fur collar of which enveloped the greater part of his face, and an old cloth cap, brought well down over his ears, made it impossible for any one to see his features.

He slunk along by the side of his companion, his two evil eyes peering out upon the long line of Princes Street, so clearly marked on that frosty night by the line of lighted lamps which ran far away into the distance.

At the Post Office his conductor called a cab, being afraid to enter the thoroughfares on foot, and in this vehicle they were driven to Newington, where they alighted to wait for the passing of the coach.

"Now, be sure to keep yourself closely muffled up," counselled the official, "and don't speak to a soul on the coach."

"Throth, and I won't," returned Hare; "but, sure now, it won't matter if I put down my cloak a bit when we get into the country, for divil a sowl knows me out of Edinburgh."

"You are known everywhere," was the reply. "Your portraits are circulating through every town and village in the kingdom, and thousands will recognise you at a glance."

---

2. incognito.

"Och, musha, but they are making a big man uv me intirely," said the wretch, with a pleased grin.

"They'll make precious short work with you if they catch hold of you, I can tell you," returned the officer sharply. "Stand clear. There's the coach."

On it came, its great flashing lamps putting the street before it all in a blaze, and at a signal made by Hare's conductor the coachman pulled up.

"Are you booked, gentlemen?" shouted the guard.

"My friend here is."

"Name?"

"Mr Black."

"All right. Jump up behind here. Quick, if you please."

Hare clambered awkwardly to the top, and his feet getting entangled in the long cloak he wore he would inevitably have fallen had not the guard grasped him by the arm.

"Take care, sir—there you are."

"Good night, *Mr Black*. A good and safe journey to you," cried the officer.

"All right," shouted the guard at the same moment, and away rattled the coach over the hard frosty road.

In little more than a minute they passed the last of the houses, and were cutting through the sharp country air. It was an intensely cold February night. Myriads of stars glittered like diamonds in the clear blue sky, and the rush of the coach over the ground created a wind of the keenest and most biting description. Snow lay deep in the fields on either side; but on the road it was beaten smooth and hard, so that the coach flew along with something like the velocity of a sledge. The long range of the Pentlands lay shrouded in their winter covering, solemn and silent under the glancing night-sky, while the great round mass of Arthur's Seat behind showed alternate streaks of snow and patches of black jagged rock.

None of the few outside passengers exchanged a word of conversation. It was much too cold to talk, and they drew their wrappings closely round them, and bent their heads to save their faces from the biting cold.

Hare sat in the back seat by himself, just in front of the guard, and he shivered and trembled in every limb, for the cloak which enveloped him was made of thin hard camlet, and did little to serve the purpose of a hap, while underneath he wore only his own ragged clothing.

His teeth chattered, his hands and feet nipped dreadfully, and his whole body shook as with ague. The cold struck upon him with dreadful severity, for though he had just come out of prison, it was not from one of the cold fireless cells, but from a warm and comfortable chamber, where, as a witness for the Crown, he had been lodged. This place he had occupied since the beginning of November—full three months—and had felt nothing of the frost which had sent suffering to the hearts and homes of thousands sunk in innocent poverty. To leave all at once, therefore, his warm quarters, and under intense frost, was a severe experience, and a thousand times during the first three hours of the journey did he wish himself back to the enjoyment of his prison comforts.

In other respects than this his position was unenviable enough. He had not a farthing in his pocket, his coach fare had been paid to Portpatrick, but once he got there he had no means of crossing to Ireland, whither he meant to go, and was trusting to fate and chance for the future.

The coach reached Noble House a little before midnight, and here the horses were changed, and twenty minutes allowed for supper in the parlour of the inn. The passengers alighted and entered the snug room, through the uncurtained window of which came the cheerful ruddy light of a blazing fire. Hare was the last to descend, and sat on his perch looking wistfully in upon the table spread for supper. Of the supper he could not partake, but he might obtain a brief shelter from the cold, and warm his shivering limbs in the heat of the room, so he ventured to slide down, and when he reached the ground his frozen feet had almost no feeling in them. But he managed to creep into the inn parlour, and still keeping his cloak muffled round his face, and his cap over his brow, sat down by himself behind the door.

An interest was felt by some of the passengers in the shy modest stranger, as they took him to be, sitting all alone in the corner, speaking to no one and asking for none of the good cheer. And one of them kindly asked him if he was not very cold back there.

"Terrible," answered Hare, through his chattering teeth.

"Then why don't you go to the fire and warm yourself?"

"I think I will," said Hare, moving at once from his seat at the door to a chair close to the blazing fire. Here with reckless imprudence he took off his cap, turned down the collar of his coat, and spread out his hands towards the heat.

A tall man was standing on the rug in front of the fire, and he, chancing casually to look round, gave a start when his eye fell upon Hare's face. Hare noticed the start, and looking furtively up at him, recognised him as one of the advocates employed against him in behalf of the mother of Daft Jamie.

In the first moment of surprise the Advocate almost burst out with an exclamation, but recollecting himself he merely shook his head menacingly, and walked to another part of the room.

All being busily engaged with supper this little pantomime was noticed by nobody, but Hare thought it as well to decamp, and again drawing the collar of his cloak round his face and slouching his cap he made his way outside, where the coach was standing with the fresh horses yoked ready to resume its journey.

There being an unoccupied seat in the inside of the coach he actually had the audacity to take it, and when the horn was blown and the passengers came out, they found him sitting in the corner.

They entered one by one, none making any objection to the stranger's presence, till the Advocate, who was the last, caught sight of him when he had his foot on the step, and starting back, exclaimed angrily to the guard, who was standing behind him—

"Take that fellow out."

"Who, sir?"

"That fellow in the corner."

"Oh, Mr Black, the outside passenger. Well, sir, if you object to his having a seat inside, and insist on him coming out—"

"I do object to his presence inside, and I do insist on him coming out," said the Advocate, indignantly.

"Very well, sir; you must go outside, Mr Black."

Without a word Hare slunk out, and clambered to his place on the top, and the lawyer took his seat amid the silence and surprised looks of the others, who thought he might have allowed the stranger the vacant inside seat on such a bitter night.

"You think that a harsh proceeding, no doubt," said the Advocate.

"Well, really, sir," said a benevolent-looking man in the corner, "it would not have inconvenienced us much to have allowed him to stay, and considering that the cold must be tremendous outside, it would have been a charity."

"And I, sir," returned the other, "would be the last to act in a churlish and unfeeling manner to any *respectable* person, however poor or friendless; but do you happen to know who that fellow is?"

"Certainly not."

"*That's Hare, the murderer!*"

Every one leapt so violently that the coach was nearly upset.

"Impossible!" said the benevolent gentleman in the corner. "Hare is not out of custody. He is to be proceeded against by Mrs Wilson for the murder of her son."

"No; the Court decided to-day that he can't be touched. I was one of the agents for Mrs Wilson, and the Court gave order for his liberation. He must be making his way to Ireland."

"Good heavens! and we were actually so near that wretch."

The excitement among the inside passengers had not subsided when the coach stopped at the next stage, and the fact was soon made known to the guard and coachman that the man in the camlet cloak was Hare. In a moment everybody in the coach knew it, and shrunk away from him as far as they could.

In the morning the coach entered Dumfries, and pulled up in front of the King's Arms. The passengers clambered out, many of them glad to be at their journey's end. The servants from the inn flocked out to take in the luggage, and the secret at once burst forth. Hare was there. The man in the camlet cloak was the notorious West Port murderer.

Hare having to go on by the Galloway coach, which did not start for a few hours, got down from his seat and made his way into the inn, aware that he was recognised, and that the knowledge of his presence was producing great excitement. In a moment the interior of the inn was in a perfect hubbub, and in the large parlour on the ground floor, into which Hare had gone, a crowd of guards, drivers, ostlers, and waiters burst, and surrounded him.

He never sought to deny his identity, and as he was at first regarded more as an object of curiosity than anything else, he was quite ready to speak to those who spoke to him, even about the West Port murders. Burke's confession had not appeared at that time, and people knew for certain nothing but what had come out at the trial, but it was sufficient to make him an object of universal loathing, detestation, and curiosity, and the coachmen handed him jugs of ale and encouraged him to talk.

Hare, devoid as usual of moral perception, grew jocose with his questioners, and with his horrible leer drank bad luck to his bad fortune. No sense of crime or guilt had he, and deeming that to those surrounding him he was some wonderful being, he got into a laughing mood at their attention, and had no objection to show himself off as he did in the jail.

"I say, Hare, ye gied Burke the twister," said one.

"Troth, and I did," answered the wretch, with his frightful leer.

"Come, tell us a' aboot it," cried another.

"Hoo mony fouk did ye kill?"

"Och, thin, sure there's no use in spaking uv that now. Didn't I do me duty in Edinburgh afore the gentlemen wid the white wigs?"

"It was a dashed shame o' ye tae murder puir Daft Jamie, though," said a big red-faced coachman, as he handed him a jug of ale.

"Musha, thin, you know it was Burke that did it."

"Gae wa' we ye, man. Dae ye think onybody believes that stuff? Burke could nae mair hae murdered Daft Jamie himsel' than he could flee tae the mune. There's nae doot ye helpit him. Was it you that held his mouth?"

"Oh, no," remarked another sarcastically. "He just sat on a chair and lookit on—sat and saw the sport."

This produced a general laugh, in which Hare heartily joined. The monster was absolutely getting merry on his West Port exploits.

"And where are you going now?" asked a gentleman who was staying at the Inn, and who had hitherto been a silent but disgusted spectator of the scene.

"To Ireland, sur," replied Hare, readily enough; "that is, yer honour, if I can get over; but I haven't a fardin.'"

Here the attention of those in the room was drawn to the fast increasing noise outside, and when some one looked forth

it was found that the wide street was densely packed with a
tumultuous crowd of excited people, who were demanding
with dreadful execrations that Hare should be set out amongst
them.

The moment the coach had arrived, the news flew through
the town that Hare had come with it, and was in the King's
Arms, and instantly the same intense wild frantic excitement
flashed out among the people of Dumfries which had manifested itself in Edinburgh and elsewhere on the appearance of
the women. The Burke and Hare murders had produced one
simultaneous shock of horror and indignation in the universal
public heart, and as we have seen wherever the murderers
appeared the irrepressible and unmitigated indignation burst
forth. It was not suggested or instigated; it was not confined
to the uneducated classes or the vulgar portion of society—it
was equally shared in by all ranks and all classes. The intelligent felt it and showed it just as fiercely as the illiterate, and
women were as fanatically indignant as men. If one touch of
nature makes the whole world kin, the desecration and sacri-
legious destruction of nature makes the whole world furious.
Here now the quiet town of Dumfries was in two hours roused
into ungovernable fury, and eight thousand of its population
surrounded the King's Arms, determined to pull Hare to
pieces. Say not that these eight thousand were roughs and
lovers of riot, or that they made up a mob whose most con-
genial element was violence and disorder. We dare say that
very few in that surging crowd had ever seen a riot in their
life, and that the immense majority were as peaceably disposed as any within the British dominions. The little town of
Dumfries could not possibly furnish at a moment's notice a
lawless, mischief-loving mob of eight thousand persons. No;
people were simultaneously and spontaneously actuated by
feelings due to outraged humanity, and felt towards Hare as
the inhabitants of a mountain village would feel towards a
wild beast which had carried off and devoured some of their
women and children.

The door of the inn was shut and barricaded, but beams
of wood were got, by which it was forced open, and in a
moment the room in which Hare sat was crammed with a
wrathful multitude, who forced him into a corner, where he
cowered in abject fear, livid and trembling.

Men and women were there, uttering a torrent of savage

imprecations, and the old cries were raised and repeated—
"Burke him!" "Hang him!"

"Hangin' is owre guid for the wretch," cried a woman
from behind, and she tried to get a poke at him with her
umbrella.

"Bring him out! bring him out!" was shouted by the
thousands who could not gain admission.

"Och musha thin, don't kill me!" whined the cowardly
murderer, clasping his hands with supplicating gesture, and
looking up with a fearful glance in the angry faces that glared
down upon him.

The fury of the crowd waxed greater every moment, and
if at this juncture two policemen had not arrived, the fate of
Hare would have been sealed. But the authorities, being now
thoroughly alarmed, sent the men to clear the inn, and they,
forcing their way into the passage, did manage to eject the
crowd, when the inn door was once more closed and barricaded.

The moment the room was cleared Hare was taken to
another apartment at the back, where a trap-door gave
entrance to a dark underground cellar. Into this the trembling
and affrighted wretch was lowered, the heavy door shut down
upon him, and a large mangle which stood in one corner
pulled forward and placed over it.

This place of safety did not promise to be very efficient,
for the crowd outside was getting more furious than ever, and
preparations were again being made to burst open the door.

CHAPTER XXIX

HARE'S FURTHER ADVENTURES

Dumfries was now in a dreadful uproar. A perfect frenzy seemed to have taken possession of the entire community; and the yard of the King's Arms Inn, with the street in front, was packed by a roaring, yelling, howling multitude, the sound of whose fury was like the ocean billows dashing on a rocky shore.

The innkeeper was naturally anxious about the safety of his premises; and he had reason, for the door had already been forced open, and the attitude of the multitude was now so threatening, that the inn itself might be destroyed, if something were not done to avert such a calamity.

But the only thing that could avert it was to have Hare removed, and to expel him at that moment was to deliver him up to instant death, for the people seemed determined to make him a speedy victim of popular vengeance.

The hour for the departure of the Galloway mail coach was drawing near, and it was resolved to put Hare inside, and, forcing a passage through the crowd, drive through the town at a furious rate, and leave the town and its excited population in the distance.

Accordingly, to effect this object, the yard of the inn was cleared, the great gates closed and fastened, and the coach brought out and placed close to the inn door. The people at once divined the intention of the authorities, and took such steps to arrest the coach as made the latter shrink from the risk of such a hazardous experiment. It was settled, therefore, that the coach should depart not only without Hare but altogether empty, and one or two passengers who were to go by it were sent forward some distance on the road in gigs till the coach should overtake them.

At the appointed hour all was ready, and the gates were thrown open, and the coach burst from the yard into the street. The crowd at first separated like a wave, and the coach dashed forward for a few yards; but, with a roar of thunder, the dense mass closed up again, and the vehicle, surrounded on all sides, was brought to a stand-still.

Instantly the doors were forced open, and two or three sprang in while the rest raised a yell of triumph, expecting now that the object of their wrath was in their hands, and that they would have the pleasure of seeing him tumble from the bridge into the river.

Great was the disappointment when the coach was found to be utterly empty. Every nook and corner was searched, the space under the seats was examined, and the boot explored. Of course all in vain; and when it became obvious that Hare was still in the inn, the crowd rolled back like an avalanche towards that building.

Meanwhile, no sooner did the coach drive out of the inn yard than Hare was brought up from the cellar, and preparations made to have him transferred to the jail, where he would be in greater security, and where the danger threatening the inn would be removed. This step was suggested by the innkeeper to the authorities of the town, and they, thoroughly alarmed at the uproar, considered it the best means of placing the wretch beyond the power of the mob, and also of bringing something like quietness and order to the place.

Hare was brought once more into the taproom, and a chaise was being got ready to take him to the jail, when a tremendous roar shook the inn to its centre. It was the return of the crowd, more furious than ever, and with all the strength of a resistless torrent the people poured again into the yard, burst open the door again, and crowded into the taproom before Hare could be got back to his hiding-place.

Once more Hare was forced into a corner, and crouched trembling there, his small red eyes nearly starting from their sockets with terror, and his gruesome face blanched with mortal fear. He was a hideous and repulsive object to look upon. Just before he was liberated from the Edinburgh jail, a phrenological cast of his head had been taken and for this purpose his hair had been cut short off, all but a fringe round the base of his skull, and this, joined to his natural ugliness, made him positively loathsome to gaze at.

He was roughly dragged from the corner and turned about in all directions, in order that the curiosity of the people might be gratified by gazing on such a monster. He was also assailed with opprobrious epithets, was asked all manner of questions about the murders, taunted, cursed, and anathematised with every degree of rage, bitterness, and angry scorn.

"Let me at him!" exclaimed a loud-voiced virago, as she struggled to get within the door of the room. "Let me get a haud o' the wretch; and if I dinna gie him a fricht, I ken mysel'."

Her words were received with loud laughter, and a way was opened for her approach, so that presently she stood face to face with him in the middle of the room. What rage and fury flashed from the woman's eyes when she suddenly found herself close to him, and scanned his fiendish countenance.

"Oh, ye wretch," she exclaimed, "ye blackguard, ye villain, ye monster, ye murderer, ye black deevil in human shape, ye—ye—"

The vocabulary of her epithets being exhausted, she closed her foaming lips, and, seizing him by the neckerchief, pulled him with all her frenzied might, shaking him to and fro, and almost strangling him. Indeed, she would have strangled him outright had not some present, giving heed to his loud appeals for mercy, interfered, and rescued him from her clutches.

"Come and I'll fecht ye," cried a slip of a stable-boy, who, no higher than Hare's elbow, sparred up in his face.

The ostlers encouraged the boy in this display, and Hare, at length taunted and jeered into anger, suddenly flared up, and looking fiercely round, roared out, squaring his arms in front of him—

"Be jabers, come on thin, any uv yez, and give me fair play."

Delighted at having goaded him to this manifestation of passion, they set the boy at him again, and encouraged him to strike him, which the fellow did with all the strength he could muster.

Driven to desperation, he caught up his bundle, and tried to make his way to the door, when an ostler intercepted him.

"Whaur are ye gaun, man?" said the latter, "or whaur can ye gang to? Hell's owre guid for ye. The very deevils, for fear o' mischief, wadna daur tae let ye in, and as for heaven, that's entirely oot o' the question."

"Faith, but yer richt, ma man," exclaimed the woman, who had nearly strangled him. "Auld Nick hasna a place het eneuch for him. He'll hae tae mak ane on purpose."

Hare, now wrought up to a pitch of reckless desperation, strove to make his way out, and had actually reached the passage, when the gentleman who had questioned him before came in his way.

"Where are you going? What do you mean to do?" he inquired.

"Och, musha, they can just do what they like wid me," returned Hare.

At this moment a strong police force made their way into the passage, and the gentleman, seizing the opportunity, thrust him into a closet just at hand.

The inn was again cleared and the doors barricaded, and another attempt made to get Hare conveyed to the jail. A chaise[1] was ostentatiously brought to the door, and a trunk buckled on, which proceeding was intended to make the people suppose he was to be sent off in that vehicle, and to divert attention from the real purpose. While all eyes were eagerly watching this chaise at the door, another chaise was got ready at the back entrance, where it was hoped he could be got off unperceived.

"Now, Hare," said the same gentleman, bringing him out of the closet; "your only chance is to reach that chaise by getting out of the back window, and making your way along the top of the wall without letting the people see you."

"Troth, then, I'll try it," returned the wretch, catching at any hope of escape.

"Away with you then; but stay a moment, you say you have no money. Now it is impossible that you can travel far while penniless—there's a sovereign for you."

This act of generosity astonished Hare into emotion, and he actually burst into tears. That bad black heart of his was not all stone. It could not be touched by remorse or repentance; but kindness, in the midst of that storm of vengeance, brought water from the rock.

As every moment was precious, he was urged to fly; so thrusting the coin into his pocket he clambered through the open window, and got upon the wall, where, like a cat, he crouched along, and kept himself out of sight of the crowd. Some boys, however, were perched on the top of an outhouse, and saw him just as he had reached the end of the wall, where the chaise stood.

"There he's! there he's!" they shouted. "They are lettin' him awa' the back way."

---

1. A light travelling carriage.

Hare heard the shouts, and knowing that he was discovered, leapt through the open door of the carriage, and called to the driver, for God's sake, to move on. The crowd heard the shouts likewise, and in a moment it was known that he was away in a carriage from the back entrance. A mighty yell burst from every throat, and the crowd instantly rushed with indescribable impetuosity down the street to intercept the chaise. There was every hope of this being effected, for the driver had to go by a circuitous path. The pace at which he went, however, was something marvellous. Once started, he knew that not Hare's safety only but his own depended on speed, and he lashed his horse like a madman, till they flew along almost like lightning. There was a sharp turn to be taken, and here, from the velocity at which it was going, the chaise ran for some yards on two wheels only. For several moments the prospect of an overturn was nearly certain, but fortunately the vehicle righted itself just as a deafening roar from behind told the driver that the crowd had caught sight of him, and was in full pursuit.

Away he shot with a recklessness which would have been sheer madness in ordinary circumstances, and never probably did vehicle dart so furiously through Dumfries or any other town. He never ceased for a moment to lash the horses, and the animals understanding, perhaps, that they were required to put forth their utmost strength, plunged forward with incredible swiftness.

The old bridge was to cross, and the people on the other side seeing the carriage dashing madly on and the crowd in its wake, understood the state of the case, and came rushing to intercept it.

Excited though they were, no one was foolhardy enough to go in the way of the prancing horses, but they shouted to the driver to stop, and put the murderer out, and when he failed to comply with their demand, they took up large stones and tried to smash the carriage in as it flew past.

Hare lay panting with terror in the bottom of the chaise, and some of the stones came crashing in with a force which, had they struck his head, would have knocked out his brains. But they failed to strike him, and the bridge being crossed, the interruptions from the people became less frequent.

Supposing that the driver meant to take the Galloway road, the pursuing thousands rushed in a mass to the end of the new bridge, hoping thereby to get in front of the carriage, but the real destination being the jail, the mistake operated in favour of the fugitive. A few moments were gained by it, which the driver did not fail to profit by, and turning another sharp corner at a break-neck pace, he entered the broad open street in which the jail stood.

Fearful as had been his pace hitherto, he here made tremendous efforts to increase it still, and with unmerciful hand lashed the poor horses till their pace became literally whirlwind speed, and in a very few minutes he dashed up to the jail door.

"Now, ye ugly deevil!" he shouted; "bung out and jump in there for yer life!"

Hare was not slow to obey this direction, and with a white pallid face he sprang out, and in two bounds was through the doorway of the jail, which was ready opened for his reception. A massive chain had been put on inside, and the instant the wretch had passed the threshold, the ponderous door was closed, the locks shut, the bolts drawn, and all the fastenings completed, just as the foremost of the crowd came panting and howling in front of the gloomy edifice.

Like a pack of hungry Russian wolves who have been pursuing a party of travellers over the snow, and have overtaken them just as they reached and had entered a secure place of refuge, the baffled, exasperated, and defeated mob threw themselves with roars of execration against the jail doors, and, made still more angry by the escape of the wretch whose capture they had deemed secure, they showed every sign of battering down the front of the prison, and, like the Porteous mob, dragging forth the object of their vengeance by main force.[2] Huge stones were flung into the courtyard, smashing the chimney cans, and making it highly dangerous for any one to peep forth from the building. The same missiles were also darted against the massive iron-bolted door; and the crashing noise thus produced from it brought forth a chorus of

---

2. A popular uprising in Edinburgh, 1736, after Captain Porteous of the City Guard directed his men to fire on a disturbance during a hanging in the Grassmarket, killing the innocent. Porteous was imprisoned, and during the "Porteous Riots" he was seized from the Tolbooth and lynched.

triumphant cheers from the assembled thousands, who expected soon to see a breach made and admission gained.

But the stout old door had been specially made for resisting assaults, and volleys of stones, however heavy, made but little impression upon it. The immense iron knocker was knocked off, the neighbouring lamps extinguished and demolished, the windows of the Court-house smashed, and an amount of damage done sufficient to cause the greatest apprehension to the authorities of the town and the occupants of the adjoining houses.

Still the massive building resisted the mob's wild and frantic attack, and at length the cry was raised to bring peats and tar barrels. This suggestion was received with shouts of acclamation, and there is no doubt that it would speedily have been carried out and the door burned if, at the moment, one hundred special constables, who had just been sworn in, had not marched with batons in their hands up to this part of the jail, and there took up a position of determined defence.

Enraged as the people were, their passions were not viciously inflamed, else a small handful of one hundred men could never have prevented them from effecting their purpose. But it was the indignant humanity within them that had roused them so, and not a wanton desire for mischief; hence the presence in opposition to them of one hundred of their fellow-citizens served to keep them from committing further violence.

For several hours longer, however, they lingered in greater or less numbers on the spot, resolved apparently to wait for another opportunity of reaching the monster whose destruction they meditated. But the night set in cold and frosty as ever, and the bitter air gradually cooled their ardour, and they departed in bands to the shelter of their homes and the repose of their beds, intending to renew their attempt on the morrow.

By one hour after midnight every individual of the mob had vanished, and not a soul remained on the street but the militia, the police, and the special constables.

This was an opportunity of getting rid of Hare which the authorities were too glad to embrace, and it was determined to send him away at once from the town. Incredible as it may seem, he had for several hours been lying in the bed of one of the cells fast asleep amid all the thundering noise and clamour. The moment he got inside the jail door his dull apathetic imbecility of mind made him imagine that now he was perfectly safe, and, being utterly worn out by the rough harassing experience of the day, he swallowed some food which was given him, threw himself on the pallet, and fell into a dead slumber.

He was in this sound sleep when, at one o'clock in the morning, the flurried officials went to rouse him and send him off. It took a good deal of shaking to bring him to consciousness, and when he did open his peeping eyes he stared in astonishment at the two turnkeys and the governor of the prison who were standing over him.

"Now then," said the latter, "you must be off as fast as you can."

"Och, thin, where am I to go to at all, at all?" he wonderingly inquired.

"Out of the town, and forward on your journey. The street is quiet now, and you may be many miles from Dumfries before daybreak."

"Sure now, can't you let me remain here?" whined the wretch. "They can't come into the jail to annoy me."

"Can't they? That's all you know about it. It's quite impossible you can remain here. We can't have the peace of the town disturbed by such as you. Come, be off, you haven't a moment to lose."

"But where am I to go to?" he querulously asked.

"Oh, that is your business, not mine. Quick now, if you don't want to fall into the hands of the people."

Roused to terror by the last suggestion, Hare got up. His clothes had not been taken off, so he was ready to go at once.

"Where's me cloak and me bundle?" he asked, as they were hurrying him from the cell.

"Don't know; they are not here. Probably you left them in the King's Arms. But you must go without them, and thank your stars that you have got off with your life, or even with a whole skin."

They brought him to the courtyard, and inquiry having been made and information obtained that the street was still clear, two policemen and a sheriff's officer were appointed to escort him from the town.

"No use in him going the Galloway road," said one of the men. "He'll be watched from every place between here and

Portpatrick. He'd better go by Hood's Loan and on to the Annan road."

"Do you hear that, Hare?" said the governor. "Would you prefer Carlisle and into England, or go on to Portpatrick?"

"Och, sure, anywhere that I would be safest," returned Hare, shivering already in the bitter night cold.

The small door leading to the street was opened, and the fugitive from popular fury passed through accompanied by his escort—the governor of the jail and the authorities of the town devoutly thankful at having got rid of him.

They went on in silence, and at a quick pace, through the deserted streets, got safely beyond the suburbs into Hood's Loan, a narrow, solitary path leading to the highway to Annan.

In going up this sequestered path the sheriff's officer spoke to Hare.

"What fearful crimes you and Burke have been guilty of. You see though you have got off at Edinburgh, how the people abhor and detest you."

"Begora, thin, this has been a terrible day for me," returned Hare, with a shudder.

"A terrible day for Dumfries, too," was the rejoinder. "The like of it I never witnessed, and all owing to your deeds in the West Port."

"Faix, thin, I see that now," muttered Hare.

"How *could* you murder these people? How could you be so cruel? Neither you nor Burke must have had any heart in you."

To this he made no reply, and the officer went on to speak of repentance and an amended life—advices which seemed to have no effect on his listener. Hare could be awakened to a sense of bodily terror by the violence and threatenings of the populace, but he seemed incapable of feeling either regret or remorse.

"I wish I knew where to go," was all he said. "It's no use going to Ireland or anywhere."

"Get into England," suggested one of the men, "and there list for India, where nobody knows you."

"Now then," said the officer, "there's the Annan road, and you had better make the best of your way wherever you mean to go; it is near two o'clock, and by daylight the people will be hunting for you."

He silently held out his hand.

"No," said the officer, "I cannot take the hand of a murderer, nor can I say good-bye or farewell. You have by your crimes put yourself beyond the pale of human sympathy or pity."

He turned round and walked away, his companions following his example, and Hare was left alone standing in the winter darkness on a road he had never before traversed to wander forward he knew not whither—to be a fugitive and a vagabond on the face of the earth.

By this time the three companions of his crimes had each experienced the full measure of their earthly retribution. His own wife had found a grave in the foaming sea; Helen M'Dougal was lying a frozen corpse under the snow-drift; and Burke had been publicly strangled on the scaffold. He was now the last of the dread quaternity, set adrift with the mark of Cain[3] upon him, an outcast from all his kind, and the object of universal scorn, rage, and disgust.

Had he been a being of average intelligence, he would, like the first murderer, have cried, "My punishment is greater than I can bear."[4] But the grief ingredients of human suffering could not enter his debased and brutified soul. Apathetic imbecility was his chief characteristic. He had little power of reflection, and less sense of moral obligation. He had, in short, no power of acute feeling, and except being gifted with a large measure of cunning, he manifested about the smallest measure of mental capacity for a man who was not absolutely an idiot.

Physical suffering was, however, a thing he could very well understand, endure, and shrink from. The pangs of hunger, the pains of cold, the weariness of travel, and terror of human vengeance were all within the compass of his capacity of suffering, and these he was now to feel to the utmost.

At three o'clock—more than an hour after the officer had left him—a farm boy, who had occasion to be on the road, saw him pass like a silent spectre, and no further trace was heard of him till near the gloaming of the following afternoon, when two men who were breaking stones on the road side,

---

3. Genesis 4:15.
4. Genesis 4:13.

within half a mile of Carlisle, found themselves joined by a
weary shivering wretch, who, apparently very much exhausted,
came trudging slowly along the road, and sat down upon the
heap of stones they had broken. He did not address them,
scarcely even looked at them, but sank down upon the stones
like one thoroughly worn out and hopeless.

"You seem to have come far, good man," remarked one of
the labourers.

"A purty long bit uv road intirely," answered Hare.

"Going into Carlisle?"

"Troth and that's just what I'm thinking uv."

Just then the mail coach drove past, and the guard saw
and knew him, as did also one of the passengers. Hare hung
his head, for he saw he was discovered, and it was not long
till a number of persons who had been made aware of his
presence came along the road to see him. It was then that the
astonished stone-breakers were made aware that their silent
companion was the notorious Hare, the murderer.

Fortunately for the wanderer, the people who now flocked
about him were more bent on gratifying their curiosity than
inclined to molest him. Only they gave him to understand
that if he went into the town of Carlisle he would be
murdered.

This roused him again, and weary, footsore, cold, and
hungry, he turned off towards Newcastle, vanishing from the
people's view amid the general darkness of approaching
night.

This was the last time that any authentic intelligence was
heard of Hare. That gloomy darkness received him entirely
out of the public sight. Numberless stories got afloat as to his
whereabouts and fate. Some say he went to Ireland, and lived
in great misery there among its solitary mountains till death
put an end to his misery. Others that he went to America and
was shot; and others that he wandered for many years in
various parts of England.

This last supposition was the true one. He did manage to
escape recognition by changing his name and altering his
appearance as far as possible; and, sometimes begging, sometimes hawking, he wandered up and down without a home,
without a friend, and without a hope.

Let him go for the present. Before our story is done we shall
find him again.

With this departure from public view the story of the Burke and Hare murders properly closes; but not so the more private tale which we have found connected with it. Our original heroine, Mary Paterson, has been swallowed up in the hideous maelstrom, and her wrongs, sins, sorrows, and sufferings have passed away; but many of the actors in the drama of her sad life are yet upon the stage; and after her death and the excitement consequent upon the discovery of the West Port murders, they were destined to play a part in further incidents of a most interesting character—incidents which came out of those we have already narrated, as effects proceed from causes; and led to more experiences, some of them sad, some of them happy; just as human life is ever made up of lights and shadows, joys and sorrows, love and hate, vice and virtue, goodness and badness.

The narrative of these further incidents we shall proceed with in the next and following chapters.

CHAPTER XXX

JOSHUA LEECH THE LAWYER MAKES RESTITUTION

Six months have passed, and summer is again shedding its glory upon the earth—bright beautiful summer, which sleeps so peacefully yet with such teeming life in the bosom of Nature. In the midst of the sunlit summer world it is difficult to realise the possibility of such dark terrible scenes as we have had to chronicle. The earth is then so fair and smiling—harmony and gladness are manifested everywhere; passion, cruelty, bloodshed, and the dark vices which deface humanity seem banished from the scene, and over heart and soul there steals a forgetfulness, savouring of incredulity of cruelties and crimes which lie like black blotches on our social annals.

"Can a world so fair be the dwelling-place of a race so vile?" murmured a tall middle-aged man, as he stood on a sultry July afternoon surveying one of the widest, sweetest, grandest scenes which Scotland can present. The solitary speaker was a tall well-formed fine-looking man, with a full open countenance, a large eye, a lofty brow, and a gentle kindly benevolent expression in his face. A stranger could not look at him without being ready to reverence and trust him. His very presence was full of assurance to the timid, and of awe to the rough and rugged in nature. This calm gentle dignity gave him a silent influence which all acknowledged according to the character of their own life. The young clung to him and loved him, the old sought his counsel, and found consolation in his guidance. The evil-minded and vicious shunned his gaze, and became outwardly meek before him, thus doing homage to the purity and power of his virtuous character.

He was the minister of a rural parish lying close to the foot of the Ochil Hills, and a minister he truly was to the people under his charge. He was like a very father to his flock, he fed them, instructed them, and faithfully led—not pointed, but *led*—them to that better land of which earth, in its highest sense, is but the shadow and the type.

It was on a summit of the Ochils that he stood, on this sultry July afternoon, when he murmured the words we have recorded. The lofty eminences reared their crests on either side and behind him, while in front of the lesser hill on which he stood lay the little town in which his church was placed, and a wide and beautiful tract of country spread itself out beyond. Away westward, past the shoulder of the Abbey Craig, could be discerned the town and Castle of Stirling, and the lofty frontiers of that fairy land which enfolds the Trossachs. From the base of the castle-crowned hill the gleaming Forth came winding like a silver thread, stretching eastward—now seen, now lost, as it followed its serpentine channel to its ocean home. On either side the noble river a vast level plain was spread, rich with the thousand tints which the year displays when in its prime. And there—far beyond in the dim distance—could be seen the shadowy outline of the Pentlands, and a speck on the horizon, which one familiar with the locality knew to be Arthur's Seat, whose lion crest keeps watch and ward over the ancient home of Scotland's monarchs, and the fair city which is Scotland's pride.

It was with pride as well as with pleasure that Mr Whitford stood gazing on the wide-spread scene within his view. He knew it well; for the spot in which he stood was one to which he often repaired both for quiet meditation and to enjoy the beauties of nature, which gave him intense delight, and which he could keenly appreciate. To his eye almost every object had its great national associations, for the whole of that extensive landscape was historical and classic ground. Even the hill on whose summit he stood was crowned by a castle, now nearly in ruins, but once a place of strength, and the home of Scottish beauty and chivalry; where fair high-born dames and valiant knights met in the dance, and loved and wooed, as men and maidens do, whether of low or high degree— where sterner doings had also been witnessed; where men at arms drew their bows on the battlements, and the war cries of deadly foes roused the echoes of the hills.

All that was over now; and the gloomy fortress, partially decayed, was left to the silence of desolation. Its position was one of great natural strength. On three sides it was securely protected by the lofty hills which rose behind for many miles; and the path which led to the plain below was steep and rugged, and fully commanded from the loop-holes in the tower; while on the right and left a very deep dell, or ravine, separated the castle from the hills around.

It was on the brow of this dell where the minister stood; and the sound of the stream murmuring in its rocky bed came up from the far depths, breaking the awful silence with softest music. The place was one where the spirit of man can hold deep and pure communion with Nature, and where influences from a higher world are most likely to stream in upon the soul. Many an effective Sabbath sermon had the good man got on that mount of meditation, and high thoughts had there flowed in upon him, which he had but to clothe in practical garments to make them understood by the rustic hearers, who hung upon his lips, and received from his ministering hand food convenient for them.

The silence and sultriness of that July afternoon was becoming oppressive, when the shadow caused by the obscuring of the sun made Mr Whitford turn his eyes to the darkened luminary, and lo! over the top of Demyat there had come a black cloud portending a thunder storm. The minister had heard it muttering in the distance several times during the afternoon, but as up to this time the sky had remained clear, he did not apprehend its near approach. Now, however, he saw that if he would get home without a wetting, he must quit the hill at once, and this he was preparing to do, when a flash of blue lightning, instantly followed by a loud reverberating peal and the falling of heavy raindrops, warned him that he could not possibly reach the village without being drenched. He therefore ran for shelter to the frowning keep, whose massive walls rose in grey stillness only a few yards away.

The place was not altogether uninhabitable. Several of the lower chambers were entire, and in one of these a shepherd with his family had taken up their abode. Here the minister would have been warmly welcomed, for the shepherd and his wife were two of his most regular hearers, but Mr Whitford, preferring to witness the grandeur of the approaching storm, ascended to the higher and untenanted chamber, at the wide loophole of which he took up his position, where he had a view of a large portion of the hills, and the opening of a glen, which began on the other side of the ravine.

In a very few minutes the storm was raging with indescribable sublimity; and a thunderstorm among the mountains is one of the grandest things in nature to him whom it does not terrify past all enjoyment. Of course the calm heart and pious mind of Mr Whitford could view the sight without being appalled, and it was with the very exultation of awe that he saw the forked lightning leap from peak to peak, and heard the crashing peals, whose numberless reverberations had not ceased when its successor burst forth, thus producing an incessant roll of heaven's artillery.

In the presence of such a war of elements in such a wild romantic place, who can but be solemnised into deepest awe, and impressed with the power of Nature's forces, and of that God whose hand directs and controls them? Unbelief must find it hard work to keep its ground under the lightning's flash and the thunder's roar; while guilt and sin must quake and tremble. But the simple-hearted believer, whose trust is in a Father who is above the thunder, and whose servant the lightning is, can witness the elemental strife without dread, and even with a subdued joy, looking on it as a manifestation of the power and majesty of Him "who rules the whirlwind and directs the storm."

So it was with Mr Whitford, as from the loophole in that ancient chamber he gazed out upon the mountain solitude, whose perpetual silence was so magnificently disturbed; and as flash after flash seemed opening the heavens, and peal after peal rolled along the sky which sent the rain down in torrents, he almost unconsciously repeated to himself the words of the twenty-ninth Psalm—

"The voice of the Lord is upon the waters, the God of glory thundereth, the Lord is upon many waters. The voice of the Lord is powerful, the voice of the Lord is full of majesty. The voice of the Lord divideth the flames of fire. The voice of the Lord shaketh the wilderness, the Lord shaketh the wilderness of Kadesh."

As he stood thus in dreamy abstraction, and when the storm was at its fiercest, his eye was caught by a dark object moving in the glen; and his attention being fixed thereon, he made it out to be a man on horseback. He was coming on at all speed, and at every blinding flash the frightened animal reared in wildest terror, and with a suddenness and violence which would have unseated any but a skilful rider. This latter qualification he seemed fully to possess, for he held the rein with a firm hand, and sat like a rock in the saddle, though he bent his head against the pouring rain, and seemed to be making every effort to reach a place of shelter.

He made direct for the ruined castle, and just as his horse had got upon the narrow path which formed the only communication between the other side of the ravine and the eminence on which the building stood, a flash more vivid than any that had preceded, or rather a series of flashes which seemed to envelope the whole hill, made the horse swerve with frantic violence; and, with a shudder of horror, Mr Whitford saw it topple on the very verge of the chasm.

"Oh, he is lost; he is lost," he shouted, bending forward till the upper half of his body hung over the wall, and there he remained in motionless suspense, expecting horse and rider to fall headlong to destruction.

They were saved, however, and as it seemed to him by a miracle. All at once the animal became conscious of its danger, and planted its hind feet upon the slope, while the intrepid rider, cool as ever in this moment of peril, struck his spurs into its sides, goading it thereby to an exercise of strength which enabled it to regain the path, when, by one bound, it cleared the peril, and was lost to view under the castle wall.

"Thank God, he is saved," ejaculated the minister, as with a long sigh of relief he drew back his head into the chamber, into which in about a minute after there entered a stout man with active steps, whose round form was enveloped in a glistening waterproof coat.

"Doctor Sharp!" exclaimed the minister in astonishment.

"Ha!—thought it was you, from the glimpse I got below. What a ride I have had."

"And what a miraculous escape. You were on the verge of destruction."

"I know I was. Had Ralph lost his hold we must have been dashed to pieces; but he's a sagacious fellow, and a surer beast never stepped. It was the lightning that did it; but, I say, it's lucky I have found you here, for I was making my way to the manse when the storm overtook me."

"Indeed! Anything wrong?"

"Yes; with your friend Leech over in Devon Cottage. He's dying."

"What—Joshua Leech?"

"Even so. A sudden illness; but it will cut him off in a few days at the most—perhaps in a few hours. When I told him, as I felt it my duty to do, he grew awfully nervous, and said he must see you immediately. My belief is, that he has something on his mind that he wishes to disclose, and as it is evidently of the greatest importance, it may be as well for you to go over at once."

Mr Whitford looked gravely out upon the storm. Severe though it was, it would not keep him from the discharge of his duty; but he was naturally concerned to think how he was to make his way over the hills under such drenching rain.

"You'll manage it easily before dark," said the doctor. "In half an hour or less the storm will have ceased, and your best and nearest road to Glen Devon is that I have just come. I would lend you Ralph if I could spare him, but I have to ride over to Alloa to-night."

"My dear sir," said the minister, with a smile, "I could no more ride Ralph over those hills than I could myself fly over them. But if the rain ceases—and I see it is already clearing in the west—I shall easily make my way on foot. Poor Joshua, much I fear that his profession of the law has not greatly conduced to a fit preparation of the heart for another world."

The doctor shrugged his shoulders, and simply remarked— "He seems to know that now."

"It is a knowledge that can never come too early, but with many comes too late. I hope it is not so with my cousin."

"If I mistake not you are his only relative. Now I should say his savings will be considerable."

"Yes; but what is a man profited if he gain the whole world—"

"And don't live to enjoy it," added the doctor, laughing. "Not much I daresay."

"That is not the end of the verse," rejoined the minister.

"I know it isn't, but, as I put it, it is more in my way. I have to do with making folks right for this life, and you for preparing them for the next. So, every man to his trade."

"A sophism, my dear Sharp, a thorough sophism," said the minister. "He who is best prepared for this life is best prepared for the next. You do your utmost to put men in the best circumstances for active existence, and I do my utmost to direct them aright in their active existence."

"Well, well, I won't dispute the point with you. We doctors are proverbially behind in theology. But see, the sun is showing again, and yonder is a most magnificent rainbow crowning the hills with glory. Isn't that grand? The sight is worth the drenching I have had."

And truly the spectacle that was to be beheld at the moment from the open space in the thick castle wall was at once beautiful and sublime. Beyond the eastern hills lay the dense black thunder cloud, and painted upon it, in hues which no human pencil could place, was an arch of light, stretching from one summit to another, and embracing in its span several lesser hills, glistening freshly with their summer baptism.

Both men stood gazing at the sight some minutes in perfect silence, till the evanescent beauty of the bow began to fade, and it gradually disappeared—melting away into the blue sky which the retreating cloud slowly revealed.

"There, 'tis gone," said the doctor, in a slightly disappointed tone. "What stuff the poet speaks when he says—'A thing of beauty is a joy for ever.' In my opinion, the most beautiful thing fades the soonest—the beauty of childhood, how soon it passes; the beauty of girlhood, that soon vanishes; flowers are hardly in bloom till they wither; a gorgeous sunset lasts but for a few moments; and that beautiful rainbow, which we could gaze on for an age, hasn't lasted ten minutes."

"Nevertheless, the poet's statement is perfectly true," returned the minister. "The joy of beauty is eternal. Doesn't a vanished childhood leave its joy for ever in the memory? and doesn't the sight of flowers, and sunsets, and rainbows produce a delight in our souls of which we can never afterwards be deprived, unless we deprive ourselves of it by vice, in which case it becomes more a bitterness than a joy."

"Ah! there you go away into metaphysics," laughed the light-hearted doctor. "Now, I'm not subtle enough for that; my work lies with the seen and temporal, yours with the unseen and eternal."

They had by this time descended to the courtyard, grass-grown and uneven with blocks of stone, which had tumbled from the decaying walls. In the most sheltered angle the doctor's horse stood in patient waiting, and his master having mounted and waved a good-bye to his friend, he trotted away with whisking tail over the narrow path, and turned down the steep road which led to the plain.

The grass was very wet after the heavy rain, but otherwise the storm had added new beauties to the scene, for from every blade there came a flash of diamond brightness, and the air was delightfully fresh and fragrant with the exhalations of the thousands of wild flowers that decked the verdant slopes.

The minister had a long although not a profitless walk along a shallow valley in the hills, through which a crystal stream meandered, growing stronger and larger as it ran from the accessions it received from the many rills which flowed into it. This valley, encircled on all sides by hills, was a spot of deep but sweet seclusion. No habitation was near it; it lay in the pure peaceful presence of Nature, quite apart from a world of sin, and care, and suffering. In traversing its silent declivity the pious soul of the pastor entered into happy communion with the holy scene, and he had many glad and beautiful thoughts suggested to his mind which would be afterwards turned into food for his hungry people.

It was approaching to sunset when he came to a farmhouse and offices at the end of the valley, and soon after he reached the beautiful and romantic glen through which the Devon flows on its way to the Forth.

Who shall adequately describe the beauties of Glen Devon, or picture the scenery traversed by that far-famed mountain stream? In that bright summer evening it looked like a region in Fairyland. The wooded sides of the ravines, presenting so many shades of living green; the dark rocky gorges, where the river became black, and where sometimes it was not seen, but only heard, as it tumbled down its rough channel, and came smiling out again in open spaces where it could laugh up to the rounded crests and sparkle in the golden light; the deep, deep green of the grassy braes, where the bluebells waved and the white gowans were about to close their eyes for the night; the dark fir clumps on the more distant uplands; the lofty summits of the neighbouring heights, the far depths of the blue sky—these several objects disposed according to the unerring taste of Nature constituted a scene which could not but fill a poetic soul with gratification and delight, and likewise pride in one's native land, that conceals in the mountain recesses such nooks of surpassing loveliness.

Turning up the broad highway which skirted the brow of the glen, Mr Whitford had not far to go when he came in sight of a well-built modern house, picturesquely situated at a turn of the glen, where a splendid view could be had both up and down. By the time the minister crossed the lawn and stood at the door, the sun had sunk behind the hill tops, and another dense cloud was gathering in the distance. It was either the same thunder-cloud which had made a circuit of the heavens and was returning, or another that had grown up out of the sultry heat and was on its thundering way to wake the echoes of the glen a second time with reverberating sounds, and illuminate them with flashes of light.

Mr Whitford had raised his hand to the knocker, when, ere he had time to let it fall, the door was opened by an elderly woman, who was the lawyer's housekeeper.

"Oh, sir, I am so glad you have come," she eagerly exclaimed, though in a suppressed voice.

"What, Mrs Oakley, is my cousin worse?"

"He is very ill, and awfully restless. He has been asking fifty times if you had not come, and fearful lest the doctor should not send you. He told me to dispatch Robert to bring you. This way, sir, he is lying in the upper bedroom."

The room into which the minister was shown was already dim with the gathering twilight, but a sharp loud voice from one corner directed him to the bed. It was a hard hurried voice, and so different from the usually soft, smooth, deliberate utterance of Joshua Leech, that the minister was startled.

"Oh, James, have you come at last. Sharp tells me I am dying. What am I to do? Come here for any sake and tell me what I am to do, for you are a minister, and must know."

"There is only one thing to do, Joshua, and if you have deferred it till now it has been a grievous mistake on your part. But, thank God, it is not too late."

"Well, what is it?—what is it?" asked the lawyer, in the same quick loud tone. "What is the one thing I must do?"

"Make your peace with God."

"Yes, yes; but how—how?"

"Confess all your sins to him."

"To him!—only to him?" cried Leech, with a peculiarity of eagerness which struck Mr Whitford as indicative of wrongs done to his fellow-men. He therefore paused a moment, and then made answer—

"Confession to God, and *reparation* to man, if you are conscious that is required."

The lawyer listened to his every word with breathless

intensity, and when he said "reparation," he started as if from a blow, and his thin hand nervously twitched at the coverlet.

"I thought so," he faltered. "I knew I must repair the wrong, as far as I can. Don't turn away from me, James. You are my heir. All that I have is yours; but I have more than I have any right to, and the reparation you counsel will make a considerable reduction in what you will get by my death."

"Joshua," said the other, solemnly, "do not let that thought for one moment intrude. Standing, as you now do, on the threshold of eternity, the vanity and worthlessness of earthly things must be apparent to you, and probably you wish at this moment you had cared less for them."

"I do, James, I do," returned Leech, with hurried tremulousness. "I loved money, and—and—sinned to obtain it."

"Then, Joshua, whatever money you have sinfully obtained can do no good either to you or your heir. Make restitution, I beseech you, to the very uttermost farthing."

"Impossible," sighed the lawyer. "I do not remember all that I obtained unjustly; but one thing haunts me, and I must make that right before—before I die. It was to tell you of it that I sent for you."

"Well, I am here to listen."

"But you will loathe—you will scorn me."

"Then would I ill represent the Master whom I profess to serve and obey. No, Joshua, speak plainly. I may pity and sorrow for you, but not despise you."

There was a silence of some minutes, during which the lawyer seemed to be undergoing an inward struggle. His thin pale face worked nervously, and his arms moved with restless uneasiness above the bed clothes. The minister patiently waited, careful not to interrupt the remorseful current of his thoughts.

At length, with a sigh, longer and heavier than any that preceded, he spoke—

"You have heard of the girl Mary Paterson, who was one of Burke and Hare's victims."

"Yes, I got the particulars from her father's minister at Kirkton. She turned out ill, left her father's house, and thus brought on a shock of apoplexy which caused his death."

"True. The old man had a small property at Kirkton; I managed his little affairs, and his savings were also in my hands. At his death I was tempted to appropriate all. I visited the house and obtained the receipts he held from me. I also forged a bond for two thousand pounds, and thus made it appear that his property was mortgaged to that amount, which was its full value. In fact, James, I took all."

The good minister was intensely shocked. A fraudulent action like this he, simple man, did not consider anybody capable of doing.

"You took all," he repeated, holding up both his hands. "And left the poor orphan girl penniless."

"Yes; God forgive me, I did, and I cannot help charging myself with the ruin of the poor girl.[1] I felt little remorse for it till I heard of her murder, and the life she had led in Edinburgh—then my conscience charged me with her destruction."

"Alas; Joshua, this is terrible," said his horrified listener; "and you have been able to retain the old man's substance for so many years. But you will restore it now—at once. To whom does it belong?"

"The girl left a child, illegitimate, so it can't inherit; but Andrew had an only sister, and she had an only son, a wild wandering youth. He is the heir, though I don't know where he is to be found."

"We can advertise for him," was Mr Whitford's ready rejoinder. "Meanwhile, you must instantly take steps to renounce the property and money, with all that it has yielded, since it came into your hands."

"With the money and its accumulations I last year bought another property, not far from Braeside, Southfield, tenanted at present by James Crawford, whose lease expires at Martinmas. He wishes it renewed, but I shrank from granting it."

"And you did right. Let its rightful owner do in that respect as he pleases."

"I trust I may live long enough to make the whole over to him," groaned the remorseful lawyer. "Let me be spared, James, as much as possible; keep the matter from the world as far as practicable."

"Joshua," said Mr Whitford, "if your repentance is sincere, and if you obtain God's forgiveness, you should now care little what the world may think or say."

---

1. The 1866 book has "ruin"; 1885 gives "murder".

This dark dishonest transaction of the lawyer having at length got to the knowledge of one honest heart, immediate measures were taken to rectify the crying wrong. Advertisements were inserted in all the principal Scottish papers for the discovery of Richard Campbell, the nephew of Andrew Paterson, and deeds prepared by which he, or whoever might turn out to be heir-at-law, should receive the inheritance.

Scarcely had the lawyer put his signature to the necessary papers when death claimed him for his prey. It could not be said that he died in peace. The fear of death, and not a feeling of genuine repentance, had prompted him to give up this particular portion of his ill-gotten gains, and in doing it he was actuated by the hope that *this* would atone for his long life of nefarious dealing. The minister laboured to bring him to a better repentance than this, but without much effect. Who knows how often before this he had stifled the better thoughts and feelings of his soul as they arose, and now when he had to confront the great mysterious future a place for repentance could not be found by him.

He died; and Mr Whitford set himself with all diligence and anxiety to find out the heir to Andrew Paterson's property.

CHAPTER XXXI

A WINDFALL

It was Saturday night in the busy bustling manufacturing town of Dundee, and the thoroughfare called the Scouringburn swarmed with its teeming population, most of whom had spent the best hours of that sultry summer day amid the noise and dust of the mills, and were now come abroad to breathe the fresh air and enjoy their recreation.

To be sure the air down in that narrow dirty street was not particularly pure and balmy—nothing like so sweet and delicious as on the sides of the "Law," whose green slopes could be seen rising at no great distance, and whose top was still glory-smitten with the golden rays of the setting sun. But it required much bodily exertion to climb to that salubrious atmosphere; and after the toils of the day the operatives had no great relish for further physical effort, besides, they had lived all their life in the Scouringburn, and had become used to its closeness and impurity. So they preferred to saunter and congregate about its doorways, and enjoy social fun and merriment.

In the centre of the street a large crowd was collected listening to the exquisite air of "Auld Lang Syne," which a young man was executing on a flute, and executing with no little degree of proficiency and expression. The bystanders listened with deep attention and evident pleasure to this charming Scottish melody; and, when it was finished, a boy who accompanied the musician received in his cap a perfect shower of coppers.

The player was Dick, to whom the reader has been already introduced in the Glasgow lodging-house, where we found him foolishly treating its inmates to a glass all round. As seen now in that summer twilight he was sober, and the intelligence of his countenance and his dashing recklessness of bearing, gave indication of a claim to move in a higher sphere than that of a wandering flute player. The very skill with which he played on his instrument showed not only natural taste, but an artistic proficiency which a vagrant origin could not impart. One saw at a glance that Dick had come down in the world; that he might have been and ought to have been occupying a better position.

His appearance was that of a youth seedy and dissipated; but his whole bearing impressed an onlooker with the idea that the pleasures of a vagabond life had enticed him from a more settled and respectable existence.

When he had finished "Auld Lang Syne" he did not strike up another air, but, satisfied apparently with the pecuniary result of his performance, he put the flute under his arm, and turned to walk away.

At this moment a woman's voice, in the outskirts of the crowd, was loudly raised in a song, and drew the general attention. She turned out to be a young woman, miserably dressed, and carrying a child in her arms. She was the picture of wretchedness and destitution, but her rags and squalor could not conceal the traces of a certain beauty which she had once possessed.

As Dick was passing his eye fell on her, and, as if struck with pity and commiseration, he paused, and stood gazing and listening. It was a plaintive song she was singing, and ever and anon her voice became tremulous and broken, as if grief and sorrow were overpowering her. At last she stopped altogether and burst out crying, carrying at the same moment the corner of her ragged shawl to her eyes to staunch the flowing tears.

"Poor soul, I pity you," said Dick, offering her a handful of the coppers he had just received.

"Oh, sir!" she exclaimed, "you are kind and generous, and heaven bless you; but you are poor like myself, and cannot afford to help me."

"Well, poor enough I am," returned Dick; "but I have only myself to keep, and you have a child to keep—is it your own?"

"Alas, yes," sighed the beggar. "I have not always been what I am now. I once had a good home, but a villain deceived me, and now I and my helpless child are poor wandering outcasts. I have no friend and no home, and neither my child nor myself have tasted food this blessed day."

This piteous tale was received with exclamations of pity and sympathy from the bystanders. None was more strongly affected by it than Dick.

"Then, for God's sake," he cried, "take these coppers and go and get food. Perhaps the good people standing here will give you a little more to help you to lodgings for to-night and to-morrow."

Instantly dozens of hands were stretched forth, and as the clink of money falling into the woman's lap was heard, Dick moved away with a smile of satisfaction on his lips.

He passed along to the West Port, and turning up the Hawkhill played there another air on his flute with a success which fully rewarded him for his act of charity. It was now wearing late, and, returning, he entered the Overgate, and, passing up Guthrie's Close, darted into one of the many dark doorways which yawned on either side of that dingy spot.

The passage was a long and dark one, dirty and damp in the extreme, and it gave access to a habitation not less dirty and disagreeable. Dick entered this latter with an air of one familiar with its interior, and passing through an outer room, where a group of beggars were squatted on the floor, he went into the apartment beyond, occupied at the moment only by two persons, with whom the reader is already acquainted—Bowser and Tibb.[1]

Bowser lounged on a settle near the faintly glowing embers of what had been a fire, with a short black pipe in his mouth, while Tibb sat close to the window, darning a pair of stockings, her immense nose coming out in bas-relief against the waning light.

"Good luck to-night, Dick?" inquired Bowser, as he slowly blew a cloud of smoke towards the ceiling.

"Fairish; I finished off with 'Auld Lang Syne,' and that never fails to bring the browns. I've sent Tom for a good supply of grub, and tipped Bet the price of a bottle of whisky. Here, too, is the week's tin for Tibb, and after all that I have got—let me see—fifteen and eightpence. 'Pon my soul, Bowser, I'm making money."

---

1. Pae locates Bowser's crew in Dundee not just as the home town of the *People's Journal*, but perhaps through its reputation as a "sink of atrocity"—as perceived by Henry Cockburn (he of the Burke and Hare trials) in his 1852 circuit journey. See Cockburn's *Circuit Journeys* (Edinburgh: David Douglas, 1889), 383.

"So you ought, Dick, for your talents are first-class. If you were only to stick close to it, you would in a few years make your fortune."

"I haven't the slightest objection to make my fortune," returned Dick, "but the slavery of the thing is more than I can bear. Look you now. I don't put the flute to my lips again till the last penny of the fifteen and eightpence is gone."

"There you go," remarked Tibb. "We never can get you to lay something past for a rainy day, and Bet is as bad. If she has come on well to-night, she'll not budge from the house till the middle of the week."

"More fool she if she does," rejoined Dick. "But here she comes to speak for herself."

And as he spoke there entered the woman who had a few minutes before been singing in the Scouringburn with the child in her arms. The child she had left in the other room, and the expression of melancholy in her had given place to a bold careless freedom.

"Well, Bet," cried Dick. "How did the dodge work?"

"Four and eleven," was the answer.

"Good. Nothing like working on the people's feelings, and showing them a good example. Like a flock of sheep, they follow in a string. Of course you don't mean to open your pipe for a day or two."

"Not likely. That child grows heavier every day. Tibb feeds it too well. He'll soon be too plump for the starving child of a starving mother, who hasn't been able to give it food for two days."

"Talking of food," laughed Dick, "there comes Tom with my supper, and I mean to pitch into it. Toss out the ham, and hand it to Tibb to fry."

Out of a piece of newspaper Tom extracted several slices of tempting bacon, which Tibb at once took away to the other room to have cooked, and Dick, throwing himself on the wooden seat beside Bowser, took up the piece of paper in which the ham had been wrapped and began listlessly to read it.

He had not lain thus for more than a minute when he gave a start and bounded half up.

"By jingo, here's a funny thing," he exclaimed. "Look here, Bowser; I'm blowed if this doesn't mean me."

"What's the row?" asked Bowser, who had nearly fallen asleep.

"I'm wanted," said Dick.

"Wanted!" repeated the other, rubbing his eyes, and looking concerned. "Why, Dick, you haven't been such a fool as bring the peelers on your track."

"My gracious! have you?" ejaculated Bet, fixing her dark eyes anxiously on the youth.

"Not I," laughed Dick; "'taint the police that want me; it's a parson."

"Oh, go along," growled Bowser, "some of your father's friends want you back to bondage. Don't be trapped, Dick— don't be trapped."

"Not such a flat; but hear what the advertisement says:—

"'If Richard Campbell, son of the late William Campbell of Lanrock, will communicate with the Rev. James Whitford, minister of Dolbeck, he will hear of something to his advantage; or if any one can give information about the said Richard Campbell, Mr Whitford will gladly receive the same. This is a matter of the very utmost importance.'

"Now, Bowser, my brick, what do you think of that?"

"Who's this parson Whitford?" asked Bowser.

"Haven't the slightest idea," replied the youth. "Dolbeck is along near the Ochils, but—"

"I know the crib well enough," said Bowser; "but what has the chap in the white choker there to do with you?"

"That's the mystery."

"Got any one to leave you a legacy?"

"Not a soul. Uncle Andrew, the godly old saint of Braeside, was the only relation who had anything, or was thought to have it, but when he died it turned out that he hadn't a rap, and that his place was mortgaged to its full value. If it hadn't been that, Burke and Hare would have done me a good turn when they murdered Mary Paterson, for I should have come in for Braeside. But that chance is gone, and devil another is there for me in the lottery of life."

"Then what can the parson want?" said Bowser.

"Who knows. Perhaps to convert me," cried the youth, with a mocking laugh, in which Bet loudly joined.

"It might be worth while to inquire though," returned Bowser. "Parsons don't put themselves to the expense of advertising in the papers for those whose souls they are

anxious about. There's a meaning in it, and if you take my
advice you'll pay him a visit."

"Haven't the least objection. Will you accompany me?"

"In course I will."

"Then let us start in the morning with a machine.[2] I'll
stand the expense to the extent of fifteen and eight, and you'll
risk the rest. If the thing turns out profitable, I'll make up
your loss."

"Agreed. I'm your man. Let us start early."

*

The summer beauty and the Sabbath peace lay upon the
village of Dolbeck and the landscape around, and the sweet
sound of the church bell floated with rich cadence on the
warm and fragrant air, as Dick and Bowser came briskly
along the dusty road in a light gig, and pulled up at the inn
door.[3] The persons of both had undergone a wonderful trans-
formation. They were dressed, if not in very good taste, yet
in a somewhat expensive fashion. Bowser sported a white hat,
a yellow vest flowered with crimson silk, white and black
trousers with a very large check, an immense shirt front pretty
clean, and a blue coat with shining brass buttons. Dick was
not so loud in his attire, but there was an approach to foppish-
ness in his appearance, otherwise he looked well, and the
people of the Scouringburn who had listened to his flute playing on the previous evening would have stared in not a little
astonishment had they seen him now sporting a cane, gloves,
and tight boots.

Giving the vehicle in charge to the ostler, and ordering
dinner to be ready at four, they strolled arm-in-arm along the
village street towards the church. The bell by this time had
ceased to ring, and the latest of the worshippers had entered
the sacred pile.

"I suppose we'll have to stand the sermon," remarked
Bowser, as he seated himself on a tombstone.

"Why, yes," drawled Dick. "That's what gentlemen have

---

2. Dick means in a horse-drawn conveyance.
3. Dolbeck appears to be fictional.

to do; and, as that's our character to-day, we must put up with its inconveniences."

"Blow me if I haven't forgot what the inside of a church is like," observed the other. "I haven't seen one for at least twenty years."

"My experience of the same thing dates back for a fourth of that period," intimated Dick. "Hilloa, it just strikes me that we haven't got books, unless that's one showing its shape through your vest pocket."

"That's Bet's song book," replied Bowser. "I brought it to amuse us on the road, but we haven't wanted it."

"Well, we shall make it do now. Hold it well down in the pew, and the people will think it is a Testament."

"All right—there they strike up the tune."

In the quiet and solemn churchyard where they sat, there came from the interior of the church the grand swelling sound of sacred music, as the people within raised their voice in praise. Dick and Bowser listened in silence to the measured strain, its natural power to soften and subdue being increased by all surrounding objects—the silent graves of the church-yard, the bright quiet summer air, the calm glad season of nature, the blue sky and the green hills lifting their heads into its holy bosom.

The two wanderers, as they listened, were impressed as they had not been for years. Their wild unregulated life had long separated them from places of Divine worship, and the sound of that psalm called up thoughts and memories of days of reverence and peace.

"That's stunning fine," observed Bowser, when the echo of the last note had melted into silence. "Of course it wouldn't do for the Overgate, but out here in the country on a Sunday morning it's natural like."

"By Jove, it would soon make me melancholy," said Dick, in whose soul it had awoke thoughts of other days, which he did not care to cherish, for they reminded him of what he once was, and what he had become.

"You don't mean that, Dick, do you?" returned the more hardened Bowser. "Melancholy! I tell you what, my boy, you want to be brought up in philosophy. Look at me now. I can remember when I used to go to church too, and go through all that sort of thing. As I said just now, that's twenty years ago; but I've never felt a want by staying away, and though it's striking a bit to hear that slow music out here, sitting like this among the graves, two or three Sundays would sicken us."

"Hadn't we better go in?" suggested Dick, "and see what the parson looks like."

"That's about the most sensible thing you've said to-day," said Bowser, rising from his seat and approaching the church door.

He opened it gently and glided in, Dick following. There was an empty seat just at hand behind two massive pillars, and here they sat down almost out of sight. They themselves had a pretty good view of the centre of the church, while, being in the deep shadow and separated from the rest of the people by the heavy masonry, they were free to observe without being observed.

It was the prayer, and the grave solemn devoutness of the people had upon them a subduing effect. The minister in the pulpit was, however, the special object of their attention. His fine, calm, reverend aspect, the sweet earnest pleading of his tone, and the rich musical sound of his voice, had something like the power of a spell upon them, and they sat in fixed attention till the Amen was pronounced, when the rustle made by the people in sitting down terminated their wrapt demeanour.

"One can't help liking a fellow like that," whispered Bowser. "If I was long near him, by Jove, he would make me uncomfortable with myself. But the sermon will put me all right, for in course he'll lecture and rail as they all do, and I can stand that—ten chances to one but I fall asleep. Don't forget to wake me, Dick, when he shuts the book."

Contrary to Bowser's expectation, Mr Whitford did not lecture or rail, but spoke in much love and tenderness, and Bowser didn't go to sleep, but sat listening with an interest which was to himself unaccountable. Dick was not so entranced, for he was busy thinking what the speaker could possibly want with him, and a whole host of conjectures chased each other through his mind.

At the close of the sermon he turned to his companion to wake him, but found there was no necessity for that, as Bowser's eyes were neither shut nor drowsy.

"You haven't slept," said the youth.

"It's the first sermon I ever remember of sitting out,"

returned the worthy. "Religion, as it comes from that man, isn't such a miserable affair as I thought. He has actually made sunshine to fall upon it. If I was young I don't know but I would take it up—but Tibb and me could make nothing of it now in the Overgate."

When the congregation dismissed, the two men sat still, and when all were gone they followed the minister into the vestry.

"It seems you want me, sir," said Dick.

This blunt address surprised the minister somewhat, and he stood for a moment looking at his strangely-dressed visitors in silent astonishment.

"May I ask who you are?" he inquired.

"Oh, yes. I'm Richard Campbell, and here's the advertisement that brought me here. I happened to see it only last night."

"Ah, you are Richard Campbell, the person referred to," said Mr Whitford.

"The very identical," returned Dick. "My father was William Campbell of Lanrock."[4]

"And your mother's name was—"

"Paterson," answered Dick. "Andrew Paterson of Braeside was my uncle."

"Just so. You seem to be the young man of whom I am in search, and will, I suppose, have no difficulty in proving your identity?"

"Oh dear no. It's just five years since I left Lanrock, and hundreds in the neighbourhood know me."

"Then call on me at the manse to-morrow morning at eleven."

"To-morrow morning at eleven!" exclaimed Dick, taken rather aback. "Couldn't the business be settled this afternoon?"

"No," returned the minister gravely. "This, as you know, is the Sabbath, and my business with you is of a secular, not a religious character."

"Very good, sir," said Bowser, speaking for the first time. "My friend and I will call on you to-morrow."

And taking Dick by the arm, he led him hurriedly from

4. Lanrock appears to be fictional.

the vestry, before he had time to put in a word of remon-
strance.

"Dick, you fool, you were about to put your foot in it," he
remarked, when they got into the churchyard.

"No; I was only going to insist on him coming to the
scratch at once."

"And that's just what he won't do. There's nothing for it
but to make ourselves jolly comfortable at the inn all night.
I'll stand everything; but in course you'll fork out for it when
you get your cash."

"What cash?"

"The cash the parson has for you. He said the business
wasn't religion. Now, the only other thing a parson has to do
with is tin, and that's worth waiting for."

Dick came to see the thing in the same light, and resolved
to do his best to curb his impatience till the following day.
Precisely at the hour appointed he and Bowser stood at the
manse door, and were at once admitted to the minister's
study.

Mr Whitford sat at a table with a few papers spread out
before him, and he motioned Dick to be seated opposite.
Bowser was left to find a chair for himself, which he did,
nearer the door.

"Young man," began the minister, "of your history and
character I know little, and have no right to inquire into
them. You are, of course, aware that by the death—murder
rather—of your cousin, Mary Paterson, you become the heir
of her father, your uncle."

"I know that well enough," returned Dick. "But it so happened that my uncle, when he died, did not leave a penny."

"So it was supposed," rejoined the minister, as the shadow
of pain and sorrow came over his face. "But I am compelled
to be the means of disclosing a fraud which was perpetrated
by—by the lawyer who managed your uncle's affairs."

"I'm blowed if I often didn't think that Leech swindled
the old simpleton," said Dick, excitedly. "And so the cheating
rascal—"

"Stay," said the minister, holding up his hand, while the
expression of pain on his face deepened—"Stay, young man;
you are speaking of the dead; and however Mr Leech
wronged your uncle and his heirs, he atoned for it as far as he
could do before he died. He confessed the fraud, and executed

deeds which enable me, his sole executor, to make restitution to you, the sole heir of your uncle."

"Oh, well, in that case, mum's the word," said Dick.

"Decidedly," added Bowser, in a very emphatic tone, betrayed unconsciously into the utterance by the absorbing nature of the information just communicated.

The minister, without noticing Bowser's expression of opinion, went on—

"At the time of your uncle's death, his property of Braeside was not only entirely his own, but he had besides a sum of money approaching to near two thousand pounds. With this sum and accumulated interest Mr Leech bought last year the adjoining property of Southfield. The two places are therefore yours, along with a sum of seven hundred pounds, which still remains; and as soon as the necessary formalities are complied with, I shall be ready to hand the titles and money over to you."

"My eye," ejaculated Bowser, utterly overwhelmed at the thought of Dick's good luck.

"Can't I have them at once?" asked Dick, his heart bounding wildly with excitement.

"One or two things require to be done first. I am personally satisfied of your identity, and, as a proof of it, I give you this ten-pound note for payment of any expense you may incur. For this you will give me your receipt. The affair must be finally settled at Lanrock, but that may be to-morrow, if you choose."

Dick did of course choose, and while on the following day Bowser returned to Dundee, he, together with Mr Whitford and a law agent, proceeded to Lanrock, where Dick had no difficulty in proving himself the nephew of Andrew Paterson; and after one or two simple forms were observed, he was put in possession of the inheritance.

This inheritance, as the reader knows, was not rightfully his after all; for, by Mary Paterson's properly executed will, it belonged to her infant boy.

CHAPTER XXXII

DICK AND BOWSER PAY A VISIT TO SOUTHFIELD, AND THERE LEARN SOMETHING THAT ASTONISHES THEM

Dick's brain was nearly turned by his good fortune. From being a penniless wandering vagabond, he had suddenly become a man of property, and was worth nearly three hundred a year. No wonder that the turning up of such a stunning trump card, as he called it, should have a strong effect upon him, and tend to a revolution of his thoughts, feelings, and ideas.

He and his friend Bowser sat in a room by themselves, in a public-house in Stirling, drinking brandy and water. They had come thus far on their journey to have a survey of Dick's possessions of Braeside and Southfield, and, rendered thirsty by the heat, had halted for a little refreshment.

Dick had already begun to think that it would be as well to get quit of Bowser, for now that he was a respectable member of society, Bowser, he thought, was no fit companion for him. He was now immensely his superior, was quite independent of him, and thought that, on the whole, it would be as well to "cut" him.

But Bowser, on his part, had no intention of being cut. With his usual acuteness he read Dick's thoughts regarding him, and knew exactly the wish and intention of his heart, just as if the youth had plainly expressed them. It did not suit him, however, to drop the acquaintance, and he was determined to stick to Dick more closely than ever. So, notwithstanding one or two attempts which the latter made to shake him off, he had insisted on accompanying him to take a survey of his inheritance, and they were thus far on their way to the accomplishment of that object.

Dick was swinging back and forward in his chair with his arms crossed, his eyes gazing on the ceiling, and a cigar between his lips, the smoke from which he seemed to be silently watching as it curled slowly upward.

Bowser was smoking likewise, but adhered to his black clay pipe; he had not come into a property of three hundred a year, and could not, therefore, afford to sport a cigar.

"By Jove, Dick, but it's jolly fine to be going to see one's estate for the first time," remarked Bowser, at the end of a considerably long silence.

"Well, yes, on the whole it is," drawled Dick.

"Two weeks ago, if anybody had told us where we were to be to-day, and for what purpose, we would have voted him a fit person for a lunatic asylum; yet here we are—you are going to see a tidy property which is all your own, and I, your most intimate and valued friend, accompanying you."

"Hem," returned Dick. "Yes, it's a wonderful change every way. Of course the past *is* past with me, and I'll have to walk according to my new position."

"In course you will, my boy: no more Saturday nights in the Overgate, agoing it on the flute, with Tom to gather in the coppers. 'Taint for Richard Campbell, Esq., to do anything of that kind, or to go seedy with empty pockets. But old friends, Dick, need'nt be shoved overboard, now that you are floating in a three hundred tunner, especially them old friends as kept you right and square when your head was in low water."

"You mean yourself, of course," rejoined Dick, as he collected a large mouthful of smoke and puffed it forth in a thick cloud.

"Just so," was Bowser's laconic reply.

"It doesn't strike me, Bowser, that I owe you anything," returned the youth. "If I lodged with you and your wife, I always paid my way."

"So you did one time or another. But it wasn't every night you had the browns to tip; and didn't Tibb and me trust you, like friends, till you were in luck?"

"And when I was in luck didn't I pay you up?" demanded the youth.

"Dick, you hurt me," rejoined Bowser. "I didn't think as how a windfall would put your head so high as to slight the man that has been a brother or even a father to you for the last five years. Many's the night and day I took care of you when you couldn't look after yourself, and you ought to remember that."

"Look ye, Bowser," said Dick, taking the cigar from his mouth. "If you want a little cash, I'll let you have it for our

past friendship; but don't you see I have got to move in different society now, and it won't do for you and me to chum it
as we have done; it would knock me up at once. I have got to
get married now, and have a house, which it wouldn't do for
you to come about. It's fate that separated us, Bowser, and
we'll just have to make up our minds for it."

"Can't see it," returned Bowser, doggedly. "I can put on
my best togs when I come to see you, and when I am in them
nobody is to know the difference between me and your fine
new friends. As to parting with you, Dick, it's not to be
thought of. I've stuck by you, my boy, when you were a
tramp, and now I mean to stick to you when you are a gentleman. Look at me; ain't I as slap-up a cove as one can clap
eyes on?"

Dick was forced to laugh, and tossing the end of his cigar
into the grate, he rose, and said they might as well be going.
So he swaggered out at the door, leaving Bowser to follow at
his leisure.

"Curse his impudence!" muttered the latter. "I may see
day about with him yet, and then won't I—but I must keep
sweet now, for he has got the tin and I haven't."

*

The sun was declining towards the west as they drove in
their gig along the road overlooking the valley, on the opposite of which lay Braeside and Southfield. In the rich lustre of
that mellow summer's evening, the valley presented a scene
of great beauty, peace, and fertility. Dark wooded clumps
here and there dotted the slopes and uplands, while smiling
fields of hay and corn lay between, at the sides of which
nestled cottage homes, from the chimneys of which the blue
smoke rose into the bluer sky. Down at the lower end of the
valley lay the village of Kirkton in sweet seclusion—the seeming abode of quiet contentment and rural felicity.

"Snug place," remarked Bowser, as his eye roved over the
delightful scene.

"Rather," assented Dick.

"You've seen it before, of course?"

"Oh, yes, often. When a boy I used to come down once a
year or so to visit uncle Andrew at Braeside yonder, on the
opposite slope; you twig the house?"

"What, the white one with the dark thatch on the roof?"

"The same. I didn't care much about the visits, for Uncle Andrew was so horrid religious. But I like the old boy now that he has left me such a snug down-sitting."

"It strikes me that you haven't him to thank for that, but Burke and Hare," laughed Bowser. "They did you a good turn at any rate. Yon brat of Hare's down in the Overgate has a claim on you, and so by the bye has Bet; she looks for marriage."

"Oh, ridiculous!" exclaimed Dick, scornfully.

"Of course it's ridiculous, but Bet doesn't think so, and she's a devil to cross. If you don't make it up in some way, she'll work her revenge."

"Pooh, what have I to fear from her?"

"The fury of an angry woman, and that's something, I can tell you."

"It's no go, Bowser, my boy; you can't frighten me," observed Dick, flourishing his whip about the horse's ears. "Bet was well enough in the Overgate; but up here at Southfield, in the house I mean to build, she would be just rather out of place. But here, I take it, is Southfield; however, to make sure, we'll ask at the bumpkin standing at yonder gate."

The gate in question was a few yards further along, where a road branched away from the main road towards a set of farm offices at no great distance. Leaning on the gate, and gazing into the field, within which grew a promising crop of wheat, was a young good-looking man, plainly, yet cleanlily dressed, and having the appearance of a comfortable well-to-do agriculturalist. At his feet sat a little boy, of some four years, gathering wild flowers.

"Hilloa, my man!" cried Dick, pulling up when opposite him. "Is that Southfield down there?"

"Yes," was the answer, accompanied with a look of inquiry at the occupants of the gig.

"All right," rejoined Dick, and he turned his horse into the road.

"I'm tenant o' Southfield, if ye hae any business wi' me," said the man, calling after them.

Dick pulled suddenly up, and looked round. "Oh, indeed; are you Crawford?"

"My name is James Crawford," said the other, drily.

"Exactly. Then you had better come along and show me the place. I am its proprietor now."

Dick, in making this announcement, drew himself up with an air of great importance; and Bowser, as the friend of the great man, drew up his shirt collar in a lofty manner.

"Oh, indeed; are ye the new laird?" rejoined James Crawford, in a respectful, yet by no means sycophantic tone. "I'm glad tae see ye, sir. I was wonderin' wha had got the place. Some folk said that it was a minister down below Alloa that was Mr Leech's heir."

"Oh, that's Whitford. No; he doesn't get Southfield or Braeside; they are both mine; and I have just come to have a look at them."

Dick moved the horse down the road at a walking pace, and James Crawford, taking the child by the hand, walked on by the side of the vehicle, scanning with a curious and somewhat anxious look the features of Dick and his friend.

"Maybe, sir," he began, "maybe ye ken that I hinna gotten a new lease o' the place. Maister Leech was aye tae get it ready, but put off, and put off; however, I hope, sir, that you and me will come to terms."

"Oh that's likely, if you give me enough for the place. I understand you have had it dirt cheap all along."

"No just that, sir," returned James. "Me and my faither hae had it sae as we could mak' a decent leevin' in it, but no muckle mair."

"Stuff; I know better. If the place goes into the market, it will bring nearly double."

"Ye may get a bigger rent, sir," answered James; "but ye may get a farmer that wad scourge the land and impoverish it, and that wad be a greater loss tae you than the extra siller wad mak' up. Noo, sir, a' body roond aboot here wull tell you that there's nae farmer looks better tae the land, or pits mair into it, than me. It's in better heart noo than it was fifty years syne."

"Well, we shall see about all that by-and-bye," said Dick, loftily. "Only let me tell you that I mean to make the most of it."

"Nice boy that of yours," remarked Bowser, who thought it was time for him to say something.

"He is a rale nice laddie, sir; but he's no mine," answered James with a sigh. "He's an orphan that I am bringing up."

"Oh, indeed. Got no family of your own?"

"No, sir; I'm no married," said James, with a still heavier sigh, as a shadow of sadness stole over his fine manly face.

"Jilted?" said Bowser, with a comic laugh.

"Made a fool of by a fickle woman, no doubt," remarked Dick. "Eh—was that it, my man?"

"I wad raither no speak on the subject," said James, his face colouring to scarlet.

"Tuts, man, don't fret your heart out about a thing of that kind. There's as good fish in the sea as ever came out of it."

"And better," added Dick. "No doubt a good-looking fellow like you could get a dozen or more of the best girls in the parish to pick and choose from. If I were you, now, I would marry right off and show the girl who jilted you that you don't mean to break your heart for her."

"She's dead," said James, in the hope that this information would cause them to quit the topic, so productive to him of sorrow and torture.

"Dead, is she?" cried Dick. "Oh, that's another thing. But time will heal the wound sooner than you think. Before a twelvemonth is over, we may see you the happy husband of a blooming nymph, who will leap at you as a cock does at a grossart."[1]

Had another dared to speak in this strain to him, James would have resented the impertinence in no measured terms, but it was his new laird who so addressed him, and as the obtaining of another lease was of very great importance, he stifled the angry feelings of his soul and kept silent. Fortunately they at this moment reached the house, and the conversation naturally took another turn, to his immense relief.

The horse being relieved of his harness, and put into the best stall of James's best stable, the visitors were ushered into the parlour, and left there by themselves till James should go and hunt up the housekeeper for refreshments.

"A sturdy fellow that," remarked Bowser, "full of genuine Scotch caution."

"Don't like him," returned Dick. "He ought to have been

---

1. The 1885 book drops the vulgar and figurative comparison to a cockerel devouring a gooseberry.

more respectful to his landlord. I've a notion that he and I won't sort. He wants the place a bargain, but, by jingo I'll put on the screw."

Meanwhile James found Peggy busy in the kitchen making porridge for the evening meal.

"Losh sake, Peggy," said the youth, "here's the new laird come tae see the place—him and anither, an aulder man. I've left them in the parlour."

"Eh, mercy," returned Peggy, holding up her mealy hands; "and the parlour is no redd up."

"Deed it disna maitter muckle, I think, for neither the young laird nor his friend seem to be gentle folks."

"Dear me," returned Peggy. "A minister is surely a gentleman."

"This is no a minister, but a young wauff-like chap, and he says that baith this place and Braeside hae fa'n tae him."

"Braeside," echoed Peggy. "Hech me, but there was robbery there, for Braeside nae mair belanged tae Maister Leech than it did tae your coo."

"That's my opinion tae, Peggy," remarked James. "But Joshua had it a' his ain way, for there was naebody tae prove him rogue; and if he wranged the faitherless, as we hae owre muckle raison tae think, he's awa' whaur count and reckonin' will be demanded o' him. But come, Peggy lass, the laird and his friend maun hae breid and cheese and a dram, for we maun speak them fair, seein' that I hinna got a lease yet; sae, bring ben the things at ance, Peggy."

"I'll dae that, James. By guid luck the parritch is ready to pour. Awa' ye go, and I'll be but[2] in a jiffy."

Peggy was as good as her word. James had little more than time to rejoin his guests when she entered, bearing a tray with bottle and glasses, a large piece of cheese of her own making, a thick wheaten scone, and a pile of oat cakes. Little Duncan was by her side, and holding firmly on by her gown.

"That's the cheese!"[3] exclaimed Bowser with much satisfaction, as he caught sight of the provisions.

---

2. "But and ben" are outer and inner rooms.
3. That's first rate.

"Ye'll find it a very guid cheese, sir," said Peggy, concluding that Bowser's remark referred specially to one article. "I
made it mysel' oot o' the best milk, and I'm aye particular tae
hae it clean."

"Had we kenned ye were comin' we wud hae had something better tae offer ye," put in James, apologetically.

"Don't mention it," said Dick. "If the whisky is the real
stuff, we are all right."

As Peggy set down the tray on the table she cast a side-long
glance at the strangers—a glance that was turned into a stare
of astonishment when she caught a glimpse of Dick's face.
She looked for some moments with inquiring intensity, then
she slowly approached the youth, still keeping her eyes fixed
on his countenance.

"Mercy me, Richard, is that you?" she at length asked.

Dick turned and regarded her with not a little astonishment.

"It's just you," added Peggy.

"To be sure it's me," returned Dick. "I have always been
myself since ever I remember, and, therefore, can't see why
the obvious fact should strike you with such astonishment. But
who the deuce are you?"

"Dae ye no ken me?" said Peggy.

"Hang me if I do."

"Losh, man, dae ye no mind o' Peggy M'Naughton, yer
uncle's housekeeper?"

Dick looked at her more attentively, and the result was a
recognition.

"So you are old Peggy!" he exclaimed; "But a deal older,
and vastly altered since I saw you last."

"There's nae doot o' that, Richard, lad. I hae gane through
a hantle sin syne. I hae had muckle grief and sorrow—yer
uncle's sudden death and puir Mary's awful end."

"Bad affairs, both, I dare say; only you see, Peggy, I'm
not in a position to feel that, since the two things together
have been the making of me."

"Eh?—the makin' o' you?" repeated Peggy, in a tone of
wonder.

"Just so. There are four people to whom I am immensely
indebted, though those deeds of theirs which made me their
debtor are looked upon by the world with detestation. First,
there was Duncan Grahame, who seduced my cousin Mary,

and made her elope,[4] to bring on her father a shock of
apoplexy causing his death. Next there was Leech, the lawyer,
who kept up my uncle's property, and sent Mary to the
streets; and lastly, there were those two eminent worthies,
Burke and Hare, who popped Mary into the hands of the
doctors, and thereby made me heir to my uncle's property,
when the fear of death caused Leech to make a clean breast of
it, and give it up. Now, I think I have made out my case;
haven't I, old lass?"

"Decidedly," observed Bowser, who was by this time helping himself to the contents of the bottle.

Peggy could only stand staring at the youth in silent bewilderment, horribly shocked at the levity of his words, but
failing to comprehend their meaning. James Crawford was
more acute.

"Did Mr Leech confess that he cheated at Andrew Paterson's death?" he eagerly asked.

"To be sure, he confessed everything; told how he forged
the bond and kept up the money. Bless your soul, it was with
the money he bought this place here, and that's how it comes
that both it and Braeside are mine."

"Yours," screamed Peggy, on whom the truth now flashed
like a sunbeam.

"Ay, mine—mine, of course. I am my uncle's heir."

Peggy literally gasped for breath, and looked with extraordinary meaning at James, who was also wildly agitated.

"Dae ye mean, Richard," she asked, in a wildly eager manner; "dae ye mean to say that Braeside and Southfield belang
tae Mary Paterson's heir?"

"Well, Mary's heir or Andrew's, it's all the same, for I
come in to get my cousin's property as well as my uncle's."

"And Leech's heirs hae gi'en them up?" screamed Peggy
in the same excited way.

"Bless me, what is the woman roaring at?" said Dick.

"One would think she was the heir instead of you,"
remarked Bowser.

"Hae they gi'en them up?" repeated Peggy.

---

4. 1885 has "induced my cousin Mary to elope", dropping mention of sexual
seduction.

"Yes, they have; the papers are all complete, and lie in the hands of Leech's agent."

"And they belong noo tae Mary's heirs?"

"Of course they do; and that means me."

"Naething o' the kind," cried Peggy. "There's no a stane, no a clod, of them yours."

"The woman's mad," ejaculated Dick.

"More likely drunk," observed Bowser.

"Neither the ane nor the ither," said James Crawford, emphatically, though Peggy's actions seemed at the moment to belie his assertion, for with wild and even frantic vehemence she had snatched up the little Duncan in her arms, and was hugging and kissing him in a most extraordinary fashion.

"Then, what the devil does it all mean?" asked Dick.

"It means, Richard Cammel," shouted Peggy, "that it's no you, but this laddie, that's the heir o' Braeside."

"Whew!" whistled Bowser, "that's a settler."

"The woman is mad," said Dick.

"Ye'll find different," said James, quietly.

"This laddie, and nae ither," repeated Peggy. "This is Mary Paterson's bairn."

"Her bastard," repeated Dick, scornfully.

"But her ain for a' that," said James Crawford, with stern tone and kindling eye; "and I warn ye, my lad, no to say a slightin' word o' Mary, for I'll no stand it."

"Hilloa! you are getting impertinent," said Dick. "That's not just the way to get a new lease."

"It wull no be frae you I'll get a new lease," retorted James. "It's as true as ye sit there, that the bairn, and no you, is heir tae the place. He couldna heir it by law; but puir Mary, haein' her suspicions, nae doot, that Leech hadna dune what was fair, and that he might tak' a remorse o' conscience and gie up the property, made a WILL by which that laddie gets a' that belonged to her."

"Eh, my bonnie bairn, but ye'll he a rich man yet," cried Peggy, as sobbing with very joy she drew the wondering and half-frightened child to her bosom. "Yer mither's richts sall yet be yours; and wha kens but I'll end my auld days at Braeside after a'."

Dick was struck dumb by the information he had received. He turned very pale, and in nervous desperation helped himself to a large glass of whisky. The fabric of his suddenly-

acquired greatness threatened to tumble into dust, and leave
him a wandering vagabond as before.

Bowser could look at the thing with more philosophic
calmness, and his quick mind began to think what the exigencies of the case required.

"Not a bad plot, Dick," he observed; "but still too clumsy
to succeed. If there's a will at all, it can't be a good one."

"No, of course not," said Dick, catching at this suggested
course of action. "It's all stuff and nonsense to say that Mary
left a will. No use trying on that dodge; you'll only get your-
selves into trouble. Be advised for your own sakes, not to go
any further with your scheme."

"Dinna vex yersel' on oor account," said James, sarcastically. "It's maybe natural for *you* tae think that it's a lee we
are tellin' you, but the will can speak for itsel', and depend
upon it, lad, the bairn shall hae its ain."

"And wha has a better right?" cried Peggy, wrathfully.
"Whate'er the law micht say, the bairn is Mary's ain bairn,
just as muckle as if she had been married. Wha then, I ask ye,
has a better richt tae his mither's property. No you, Richard
Cammel, that was aye a neer-dae-weel, and broke yer
pawrents' hearts, and that's been gaun wanderin' the kintra
like a vagabond, consortin' wi' beggars and blackguards. A
bonny like thing it wad be for you tae come in afore Mary's
ain flesh and bluid. What a mercy it was that the puir lassie
was guided tae mak oot this paper, or wae's me the property
o' Braeside wad hae gaen a black gate."

"Can't you stop the old fool's tongue, Dick?" observed
Bowser.

"Look ye, sir," said James, rising and striding towards the
speaker, "I dinna ken wha ye are; I hae nae great broo' o' ye
by yer looks, but whatever ye are, ye hae nae richt tae speak
a word in my house, and if ye dare tae gie either Peggy or me
ony mair impidence, I'll tak ye by the shouthers an' pit ye
oot at the door."

This sturdy speech disconcerted Bowser somewhat. He
glanced his eye over the strong frame of the young farmer,
and saw it would not be safe to provoke a physical contest.

"Don't fire up in that way, man," he quietly said; "I'm
Dick's friend, and am interested in his rights; of course it's not
for me to dictate what he should do, but if I were him I would
demand a sight of this extraordinary will."

"So I do," exclaimed Dick. "If there is such a will, show
it me?"

"Hech, man, that's easy dune," said Peggy, setting down
the boy, and going to an old-fashioned chest of drawers that
stood in a corner of the room. "I put the paper in here the
very nicht I got it, and it has lain there ever sin' syne. Neither
James nor me ever said anything aboot it tae anybody, for
we never thocht it wad come to be o' use; but, my certie, time
has tel't us a different tale."

The chest of drawers had a slanting top like a bureau, and
this was fastened down with a brass lock. Having opened it
with one of a bundle of keys which she took from her pocket,
there was then a range of small drawers within, and from
the centre one, which she opened with another key, she took a
folded parchment.

Bowser watched all her motions with a keen eye, though
he *pretended* to be wholly occupied, as Dick *really* was, with
swallowing another glass of liquor.

"There, Jimes, show them the paper," said Peggy, handing
the parchment to the youth, who took it and spread it out
on the table. Dick bent over it with unsteady eyes, and Bowser
looked over his shoulder with a much cooler gaze. The short
document was easily scanned, and Bowser saw at a glance
that it was perfectly valid.

"I don't know much about these things," said Dick. "It
may be right or wrong for anything I can see."

"It's devilish wrong for you, at any rate," whispered his
companion. "The paper is as safe as the bank, but don't own
that."

"I'll try what the law can do, at any rate," said Dick,
aloud. "The bastard shan't take the ground from under my
feet if I can help it. Oh, my man, don't flush up so red; you
can't deny that this brat *is* a bastard."[5]

"If ye hae read the paper," said James, striving to command himself, "ye will see that his mother appoints me trustee
for the bairn, sae he is under my protection till he comes o'
age, and depend upon it I'll see him righted. Gang tae law if

---

5. 1885 book changes "The bastard" to "That child", and "this brat *is* a bastard" to "is not quite the thing", dropping impolite terms about illegitimacy.

ye like, I'll meet ye there though I sud spend every farden I
hae in the world."

"And me tae!" exclaimed Peggy.

"And when I win, as I am sure to do," said Dick, "don't
look for a new lease, for by the Lord Harry, you'll not get it.
Come, Bowser, let us go."

Bowser gulped up his glass, and followed Dick from the
room.

James in silence helped them to harness the horse and put
him into the gig, when, without a word, they sprang in, and
the animal, under the furious lashing of the disappointed
youth, bounded forward at a pace which soon carried the
vehicle out of sight.

CHAPTER XXXIII

THE MIDNIGHT THEFT

Two miles from Southfield, on the borders of the great moor, stood a lonely roadside inn, and there, in about a quarter of an hour after Dick and Bowser departed from the farmhouse, they alighted from their gig, threw the reins to the landlord, who waited in person, and entered the little sanded parlour—the only travellers who had made their appearance for several weeks.

Not one word had yet been spoken by either to the other, and their stoppage at that place was not the result of a mutual arrangement, but was simply effected by Bowser, who, as soon as he saw what kind of a place the solitary building was, gave a firm pull at the slack rein, which Dick held carelessly in his one hand, and the horse, in obedience to the summons, came to a stand-still at the inn door.

Dick made not the slightest objection to this step, but with ready, though silent, alacrity, followed Bowser into the room, and threw himself into the first chair he saw.

The landlady, a big, bouncing, ruddy-faced woman, presented herself on the threshold, and smilingly waited to receive the orders of her guests.

"House full to-night, Mrs Fraser?" inquired Bowser, who knew this to be her name from seeing it above the door.

"Na, sir, no just that," returned the landlady in a strong Highland accent.

"Got many guests?"

"No very mony," answered the woman, who, with the usual pride of her race, was not willing to confess that the inn was at the time entirely deserted.

"How many?" asked her persistent questioner.

"Twa," was the slow rejoinder, as the woman gave a glance first at one, then at the other.

"Two, only two; of what sort, male or female?"

"Baith men."

"Ah, indeed; young or old?"

"Ane auld, ane young."

"What like are they?"

"Hoots, sir," answered the landlady, seeing it useless to conceal the truth, "ye sud ken a' that better than me, since the twa travellers are just yersells."

"Ha, so we are your only guests?"

"Deed aye, sir. This house was a stirrin' place ance, afore the post road was changed; but wae's me, there's little traffic on it noo."

"Oh, never mind," interrupted Bowser, very unceremoniously. "Just come and show me our bed-room. I like always to choose that myself."

Bowser and the woman were gone for a minute or two, when they returned, the latter bearing a supply of whisky, which she set upon the round oaken table and retired.

Bowser sat down in a chair opposite to Dick, folded his arms across his chest, and steadily looked at his companion. It was, in the circumstances, a strange and unaccountable look. There was even a gleam of satisfaction in his little grey eyes, and a half-suppressed smile upon his shut lips.

Since he sat directly over against Dick, the latter could scarcely forbear looking at him in return—and he did.

"Well?" remarked the youth.

"Oh, it's *well*, is it?" returned Bowser. "In that case we've got nothing to do but let well alone. So we'll go to bed and have a jolly sleep."

"Confound your nonsense," said Dick, angrily. "This is the most cursed ill luck that ever happened me."

"That's better," rejoined Bowser, with a nod of approval. "That's more natural like. It is, out and out, a piece of desperate bad luck for you; but as it befriends me, I haven't the least desire to quarrel with it."

"What the deuce do you mean?" cried Dick, with a stare of surprise.

"I'll tell you. You were about to give me the go by, Dick. Your good fortune was making you proud and ungrateful, and you didn't mean to let me have any share in it. I felt this on the part of an old friend that I've helped along many a time, only I didn't see well how I was to help myself. *But I do now.*"

Bowser smiled complacently, poured out two glasses of liquor, and placed one before his companion, remarking—

"Take it off, it will bring your spirits up again."

Dick emptied the glass at a gulp.

"You see now how you can help yourself," he bitterly observed. "Of course you can help yourself in having me back for a lodger. Hang it, Bowser, isn't this a shabby trick the jade Fortune has played me? Who'd have thought that little brat of a bastard was to kick me out of the inheritance that I thought myself so sure of?"[1]

"Wait a bit, Dick," remarked Bowser. "Before you discuss the state of affairs, let us settle personal matters. I suppose your mind has changed a bit about our relation to one another. You've come to see, I fancy, that it will be as well for us to swim in the same boat."

"Didn't I always see that?" returned Dick.

"No, you didn't," replied the candid Bowser.

"You saw different this afternoon down at Stirling. You've seen different since yon day at Whitford's manse, when he told you that you were a rich man. You meant to cut me, Dick, and I tell you again I'm not sorry at what has happened, for it gives me a share in the pie."

"Don't be too sure of that," exclaimed Dick, firing up, "I can tramp it out without you, and would not think two minutes about going off by myself."

"Just so," rejoined Bowser, "you can *tramp* without me, and live a vagabond; but without me you can't be a gentleman."

"A gentleman," echoed Dick, with a scornful laugh. "A pretty gentleman you'll help me to become."

"I will," said Bowser, quite gravely, "at least as good a gentleman as—*two hundred a year* can make you."

"You've taken too much whisky, Bowser; you're drunk," said Dick, disdainfully.

"Not a bit of it; it's you that's a noodle, for nobody but a noodle would sit down and do nothing to get such a pretty inheritance."

"What can I do?" asked Dick, hopelessly. "The will is all right, there's no overturning it."

"Perhaps not, but there is such a thing as—*destroying* it."

The idea whispered across the table made Dick start and prick up his ears. The possibility of such a thing had not before entered his mind, but now that it was presented he grasped at it eagerly.

---

1. Mention of bastard is again dropped from the 1885 book.

"Ah," he exclaimed, "if *that* could be done I'm all right—but *can* it?"

"That depends a good deal upon yourself," suggested Bowser.

"Ah, there it is," returned the youth. "I haven't nerve for such an enterprise."

"I know you haven't, and that's just why you'll want me."

"Bowser, will you do it, and save me?" cried Dick, excitedly.

"I will."

"You're a good soul—a capital brick of a fellow. But how will you manage it? What is your plan?"

"Stop a bit. Let us first settle our shares of the proceeds. I don't work in the matter for you alone, but also for myself. Now I may as well state my terms at once."

"Do," said Dick.

"One-third," returned Bowser.

"My gracious!" ejaculated the youth fairly aghast, "one-third of the whole property!"

"Of the income from it. It brings three hundred. I must have one hundred a year."

"My eye, Bowser, that's a draw," said Dick, altogether taken aback by the other's proposition.

"Think so," rejoined Bowser, as with great composure he poured out another glass. "Well, we'll say no more about it, and the sooner we get back to Dundee and settle down in our old life the better. I think I'll go to bed and be ready to start in the morning."

"Be reasonable now, Bowser," said Dick, forcing a laugh. "Say something less than that, and let us set to work at once."

"Not a farthing less, Dick; and you might be thankful I didn't say more. Why, look ye, I might have claimed the half just as well as the third, for without me you couldn't get a farthing of the cash."

"Well, let us say done then," cried the youth, hurriedly.

"A hundred a year for me?" said Bowser.

"Yes," returned Dick.

"All right."

"Now for your plan," said the other, breathlessly.

"We must get the will into our hands this very night. To-morrow will be too late; of course that young fellow Crawford starts in the morning to put it in force."

"But how are we to get it?" asked Dick, who shrunk from the thought of a burglary.

"Easily enough," was Bowser's reply. "The moment the old woman spoke of the will I saw what was wanted, and began to prepare for it. I asked a sight of the will, not because I thought it might be a bad one, but that we might know where she kept it. We have got that knowledge. Then I looked at the room, and saw that we could get in by the back window; and next I pulled up here, for it is far enough away from the farmhouse. I have selected a bed-room for us both at the rear of the place, where we can get out and in without discovery. Now we go up as if to bed, and as soon as the old folks are gone to sleep we make our way out, and half-an-hour's walk brings us to Southfield. We creep into the parlour there, get the will from the drawer, return here to sleep for an hour or two, then bolt. You take possession as if you had heard nothing about a will; they'll not be able to produce it, and fortunately no one but themselves know it ever existed, so they will have no means of proving it. There, my boy, there's my programme. Ain't it perfect?"

"Wants one material thing," said Dick.

"What's that?" cried Bowser sharply.

"It don't contain the *destruction* of the will."

"Of course not," sneered Bowser. "I hope, Dick, you don't take me for a fool. If the will was destroyed where would we lay hold upon you? No, no; I *keep* the will to secure my hundred a year."

"Can't you trust me?" asked Dick, biting his lips.

"No. I'd rather make sure work, and hold a hank in my own hand."[2]

"Be it so," said Dick, who had no course left but to acquiesce. "Only it might be as well to take nobody into our confidence—not even Tibb or Bet."

"When I'm tired of the hundred a year I'll trust Bet; not till then," said Bowser significantly. "Now to bed, for it wears late, and we have got our work to do."

Shortly after midnight, when all was quiet and still in and about the little roadside inn, a window at the rear of the building was pushed stealthily up, and, without making the

---

2. From weaving: have a bird in the hand; hold my advantage.

least noise, Bowser and Dick crept from the aperture, and dropped upon the soft earth beneath. Crossing a little garden, they entered a grass field, and walked on under the shadow of the tall hedge which separated them from the white dusty highway. It was a beautiful moonless summer night, and perfect silence rested on the sleeping earth. The very atmosphere was warm with the hot sun of the previous day, for not a breath of air stirred the leaves or moved the branches. Overhead the sky seemed thinly strewn with stars that dimly showed themselves through the sultry haze, and a rosy tint already appeared above the eastern horizon, foretelling the approach of early morn.

Neither Bowser nor Dick were able to realise much of the soft peacefulness and still beauty of the scene. The errand on which they were bent was nowise in harmony with the truth and purity of the nature which lay around them, and filled with their bad thoughts and guilty purposes they walked silently forward till the farm offices of Southfield could be discerned lying like a deep shadow upon the slope.

"We must not lose any time," observed Bowser, in a low whisper. "In an hour or so it will be light, and people will be abroad; and it is of the utmost importance that we should get back unseen."

"It will be a devil of a business if we can't get the paper."

"It will," resumed Bowser. "But if the old hag has put it back into the drawer we are sure to nab it. We had better go in by this gate and get to the back of the house, and keep as still as mice for fear of rousing the dog. If once the brute begins to bark our game's up."

To effect this purpose of getting to the rear of the premises, they required to make a considerable circuit, and, as the course of the night had made visible progress towards dawn, therefore every passing moment became of increasing importance.

In the house and about the premises of Southfield all was still as elsewhere; and when Bowser cautiously raised his head and peered in at the back window of the parlour, he had the satisfaction of finding that it was empty.

In that rural place window fastenings were in those days considered unnecessary. He had, therefore, no difficulty in raising the sash far enough to admit his person. The sill was quite low, he did not need to climb; but, pressing his hands upon the wooden frame, he slowly, silently, and successfully crept through, and stood in the little apartment.

Dick followed. This kind of work was new to him, and he felt tremulous; but the importance of what was at stake emboldened him, and he unhesitatingly followed his leader.

Most unfortunately, yet with a negligence pardonable under the excitement, Peggy had left her keys hanging in the lock of the upper drawer, and Bowser absolutely chuckled with delight when his hands touched them and they chinked.

"That saves us a world of time and trouble," he muttered; "and we are very much obliged to the old woman for her consideration."

"Have you got it?" whispered Dick.

"Not just yet; but here goes."

A faint click told that the drawer was being opened, and presently a suppressed exclamation of satisfaction from Bowser intimated that he had got his hands on the will.

"Right as a trivet,"[3] Dick heard him say. "Two hundred to you, and one to me, ain't a bad night's work. Come on."

The drawer was locked, and the keys left as they were. They also closed the window behind them, made the same circuit of a field, gained the high road, and reached their bedroom in the inn without a sound, just as the first streaks of sunrise were shot up from the blue waters of the sea.

Bowser's nefarious scheme had been perfectly successful. The important document was now in their hand, and Dick was again the possessor of the two properties of Braeside and Southfield.

They lost not a moment in undressing, and as the room was a double-bedded one, Bowser went into one, while Dick laid himself down in the other.

Bowser fell asleep almost immediately, but not so Dick. His rushing thoughts and excited feelings kept him wakeful, and when he heard Bowser's deep-measured breathing he began to think that the best thing he could do was to get the will into his own possession and be an independent man.

One hundred a year he argued was a large sum to lose. Bowser's power to force it from him lay in his holding the

---

3. From three-legged trivet for pots: secure; steady; just right.

parchment. Let that be destroyed, and he was the full and entire master of his uncle's property.

Dick rose to his elbow, and looked towards the bed in which Bowser lay. His grisly hair and sunburnt countenance appeared above the white counterpane, and by his closed eyes and the calmness of his features he seemed to be in a profound slumber.

The youth knew that the will was under his pillow, for he saw him put it there, and after a minute or two's meditation he stealthily left his own couch, and with bated breath and cat-like cunning approached that of his confederate.

He bent over the shaggy, motionless head, and made himself certain that Bowser was in a profound sleep, then, with all-careful dexterity he slipped his hand under the pillow and it touched what he sought. The blood went with a great bound to his heart as his fingers touched the paper, and a thrill of triumph rushed through his soul as in imagination he deemed himself free. Quietly, yet not without a little nervous trembling, he began to draw forth the precious packet, when to his intense dismay he felt a grasp upon his wrist like the hold of a vice, and Bowser, opening his small grey eyes, said with all coolness, but with terrible emphasis—

"*No you don't.*"

Dick leapt several inches off his feet, and would have recoiled to the other side of the room, if Bowser's gripe had not kept him by the side of the bed.

"Oh, Lord, Bowser!" he exclaimed. "Quit your hold; you'll break my wrist."

"Don't matter much," said the other savagely. "So," he added, "you meant to do me."

"Oh, no," stammered the youth. "I—I only wanted to see if you had brought away the right paper."

"That's a lie; and you shouldn't lie when it doesn't serve your purpose. I never do. I suspected you would try that trick, and shammed a snore. But you might have learned by this time that you aint no match for me. Now, look ye here, Dick, I don't like that sort of doing between friends. It's not the cheese, by no manner of means; and if you try it again, I may happen to do something to astonish you. As to getting the better of me, that's a sheer impossibility; but you may tempt me to have revenge both on myself and you."

Dick forced a laugh, and saying nothing more, went back

to bed, and covering himself up with the clothes, fell asleep, and slept very soundly till a rough shake of the shoulder roused him. He looked confusedly up, and saw it was Bowser, who was already dressed.

"Come along, Dick; it's time we were on the road."

The youth needed no further bidding, but rubbed his eyes, yawned, and got up at once. Bowser left him to dress, saying he would go and look after breakfast, both for themselves and the horse.

When the youth descended to the parlour, he was met by both landlord and landlady in the passage, with an extraordinary show of respect.

"I wush ye joy, sir," said the first.

"And lang may ye live tae enjoy it," added the second, with a low curtsey.

"That blackguard, Leech," ejaculated the landlord, "tae keep back the property frae the puir orphan."

"And send her tae Embro' to be murdered," followed up the landlady.

Dick was puzzled for a moment, but catching sight of Bowser seated in the parlour, he received a sign from that worthy which made him understand the state of matters, and with a shrewd appreciation of his part, he at once assumed it.

"Oh, I see my friend has informed you that I am the nephew of Andrew Paterson, and heir to his property," he observed. "Yes, it was a villainous piece of business to keep poor Mary out of it. We were along at Southfield last night having a view of that property which Leech bought with the money he filched."

"And egad," observed Bowser, "the fellow who is tenant there wasn't over civil. He told us some absurd story of a little boy he has yonder, and declared that he is the proper heir."

"Oh, puir man, Jimes Crawford is sair tae be pitied," said the landlady. "Mary Paterson and him were sweethearts ance, and sud hae been married, but a neer-dae-weel young doctor chield got the better o' her, and sent her tae ruin. The news o' her murder put Jimes in a sair way; and I dinna think he has been richt in the head sin' syne."

"Ah, that explains his strange conduct," said Bowser. "He grew dreadfully excited, and even went so far as to say that he had a will in his possession which made the girl's child the heir to the property. He couldn't show us the will, though."

"Puir chield, he wadna ken what he was sayin'," said the landlord, compassionately. "He's a dacent, weel-daein' lad, Jimes Crawford; but the loss o' Mary took haud o' his brain."

"And set him mad?" suggested Bowser.

"Deed—next door tae mad. They say he was crazy a'thegither at the hangin' o' Burke, and gaed on like a man demented."

"We are all safe now," said Bowser to Dick, as at a rattling pace they flew along the dusty road. "The idea held by the people that Crawford has to some extent lost his reason will work in our favour and cause his story of the will and its loss to be looked upon as a pure invention of his mad brain."

"He's dangerous, though, and must quit Southfield at Martinmas," said Dick.

"Of course. Our game is to get rid of him, and send him to the devil."

While this vile plot was being so successfully carried out, during the course of that brief summer night, those whom it so much affected were sleeping the sleep of innocence and peace. Peggy M'Naughton and the child lay in a bed in the kitchen, and James himself slept in a room which looked out upon the stables. They all three slumbered on till the usual hour of rising, quite unconscious of the visit that was paid to their abode by the unscrupulous pair.

Peggy and the young man were early astir, for James was that day to ride down to Stirling, and he required to see his men at their labours before he started. The object of his journey was to put the will into the hands of a lawyer, and instruct him to take the necessary steps towards securing the property for the boy.

At eight o'clock he had got breakfast and was ready to set out.

"Noo, Peggy lass," he said, "bring but the wull, and let me go."

Peggy went to the parlour, and was some moments there, when she uttered an exclamation which made James run to see what was the matter.

"The wull—The wull!" screamed Peggy. "It's gane. Mercifu' po'ors, Jimes, it's gane."

"Hout, Peggy woman; ye've puttin' it into some ither drawer," said James with a smile.

"I've lookit every drawer," cried the agitated Peggy; "but I didna need, for I mind o' puttin' it back into the place whaur it has lain sin' e'er it cam' here."

"And is it no there now?" asked James, beginning to get concerned.

Peggy could only answer by pointing to the open drawer, which contained nothing.

"Gane—lost?" shouted James in amazement. "It's impossible; hoo can it be lost?"

They stood looking at each other for some moments in utter consternation; then all at once James ran to the back window and examined it. There were clay marks on the sill and the floor, which only too significantly confirmed his suspicions. He lifted the window with great energy, and bent over. The grass outside was soiled and trampled.

Then he knew that the will was stolen, and he knew also who had stolen it.

CHAPTER XXXIV

THE HATE OF LOVE

Tibb sat in the inner room of the lodging-house in Guthrie's Close, and Bet sat beside her. The former was busy with her knitting, but Bet sat idly looking at the dull red ashes of the expiring fire.

"So you don't mean to go out to-night," said Tibb, in somewhat of a dissatisfied tone.

"No, indeed," answered Bet. "I don't expect to have to go out any more."

"You seem to look for great things from Dick," returned Tibb.

"Of course I do," replied the young woman. "Isn't Dick a rich man now? And what for should I go out singing and begging when he can keep me without it?"

"Take care you don't disappoint yourself," observed Tibb with a suggestive nod. "Dick's prosperity may have made him change his mind a bit, and you may not find him just the man he has been."

"Now, you just stop that, Tibb, for I won't hear it," cried Bet angrily. "It's not for the likes of you to speak a wrong word against Dick. He has promised to marry me; and he's not the man to break his word."

"To marry you!" exclaimed Tibb. "You really expect that he will marry you?"

Bet's brown face flushed red and her eyes flashed brightly, while she pressed her lips together for some moments to suppress the passion that struggled to burst forth.

"If anybody but you, Tibb, had dared to be impudent to me like that, I would have torn their eyes out," she said in a low hoarse tone. "Marry me? Of course he'll marry me; and why shouldn't he? Aint I as good as he is? Wasn't my mother a farmer's daughter; and wasn't I brought up as well as him?"

"That's all true," rejoined Tibb quietly. "But now that he's got an estate and a deal of money, he may want a wife that has the same."

"But I tell you I have his promise," said Bet vehemently; "and that settles the matter."

Tibb smiled, and remained silent for a little.

"That child," she remarked again; "what am I to do with him? It was for you I got him; and if you give up work he'll be a dead loss on my hands."

"Stuff," returned Bet. "You'll get plenty girls to go out as I do, only they'll find the brat precious heavy. If I were you I'd make him walk; he's old enough. And what a vicious little wretch he's got to be; kicks and cuffs only make him worse. You feed him too well, you do."

"It's the kind he's come of," remarked Tibb. "He has got the bad murderer's blood in him, and won't tame. But he has paid himself to both of us. You have made a deal out of him, Bet, and might have made more if you hadn't kept the house so much."

"I'm not such a fool as to go out when I don't need. Dick said I was right. My eye! hear to the brat squalling."

The violent screaming of a child in the outer room, which for several minutes had been annoying, had become absolutely deafening, when, above the din, a loud rough voice was heard growling,

"Stop that imp's pipe, will ye; or I'll knock his brains out."

"There's Bowser!" exclaimed Tibb.

"And Dick will be with him," cried Bet, as in great animation she rose to her feet just as the door of the inner room opened and Bowser appeared—alone.

"Here I am all alive, and hungry as a hawk," he exclaimed. "Come, Tibb, my lass, stir yourself and get supper, and let it be a good 'un. There's a crown to do the stylish on."

"Where's Dick?" asked Bet, when she saw that the youth did not make his appearance.

"Along at the White Horse," replied Bowser.

"What's he doing there?"

"Putting up, of course, like any other gentleman; and, my eye! don't he come the gent real nobby."

"He'll be up to supper, I suppose?" observed Bet.

"What—here? Not likely. He has ordered the best that's to be had in the White Horse. Here! 'Taint likely Dick will show face in this crib again."

"Thought so," muttered Tibb, as she moved away to make ready the supper her lord had demanded.

"Did he say I was to hurry?" asked Bet, as she moved to

the door of a little closet which had its entrance from the passage.

"Hurry?" repeated Bowser. "Haven't you been out to-night yet? It's too late now; the coppers don't come well in at this hour."

"I mean, when does Dick want me at the White Horse," returned Bet impatiently.

"Dick doesn't want you at the White Horse at all," was the answer. "How did you ever come to think so?"

"Then where am I to see him?"

"I don't suppose you will see him at all. He's to be off for Edinburgh in the morning, and it's hard to say if he's ever in Dundee again."

"And he's going without seeing me," said Bet, returning to the middle of the room she was about to quit, and confronting Bowser with an ominous frown upon her countenance.

"Pooh, Bet, don't put on an air like that. Dick ain't the chap he was. He has got an esquire tacked to his name now— Richard Campbell, Esquire; that's about the sound of it. Now what has a man of his position to do with the likes of you? You might have sense to know that your acquaintance with him must drop."

Bet answered not a word; but by the flash which her eyes again emitted Bowser was aware of the passion stirring in her heart. But silently she turned away, and, entering the little closet which held her bed and her scanty articles of clothing, she quickly arrayed herself in her best dress, muttering wildly all the time she did so.

"He never would be so base as desert me. He has said a thousand times he would marry me; and now that he can afford to do it, he would not be false enough to draw back. If he is, my deepest vengeance shall fall upon him, my bitterest curse shall—no, no, what am I saying? Dick will not be false to me. I will not believe it. I know him better than think that the money he has got has made him proud. No—he will raise me with himself: and we shall have such a jolly life of it. He might have sent for me though; and I'll not forget to tell him that."

The last gleams of the fading western light came through a very small window in the closet, and revealed Bet's face, varying in expression from fiercest wrath to quiet confidence. When the thought of Dick's deserting her, as suggested by

Bowser, rushed across her mind, the passion that was for some moments indexed in her countenance was positively frightful. All womanly softness vanished entirely, and in its stead there was a most vengeful and vindictive expression, which showed that the love she now had for Dick, if slighted, would curdle into direst hate—for what is the truest and deadliest hate but curdled love? In some natures love cannot thus pass through its natural change and become boundless wrath. When pure and unfeigned, and dwelling in a heart which it has sanctifyingly permeated, it never, even amid slights and wrongs, loses its gentleness and sweet forgiving character; but when it possesses a heart where other passions also dwell, and where it has not subdued all things to itself—then, when it suffers at the hand of the object of its affection, these passions kindle up, and it but gives them fuel to burn the fiercer. Bet had a heart of this latter kind—a heart in which the strongest passions largely dwelt, and made her love itself fiercely jealous in its strength. For Dick she was ready to make any sacrifice. For him she had given up all that a woman can give up, and she was ready to endure any hardship, if, thereby, she could minister to his comfort. But in return she demanded his entire devotion, and would blaze up into fury at the slightest appearance of his bestowing favour upon another, which Dick sometimes pretended to do, that he might have the pleasure of raising her into anger.

Hitherto their connection, however disreputable, had been characterised by strong affection on her side, and by unwavering preference on his. Dick liked Bet more than he liked any other, and this was all that his selfish nature could attain to. So long as his relation to her did not interfere with his own interests he had no thought of leaving her; but now in his changed circumstances he looked upon their separation as a matter of course, so much so that he did not intend to see her again.

Unconscious of this, and scornfully rejecting Bowser's suggestion of it, Bet, arrayed in her best, made her way to the inn at which she was told Dick had taken up his quarters. Dressed as she now was, she was far from being ill-favoured or unprepossessing. She had a beauty of person which originally caused the temptation by which she first fell from virtue, and which had subsequently taken the fancy of Dick when they were first thrown together in their vagrant life. This bold beauty, discernible even under her rags, was more conspicuous now in her decent though somewhat gaudy attire, and no one whom she passed would have identified her as the starving mother of a starving child, who was to be seen and heard singing for charity in the streets.

Arrived at the inn, she had no difficulty in discovering him she sought. Dick had secured a room all to himself, and sat entertaining himself highly with the thoughts and prospects of his new position, as a man with an income of three—no, *two* hundred a year. This fact lay like a shadow on his view—the fact that he had been compelled to give up one hundred to Bowser. This was a bitter pill to swallow, but without Bowser's help he would have lost all, and it was his best policy to sacrifice one hundred in order to secure two. Nevertheless it was an unpleasant drop in the cup of his enjoyment, and, as we have said, cast a shadow over prospects otherwise bright and pleasant.

When Bet entered he had just finished a sumptuous supper, and was washing it down with his favourite beverage, brandy and water. He heard the door open well enough, and was not oblivious to the entrance of some one, but supposing it to be a servant come to remove the dishes, he did not look round. Bet had therefore the opportunity of taking a few moments' silent observation, and she did it. Dick, she thought, was decidedly handsome in his fashionable dress, and looked the gentleman he had become uncommonly well. His appearance made her proud, only the glance of her eye changed somewhat when she saw he had eaten his supper without sending for her to share with him, as she considered it the most natural thing in the world for him to do.

As there did not seem any prospect of the youth turning round, and so becoming aware of her presence, Bet grew impatient, and spoke:

"You have got snug quarters here, Dick," she remarked.

This had all the effect she intended, for with a great start Dick wheeled round, and stared at her with unmitigated surprise.

The surprise soon gave place to a frown.

"Who sent you here?" he angrily demanded.

"Nobody sent me," answered Bet.

"That's a lie!" growled Dick. "It was Bowser."

"Bowser didn't," she rejoined. "He only told me you were here, and I came. Didn't you expect me?"

"Expect you—not likely. This is not just the place for you to come to."

"Well, no; perhaps not. But I wished to congratulate you on your good fortune."

"Oh, well, that's all right enough," returned Dick, his natural vanity getting the better of his anger. "Yes," he added, "this is rather a good thing that has turned up for me. It's rather jolly to be sure of one's bread and butter, without having the trouble of working for it."

"Wasn't I glad when Bowser told me," observed Bet. "But I say, Dick, you might have told him to tell me to come along and have supper with you. You know I don't have such a stunning turn up in Tibb's."

"Didn't think of it," said Dick, coldly.

"Had it been me, I should not have forgot you," returned Bet, in a tone of reproach.

"Oh, yes, you would. You would just have seen the thing as I do."

"Seen what?" she rejoined. "Who's to know here that I came from a lodging-house in the Overgate, and that I go out singing? Haven't you said yourself, Dick, when I got on my best togs, that I looked prime, and could show off with the best of them?"

"You are well enough, I daresay," was Dick's careless reply, "and I might have said that when things were as they were. But that's altered now, and as we can't live together any more, it's no use you seeking me. Bowser might have told you so, and kept you from coming."

Had Dick been looking at Bet when he said this, he must have quailed beneath her enraged eyes. The passion which in a moment distorted her face was terrible to behold, and it declared the *curdling* process to be fearfully imminent. But he was not looking at her. Selfish though he was, he was rather ashamed to meet the gaze of the woman he was casting off.

"Dick," said Bet, making an effort to speak calmly, "it has long been settled between us that we should be married when good luck came. It has come now. You'll want a little time to get things settled in your new place, and then I suppose we shall go together."

"You don't need to suppose anything of the kind," returned Dick, with brutal bluntness. "Married to you *now*! What a preposterous idea! That was well enough when you and I

made our living in the streets; but when I have come in for
three hundred a year it is quite out of the question, and the
sooner you understand that the better. It's quite natural, of
course, for you to want to stick to me; but I'm not such a fool
as throw myself away. I've got the command of the market
now, and it's my chance to make the best of it. So let us say
good-bye and part friends."

"Have a care, Dick," said Bet, still in a voice which, though
calm, bordered on ungovernable passion. "You mean what
you say for a joke, but a joke of that kind don't take well, and
I'd advise you not to carry it further."

"A joke!" echoed Dick, with a laugh. "You think it a joke,
do you? You really dreamt it possible that I should be green
enough to throw myself and my three hundred a year away
on you, when I have the power to make an advantageous and
respectable marriage? Oh, come, come, Bet, *you* are joking
now!"

"And so you *are* in earnest," she said, isolating every word,
and uttering the sentence with a peculiar emphasis.

"Never was more so in my life."

"You will be false to your promise?"

"Circumstances have changed."

"And faithless to your love?"

"Love! Pooh! There was no great love lost between us."

"You said you loved me, Dick."

"I might—I liked you better than I liked any other girl; that
was all."

"And you have no pity for me. You cast me off without a
thought of my fate. You leave me to my life of poverty and
want—me who have sacrificed all for you. My love, my devotion to you are nothing in your eyes. You can go to live in
luxury, and care not what comes of the poor girl that made
your life of poverty as sweet as she could."

"Oh, well," resumed Dick, "if you put it in that way I
may do a little for you. For the sake of the past, I don't care
if I do give you a small sum. Let me see. I think I have a few
shillings in my purse, and I shall let you have them, only you
must not annoy me any more, for I am determined not to—"

He had taken his purse from his pocket—Dick carried a
purse now—and was proceeding to count out its silver contents, when his hand was arrested by Bet, who seized his arm
with a gripe of concentrated strength.

"Money for *me!*" she hissed, while her eyes blazed like two living coals. "Money instead of the fulfilment of your promise! Think you my honour, my love, is to be paid for by a few paltry coins? Am I a hireling, then, whose claim to be your wife is to be met by throwing silver in my face, and bidding me begone, as if I was a dog? Mark me, Dick; henceforth there is hate, eternal hate, between us. This night's insult shall never be forgotten, and I live only for revenge."

"Spit away, you vicious she-tiger," said Dick contemptuously. "Send out your venom in the worst words you can find; it's the only way you have of getting quit of it. As for your threats, I don't care one pin for them, for though you have the will you haven't the power to harm me."

"Don't be too sure of that. A woman like me, whose love has been turned to hate, is sure to find the means of working out her revenge; and with her there can be no forbearance— no mercy. The most venomous serpent in the world, coiled in your bosom, would not be a more deadly enemy than I am."

"That's right," said Dick, snapping his fingers. "Make your mouth a safety-valve for the escape of your rage, or you may burst. And now, having done your worst by spending all that wind on me, you can take yourself off, if you don't want a policeman to be sent for."

She released his arm, drew herself up to her full height, and with an expression of the most bitter intensity and vindictive passion, whispered in tones low, but terribly distinct—

"The day is coming when you will rue as man seldom rues this night's heavy wrong and heartless cruelty to me. When you find yourself plunged in ruin, and learn that my hand has accomplished your downfall, you will then repent with hopeless regret the deed that made me loathe and curse you, as I now do, and swear to accomplish your destruction. Farewell, Dick; be sure we shall meet again, when it shall be my turn to triumph, and yours to howl in despair."

"By Jove, but you are ten times as spiteful as I ever thought you," sneered Dick. "However, it's as well for you to go the whole hog as you are at it, and I hope you'll sleep sounder after getting rid of that black bellyful. As to our meeting again, that's not unlikely. I may come across you singing in the streets sometimes, and throw a copper to you as I pass. It's like ye'll be more respectful then than you are now. But harkee, my spitting cockatrice, if you don't quit this room in

two seconds, I'll ring the bell, and order the waiter to kick
you out. Now, take your mind of it."

Bet uttered not another word, but gathering into her countenance the essence of unspeakable fury, hate, and scorn, she
bent her eye steadily on his, moved slowly backwards towards
the door, and never took her gaze from his face till she had
gained the threshold, then flinging upon him one last withering glance, she turned quickly round and vanished from his
view.

"What a malicious she-devil Bet is, to be sure," said Dick
as he took a long pull at his tumbler of brandy and water. "If
I was weak enough now, her angry words would make me
uncomfortable; but as I know them to be nothing more than
idle breath, they are only fit to be laughed at. What presump-
tion in the wench to expect that I should marry her after what
has turned up. It would be snug down-sitting for her, no
doubt, but a pretty clipping of my wings. No, I flatter myself
I shall be able to do a deal better than that; I'll make up to
some laird's daughter who has got a lot of tin, and make my
two hundred a year four or five. *Two* hundred—only two,
when I ought to have three. Curse that fellow Bowser; how
cleverly he has managed to get a fat share of my inheritance.
If I could only manage to get the will out of his possession,
wouldn't I snap my fingers at him, and pocket the whole rent
roll. I suppose there's not the slightest chance of that, though.
Bowser is not such a flat as to let out of his fingers the precious
document that brings him a hundred a year."

While the unscrupulous and unprincipled youth mused thus,
the woman he had so unceremoniously cast off was wandering
wildly through the streets, she knew not whither. In her aimless
progress she passed along the Nethergate, and turning down an
opening to the left, she came upon the quiet and solitary bank
of the river. The summer night had now settled softly down upon
the landscape, and in the blue waters of the Tay the starry
canopy above was placidly reflected. The shadowy woods and
rich fertile fields and swelling eminences of the opposite shore
lay dark against the hazy southern sky, while far westward
and lost in dim distance was the far-famed Carse of Gowrie,
bearing on its generous bosom the promise of a plenteous
harvest. Down towards the east the black tapering masts and
netted cordage of the ships in the harbour rose into the silent
air, and behind was the wooded slope, not so thickly planted

with villas as now, yet dotted here and there with comfortable mansions, where reposed in ease and affluence the more favoured sons and daughters of the earth.

It was a scene of great beauty and peace, brooded over by the stillness of the calm and sultry night. A very gentle and most refreshing breeze was wafted down the river, bringing with it the fragrance of flowers and meadows, and faintly stirring with delicious gentleness the hot flushed cheek of the wandering girl, in whose raging heart a fever of passion rushed and swayed like a whirlwind. How different the serenity without from the tumult within her bosom. It was a scene calculated to soothe and calm the wildest storm of human feeling, but on Bet it had no such influence. She was, indeed, but dimly conscious of surrounding objects, and gave herself up unrestrainedly to the fury of her thoughts and the vengefulness of her desires. The threats she had hurled in her anger against Dick were threats which—however boldly and specifically delivered—she knew no means of accomplishing; and her very impatience to work out the vengeance she panted for made her rage and fury all the more consuming. To accomplish Dick's destruction was her intense desire and settled purpose, but the method was as yet unperceived by her. Her love—curdled now into a hate that was measureless and implacable, was unable to see an issue to its wish for vengeance, or any means for securing an adequate triumph, and when, after wandering to and fro for nearly an hour, like a spectre or a shadow, she returned into the town, the only thought which had flitted through her mind and returned thither again was of a plan to wait till Dick had settled in his property and then burn his house to the ground, a scheme which did very little to meet and satisfy the passion of her heart.

She entered the outer room in the lodging-house just as Tibb—having concluded the superintendence of preparing supper for her several lodgers—entered the inner room, where sat Bowser, content now and good-natured, for he had by this time finished the substantial and savoury meal which his "helpmeet" had prepared for him. Tibb did not perceive the entrance of Bet, and the latter being in no mood to enter the society of Tibb and Bowser that night, slipped quietly into the closet which she and Dick had been accustomed to occupy together, intending there to undress and go quietly to bed.

She was busy removing her upper garments, when a conversation between Tibb and Bowser, which was taking place
in the adjoining room, and which she heard distinctly through
the thin and dilapidated partition, made her pause to listen
with breathless interest.

"Wherever can Bet have gone to?" she heard Tibb remark.
"It's about twelve, and she aint come in."

"I know where she is," replied Bowser. "She's along at the
White Horse seeing Dick. The fool thinks he'll marry her."

"And won't he?"

"Won't he? My eye, have you to ask that question? Aint
Dick a gentleman now?"

"Suppose he is. Gentlemen sometimes marry poor girls;
and then, you know, it was all settled between Dick and her
before."

"Oh, that was when Dick had no thought of this golden
turn-up. That has made a precious difference with him, I can
tell you. It has made him as proud as Lucifer, and he'd as
soon marry old Kirsty ben the house as take Bet."

"It's my opinion Dick's good luck is bad luck for us,"
returned Tibb. "The profit we had out of him is done, and he
looks as if he didn't mean to seek our company any more,
for as good friends as we have been to him."

"That's a fact, Tibb," said Bowser. "Dick did just mean
that same; and but for a lucky chance he would have cut me
as clean as he would cut a turnip. But I've got the whip-hand
of him; and to let you into a secret, old lass, our luck is almost
as good as his."

"Bowser, you've been drinking too much," said Tibb in a
severe tone.

"What! you think me slushey, do you? Ha, ha! that's good.
Tibb, what would you think of you and me having a hundred
a year to live on?"

"Bah, don't be a fool," said Tibb impatiently. "Go to bed
and sleep off the whisky."

"Whisky! Bless the woman, I'm as sober as ever I was in
my life; and I tell you, Tibb, in right down earnest, that we
have a hundred a year. One-third of Dick's windfall is ours;
'cause why?—Dick hasn't no more claim to his uncle's property than you have. There's a will that keeps him out of
it."

"A will," echoed Tibb in astonishment.

"Ay, a will made by Mary Paterson, making over all that was hers to her child. Now, I've got that will; and for keeping it secret, Dick has made a bargain to pay me a hundred a year. You twig the thing now?"

"Why didn't he destroy the will?" asked Tibb.

"Because he hasn't got it," returned Bowser; "he tried his best to do me out of it, but found I was too many for him."

"I see," said Tibb, nodding her head with an air of satisfaction. "You keep the will as security for the cash."

"Just so; and as it wouldn't be safe for me to carry it about, I've put it *there*—do you see?" and he pointed to a particular corner of the room.

"All right," said Tibb. "It's safe enough; no one will ever come on it there. A whole hundred a year! Gracious me, Bowser, we'll not need to keep a lodging-house any more."

"Of course we won't; our fortune is made, old lass. Let us go to bed and dream of it, and Bet may come in when she likes."

Little did the speakers imagine that Bet was on the other side of the partition, and had heard every word that had been spoken. As she listened and comprehended the state of the case, her temples throbbed with the vehemence of her frantic joy. By the knowledge of which she had so unexpectedly become possessed, the means were given her of working out the revenge for which her raging heart panted; and as she saw how completely Dick was in her power, her brain reeled with the intensity of her fondest joy, and it was only by a terrible effort that she could refrain from shrieking forth her unbounded satisfaction.

"That will," she gasped, with feverish agitation. "I must secure that will. Then, Dick—then shall you find what it is to have wronged and deserted me."

CHAPTER XXXV

LIGHT OUT OF DARKNESS AND SUNSHINE
AFTER SHADOW

The feelings of James Crawford and Peggy M'Naughton on discovering that the will was stolen may be better imagined than described. First consternation and dismay, then indignation and rage, filled their hearts. They had no doubt as to who had abstracted the document, and charged themselves with stupidity and carelessness in allowing such an important paper to slip from their possession. Without it, they were well aware, little Duncan could not get his inheritance; for however certain *they* were that such a document once existed, they had no means of proving it to the world. They had hitherto carefully kept it in their possession as if it had been an important secret—never mentioning it to a living soul, because never dreaming that it would come to be of use.

It was doubly mortifying, therefore, to have lost it as they had done. Knowing well by whom it had been stolen from them, they were powerless to bring the theft home to Dick and Bowser, and were besides utterly unable to rectify the evil by producing any evidence at all to show that such a will had been made. They had not even noticed the name of the lawyer who had drawn out the deed, or of those who had witnessed it; and Jessie Brown—who now lived in a little cottage in the village of Kirkton, and maintained herself sewing—could give no information on these important points. When poor Mary gave her the packet to keep she did not tell her what it contained; the will, therefore, Jessie had never seen or even heard about—and however anxious she was to see its purpose served, she could, alas, render no assistance towards that end.

Neither James nor Peggy, however, could think of remaining silent. If nobody knew such a will had existed, they did; and the truth they should tell, however unable they were to establish it. And they did tell it; they told how a will executed by Mary had come into their possession, how they had shown it to Dick and his companion the evening they were at Southfield, and how on the following morning when they went to the drawer in which it was laid they found it gone, and found footmarks close to the window of the room where it lay. They were not imprudent enough to say whom they suspected; but their story so naturally suggested to others the suspicion which filled their own minds, that, without naming it, Dick and his companion were publicly suspected of the act—if indeed there was truth in the story at all.

Here, however, circumstances combined to make people to think that the whole matter was a myth. The strange and extravagant conduct of James Crawford at the time of Burke's execution caused it to be generally considered that the loss and murder of his sweetheart had unsettled his reason, and it was now believed that the story of the will was an invention of his diseased mind, and had no existence whatever in fact. And to prove most incontestibly that Dick and Bowser could not have entered the farmhouse of Southfield on the night in question to steal the document, the landlord and landlady of the little wayside inn testified to their having slept there all night, and departed in their vehicle in the morning.

It came to pass, therefore, that with very little trouble on his part, Dick was enabled to defy James and Peggy, and without opposition he entered on possession of his uncle's property; and people were inclined on the whole to sympathise with him. James and Peggy, it was thought, had made an attempt to deprive him of that which was legally his, and public feeling was enlisted on his behalf. He even became rather popular in the neighbourhood, for he had a speciousness in his manner which made him shine in the society into which his position enabled him to enter; and then the facts that he was young, good-looking, and rich, made him welcome in those households where marriageable daughters resided. His past character was not untainted—his vagrant life for the five preceding years was not unknown; but money, like charity, covers a multitude of sins, and these things were all overlooked.

As was to be expected, James Crawford did not get a new lease of Southfield. He did not even ask it, not only because he knew that it would be insolently refused, but because he was too upright and indignant to take a lease from a usurper such as he knew Dick to be. Therefore it was settled that he should leave the farm at Martinmas; and no surprise was manifested

when this was known—from the circumstances of the case
nothing else was to be expected.

It was a sore trial, however, for James to quit his home.
The family of Crawford had been in Southfield for many generations, and he had looked forward to spending there a long
and happy life. But this was not now to be. He must go and
seek another home among strangers; he must break the old
ties and form new ones; he must leave the dear familiar scenes
of his childhood and youth and go to some place as yet
unknown. And to make the matter more bitter, he knew that
this need not have been. If truth and justice had been
observed he would not needed to have quitted Southfield, but
villany and wrong-doing had triumphed, and of these he was
the victim.

In sadness and despondency he began to lay plans and take
steps for the future. His first thought was to emigrate; to go
and become a Canadian farmer or an American backwoods-
man, and but for a seeming accident he might have departed
to a foreign land. Providence, however, was working in the
matter, and guiding him from the cloud which had long over-
shadowed him to a brighter and happier life. James had
deemed that happiness could not now be in store for him on
earth, and that he must carry his burden of sorrow to the
grave; but a kinder better fate was awaiting him, and even
through new and deeper darkness he was being led to it.

One day, in looking over the *Courant*, his eye fell on the
advertisement of a farm to let on the east coast, and the
thought occurred to him that he might give an offer for it. It
was a thought born as it seemed of an impulse, and in his
present frame of mind was likely to leave him ere it had well
been presented; but it did not. On the contrary, it stuck to
him; and the desire to take a farm in Scotland, and forego his
purpose of emigration, so grew in his heart that he resolved
to go at once and see this place by the sea.

So on a radiant summer day he journeyed to the place,
and the coach put him down at the inn-door of a country
village, in front of which and at no great distance was the far-
stretching blue sea. James was in better spirits than he had
been for years. The journey on the top of the coach had done
him much good—for he had been carried through a beautiful
and fertile tract of country, and as it was now near to harvest,
his agricultural eye was pleased by the abundance of the

crops and with the high farming which everywhere met his view.

He had dinner at the inn, and having bespoken a bed there for the night, and inquired the road to Redlaw, he was directed to a path which winded away towards the sea. How that mighty sleeping sea impressed him as he approached the top of the cliffs whose base it kissed with a gentle murmur! Having all his days resided inland, he had seen the ocean but seldom, and that only at Granton or Leith. Never had he beheld such a wide expanse of blue and glassy water as now lay before him, stretching on and on till in the far horizon it joined the sky, meeting as it were heaven and earth together, and making a covenant of peace between them. Neither had he before witnessed such rocky crags and lofty precipices as here formed the boundary of the rugged and indented coast— frowning in awful strength and towering altitude on the bosom of the deep; peaceful *then*, under the calm summer sun, but turbulent and tempest-tossed at other times, when the howling north wind blew in its fury, bearing on its wings the Spirit of the Storm. Then these rocky sentinels of the coast seemed in nowise too strong for the foaming billows that dashed madly to the shore and hurled themselves in thunder and spray against the cliffs.

No sign of this madness of wrath now, however, as James Crawford gazed for the first time on the peaceful sea and frowning shore, where rest and silence reigned; and the scene had for him a peculiar charm. Altogether the desire grew stronger in him that he should come to reside in a spot so romantic and grand.

The road led him into a little fishing village, where, on a grassy eminence on the very verge of the cliffs, hardy weather-beaten men were spreading their nets, and brown, healthy children of both sexes rolled and sported in childish glee, dangerously near to the beetling precipice, from which there was no protection. Passing this little hamlet—for it was little more—perched on the bluff and breezy height, James proceeded on his way, following the road till it led him to the end of a dark tunnel cut in the soft sandstone rock into the heart of a lofty hill. As this was evidently the regularly used path, he boldly entered its gloomy shadow, and after traversing its subterraneous windings for perhaps a hundred yards, he reached the opposite opening, and to his surprise found himself in a secluded harbour, shut in on the landward side by beetling cliffs. Here he was brought to a stand-still, for the road went no further—and the tunnel in the rock had been cut to give access to this natural basin, where a number of fishing boats lay in perfect security, sheltered by the hills behind and shelving rocks in front. At the base of the precipice and close to the beach stood one or two curing-houses, from which columns of smoke slowly rose, and were dispersed against the sides of the lofty crags.

Seeing there was nothing for it but to retreat, James retraced his steps, and emerging again from the tunnel he was not long in coming to a place where the road branched away up the slope. This was the path he should have taken before; but not sorry that his error should have led him to a place so romantic, he took it now, and once more found himself on the table-land above. Walking forward, the road descended by a long slope into a ravine opening from the sea, which received from the depths of its wooded sides a crystal stream fresh from the hills. Here, to the youth's surprise and admiration, he beheld down in the valley, and near to the low sea beach, a mill, whose busy wheel was making music with the burn, while its noisy clapper kept joyous time to the rushing sound. It was the same scene we described in a former chapter of this story, when we related the sad fate of Joe the miller's son. Strangely enough, the farm which James Crawford had come to see was the farm occupied in that former time by the father of Lizzy Fairbairn, whom Joe was to have married. Mr Fairbairn had died the previous year, and poor Lizzy, being left alone, was not able to continue in the place, so the lease having expired, it was now in the market, and at the following Martinmas she must leave it.

Knowing nothing of these more private particulars, James Crawford entered the open door of the mill, and encountering there a young ruddy-faced man, white from head to foot with flour, he asked, not without difficulty amid the noise, the way to Redlaw.

The miller—a free, frank, manly young fellow—came outside and pointed to a path to the east which went zigzag up the heights, and told him that by following it the first place he would reach would be the place for which he sought. With thanks for the information, James pursued his way; and the moment he came again upon the table-land he saw the house and farm offices at a little distance up the slope.

It was Lizzy who received him; and when she came to the door in her dark mourning dress, James was particularly struck by her sad yet sweet appearance. She was pretty still. Nay, grief and sorrow had added a new charm to her beauty, which was all the more appreciated by one who had himself known sorrow, and that of a kindred character.

Their interview was short, but agreeable on both sides. Lizzy seemed to be pleased with James as much as he was with her. Was it instinctive sympathy of soul that drew them towards each other? Did the face of the one betray to the eye of the other a reflection of the same experience? We may not determine, but assuredly Lizzy regarded the young stranger with unwonted pleasure, and expressed a hope that he might be her father's successor in the farm. And curiously enough the interest so sweetly expressed made James all the more anxious to get the place. The "grieve," being commissioned to show the youth over the lands, and give him all requisite information, executed his task with much civility, and the result was that James, on descending the slope in the evening on his way to the inn, was resolved to send in his offer immediately. It was a large farm, and in capital order. The crops which at the moment waved on its swelling uplands were heavy, the pasturage was rich, and all things betokened comfort and fertility. But above and beyond even these inducements was a strange undefined attraction in the person of Lizzy Fairbairn. The young man's thoughts ran constantly back to her, and despite the fact that she was about to leave the farm, his wish to take it was closely associated with her presence there. The interest he felt in her was something wonderful, because such interest in any girl was for him altogether unusual. Since the loss of Mary, his mind had never once been taken up or his fancy impressed by one of her age and sex, and it had been a settled idea with him that the affections of his heart were withered up for ever. Hence the singularity of his feelings now in regard to Lizzy Fairbairn.

The interest he felt awakened of course a corresponding curiosity, and he longed to know something about her. "There's something by common in yon lassie," he muttered to himself. "There's nae licht-heidedness or haverel daffin' aboot her, but a serious sweetness and a modest common sense that ane seldom meets wi'; and she's bonnie, tae—bonnie and weel-faured, and sae nice and auld-fashioned. I wad like real weel tae ken something aboot her. Dod, yonder's the miller stannin' at the side o' the burn. I wadna care tae ask him, for he's sure tae ken a' aboot her, and he's a frank ceevil chiel."

With all the ease which country people have in accosting each other, James left the road and crossed the bit of grassy ground which lay between him and the stream, on the banks of which the miller stood with a pipe in his mouth. The mill was now quiet and at rest. The wheel stood still, the clapper had ceased its noise, and the stream kept in peace its rippling course to the sea, so close at hand.

"Man, this is a bonny place o' yours," remarked James.

"No amiss," responded the miller, who being more familiar with its beauties, was less enraptured with them than the stranger.

"Eh, I think it's grand," continued the latter. "For my part, I never saw the like o't."

"Weel, I daursay it's no mony places alang the coast that's sae high and rocky," observed the miller. "But it's gey dull and eerie, especially in the winter time. It's pleasant eneuch enoo, when the days are lang, and the weather fine, but in a winter's night, when there's a sea on, and a scud o' rain or snaw frae the north, it's fearsome eneuch. Ye wadna like it sae weel then, I'm thinkin'."

"I dinna ken," returned James. "This is a place I think I wad like at ony time. I've just been up lookin' at Redlaw."

"Ay," said the miller, with some interest. "Are ye thinkin' o' giein' an offer for it?"

"Weel, I dinna ken but I may. It seems raither a nice place."

"Capital—few better," returned the miller emphatically. "Maister Fairbairn was amang the best farmers round about."

"That will be his dauchter I saw up bye at the hoose, I fancy," observed James.

"Ay, it wad be Lizzy, puir thing."

"She seems tae tak' on sair for the loss o' her faither."

"No for her faither a'thegither," returned the miller. "It's a waesome story hers. Of course ye hae heard o' the awfu' Burke and Hare murders?"

James started violently, and became pale and agitated.

"My gracious me!" he ejaculated. "What had she tae dae wi' them?"

"Her sweetheart was ane o' the victims."

The youth actually staggered, and his emotion became extreme.

"The man that had this mill afore me had a son ca'd Joe—a weel-faured, guid-hearted chiel as ever lived, and Lizzy and he were tae be married. But Joe had just ae faut, and a sair ane it was—he was muckle gi'en to the dram; and it got sae bad that Lizzy had tae gie him up. So the puir chap set off, naebody kenned where. But Burke, afore he was hanged, confessed that he was ane o' them that him and Hare had murdered. The news maist killed Lizzy a'thegither, and she's ne'er been seen to lauch sin syne. Mony's the ane she could hae married in the neebourhood; but she couldna forget puir Joe, and I believe she thinks o' him yet. It's a great pity, for Lizzy wad mak' the best o' wives, and noo that her faither is awa she'll be very lanely hersel."

The miller would have prolonged the conversation further, but James was utterly unable to bear it. The information he had received was such as to send a rush of strongest feeling through his heart, and feeling that he must soon utterly break down, he wished to reach a solitary place where his emotion would be unseen. So be bade the miller good night, and walked hastily away.

"Maybe we'll be gettin' you for a neebour yet?" cried the miller after him, in his frank, cheery tones.

James nodded, waved his hand in token of assent, and without trusting himself to speak, leapt over the burn, and pressed up the westward slope.

Soon a turn of the road shut out the mill and the valley in which it lay, and James, vaulting over the stone fence, climbed the neighbouring height, and found himself upon the brow of a rocky precipice with the sea gleaming far below. Here, unseen by mortal eye, he threw himself on the green sward, buried his face among the thick grass, and sobbed in the excess of his emotion. It was not bitter grief that so unmanned him; it was a burst of tender sympathetic sorrow. His strange deep interest in Lizzy Fairbairn was all explained now. She had suffered as he had done, and he knew so well how heavy and painful the suffering was that he felt as if he could fold the lonely desolate girl to his heart, and give her comfort. She was no stranger to him in the true sense of the word, though he had seen her that day for the first time; their common grief made her like a sister or a friend. He understood her heart and soul as he understood the heart and soul of none other in the world, for his own experience was the interpreter.

The strength of his emotion was overpowering only at first. He very speedily grew calm, and raising his head, looked down upon the calm sea, lost in thought—thought not unpleasant, but tenderly sweet. There was now an object in the world which had awakened a feeling in his heart, such as he thought he should never experience more; and his life again seemed desirable, and tinged with promise. It seemed as if in the dark cloud which had so long shrouded his sky a rainbow had appeared, giving token of a sunshine that was yet to come.

Long he lay on that secluded table-land, lulled and soothed by the tender current of his new thoughts, and the soft murmur of the ocean beneath, till the twilight drew its curtain over earth and sky, and the stars came forth one by one to hold silent vigil over reposing nature and a sleeping world. Then he rose, and returning to the path, pursued it till he reached the village inn, where he slept for the night, and dreamed of Lizzy Fairbairn.

*

In less than a month James Crawford was the accepted tenant of Redlaw. He pled with Peggy M'Naughton to remove thither with him, and be his housekeeper still, but this proposal Peggy steadily though kindly refused to entertain.

"Na, Jimes, lad," she rejoined; "I'm owre auld noo tae leave the kintra side where I've been sae lang. It wad pit me sair aboot tae gang amang strange folk and pit up wi' strange ways, sae I'll just live butt and ben[1] wi' Jessie Broon doon at Kirkton, and set mysel' tae bring up the puir laddie, Duncan, that's sae sinfully keepit oot o' his ain; and ye'll no miss me muckle, Jimes, at least no lang, for it's borne in upon me that you and Lizzy Fairbairn are fated tae be man and wife. And

---

1. In a two-room cottage, close together; or a main house with addition.

rale gled am I tae think sae. There's nae doot Providence
has custin' you thegither, and if I was you, Jimes, I wadna pit
aff. Sae gang yer gate, my bonny man, and may the blessin'
o' heaven follow and rest on ye."

And so it was settled that Peggy and the boy should go to
live with Jessie Brown down at Kirkton. Had James been the
same desolate being he had been for years, she would unques-
tionably have accompanied him, and for his sake braved the
strange people and customs of the place; but with the shrewdness of an old woman in such matters, she saw the impression
Lizzy Fairbairn had made on the young man's mind, and
piecing his garrulous reports together, formed the idea that in
a little while James would require no housekeeper at all—a
circumstance which she greatly rejoiced at, for it had often
been her wish to see James married to one worthy of and
suited to him, and, from all she could gather, Lizzy Fairbairn
was this proper one.

Between harvest and Martinmas it was necessary that
James should visit Redlaw, but he made these visits more
frequently than *necessity* required. He found a peculiar and
growing pleasure in going there—the pleasure of seeing Lizzy,
and deepening his acquaintance with her. The more he associated with her, the better he liked, the more ardently he
admired her. It was, in fact, the old love sprung up anew. In
Lizzy he found a second Mary, nay, better even in many
respects than the first. A sorrowful experience had sweetened
and made still more tender a disposition naturally gentle and
affectionate. Lizzy had all Mary's beauty and attractions,
without her wilfulness and impetuosity of temper, and the
school of affliction had perfected her fine qualities of heart
and mind, till she had become a woman who could not but be
loved by those who could appreciate her character.

It soon became evident, also, that with James she was
greatly pleased. She treated him with an attention which she
had bestowed on no young man since the loss of Joe, and her
eye sparkled and a smile broke upon her lips when he made
his appearance at the farm.

Still, James cherished fears as to the issue. Having made
the discovery that he deeply, truly, and strongly loved her,
like all true manly souls, he did not think he was worthy of
her, and durst not entertain the hope that he had inspired her
with affection for him in return. It was true she was kind to

him, and seemed pleased with his company; but this might arise only from her natural sweetness of disposition, and be nothing more than the treatment she would have extended to any other man in the circumstances. And so James worried himself with gloomy conjectures, till he fairly made up his mind to break the ice, and know the truth in its best and worst.

It was on a breezy October evening when the momentous words were spoken. James was to leave on the morrow, and he stayed later at the farmhouse than usual. Lizzy and he sat in the parlour alone. The candles were not lighted, and the great red round moon had risen from the sea and lighted up the hills and rocky crags which formed the view from the window. They had been silent for some time, and both gazed out upon the weird beauty of the scene. At length, in low, tremulous tones, James spoke of what was uppermost in his heart. At first his words were broken and faltering, but as Lizzy did not interrupt him, and did not show any sign of pain or displeasure, he gathered courage, and grew warm and eloquent. And, for the first time, he spoke to her of the past—both her past and his own—spoke of Joe and Mary. The revelation regarding the latter amazed Lizzy, and unsealed in a moment the fountain of love which had already formed in her heart for the youth. She felt towards him much as he had felt towards her when told by the miller of her sorrow, only as there was no solitude for her to go to that she might find vent for her emotion, she did what was most natural in her state of feeling—she suddenly turned to the impassioned speaker, and threw herself sobbing and weeping on his bosom.

This conveyed to James the rapturous intelligence of her love a thousand times better than words could have done, and, as a thrill ran through all his being, produced by the delicious knowledge that she was his, he folded his strong yet trembling arms around her, and the full-orbed moon looked in through the window panes upon a scene as pure and holy as earth ever presents.

It was a scene over which we let the silence and sacredness of night rest, and only add that when an hour later James left the house, Lizzy accompanied him to the brow of the valley in which lay the mill, and there in sight of the house of her first lover she plighted troth without a shadow of crime to another.

Could Joe and Mary have looked down upon them at that moment from the spirit land, they would have smiled in approbation of the deed; and James and Lizzy, conscious on their part that they were in no wise unfaithful to the dead, lifted their joyous faces to the bending heaven, and standing at last from out the shadow of their long and heavy sorrow, they met the dawn of a new, bright day bursting forth upon the sky of their life.

CHAPTER XXXVI

BET MAKES AN UNSUCCESSFUL SEARCH FOR THE WILL—HER STRATAGEM AND DISCOVERY—THE DESERTED INN

Never did mortal curse so vehemently the intervention of lath and plaster as did Bet, when it was of such importance to her to see into the next room, and she could not because of the partition of the little closet which separated her from the speakers, whose conversation she had been so eagerly listening to.

From what she heard she understood that Bowser had concealed the will somewhere about the next room, and the exact spot he pointed out to Tibb, but where it was she could not see. She strained her eyes everywhere to discover an open chink in the partition, but her search proved vain, and though she chafed fiercely at the disappointment, she could do nothing but sit silently down on the side of her bed and think.

That will she must possess. By fraud or wile, she must secure it, and with it she had in her hand an engine of direct vengeance which should crush Dick as completely as her vindictive heart could wish. How that slighted woman's heart of her's leapt in mad joyous fury as she contemplated the use of such power as she would soon obtain. How she would gloat over Dick's downfall as effected by herself. With what luxury of satisfaction would she witness his dismay at the production of the parchment which made him a beggar. With what intense enjoyment would she watch his mortification, confusion, and despair, increasing all three and crowning her own triumph by telling him that she it was who had effected his overthrow—she, the woman he had despised, insulted, cast off. Oh, the sweetness to Bet of this hour of anticipated triumph. There she sat in the darkness of the closet, with heaving heart and clenched hand, and an expression of face which would have been frightful to any beholder. She sat till the light of the summer morning had broke over the silent city, then, only partially undressing, she threw herself on the bed, and slept and dreamed—her dreams being but an extension of her waking thoughts.

It was late when she rose, but Tibb and Bowser had been late likewise, and were seated at breakfast when she entered the adjoining room—a room which she and Dick alone, of all the lodgers, had a right to enter, the others being kept in the outer apartment.

"There you are," remarked Bowser briskly. "What came over you last night?"

"I was seeing Dick,' answered Bet, quite calmly, though a tightness of the lips betrayed that the calmness was the result of effort.

"Seeing Dick; I thought so," returned Bowser. "And what's the upshot? Was he pleased with your visit? Have you settled the marriage day?"

The last question he accompanied with a loud bantering laugh, in which Tibb heartily joined. This exasperated Bet almost to the point of explosion, but the secret purpose of her soul requiring her to keep calm, she managed to do so, and in a steady voice replied—

"Dick has proved a villain."

"In other words, he won't marry you."

"No."

"Of course not. I told you so, and you were a fool to expect it."

"Why?" asked Bet, her dark eye emitting one lurid flash. "Hadn't he promised to marry me whenever he could?"

"That was before the night he twigged the advertisement in the paper."

"It was; but what difference is there between then and now? I am as good as I was, and he is no better."

"Yes, he is," replied Bowser. "He is—three hundred a year better."

"And," resumed Bet, "didn't that give him the chance to make his promise good? Couldn't he and I have lived very snugly on three hundred a year?"

Bet was strongly tempted to add, "or even *two* hundred," but she prudently refrained from saying anything to indicate that she had heard last night's conversation.

"I should think you could have lived very snugly on three hundred a year," returned Bowser, with another loud laugh.

"Uncommon jolly," chimed in Tibb, with a gleeful treble.

"But," added Bowser, "as Dick's three hundred gives him the chance of marrying to other three, or perhaps more, he

would be the most precious fool that ever walked in leather
if he threw that chance away. You don't see that, of course;
it's not natural you should; but any other body does. I don't
deny that it is a bit hard on you to give up Dick this way.
And he won't forget you altogether if you aint bumptious.
Perhaps you got a couter or two out of him last night?"

"Not a farthing," returned Bet. "He offered me a few
shillings, which I threw in his face."

"Only a few shillings!" repeated Bowser. "Well, I must
say that was too bad. A fiver was the least he could tip in the
circumstances."

"It would have been all the same," said Bet, her voice
getting fiercely bitter in spite of her efforts to control it. "It
wasn't money I wanted: it was marriage, and I wouldn't have
taken the insult he has offered me at any price."

"You are too proud, Bet," observed Tibb. "As Bowser says,
it was all nonsense of you to expect Dick to marry you, now
that he's a landed gentleman; and if you had spoken him fair,
I have no doubt but he would have given you something
handsome for what is past between you. You can't afford to
throw even a few shillings over your shoulder."

"I wouldn't take a farthing from him if I was perishing,"
was Bet's vehement rejoinder.

"And that's just what you'll soon be, if you don't bestir
yourself," retorted Tibb. "You haven't been out for some
days, and every halfpenny you had is gone."

"I'll go out to-day," said Bet, getting calm again. "But,"
she added, "the time may come when Dick shall rue having
made me his enemy."

"Then you'd harm him if you could?" sneered Bowser.

"Wouldn't I," said Bet, setting her teeth.

"And much he need to care for that," cried Tibb. "Though
you and him should both live to the age of Methuselah you
couldn't do a pin's point worth of ill to him."

Bet in return only smiled, but said nothing. She took her
breakfast in silence, looked furtively but keenly round the
room all the while, to see if she could detect the place where
the will was concealed. She particularly inspected the hearth-
stone, to see if it had been recently disturbed, but to all
appearance it was firmly imbedded among the dirt and ashes
of years. The most minute scrutiny she was able to make failed
to bring before her any likely spot, and she was at length

obliged to rise and depart, with the firm resolution, however, of watching every movement of Tibb and Bowser, and taking the first opportunity to search for herself.

Weeks and months passed on, however, without her being able to effect her object. She pierced a small hole in the partition of her closet, through which she could peep, and observe all that went on in the adjoining room; and often would she, on the pretence of being unwell, retire to her dormitory, where, while those she watched imagined her in bed, she was in reality placed at her post of observation, and with patient, unflagging watchfulness, keeping a close eye on their every movement.

In vain; neither by word nor sign did either Bowser or Tibb indicate the place where the will was hidden. It was often alluded to—at least the advantage which its possession gave them; and through the conversations which she overheard, Bet learned a good deal of Dick's movements in his new sphere. She made out that James Crawford had left Southfield, and, lest she should forget the name of the place to which he had gone, she marked it on a slip of paper, for he was the party she knew, to whom she must go with the will when she procured it. She also made out that Dick had taken up his abode at Southfield, where he was building a fine house, and living a jolly life among the gentry of the neighbourhood. This latter information she obtained through the medium of a conversation held by Bowser and Tibb, one evening when the former had returned to the Overgate, after an absence of two days. Bet knew where he had been during that time, for on the evening previous to his departure she had overheard the pair speaking of his intended journey, and the object of it. It was the Martinmas term, when Dick would receive his first half-year's rents, and Bowser was going to get his share of the same—viz, fifty pounds. On the following day, after he was gone, Bet was on the watch—remained in the house—and whenever Tibb went to the other room, and she was left alone, she made diligent search everywhere in the apartment for the will. She sought in every conceivable place, tried every plank of the floor to find one loose, tapped the plaster all round the walls, in short, examined everything she could think of, and still in vain.

To Bet's passionate nature it was tantalising and irritating in the extreme to know that the means of vengeance was at her very hand and yet she could not grasp it, and it taxed her powers of acting to the utmost to simulate a quiet, indolent, and indifferent seat by the fire, when Tibb returned to the chamber.

It was pretty late on the evening of the second day when Bowser returned, and Bet, thinking she would be sure to hear something important if he and Tibb were left to themselves, speedily repaired to her closet, and in a twinkling brought eye and ear to the watch. Then it was that she obtained the information we have mentioned regarding Dick. Bowser also gave Tibb to understand that he had got the fifty pounds; but on this occasion, as on all others, the place where the will was hid was not alluded to, so Bet made nothing of it, and her fierce spirit chafed the more impatiently.

Not for a moment, however, did she go off the watch. Day after day she was on the alert. It was the one purpose of her existence to obtain the all-important document, and she devoted herself to it with a zeal and assiduity which knew no weariness, except the weariness arising from failure. Again weeks and months passed on—the dark days of winter, the cold weeks of spring—and Bet was regularly in the streets with the child in her hand. Misery and want, vice and crime, were there alongside of her; real destitution and knavish mendicancy sought to win the pity and the charity of the passers-by. Bet fared better than many of her class. She sung well, in a loud clear street voice, and coppers were given to her when mere beggars who held out a trembling hand and asked alms were passed by.

And she grew careful now and economical with her winnings. She did not, as formerly, waste the money she got on riotous living, and loiter in-doors till all was gone, but daily she went her rounds, and nightly she spent only what was necessary. This thrift elicited Tibb's unqualified approbation. She thought it was the result of her often-repeated advice to "save something for a sore foot"; but the purpose for which it was done was not exactly that which Tibb supposed.[1] Bet, who never lost the hope that one day or other the will would fall into her hands, thought that it would facilitate her course consequent on that if she had a little money in her possession,

---

1. Proverbial: lay up store as insurance against shortage or injury.

and it was in order to have this that she was working hard and saving up now.

Spring passed, and the bright cheerful Whitsuntide approached. Bet was still baffled in her efforts to find the will, and growing every day more fiercely impatient at the disappointment. The thought that Dick was enjoying himself to the full all the time, living on the fat of the land,[2] when the production of the deed would hurl him from his position, was galling to her heart, now so full of hatred against him; and she chafed in the bitterness of passion against the delay, for the baffled soul of an angry woman contains the very essence of storm and whirlpool. She did sometimes feel a consolation in her disappointment, and it was derived from the idea that the months which were passing would be accustoming Dick more to the fine life he was leading, and that, therefore, his downfall, though protracted, would on this very account be the greater punishment; and in the intensity of her hate this thought gave her pleasure, and made her more patient in her as yet fruitless efforts.

One night she was at her post as usual in the closet, with her eye at the small hole she had made, and her ears on the stretch to hear any words that might pass between Bowser and Tibb. Of late her nightly watchings had been utterly unproductive. Nothing had been said by either of the two on the subject which was to her of all-absorbing interest. But on this night her patience was destined to be partially rewarded.

Bowser sat smoking by the fire, and Tibb, with her accustomed thrift, was knitting by the dim light of a small lamp. Quietness had settled down on the outer room, where the lodgers had retired to rest, and Bet was supposed to be asleep likewise in her closet.

"What day is this, Tibb?" asked Bowser, after a long spell of silent smoking.

"Tuesday," replied the other.

"I know that; but what's the day of the month?"

"Let me see," answered Tibb, reflectively. "It must be getting on in the twenties."

She laid her knitting on the table, and taking down a dirty almanac from a shelf above the fireplace, she began to examine it.

---

2. Genesis 45:17–18.

"It's the twenty-fourth," she said.

"Thought so," said Bowser. "Then I'm off the day after to-morrow."

"To see Dick?" said Tibb, in a tone of interested interrogation.

"Of course. Thursday is rent day, and I must bag my fifty. I have just been thinking, Tibb, that we might be making a change soon. I'm tired of the lodging-house, and I don't see why we should keep it on when we can do better."

"It's a worrying business," observed Tibb; "it keeps one drudging from morning till night, and often you get nothing but abuse from the dirty, ungrateful, drunken wretches. It would be a deal pleasanter to have something easy and quiet."

"We needn't have anything at all," rejoined Bowser. "A hundred a year will keep us as snug as a trivet, and we can be our own master, to go where we like, and out and in when it suits us. I vote for a house in the country. I was always fond of freedom, and it wasn't taste but business that made me stick in this dark den, where one can see only an inch or two of the sky and not a single tree leaf."

"We'd have the house to furnish," suggested Tibb.

"Well, haven't you saved a bit of money, and isn't there the fifty I got from Dick at Martinmas lying beside the will never touched? Then I'll get other fifty on Thursday, and if that doesn't set us respectably on our feet it should, that's all."

"And it will too," said Tibb. "The tramps will wonder at us giving up. I shouldn't wonder but Bet might want to keep on the house."

"Nothing more likely. But mark you this, Tibb. Wherever we go, neither Bet nor any of them must know, or they'll come annoying us, and that wouldn't do at all."

"No more it would," acquiesced Tibb.

Here Bowser yawned and tumbled into bed, which terminated the conversation, every word of which had been listened to by Bet with feelings not to be described.

They were going to give up the lodging-house, when all chance would be lost of obtaining the will; and there the deed was still in its secret repository, and, what was more, the sum of fifty pounds was lying beside it. If she could get the one, she could get both.

Long she sat on the edge of her bed that night a prey to consuming thoughts. The prospect of utter failure was before her—a prospect, the contemplation of which was like to make her frantic. If she did not obtain the will very soon she would not get it at all, and the power of vengeance, almost within her grasp, would vanish away for ever.

"This must not be," she vehemently muttered through her set teeth, while her clenched hands seized the coverlet with a convulsive grip. "The will I must have—must—shall. But how, how? Oh, that I could think of some plan."

For a long time she kept her feverish brain at work, trying to devise a stratagem by which she might get to know where the will lay, since she had failed in the search. At length she did hit upon a method that seemed promising. It was bold, however, and risky, and would either result in success or complete failure. Nevertheless, it was the only hope, and the venture must be run.

On the following night Bet had supper along with Bowser and Tibb, and while she was casting about in her mind for a pretext by which she might naturally introduce what she meant to say, Bowser himself fortunately led the way to it.

"Would you like to become the mistress of a lodging-house?" asked the latter, with an abruptness which made Bet start.

"That would depend on what sort of a house it was," she replied.

"Well, then, this house," rejoined Bowser. "Tibb and me are thinking of giving up, for we are getting old and—"

"And don't need to keep lodgers any more," said Bet, quickly. "Your fortune's made."

"How quick you run on," returned the other. "Fortunes are not so easy made—leastways not in lodging-houses. But Tibb and I have been careful, and we have managed to lay by a little bit—just as much as will keep us moving to the end of our days. It ain't much, but as we have nobody but our-selves to look to, we are not particularly greedy, and she and I have come to think that what we have saved together will—"

"Gammon! You can't deceive me," said Bet. "What you've saved from the lodging-house couldn't keep you. I know that well enough. You've got something else to look to, and I know what it is."

"What's the wench raving at?" replied Bowser, with an air of astonishment not altogether affected.

"I tell you, you can't deceive me," continued Bet. "I know more than you think."

"What the devil do you know?" roared Bowser, fairly taken aback, and not a little alarmed.

"I know that Dick's good luck has been your good luck too, and this is how you have got your nest feathered. But don't count too much upon it—don't be in a hurry in giving up your lodging-house. I have sworn to be revenged on Dick, and my hour will come. My power is greater than he or you think."

And delivering herself thus—which was in reality making the venture on which all her hope rested—she swept loftily from the room with an air of leisurely dignity; but the moment she had closed the door behind her, she rushed into the closet and sprang to her post of observation, there breathlessly to await the issue, and see whether her shot had struck or missed its mark.

When she got her eye to the aperture, Bowser and Tibb had not recovered from their consternation, but sat looking at each other in silent amazement.

"In the name of all the fiends, what does that mean?" said Bowser, as he drew a long breath.

"Not a bit of me knows," responded Tibb.

"You haven't been fool enough to tell her anything?"

"Me! Not a word. I'm not mad."

"Then she has found it out some way. By heaven, perhaps she has got hold of the will."

And as this thought occurred to him, Bowser sprang to his feet in a frenzy, and went to a corner of the room where stood an old worm-eaten eight-day clock that had not gone for many a day. The inside of that clock Bet had examined more than once, but could find no cavity there which could contain the will.

"Keep your back against the door, and don't let anybody in," whispered Bowser, pausing for a moment and looking round.

Tibb did as she was bid, and took her position close to the door of the chamber.

Deeming that thus they were secure from observation, and altogether unconscious that Bet's eye was glaring upon his very motion, Bowser took up the poker, and inserting it between the clock and wall, used it there for the purpose of a lever, when with the low harsh sounds as of nails wrenched from their place, the clock was brought away from the wall revealing a cavity in the latter, which was *not* empty.

"Safe—all safe," said Bowser, in great excitement, as darting in his hand he brought out two packets. The one was the will, the other a bundle of bank notes.

"I was sure they would be safe," said Tibb, with the air, however, of one who was immensely relieved. "Nobody could get there."

"What a devil of a fright Bet gave me though. She must have been stumping when she talked of her power to harm Dick. She would do it if she could; but there's only one way in which she could, and that is by getting hold of the will—a thing she does not know even exists. Bah! I was an idiot to be taken in with her boasting threats—might have known it was a gag. Just stand there a little longer, Tibb, till I put these things back again."

The will, together with the fifty pounds, was put back into the cavity in the wall, and the clock placed against it and fixed as before. Then Tibb left her place behind the door, and Bowser and she resumed their seats by the fireside.

Bet's heart throbbed as if it would burst, and in the wildness of her joy she felt an almost irresistible temptation to shriek out her triumph. For some minutes her will was on the point of abdicating its place, and self-control was nearly lost.

At last then, at last, she had effected her purpose. She knew now where the will lay, and had but to watch her opportunity to obtain it, and along with it the fifty pounds. The near realisation of her long-baffled desire was as exciting as her former disappointment had been irritating.

But Bet was naturally a strong-minded, firm-natured woman, and it was not long ere her will regained its ascendancy, and took again the command of her thoughts and feelings. She had accomplished much, but had not yet gained all. The will was not in her possession, and it might be extremely difficult to get it. Her plan must be laid for this object, and that at once.

So, when she gained something like calmness after her discovery, she set herself to think over that important matter. And as she thought, the case unfolded itself to her view in more than one aspect, and she had to make her choice. Thus:—

It would be no easy matter to be alone in the adjoining room long enough to enable her to abstract the will. It would require some time—a few minutes at least, and Tibb and Bowser were rarely absent from the house together. Clearly her best chance would be got during Bowser's absence on the following day. Tibb went regularly out in the afternoon for the purchase of provisions for her lodgers, and in her absence she could effect her object. But here a temptation was presented to her mind. By waiting till after Bowser's return she might secure along with the will one hundred pounds instead of fifty. In all likelihood Bowser would place the fifty he was going for beside the rest, and so Bet might bag the whole.

This was to her a tempting object, but would it be prudent? Bowser might *not* put the second fifty there; or he might remove the will and the cash to some other secret place altogether, or she might never again have the same opportunity. On the whole, therefore, she concluded it was better to sacrifice the second fifty than to run the risk of losing the whole, and her final resolution was to obtain the will on the following day, and decamp ere Bowser returned.

*

Let us shift the scene for a moment to the quiet serene country, whose summer loveliness was beginning to be developed by the progress of the advancing year. Blooming May was ready to give place to blushing June. The hedgerows were white with hawthorn blossom, which set forth a most delicious fragrance in the dewy evening, as Bowser drove slowly along towards the little wayside inn, where he and Dick put up on the night when they stole the will from James Crawford's cottage.

It was at this little inn where they had always met since, when they had their peculiar business to transact; and by previous appointment they were to see each other there on that particular evening of the 26th of May. This had been arranged six months before, and they had neither seen nor heard anything of each other in the interval. Bowser knew that Dick had no desire for his society, and so long as he got his share of the plunder, he had no desire to press it upon him

The sun had just set in great splendour behind the western hills as Bowser drove his horse at a walking pace towards the place of meeting.

He had left the main highway, and entered on the narrow and less frequented road which led past the public-house in question, and so further on to Southfield. As he proceeded, he began to think he had taken the wrong path, for the road seemed as if all the traffic had departed from it. The marks left by the wheels of his own vehicle were the only fresh marks which it bore, and tufts of green untrodden grass grew in the old cart-ruts.

These signs of a byepath increased as he proceeded, Bowser began to make himself certain that he was in the wrong road, and was about to turn back, when, in the distance before him, he saw a building, which he recognised as the inn to which he was bound.

"By Jove, I'm right enough after all," he muttered; "but it looks as if I was the first traveller that's come along here for months. That poor devil of a landlord must make a miserable living of it now. I don't think I shall find his wife so fat as she was."

He went on, and drew up at the grass-grown door, without observing a single soul moving about the place, and to his further surprise he found the sign down, and the windows and doors shut and fastened.

"Starved out," he muttered. "Well, I don't wonder at it. But what am I to do? The beast is tired and needs food and rest, and egad so do I. I'm blessed if I don't go on to South-field, and beat up Dick in his own quarters."

He had raised the whip to urge his beast forward, when looking along the road he saw a horseman approaching at a smart gallop, and recognised the form of Dick. In a minute or less he had cantered up, and drew rein abreast of Bowser's gig.

Dick was vastly improved in outward appearance since last we saw him. He was dressed in better taste, was stouter and ruddier in complexion, and had lost in a measure the jaunty air which formerly had characterised him.

"What's the meaning of this?" asked Bowser, pointing to the closed inn.

"A new road is opened a few miles along from this, and joins the main highway," replied Dick, "and this has diverted the traffic entirely from here, and the consequence is that this house has become as solitary as the grave. Frazer had to evacuate, and has gone to a new inn about four miles off."

"Then the house is to let?" returned Bowser.

"It will never be let," returned Dick. "The opening of that new road has placed it as much in a wilderness as if it were planted in the centre of yon trackless moor."

"Good," said Bowser with satisfaction. "It's the very thing for me. I'll take it."

"You!" exclaimed Dick in amazement.

"Yes. Tibb and I have got a notion that we shall give up the lodging-house in the Overgate, and live in some quiet place in the country. This house is the very thing."

Dick bit his lips, and looked anything but pleased with this idea.

"Nonsense," he returned; "You'd fret yourself to death there in no time."

"Not a bit of it. It will suit us to a 'T'. But I say, what am I to do in the meantime? Got any up-putting for me at Southfield?"

"Well—no," answered Dick. "Everything is in confusion there. You'll have to go back till you reach the highway again, then trot on for four miles, and you'll come to Frazer's new place."

"Oh, very well," said Bowser. "Tip me the fifty couter and I'm off."

Dick drew from his breast a pocket-book, and took from it a bundle of notes, which he handed to the other.

"You may count them if you choose," he remarked; "but they are all right."

"Maybe so, but I'll just see for myself," muttered Bowser, and deliberately he counted and examined them. The inspection was satisfactory, for he folded them up and put them in his pocket.

The two associates remained for a little longer together in conversation, then separated. Dick returning to Southfield, and Bowser retracing his way in search of Frazer's Inn. He found it in less than an hour, put up for the night, and departed in the morning for Dundee, little dreaming of the catastrophe which had taken place there in his absence.

CHAPTER XXXVII

BET SECURES THE WILL—BOWSER IS BURNED OUT

On the morning of Bowser's departure to meet with Dick, Bet was purposely late in rising. She had slept little or none, being too thoroughly excited and nervously restless to compose herself for slumber. She heard Bowser rise and leave the house, and for some time before she left her closet she stood watching Tibb, who was now the only occupant of the adjoining room, and the old useless clock standing like a skeleton against the wall.

What a fascination that clock had for Bet now. Behind it was the means of that revenge for which she panted. The secret of months, which it had kept so well, was known to her at last, and she looked on it now as connected with the great crisis of her life. The will which was so snugly ensconced at the back of it she must secure that day *at whatever hazard.* These were her own emphasised words, muttered to herself again and again, *"at whatever hazard."* Nothing earthly should stand in the way between her and the possession of the document within the next twenty-four hours. She would try to obtain it stealthily, but if unable to do that, then by force—by crime. She was prepared for the very worst course—ay, the worst—even murder—the murder of Tibb. What was Tibb's life to the failure of her mighty revenge?

She stayed in the house all the forenoon, waiting and watching for an opportunity which, after all, she did not expect to get, for Tibb seldom or never went out till after dinner, and though she was frequently engaged in the outer room, still she might enter the inner apartment at any moment, and come upon Bet busy tampering with the clock.

"Don't mean to go out to-day, Bet?" asked Tibb, rather surprised to find her lodger, who had recently become so industrious, loitering in the house.

"Yes, in the afternoon," was the answer, "but I don't want Pat to-day, he's so tiresome. You can send him out with some of the others."

After dinner Bet was as good as her word, and went out

alone. She had not Hare's child with her. It did not suit her purpose to be in any way trammelled in her action. She did not go far, only to the mouth of the close, and across the Overgate to an entry a little further along, from which she commanded a full view of the entrance to the close she had just quitted. Here she took up her position, and never took her dark glittering eyes from the one spot.

More than half an hour passed in patient, motionless watching, when at length the tall form of a woman emerged from Guthrie's Close and went eastward along the street.

It was Tibb; and Bet startled violently when she saw her, though her appearance was what she expected—what she was waiting and longing for.

Tibb carried a basket in her hand, and went on till she turned a corner and was lost to view. The moment she did so Bet started from the mouth of the entry, crossed the Overgate at a swift pace, and darting into Guthrie's Close, made at once for the lodging-house.

The door, leading from the passage into the outer room was on the latch, which she noiselessly raised, and slowly, silently opened the door. An old beggar woman was the only person in that outer room—an old paralytic creature called Kirsty, and she sat by the fire, apparently asleep.

Bet glided in with the stealthy step of a cat. The door to the inner room was shut, and she feared it might be locked. It was locked; but the key was left in the outside, and all that Bet had to do to gain admission was to turn it round. She did so; and she looked nervously round to see if the noise had awoke old Kirsty. Little fear of that. The crone was deaf, and dozed over the fire utterly oblivious of what was taking place.

Entering the inner room, Bet, with a shaking hand, closed the door behind her, and went to work without a moment's delay. The poker which Bowser had used on the previous evening lay among the ashes. This she grasped, and inserting it between the clock and the wall, as she had seen him do, she pulled. There was a slight crash, and with a sudden jerk the clock swung round, showing her the aperture containing what she sought.

Uttering an exclamation which she could not suppress, she clutched the will and the bundle of notes and thrust them into her bosom. Then laying the poker in the very spot where she had picked it up, she replaced the old rickety clock against the wall, and pressed against it to send the nails into their places—all as she had seen Bowser do the night before.

The moment she found it somewhat firm, she returned with the same swift stealthy step to the outer room, turned the key in the lock, gave one glance at the still sleeping Kirsty, darted noiselessly to the outer door, closed it behind her, and vanished through the close.

All this was the work of a very few minutes; and once in the Overgate she went with rapid strides towards the West Port and turned into Brown Street.

The will was in her possession now. She had it in her bosom. Her hand grasped it through her dress; and the grasp sent a thrill of wild excitement to her bounding heart.

Her brain almost reeled under its frantic joy, and again, as on the previous night, she felt impelled to shriek aloud in her mad delirium.

As an outlet for her bursting feelings, she began to sing; and never, we venture to say, was a song sung with such wild vehemence in the streets of Dundee. Her voice rang far and near, and the notes seemed to pierce the very air and roll one upon another with a fierce triumphant rush that made the performance something for people to stand and wonder at.

Even Tibb was amazed, as she passed slowly along upon the pavement on her way back to the lodging-house. She had often heard Bet sing well outside, but never with a spirit like this; and she smiled approval to Bet's flashing glance of recognition, and passed into the Overgate.

The singer did not wait to receive coppers. It was not for coppers she sang then—it was for relief to her rushing heart and reeling brain. Hitherto she had sung on the streets to please others, now it was to please herself. Coppers! What did she care for coppers just then? Had she not fifty pounds lying in her bosom beside the will—whole fifty pounds, which was to her wealth?

Heedless, therefore, of the admiration she excited, and waiting not for the offer of pence, Bet hurried on, giving vent to her wild startling music as she proceeded, and neither stopped in her walk nor her singing till she had gained the suburbs. Here, quickening her pace, she pushed westward along the Lochee Road, then—still walking very fast—turned to the

right, and ascended a steep path towards the Law, whose
round crest rose green and bold before her.

Bet was much heated as she pressed up the ascent; but
neither heat nor fatigue seemed to be felt by her. She wished
to be away in solitude that she might get vent to her feelings
unseen and unheard—that she might also reflect on the course
she would now take.

She paused on one of the knolls of the hill, and, raising
her arms wildly above her head, there rang through the solitary air shrieks of mad mocking laughter, whose echoes ran
over the secluded heights, and died away in the wide atmosphere ere they could fall upon a human ear.

For several minutes Bet seemed like one seized by madness,
or moved by a fiend, so frantic were her screams and extravagant her gesticulations; while everything human had, to all
appearance, gone out of her, and given place to a vindictive
spirit of evil, whose natural home was not on earth but in hell.
She snatched the will and the notes from her bosom, and holding them aloft in her two hands, she wildly waved her bare
arms to and fro, while again and again the peals of demoniac
laughter startled the solitude.

"Mine—mine!" she screamed, "the power is mine to crush
him, to send him to a felon's doom, to take him from his fine
mansion and make him a beggar again, ha, ha! He shall yet
writhe before the woman he cast off. He who had no mercy
for me shall get none from me—none, none! No whining, no
pleading, shall avail. I shall be pitiless, for has he not turned
my heart to stone—to hate? Once I would have sacrificed all
to save him. I would have died to save him—now, my dearest
wish is to gloat over his ruin and despair."

An excited mind, and a fierce indomitable will, exacts
extraordinary service from the physical energies; but there is a
limit beyond which these refuse to be commanded, and when
Bet gave vent to this torrent of passionate vehemence she
threw herself upon the grass fairly exhausted. The bodily
fatigue she had undergone served at length to calm in some
degree her mental excitement, and now for a time she lay
panting and silent, looking out upon the wide scene which
spread itself below and forward in mighty magnificence to the
distant horizon. The town with its smoke, through which rose
the factory chimneys and the church spires, the gleaming
river, the shipping in the harbour, the limitless sea, and the

varied beauties of the southern landscape, made up a scene of such interest and grandeur as can rarely be beheld yet. Bet saw nothing of it; she was utterly absorbed in the passionate workings of her dark heart, and in the feverish enjoyment of an anticipated revenge.

She opened the will and perused it. It was short and soon read; and she was the more confirmed in her idea that James Crawford was the proper party to whom it should be taken. Him, therefore, she would seek out in his new farm; but as she knew that was a long distance from Dundee, she debated within herself whether to depart at once or start early on the following morning. It was now wearing towards sunset, and were she to start immediately, night would speedily interrupt her journey. On the other hand, if she were to remain till the morning in the Overgate, it might be discovered that she had stolen the will; and yet she thought to herself, how could it? Bowser would not return till the following night, when she would be far enough away beyond his power to trace her, and there was no likelihood of Tibb looking in the recess behind the clock.

On the whole she thought she would risk it, and this resolution being formed, she took her way down the hill, and entered the town at dusk. It was as yet early enough to repair to the lodging-house, and she began to sing in the crowded thoroughfare of the Scouringburn, whose population was now about to enjoy their usual evening merriment.

As she sung she called to mind how often the strains of Dick's flute had charmed the ears of the frequenters of that noted locality, and specially she remembered the evening on which, with affected commiseration, he gave her a handful of coppers on the very spot where she now stood, and so drew forth the charity of the passers-by. That was the night on which he first had tidings of the property that waited his appearance to be possessed. It was therefore the date of that change in his conduct towards her which had led to the bitter hatred she now cherished towards him.

Still under the influence of excited feeling, Bet sang with great vigour and animation, and coppers came freely in, which she accepted with an air of careless indifference, for had she not an almost exhaustless treasure in her bosom, making the halfpence which formerly she prized paltry and worthless in her sight?

On coming into the West Port she ceased her singing, and gliding into a dark corner to secure the will and the notes safely in her bosom, she proceeded, not without some nervous trepidation, to Guthrie's Close.

The outer room was pretty full when she entered, and Tibb was there superintending the preparation of supper for her numerous and motley guests. One glance of Bet's piercing eye served to show that all was right. Tibb was in possession of her wonted calmness, and was more than usually good-humoured; made so no doubt by the prospect she had of soon retiring from the worrying cares of lodging-house keeping, and living for the rest of her life in ease and affluence.

Without speaking to any one, Bet went into the inner room, and being tired threw herself on the long wooden settle near the fire, which was Bowser's accustomed seat. She cast a hasty furtive look at the clock, which to her satisfaction she found showed no suspicious appearance of having been moved.

Tibb soon followed, and brought in her hand an abundant and tempting supper.

"My eye, Bet, but yon was stunning singing," she exclaimed.

"Wasn't it," returned Bet, with a peculiar smile.

"Uncommon tip-top," said Tibb, "I was glad to see you in such spirits. You've moped and sulked every day since Dick left you; but I'm glad to see you are getting over that disappointment. It's one of those things that was to be looked for; and though it was hard to bear at first, you'll have come to see now that Dick could not do any other thing. You were joking in what you said last night—weren't you? You wouldn't harm Dick if you had the power, which of course you haven't."

"Oh, I don't want to speak about that now," returned Bet. "I'm both hungry and tired, and as soon as I bolt my supper I'll away to bed, for I mean to be off on the tramp in the morning."

"On the tramp!" repeated Tibb, in astonishment.

"Yes; I want a change. I haven't been over the country for a long time, and now that the good weather has come, I've taken a longing for the green fields."

"And how long will you be away?" asked Tibb, not at all pleased at this move on the part of her most profitable lodger.

"Don't know. Till I'm tired, I suppose," was Bet's vague and unsatisfactory reply.

Knowing from the wilful nature of the woman that it was no use to try to persuade her to abandon this purpose, Tibb wisely said no more, and Bet, having finished her supper, went to bed in the closet, with the will and the notes carefully placed in her bosom, and both her hands tightly pressed upon them.

She was very tired, and soon became drowsy, notwithstanding the noisy doings that were going forward in the outer room. The lodgers were on that evening more than usually disorderly. Bowser was known to be absent, and though Tibb ruled among them with a pretty stern hand, she was but a woman, and some of the rougher and more turbulent spirits were not to be quite subdued by her.

Shortly after midnight, however, the house grew quiet, and long before this Bet was fast asleep. Worn out nature was claiming for itself the necessary repose, and the overtaxed energies, both of mind and body, were recruiting after the strain which had been put upon them.

Bet was awoke by some one pulling her roughly by the arm, and the first thought of her returning reason was of the will.

"You shall not have it. You shall kill me first!" she shouted, clutching frantically at the packet in her bosom.

"You'll die if you lie there any longer," said a voice, which she recognised as belonging to one of the lodgers. "Get up this minute; the house is on fire!"

"Fire!" screamed Bet, springing half up in bed, and feeling for the first time that the closet was full of smoke.

"Ay, fire. Quick, or you'll be roasted to death!"

"Mercy, it is true!" gasped Bet, as through the volumes of smoke which poured through the open door of the closet she saw bright flames in the next room.

She sprang to her feet, and mechanically caught up the bundle of clothes she had made up for her departure. With this in one hand, and the other pressed on the precious packet in her bosom, she darted out to confront the mass of flame in which the beds and furniture of the outer room were enveloped.

All was uproar and confusion. Wild shrieks of terror burst from despairing lips, and these, combined with the roar of the fire, the glare of the flames, and the blinding suffocating smoke, made the scene awfully appalling. The fire had already gained the mastery over the few articles of wood and straw which made up the scanty furniture of the room, and it required the utmost firmness of nerve to cross to the opposite passage. But Bet, knowing that life and all was at stake, sprang wildly forward and gained the passage, and staggered breathless and bewildered into the arms of a policeman, who with several others had already been attracted to the spot.

"Any more in the house?" asked the officer in a loud voice.

"Yes, Tibb—Tibb," shouted several of the lodgers.

"Fiddler Jim has gone to rouse her," exclaimed another.

Fiddler Jim was the man who had awaked Bet, and the moment he saw her fly he burst into the inner room where Tibb lay alone. It was some time ere, blinded by the smoke and confused by the darkness, he could find the bed; but he shouted at the utmost pitch of his voice, and a gurgling sound directed him to where Tibb was. He rushed forward and found her helpless and gasping for breath, so without a moment's hesitation he lifted her in his strong arms and bore her through smoke and flame to the passage, where his appearance was hailed with loud huzzahs.

Had he been a moment later neither he nor Tibb could have escaped destruction, for the wooden partition, which had been burning for some time, fell down with a loud crash, piling up a heap of blazing deals, which effectually obstructed all communication between the outer and inner rooms—the latter of which was very speedily wrapt in flame also.

It was a minute or two ere Tibb recovered so far as to comprehend the nature of the calamity, but no sooner did she understand that the house was burning beyond all hope of saving it, than she became like a woman distracted, and with a piercing scream sprang back into the blazing mass.

The policeman flew after her, and forcibly dragged her back, extinguishing as he did so the flames of her night dress, which had caught fire.

"Woman, are you mad?" he demanded, as he dragged her out into the close.

"Don't hold me; I must get it. There is something in the house that must be saved," shrieked Tibb, struggling with all her might to free herself from the policeman's grasp, and return into the interior.

"You can't get in," he gruffly rejoined. "Everything is in a blaze now, and you would only lose your life."

"I tell you I must," shrieked Tibb, more excited than before, and with a strength which the officer little looked for, she burst from his gripe, and flew again into the passage of the burning house.

"Confound the woman," growled the officer, as again he darted in after her, and came upon her on the threshold of the outer room, where she had fallen overpowered by the smoke. Seizing her once more in his arms, he carried her out right into the Overgate, where her half-dressed lodgers were huddled together in the centre of an excited crowd, which was increasing every moment. There too was Bet—the only one who knew the cause of Tibb's distraction.

"It's the will and the notes she wants," she said to herself with a chuckle. "No wonder she is bad at the loss of them. But this is more good luck for me, for she and Bowser will think they have been burnt."

The lodging-house was an old, low building, which stood between two higher erections, but had no communication with them. The fire was, therefore, prevented from spreading, but the lodging-house itself was entirely consumed, and in less than an hour was only a heap of glowing ashes.

Like most fires of a like nature, its origin was not clearly known. There was a whisper among the lodgers that some of them had been smoking and drinking among the straw, and that a spark from a pipe had been the cause of the conflagration. But the fact could not be established, and as the loss had not been great, nor the property destroyed valuable, the matter was not minutely inquired into. The house was in a dilapidated condition, and its owner half intended to take it down—an intention which was now made a necessity, and not in the circumstances a very grievous one. The contents of the house had also been of little value, and it was not considered by anybody that Bowser had lost much.

Some of the lodgers lost a few of their rags, and as they all stood in a group, half-naked and houseless, they became the objects of general sympathy—a sympathy which, with their characteristic cunning, they took advantage of to solicit the charity of the feeling-hearted, and with such success that the fire proved to them a piece of good luck.

In a few hours they had squandered themselves over the

town, and ere the following night other lodging-houses had received them into their shelter—all but Bet, who, at an early hour in the morning, had crossed the ferry, and entered on her journey southward.

In the afternoon of that same day, Tibb, almost half naked, left the town by the Perth Road, and wandered on till she was beyond the houses in the outskirts, and had reached a solitary part, where a wood grew on one side and a cornfield lay on the other. Here, on a large stone she sat down, and drawing her thin rag of a shawl round her shoulders, laid her arms on her knees, bent the upper part of her body forward till her chin and her knees nearly met, and there, in that position, rocked to and fro like one prostrate with grief.

Occasionally she slowly lifted her head and looked westward along the road as if watching some one's approach.

She had sat there a long time, and the sun had nearly set, when in the distance a gig came into sight, in which the figure of one man could be discerned against the western light.

It was Bowser, and as he came forward he noticed the woman sitting on the stone, but thinking it only a wandering beggar resting herself, and not wishing to be recognised by her, he laid his whip about the horse's ears, intending to gallop past.

But Tibb rose, and throwing the handkerchief off her head, came into the middle of the road, and stood there. Then Bowser had to look at her, and beyond description was his amazement when he saw who it was. He pulled up the horse, and sat silently staring at her.

"Bowser, we are ruined!" burst out Tibb, wringing her hands.

"Heaven and earth, what's the matter?" he ejaculated.

"Ruined—ruined!" repeated Tibb, with a piteous wail. "The house was burned down last night!"

"Gracious, you don't say so?" he cried. "But you saved the—the will."

"I saved nothing," she cried.

"Perdition!" he roared. "Is the will burned and the fifty pounds?"

"Both gone," she mournfully replied.

"Idiot! Why didn't you save *them*?" he shouted, frantic with rage.

"I could not. It was in the night time, and they carried

me out half asleep. As soon as I came to myself I flew back and the smoke overpowered me. When I got round again they had me outside, and the roof had fallen in."

"Curses on it, then we are ruined!" shouted Bowser in a fearful passion. "Did you go and look among the rubbish?"

"No, I didn't; what use is there in doing that? Everything is burnt, I tell you—everything but the bare walls."

Without a word of explanation, Bowser brought the whip with a tremendous whack upon the horse's head, and the animal bounded forward with a suddenness which nearly upset Tibb. The wheel just grazed her arm as it rolled by, and Bowser, as he galloped off, roared over his shoulder—

"Come to Kelly's in the Hawkhill, you'll find me there."

In less than a minute the vehicle had vanished in the gathering twilight, and Tibb slowly retraced her steps to the town.

Bowser, however, reached it long before her, and delivering horse and gig to their owner, and paying for their hire, he lost not a moment in repairing to the Overgate. A crowd of curious people were assembled at the mouth of Guthrie's Close, eager to see the blackened walls of the burnt building. But a policeman was stationed there to keep them back.

When Bowser went forward the policeman recognised him.

"Bad business this for you," he observed.

"A piece of the most cursed luck I ever met with," returned the burned-out lodging-house keeper. "Give me your lantern a minute till I go and see if anything is to be picked up."

"Lord bless you, there's nothing but stones there that's not burned," answered the officer.

"I'll look though," said Bowser, as he took the lantern and entered the close.

The ashes had ceased to smoke, but they were still warm. Tibb had told him truly. Nothing but the walls remained, and they enclosed only desolation.

He made his way over the charred rubbish to the corner where he knew the clock had stood, and had no difficulty in finding the cavity in the wall which it had concealed. It was concealed no longer, and eagerly he groped in it with his hand. It was empty.

Then he bent down, and with the poker which he got in the fireplace he turned over the rubbish in the corner.

The search, however, was a vain one. He came upon the clock weights and a few wheels, but found no trace of the important document he sought.

"We must swear to Dick that the will was saved," he muttered, as he retraced his steps over the blackened rubbish.

CHAPTER XXXVIII

BET MADE PRISONER

Not far from James Crawford's new farm of Redlaw, the high road crossed a very deep and thickly-wooded ravine, and this ravine was crossed by a bridge of extraordinary height—so extraordinary was its height that at the time of which we write it was among the highest, if not actually the highest in Scotland. It has lost this pre-eminence now, for the railways, in their intersections of the country, have reared arches and viaducts which outvie in magnificence and altitude anything which the requirements of turnpikes had brought into being.

Nevertheless, the bridge of which we speak now is still a "sight," and is visited by hundreds in the course of every season. Looked at from the bottom of the ravine it seems a wonderful structure; as, standing on its lofty arches, it unites the rocky sides of the rugged gorge, and rises far above the tall old trees that hide with their foliage the clefts and precipices, and whose branches bend gracefully over the clear wimpling burn that murmurs beneath their shadow on its way to the ocean near at hand. Gazing up at that narrow airy line we cannot imagine that its upper surface is broad enough to form a highway; yet over its solid masonry did the mail coaches run for many years, and when you ascend by the steep and difficult pathway, and stand between its parapets, you find that there is room enough and to spare. To climb upon one of these parapets, and gaze down into the depths of the ravine, how grand and romantic is the sight! The tree tops are all beneath you, and if it is summer time the rich many-shaded foliage, as it waves gently to and fro, stirred by the light breeze that is wafted down the plain, is beautiful to behold. The sternness and loveliness of nature combine to constitute a scene which human art has enhanced and made doubly romantic by throwing across the wooded gulf a structure so imposing.

Upon this lofty bridge Bet found herself on the afternoon of a golden day in May. She had nearly reached the end of her journey. At the inn, a mile or two off, she had been told that James Crawford's farm was at no great distance beyond the bridge, and that she could reach it either by keeping the highway or by taking the less frequented path close to the sea. She preferred the former course, and having reached the bridge she paused to rest and to gaze over upon the ravine whose romantic beauty had a charm even for her.

Let men or women abandon themselves to vice as they will, they never get entirely free from the power of nature. Flowers and woods and streams exert an influence on the hardest and foulest of hearts, and Bet, despite the hate and passion in her soul, was strangely subdued by the solitary grandeur over which she hung. It carried her thoughts further away from her expected vengeance than they had been for months; and a vague melancholy regretfulness stole over her spirit like a faint whisper of sorrow from the sad ruins of her life.

But this softening impression remained only while she gazed. When she left the bridge and resumed her journey, it speedily vanished, and the old, fierce, vindictive thoughts returned.

Half a mile further on she came to a few houses standing by the wayside, and there, in answer to her inquiries after Redlaw, she was directed to a path leading from the high road down towards the sea. This path she followed for some time till it diverged into two, and she was at a loss which to take. As usual in such a case, she took the wrong one; a fact of which she began to be suspicious when, after a long walk, she saw herself approaching the top of the cliffs, with no buildings in sight but a grey, shapeless pile, which had every appearance of being a ruin. She hesitated whether to approach it or to turn and seek for Redlaw in another direction, but curiosity eventually impelled her to go forward and examine a ruin which stood in a spot so secluded and lonely. To her great surprise she found on reaching it that it was the ruin of a church or chapel, surrounded by a small graveyard, and the whole enclosed by a low stone wall, which in some places was broken down. She passed through one of these gaps, and stood in that rural place of graves. There the long grassy mounds clustered at her feet, and here the quaint, rude tombstones were strewn all around. Some stood upright at the head of the lowly sleepers, others lay flat and covered the whole grave, while others again were massive slabs of sandstone, raised on pillars high enough to enable a man to crouch underneath.

Bet stepped over the moss-covered stones, and stood close

under the crumbling wall of the chapel. Once it had been a place of architectural beauty, for the remains of fine Gothic arches and ornamental windows showed themselves. But the shadow of desolation and decay now rested over all. A deep silence and intense solitude brooded over the spot, and these were deepened, not relieved, by the murmur of the ocean on the beach below, and the shrill scream of the sea bird as it wheeled here and there in its aerial flight.

Bet's fierce passionate nature was subdued, and even awed, in a place over which such weird solitude reigned, and she stood gazing at the crumbling walls of the ancient pile, and rude quaint grave-stones, with a quiet wonder and a feeling of mingled sadness and fear. A churchyard on that secluded table-land, far from human habitation, and overlooking the boundless sea, was something to produce a melancholy sensation even on her hardened nature, and to awake the superstition which slumbered there, as it slumbers more or less in all natures. She was alone with the dead. The rude forefathers of the hamlet slept at her feet, while above was the great blue silent canopy of heaven, and around her the bare crests of the rocky heights, and beneath the illimitable plain of ocean. So powerful was the impression which the scene produced, that she sat down upon one of the horizontal stones and mused.

For the first time for years, she thought of her wasted life—of the home and the innocence she had left long years ago, and of the bleak almost hopeless prospect which lay before her. Her revenge accomplished—what next? Would Dick's ruin do her any positive benefit? She had reflection enough to see that the fifty pounds would not last her very long, and when the money was spent, her vagrant life must be resumed, and again must she wander through the country begging her bread—a most cheerless, hopeless life.

Musing thus, the thought suddenly occurred to her that the possession of the will gave her power to make terms for herself. Bowser had made a first rate bargain with Dick, and she might do so too. Rather than lose all, he would marry her, and, as his wife, her luck was secured; while the destruction of the will the moment the ceremony was performed, would enable them both to defy Bowser, and keep the whole rents for themselves.

Bet was excessively pleased with this idea, and the more

she thought of it, she was pleased with it the more. True, Dick had insulted her in the very worst manner, and deserved no consideration; but her own interests pointed to a compromise, and when she was Dick's wife, she would have the power of paying him back for his injustice and wrong on the night when last they met in Dundee.

Long she sat revolving her plan in her mind, and when at last she rose from her seat, the sun was just setting behind the far western horizon, amid a cloudy mass of purple and gold, the splendour of which no painter's pencil could depict.

In following out the resolution to which she had come, Bet did not lose prudence or caution. She knew Dick and Bowser too well now to trust them, and concluded not to have the will on her person when she went to make her terms, for in that case Dick might take it from her by force, and thus take her power away. No; she would deposit the will in some secure place where no one could get it but herself, and communicate the secret of its hiding place to Dick, when he had fulfilled the only conditions on which she would hand it up.

But where was this safe hiding place to be found? As Bet pondered over this, her eye rested on the moss-covered gravestone on which she had just sat, and it flashed upon her mind that there was the very repository she required. To that solitary spot very few people would come, and who of those few would by chance examine the crevices of that ancient urn, which had seemed undisturbed for many years?

She approached close to the stone, and carefully examined it. It was a thick grey slab, laid upon square pillars of the same sandstone, and the spaces between the pillars were closed up by thinner slabs, cemented with lime. In some of these seams the lime had partly decayed, and a crust of green moss had gathered over their surface. From one of them Bet picked the crust away to the extent of about six inches, and behind was a crevice a quarter of an inch broad. Gazing round in all directions to see that no one was observing her, she took the will from her bosom and inserted it within the crevice, close to the foot of the stone. Then she replaced the crust of moss, by which it was entirely concealed, and nothing whatever appeared to the eye to indicate that the moss had been removed.

The twilight was now gathering, and as she required to seek some shelter for the night, she slowly left the churchyard, with its melancholy ruin, and retraced her steps towards the high road.

She missed her way, and in the gathering darkness was unable to make out the direction in which she was going. She did indeed come upon a half-beaten road leading across the fields, and believing that it would sooner or later bring her to some human habitation she followed it.

In a quarter of an hour she found herself before a group of farm offices, and from the window of what seemed to be the farmer's dwelling the bright fitful fire-light streamed and flickered. Bet approached the window and peered through the panes upon a scene calculated to fill the wanderer's heart with envy. It was a well-furnished parlour, and on the cosy hearth, before a blazing coal fire, sat close together a youth and a girl, whose beaming faces and soft glances told of the deepest mutual affection. The youth had his manly arm passed round the girl's waist, and she lay with her head upon his heart, looking with a joyous happy smile into the honest noble face that was bent down to meet her upturned gaze. They were speaking together in the low sweet accents of affection, so that the words of their conversation did not reach the listener's ears, but Bet saw that they were enjoying the deep communion of harmonious hearts, and their evident felicity, contrasted with the jarring discord of her own unhallowed life, made her dislike—nay, almost hate them.

"That must be the man Crawford I have come all this length to see?" she muttered in a tone of bitterness. "And that pale thing beside him will be his young wife. Why shouldn't Dick and I be sitting together in the same fashion? We shall soon, I expect, when I won't have to stand a houseless wanderer, looking in upon any one's comforts."

False hope. Bet and Dick could never sit as James Crawford and Lizzy are sitting now, for they have never known either true love or true sorrow. Their hearts are steeped in vice; they are subject to no moral principle, the elements of pure enjoyment are not in their natures; therefore, though married to-morrow, it would be but an outward connection and no true union of soul, and for this reason the pure sweet joys of wedded life could not be theirs. Such joys rest not in passion or in fraud; and Bet was proposing to base her wedded life on these. Again we say she cherished a false hope, and the scene on which she now gazed with a bitter envy could never by her be realised, unless, indeed, she passed through the transforming discipline of sorrow and repentance, and entered upon the experience of a new and better life, a contingency which though not impossible is as yet no ways in prospect.

Since the village on the highway was a considerable distance off, and as Bet was both tired and hungry, while the hour was wearing late, she went round to the kitchen door, and solicited shelter for the night. This was readily granted, and Lizzy, who was passing to the kitchen at the moment, gave orders that the wanderer, before being put into the barn, where all such vagrants were quartered, should receive a liberal supply of porridge and milk—a supper which was very welcome to Bet, and which she did ample justice to. In the morning she was up betimes, and began her journey to Southfield.

And to this latter place we shall now change the scene.

*

The young proprietor of Braeside and Southfield was now much courted in the district, especially by those families in which there were daughters to marry. By all such he was considered a great catch, and there was a general emulation to please and captivate him. Dick understood the game perfectly, and inasmuch as it was his game likewise, he played his cards to the best of his ability. If it was the object of the young girls to gain for their husband the young proprietor of lands which yielded £300 a year, it was Dick's object, on the other hand, to make the very best of his position, and marry the richest girl that came within his grasp. He was not the man to make what is called a romantic marriage. No dowerless maiden would he wed, but one who would add a duplicate of his own income at least, or more if possible.

Both sides, of course, cunningly concealed their object. Dick was professedly taken out for his personal qualities, and he spouted sentiment of the most generous and disinterested character, keeping his eye open all the time to make the best match which turned up.

His hopes and intentions settled at last upon Kate Sutherland, who, with her father, Captain Sutherland, had recently come to reside in a picturesque cottage at no great distance from Southfield. They were strangers in the place, but had every appearance of being wealthy. The Captain kept an open table, and lived extravagantly. Kate was his only daughter, and made herself very agreeable, especially to Dick, who thought he had found in her just the heiress he sought. That she was an heiress everybody concluded, for was not she the Captain's only child, and he, it was known, was wealthy—she would therefore inherit all his money.

Dick, once resolved, began the siege with earnestness and energy, and, truth to say, Kate gave him every encouragement. Things had not gone on thus for very long, when Dick thought he would, as he called it, strike the iron while it was hot, and one night made up his mind to go up to Woodard Cottage and propose for the hand of his charmer.

He went, sought an interview with Kate, made his offer, and was blushingly accepted. The Captain was called to the conference, was made acquainted with the state of matters, and graciously gave his consent, declaring that Dick was the only one in the world to whom he would have given his darling Kate.

Dick left the cottage at a late hour, full of ecstasy. He had won the heiress, and his two hundred a year had swelled out to a sum the greatness of which he could not estimate. Had man ever such luck as his? A few months ago he was a wandering vagabond; now he was a popular landed proprietor, engaged to be married in a month to a captain's only daughter.

Full of the most pleasant thoughts, Dick went homewards whistling one of his favourite airs—an air which he had often executed on the flute to admiring listeners on the street.

In a hollow, where the road passed through a wood, a dark figure glided silently from the side of the path and stood before him. It was just light enough for Dick to see that it was a woman, and too dark for him to discern her features. He stopped his whistling, and stood still. He could not well do any other thing, for the woman stood right in his way.

"Hillo! who are you—what do you want?" he asked.

"Don't you know me, Dick?" asked the figure in a voice which he recognised only too well.

"Confound it, Bet, is it you?" he said in an angry tone. "What the devil has brought you here?"

"To see you," she returned.

"And what was the use of that after the way we parted. I

told you then that everything was done between us, and you gave me a mighty deal of abuse."

"And didn't you merit it?" asked Bet. "Didn't you use me worse than a dog; and didn't I say I would have my revenge?"

"Oh yes, you raved a deal of stuff of that kind, for which I didn't care one straw, but which I also haven't forgot. If you have come here thinking to get anything from me, you are mightily mistaken, and can just take your way back again."

He pushed past her, and would have passed on, but she grasped him by the arm.

"Hands off, I tell you," he shouted, "or, by heaven, I'll knock you down!"

"Wait a bit," said Bet, with wonderful calmness; "I haven't sought you to beg, but to demand. I could have revenge, but I choose rather to use my power to the best advantage for us both. Dick, you must marry me."

"Must!" he echoed, scornfully.

"Ay, must—or be ruined."

"Ruined! Well, I think I just should be ruined if I did marry you. Woman, you are mad. The authorities should confine you. There, let me go. I won't stand any of your foolish nonsense."

"Don't talk so big, Dick," resumed Bet, "or you may tempt me to do that which shall hurt both of us. Listen—I have got Mary Paterson's will. Ha! that makes you start. I knew it would."

Dick did indeed start, and stood for some moments thunderstruck. Her words were so unexpected, and their import so alarming that he might well be struck dumb. But presently he recovered, for he believed that what she said could not be true. She must know something about the will, but could not possibly have it—Bowser would take good care of that.

"That's a bold move of yours, Bet," he at last observed— "a very bold move; but it doesn't frighten me. You may have overheard something at Bowser's but—"

"I overheard everything," said Bet, hurriedly. "You know as well as I do that every word spoken in the inner room can be heard in the closet."

"So it can; and that's how you got your information. Bowser, I know, was idiot enough to tell Tibb all about it;

but the will itself he has kept safe in his possession. So your knowledge avails you nothing. You may tell what you like, nobody will believe you, and you have no proof of what you say."

"I have the best of all proof—I have the will," rejoined Bet. "Bowser had it hidden behind the old clock, and with it the fifty pounds he got from you six months ago. I bagged both that night the house was burned. Bowser and Tibb think the will is consumed; but it isn't. I have it safe, and mean to make my own of it—marriage or revenge. Make me your wife, Dick, and the will shall be destroyed the moment the priest joins us, when Bowser may whistle on his thumb for his hundred a year. It is out of no love for you that I make you this offer, for you destroyed my love when you cast me off. But I have a liking for a good living as well as you, and that's why I make the offer. Refuse, and I go at once and give the will to James Crawford."

Dick listened keenly to every word she uttered. It might be true that she had the will, and in that case he was wholly in her power. Bowser had said to him that he still had it in his possession—that Tibb had saved it from the flames, but that assertion went for nothing. Bowser could easily tell a lie to serve himself. What was to be done? He was in a fix and must temporise. A bold course—a desperate step was necessary, and he resolved to take it. To marry Bet was impossible, for he had that very night engaged to go to the altar with another within a month; but if she produced the will he was doubly ruined. There was one way to prevent this terrible catastrophe. Bet was there; she must be secured and the will taken from her. Now it was that he was mentally thankful for a circumstance of the day before, which had annoyed him most grievously, for that circumstance would now enable him to avoid the ruin which had so suddenly threatened.

It took a minute or two for Dick to run over these matters in his mind, to reach the conclusion to which he had come, and during these minutes he and Bet remained silent. The latter, supposing that he was making up his mind to close with her offer, and little aware of the plot he was hatching, waited patiently for the favourable issue to which she was sure his thoughts would come; and as she waited her bosom swelled with expected triumph.

At length Dick spoke—

"If what you say be true, you have played a clever game, and you hold what is like to be a winning card. But, of course, I must have till the morning to consider."

"I give you that time," said Bet. "Go and think about it, but don't forget what will follow if you reject my terms. Money won't tempt me to turn from my purpose. Your wife I must be, or I will crush you with all the joy which the hate I now have for you produces. I swore to have revenge, and I shall if you defy me."

"I shan't forget the pleasant alternative," returned Dick, with an ill-concealed sneer. "Meanwhile, where are you to pass the night?"

"Oh! I shall do well enough," answered Bet. "You and I have slept in the fields on a worse night than this, and though you have of late been used to luxury, I have not. This wood will afford me shelter enough."

"Oh, nonsense!" rejoined Dick, "you must have a bed somewhere. The village is a long way off, or you could go there. Let me see now. There is a little inn at no great distance. Come and I will get you up-putting there for the night."

Bet was softened a little by what she thought was, on his part, a consideration for her comfort, and willingly agreed to accompany him to the place he referred to. So they walked on together, speaking very little, for Dick was busy with his counter-working plans, and Bet, in her fancied security, was willing to remain silent.

After half an hour's walking through the mild and silent night, they turned from the highway into a narrower and less beaten path, and for a moment a vague suspicion crossed Bet's mind.

"This is a bye-road," she remarked. "Surely there can't be an inn here."

"Oh, yes, there is," remarked Dick, quite readily; "and a busy inn it was a little while ago, but the road was changed a few months since, and it has been left in the lurch. Yonder it is."

Bet looked along the road and saw a dark outline of a group of buildings. Her suspicion had vanished with Dick's explanation, and she proceeded by his side with no thought of foul play.

At a considerable distance from the house Dick paused.

"Just stay here," he said, "till I go on and explain the matter to the landlord. He knows me well enough; but you are not the sort of party he is in the habit of taking in, and a word or two will be necessary."

She made no objection, but, being tired she sat down by the road side, and Dick walked forward. He was gone much longer than she expected, and she grew impatient, and had risen to walk forward alone when she saw his dark form returning.

"What a time you have been," she remarked. "You've surely had a difficulty in getting the landlord to house me."

"I have," he replied. "He's a cautious old Scotchman, and had to be persuaded a bit; but it's all right. You'll get a bed now, and I have ordered a hot supper to be got ready for you; so come along."

They approached the house, where all was dark, but when Dick opened the front door a candle glimmered in the passage, and taking this up he ascended the stair, Bet closely following him. About the middle of the stair they came to a long narrow passage leading towards the rear of the building. Dick took this passage, and followed it through various windings till he reached a door which he opened, and he and Bet entered a small room with little or no furniture in it. A table in the middle of the floor, with a chair on either side of it, was literally all that it contained. Floor and walls were both bare, the window was boarded up on the outside, and a damp close smell indicated that the chamber had not been used for some time.

Dick set the candle on the table, and sat down on one of the chairs, pointing to Bet to take the other, which stood with its back to the door. The tired wanderer seated herself in it at once, and surveyed Dick by the light which the candle gave.

"My eye, how smart you are," she observed, running her eye over him from head to foot.

"I've got to be a little stylish now," returned Dick. "But tell me, how did you come to meet me in the road?"

"Because I had been along at your fine house, and they told me that you were out seeing some of your fine friends; they also told me the road you would come. Oh, don't frown and look savage, I didn't show myself. It was dark, and I kept in the shadow, and they couldn't see what like I was. So you see I haven't disgraced you."

"Ah! And so Bowser was burned out when he got back. How did it happen? Was it a card of your playing?"

"No it wasn't. Some of them were drunk in the outer room, and were smoking among the straw. It was lucky for me though, for I got off with the will without suspicion, and—"

Bet suddenly paused, for she heard behind her the harsh grating sound caused by some one locking the chamber door.

She started up in alarm, wheeled suddenly round, and to her amazement found herself face to face with—Bowser.

The truth flashed upon her in an instant. She had been betrayed. The place was no inn, but a lonely house in an unfrequented place, and Bowser and Dick had her completely in their power.

CHAPTER XXXIX

BET IN PERIL—A WONDERFUL DISCOVERY

Dick had likewise sprung up when Bowser made his appearance, and Bet was thus placed between them. She did not once think of resistance, for she knew that would be useless. There was no help at hand, and what strength had she in the hands of these strong men? With what intense mental satisfaction did she at the moment congratulate herself on her prudence in not bringing the will with her.

"So, you've been a-robbing me, it seems," said Bowser, with a peculiar smile and tone.

"It's no great robbery when you daren't give me in to the police for it," returned Bet, with a sneer.

Her coolness and firmness had now quite returned, and a bitterly savage expression spread over her countenance, as she turned a withering glance on Dick.

"And you have betrayed me and made choice of ruin for yourself," she hoarsely remarked. "Be it so. I shall trust you no more. I would not now save you even to save myself. You have brought your doom upon your own head."

"Fine words and big, my caged she-tiger," retorted Dick. "You would bite if you could, I don't doubt, but you don't think we mean to let you go without drawing your teeth. Now, then, give up the will."

"Ay, give it to me," said Bowser, taking a sudden step forward, and eagerly thrusting forth his hand.

"Oh, you want to secure your hundred a year," said Bet, with a scornful smile.

"It don't matter to you what I want," roared Bowser, in anger. "It was from my house you stole it, and to me it must be returned."

"Stole it!" repeated Bet, with another bitter, scornful smile. "And who stole it first? Who sneaked in at James Crawford's window, under night, and took it out of his drawer?"

"I did," said Bowser, "and that's why I claim it now."

"Oh, indeed!" sneered Bet. "You have a right to it because you stole it."

"Exactly."

"Then so have I," she added.

"So you have—that is, if you had the power to keep it. But you forget that you are here in our power, and should know us too well to think we will let you go before we have got it. Now, I would advise you to give it up quietly; it will be the better for you."

"Yes," cried Dick. "And you can keep the fifty pounds you took along with it."

Bet smiled disdainfully, and sat down again in the chair.

"Quick now," roared Bowser. "I am in no humour to wait. Out with it, or I'll take it from you in two minutes."

"You'll be a very clever man if you do," was Bet's quiet rejoinder.

"Why, you are not going to be such a fool as defy us. You don't think as how you'll be able to hinder us from taking it from you."

"Not if I had it here," returned Bet: "But I haven't."

"Haven't," repeated Bowser.

"Haven't," echoed Dick in alarm.

"No," rejoined Bet. "As you said just now, I'm not a fool; and before trusting myself too near Dick, I left the will in a safe place."

"That's gammon," exclaimed Bowser. "There's something in your bosom."

And with sudden roughness he dashed his hand into Bet's breast and pulled out a small packet which turned out to be a bundle of bank notes.

"There's the couter at any rate," exclaimed Bowser, triumphantly.

Dick with great eagerness thrust his hand also into Bet's bosom in the expectation of getting the will, but the moment he did so Bowser sprang upon him, and with a fierce oath and a vigorous sweep of his strong arm knocked him away with a violence that sent him staggering against the wall.

"None of your cursed nonsense with me," shouted Bowser, in a fearful rage. "If you try to get the will for yourself and destroy it as you once did, I'll knock your brains out. Here, Bet, if you value a whole skin, hand it out to me this moment."

"I have told you both I haven't got it," said Bet, with provoking coolness.

"But I know better," said Bowser. "You weren't such an idiot as part with it to any one."

"Of course I wasn't. But I hid it."

"Where?"

"Where nobody but myself will find it."

"Don't believe a word of that," growled Bowser savagely.

"Well, search me," said Bet; "or if Tibb is here she can do it."

"Ay, Tibb shall search you to the skin," cried Bowser, and unlocking the door he was about to shout for Tibb to come up, but he was saved that trouble by the appearance of the latter at the threshold of the open door.

"Oh, you cunning and ungrateful wretch!" exclaimed Tibb, as she stalked into the room and confronted Bet. "To think that you would go and be a spy on Bowser and me, and listen to everything we said, and then rob us. I've a good mind to tear every hair out of your head. But we have you safe now, my lass, and all your cunning will do you no good."

"She says she hasn't got the will here; just you search her," growled Bowser.

With no gentle hand Tibb proceeded with the task entrusted to her, the others standing by in the full hope that she would find the will. But, of course, they were all disappointed, for, as we know, the will was deposited in a secret place twenty miles away.

"Curse her, she hasn't got it," said Tibb, in great wrath, after she had searched so completely that there could be no doubt of the fact.

"Didn't I tell you so?" observed Bet, with a smile of triumph.

"Then, where is it? tell us that," roared Bowser.

"I'll not tell," answered Bet, firmly.

"I'll make you tell," he shouted again.

"You can't and never will," was Bet's dogged rejoinder.

"I'll starve you—torture you, till you tell," roared Bowser, with savage ferocity, and he fully looked the man to do what he said.

"You may torture me to death, but you'll never get a word out of me."

"Don't be obstinate, Bet," counselled Tibb. 'You know Bowser will do what he says, and it's no use standing out. So you had just better say at once where you've hid the will."

"And I'll give you back the couter," added Bowser.

"And I'll give you fifty pounds more," said Dick, who had by this time recovered a little from the shock he had received.

Bet turned towards him with flashing eyes—eyes gleaming with vindictive passion and hate.

"Five thousand wouldn't buy me," she vehemently answered. "To-night I offered you the only terms on which I would give up the will, and while pretending to consider them, you basely betrayed me hither. For this second wrong nothing will atone. No, not if you would make me your wife to-morrow would I forego my purpose. Revenge now, nothing but revenge shall I have. I shall be satisfied only when I see you back to beggary, or, better than that, transported for robbery—you and Bowser. Ha! ha! my time for triumph is coming."

"Twenty-four hours fasting may make you change your tune," roared Bowser. "We'll leave you for that time, and when we come back it's like we'll find your obstinacy brought down a peg or two."

He took up the light as he spoke, and handed it to Tibb, who, along with Dick, quitted the room. Bowser came last, and he carefully closed and locked the door.

Bet was now alone and in darkness. She heard their footsteps die away in the long passage, and their voices grow fainter and fainter, till they failed to reach her ear. Then silence was added to darkness and solitude, and she was free to indulge in her own reflections.

These were bitter and gloomy enough. Her fierce passionate heart chafed terribly at the trick which Dick had played on her, in luring her to captivity under pretence of finding her shelter for the night. She was angry with herself for being so easily deceived. One thing alone was a source of satisfaction—viz., the thought that the will was safe from their reach. It was impossible that they should ever discover its hiding-place, but of her own safety she was by no means so sure. She well knew that Bowser was a man of terrible determination, and he might be cruel enough to keep his word, in which case her position was anything but enviable. One thing was certain, she would never, while her senses remained, inform them where the will was. She would suffer anything—death even—rather than be baulked of her revenge.

She was both hungry and weary, and bitterly she thought of how Dick was mocking her when he spoke of the supper that was preparing. They had deprived her of food, but they could not deprive her of sleep, though she had only the hard wooden boards to lie on. So she laid herself down in a corner of the room and fell asleep.

She slept like a stone, and that for many hours, for when she awoke the light of day shone in streaks across the floor, passing in through the chinks between the boards which covered the window on the outside. Bet got up and approached the window to see if there was any chance of escape by it, or of making a signal for help from it. Her heart sank within her when she saw there was no chance either of the one or the other. The boards were rough strong deals, securely nailed, and the window looked out upon the roofs of stables, so that a signal hung from it could be seen by no one.

To Bet, who had for years been a restless wanderer, it was irksome in the extreme to sit inactive in that darkened room, subjected to the pangs of hunger and a prey to her own bitter thoughts. A perfect silence reigned within and without the house. Not a bark of a dog nor the rumble of a cart was heard, nor any sound to break the wearisome monotony of imprisonment. She either paced the chamber to and fro, or sat on a chair, with her head leaning upon the table, her passionate spirit resolute and determined as ever.

Meanwhile, during the hours of that same day, Dick and Bowser were not idle. They suspected that Bet had hid the will in the wood where she had met Dick the previous evening, and they went in company and spent many hours in searching there for it. They were, of course, unsuccessful, and their failure irritated them still further against Bet.

At night they went all three to the room in which she was confined, and found her sitting just as they had left her.

"Well," cried Bowser, "I hope you have now thought better of it. Come, tell us where the will is, and Tibb will bring you up some supper. You must feel hungry."

"Yes, I am hungry," replied Bet, "but hunger will not make me yield. I have told you nothing will."

"That's your answer, is it?"

"Yes."

They left her, and the door was again locked.

Bowser and his companions descended to the kitchen, which

was the only furnished apartment in the house. Here a large
fire blazed in the ample grate, and bottles and glasses were set
out upon the table.

"What's to be done?" asked Dick. "Bet is as obstinate as
the devil. She'll never yield. She'll die first."

"Then let her die!" said Bowser, ferociously.

"Murder is an ugly thing," said the youth.

"Bah; who's to know anything about it here? Nobody saw
her come, and she hasn't a soul in the world to ask after
her."

"Yet murder is murder," observed Tibb, "and I wouldn't
like to have the weight of blood on my conscience."

"Nor I," added Dick, with a shudder.

"Nor I if I can help it," growled Bowser. "But either she
or we must knock under. Let her go and we are beggars, every
one of us, in less than a week. *Do* for her and we are safe."

"Perhaps not," said Dick. "Some one may stumble by
accident on the place where she has put the will, and where
are we?"

"Couldn't we frighten her into telling us?" suggested Tibb.

"Not a bad idea," rejoined Bowser. "We'll pretend that
we are going to murder her, and if that don't make her give
in, nothing will."

The following morning, as Bet lay on the floor, she heard
the door of her room opened, and looking up, saw Tibb
enter with a basin in one hand and a slice of bread in the
other.

"Here's some tea for you. Sit up and take it—quick. Bowser
don't know I've brought it, and if he comes up and finds what
I've done, he'll be in a fine rage."

Without a word, Bet sat up and ate voraciously.

"Ain't you going to tell us where the will is yet?" asked
Tibb, as she took back the empty basin.

"No," was Bet's laconic answer.

"Then your doom is sealed!" said Tibb, with awful emphasis. "You'll get one chance more to-night, and if you still
refuse, *they'll murder you!*"

"That's more than they dare," said Bet, in a firm tone,
though Tibb's keen eye saw that she turned pale.

"Dare! Dick and Bowser will dare anything rather than lose
the property. Just you think better of it, and save your life
by giving up the will."

Having given this advice, and accompanied it with a significant shake of the head, Tibb withdrew, securing the door as she went.

Bet passed another weary day in her silent prison, watching the streaks of light across the floor, and upon the walls, and cherishing with greater intensity the regretful thoughts she entertained for having been induced to depart from her purpose of putting the will into the hands of James Crawford. It was a vain dream of ambition which had caused her to change her course, and the consequence threatened to be serious enough.

At night she again heard the well-known footsteps in the passage, and Dick and Bowser entered without Tibb. Dick carried the light, and Bowser had a thick cord over his arm. He locked the door in the inside, and put the key into his pocket.

"Have you made up your mind to be reasonable yet, Bet?" demanded Bowser, in a gruff tone.

"My mind is just the same as it was," she coldly replied.

"And you still refuse to tell us where the will is?"

"Yes."

"Sorry for it—on your account. The fact is, Bet, Dick and I have come to the conclusion that we must have the will or take your life."

"Oh, you've come to frighten me, have you?" said Bet, with a sneer.

"No; only to allow you your last choice. We don't want to murder you—if we can help it, but since you insist on ruining us, you force us to do it."

"Come, be wise, Bet, and save yourself," counselled Dick. "What's your revenge, as you call it, compared with your life?"

"What's three hundred a year compared with the hangman's rope?" retorted Bet.

"Pooh! The hangman's rope wont touch us," said Bowser. "We'll make all square so that the thing will never be found out. Now, then, once more, where is the will?"

Bet was silent.

"Won't you answer?"

"No."

Bowser grinned with savage ferocity, and glanced to the ceiling where a strong beam went across the apartment. He drew the table under it, set a chair on the table, and mounting on both began deliberately to fasten the rope round the wood. The expression of his countenance was something fiendish, even to Dick, who understood him not to be in earnest. Bet tried not to look at him, and to appear unconcerned; but, do as she would, her eyes were drawn upon his movements as by a spell, and it required all the strength of her iron will to refrain from shuddering at sight of the diabolic ferocity pictured in his face. With great care he securely fixed the rope, adjusted its length by his own height, and cast upon it a running noose. Then he tested the strength of the rope and its fastenings by grasping it with both hands and swinging from it. It creaked, but was perfectly firm.

Next he slowly descended, and taking a smaller cord from his pocket approached Bet. The latter uttered a piercing shriek, and rushed to the far corner of the room.

"Not a bit of use in howling," said Bowser. "There's not a soul but ourselves within two miles of this."

As he spoke he sprung upon her for the purpose of binding her arms. Bet shrieked again, and struggled desperately.

"Lend a hand here, Dick," roared Bowser, and the youth, rushing to his assistance, Bet's arms and legs were securely bound, and she lay helpless on the floor.

Bowser raised her in his strong arms, and with Dick's help they set her upright on the table, and put the noose of the rope round her neck. All that was wanting now to complete the tragedy was the removal of the table from beneath her, when she would be suspended and suffocated. Dick and Bowser were, however, acting on the understanding that this should not be done. If Bet remained obstinate even in the circumstances it was clear she would die rather than reveal her secret, and there would be nothing for it but to take her down again, and unloose the cords that bound her.

As yet she was firm and unyielding as ever. She had ceased to scream, but stood upon the table, with her eyes glaring upon Dick, her lips firmly compressed, and her face as pale as ashes.

"Now, Bet, this is your last chance," cried Bowser. "If you still refuse to tell, you will in a moment or two be swinging in the air. Where is the will?"

"For God's sake tell us, and save your life," exclaimed Dick.

There were some moments of terrible silence, broken only by Bet's quick and laboured breathing. Dick hoped she was broken at last, and would through terror divulge the secret, and he stood by the side of the table in breathless expectation. Bowser waited with ill-suppressed impatience, and was not long in repeating his question.

"Won't you tell?"

"No," answered Bet huskily through her parched lips.

"I'll count three before I turn you off."

"One!"

No response from Bet.

"Two!"

Still no signs.

Bowser waited for some seconds before pronouncing the last number, and the diabolical expression of ferocity deepened on his countenance.

"Three!" he shouted, then with an oath he kicked the table away, and Bet hung writhing in the rope.

Dick uttered an exclamation of horror, and, springing forward, supported her in his arms.

"Bah! let her hang!" said Bowser, in a tone of savage brutality, as, grasping Dick's arm, he tried to pull him from the chamber.

"No, no," cried the youth. "For God's sake cut the rope, Bowser; quick, quick! she'll be suffocated."

"Let her; it's our only safety. Come on."

And with a hurried step Bowser went to the door, opened it, and rushed out.

"Bowser, come back," shouted Dick at the uttermost pitch of his voice, and still supporting Bet in his arms.

But the monster heeded not, for his heavy footsteps were heard clattering down the stair.

The youth, who to do him justice, had no intention of committing murder, stood holding his burden in his trembling arms, the perspiration running down his cheeks in a stream. He looked up at Bet's face, and saw that it had become black.

"My God! she will be strangled," he wildly exclaimed, and at the same moment Tibb flew into the room with a knife in her hand.

"Up and cut the rope!" shouted Dick.

Tibb needed no second bidding, but, leaping on a chair,

she cut the rope so suddenly that both Dick and his burden
fell on the floor. The rope round Bet's neck was slackened in a
moment, but she lay motionless.

"Oh, she's dead—she's dead!" groaned Dick.

"Whatever tempted Bowser to do it?" cried Tibb, in great
agitation.

"Run for water, run; we may revive her yet!"

Tibb flew from the room, and during her absence Dick
hung over Bet's inanimate form in an agony of terror. Not for
her but for himself he was in fear, for he knew that murder
seldom escaped detection.

Every moment seemed an age till Tibb returned. At last
she appeared, bearing a large jug of cold water.

Dick dashed a quantity in Bet's face, and watched the result
with breathless anxiety. Still she lay heavy and motionless as
a stone. At Tibb's suggestion Dick cut the cords that bound
her limbs. Then, to their great joy, they saw the dark purple
on her face begin to diminish; and Tibb, who had her hand
on her breast, declared that she felt her heart beat.

The youth dashed another quantity of water in Bet's face,
which seemed to send a shock through all her body. Then her
lips worked convulsively, and she made one or two gasps for
breath. They immediately raised her head, and held the water
to her lips. Her mouth opened with a jerk, and closing again,
her teeth seized the rim of the jug, and held it as in a vice.
Dick elevated the dish, and let a little of the water flow down
her throat, which was mechanically swallowed, and in a little
after the death-like stare of the eyes gave place to intelligence,
and she looked up in a strange bewildered way at the two
faces bent over her.

Seeing that she was now in a fair way of recovery, Dick,
overcome by a sickening sensation, rushed away from the
apartment, and down stairs to the kitchen. Bowser was there
with the brandy bottle before him, and Dick, pouring out a
large glass, drank it off at a gulp.

"Well, is she dead?" asked Bowser, in the most careless tone
imaginable.

"No, thank goodness. Tibb and I have managed to revive
her."

"More fools you."

"You nearly had us in for murder, Bowser."

"Suppose I had, who'd have ever known of it? It's clear

now that Bet's determined not to give in, and what's to be done with her? If we let her go you'll be kicked out of the property in less than a week."

"Then we must keep her," said Dick.

"Ay, there's the bother. We'll have her to look after, and who's to pay for that?"

"Come, be reasonable, Bowser," returned Dick. "Your hundred a year will afford a little strain on it, and who knows but ere long we shall get the secret out of Bet."

Bowser merely growled, and Dick, swallowing some more drink to recover his shaken nerves, took his leave.

"My only chance is this marriage," he muttered, as he made his solitary way through the darkness to Southfield. "If that cursed will turns up before the month is out I am done for. If the knot is tied, I'm safe so far. The captain's rhino will keep Kate and me pretty snug, but of course the thing will be blown to the winds if I lose the property.[1] A month! Let a month pass and I am safe. What an obstinate she-devil Bet is to be sure, and what a near miss of hanging she had."

*

Away back we go to the sea-beaten cliffs and breezy table-land on which is situated James Crawford's farm of Redlaw. It is now near the close of June, and on one of the brightest of mornings James stood on the brow of one of the precipices which overhung the sea, gazing with delight at the far stretch of waters flashing under the rays of the unclouded sun.

He had been to the height where his sheep were grazing, and having seen that they were all right, he was slowly return-ing home to breakfast, but had paused for a few moments to view the grand and glorious scene stretched out before him. Far away in the distance was the blue Fife coast, and between it and the spot on which he stood was the wide entrance to the Frith[2] of Forth, towards which several ships were moving, their white sails unfurled to catch the soft morning breeze, which was so gentle as scarcely to ruffle the surface of the glassy deep.

---

1. Rhino: money.
2. Local for Firth.

While standing thus, with his sagacious sheep-dog crouching at his feet, the sound of voices from behind reached his
ear, and looking round he saw two men entering the little
churchyard which surrounded the ruin. One of them was the
grave-digger, and he carried a shovel and mattock; the other
was a mason from the village. As James knew them both, he
sauntered towards the ruin, and entered the solitary place of
graves.

The two men had taken off their coats, and laying them
on the top of a flat stone, turned their attention to another
which was close by.

"Guid morning, lads," quoth James; "what are ye gaun to
be after here the day?"

"Something that I dinna dae aften noo adays," responded
the grave-digger. "The maist o' the folks round aboot hae
taen into their heads to bury along by at the parish kirk. It's
only when an auld residenter pops awa' that I get a job here;
for the auld folk that hae friends here a'ready like to be puttin'
aside them."

"And who is it that's dead up in the village?"

"It's auld Shusey Swanston; but aiblins ye'll no ken her,
for she's been bedridden sin' ye cam' here, and lang afore
that. The Swanstons were ance great folks here awa', but they
have been a' deid but Shusey for mony a year. This is their
throuch, and as it is a heavy one, I've broucht Tammas alang
tae help me tae lift it."

The gravestone which was required to be removed was
indeed a heavy one, and seemed to have been in its place for a
generation. Its sides were overgrown with tall rank grass,
above which grew grey moss, stuck in clustering spots, over
the face of the sandstone, and in the seams and joints. The old
man and his assistant had great difficulty in getting the
massive top to move, and James willingly lent his assistance.
With his powerful aid the slab was at length raised out of its
socket, and set carefully on its edge against the broken walls
of the ruin. James then sat down on the neighbouring stone,
and looked on while the others took out the sides and dug up
the pillars.

When the side next where he sat was extracted, something
white fell to the ground.

"Guid guide us, what's this?" ejaculated the grave-digger,
as with something of a superstitious feeling he picked it up.

"It seems a paper o' some kind," observed James.

"A paper. Wha can hae puttin' a paper there; or what can it be about?"

"Ye had better look and see," suggested James, as the grave-digger turned it round and round, regarding it all the time with a look amounting to dread.

"Maybe it's no canny," said the other, with a prudent shake of the head.

"Hoots man," remarked the mason, "what's no canny aboot it? It disna seem tae hae been hidden there lang, for it's quite clean and fresh. Let me see it, if ye winna open it."

"Maybe some o' thae smugglin' deevils has puttin' it there," said the grave-digger, as he handed it to his companion, who very speedily unfolded the parchment.

"By Jingo, it's a will!" exclaimed the mason.

"A will hidden in a throuch!"

"It's as fack as death."

"Wha's will, then? Is it Shusey Swanston's?"

"What name is that at the bottom—*Mary Paterson*."

With an instantaneous bound James Crawford sprang from his seat upon the stone, and snatching the parchment out of the mason's hand, looked at it with frantic eagerness.

What was his indescribable amazement to behold the stolen will—the very paper which Dick and Bowser stole from the drawer at Southfield. He could not believe the testimony of his eyes, but stood staring at the paper in speechless bewilderment.

The other two looked at him in astonishment. To them he had the appearance of one who had suddenly lost his senses.

"Weel, if that disna bate every green thing," he at length ejaculated.

"Is it your paper?" asked the grave-digger.

"Yes, it's my paper," replied James. "It's a paper that I lost—that was steal'd oot o' my hoose a year syne; and hoo it has come there dear a bit o' me kens. But it's the wull sure eneuch; and that vagabond wull be turned oot o' the place, and the puir laddie will get his ain at last."

"And in the name o' a' that's guid, hoo cam' the paper there?" asked the wondering grave-digger.

"It's the daein's o' Providence," cried James, joyfully. "Little ken ye, lads, hoo happy the possession o' this paper makes me. Though ony body had gi'en me a thousand pounds

this mornin' I wadna hae been sae glad. It's no for mysel'
but for a puir orphan laddie that has been keepit oot o' his
ain for the want o' this paper. Here's a guinea—divide it
atween ye; and noo, guid mornin', for I hae gotten wark tae
dae that winna bide a moment's delay."

And throwing down the piece of gold upon the stone on
which he had just sat, James jumped over the grassy graves,
cleared the churchyard wall at a bound, and, followed by his
dog, scampered across the heights towards the house, with
the precious paper so mysteriously restored, tightly grasped in
his hand.

CHAPTER XL

HAPPINESS AT KIRKTON[1]

About the middle of the long street which constituted the principal portion of the village of Kirkton was the low red-tiled house occupied by Jessie Brown and Peggy M'Naughton. The house consisted of two pretty large apartments, with a closet and coal-place behind each; and though one end of the building was nominally Peggy's and the other Jessie's, they went back and forward with the utmost freedom, and lived more like a single family in the house than as two separate tenants.

And very happily they lived together—Jessie, Peggy, and the little Duncan, now a sharp, intelligent fellow, four years of age. Jessie, by her own efforts, by the kindly aid of others, and by the help of the great loving Father who delights to help his erring and repentant children on their way back to virtue, was now reclaimed from her past lost life, and respectably maintained herself by honest industry. No one in the village but Peggy knew her past history; and in *that* bosom it lay in perfect silence, surrounded by the memory of a sad and sacred sympathy. Jessie, at the worst, had been a companion of her poor lost Mary, and as such was dear to the old woman's heart. The generous girl never said so, but Peggy understood only too well that Mary had become the most abandoned of the two; and in the extenuating thoughts in which Peggy's love prompted her to indulge, Jessie had thus her full share. She received her at first with compassionate forbearance on poor Mary's account, but very soon she learnt to love her for herself. Jessie, now that she was delivered from her life of debauchery and debasement, was a sweet, gentle, considerate being, intensely grateful to those who had rescued her, and ever ready to assist Peggy in all possible ways. She was always cheerful and happy, but her cheerfulness was always characterised by a marked gravity, and her happiness

---

1. See Textual Essay for how these last four chapters become two in the *Sheffield Daily Telegraph* and in both editions of the book.

was ever subdued and restrained. The shadow of a sad in-
effaceable memory lay upon her spirits, making her humble
and lowly.

Jessie soon became a favourite in the village, and had
always as much work as she could perform. The young men
were likewise ready at all times to court her company and
gain her smile; but Jessie, while affable and kind in her
manners to all, gave no encouragement to those who desired a
closer intimacy. One young man, a respectable, well-doing
youth, drawn on by his feelings, asked her to be his wife; but
this Jessie at once firmly and decisively refused. Peggy thought
she was rash in this. The youth was in all respects unexcep-
tionable, and had it in his power to give a wife a good comfortable home, and the good old soul took it upon her to advise
Jessie to think better of it.

Jessie sadly shook her head and answered—

"No, Peggy, I shall never marry. I shall never bring shame
to the home and the heart of an honest man. He knows not
what I once was, but I can never forget it myself, and the
knowledge would cast a shadow between us for ever. I have
forfeited for ever the honoured name and place of wife, and
shall remain as I am, for I am very happy—far happier than
I deserve."

Peggy listened to her words, wiped her eyes in silence, and
had not the heart to make any reply. So the ark that offered
its shelter against the storms of life's ocean was allowed to go
its way, and Jessie resumed her work without a sigh or a
regret for her act of self-denial.[2]

On a bright, bright June day, when the sun was little past
the meridian, Jessie and Peggy sat together in the little room
of the former. Both were busily at work, Jessie upon a dress
that required to be sent home that evening, and Peggy at her
old unceasing occupation of stocking knitting. Duncan was
playing in the warm sunshine outside the open door, and
occasionally his merry shout of glee reached the ears of his
loving friends within.

All at once his noise ceased for some moments, then
suddenly he uttered a loud delighted scream, and clapping his
hands in an ecstasy of joy—

---

2. The 1885 book breaks the chapter here, before continuing.

"Uncle Dim, Uncle Dim," he shouted, his large blue eyes dancing with the most joyous excitement, and in a moment was off again as fast as his little legs could carry him.

"Losh me, can it railly be James?" cried Peggy, looking with great interest through the open door into where the little fellow has just disappeared.

"I wasna expectin' him just the noo," she added; "but that mak's his veesit a' the mair welcome."

Jessie had laid down her work likewise, and gazed at the entrance of the chamber with eager glistening eyes. She almost adored and worshipped James Crawford, for he it was who had saved her from her life of vice and shame, and her purified heart went out in gushing thankfulness towards him, therefore the hope of seeing him now was as pleasurable as it was unexpected.

A few moments of breathless silence passed, then Duncan's crow of delight was again heard, and a firm manly tread sounded along the silent village street.

"It's him, it's just him," cried Peggy, throwing down her spectacles and hurrying towards the passage; but ere she got to the threshold of the chamber the passage was darkened by a moving shadow, and James Crawford marched in, bearing on his shoulders the little fellow, whose happiness knew no bound.

"Eh, my bonny man," exclaimed Peggy, holding up both her arms.

"Weel, Peggy, lass, hoo's a' wi' ye?" cried James, in a hearty tone, and, setting Duncan on the floor he caught the happy old woman in his arms and warmly embraced her.

"I'se wager ye didna expect to see me here the day, auld freend," he gaily exclaimed.

"Atweel, that's true; but oh, man, we are glad tae see you."

"Weel, Jessie, hoo's a' wi' *you*?" said James, as, freed from Peggy's embrace his eye lighted on the bright pleased face that was watching his own, and advanced to shake Jessie warmly by the hand.

Jessie did not in words reply to James' kind enquiry; but the fervent pressure of his hand, and the beaming grateful glance she cast up to him, told that she was well and happy.

"How is Mrs Crawford?" she asked.

"Ay, hoo is Lizzy?" cried Peggy.

"Brawly," returned James, as again he caught up the delighted Duncan in his arms, and held him high above his head till the clustering curly locks touched the low ceiling.

"Little did I think yesterday mornin' afore breakfast that I was tae be here the day," James continued. "But, my certie, Peggy, I bring braw news wi' me—grand news—glorious news. This little prince will get his ain at last. Look at him, Peggy; look at him, Jessie. There's the laird o' Braeside and Soothfield. Hurrah! hurrah!! hurrah!!!"

"Mercy me, Jimes, what's happened?" asked Peggy, thrown into much perturbation by his extravagant language and still more extravagant action.

"Happened!" echoed James; "the best thing that ever happened in this world. Look at that, Peggy. There's the wull. There's the precious bit o' paper that maks Duncan a rich young laird—there's the document that was stealed frae us yon night at Soothfield."

And James struck Peggy utterly dumb by throwing upon the table Mary Paterson's will.

Peggy snatched it up and her spectacles along with it. The latter, in her nervous haste, she put on upside down, and it was some moments ere her trembling fingers could get them properly adjusted on her nose. But she did at length manage this essential operation, when a few moments' inspection sufficed to satisfy her that it was indeed the lost will.

"My guid gracious, James, where or hoo did ye get it?" she ejaculated.

"In the last place in this yirth where I wad hae thoucht o' lookin' for it," answered James. "It's a Providence, Peggy, a rale even-doun Providence, and there's nae sic a thing as understandin' it. It's a mystery tae me; abune my comprehension a'thegither. I hae puzzled my brain aboot it for this last twenty-four hoors without makin' an inch o't, and I wad puzzle them for as mony years without gettin' a bit farer forrit. But never mind, that's the wull, and if I dinna ken hoo it cam' I ken what tae dae wi' it."

And forthwith James told his eager listeners the wonderful way in which the will came into his possession. The matter was of course as mysterious to them as to him, but Peggy firmly believed that it had been restored by some agency from the other world, and she laid down the paper with a great and wondering care that strongly partook of the superstitious.

But the mystery attending its recovery was speedily forgot in the happiness which its recovery brought, and little Duncan was, to his no small surprise, caught up by Peggy and smothered with kisses.

"My certies!" she vigorously exclaimed, "but that young blackguard will hae tae march frae Soothfield noo. A fine time he has had o't for this while back. The hail kintry side has been haudin' their haunds aboot him, and among the young hizzies it was wha tae be first tae catch him. A bonny galravish he's had up at Soothfield, tae. His braw hoose is finished noo, and he has gotten grand plenishin' for it, and this is his marriage nicht, and—"

"He's tae be married the nicht?" broke in James, excitedly.

"Ay, is he, on a captain's dochter, wha thinks, nae doot, she's gettin' a great bargain. But her tack o' the braw hoose winna be a lang ane, and she'll get her blackguard o' a gudeman tae keep."

"Peggy, she maun ne'er come to Soothfield ava," said James, "and the marriage itsel' maunna take place without the lassie kennin' that she's takin' a beggar."

"And a thief and a vagabond," added Peggy, emphatically.

"He's a' that, I hae nae doot," returned James, "but as we hae nae proof that he stole the wull, we'll no daur say sae."

"He did it though, for a' that," cried Peggy, stoutly. "And what dae ye think, James, yun ither blackguard that was wi' him has come tae live at Willie Frazer's auld hoose. Nae doot Richard will hae him tae pay weel for the help he gied him."

"Dod, I mind weel o' him," said James, with a frown; "an impudent, ugly, vulgar, and angersome fellow he was. He lives there, ye say? I'll ca' on him as I gang by, just tae hae the pleasure o' paying him back for his impudence yon nicht."

"Tak' care o' him though, Jimes," counselled Peggy. "He's a muckle strong fellow, and might fell ye."

"Let him try it," said James, with a swelling bosom, and a determination in his face which indicated the pleasure he would have in a personal encounter with Bowser.

"And noo," he added, "whaur is this great marriage tae come aff?"

"Up by, at Wudend," answered Peggy.

"Guide us, that's a lang gate," rejoined the youth, "and it's time I was stappin'."

"Surely you will take some dinner before ye go," said Jessie.

"Tae be shure he wull," cried Peggy, "he's no gaun his fit length owre the door till he gets meat. Hech me, but, I am a happy woman this day, and wha kens but I may end my days in the auld hoose at Braeside after a'?"[3]

---

3. The book chapter 40 (1866 and 1885) continues on until the gossip about the wedding debacle has "spread over the entire district" (end of newspaper ch. 41).

CHAPTER XLI

TRIUMPH

The sun was verging towards the west as James Crawford came to a byepath in the wood in sight of the solitary wayside inn. He carried a stout oaken cudgel in his hand, and his tread was firm and manly, for his bosom swelled with feelings of pride and satisfaction. Recollecting as he did the insolence he had to submit to from Bowser and Dick on the night they arrived at Southfield, he had a peculiar gratification in mortifying them now, and he experienced something like a stern eager joy in the fulfilment of the mission on which he was now bent.

When he got up to the house the door was shut, but on raising the latch it yielded, and opening it he went in. The kitchen door stood wide, and as he entered it Tibb was standing by the fire in the attitude of one who had risen from a seat in alarm on hearing a footstep. Bowser lay upon a settle, in front of the bed, fast asleep.

James quietly marched forward and stood in the middle of the floor, surveying Bowser with a grim satisfaction.

Tibb, mistaking him for some one who had come in for refreshment, hastened to say, "You have come wrong, sir, this is not an inn now."

"So I understand," responded James. "But I havena come far wrang, for there lies the man that I hae some little business wi'. His name, I think, is Bowser."

"Who wants me?" asked the latter, rousing up at the sound of his name.

"I want you," replied James, in a tone which made Bowser open his eyes in a wide stare. The moment he saw who it was standing in the kitchen he started up in alarmed surprise.

"Ye ken me, I think," said James, with a meaning smile.

"Of course I do," responded Bowser. "You are young Crawford. What want you here?"

"To return a veesit that you ance paid tae me," answered the youth with dry humour. "In fact I should say twa veesits," added James, "though I saw ye only the first time."

"What the devil do you mean?" growled Bowser.

"Ye ken brawly what I mean," retorted James. "A fine pliskey you and your friend Dick played us when ye cam' in at the back window and took the will oot o' the drawer. Eh, but yer a nice pair o' swindlers."

Bowser sprang to his feet in a rage. "Out of this house, fellow," he roared, "or I'll kick you to the door."

"Wull ye railly?" said James, grasping his cudgel very hard. "Juist you keep a calm sough, if ye dinna want yer heid and my stick tae become acquent. If ye offer tae lay a hand on me I wad think nae mair o' clourin' yer croon than a butcher dis o' fellin' an ox. Ye had the better o' me yon time, but my fagues its my turn tae craw noo. See, dae ye ken that?"

And James took the will from his bosom, and triumphantly held it up before Bowser.

Bowser leapt forward a step, and so did Tibb.

"Stand back!" roared James. "If ye daur—either the ane or the other o' ye—tae pit yer fingers on that paper, I'll knock ye doon as shure as the sun is sinkin' in the west; and that minds me that I should be gaun, for they tell me yer friend Dick is tae be married the nicht, and I want tae let it spunk oot that he is no a laird afore the knot is tied. Sae, my man, if ye hae ony pickin' aff Dick, baith his guid time and yours is at an end. Guid day tae ye, ye blackguard, and—"

Bowser, growing desperate in his rage, made a dash forward as James was retreating to the door, and Tibb prepared to back him in his evident attempt to take the paper from the youth by force.

A fierce flash blazed for a moment in James' eye, and swift as lightning the stick ascended in the air and fell with fearful force on Bowser's right arm.

He gave a roar like the bellow of a bull, and Tibb echoing it, though in a shriller key, rushed forward as her lord staggered back.

"Haud aff," shouted James. "Though ye're a woman I'll gie ye the same if ye daur tae assail me! A' the fiends in hell wadna tak' the will frae me!"

"Curse you," roared Bowser, gnashing his teeth with rage and pain.

"Ay, curse awa'. That's a' ye'll be guid for for some time tae come, I'm thinking. Guid day wi' ye, ye blackguard, and I'll send yer precious friend tae condole wi' ye."

At this moment, and just as James was about to quit the

house, a loud knocking was heard on a door above, and a woman's voice exclaiming in frantic tones—

"Help! help! oh, help!"

It flashed upon the mind of James that this must be a prisoner which Bowser had confined in that lonely house; and fired with the desire to liberate her if it was really so, he bounded up the stair, and was guided to the room by the loud knocking and louder cries.

The door was locked, but the key was in the outside, James had therefore nothing to do but turn it, when he opened the door, and stood face to face with Bet. In the dimness of the darkened room he could only see that it was a woman.

"Oh, save me, Mr Crawford! Protect and take me from this place," pleaded Bet.

"Bless us a', how dae ye ken me?" asked James, in great surprise.

"I heard your voice and the words you spoke," answered Bet, speaking very fast. "You have got the will?"

"My gracious—yes. What ken ye about it?"

"I hid it in the tombstone. I am the woman who got shelter at your place a month ago. Bowser and Dick have kept me a prisoner here ever since, because I would not tell them where I put the will."

"Oh, oh!" said James, to whose mind the mystery was being unfolded. He was about to say something more when an exclamation from Bet, and the pointing of her finger, warned him that danger was approaching. He was in the act of wheeling round to see what it was, when he felt himself violently pushed forward, and the next moment the door was shut and locked, and he and Bet were prisoners together.

Like a caged lion, the youth threw himself against the door with a force so terrific that he smashed it in pieces, and encountered Bowser and Tibb on the landing.

"So this is some mair o' yer black work," he cried, as brandishing his cudgel he advanced upon them. They durst not await his approach, but fled in terror down the stair.

"Noo, then, if ye want liberty follow me," exclaimed the youth, and with sturdy step he too went along the winding passage and down the steps, Bet following close at his heels.

The outer door stood open, and their exit being unimpeded,

they were next moment in the open air, under the bright
golden rays of the sinking sun.

*

We change the scene to the largest room in Woodend
Cottage, where a company more select than numerous had
assembled to witness the marriage of Dick and Kate Sutherland. The minister had come, and the captain and his guests
sat waiting the entrance of the bride for the ceremony to be
performed.

Dick was full of self-gratulation: Kate was now as good as
his, and her fortune too. In a few minutes the ceremony would
be observed which indissolubly united them, and he was thus
made safe from the worst that could happen. He stood at one
of the windows by himself, too excited with his own thoughts
to engage in the conversation that was going forward; but, of
course, everybody excused him, for a waiting bridegroom is
generally excused from social activity.

It was a gorgeous evening. The glare and heat of the
summer day had given place to a cool and mellow radiance,
and wood and field lay bathed in the rich clear light which
preceded sunset.

Dick's eyes wandered vacantly over the beautiful scene.
He had no great perception of Nature's loveliness at any time;
but, in present circumstances, less than ever. He was busy in
conjectures about the extent of Kate's fortune. He had as yet
made no inquiries on this point, deeming it impolitic to do so;
but never doubting it would be large. The Captain had never
talked of a settlement, so that, whatever amount it might be,
he would have full command of it.

At length, and when every person had become impatient,
Kate and her bridesmaids appeared—the former sailing into
the room in her bridal dress, like a vision of dazzling light.
Her father led her by the hand, and Dick stepping forward,
the happy pair took up a position side by side before the
clergyman.

The others stood round in a circle, and the ceremony
began.

Dick was asked in due form and at the proper time if he
took Kate to be his lawful wife, and in a clear firm voice he
answered, "Yes."

Kate was next asked if she, of her own free will and consent, took Dick to be her lawful husband, and she had just opened her mouth to pronounce the same irrevocable word when the door of the room suddenly flew open, and James Crawford and Bet stood together on the threshold.

The sensation produced by their appearance was great and universal. Dick turned round with the others, and the moment his eye fell on the intruders he knew that all was lost, and, in the intensity of his bitter rage and disappointment, he uttered through his grinding teeth,

"Damnation!"

"Are we owre late?" cried James. "Is the marriage owre?"

"What means this intrusion?" demanded the Captain, advancing from the astonished group. "By what right do you come here and break in unannounced at such a moment?"

"Richt!" returned James, slowly. "I'm no shure that we had ony great richt. But the maist o' the leddies and gentlemen here ken me, and I made bold tae enter tae tell ye that the man ye are takin' for a son-in-law, and yer dochter for a husband, isna what he gi'es oot tae be. Ye look upon him, nae doot, as the Laird o' Soothfield and Braeside; but he's no, and he's a doonricht blackguard into the bargain."

Kate here gave a short scream, and turning very faint, was by the minister set upon a chair—everybody but him being engrossed by the extraordinary scene.

The Captain turned to Dick with an amazed and questioning look, and seeing then his extreme confusion, and, coupling that with the exclamation which had escaped him, he perceived that there was truth in the incredible statement which the stranger had made.

"Mr Campbell, is this true, sir?" he angrily said. "Speak, and say that it is false."

"He cannot, for he knows it is the truth," said Bet, speaking for the first time, and advancing into the room with a triumphant air, and fixing her gleaming eyes upon Dick alone. "And so this is why you refused to marry me?" she scornfully said. "You had engaged yourself to another, and rejected me, who had the strongest claim on you. See now how your baseness has brought ruin upon your head. I swore to be revenged, and I have accomplished my oath. You are again a beggar. James Crawford has the will you stole. If your fine dame takes you after knowing that, she is welcome to do so for me."

"Tell me, sir," demanded the Captain, now very wroth; "tell me if what the woman says is true. Are you the unprincipled villain she declares?"

"Here is proof sae far, at ony rate," said James, holding the open will before the Captain's face.

A glance was enough to show the latter what the document was; and Dick's mortification being too extreme to allow him to brave the matter out, he stood speechless.

"Begone, villain," shouted the Captain, now in an ungovernable rage. "Quit this house instantly, or I may be tempted to demean myself by laying hands on a scoundrel whose touch is pollution."

With an oath too terrible to repeat, Dick gave a vehement stamp with his foot, and brandishing his arms with rage, rushed at headlong speed from the room, followed by the loud, mocking triumphant laughter of Bet.

Kate now made as if to faint, and cried—

"Oh, father, lead me to my chamber."

The Captain strode forward and supported her from the room, waving back the bridesmaid, who was following to render assistance.

The moment she was within the sanctuary of her bedchamber her bearing changed, and standing erect, father and daughter confronted each other.

"What a dreadful discovery," said Kate.

"Be thankful it did not take place a moment later," observed the Captain.

"Oh! horrible," said Kate. "I should have then been the wife of a beggar and a wretch. Thank goodness, I am at least saved from that, though our hopeful scheme has failed. My chance is gone for ever."

"Nonsense," returned her father hastily; "we must go to some other part of the country where we are unknown, and try again. The next game won't turn out so badly. Now, I must go down stairs and get rid of these people as best I can."

When he got down most of the guests were gone, and that night the astounding news was spread over the entire district.

CHAPTER XLII

AFTER TWENTY YEARS

Our story may be said to have closed with the denouement recorded in last chapter; and so far as the sequence of incident is concerned it did close then, for with the production of the will by James Crawford, and the exciting scene at Woodend Cottage, all the plans and plottings of Bowser and Dick came to an end. Indeed, so complete and hopeless was their failure that these worthies disappeared altogether; and it was conjectured that, to avoid being brought to account for the fraud they had practised, they fled from the country. This idea seems to have been the correct one, for from that night neither the one nor the other was heard of. The next day, or the day after, the lonely house where Bowser and Tibb had taken up their abode was found to be deserted, and from that time forward all trace of them was lost.

It was a consciousness of their evil deserts, and nothing more, that caused them to decamp, for James Crawford, finding the genuineness and force of the will undisputed, and the boy's right to his mother's property unopposed, was not inclined to prosecute Dick and Bowser for their crime. Calling in the assistance of a law agent, the proper forms were gone through; and James, as the child's trustee, entered on the possession and management of the property. He retained his own farm of Redlaw, and let Southfield and Braeside to one tenant, with this stipulation—that Peggy M'Naughton, with Duncan and Jessie, should inhabit the old house at Braeside.

These arrangements were effected, and the dearest wish of Peggy's heart was accomplished—she spent her last days under the old roof where she had known so much happiness as Andrew Paterson's housekeeper. The evening of her life here was long and serene. Her heart was bound up in the boy, who grew up in much danger of being spoiled; but a natural disposition leaning to amiability, fostered by the more judicious care of Jessie Brown, kept him from being overtaken by this calamity, and he grew up into a fine, intelligent, open-hearted boy—the favourite of all who knew him.

For years before she died, Peggy was infirm and almost

helpless; and in this condition she was ministered to by Jessie with all the care, devotion, and love of a daughter. Her every want was attended to, and every wish gratified as far as possible. The querulousness of age and infirmity was patiently borne with, and Peggy herself was deeply sensible of Jessie's unwearied devotion.

At length she died—died in the room which was once poor Mary's, with her hand clasped in Duncan's, and her aged eyes fixed lovingly on his as the film of death grew over them. The grieved boy wept long and sore when the hand he held grew cold and stiff, and when the face on which he gazed had taken on the awful hue and aspect of death. It was his first real sorrow, and as such was to him overwhelming. After the funeral James Crawford took him to reside with himself at Redlaw, and in the cheerful, active life to which he was there introduced, his young buoyant heart overcame its grief, and in due time he became engaged and interested in the serious duties of existence.

James and Lizzy had but one child, a daughter, and with mutual consent she had been named *Mary*. She was four years younger than Duncan, and as most natural in the circumstances they "fell in love." Mary inherited her mother's sweetness and beauty, and the honest uprightness of both her parents, who beheld with pleasure and satisfaction the attachment between her and Duncan. In this instance Shakespeare's rule was not verified, for with them the course of true love did from first to last run smooth and in the June of 1851 they were united, amid much happiness and rejoicing.

A marriage jaunt was resolved upon, and as both James and Duncan were deeply interested in the state and prospects of agriculture in Ireland, they resolved on taking a short journey through that country. This was not decided on without the settlement of a counter proposition. There was the attraction of the Great Exhibition,[1] and it was a matter of some discussion whether London or Ireland should be the scene of their jaunt, but Ireland was finally decided on, and they set off.

James strove hard to get Lizzy to accompany them, but

---

1. The Great Exhibition at the Crystal Palace in Hyde Park, London, ran from 1 May to 11 October 1851.

Lizzy would not go. She was too old, she said, to travel so
far from home. Old! yes, Lizzy was getting old now, and so
was James for that matter. Remember, twenty years have
come and gone since the enactment of the drama in life in
which they had played their parts, and twenty years make an
important change on everyone, Our two friends, James and
Lizzy, had by this time reached the mature age of fifty, and
though he would not allow that he had got beyond his prime,
or that the advance of years had told much on the form of
her he loved so strongly, she smiled and shook her head as a
negative to all his entreaties. Nor when these were combined
with the solicitations of Mary and Duncan would she consent,
but laughingly said that while they were away she must stay
to look after the farm, so they had ultimately to go without
her.

Their journey through Ireland was most delightful. Everything was strange and novel, the country was picturesque and
highly beautiful, the people kind and courteous, and their
ways, manners, habitations, and speech, presented unceasing
subjects for wonder, amusement and delight.

They penetrated as far as Munster,[2] and one afternoon
when travelling through the wilder parts of that wild district,
they entered a village which seemed to be in extreme commotion, for the inhabitants—mostly women—were going
about in great excitement, and talking together with great
gesticulation.

"There's surely something wrang here," said James, as they
rattled along in their car through the dirty street.

"What's the matter with the people, Mike?" asked Duncan
at their driver.

"Sure, thin, and it's meself that doesn't know," was the
answer. "Maybe there's been a fight, and some o' the boys
has got kill't."

He pulled suddenly up opposite a group, and inquired the
cause of the disturbance.

"Och, muscha, hasn't Pat O'Rooney gone and kill't the
doctor, and ran off to the bog, where the boys are seekin' for
him."

---

2. In the south-west, and therefore as far from Scotland and "civilisation" as
possible.

The driver received this information with great equanimity, as if it was a matter of so common occurrence as to make it familiar. But not so the party who sat in his car. James and his companions were greatly shocked. They had heard much of the wild lawless character of the people of the district, but had not yet seen anything of it. But here, evidently, a murder had been perpetrated in the open day, and the people were seeking for the criminal, either to wreak their vengeance on him, or—as Mike suggested—more probably to screen him from justice.

They had left the village some distance behind, and were jolting over the rough road which skirted the edge of an immense morass or peat bog, as it is there called. Its surface was covered with clumps of grass, and low scraggy bushes, and here and there large water-holes gleamed in the sun, At one part of the bog, a long way from the edge, the forms of many men could be seen, and a few stragglers were making their way towards them in much haste. One man only was making his way out of the bog, and as he had almost cleared it he encountered a tall woman standing alone, gazing earnestly across the morass, with her hand above her eyes to shade them from the fierce summer glare. The man spoke to this woman for a few moments, and his communication seemed to be of intense interest, for while he was speaking his gestures were rapid and excited, and the woman raised her arms above her head as deeply moved by his information.

Then the man, who appeared to be in a great hurry, left her and made for the road, when he ran at great speed towards the village.

Mike pulled up as he approached.

"Have the boys got hould of Pat O'Rooney?" he shouted.

"Och, sure, and that's what they'll never do," was the answer. "He's gone clane down into the Garcar's Hole, and will never be got either to be waked or buried."

"Or hanged," added Mike, with a nod.

"Is it hanged, ye said?" returned the other. "Sure, thin, it was to save him from that the boys were afther him. Their manein' was to have him away to the mountains afore the constables come over from Callymash; but the poor boy didn't understand that, and went into the bog to be drowned."

And having delivered himself thus, the man gathered the

long tails of his ragged coat under his arms, and started off
again at full speed for the village.

Mike drove slowly on, and the attention of those in his car
were fixed on the tall woman, who had now also reached the
road, and was slowly approaching them. She was a middle-
aged woman, with black hair, large dark eyes, and strong,
almost masculine features. Neither her figure or countenance
were like those of an Irishwoman, and so marked was the
difference between her and the women they had hitherto seen
in the country that they all three fixed their eyes on her as
she came near.

As James gazed on her face, which was calmly confronting
theirs, he thought it was not entirely unfamiliar to him. He
had a dim recollection of having seen those features before,
but where, when, or in what circumstances he could not
determine.

As he earnestly gazed upon her, the woman's eye was
caught by his steadfast look, and as she returned it she started,
and cast upon him a glance of piercing inquiry. At length
when they were opposite each other she stood still and
exclaimed—"James Crawford!"

Duncan and Mary stared in amazement, and Mike stopped
his horse at once.

"Guid guide us, wha are ye?" ejaculated James, "I thoucht
I should ken ye, and ye seem to ken me."

"'Tis twenty years since we met," returned the woman,
"and that only once; but the circumstances were such as to
impress your face indelibly on my memory. You remember
the restored will, and Bowser and Dick?"

"I hae ye noo," cried James, slapping his hand emphatically on the side of the car. "Ye are the woman that I got oot
o' Bowser's clutches, and that went wi' me tae Woodend tae
hinder Dick's marriage."

"The same," returned the woman, who was no other than
Bet.

"And what in a' the world are ye daein' here?"

"I keep the public-house doun in the village, and have
up-puttin' for travellers. If you would honour me so far as to
remain at my place all night I shall be proud to do my best to
serve you."

"Faith and we will," responded James. "Ye'll no ken thir
twa," he added, pointing with a sly smile to Duncan and

Mary. "That chap was the bairn twenty year syne that the wull made richt."

"Mary Paterson's son," said Bet, with a start.

"Deed aye, and the lassie is my ain dochter. The twasome are just married, and we are here on the marriage jaunt."

"How wonderful that we should meet at this particular time," said Bet. "Of course you heard of the murder as you came through the village?"

"Aye, and o' the death o' the murderer in that peat moss," responded James.

"Then I have a story to tell in connection with both that has a particular interest for you, and, again I say, it is most wonderful that you should have come here at this time."

Mike was only too glad to have no further to drive that night, and turning his horse's head they returned to the village, in the centre of which was Bet's public-house—a place wonderfully large, airy, respectable, and clean, considering the spot in which it was located.

Here the travellers alighted, and ere long an abundant and most welcome supper smoked before them. Having done ample justice to this, Bet made her appearance in the parlour, and related to them her promised story. We shall, in our turn, relate it to the reader in our own words, and it will be found to form a natural conclusion to the tale.[3]

---

3. This concluding clause: "and it will be found to form a natural conclusion to the tale", is dropped in the 1866 and 1885 books, which also lack a chapter break here.

CHAPTER XLIII

THE FATE OF HARE—CONCLUSION

Bet having accomplished her revenge on Dick by frustrating his marriage and depriving him of the property, did not wait to receive from James Crawford the thanks which she knew she did not deserve, but fled on and on through that summer night till, through sheer exhaustion, she dropped down upon the road, and, crawling into a wood, she found there an old wooden shed, and there slept till late on the following day. She then made her way back to Dundee, and obtaining Hare's child, which she had left in a lodging-house there, went away to wander she knew not whither. She was again penniless. Bowser had possessed himself not only of the fifty pounds which she got beside the will, but also of the few pounds of her own savings which she carried in the same pocket. Bet was, however, used with being penniless, and did not much mind. Her vocal powers she knew could always gain her food and lodging, and for anything more she did not at that time much care.

She had now come to realise this truth, that revenge is only sweet in anticipation. Now that she had got her wish fully accomplished, and Dick humbled and crushed, she somehow did not feel the satisfaction she expected. She had no pleasure in thinking of his downfall, and of the unknown hardships he might then be enduring. The fire of her hate had gone down considerably when the fuel that kept it up was burned away, and the love she once had for Dick revived in the form of mingled pity and remorse.

She left Scotland and went to Ireland, where for years she wandered, the boy still with her, till finally, after experiencing many vicissitudes, she was enabled to settle down in a public-house, in one of the little villages of Munster, where the people were fierce, wild, and lawless, and ready for all kinds of outrage.

The boy she still kept with her, and named him Pat O'Rooney. Pat grew up a thorough Irish boy, and was the foremost in any lawless adventure. Bet had no great affection, or even liking for him; but he was useful in the public-house, and brought many a riotous party to spend money in it.

A few weeks before the time at which James Crawford and his travelling companions had arrived at the village it became known that a strange being had taken up his residence among the neighbouring hills. He was an old man, and the few who had casually seen him told how unearthly was his appearance. He shunned all human society, and obtained food no one knew how. He was dirty, haggard, and wild-looking in the extreme, and on the appearance of any one in his neighbourhood he would slink away and hide himself.

Who he was, or what he was, no one knew; but the people, fierce and lawless though they were, looked upon him with superstitious terror, and did not care to approach the hills where he had taken up his abode.

One day the doctor of the village had occasion to cross the hills to see a patient, and on his way back a thunder-storm suddenly came on, and the rain fell in torrents. There was no place of shelter near; but looking round he observed an aperture under an overhanging rock, which promised to afford a protection from the rain, and he ran towards it, and entered what, to his surprise, he found to be a small natural cave. Nor was it untenanted, for on a heap of dried grass lay a human figure, which the doctor at once concluded to be the unknown wanderer of whom he had heard the villagers speak.

A more repulsive face, a more squalid form, the doctor had never seen. The man looked at him in terror, but was too weak to fly. Gaunt hunger showed itself on his fleshless face, his low sloping forehead was bare and dry as a skull; but what struck the doctor most was his small oval eyes, set far apart above his projecting cheek bones. Those eyes woke up a long past memory, dim at first, but growing clearer and clearer, till he fully remembered them and the repulsive face in which they were set.

"You seem weak and ill," said the doctor, going nearer to him.

" 'Throth and I'm just that same," was the answer, in a hollow husky voice.

"Why don't you go down to the village?"

The man did not answer, but he shuddered. The doctor went closer to him still, bent down till his face was on a level with the man's, and after a few moments scrutiny, said:

"*You are Hare.*"

The wretch started as if he had received a shock from a galvanic battery, and the look of terror deepened on his inhuman countenance.

"I knew it," continued the doctor. "I have seen you too often in Knox's hall in Surgeons' Square to forget your face. Where on earth have you been for the last twenty years?"

"Living like a wild beast," returned Hare, with great bitterness, for seeing that the doctor fully recognised him, he did not attempt to deny the fact that he was the notorious West Port murderer. "I've been hunted over the whole counthry," he went on to say, "and devil a bed have I ever slept in at all at all. I durst not even go into a house, for fear they might know me and tear me to pieces. Ochone! but it's the weary life I've had of it entirely."

"And didn't you deserve it?" asked the doctor, with a loathing look.

"Bedad, thin, it isn't for the likes uv you to say so," growled Hare. "If ye are one o' the doctors that tuk in the bodies, didn't ye give us the encouragement? Sure if ye hadn't bought the shots uv us, we wouldn't ha' brought them; and devil a word ye axed us how we came by them."

"Oh, it's no use talking about that now," said the doctor. "It was a bad business for Knox and us all, and the senseless Edinburgh idiots would have it that we knew all about it. And so it was these long bony fingers of yours that clutched the throat of Daft Jamie and—and Mary Paterson, and the rest, you infernal monster!"

"I've suffered for it any how," muttered Hare. "I wish I had been hanged with Burke."

"You may have that wish gratified any day you like," returned the doctor. "Just go down among the rough boys here, and say you are Hare, and faith you'll find a rope about your neck in five minutes."

"Oh, don't tell them, Doctor, dear. For the love o' the Virgin, don't tell them it's me," whined the wretch, in the extremity of terror.

The doctor promised not to disclose the secret; and the storm being now over he left the cave and descended to the village. He fully intended to keep his promise, but landing in Bet's public-house, where a noisy group of "boys" sat smoking, he was induced to join them, for intemperance was a vice to which he had given himself wholly up, and in his drunken loquaciousness he let out the secret.

It fell like a spark upon tinder, and, a few minutes after a shouting, yelling party, headed by Pat O'Rooney, was on their way to the cave in the hill where Hare lay.

They found him lying as the doctor had left him, and with yells and curses dragged him from the cave to the foot of a rock, over which grew the trunk of a gnarled thorn. Here a rope which Pat O'Rooney had brought with him was fastened round Hare's neck, in spite of his shrieks of terror, and Pat, climbing like a cat up the face of the rock, put the end of the rope round the thorn, and with a savage shout of triumph pulled Hare up from the ground. The struggling wretch tried to wrench away the cord with his bony fingers, but was too weak to succeed, and he writhed and struggled in the death agony, surrounded by the leaping, shouting, frantic mob, who pelted him with stones till long after he was dead.

Then Pat quitted his hold of the rope, when the lifeless, battered body rolled upon the ground, and was quickly buried under a heap of stones; after which the mob returned to the village with the news of what they had done.

Bet had not heard of the doctor's revelation till the party had departed on their errand of vengeance, but no sooner had they returned and given an account of the hanging, and the share each had taken in the deed, than she called Pat O'Rooney into a back room, and transfixed him with astonishment and horror by telling him Hare was *his own father*.

The youth listened in motionless silence to the story of his infancy, then at the close he uttered a yell of despair, and flinging his arms wildly above his head, he rushed out and fled at utmost speed from the village.

That night he did not return, and nothing more was seen of him till near noon of the following day, when he was observed climbing in by the window of the doctor's bed-room. The doctor lay there sleeping off his previous night's debauch, and proved an easy victim to the young murderer. There was the sound of blows, cries, and deep groans, and when the doctor's housekeeper rushed into the room, it was just in time to see Pat leap from the window, holding in his hand the bloody shilellah[1] with which he had smashed in the doctor's skull.

The doctor was quite dead, and his head and face battered past recognition. Pat's first or second blow had made him helpless and insensible, and the savage ruffian had dealt many strokes after his victim was dead. Escaping by the window through which he had entered, he fled into the marshes, there to find concealment, and there it was, that seeing the villagers following him to hand him up to justice, as he supposed, he sped on further and further into the treacherous bog, till a stagnant pool of unknown depth received him out of sight, and brought suddenly upon him the murderer's doom.

Such was the substance of Bet's story, and her three listeners sat entranced by its recital. James Crawford was particularly struck, and even agitated by the tragic facts, and when Bet had done, he bent forward and asked with unsteady lips:—

"What was the doctor's name?"

"Doctor Grahame," answered Bet.

James held up his hands, and Duncan, starting up, exclaimed:—

"My father!"

It was even so. The betrayer and seducer of Mary Paterson had finished an obscure and dissipated life by a bloody and violent death. The hopes and prospects of his youth had never been realised. His cruel sin had found him out. When repudiated and cast off by his wife, he had sunk lower and lower in the social scale, till he had become the poverty-stricken and intemperate doctor of this obscure Irish village, wrecked in character, fortune, and hope, unhonoured in life; unwept in death.

Poor Mary! Her wrongs were now avenged as far as earthly retribution could go. She was the first victim of that fatal error which was committed in yielding to the tempter. The first but not the last. The tempter at length was overtaken by the fearful consequences which followed the sin, and a fierce and bloody hand forced him through the door of death into the awful future.

Thus, too, perished Hare, the last of the four West Port murderers. Like Cain, his punishment had been verily greater

---

1. Irish: stick or cudgel with a knob at the end.

than he could bear, and after twenty years' endurance of the most terrible suffering, he met the fate to which he had without compunction consigned so many victims; and as the very acme of poetical justice, the chief instrument of his strangulation was his own son. Where shall we find a more perfect illustration of what the Psalmist says of the evil man—"He made a pit and digged it, and is fallen into the ditch which he made. His mischief shall return upon his own head, and his violent dealing shall come down upon his own pate."[2]

James Crawford and his two companions were so shocked by what they had seen and heard in this Irish village, that they proceeded no further, but returned at once to Scotland, where they settled down to their calm life of honest industry, and in time forgot the sufferings and trials through which they had passed.

And so, kind reader, we bring this "owre true tale" to a close. It has led us into a very dark region of human cruelty and depravity. We have had to chronicle deeds and depict scenes which must have made the flesh creep and the blood run cold. Our sympathy, our pity, our indignation have all been stirred; but have we not, even in this dark and murky sphere of human crime, obtained glimpses also of human love and goodness, and have we not seen, on the whole, the workings of justice and mercy; teaching us that for wrong-doing there is punishment, and for right-doing ultimate peace and prosperity—that there is for repentance forgiveness, and for brave and patient endurance deliverance and rest. Let us learn these various lessons, and live and act under their influence, never forgetting to offer, in utmost earnestness of soul, the daily petition—"LEAD US NOT INTO TEMPTATION, BUT DELIVER US FROM EVIL."

THE END

---

2. Psalm 7:15–16.

Historical Figures

The Edinburgh sections of the novel, relating to Burke and Hare, draw extensively and accurately on the criminal record in Buchanan's account for Burke's trial and the civil prosecution against Hare, and the press documents and folk materials of its appendices. Those documents are occasionally at odds. See Rosner and McCracken-Flesher for extensive recent information, and Edwards for a speculative yet logical portrait of Burke and Hare. Amounts paid for victims are from Burke's confessions in Buchanan.

Alison, Archibald: lawyer and advocate-depute, Alison cross-examined for the crown against Burke and was counsel for the Crown in the civil action against Hare.

Black, [Alexander]: "surgeon to the Edinburgh Police establishment". He went to Burke's house with Fisher and later examined Mrs Docherty's body. He testified to her swollen face and eyes, and that she had died by violence (Buchanan, 4, 87, 118).

Broggan, uncle Barney: John Broggan senior was paid off when he found a body in a box in his house, and promptly decamped (Buchanan, Appendix, 41).

Broggan, John: the son "in the employment of John Vallance ... carter" (Buchanan, 4). Brogan/Broggan was arrested with Burke, but released despite Hare's attempt to implicate him.

Brown, Jessie: appears in the list of witnesses as "Janet Brown, now or lately servant to and residing with Isabella Burnet or Worthington, now or lately residing in Leith Street" (Buchanan, 4). She was not called to testify given that Burke was tried for Docherty, but her experience is described (Buchanan, Appendix, 14).

Burke, Constantine, and Mrs Burke: "Elizabeth Graham or Burke, wife of Constantine Burke, now or lately scavenger in the employment of the Edinburgh Police, and ... residing in Gibb's Close" (Buchanan, 4).

Burke, William: 36 at the time of his death (Buchanan, Appendix, 44). Donegal militia man and immigrant who worked on the Union canal, consorted with Helen McDougal, and with Hare murdered sixteen people, mostly by suffocation, then sold them to Dr Knox. See Edwards.

cinder sifter: Effy, who occasionally supplied Burke with small pieces of leather she found (Buchanan, Appendix, 39). £10.

Cockburn, Henry: Whig advocate. Cockburn remembered being "drawn into the case by the junior counsel" and noted that "Except that he murdered, Burke was a sensible, and what might be called a respectable, man", *Memorials of his Time* (Edinburgh: Adam and Charles Black, 1856), 456, 458.

Connaway, Mrs (spelling varies): "Ann Black or Connaway ... residing in Portsburgh". She testified that her husband, ex-army and who had served in Ireland, had chatted with Mrs Docherty about her Irish origins, and recognised where she came from (Buchanan, 4, 55).

Curator: see "keeper".

Daft Jamie: well known about Edinburgh, brought home by Mrs Hare or Burke and disposed of with difficulty, his belongings purloined (Buchanan, Appendix, 35, 14; 40, 15). May have been recognised at Knox's; his hands and feet were dissected early. £10.

Docherty, Mrs (also Margery Campbell or McGonagal): Irish; evidence at trial gave her as from Inishowen in Donegal; met Burke in Rymer's; the last victim (Buchanan, Appendix, 1–3, 36). Part payment, £5.

Donald, the old soldier who died of natural causes owing money to Burke: described in Burke's 3 January confession (Buchanan, Appendix, 32). £7.10.

Fisher, policeman: "one of the criminal officers of the Edinburgh police establishment" (Buchanan, 4). David Paterson termed him "Lieutenant of Police" (70). His evidence suggests he cajoled the criminals into thinking he believed the charges to be based on spite to get them to the police office (4, 86).

Gilmerton, the old woman from: Burke describes her as a lodger. Hers was the body Knox welcomed as "fresh" (Buchanan, Appendix, 33). Burke's *Courant* confession names her Abigail Simpson and gives the date of her murder as 12 February 1828 (Buchanan, Appendix, 38). £10.

Gray, William and Rose: "James Gray ... labourer ... residing in the Grassmarket"; "Ann McDougall or Gray, wife" (also called Elizabeth) was a townswoman of Helen's, and related to her—Helen had two children by Ann's father. Gray later said he suspected he and his wife had been destined as victims (Buchanan, 4, Appendix, 59).

Mrs O'Shea and grandson: unnamed lodgers disposed of together in a herring barrel (Buchanan, Appendix, 34, 39, 15). £16.

Haldane, Margaret (or Peggy): Mrs Haldane's daughter, disposed of some time after her mother (Buchanan, Appendix, 35). £8.

Haldane, Mary, the elder: fell asleep in Hare's stable and was murdered (Buchanan, Appendix, 34, 41).

Hare, Mrs: Margaret Logue, or Laird, a widow who had married Hare. Edwards gives an expansive biography, 67–72.

Hare's infant (Pat O'Rooney): a "yellow, 'yammering' infant, (the image of its father)" observed by Christopher North (*Blackwood's*, March 1829: 384). Cockburn notes that "every attack [of whooping cough] seemed to fire [the mother] with intenser anger and impatience; till at last the infant was plainly used merely as an instrument for delaying or evading whatever question it was inconvenient for her to answer" (Buchanan, 182). Further life unknown.

Hare, William: Irish boatman, labourer and fish seller, resident in Scotland ten years; knew Burke a year; testified against him (Buchanan, 87–96; 105–10). Later acknowledged involvement in murders (Buchanan, Appendix, 3).

Hare's separate victim: described (Buchanan, Appendix, 39).

horse: Burke described the recalcitrant and injured horse (Buchanan, Appendix, 39).

Jeffrey, Francis: whig lawyer and editor of the *Edinburgh Review*, prosecutor on behalf of Daft Jamie's mother.

Joe the Miller: described as ill; fearing contagion in the house, Burke and Hare murdered him (Buchanan, Appendix, 33–34). £10.

"keeper of the doctor's rooms": David Paterson (no relation to Mary). For the controversy over his involvement, see Buchanan, 25–31.

Knox, Robert: charismatic anatomist who received bodies from Burke and Hare. See Rosner.

Lord Advocate, William Rae: the chief legal representative of the Crown in Scotland, and chief prosecutor.

Lord Justice-Clerk David Boyle: second most senior justice in Scotland.

Lord McKenzie: a Lord ordinary, would normally preside over a jury court of first instance. For Burke, the luminaries of Scots law assembled in one hearing.

Lord Meadowbank (Alexander Maconochie): Solicitor General for Scotland in 1828 (deputy to the Lord Advocate and responsible for the Crown Office and Procurator Fiscal Office—the criminal prosecution arm of justiciary).

Lord Pitmilly (David Monypenny): a Lord of Session (the supreme civil court in Scotland), thus also sat for the High Court of Justiciary, before which Burke was tried.

McCulloch, the porter: "John McCulloch ... porter ... residing in Allison's Close, Cowgate", testified that he knew the box held a body because he felt something like hair when he picked it up (Buchanan, 4, 83).

McDougal, Helen: Burke's common law wife for ten years, Burke said she knew nothing (Buchanan, Appendix, 44).

McNeill, Duncan: advocate, later Lord President of the Court of Session. He filed in behalf of Hare against prosecution on behalf of Daft Jamie's mother, Mrs Wilson.

Moncrieff, [James W.]: Dean of the Faculty of Advocates 1826, cross-examined Mrs Connoway.

Munro (spelling varies), Alexander III (Tertius): the third generation of medical Munros, considered a poor professor. Burke's confession states they were looking for Munro to dispose of Donald when a student directed them to Knox (Buchanan, Appendix, 33).

Paterson, David: see "keeper".

Paterson, Mary [or Mitchell]: met in Constantine Burke's house and murdered, or intercepted on 9 April when discharged from the Canongate watch-house (Buchanan, Appendix, 35, 40, 14). Burke claimed a student recognised her (Buchanan, Appendix, 39). £8.

Priest who visits Burke in jail: see Edwards, 282.

Robertson, Mr P. (Patrick or "Peter"): advocate in the Court of Session.

Rymer's: "David Rymer ... grocer and spirit-dealer in Portsburgh". Hare testified to being in Rymer's when Burke told him he had decoyed Mrs Docherty home, and that Burke had got a box to transport her from Rymer's (Buchanan, 4, 88, 94). Rymer's shop boy testified to Burke meeting Mrs Docherty there, and later buying a tea chest (51–52).

Simpson, Jenny: daughter of the old woman from Gilmerton, mentioned, but not by name, in Burke's confession (Buchanan, 38).

student who recognises Mary: "William Ferguson ... surgeon ... residing in Charles Street" (Buchanan, 4). Edwards speculates on his involvement, 89.

Superintendent of police (Captain James Stewart): interim appointment from 1827; Superintendent from 1828.

washerwoman: Mrs Hostler, disposed of in September or October (Buchanan, Appendix, 35; Edwards, 109).

Williams, Thomas: the Edinburgh hangman, and ex-military like Burke and Hare's first victim. He died lamented in 1833, after twelve years in the job. A broadside elegy celebrated his "strae-bed death" and rhymed: "Here lies TAM WILLIAMS, our city Dempster, / At times he was right social good; / He was the Prince of ony Hemp-ster". Online at digital.nls.uk/broadsides/broadside.cfm/id/14616

Wilson, John, Professor: lawyer, writer for *Blackwood's Edinburgh Magazine* as "Christopher North", and professor of Moral Philosophy from 1820.

Glossary

abune: above
alanna: Irish, dear
ane: one
arrah: Irish, ejaculation
ava: at all
avourneen: Irish, sweetheart
ax: Irish pronun., ask
bedad: Irish, oath euphemistic for "by God"
bejabers: Irish, oath euphemistic for "by Jesus" (also "be jabers" and "by jabers")
begorra: Irish, oath euphemistic for "by God" (also "be gorra")
boughal: Irish, from buachaill; boy, herd
braw: brave; handsome
broo: good opinion
broth of a boy: Irish, fine fellow
caddy: messenger, errand boy or porter
Caed mille failthe: Irish, a hundred thousand welcomes
calker: (stand a calker), a drink
canty: cheerful
cauldrif: chilly
certie; my certie: surely; to be sure
chield: child; fellow
clour: dent; damage
cog: wooden vessel
colleen: Irish, girl
couter: pounds sterling
craythur, etc.: Irish pronun., creature; person
cruskin: jar, pot
cushla machree: Irish, pulse of my heart; dear one
custin: cast (past tense)
daffing: foolish playfulness
dawtie: darling, pet
dod: exclamation
douce: sweet, respectable (biddable)
enoo: at present
fack: sure; certain
faix: Irish, a corruption of "faith"
faugh shana nis: Irish, exclamation of disgust
fecht: fight

forfouchten: exhausted
fremmed: made strangers, foreign
galravish: make an uproar, live riotously
glaikitness: silliness, flirtatiousness
grieve: steward or estate manager
gudeman: term of respect to a male equal; husband
hantle: handful; a lot
haud: hold
haveral: DSL haiverel; foolish chatting
hech: expression of surprise or sorrow
limmer: female scoundrel
losh sake: exclamation
macree aisthig: my heart's
maun: must; maunna: must not
muckle: much
musha: Irish interjection
my fagues (fegs, etc.): my faith
ochone: Irish, expression of sorrow
ony: any
pickle: a little; small amount
plenishing: equipment, stock, furnishing
pliskey: trick
potheen: home-distilled liquor
prattie: Irish colloquial; potato
redd up: tidied up
richt: right
sin syne: since then
skalteen: or scaltheen; an Irish drink, made with scorched
    butter and whiskey
sough: fevered brain (of animals)
spache: Irish pronun., speech
spalpeen: Irish, rascal
spunk: spark
swaff: swept (swaffed awa, passed away)
tack: tenancy
thole: endure, bear
throth: Irish, "in truth"
throuch: DSL throch: tombstone; slab laid over a tomb
unco: very; strange; out of sorts; shy
wauff-like: uncertain; wandering; unreliable
wirra: Irish; utterance of lament

Chapter Equivalences

Mary Paterson in the Dundee *People's Journal*, *Sheffield Daily Telegraph*, and book form.

The Dundee *People's Journal* published *Mary Paterson* weekly, on Saturdays.

The *Sheffield Daily Telegraph* ran it in the Saturday supplement, priced one penny; it became known by its subtitle, *The Fatal Error*, as the series progressed. I find no evidence that the serial was pulled from the *ST*, although it is reported as pulled from a Yorkshire paper in Alexander Andrews (ed.), *The Newspaper Press: A Medium of Intercommunication Between All Parties Associated with Newspapers and a Record of Journalistic Lore* (London: E. W. Allen, 1867), 177.

Column length is given as approximately, recognising full and half pages, and increments in between with −/+.

Dundee PJ	page, number of columns, chapter	Sheffield DT	chapter	book: 1866 and 1885
9 July 1864	2:2 − (pref. & ch. 1)	28 October 1865		1866 has preface; 1885 has ch. 1 only
16 July	2:2 (ch. 2)	4 November		
23 July	2:2+ (ch. 3)	11 November		
30 July	2:2 (ch. 4)	18 November	begins at break in ch. 3; continues until break in ch. 4	
6 August	2:2+ (ch. 5)	25 November		
13 August	2:2+ (ch. 6)	2 December	MP moves into second position after new serial *Wadsley Jack*	
20 August	2:2+ (ch. 7)	9 December		
27 August	2:2+ (ch. 8)	16 December	begins at ch. 7 "The tea chest was now brought in"	

Dundee PJ	page, number of columns, chapter	Sheffield DT	chapter	book: 1866 and 1885
3 September	2:2+ (ch. 9)	23 December		
10 September	2:2+ (ch. 10)	30 December	ch. 9 and part 10	
		6 January 1866	ch. 10 cont.	
17 September	2:2+ (ch. 11)	13 January		
24 September	2:2+ (ch. 12)	20 January		
1 October	2:2 − (ch. 13)	27 January		
8 October	2:2+ (ch. 14)	3 February		
15 October	2:2+ (ch. 15)	10 February		
22 October	2:2+ (ch. 16)	17 February		
29 October	2:2+ (ch. 17)	24 February		
5 November	2:2 − (ch. 18)	3 March		
12 November	2:2+ (ch. 19)	10 March		
19 November	2:1.5 (ch. 20)	17 March		
26 November	2:2+ (ch. 21)	24 March		
3 December	2:2+ (ch. 22)	31 March		
10 December	2:2+ (ch. 23)	7 April		
17 December	2:2+ (chs 24 & 25)	14 April	ch. 24	
		21 April	chs 25 & 26 (?) retitled: "The Fate of Helen McDougal"	
24 December	2:2.5 (ch. 26)			
31 December	2:2+ (ch. 27)	28 April		
7 January 1865	2:2+ (ch. 28)	5 May		
14 January	2:2+ (ch. 29)	12 May		
21 January	2:2+ (ch. 30)	19 May		
28 January	2:2 (ch. 31)	26 May		
4 February	2:2+ (ch. 32)	2 June		
11 February	2:2 (ch. 33)	9 June		

Dundee PJ	page, number of columns, chapter	Sheffield DT	chapter	book: 1866 and 1885
18 February	2:2+ (ch. 34)	18 June		
25 February	2:2+ (ch. 35)	30 June		
4 March	2:2+ (ch. 36)	7? July		
11 March	2:2+ (ch. 37)	14 July		
18 March	2:2+ (ch. 38)	21? July		
25 March	4:2.5 (ch. 39)	27? July		
1 April	2:1 — (ch. 40)	28 July	retitled "Triumph"; moves back to front page	40 and 41 become 40: "Triumph"
8 April	2:1+ (ch. 41)	4 August	chs 41, 42, 43 pub. together	42 and 43 become 41; titles combined
15 April	2:1+ (ch. 42)			
22 April	2:1+ (ch. 43)			

Selected Bibliography

Anon. *Fortunes Made in Business: or the Life Struggles of Successful People.* London: Amalgamated Press, n.d. 313–19.

Buchanan, Robert. *Trial of William Burke and Helen M'Dougal before the High Court of Justiciary at Edinburgh on Wednesday, December 24, 1828 for the murder of Margery Campbell or Docherty.* Edinburgh: Robert Buchanan, William Hunter, John Stevenson, Baldwin & Cradock, 1829. Also *Supplement ... containing the Whole Legal Proceedings against William Hare, with an Appendix.*

Donaldson, William. *Popular Literature in Victorian Scotland.* Aberdeen: Aberdeen University Press, 1986.

Edwards, Owen Dudley. *Burke and Hare.* Edinburgh: The Mercat Press, 1993.

Ireland, Thomas. *West Port Murders: or an Authentic Account of the Atrocious Murders Committed by Burke and Hare and His Associates.* Edinburgh: Thomas Ireland, Junior, 1829.

Law, Graham. *Serializing Fiction in the Victorian Press.* Houndsmills: Palgrave, 2000.

Lecky, William. *A History of England in the Eighteenth Century,* 7 vols (New York: D. Appleton, 1892).

Leighton, Alexander. *The Court of Cacus: The Story of Burke and Hare.* Edinburgh: W. P. Nimmo, 1861.

Maunder, Andrew. "Mapping the Victorian Sensation Novel: Some Recent and Future Trends", *Literature Compass,* 2.6 (2005): 1–33.

McCracken-Flesher, Caroline. *The Doctor Dissected: A Cultural Autopsy of the Burke and Hare Murders.* Oxford: Oxford University Press, 2012.

McGowan, John. *Policing the Metropolis of Scotland: A History of the Police and Systems of Police in Edinburgh and Edinburghshire, 1770–1833.* Minneapolis: BPR, 2010.

Pae, David. *Lucy, The Factory Girl, or, The Secrets of the Tontine Close.* 1858–59. Ed. Graham Law. Hastings: The Sensation Press, 2001.

Rosner, Lisa. *The Anatomy Murders: Being the True and Spectacular History of Edinburgh's Notorious Burke and Hare and of the Man of Science Who Abetted Them in the Commission of Their Most Heinous Crimes.* Philadelphia: University of Pennsylvania Press, 2010.

Royal Commission on the Ancient and Historical Monuments of Scotland. Online canmore.rcahms.gov.uk/